CHARLES DICKENS

MR. DOMBEY AND HIS "CONFIDENTIAL AGENT."

CHARLES DICKENS

❧

DOMBEY AND SON

VOLUME II

WITH ILLUSTRATIONS BY

HABLÔT KNIGHT BROWNE ('PHIZ')

❧

WALTER J. BLACK, INC.

NEW YORK

PRINTED IN THE UNITED STATES OF AMERICA

CONTENTS

ILLUSTRATIONS

DOMBEY AND SON

DOMBEY AND SON

CHAPTER XXXI

THE WEDDING

DAWN, with its passionless blank face, steals shivering to the church beneath which lies the dust of little Paul and his mother, and looks in at the windows. It is cold and dark. Night crouches yet, upon the pavement, and broods, sombre and heavy, in nooks and corners of the building. The steeple-clock, perched up above the houses, emerging from beneath another of the countless ripples in the tide of time that regularly roll and break on the eternal shore, is greyly visible, like a stone beacon, recording how the sea flows on; but within doors, dawn, at first, can only peep at night, and see that it is there.

Hovering feebly round the church, and looking in, dawn moans and weeps for its short reign, and its tears trickle on the window-glass, and the trees against the church-wall bow their heads, and wring their many hands in sympathy. Night, growing pale before it, gradually fades out of the church, but lingers in the vaults below, and sits upon the coffins. And now comes bright day, burnishing the steeple-clock, and reddening the spire, and drying up the tears of dawn, and stifling its complaining; and the scared dawn, following the night, and chasing it from its last refuge, shrinks into the vaults itself and hides,

1

with a frightened face, among the dead, until night returns, refreshed, to drive it out.

And now, the mice, who have been busier with the prayer-books than their proper owners, and with the hassocks, more worn by their little teeth than by human knees, hide their bright eyes in their holes, and gather close together in affright at the resounding clashing of the church-door. For the beadle, that man of power, comes early this morning with the sexton; and Mrs. Miff, the wheezy little pew-opener— a mighty dry old lady, sparely dressed, with not an inch of fulness anywhere about her—is also here, and has been waiting at the church-gate half an hour, as her place is, for the beadle.

A vinegary face has Mrs. Miff, and a mortified bonnet, and eke a thirsty soul for sixpences and shillings. Beckoning to stray people to come into pews, has given Mrs. Miff an air of mystery; and there is reservation in the eye of Mrs. Miff, as always knowing of a softer seat, but having her suspicions of the fee. There is no such fact as Mr. Miff, nor has there been, these twenty years, and Mrs. Miff would rather not allude to him. He held some bad opinions, it would seem, about free seats; and though Mrs. Miff hopes he may be gone upwards, she couldn't positively undertake to say so.

Busy is Mrs. Miff this morning at the church-door, beating and dusting the altar-cloth, the carpet, and the cushions; and much has Mrs. Miff to say, about the wedding they are going to have. Mrs. Miff is told, that the new furniture and alterations in the house cost full five thousand pound if they cost a penny; and Mrs. Miff has heard, upon the best authority, that the lady hasn't got a sixpence wherewithal to bless herself. Mrs. Miff remembers, likewise, as if it had happened yesterday, the first wife's funeral, and then the christening, and then the other funeral; and Mrs. Miff says, by the bye she 'll soap-and-water that 'ere tablet presently, against the company arrive. Mr. Sownds, the beadle, who is sitting in the sun upon the church steps all this time (and seldom does anything else, except, in cold weather, sitting by the fire), approves of Mrs. Miff's discourse, and asks if Mrs. Miff has heard it said, that the lady is uncommon handsome? The information Mrs. Miff has received, being of this nature, Mr. Sownds the beadle, who, though orthodox and corpulent, is still an admirer of female beauty, observes, with unction, yes, he hears she is a spanker—an expression that seems somewhat forcible to Mrs. Miff, or would, from any lips but those of Mr. Sownds the beadle.

In Mr. Dombey's house, at this same time, there is great stir and bustle, more especially among the women: not one of whom has had a wink of sleep since four o'clock, and all of whom were full dressed before six. Mr. Towlinson is an object of greater consideration than usual to the housemaid, and the cook says at breakfast-time that one wedding makes many, which the housemaid can't believe, and don't think true at all. Mr. Towlinson reserves his sentiments on this question; being rendered something gloomy by the engagement of a foreigner with whiskers (Mr. Towlinson is whiskerless himself), who had been hired to accompany the happy pair to Paris, and who is busy packing the new chariot. In respect of this personage, Mr. Towlinson admits, presently, that he never knew of any good that ever come of foreigners; and being charged by the ladies with prejudice, says, look at Bonaparte who was at the head of 'em, and see what *he* was always up to! Which the housemaid says is very true.

The pastry-cook is hard at work in the funereal

room in Brook Street, and the very tall young men are busy looking on. One of the very tall young men already smells of sherry, and his eyes have a tendency to become fixed in his head, and to stare at objects without seeing them. The very tall young man is conscious of this failing in himself; and informs his comrade that it's his 'exciseman.' The very tall young man would say excitement, but his speech is hazy.

The men who play the bells have got scent of the marriage; and the marrow-bones and cleavers too; and a brass band too. The first, are practising in a back settlement near Battle Bridge; the second, put themselves in communication, through their chief, with Mr. Towlinson, to whom they offer terms to be bought off; and the third, in the person of an artful trombone, lurks and dodges round the corner, waiting for some traitor tradesman to reveal the place and hour of breakfast, for a bribe. Expectation and excitement extend further yet, and take a wider range. From Balls Pond, Mr. Perch brings Mrs. Perch to spend the day with Mr. Dombey's servants, and accompany them, surreptitiously, to see the wedding. In Mr. Toots's lodgings, Mr. Toots attires himself as if he were at least the bridegroom; determined to behold the spectacle in splendour from a secret corner of the gallery, and thither to convey the Chicken: for it is Mr. Toots's desperate intent to point out Florence to the Chicken, then and there, and openly to say, 'Now, Chicken, I will not deceive you any longer; the friend I have sometimes mentioned to you is myself; Miss Dombey is the object of my passion; what are your opinions, Chicken, in this state of things, and what, on the spot, do you advise?' The so-much-to-be-astonished Chicken, in the meanwhile, dips his beak into a tankard of strong beer, in Mr.

Toots's kitchen, and pecks up two pounds of beef-steaks. In Princess's Place, Miss Tox is up and doing; for she too, though in sore distress, is resolved to put a shilling in the hands of Mrs. Miff, and see the ceremony which has a cruel fascination for her, from some lonely corner. The quarters of the wooden midshipman are all alive; for Captain Cuttle, in his ankle-jacks and with a huge shirt-collar, is seated at his breakfast, listening to Rob the Grinder as he reads the marriage service to him beforehand, under orders, to the end that the captain may perfectly understand the solemnity he is about to witness: for which purpose, the captain gravely lays injunctions on his chaplain, from time to time, to 'put about,' or to 'overhaul that 'ere article again,' or to stick to his own duty, and leave the Amens to him, the captain; one of which he repeats, whenever a pause is made by Rob the Grinder, with sonorous satisfaction.

Besides all this, and much more, twenty nursery-maids in Mr. Dombey's street alone, have promised twenty families of little women, whose instinctive interest in nuptials dates from their cradles, that they shall go and see the marriage. Truly, Mr. Sownds the beadle has good reason to feel himself in office, as he suns his portly figure on the church steps, waiting for the marriage hour. Truly, Mrs. Miff has cause to pounce on an unlucky dwarf child, with a giant baby, who peeps in at the porch, and drive her forth with indignation!

Cousin Feenix has come over from abroad, expressly to attend the marriage. Cousin Feenix was a man about town, forty years ago; but he is still so juvenile in figure and in manner, and so well got up, that strangers are amazed when they discover latent wrinkles in his lordship's face, and crows' feet in his eyes; and first observe him, not exactly certain when he walks across a room, of going quite straight to where he wants to go. But cousin Feenix, getting up at half-past seven o'clock or so, is quite another thing from cousin Feenix got up; and very dim, indeed, he looks, while being shaved at Long's Hotel, in Bond Street.

Mr. Dombey leaves his dressing-room, amidst a general whisking away of the women on the staircase, who disperse in all directions, with a great rustling of skirts, except Mrs. Perch, who, being (but that she always is) in an interesting situation, is not nimble, and is obliged to face him, and is ready to sink with confusion as she curtseys;—may Heaven avert all evil consequences from the house of Perch! Mr. Dombey walks up to the drawing-room, to bide his time. Gorgeous are Mr. Dombey's new blue coat, fawn-coloured pantaloons, and lilac waistcoat; and a whisper goes about the house, that Mr. Dombey's hair is curled.

A double knock announces the arrival of the major, who is gorgeous too, and wears a whole geranium in his buttonhole, and has his hair curled tight and crisp, as well the native knows.

'Dombey!' says the major, putting out both hands, 'How are you?'

'Major,' says Mr. Dombey, 'how are You?'

'By Jove, sir,' says the major, 'Joey B. is in such case this morning, sir,'—and here he hits himself hard upon the breast—'in such case this morning, sir, that, damme, Dombey, he has half a mind to make a double marriage of it, sir, and take the mother.'

Mr. Dombey smiles; but faintly, even for him; for Mr. Dombey feels that he is going to be related to the mother, and that, under those circumstances, she is not to be joked about.

'Dombey,' says the major, seeing this, 'I give you joy. I congratulate you, Dombey. By the Lord, sir,' says the major, 'you are more to be envied, this day, than any man in England!'

Here again Mr. Dombey's assent is qualified; because he is going to confer a great distinction on a lady; and, no doubt, she is to be envied most.

'As to Edith Granger, sir,' pursues the major, 'there is not a woman in all Europe but might—and would, sir, you will allow Bagstock to add—and would give her ears, and her ear-rings, too, to be in Edith Granger's place.'

'You are good enough to say so, major,' says Mr. Dombey.

'Dombey,' returns the major, 'you know it. Let us have no false delicacy. You know it. Do you know it, or do you not, Dombey?' says the major, almost in a passion.

'Oh, really, major—'

'Damme, sir,' retorts the major, 'do you know that fact, or do you not? Dombey! Is old Joe your friend? Are we on that footing of unreserved intimacy, Dombey, that may justify a man—a blunt old Joseph B., sir—in speaking out; or am I to take open order, Dombey, and to keep my distance, and to stand on forms?'

'My dear Major Bagstock,' says Mr. Dombey, with a gratified air, 'you are quite warm.'

'By Gad, sir,' says the major, 'I am warm. Joseph B. does not deny it, Dombey. He is warm. This is an occasion, sir, that calls forth all the honest sympathies remaining in an old, infernal, battered, used up, invalided, J. B. carcase. And I tell you what, Dombey—at such a time a man must blurt out what he feels, or put a muzzle on; and Joseph Bagstock tells you to your face, Dombey, as he tells his club behind your back, that he never will be muzzled when Paul Dombey is in question. Now, damme, sir,' concludes the major, with great firmness, 'what do you make of that?'

'Major,' says Mr. Dombey, 'I assure you that I am really obliged to you. I had no idea of checking your too partial friendship.'

'Not too partial, sir!' exclaims the choleric major. 'Dombey, I deny it.'

'Your friendship I will say then,' pursues Mr. Dombey, 'on any account. Nor can I forget, major, on such an occasion as the present, how much I am indebted to it.'

'Dombey,' says the major, with appropriate action, 'that is the hand of Joseph Bagstock: of plain old Joey B., sir, if you like that better! That is the hand of which His Royal Highness the late Duke of York did me the honour to observe, sir, to His Royal Highness the late Duke of Kent, that it was the hand of Josh.: a rough and tough, and possibly an up-to-snuff, old vagabond. Dombey, may the present moment be the least unhappy of our lives. God bless you!'

Now enters Mr. Carker, gorgeous likewise, and smiling like a wedding-guest indeed. He can scarcely let Mr. Dombey's hand go, he is so congratulatory; and he shakes the major's hand so heartily at the same time, that his voice shakes too, in accord with his arms, as it comes sliding from between his teeth.

'The very day is auspicious,' says Mr. Carker. 'The brightest and most genial weather! I hope I am not a moment late?'

'Punctual to your time, sir,' says the major.

'I am rejoiced, I am sure,' says Mr. Carker. 'I was afraid I might be a few seconds after the appointed time, for I was delayed by a procession of waggons; and I took the liberty of riding round to Brook Street'—this to Mr. Dombey—'to leave a few poor rarities of flowers for Mrs. Dombey. A man in my position, and so distinguished as to be invited here, is proud to offer some homage in acknowledgment of his vassalage: and as I have no doubt Mrs. Dombey is overwhelmed with what is costly and magnificent'; with a strange glance at his patron; 'I hope the very poverty of my offering, may find favour for it.'

'Mrs. Dombey, that is to be,' returns Mr. Dombey, condescendingly, 'will be very sensible of your attention, Carker, I am sure.'

'And if she is to be Mrs. Dombey this morning, sir,' says the major, putting down his coffee-cup, and looking at his watch, 'it's high time we were off!'

Forth, in a barouche, ride Mr. Dombey, Major Bagstock, and Mr. Carker, to the church. Mr. Sownds the beadle has long risen from the steps, and is in waiting with his cocked hat in his hand. Mrs. Miff curtseys and proposes chairs in the vestry. Mr. Dombey prefers remaining in the church. As he looks up at the organ, Miss Tox in the gallery, shrinks behind the fat leg of a cherub on a monument, with cheeks like a young Wind. Captain Cuttle, on the contrary, stands up and waves his hook, in token of welcome and encouragement. Mr. Toots informs the Chicken, behind his hand, that the middle gentleman, he in the fawn-coloured pantaloons, is the father of his love. The Chicken hoarsely whispers Mr. Toots that he's as stiff a cove as ever he see, but that it is within the resources of Science to double him up, with one blow in the waistcoat.

Mr. Sownds and Mrs. Miff are eyeing Mr. Dombey from a little distance, when the noise of approaching wheels is heard, and Mr. Sownds goes out, Mrs. Miff, meeting Mr. Dombey's eye as it is withdrawn from the presumptuous maniac upstairs, who salutes him with so much urbanity, drops a curtsey, and informs him that she believes his 'good lady' is come. Then there is a crowding and a whispering at the door, and the good lady enters, with a haughty step.

There is no sign upon her face, of last night's suffering; there is no trace in her manner, of the woman on the bended knees reposing her wild head, in beautiful abandonment, upon the pillow of the sleeping girl. That girl, all gentle and lovely, is at her side —a striking contrast to her own disdainful and defiant figure, standing there, composed, erect, inscrutable of will, resplendent and majestic in the zenith of its charms, yet beating down, and treading on, the admiration that it challenges.

There is a pause while Mr. Sownds the beadle glides into the vestry for the clergyman and clerk. At this juncture, Mrs. Skewton speaks to Mr. Dombey: more distinctly and emphatically than her custom is, and moving at the same time, close to Edith.

'My dear Dombey,' says the good mamma, 'I fear I must relinquish darling Florence after all, and suffer her to go home, as she herself proposed. After my loss of to-day, my dear Dombey, I feel I shall not have spirits, even for her society.'

'Had she not better stay with you?' returns the bridegroom.

'I think not, my dear Dombey. No, I think not. I shall be better alone. Besides, my dearest Edith will be her natural and constant guardian when you return, and I had better not encroach upon her trust, perhaps. She might be jealous. Eh, dear Edith?'

The affectionate mamma presses her daughter's

arm, as she says this; perhaps entreating her attention earnestly.

'To be serious, my dear Dombey,' she resumes, 'I will relinquish our dear child, and not inflict my gloom upon her. We have settled that, just now. She fully understands, dear Dombey. Edith, my dear,—she fully understands.'

Again, the good mother presses her daughter's arm. Mr. Dombey, offers no additional remonstrance; for the clergyman and clerk appear; and Mrs. Miff and Mr. Sownds the beadle, group the party in their proper places at the altar rails.

' "Who giveth this woman to be married to this man?" '

Cousin Feenix does that. He has come from Baden-Baden on purpose. 'Confound it,' cousin Feenix says—good-natured creature, cousin Feenix —'when we *do* get a rich City fellow into the family, let us show him some attention; let us do something for him.'

'*I* give this woman to be married to this man,' saith cousin Feenix therefore. Cousin Feenix, meaning to go in a straight line, but turning off sideways by reason of his wilful legs, gives the wrong woman to be married to this man, at first—to wit, a bridesmaid of some condition, distantly connected with the family, and ten years Mrs. Skewton's junior —but Mrs. Miff, interposing her mortified bonnet, dexterously turns him back, and runs him, as on castors, full at the 'good lady': whom cousin Feenix giveth to be married to this man accordingly.

And will they in the sight of heaven—?

Aye, that they will: Mr. Dombey says he will. And what says Edith? *She* will.

So, from that day forward, for better for worse,

for richer for poorer, in sickness and in health, to love and to cherish, till death do them part, they plight their troth to one another, and are married.

In a firm, free hand, the bride subscribes her name in the register, when they adjourn to the vestry. 'There an't a many ladies comes here,' Mrs. Miff says with a curtsey—to look at Mrs. Miff, at such a season, is to make her mortified bonnet go down with a dip —'writes their names like this good lady!' Mr. Sownds the beadle thinks it is a truly spanking signature, and worthy of the writer—this, however, between himself and conscience.

Florence signs too, but unapplauded, for her hand shakes. All the party sign; Cousin Feenix last; who puts his noble name into a wrong place, and enrols himself as having been born that morning.

The major now salutes the bride right gallantly, and carries out that branch of military tactics in reference to all the ladies: notwithstanding Mrs. Skewton's being extremely hard to kiss, and squeaking shrilly in the sacred edifice. The example is followed by cousin Feenix, and even by Mr. Dombey. Lastly, Mr. Carker, with his white teeth glistening, approaches Edith, more as if he meant to bite her, than to taste the sweets that linger on her lips.

There is a glow upon her proud cheek, and a flashing in her eyes, that may be meant to stay him; but it does not, for he salutes her as the rest have done, and wishes her all happiness.

'If wishes,' says he in a low voice, 'are not superfluous, applied to such a union.'

'I thank you, sir,' she answers, with a curled lip, and a heaving bosom.

But, does Edith feel still, as on the night when she knew that Mr. Dombey would return to offer his alliance, that Carker knows her thoroughly and reads her right, and that she is more degraded by his knowledge of her, than by aught else? Is it for this reason that her haughtiness shrinks beneath his smile, like snow within the hand that grasps it firmly, and that her imperious glance droops in meeting his, and seeks the ground?

'I am proud to see,' says Mr. Carker, with a servile stooping of his neck, which the revelations making by his eyes and teeth proclaim to be a lie, 'I am proud to see that my humble offering is graced by Mrs. Dombey's hand, and permitted to hold so favoured a place in so joyful an occasion.'

Though she bends her head, in answer, there is something in the momentary action of her hand, as if she would crush the flowers it holds, and fling them, with contempt, upon the ground. But, she puts her hand through the arm of her new husband, who has been standing near, conversing with the major, and is proud again, and motionless, and silent.

The carriages are once more at the church door. Mr. Dombey, with his bride upon his arm, conducts her through the twenty families of little women who are on the steps, and every one of whom remembers the fashion and the colour of her every article of dress from that moment, and reproduces it on her doll, who is for ever being married. Cleopatra and cousin Feenix enter the same carriage. The major hands into a second carriage, Florence, and the brides-maid who so narrowly escaped being given away by mistake, and then enters it himself, and is followed by Mr. Carker. Horses prance and caper; coachmen and footmen shine in fluttering favours, flowers, and new-made liveries. Away they dash and rattle through the streets: and as they pass along, a thou-sand heads are turned to look at them, and a thousand sober moralists revenge themselves for not being married too, that morning, by reflecting that these people little think such happiness can't last.

Miss Tox emerges from behind the cherub's leg, when all is quiet, and comes slowly down from the gallery. Miss Tox's eyes are red, and her pocket-handkerchief is damp. She is wounded, but not exasperated, and she hopes they may be happy. She quite admits to herself the beauty of the bride, and her own comparatively feeble and faded attractions; but the stately image of Mr. Dombey in his lilac waistcoat, and his fawn-coloured pantaloons, is present to her mind, and Miss Tox weeps afresh, behind her veil, on her way home to Princess's Place. Captain Cuttle, having joined in all the amens and responses, with a devout growl, feels much improved by his religious exercises; and in a peaceful frame of mind, pervades the body of the church, glazed hat in hand, and reads the tablet to the memory of little Paul. The gallant Mr. Toots, attended by the faithful Chicken, leaves the building in torments of love. The Chicken is as yet unable to elaborate a scheme for winning Florence, but his first idea has gained possession of him, and he thinks the doubling up of Mr. Dombey would be a move in the right direction. Mr. Dombey's servants come out of their hiding-places, and prepare to rush to Brook Street, when they are delayed by symptoms of indisposition on the part of Mrs. Perch, who entreats a glass of water, and becomes alarming; Mrs. Perch gets better soon, however, and is borne away; and Mrs. Miff, and Mr. Sownds the beadle, sit upon the steps to count what they have gained by the affair, and talk it over, while the sexton tolls a funeral.

Now, the carriages arrive at the bride's residence, and the players on the bells begin to jingle, and the band strikes up, and Mr. Punch, that model of connubial bliss, salutes his wife. Now, the people run and push, and press round in a gaping throng, while Mr. Dombey, leading Mrs. Dombey by the hand, advances solemnly into the Feenix halls. Now, the rest of the wedding party alight, and enter after them. And why does Mr. Carker, passing through the people to the hall-door, think of the old woman who called to him in the grove that morning? Or why does Florence, as she passes, think, with a tremble, of her childhood, when she was lost, and of the visage of Good Mrs. Brown?

Now, there are more congratulations on this happiest of days, and more company, though not much; and now they leave the drawing-room, and range themselves at table in the dark-brown dining-room, which no confectioner can brighten up, let him garnish the exhausted negroes with as many flowers and love-knots as he will.

The pastry-cook has done his duty like a man, though, and a rich breakfast is set forth. Mr. and Mrs. Chick have joined the party, among others. Mrs. Chick admires that Edith should be, by nature, such a perfect Dombey; and is affable and confidential to Mrs. Skewton, whose mind is relieved of a great load, and who takes her share of the champagne. The very tall young man who suffered from excitement early, is better; but a vague sentiment of repentance has seized upon him, and he hates the other very tall young man, and wrests dishes from him by violence, and takes a grim delight in disobliging the company. The company are cool and calm, and do not outrage the black hatchments of pictures looking down upon them, by any excess of mirth. Cousin Feenix and the major are the gayest there; but Mr.

Carker has a smile for the whole table. He has an especial smile for the bride, who very, very seldom meets it.

Cousin Feenix rises, when the company have breakfasted, and the servants have left the room; and wonderfully young he looks, with his white wristbands almost covering his hands (otherwise rather bony), and the bloom of the champagne in his cheeks.

'Upon my honour,' says cousin Feenix, 'although it's an unusual sort of thing in a private gentleman's house, I must beg leave to call upon you to drink what is usually called a—in fact a toast.'

The major very hoarsely indicates his approval. Mr. Carker, bending his head forward over the table in the direction of Cousin Feenix, smiles and nods a great many times.

'A—in fact it's not a—' Cousin Feenix beginning again, thus, comes to a dead stop.

'Hear, hear!' says the major, in a tone of conviction.

Mr. Carker softly claps his hands, and bending forward over the table again, smiles and nods a great many more times than before, as if he were particularly struck by this last observation, and desired personally to express his sense of the good it has done him.

'It is,' says cousin Feenix, 'an occasion in fact, when the general usages of life may be a little departed from, without impropriety; and although I never was an orator in my life, and when I was in the House of Commons, and had the honour of seconding the address, was—in fact, was laid up for a fortnight with the consciousness of failure—'

The major and Mr. Carker are so much delighted by this fragment of personal history, that cousin

Feenix laughs, and addressing them individually, goes on to say——

'And in point of fact, when I was devilish ill— still, you know, I feel that a duty devolves upon me. And when a duty devolves upon an Englishman, he is bound to get out of it, in my opinion, in the best way he can. Well! our family has had the gratification, to-day, of connecting itself, in the person of my lovely and accomplished relative, whom I now see —in point of fact, present—'

Here there is general applause.

'Present,' repeats cousin Feenix, feeling that it is a neat point which will bear repetition,—'with one who—that is to say, with a man, at whom the finger of scorn can never—in fact, with my honourable friend Dombey, if he will allow me to call him so.'

Cousin Feenix bows to Mr. Dombey; Mr. Dombey solemnly returns the bow; everybody is more or less gratified and affected by this extraordinary, and perhaps unprecedented, appeal to the feelings.

'I have not,' says cousin Feenix, 'enjoyed those opportunities which I could have desired, of cultivating the acquaintance of my friend Dombey, and studying those qualities which do equal honour to his head, and, in point of fact, to his heart; for it has been my misfortune to be, as we used to say in my time in the House of Commons, when it was not the custom to allude to the Lords, and when the order of parliamentary proceedings was perhaps better observed than it is now—to be in—in point of fact,' says cousin Feenix, cherishing his joke, with great slyness, and finally bringing it out with a jerk, ' "in another place"!'

The major falls into convulsions, and is recovered with difficulty.

'But I know sufficient of my friend Dombey,' resumes cousin Feenix in a graver tone, as if he had suddenly become a sadder and wiser man, 'to know that he is, in point of fact, what may be emphatically called a—a merchant—a British merchant—and a —and a man. And although I have been resident abroad for some years (it would give me great pleasure to receive my friend Dombey, and everybody here, at Baden-Baden, and to have an opportunity of making 'em known to the Grand Duke), still I know enough, I flatter myself, of my lovely and accomplished relative, to know that she possesses every requisite to make a man happy, and that her marriage with my friend Dombey is one of inclination and affection on both sides.'

Many smiles and nods from Mr. Carker.

'Therefore,' says cousin Feenix, 'I congratulate the family of which I am a member, on the acquisition of my friend Dombey. I congratulate my friend Dombey on his union with my lovely and accomplished relative who possesses every requisite to make a man happy; and I take the liberty of calling on you all, in point of fact, to congratulate both my friend Dombey and my lovely and accomplished relative, on the present occasion.'

The speech of cousin Feenix is received with great applause, and Mr. Dombey returns thanks on behalf of himself and Mrs. Dombey. J. B. shortly afterwards proposes Mrs. Skewton. The breakfast languishes when that is done, the violated hatchments are avenged, and Edith rises to assume her travelling dress.

All the servants in the meantime, have been breakfasting below. Champagne has grown too common among them to be mentioned, and roast fowls, raised pies, and lobster-salad, have become mere drugs.

The very tall young man has recovered his spirits, and again alludes to the exciseman. His comrade's eye begins to emulate his own, and he, too, stares at objects without taking cognisance thereof. There is a general redness in the faces of the ladies; in the face of Mrs. Perch particularly, who is joyous and beaming, and lifted so far above the cares of life, that if she were asked just now to direct a wayfarer to Balls Pond, where her own cares lodge, she would have some difficulty in recalling the way. Mr. Towlinson has proposed the happy pair; to which the silver-headed butler has responded neatly, and with emotion; for he half begins to think he *is* an old retainer of the family, and that he is bound to be affected by these changes. The whole party, and especially the ladies, are very frolicsome. Mr. Dombey's cook, who generally takes the lead in society, has said, it is impossible to settle down after this, and why not go, in a party, to the play? Everybody (Mrs. Perch included) has agreed to this: even the native, who is tigerish in his drink, and who alarms the ladies (Mrs. Perch particularly) by the rolling of his eyes. One of the very tall young men has even proposed a ball after the play, and it presents itself to no one (Mrs. Perch included) in the light of an impossibility. Words have arisen between the housemaid and Mr. Towlinson; she, on the authority of an old saw, asserting marriages to be made in heaven: he, affecting to trace the manufacture elsewhere; he, supposing that she says so, because she thinks of being married her own self: she, saying, Lord forbid, at any rate, that she should ever marry *him*. To calm these flying taunts, the silver-headed butler rises to propose the health of Mr. Towlinson, whom to know is to esteem, and to esteem is to wish well settled in life with the object of his choice, wherever (here the silver-headed butler eyes the housemaid) she may be. Mr. Towlinson returns thanks in a speech replete with feeling, of which the peroration turns on foreigners, regarding whom he says they may find favour, sometimes with weak and inconstant intellects that can be led away by hair, but all he hopes, is, he may never hear of no foreigner never boning nothing out of no travelling chariot. The eye of Mr. Towlinson is so severe and so expressive here, that the housemaid is turning hysterical, when she and all the rest, roused by the intelligence that the bride is going away, hurry upstairs to witness her departure.

The chariot is at the door; the bride is descending to the hall, where Mr. Dombey waits for her. Florence is ready on the staircase to depart too; and Miss Nipper, who has held a middle state between the parlour and the kitchen, is prepared to accompany her. As Edith appears, Florence hastens towards her, to bid her farewell.

Is Edith cold, that she should tremble? Is there anything unnatural or unwholesome in the touch of Florence, that the beautiful form recedes and contracts, as if it could not bear it? Is there so much hurry in this going away, that Edith, with a wave of her hand, sweeps on, and is gone?

Mrs. Skewton, overpowered by her feelings as a mother, sinks on her sofa in the Cleopatra attitude, when the clatter of the chariot wheels is lost, and sheds several tears. The major, coming with the rest of the company from the table, endeavours to comfort her; but she will not be comforted on any terms, and so the major takes his leave. Cousin Feenix takes his leave, and Mr. Carker takes his leave. The guests all go away. Cleopatra, left alone, feels a little giddy from her strong emotion, and falls asleep.

Giddiness prevails below-stairs too. The very tall young man whose excitement came on so soon, appears to have his head glued to the table in the pantry, and cannot be detached from it. A violent revulsion has taken place in the spirits of Mrs. Perch, who is low on account of Mr. Perch, and tells cook that she fears he is not so much attached to his home, as he used to be, when they were only nine in family. Mr. Towlinson has a singing in his ears and a large wheel going round and round inside his head. The housemaid wishes it wasn't wicked to wish that one was dead.

There is a general delusion likewise, in these lower regions, on the subject of time; everybody conceiving that it ought to be, at the earliest, ten o'clock at night, whereas it is not yet three in the afternoon. A shadowy idea of wickedness committed, haunts every individual in the party; and each one secretly thinks the other a companion in guilt, whom it would be agreeable to avoid. No man or woman has the hardihood to hint at the projected visit to the play. Any one reviving the notion of the ball, would be scouted as a malignant idiot.

Mrs. Skewton sleeps upstairs, two hours afterwards, and naps are not yet over in the kitchen. The hatchments in the dining-room look down on crumbs, dirty plates, spillings of wine, half-thawed ice, stale discoloured heel-taps, scraps of lobster, drumsticks of fowls, and pensive jellies, gradually resolving themselves into a lukewarm gummy soup. The marriage is, by this time, almost as denuded of its show and garnish as the breakfast. Mr. Dombey's servants moralise so much about it, and are so repentant over their early tea, at home, that by eight o'clock or so, they settle down into confirmed seriousness; and Mr. Perch, arriving at that time from the City, fresh and

jocular, with a white waistcoat and a comic song,
ready to spend the evening, and prepared for any
amount of dissipation, is amazed to find himself
coldly received, and Mrs. Perch but poorly, and to
have the pleasing duty of escorting that lady home
by the next omnibus.

Night closes in. Florence having rambled through
the handsome house, from room to room, seeks her
own chamber, where the care of Edith has surrounded
her with luxuries and comforts; and divesting herself
of her handsome dress, puts on her old simple mourning for dear Paul, and sits down to read, with
Diogenes winking and blinking on the ground beside her. But Florence cannot read to-night. The
house seems strange and new, and there are loud
echoes in it. There is a shadow on her heart: she
knows not why or what; but it is heavy. Florence
shuts her book, and gruff Diogenes, who takes that
for a signal, puts his paws upon her lap, and rubs
his ears against her caressing hands. But Florence
cannot see him plainly, in a little time, for there is a
mist between her eyes and him, and her dead brother
and dead mother shine in it like angels. Walter,
too, poor wandering shipwrecked boy, oh, where is
he?

The major don't know; that's for certain; and
don't care. The major, having choked and slumbered, all the afternoon, has taken a late dinner at
his club, and now sits over his pint of wine, driving
a modest young man, with a fresh-coloured face, at
the next table (who would give a handsome sum to
be able to rise and go away, but cannot do it), to the
verge of madness, by anecdotes of Bagstock, sir, at
Dombey's wedding, and old Joe's devilish gentlemanly friend, Lord Feenix. While cousin Feenix,
who ought to be at Long's, and in bed, finds himself,

instead, at a gaming-table, where his wilful legs have taken him, perhaps, in his own despite.

Night, like a giant, fills the church, from pavement to roof, and holds dominion through the silent hours. Pale dawn again comes peeping through the windows; and, giving place to day, sees night withdraw into the vaults, and follows it, and drives it out, and hides among the dead. The timid mice again cower close together, when the great door clashes, and Mr. Sownds and Mrs. Miff, treading the circle of their daily lives, unbroken as a marriage ring, come in. Again, the cocked hat and the mortified bonnet stand in the background at the marriage hour; and again this man taketh this woman, and this woman taketh this man, on the solemn terms—

'To have and to hold, from this day forward, for better for worse, for richer for poorer, in sickness and in health, to love and to cherish, until death do them part.'

The very words that Mr. Carker rides into town repeating, with his mouth stretched to the utmost, as he picks his dainty way.

CHAPTER XXXII

THE WOODEN MIDSHIPMAN GOES TO PIECES

HONEST Captain Cuttle, as the weeks flew over him in his fortified retreat, by no means abated any of his prudent provisions against surprise, because of the non-appearance of the enemy. The captain argued that his present security was too profound and wonderful to endure much longer; he knew that when the wind stood in a fair quarter, the weathercock was seldom nailed there; and he was too well acquainted with the determined and dauntless character of Mrs. MacStinger, to doubt that that heroic woman had devoted herself to the task of his discovery and capture. Trembling beneath the weight of these reasons, Captain Cuttle lived a very close and retired life; seldom stirring abroad until after dark; venturing even then only into the obscurest streets; never going forth at all on Sundays; and both within and without the walls of his retreat, avoiding bonnets, as if they were worn by raging lions.

The captain never dreamed that in the event of his being pounced upon by Mrs. MacStinger, in his walks, it would be possible to offer resistance. He felt that it could not be done. He saw himself, in his mind's eye, put meekly in a hackney-coach, and carried off to his old lodgings. He foresaw that, once immured there, he was a lost man; his hat gone; Mrs. MacStinger watchful of him day and night; reproaches heaped upon his head, before the infant family; himself the guilty object of suspicion and distrust; an ogre in the children's eyes, and in their mother's a detected traitor.

A violent perspiration, and a lowness of spirits always came over the captain as this gloomy picture presented itself to his imagination. It generally did so previous to his stealing out of doors at night for air and exercise. Sensible of the risk he ran, the captain took leave of Rob, at those times with the solemnity which became a man who might never return: exhorting him, in the event of his (the captain's) being lost sight of, for a time, to tread in the paths of virtue, and keep the brazen instruments well polished.

But not to throw away a chance; and to secure to himself a means, in case of the worst, of holding communication with the external world; Captain

Cuttle soon conceived the happy idea of teaching Rob
the Grinder some secret signal, by which that adherent might make his presence and fidelity known to
his commander, in the hour of adversity. After
much cogitation, the captain decided in favour of in-
structing him to whistle the marine melody, 'Oh
cheerily, cheerily!' and Rob the Grinder attaining a
point as near perfection in that accomplishment as a
landsman could hope to reach, the captain impressed
these mysterious instructions on his mind—

'Now, my lad, stand by. If ever I'm took—'

'Took, captain!' interposed Rob, with his round
eyes wide open.

'Ah!' said Captain Cuttle darkly, 'if ever I goes
away, meaning to come back to supper, and don't
come within hail again twenty-four hours arter my
loss, go you to Brig Place and whistle that 'ere tune
near my old moorings—not as if you was a meaning
of it, you understand, but as if you'd drifted there,
promiscuous. If I answer in that tune, you sheer
off, my lad, and come back four-and-twenty hours
arterwards; if I answer in another tune, do you stand
off and on, and wait till I throw out further signals.
Do you understand them orders, now?'

'What am I to stand off and on of, captain?' inquired Rob. 'The horse-road?'

'Here's a smart lad for you!' cried the captain,
eyeing him sternly, 'as don't know his own native
alphabet! Go away a bit and come back again alternate—d' ye understand that?'

'Yes, captain,' said Rob.

'Very good, my lad, then,' said the captain, relenting. 'Do it!'

That he might do it the better, Captain Cuttle
sometimes condescended of an evening, after the shop
was shut, to rehearse this scene: retiring into the par-

lour for the purpose, as into the lodgings of a sup-
posititious MacStinger, and carefully observing the
behaviour of his ally, from the hole of espial he had
cut in the wall. Rob the Grinder discharged himself of his duty with so much exactness and judgment, when thus put to the proof, that the captain
presented him, at divers times, with seven sixpences,
in token of satisfaction; and gradually felt stealing
over his spirit the resignation of a man who had made
provision for the worst, and taken every reasonable
precaution against an unrelenting fate.

Nevertheless, the captain did not tempt ill-fortune,
by being a whit more venturesome than before.
Though he considered it a point of good breeding in
himself, as a general friend of the family, to attend
Mr. Dombey's wedding (of which he had heard from
Mr. Perch), and to show that gentleman a pleasant
and approving countenance from the gallery, he had
repaired to the church in a hackney cabriolet with
both windows up; and might have scrupled even to
make that venture, in his dread of Mrs. MacStinger,
but that the lady's attendance on the ministry of the
Reverend Melchisedech rendered it peculiarly unlikely that she would be found in communion with
the Establishment.

The captain got safe home again, and fell into the
ordinary routine of his new life, without encounter-
ing any more direct alarm from the enemy, than was
suggested to him by the daily bonnets in the street.
But other subjects began to lay heavy on the captain's mind. Walter's ship was still unheard of. No
news came of old Sol Gills. Florence did not even
know of the old man's disappearance, and Captain
Cuttle had not the heart to tell her. Indeed the captain, as his own hopes of the generous, handsome,
gallant-hearted youth, whom he had loved, according

to his rough manner, from a child, began to fade, and faded more and more from day to day, shrunk with instinctive pain from the thought of exchanging a word with Florence. If he had had good news to carry to her, the honest captain would have braved the newly decorated house and splendid furniture—though these, connected with the lady he had seen at church, were awful to him—and made his way into her presence. With a dark horizon gathering around their common hopes, however, that darkened every hour, the captain almost felt as if he were a new misfortune and affliction to her; and was scarcely less afraid of a visit from Florence, than from Mrs. Mac-Stinger herself.

It was a chill dark autumn evening, and Captain Cuttle had ordered a fire to be kindled in the little back-parlour, now more than ever like the cabin of a ship. The rain fell fast, and the wind blew hard; and straying out on the house-top by that stormy bedroom of his old friend, to take an observation of the weather, the captain's heart died within him, when he saw how wild and desolate it was. Not that he associated the weather of that time with poor Walter's destiny, or doubted that if Providence had doomed him to be lost and shipwrecked, it was over, long ago; but that beneath an outward influence, quite distinct from the subject-matter of his thoughts, the captain's spirits sank, and his hopes turned pale, as those of wiser men had often done before him, and will often do again.

Captain Cuttle, addressing his face to the sharp wind and slanting rain, looked up at the heavy scud that was flying fast over the wilderness of house-tops, and looked for something cheery there in vain. The prospect near at hand was no better. In sundry tea-chests and other rough boxes at his feet, the pigeons of Rob the Grinder were cooing like so many dismal breezes getting up. A crazy weathercock of a midshipman, with a telescope at his eye, once visible from the street, but long bricked out, creaked and complained upon his rusty pivot as the shrill blast spun him round and round, and sported with him cruelly. Upon the captain's coarse blue vest the cold raindrops started like steel beads; and he could hardly maintain himself aslant against the stiff nor'-wester that came pressing against him, importunate to topple him over the parapet, and throw him on the pavement below. If there were any Hope alive that evening, the captain thought, as he held his hat on, it certainly kept house, and wasn't out of doors; so the captain, shaking his head in a despondent manner, went in to look for it.

Captain Cuttle descended slowly to the little backparlour, and, seated in his accustomed chair, looked for it in the fire; but it was not there, though the fire was bright. He took out his tobacco-box and pipe, and composing himself to smoke, looked for it in the red glow from the bowl, and in the wreaths of vapour that curled upward from his lips; but there was not so much as an atom of the rust of Hope's anchor in either. He tried a glass of grog; but melancholy truth was at the bottom of that well, and he couldn't finish it. He made a turn or two in the shop, and looked for Hope among the instruments; but they obstinately worked out reckonings for the missing ship, in spite of any opposition he could offer, that ended at the bottom of the lone sea.

The wind still rushing, and the rain still pattering, against the closed shutters, the captain brought to before the wooden midshipman upon the counter, and thought, as he dried the little officer's uniform with his sleeve, how many years the midshipman had seen, during which few changes—hardly any—had transpired among his ship's company; how the changes had come all together, one day, as it might be; and of what a sweeping kind they were. Here was the little society of the back-parlour broken up, and scattered far and wide. Here was no audience for Lovely Peg, even if there had been anybody to sing it, which there was not, for the captain was as morally certain that nobody but he could execute that ballad, as he was that he had not the spirit, under existing circumstances, to attempt it. There was no bright face of 'Wal'r' in the house;—here the captain transferred his sleeve for a moment from the midshipman's uniform to his own cheek;—the familiar wig and buttons of Sol Gills were a vision of the past; Richard Whittington was knocked on the head; and every plan and project, in connection with the midshipman, lay drifting, without mast or rudder, on the waste of waters.

As the captain, with a dejected face, stood revolving these thoughts, and polishing the midshipman, partly in the tenderness of old acquaintance, and partly in the absence of his mind, a knocking at the shop-door communicated a frightful start to the frame of Rob the Grinder, seated on the counter, whose large eyes had been intently fixed on the captain's face, and who had been debating within himself, for the five hundredth time, whether the captain could have done a murder, that he had such an evil conscience, and was always running away.

'What 's that!' said Captain Cuttle, softly.

'Somebody's knuckles, captain,' answered Rob the Grinder.

The captain, with an abashed and guilty air, immediately sneaked on tiptoe to the little parlour and locked himself in. Rob, opening the door, would have parleyed with the visitor on the threshold if the visitor

had come in female guise; but the figure being of the
male sex, and Rob's orders only applying to women,
Rob held the door open and allowed it to enter: which
it did very quickly, glad to get out of the driving
rain.

'A job for Burgess and Co. at any rate,' said the
visitor, looking over his shoulder compassionately at
his own legs, which were very wet and covered with
splashes. 'Oh, how-de-do, Mr. Gills?'

The salutation was addressed to the captain, now
emerging from the back-parlour with a most transparent and utterly futile affectation of coming out by
accident.

'Thankee,' the gentleman went on to say in the
same breath; 'I 'm very well indeed, myself, I 'm much
obliged to you. My name is Toots,—*Mister* Toots.'

The captain remembered to have seen this young
gentleman at the wedding, and made him a bow. Mr.
Toots replied with a chuckle; and being embarrassed,
as he generally was, breathed hard, shook hands with
the captain for a long time, and then falling on Rob
the Grinder, in the absence of any other resource,
shook hands with him in a most affectionate and cordial manner.

'I say; I should like to speak a word to you, Mr.
Gills, if you please,' said Toots at length, with surprising presence of mind. 'I say! Miss D. O. M.
you know!'

The captain, with responsive gravity and mystery,
immediately waved his hook towards the little parlour,
whither Mr. Toots followed him.

'Oh! I beg your pardon though,' said Mr. Toots,
looking up in the captain's face as he sat down in a
chair by the fire, which the captain placed for him;
'you don't happen to know the Chicken at all; do you,
Mr. Gills?'

'The Chicken?' said the captain.

'The Game Chicken,' said Mr. Toots.

The captain shaking his head, Mr. Toots explained that the man alluded to was the celebrated public character who had covered himself and his country with glory in his contest with the Nobby Shropshire One; but this piece of information did not appear to enlighten the captain very much.

'Because he 's outside: that 's all,' said Mr. Toots. 'But it 's of no consequence; he won't get very wet, perhaps.'

'I can pass the word for him in a moment,' said the captain.

'Well, if you *would* have the goodness to let him sit in the shop with your young man,' chuckled Mr. Toots, 'I should be glad; because, you know, he 's easily offended, and the damp 's rather bad for his stamina. *I* 'll call him in, Mr. Gills.'

With that, Mr. Toots repairing to the shop-door, sent a peculiar whistle into the night, which produced a stoical gentleman in a shaggy white great-coat and a flat-brimmed hat, with very short hair, a broken nose, and a considerable tract of bare and sterile country behind each ear.

'Sit down, Chicken,' said Mr. Toots.

The compliant Chicken spat out some small pieces of straw on which he was regaling himself, and took in a fresh supply from a reserve he carried in his hand.

'There an't no drain of nothing short handy, is there?' said the Chicken, generally. 'This here sluicing night is hard lines to a man as lives on his condition.'

Captain Cuttle proffered a glass of rum, which the Chicken, throwing back his head, emptied into himself, as into a cask, after proposing the brief sentiment, 'Towards us!' Mr. Toots and the captain returning then to the parlour, and taking their seats before the fire, Mr. Toots began—

'Mr. Gills—'

'Awast!' said the captain. 'My name's Cuttle.'

Mr. Toots looked greatly disconcerted, while the captain proceeded gravely.

'Cap'en Cuttle is my name, and England is my nation, this here is my dwelling-place, and blessed be creation—Job,' said the captain, as an index to his authority.

'Oh! I couldn't see Mr. Gills, could I?' said Mr. Toots; 'because—'

'If you could see Sol Gills, young gen'l'm'n,' said the captain, impressively, and laying his heavy hand on Mr. Toots's knee, 'old Sol, mind you—with your own eyes—as you sit there—you'd be welcomer to me, than a wind astern, to a ship becalmed. But you can't see Sol Gills. And why can't you see Sol Gills?' said the captain, apprised by the face of Mr. Toots that he was making a profound impression on that gentleman's mind. 'Because he's inwisible.'

Mr. Toots in his agitation was going to reply that it was of no consequence at all. But he corrected himself, and said, 'Lor bless me!'

'That there man,' said the captain, 'has left me in charge here by a piece of writing, but though he was a'most as good as my sworn brother, I know no more where he's gone, or why he's gone; if so be to seek his nevy, or if so be along of being not quite settled in his mind; than you do. One morning at daybreak, he went over the side,' said the captain, 'without a splash, without a ripple. I have looked for that man high and low, and never set eyes, nor ears, nor nothing else, upon him, from that hour.'

'But, good gracious, Miss Dombey don't know—' Mr. Toots began.

'Why, I ask you, as a feeling heart,' said the captain, dropping his voice, 'why should she know? why should she be made to know, until such time as there warn't any help for it? She took to old Sol Gills, did that sweet creetur, with a kindness, with a affability, with a—what's the good of saying so? you know her.'

'I should hope so,' chuckled Mr. Toots, with a conscious blush that suffused his whole countenance.

'And you come here from her?' said the captain.

'I should think so,' chuckled Mr. Toots.

'Then all I need observe, is,' said the captain, 'that you know a angel, and are chartered *by* a angel.'

Mr. Toots instantly seized the captain's hand, and requested the favour of his friendship.

'Upon my word and honour,' said Mr. Toots, earnestly, 'I should be very much obliged to you if you'd improve my acquaintance. I should like to know you, captain, very much. I really am in want of a friend, I am. Little Dombey was my friend at old Blimber's, and would have been now, if he'd have lived. The Chicken,' said Mr. Toots, in a forlorn whisper, 'is very well—admirable in his way—the sharpest man perhaps in the world; there's not a move he isn't up to, everybody says so—but I don't know—he's not everything. So she *is* an angel, captain. If there is an angel anywhere, it's Miss Dombey. That's what I've always said. Really though, you know,' said Mr. Toots, 'I should be very much obliged to you if you'd cultivate my acquaintance.'

Captain Cuttle received this proposal in a polite manner, but still without committing himself to its acceptance; merely observing, 'Aye, aye, my lad.

We shall see, we shall see'; and reminding Mr. Toots of his immediate mission, by inquiring to what he was indebted for the honour of that visit.

'Why the fact is,' replied Mr. Toots, 'that it 's the young woman I come from. Not Miss Dombey—Susan you know.'

The captain nodded his head once, with a grave expression of face, indicative of his regarding that young woman with serious respect.

'And I 'll tell you how it happens,' said Mr. Toots. 'You know, I go and call sometimes, on Miss Dombey. I don't go there on purpose, you know, but I happen to be in the neighbourhood very often; and when I find myself there, why—why I call.'

'Nat'rally,' observed the captain.

'Yes,' said Mr. Toots. 'I called this afternoon. Upon my word and honour, I don't think it 's possible to form an idea of the angel Miss Dombey was this afternoon.'

The captain answered with a jerk of his head, implying that it might not be easy to some people, but was quite so to him.

'As I was coming out,' said Mr. Toots, 'the young woman, in the most unexpected manner, took me into the pantry.'

The captain seemed, for the moment, to object to this proceeding: and leaning back in his chair, looked at Mr. Toots with a distrustful, if not threatening visage.

'Where she brought out,' said Mr. Toots, 'this newspaper. She told me that she had kept it from Miss Dombey all day, on account of something that was in it, about somebody that she and Dombey used to know; and then she read the passage to me. Very well. Then she said—wait a minute; what was it, she said though?'

Mr. Toots, endeavouring to concentrate his mental powers on this question, unintentionally fixed the captain's eye, and was so much discomposed by its stern expression, that his difficulty in resuming the thread of his subject was enhanced to a painful extent.

'Oh!' said Mr. Toots after long consideration. 'Oh, ah! Yes! She said that she hoped there was a bare possibility that it mightn't be true; and that as she couldn't very well come out herself, without surprising Miss Dombey, would I go down to Mr. Solomon Gills the instrument-maker's in this street, who was the party's uncle, and ask whether he believed it was true, or had heard anything else in the City. She said, if he couldn't speak to me, no doubt Captain Cuttle could. By the bye!' said Mr. Toots, as the discovery flashed upon him, 'you, you know!'

The captain glanced at the newspaper in Mr. Toots's hand, and breathed short and hurriedly.

'Well,' pursued Mr. Toots, 'the reason why I 'm rather late is, because I went up as far as Finchley first, to get some uncommonly fine chickweed that grows there, for Miss Dombey's bird. But I came on here, directly afterwards. You 've seen the paper, I suppose?'

The captain, who had become cautious of reading the news, lest he should find himself advertised at full length by Mrs. MacStinger, shook his head.

'Shall I read the passage to you?' inquired Mr. Toots.

The captain making a sign in the affirmative, Mr. Toots read as follows from the Shipping Intelligence—

' "Southampton. The barque Defiance, Henry James, commander, arrived in this port to-day, with a cargo of sugar, coffee, and rum, reports that being becalmed on the sixth day of her passage home from

Jamaica, in"—in such and such a latitude, you know,' said Mr. Toots, after making a feeble dash at the figures, and tumbling over them.

'Aye!' cried the captain, striking his clenched hand on the table. 'Heave ahead, my lad!'

'—latitude,' repeated Mr. Toots, with a startled glance at the captain, 'and longitude so-and-so,—"the look-out observed, half an hour before sunset, some fragments of a wreck, drifting at about the distance of a mile. The weather being clear, and the barque making no way, a boat was hoisted out, with orders to inspect the same, when they were found to consist of sundry large spars, and a part of the main rigging of an English brig, of about five hundred tons burden, together with a portion of the stern on which the words and letters 'Son and H—' were yet plainly legible. No vestige of any dead body was to be seen upon the floating fragments. Log of the Defiance states, that a breeze springing up in the night, the wreck was seen no more. There can be no doubt that all surmises as to the fate of the missing vessel, the Son and Heir, port of London, bound for Barbados, are now set at rest for ever; that she broke up in the last hurricane; and that every soul on board perished." '

Captain Cuttle, like all mankind, little knew how much hope had survived within him under discouragement, until he felt its death-shock. During the reading of the paragraph, and for a minute or two afterwards, he sat with his gaze fixed on the modest Mr. Toots, like a man entranced; then, suddenly rising, and putting on his glazed hat, which, in his visitor's honour, he had laid upon the table, the captain turned his back, and bent his head down on the little chimney-piece.

'Oh, upon my word and honour,' cried Mr. Toots,

whose tender heart was moved by the captain's unexpected distress, 'this is a most wretched sort of affair
this world is! Somebody's always dying, or going
and doing something uncomfortable in it. I'm sure
I never should have looked forward so much, to coming into my property, if I had known this. I never
saw such a world. It's a great deal worse than
Blimber's.'

Captain Cuttle, without altering his position, signed
to Mr. Toots not to mind him; and presently turned
round, with his glazed hat thrust back upon his ears,
and his hand composing and smoothing his brown face.

'Wal'r, my dear lad,' said the captain, 'farewell!
Wal'r my child, my boy, and man, I loved you! He
warn't my flesh and blood,' said the captain, looking
at the fire—'I an't got none—but something of what
a father feels when he loses a son, I feel in losing
Wal'r. For why?' said the captain. 'Because it an't
one loss, but a round dozen. Where's that there
young schoolboy with the rosy face and curly hair,
that used to be as merry in this here parlour, come
round every week, as a piece of music? Gone down
with Wal'r. Where's that there fresh lad, that nothing couldn't tire nor put out, and that sparkled up and
blushed so, when we joked him about Heart's Delight, that he was beautiful to look at? Gone down
with Wal'r. Where's that there man's spirit, all
afire, that wouldn't see the old man hove down for a
minute, and cared nothing for itself? Gone down
with Wal'r. It an't one Wal'r. There was a dozen
Wal'rs that I know'd and loved, all holding round
his neck when he went down, and they're a holding
round mine now!'

Mr. Toots sat silent: folding and refolding the
newspaper as small as possible upon his knee.

'And Sol Gills,' said the captain, gazing at the

fire, 'poor nevyless old Sol, where are *you* got to?
You was left in charge of me; his last words was,
"Take care of my uncle." What came over *you*, Sol,
when you went and gave the go-by to Ned Cuttle?
and what am I to put in my accounts that he's a
looking down upon, respecting you! Sol Gills, Sol
Gills!' said the captain, shaking his head slowly, 'catch
sight of that there newspaper, away from home, with
no one as know'd Wal'r by, to say a word; and broad-
side to you broach, and down you pitch, head foremost!'

Drawing a heavy sigh, the captain turned to Mr.
Toots, and roused himself to a sustained consciousness of that gentleman's presence.

'My lad,' said the captain, 'you must tell the young
woman honestly that this here fatal news is too correct. They don't romance, you see, on such p'ints.
It's entered on the ship's log, and that's the truest
book as a man can write. To-morrow morning,' said
the captain, 'I'll step out and make inquiries; but
they'll lead to no good. They can't do it. If you'll
give me a look-in in the forenoon, you shall know what
I have heerd; but tell the young woman from Cap'en
Cuttle, that it's over. Over!' And the captain,
hooking off his glazed hat, pulled his handkerchief
out of the crown, wiped his grizzled head despairingly,
and tossed the handkerchief in again with the indifference of deep dejection.

'Oh! I assure you,' said Mr. Toots, 'really I am
dreadfully sorry. Upon my word I am, though I
wasn't acquainted with the party. Do you think Miss
Dombey will be very much affected, Captain Gills—
I mean Mr. Cuttle?'

'Why, Lord love you,' returned the captain, with
something of compassion for Mr. Toots's innocence.

'When she warn't no higher than that, they were as fond of one another as two young doves.'

'Were they though?' said Mr. Toots, with a considerably lengthened face.

'They were made for one another,' said the captain, mournfully; 'but what signifies that now?'

'Upon my word and honour,' cried Mr. Toots, blurting out his words through a singular combination of awkward chuckles and emotion, 'I 'm even more sorry than I was before. You know, Captain Gills, I—I positively adore Miss Dombey;—I—I am perfectly sore with loving her'; the burst with which this confession forced itself out of the unhappy Mr. Toots, bespoke the vehemence of his feelings; 'but what would be the good of my regarding her in this manner, if I wasn't truly sorry for her feeling pain, whatever was the cause of it? Mine an't a selfish affection, you know,' said Mr. Toots, in the confidence engendered by his having been a witness of the captain's tenderness. 'It 's the sort of thing with me, Captain Gills, that if I could be run over—or—or trampled upon—or—or thrown off a very high place —or anything of that sort—for Miss Dombey's sake, it would be the most delightful thing that could happen to me.'

All this, Mr. Toots said in a suppressed voice, to prevent its reaching the jealous ears of the Chicken, who objected to the softer emotions; which effort of restraint, coupled with the intensity of his feelings, made him red to the tips of his ears, and caused him to present such an affecting spectacle of disinterested love to the eyes of Captain Cuttle that the good captain patted him consolingly on the back, and bade him cheer up.

'Thank 'ee, Captain Gills,' said Mr. Toots, 'it 's

kind of you, in the midst of your own troubles, to say
so. I'm very much obliged to you. As I said before, I really want a friend, and should be glad to
have your acquaintance. Although I am very well
off,' said Mr. Toots, with energy, 'you can't think
what a miserable beast I am. The hollow crowd, you
know, when they see me with the Chicken, and characters of distinction like that, suppose me to be happy;
but I'm wretched. I suffer for Miss Dombey, Captain Gills. I can't get through my meals; I have
no pleasure in my tailor; I often cry when I'm alone.
I assure you it 'll be a satisfaction to me to come back
to-morrow, or to come back fifty times.'

Mr. Toots, with these words, shook the captain's
hand; and disguising such traces of his agitation as
could be disguised on so short a notice, before the
Chicken's penetrating glance, rejoined that eminent
gentleman in the shop. The Chicken, who was apt
to be jealous of his ascendancy, eyed Captain Cuttle
with anything but favour as he took leave of Mr.
Toots; but followed his patron without being otherwise demonstrative of his ill-will: leaving the captain
oppressed with sorrow; and Rob the Grinder elevated
with joy, on account of having had the honour of
staring for nearly half an hour, at the conqueror of
the Nobby Shropshire One.

Long after Rob was fast asleep in his bed under
the counter, the captain sat looking at the fire; and
long after there was no fire to look at, the captain
sat gazing on the rusty bars with unavailing thoughts
of Walter and old Sol crowding through his mind.
Retirement to the stormy chamber at the top of the
house brought no rest with it; and the captain rose
up in the morning, sorrowful and unrefreshed.

As soon as the City offices were open, the captain

issued forth to the counting-house of Dombey and Son. But there was no opening of the midshipman's windows that morning. Rob the Grinder, by the captain's orders, left the shutters closed, and the house was as the house of death.

It chanced that Mr. Carker was entering the office, as Captain Cuttle arrived at the door. Receiving the manager's benison gravely and silently, Captain Cuttle made bold to accompany him into his own room.

'Well, Captain Cuttle,' said Mr. Carker, taking up his usual position before the fireplace, and keeping on his hat, 'this is a bad business.'

'You have received the news as was in print yesterday, sir?' said the captain.

'Yes,' said Mr. Carker, 'we have received it! It was accurately stated. The underwriters suffer a considerable loss. We are very sorry. No help! Such is life!'

Mr. Carker pared his nails delicately with a penknife, and smiled at the captain, who was standing by the door looking at him.

'I excessively regret poor Gay,' said Carker, 'and the crew. I understand there were some of our very best men among 'em. It always happens so. Many men with families too. A comfort to reflect that poor Gay had no family, Captain Cuttle!'

The captain stood rubbing his chin, and looking at the manager. The manager glanced at the unopened letters lying on his desk, and took up the newspaper.

'Is there anything I can do for you, Captain Cuttle?' he asked, looking off it, with a smiling and expressive glance at the door.

'I wish you could set my mind at rest, sir, on something it 's uneasy about,' returned the captain.

'Aye!' exclaimed the manager, 'what's that? Come, Captain Cuttle, I must trouble you to be quick, if you please. I am much engaged.'

'Look 'ee here, sir,' said the captain, advancing a step. 'Afore my friend Wal'r went on this here disastrous voyage—'

'Come, come, Captain Cuttle,' interposed the smiling manager, 'don't talk about disastrous voyages in that way. We have nothing to do with disastrous voyages here, my good fellow. You must have begun very early on your day's allowance, captain, if you don't remember that there are hazards in all voyages whether by sea or land. You are not made uneasy by the supposition that young what's-his-name was lost in bad weather that was got up against him in these offices—are you? Fie, captain! Sleep, and soda-water, are the best cures for such uneasiness as that.'

'My lad,' returned the captain, slowly—'you are a'most a lad to me, and so I don't ask your pardon for that slip of a word,—if you find any pleasure in this here sport, you an't the gentleman I took you for, and if you an't the gentleman I took you for, may be my mind has call to be uneasy. Now this is what it is, Mr. Carker.—Afore that poor lad went away, according to orders, he told me that he warn't a going away for his own good, or for promotion, he know'd. It was my belief that he was wrong, and I told him so, and I come here, your head governor being absent, to ask a question or two of you in a civil way, for my own satisfaction. Them questions you answered—free. Now it'll ease my mind to know, when all is over, as it is, and when what can't be cured must be endoored—for which, as a scholar, you'll overhaul the book it's in, and thereof make a note—to know once more, in a word, that I warn't mistaken; that I warn't back'ard in my duty when I didn't tell the old man what Wal'r told me; and that the wind was truly in his sail, when he highsted of it for Barbados Harbour. Mr. Carker,' said the captain, in the goodness of his nature, 'when I was here last, we was very pleasant together. If I ain't been altogether so pleasant myself this morning, on account of this poor lad, and if I have chaf'ed again any observation of yours that I might have fended off, my name is Ed'ard Cuttle, and I ask your pardon.'

'Captain Cuttle,' returned the manager, with all possible politeness, 'I must ask you to do me a favour.'

'And what is it, sir?' inquired the captain.

'To have the goodness to walk off, if you please,' rejoined the manager, stretching forth his arm, 'and to carry your jargon somewhere else.'

Every knob in the captain's face turned white with astonishment and indignation; even the red rim on his forehead faded, like a rainbow among the gathering clouds.

'I tell you what, Captain Cuttle,' said the manager, shaking his forefinger at him, and showing him all his teeth, but still amiably smiling, 'I was much too lenient with you when you came here before. You belong to an artful and audacious set of people. In my desire to save young what's-his-name from being kicked out of this place, neck and crop, my good captain, I tolerated you; but for once, and only once. Now, go, my friend!'

The captain was absolutely rooted to the ground, and speechless.

'Go,' said the good-humoured manager, gathering up his skirts, and standing astride upon the hearth-rug, 'like a sensible fellow, and let us have no turning out, or any such violent measures. If Mr. Dom-

bey were here, captain, you might be obliged to leave
in a more ignominious manner, possibly. I merely
say, Go!'

The captain, laying his ponderous hand upon his
chest, to assist himself in fetching a deep breath,
looked at Mr. Carker from head to foot, and looked
round the little room, as if he did not clearly understand where he was, or in what company.

'You are deep, Captain Cuttle,' pursued Carker,
with the easy and vivacious frankness of a man of the
world who knew the world too well to be ruffled by
any discovery of misdoing, when it did not immediately concern himself; 'but you are not quite out of
soundings, either—neither you nor your absent friend,
captain. What have you done with your absent
friend, hey?'

Again the captain laid his hand upon his chest.
After drawing another deep breath, he conjured himself to 'stand by!' But in a whisper.

'You hatch nice little plots, and hold nice little
councils, and make nice little appointments, and receive nice little visitors, too, captain, hey?' said Carker,
bending his brows upon him, without showing his
teeth any the less: 'but it's a bold measure to come
here afterwards. Not like your discretion! You
conspirators and hiders, and runners-away, should
know better than that. Will you oblige me by
going?'

'My lad,' gasped the captain, in a choked and
trembling voice, and with a curious action going on
in the ponderous fist; 'there's a many words I could
wish to say to you, but I don't rightly know where
they're stowed just at present. My young friend,
Wal'r, was drownded only last night, according to
my reckoning, and it puts me out, you see. But you
and me will come alongside o' one another again, my

lad,' said the captain, holding up his hook, 'if we live.'

'It will be anything but shrewd in you, my good fellow, if we do,' returned the manager, with the same frankness; 'for you may rely, I give you fair warning, upon my detecting and exposing you. I don't pretend to be a more moral man than my neighbours, my good captain; but the confidence of this house, or of any member of this house, is not to be abused and undermined while I have eyes and ears. Good day,' said Mr. Carker, nodding his head.

Captain Cuttle, looking at him steadily (Mr. Carker looked full as steadily at the captain), went out of the office and left him standing astride before the fire, as calm and pleasant as if there were no more spots upon his soul than on his pure white linen, and his smooth sleek skin.

The captain glanced, in passing through the outer counting-house, at the desk where he knew poor Walter had been used to sit, now occupied by another young boy, with a face almost as fresh and hopeful as his on the day when they tapped the famous last bottle but one of the old Madeira, in the little back-parlour. The association of ideas, thus awakened, did the captain a great deal of good; it softened him in the very height of his anger, and brought the tears into his eyes.

Arrived at the wooden midshipman's again, and sitting down in a corner of the dark shop, the captain's indignation, strong as it was, could make no head against his grief. Passion seemed not only to do wrong and violence to the memory of the dead, but to be infected by death, and to drop and decline beside it. All the living knaves and liars in the world, were nothing to the honesty and truth of one dead friend.

The only thing the honest captain made out clearly,

in this state of mind, besides the loss of Walter was, that with him almost the whole world of Captain Cuttle had been drowned. If he reproached himself sometimes, and keenly too, for having ever connived at Walter's innocent deceit, he thought at least as often of the Mr. Carker whom no sea could ever render up; and the Mr. Dombey, whom he now began to perceive was as far beyond human recall; and the 'Heart's Delight,' with whom he must never foregather again; and the Lovely Peg, that teak-built and trim ballad, that had gone ashore upon a rock, and split into mere planks and beams of rhyme. The captain sat in the dark shop, thinking of these things, to the entire exclusion of his own injury; and looking with as sad an eye upon the ground, as if in contemplation of their actual fragments as they floated past him.

But the captain was not unmindful, for all that, of such decent and respectful observances in memory of poor Walter, as he felt within his power. Rousing himself, and rousing Rob the Grinder (who in the unnatural twilight was fast asleep), the captain sallied forth with his attendant at his heels, and the door-key in his pocket, and repairing to one of those convenient slop-selling establishments of which there is abundant choice at the eastern end of London, purchased on the spot two suits of mourning—one for Rob the Grinder, which was immensely too small, and one for himself, which was immensely too large. He also provided Rob with a species of hat, greatly to be admired for its symmetry and usefulness, as well as for a happy blending of the mariner with the coal-heaver, which is usually termed a sou'wester; and which was something of a novelty in connection with the instrument business. In their several garments, which the vendor declared to be such a miracle in point of fit as nothing but a rare combination of fortuitous circumstances ever brought about, and the fashion of which was unparalleled within the memory of the oldest inhabitant, the captain and Grinder immediately arrayed themselves: presenting a spectacle fraught with wonder to all who beheld it.

In this altered form, the captain received Mr. Toots. 'I 'm took aback, my lad, at present,' said the captain, 'and will only confirm that there ill news. Tell the young woman to break it gently to the young lady, and for neither of 'em never to think of me no more—'special, mind you, that is—though I will think of them, when night comes on a hurricane and seas is mountains rowling, for which overhaul your Doctor Watts, brother, and when found make a note on.'

The captain reserved, until some fitter time, the consideration of Mr. Toots's offer of friendship, and thus dismissed him. Captain Cuttle's spirits were so low, in truth, that he half determined, that day, to take no further precautions against surprise from Mrs. MacStinger, but to abandon himself recklessly to chance, and be indifferent to what might happen. As evening came on, he fell into a better frame of mind, however; and spoke much of Walter to Rob the Grinder, whose attention and fidelity he likewise incidentally commended. Rob did not blush to hear the captain earnest in his praises, but sat staring at him, and affecting to snivel with sympathy, and making a feint of being virtuous, and treasuring up every word he said (like a young spy as he was) with very promising deceit.

When Rob had turned in, and was fast asleep, the captain trimmed the candle, put on his spectacles— he had felt it appropriate to take to spectacles on entering into the instrument trade, though his eyes

were like a hawk's—and opened the prayer-book at
the Burial Service. And reading softly to himself,
in the little back-parlour, and stopping now and then
to wipe his eyes, the captain, in a true and simple
spirit, committed Walter's body to the deep.

CHAPTER XXXIII

CONTRASTS

TURN we our eyes upon two homes; not lying side
by side, but wide apart, though both within easy
range and reach of the great city of London.

The first is situated in the green and wooded country near Norwood. It is not a mansion; it is of no
pretensions as to size; but it is beautifully arranged,
and tastefully kept. The lawn, the soft, smooth
slope, the flower-garden, the clumps of trees where
graceful forms of ash and willow are not wanting,
the conservatory, the rustic verandah with sweet
smelling creeping plants entwined about the pillars,
the simple exterior of the house, the well-ordered
offices, though all upon the diminutive scale proper to
a mere cottage, bespeak an amount of elegant comfort within, that might serve for a palace. This indication is not without warrant; for within it is a
house of refinement and luxury. Rich colours, ex-
cellently blended, meet the eye at every turn; in the
furniture—its proportions admirably devised to suit
the shapes and sizes of the small rooms; on the walls;
upon the floors; tinging and subduing the light that
comes in through the odd glass doors and windows
here and there. There are a few choice prints and
pictures too; in quaint nooks and recesses there is no
want of books; and there are games of skill and

chance set forth on tables—fantastic chess-men, dice, backgammon, cards, and billiards.

And yet amidst this opulence of comfort, there is something in the general air that is not well. Is it that the carpets and the cushions are too soft and noiseless, so that those who move or repose among them seem to act by stealth! Is it that the prints and pictures do not commemorate great thoughts or deeds, or render nature in the poetry of landscape, hall, or hut, but are of one voluptuous cast—mere shows of form and colour—and no more? Is it that the books have all their gold outside, and that the titles of the greater part qualify them to be companions of the prints and pictures? Is it that the completeness and the beauty of the place are here and there belied by an affectation of humility, in some unimportant and inexpensive regard, which is as false as the face of the too truly painted portrait hanging yonder, or its original at breakfast in his easy chair below it? Or is it that, with the daily breath of that original and master of all here, there issues forth some subtle portion of himself, which gives a vague expression of himself to everything about him?

It is Mr. Carker the manager who sits in the easy chair. A gaudy parrot in a burnished cage upon the table tears at the wires with her beak, and goes walking, upside down, in its dome-top, shaking her house and screeching; but Mr. Carker is indifferent to the bird, and looks with a musing smile at a picture on the opposite wall.

'A most extraordinary accidental likeness, certainly,' says he.

Perhaps it is a Juno; perhaps a Potiphar's Wife; perhaps some scornful Nymph—according as the picture dealers found the market, when they christened it. It is the figure of a woman, supremely handsome, who, turning away, but with her face addressed to the spectator, flashes her proud glance upon him.

It is like Edith.

With a passing gesture of his hand at the picture —what! a menace? No; yet something like it. A wave as of triumph? No; yet more like that. An insolent salute wafted from his lips? No; yet like that too—he resumes his breakfast, and calls to the chafing and imprisoned bird, who coming down into a pendent gilded hoop within the cage, like a great wedding-ring, swings in it, for his delight.

The second home is on the other side of London, near to where the busy great north road of bygone days is silent and almost deserted, except by wayfarers who toil along on foot. It is a poor, small house, barely and sparely furnished, but very clean; and there is even an attempt to decorate it, shown in the homely flowers trained about the porch and in the narrow garden. The neighbourhood in which it stands has as little of the country to recommend it, as it has of the town. It is neither of the town nor country. The former, like the giant in his travelling boots, has made a stride and passed it, and has set his brick-and-mortar heel a long way in advance; but the intermediate space between the giant's feet, as yet, is only blighted country, and not town; and, here, among a few tall chimneys belching smoke all day and night, and among the brickfields and the lanes where turf is cut, and where the fences tumble down, and where the dusty nettles grow, and where a scrap or two of hedge may yet be seen, and where the bird-catcher still comes occasionally, though he swears every time to come no more—this second home is to be found.

She who inhabits it, is she who left the first in her devotion to an outcast brother. She withdrew from that home its redeeming spirit, and from its master's breast his solitary angel: but though his liking for her is gone, after this ungrateful slight as he considers it; and though he abandons her altogether in return, an old idea of her is not quite forgotten even by him. Let her flower-garden, in which he never sets his foot, but which is yet maintained, among all his costly alterations, as if she had quitted it but yesterday, bear witness!

Harriet Carker has changed since then, and on her beauty there has fallen a heavier shade than Time of his unassisted self can cast, all-potent as he is—the shadow of anxiety and sorrow, and the daily struggle of a poor existence. But it is beauty still; and still a gentle, quiet, and retiring beauty that must be sought out, for it cannot vaunt itself; if it could, it would be what it is, no more.

Yes. This slight, small, patient figure, neatly dressed in homely stuffs, and indicating nothing but the dull, household virtues, that have so little in common with the received idea of heroism and greatness, unless, indeed, any ray of them should shine through the lives of the great ones of the earth, when it becomes a constellation and is tracked in Heaven straightway—this slight, small, patient figure, leaning on the man still young but worn and grey, is she his sister, who, of all the world, went over to him in his shame and put her hand in his, and with a sweet composure and determination, led him hopefully upon his barren way.

'It is early, John,' she said. 'Why do you go so early?'

'Not many minutes earlier than usual, Harriet. If I have the time to spare, I should like, I think—it's a fancy—to walk once by the house where I took leave of him.'

'I wish I had ever seen or known him, John.

'It is better as it is, my dear, remembering his fate.'

'But I could not regret it more, though I had known him. Is not your sorrow mine? And if I had, perhaps you would feel that I was a better companion to you in speaking about him, than I may seem now.'

'My dearest sister! Is there anything within the range of rejoicing or regret, in which I am not sure of your companionship?'

'I hope you think not, John, for surely there is nothing!'

'How could you be better to me, or nearer to me then, than you are in this, or anything?' said her brother. 'I feel that you did know him, Harriet, and that you shared my feelings towards him.'

She drew the hand which had been resting on his shoulder, round his neck, and answered, with some hesitation.

'No, not quite.'

'True, true!' he said; 'you think I might have done him no harm if I had allowed myself to know him better?'

'Think! I know it.'

'Designedly, Heaven knows I would not,' he replied, shaking his head mournfully; 'but his reputation was too precious to be perilled by such association. Whether you share that knowledge, or do not, my dear—'

'I do not,' she said quietly.

'It is still the truth, Harriet, and my mind is lighter when I think of him for that which made it so much heavier then.' He checked himself in his tone of melancholy, and smiled upon her as he said 'Goodbye!'

'Good-bye, dear John! In the evening, at the old

time and place, I shall meet you as usual on your way
home. Good-bye.'

The cordial face she lifted up to his to kiss him,
was his home, his life, his universe, and yet it was a
portion of his punishment and grief; for in the cloud
he saw upon it—though serene and calm as any radiant cloud at sunset—and in the constancy and devotion of her life, and in the sacrifice she had made of
ease, enjoyment, and hope, he saw the bitter fruits
of his old crime, for ever ripe and fresh.

She stood at the door looking after him, with her
hands loosely clasped in each other, as he made his
way over the frowzy and uneven patch of ground
which lay before their house, which had once (and not
long ago) been a pleasant meadow, and was now a
very waste, with a disorderly crop of beginnings of
mean houses, rising out of the rubbish, as if they had
been unskilfully sown there. Whenever he looked
back—as once or twice he did—her cordial face shone
like a light upon his heart; but when he plodded on
his way, and saw her not, the tears were in her eyes
as she stood watching him.

Her pensive form was not long idle at the door.
There was daily duty to discharge, and daily work to
do—for such commonplace spirits that are not heroic,
often work hard with their hands—and Harriet was
soon busy with her household tasks. These discharged, and the poor house made quite neat and
orderly, she counted her little stock of money, with
an anxious face, and went out thoughtfully to buy
some necessaries for their table, planning and con-
triving, as she went, how to save. So sordid are the
lives of such low natures, who are not only not heroic
to their valets and waiting-women, but have neither
valets nor waiting-women, to be heroic to withal!

While she was absent, and there was no one in the

house, there approached it by a different way from
that the brother had taken, a gentleman, a very little
past his prime of life perhaps, but of a healthy florid
hue, an upright presence, and a bright clear aspect,
that was gracious and good-humoured. His eyebrows were still black, and so was much of his hair;
the sprinkling of grey observable among the latter,
graced the former very much, and showed his broad
frank brow and honest eyes to great advantage.

After knocking once at the door, and obtaining no
response, this gentleman sat down on a bench in the
little porch to wait. A certain skilful action of his
fingers as he hummed some bars, and beat time on the
seat beside him, seemed to denote the musician; and
the extraordinary satisfaction he derived from humming something very slow and long, which had no
recognisable tune, seemed to denote that he was a
scientific one.

The gentleman was still twirling a theme, which
seemed to go round and round and round, and in and
in and in, and to involve itself like a corkscrew twirled
upon a table, without getting any nearer to anything,
when Harriet appeared returning. He rose up as she
advanced, and stood with his head uncovered.

'You are come again, sir!' she said, faltering.

'I take that liberty,' he answered. 'May I ask for
five minutes of your leisure?'

After a moment's hesitation, she opened the door,
and gave him admission to the little parlour. The
gentleman sat down there, drew his chair to the table
over against her, and said, in a voice that perfectly
corresponded to his appearance, and with a simplicity
that was very engaging—

'Miss Harriet, you cannot be proud. You signified to me, when I called t' other morning, that you
were. Pardon me if I say that I looked into your

A VISITOR OF DISTINCTION.

face while you spoke, and that it contradicted you.
I look into it again,' he added, laying his hand gently
on her arm, for an instant, 'and it contradicts you
more and more.'

She was somewhat confused and agitated, and
could make no ready answer.

'It is the mirror of truth,' said her visitor, 'and gentleness. Excuse my trusting to it, and returning.'

His manner of saying these words, divested them
entirely of the character of compliments. It was so
plain, grave, unaffected, and sincere, that she bent
her head, as if at once to thank him, and acknowledge
his sincerity.

'The disparity between our ages,' said the gentleman, 'and the plainness of my purpose, empower me,
I am glad to think, to speak my mind. That is my
mind; and so you see me for the second time.'

'There is a kind of pride, sir,' she returned, after
a moment's silence, 'or what may be supposed to be
pride, which is mere duty. I hope I cherish no other.'

'For yourself,' he said.

'For myself.'

'But—pardon me—' suggested the gentleman.
'For your brother John?'

'Proud of his love, I am,' said Harriet, looking full
upon her visitor, and changing her manner on the
instant—not that it was less composed and quiet, but
that there was a deep impassioned earnestness in it
that made the very tremble in her voice a part of her
firmness, 'and proud of him. Sir, you who strangely
know the story of his life, and repeated it to me when
you were here last—'

'Merely to make my way into your confidence,' interposed the gentleman. 'For Heaven's sake, don't
suppose—'

'I am sure,' she said, 'you revived it, in my hearing,

with a kind and good purpose. I am quite sure of it.'

'I thank you,' returned her visitor, pressing her hand hastily. 'I am much obliged to you. You do me justice, I assure you. You were going to say, that I, who know the story of John Carker's life—'

'May think it pride in me,' she continued, 'when I say that I am proud of him! I *am*. You know the time was, when I was not—when I could not be—but that is past. The humility of many years, the uncomplaining expiation, the true repentance, the terrible regret, the pain I know he has even in my affection, which he thinks has cost me dear, though Heaven knows I am happy, but for his sorrow!—oh, sir, after what I have seen, let me conjure you, if you are in any place of power, and are ever wronged, never, for any wrong, inflict a punishment that cannot be recalled; while there is a GOD above us to work changes in the hearts He made.'

'Your brother is an altered man,' returned the gentleman, compassionately. 'I assure you I don't doubt it.'

'He was an altered man when he did wrong,' said Harriet. 'He is an altered man again, and is his true self now, believe me, sir.'

'But we go on,' said her visitor, rubbing his forehead, in an absent manner, with his hand, and then drumming thoughtfully on the table, 'we go on in our clockwork routine, from day to day, and can't make out, or follow, these changes. They—they 're a metaphysical sort of thing. We—we haven't leisure for it. We—we haven't courage. They 're not taught at schools or colleges, and we don't know how to set about it. In short, we are so d—d business-like,' said the gentleman, walking to the window, and back, and sitting down again, in a state of extreme dissatisfaction and vexation.

'I am sure,' said the gentleman, rubbing his forehead again; and drumming on the table as before, 'I have good reason to believe that a jog-trot life, the same from day to day, would reconcile one to anything. One don't see anything, one don't hear anything, one don't know anything; that's the fact. We go on taking everything for granted, and so we go on, until whatever we do, good, bad, or indifferent, we do from habit. Habit is all I shall have to report, when I am called upon to plead to my conscience, on my death-bed. "Habit," says I; "I was deaf, dumb, blind, and paralytic, to a million things, from habit." "Very business-like indeed, Mr. What's-your-name," says Conscience, "but it won't do here!"'

The gentleman got up and walked to the window again and back: seriously uneasy, though giving his uneasiness this peculiar expression.

'Miss Harriet,' he said, resuming his chair, 'I wish you would let me serve you. Look at me; I ought to look honest, for I know I am so, at present. Do I?'

'Yes,' she answered with a smile.

'I believe every word you have said,' he returned. 'I am full of self-reproach that I might have known this and seen this, and known you and seen you, any time these dozen years, and that I never have. I hardly know how I ever got here—creature that I am, not only of my own habit, but of other people's! But having done so, let me do something. I ask it in all honour and respect. You inspire me with both, in the highest degree. Let me do something.'

'We are contented, sir.'

'No, no, not quite,' returned the gentleman. 'I think not quite. There are some little comforts that might smooth your life, and his. And his!' he repeated, fancying that had made some impression on

her. 'I have been in the habit of thinking that there
was nothing wanting to be done for him; that it was
all settled and over; in short, of not thinking at all
about it. I am different now. Let me do something
for him. You too,' said the visitor, with careful delicacy, 'have need to watch your health closely, for his
sake, and I fear it fails.'

'Whoever you may be, sir,' answered Harriet, raising her eyes to his face, 'I am deeply grateful to you.
I feel certain that in all you say, you have no object
in the world but kindness to us. But years have
passed since we began this life; and to take from my
brother any part of what has so endeared him to me,
and so proved his better resolution—any fragment of
the merit of his unassisted, obscure, and forgotten
reparation—would be to diminish the comfort it will
be to him and me, when that time comes to each of
us, of which you spoke just now. I thank you better
with these tears than any words. Believe it, pray.'

The gentleman was moved, and put the hand she
held out, to his lips, much as a tender father might
kiss the hand of a dutiful child. But more reverently.

'If the day should ever come,' said Harriet, 'when
he is restored, in part, to the position he lost—'

'Restored!' cried the gentleman, quickly. 'How
can that be hoped for? In whose hands does the
power of any restoration lie? It is no mistake of
mine, surely, to suppose that his having gained the
priceless blessing of his life, is one cause of the an-
imosity shown to him by his brother.'

'You touch upon a subject that is never breathed
between us; not even between us,' said Harriet.

'I beg your forgiveness,' said the visitor. 'I should
have known it. I entreat you to forget that I have
done so, inadvertently. And now, as I dare urge
no more—as I am not sure that I have a right to do

so—though Heaven knows, even that doubt may be habit,' said the gentleman, rubbing his head, as despondently as before, 'let me; though a stranger, yet no stranger; ask two favours.'

'What are they?' she inquired.

'The first, that if you should see cause to change your resolution, you will suffer me to be as your right hand. My name shall then be at your service: it is useless now, and always insignificant.'

'Our choice of friends,' she answered, smiling faintly, 'is not so great, that I need any time for consideration. I can promise that.'

'The second, that you will allow me sometimes, say every Monday morning, at nine o'clock—habit again—I must be business-like,' said the gentleman, with a whimsical inclination to quarrel with himself on that head, 'in walking past, to see you at the door or window. I don't ask to come in, as your brother will be gone out at that hour. I don't ask to speak to you. I merely ask to see, for the satisfaction of my own mind, that you are well, and without intrusion to remind you, by the sight of me, that you have a friend—an elderly friend, grey-haired already, and fast growing greyer—whom you may ever command.'

The cordial face looked up in his; confided in it; and promised.

'I understand, as before,' said the gentleman, rising, 'that you purpose not to mention my visit to John Carker, lest he should be at all distressed by my acquaintance with his history. I am glad of it, for it is out of the ordinary course of things, and—habit again!' said the gentleman, checking himself impatiently, 'as if there were no better course than the ordinary course!'

With that he turned to go, and walking, bare-

headed, to the outside of the little porch, took leave
of her with such a happy mixture of unconstrained
respect and unaffected interest, as no breeding could
have taught, no truth mistrusted, and nothing but a
pure and single heart expressed.

Many half-forgotten emotions were awakened in
the sister's mind by this visit. It was so very long
since any other visitor had crossed their threshold;
it was so very long since any voice of sympathy had
made sad music in her ears; that the stranger's figure
remained present to her, hours afterwards, when she
sat at the window, plying her needle; and his words
seemed newly spoken, again and again. He had
touched the spring that opened her whole life; and if
she lost him for a short space, it was only among
the many shapes of the one great recollection of which
that life was made.

Musing and working by turns; now constraining
herself to be steady at her needle for a long time
together, and now letting her work fall, unregarded,
on her lap, and straying wheresoever her busier
thoughts led, Harriet Carker found the hours glide
by her, and the day steal on. The morning, which
had been bright and clear, gradually became over-
cast; a sharp wind set in; the rain fell heavily; and
a dark mist drooping over the distant town, hid it
from the view.

She often looked with compassion, at such a time,
upon the stragglers who came wandering into London, by the great highway hard by, and who, foot-
sore and weary, and gazing fearfully at the huge
town before them, as if foreboding that their misery
there would be but as a drop of water in the sea, or
as a grain of sea-sand on the shore, went shrinking
on, cowering before the angry weather, and looking
as if the very elements rejected them. Day after

day, such travellers crept past, but always, as she thought, in one direction—always towards the town. Swallowed up in one phase or other of its immensity, towards which they seemed impelled by a desperate fascination, they never returned. Food for the hospitals, the churchyards, the prisons, the river, fever, madness, vice, and death,—they passed on to the monster, roaring in the distance, and were lost.

The chill wind was howling, and the rain was falling, and the day was darkening moodily, when Harriet, raising her eyes from the work on which she had long since been engaged with unremitting constancy, saw one of these travellers approaching.

A woman. A solitary woman of some thirty years of age; tall; well-formed; handsome; miserably dressed; the soil of many country-roads in varied weather—dust, chalk, clay, gravel—clotted on her grey cloak by the streaming wet; no bonnet on her head, nothing to defend her rich black hair from the rain, but a torn handkerchief; with the fluttering ends of which, and with her hair, the wind blinded her so that she often stopped to push them back, and look upon the way she was going.

She was in the act of doing so, when Harriet observed her. As her hands, parting on her sun-burnt forehead, swept across her face, and threw aside the hindrances that encroached upon it, there was a reckless and regardless beauty in it: a dauntless and depraved indifference to more than weather: a carelessness of what was cast upon her bare head from heaven or earth: that, coupled with her misery and loneliness, touched the heart of her fellow-woman. She thought of all that was perverted and debased within her, no less than without: of modest graces of the mind, hardened and steeled, like these attractions of the person; of the many gifts of the Creator flung to the winds like the wild hair; of all the beautiful ruin upon which the storm was beating and the night was coming.

Thinking of this, she did not turn away with a delicate indignation—too many of her own compassionate and tender sex too often do—but pitied her.

Her fallen sister came on, looking far before her, trying with her eager eyes to pierce the mist in which the city was enshrouded, and glancing, now and then from side to side, with the bewildered and uncertain aspect of a stranger. Though her tread was bold and courageous, she was fatigued, and after a moment of irresolution, sat down upon a heap of stones; seeking no shelter from the rain, but letting it rain on her as it would.

She was now opposite the house; raising her head after resting it for a moment on both hands, her eyes met those of Harriet.

In a moment Harriet was at the door: and the other, rising from her seat at her beck, came slowly, and with no conciliatory look, towards her.

'Why do you rest in the rain?' said Harriet, gently.

'Because I have no other resting-place,' was the reply.

'But there are many places of shelter near here. This,' referring to the little porch, 'is better than where you were. You are very welcome to rest here.'

The wanderer looked at her, in doubt and surprise, but without any expression of thankfulness; and sitting down, and taking off one of her worn shoes to beat out the fragments of stone and dust that were inside, showed that her foot was cut and bleeding.

Harriet uttering an expression of pity, the traveller looked up with a contemptuous and incredulous smile.

'Why, what's a torn foot to such as me?' she said.
'And what's a torn foot in such as me, to such as
you?'

'Come in and wash it,' answered Harriet, mildly,
'and let me give you something to bind it up.'

The woman caught her arm, and drawing it before
her own eyes, hid them against it, and wept. Not
like a woman, but like a stern man surprised into that
weakness; with a violent heaving of her breast, and
struggle for recovery, that showed how unusual the
emotion was with her.

She submitted to be led into the house, and, evidently more in gratitude than in any care for herself,
washed and bound the injured place. Harriet then
put before her fragments of her own frugal dinner, and when she had eaten of them, though spar-
ingly, besought her, before resuming her road (which
she showed her anxiety to do), to dry her clothes before the fire. Again, more in gratitude than with
any evidence of concern in her own behalf, she sat
down in front of it, and unbinding the handkerchief
about her head, and letting her thick wet hair fall
down below her waist, sat drying it with the palms
of her hands, and looking at the blaze.

'I dare say you are thinking,' she said, lifting her
head suddenly, 'that I used to be handsome, once. I
believe I was—I know I was. Look here!'

She held up her hair roughly with both hands;
seizing it as if she would have torn it out; then, threw
it down again, and flung it back as though it were a
heap of serpents.

'Are you a stranger in this place?' asked Harriet.

'A stranger!' she returned, stopping between each
short reply, and looking at the fire. 'Yes. Ten or
a dozen years a stranger. I have had no almanack
where I have been. Ten or a dozen years. I don't

know this part. It's much altered since I went away.'

'Have you been far?'

'Very far. Months upon months over the sea, and far away even then. I have been where convicts go,' she added, looking full upon her entertainer. 'I have been one myself.'

'Heaven help you and forgive you!' was the gentle answer.

'Ah! Heaven help me and forgive me!' she returned, nodding her head at the fire. 'If man would help some of us a little more, God would forgive us all the sooner perhaps.'

But she was softened by the earnest manner, and the cordial face so full of mildness and so free from judgment of her, and said, less hardily—

'We may be about the same age, you and me. If I am older, it is not above a year or two. Oh think of that!'

She opened her arms, as though the exhibition of her outward form would show the moral wretch she was; and letting them drop at her sides, hung down her head.

'There is nothing we may not hope to repair; it is never too late to amend,' said Harriet. 'You are penitent—'

'No,' she answered. 'I am not! I can't be. I am no such thing. Why should I be penitent, and all the world go free. They talk to me of my penitence. Who's penitent for the wrongs that have been done to me!'

She rose up, bound her handkerchief about her head, and turned to move away.

'Where are you going?' said Harriet.

'Yonder,' she answered, pointing with her hand. 'To London.'

'Have you any home to go to?'

'I think I have a mother. She's as much a mother, as her dwelling is a home,' she answered with a bitter laugh.

'Take this,' cried Harriet, putting money in her hand. 'Try to do well. It is very little, but for one day it may keep you from harm.'

'Are you married?' said the other, faintly, as she took it.

'No. I live here with my brother. We have not much to spare, or I would give you more.'

'Will you let me kiss you?'

'Seeing no scorn or repugnance in her face, the object of her charity bent over her as she asked the question, and pressed her lips against her cheek. Once more she caught her arm, and covered her eyes with it; and then was gone.

Gone into the deepening night, and howling wind, and pelting rain; urging her way on towards the mist-enshrouded city where the blurred lights gleamed; and with her black hair, and disordered head-gear, fluttering round her reckless face.

CHAPTER XXXIV

ANOTHER MOTHER AND DAUGHTER

In an ugly and dark room, an old woman, ugly and dark too, sat listening to the wind and rain, and crouching over a meagre fire. More constant to the last-named occupation than the first, she never changed her attitude, unless, when any stray drops of rain fell hissing on the smouldering embers, to raise her head with an awakened attention to the whistling and pattering outside, and gradually to let it fall again lower and lower and lower as she sunk into a brooding state of thought, in which the noises of the night were as indistinctly regarded as is the monotonous rolling of a sea by one who sits in contemplation on its shore.

There was no light in the room save that which the fire afforded. Glaring sullenly from time to time like the eye of a fierce beast half asleep, it revealed no objects that needed to be jealous of a better display. A heap of rags, a heap of bones, a wretched bed, two or three mutilated chairs or stools, the black walls and blacker ceiling, were all its winking brightness shone upon. As the old woman, with a gigantic and distorted image of herself thrown half upon the wall behind her, half upon the roof above, sat bending over the few loose bricks within which it was pent, on the damp hearth of the chimney—for there was no stove—she looked as if she were watching at some witch's altar for a favourable token; and but that the movement of her chattering jaws and trembling chin was too frequent and too fast for the slow flickering of the fire, it would have seemed an illusion wrought by the light, as it came and went, upon a face as motionless as the form to which it belonged.

If Florence could have stood within the room and looked upon the original of the shadow thrown upon the wall and roof, as it cowered thus over the fire, a glance might have sufficed to recall the figure of Good Mrs. Brown; notwithstanding that her childish recollection of that terrible old woman was as grotesque and exaggerated a presentment of the truth, perhaps, as the shadow on the wall. But Florence was not there to look on; and Good Mrs. Brown remained unrecognised, and sat staring at her fire, unobserved.

Attracted by a louder sputtering than usual, as the
rain came hissing down the chimney in a little stream,
the old woman raised her head, impatiently, to listen
afresh. And this time she did not drop it again; for
there was a hand upon the door, and a footstep in the
room.

'Who's that?' she said, looking over her shoulder.

'One who brings you news,' was the answer, in a
woman's voice.

'News? Where from?'

'From abroad.'

'From beyond seas?' cried the old woman, starting up.

'Aye, from beyond seas.'

The old woman raked the fire together, hurriedly,
and going close to her visitor who had entered, and
shut the door, and who now stood in the middle of
the room, put her hand upon the drenched cloak, and
turned the unresisting figure, so as to have it in the
full light of the fire. She did not find what she
had expected, whatever that might be; for she let
the cloak go again, and uttered a querulous cry of
disappointment and misery.

'What is the matter?' asked her visitor.

'Oho! oho!' cried the old woman, turning her face
upward, with a terrible howl.

'What is the matter?' asked the visitor again.

'It's not my gal!' cried the old woman, tossing up
her arms, and clasping her hands above her head.
'Where's my Alice? Where's my handsome daughter? They've been the death of her!'

'They've not been the death of her yet, if your
name's Marwood,' said the visitor.

'Have you seen my gal, then?' cried the old woman.
'Has she wrote to me?'

'She said you couldn't read,' returned the other.

'No more I can!' exclaimed the old woman, wringing her hands.

'Have you no light here?' said the other, looking round the room.

The old woman, mumbling and shaking her head, and muttering to herself about her handsome daughter, brought a candle from a cupboard in the corner, and thrusting it into the fire with a trembling hand, lighted it with some difficulty and set it on the table. Its dirty wick burnt dimly at first, being choked in its own grease; and when the bleared eyes and failing sight of the old woman could distinguish anything by its light, her visitor was sitting with her arms folded, her eyes turned downwards, and a handkerchief she had worn upon her head lying on the table by her side.

'She sent to me by word of mouth then, my gal, Alice?' mumbled the old woman, after waiting for some moments. 'What did she say?'

'Look,' returned the visitor.

The old woman repeated the word in a scared uncertain way; and, shading her eyes, looked at the speaker, round the room, and at the speaker once again.

Alice said, 'Look again, mother'; and the speaker fixed her eyes upon her.

Again the old woman looked round the room, and at her visitor, and round the room once more. Hastily seizing the candle, and rising from her seat, she held it to the visitor's face, uttered a loud cry, set down the light, and fell upon her neck!

'It's my gal! It's my Alice! It's my handsome daughter, living and come back!' screamed the old woman, rocking herself to and fro upon the breast that coldly suffered her embrace. 'It's my gal! It's my Alice! It's my handsome daughter, living and come back!' she screamed again, dropping on the floor before her, clasping her knees, laying her head against them, and still rocking herself to and fro with every frantic demonstration of which her vitality was capable.

'Yes, mother,' returned Alice, stooping forward for a moment and kissing her, but endeavouring, even in the act, to disengage herself from her embrace. 'I am here, at last. Let go, mother; let go. Get up, and sit in your chair. What good does this do?'

'She's come back harder than she went!' cried the mother, looking up in her face, and still holding to her knees. 'She don't care for me! after all these years, and all the wretched life I 've led!'

'Why, mother!' said Alice, shaking her ragged skirts to detach the old woman from them: 'there are two sides to that. There have been years for me as well as you, and there has been wretchedness for me as well as you. Get up, get up!'

Her mother rose, and cried, and wrung her hands, and stood at a little distance gazing on her. Then she took the candle again, and going round her, surveyed her from head to foot, making a low moaning all the time. Then she put the candle down, resumed her chair, and beating her hands together to a kind of weary tune, and rolling herself from side to side, continued moaning and wailing to herself.

Alice got up, took off her wet cloak, and laid it aside. That done, she sat down as before, and with her arms folded, and her eyes gazing at the fire, remained silently listening with a contemptuous face to her old mother's inarticulate complainings.

'Did you expect to see me return as youthful as I went away, mother?' she said at length, turning her eyes upon the old woman. 'Did you think a

foreign life, like mine, was good for good looks?
One would believe so, to hear you.'

'It an't that!' cried the mother. '*She* knows it!'

'What is it then?' returned the daughter. 'It had
best be something that don't last, mother, or my way
out is easier than my way in.'

'Hear that!' exclaimed the mother. 'After all
these years she threatens to desert me in the moment
of her coming back again!'

'I tell you, mother, for the second time, there have
been years for me as well as you,' said Alice. 'Come
back harder? Of course I have come back harder.
What else did you expect?'

'Harder to me! To her own dear mother!' cried
the old woman.

'I don't know who began to harden me, if my own
dear mother didn't,' she returned, sitting with her
folded arms, and knitted brows, and compressed lips
as if she were bent on excluding, by force, every
softer feeling from her breast. 'Listen, mother, to
a word or two. If we understand each other now,
we shall not fall out any more, perhaps. I went
away a girl, and have come back a woman. I went
away undutiful enough, and have come back no better, you may swear. But have you been very dutiful to me?'

'I!' cried the old woman. 'To my own gal! A
mother dutiful to her own child!'

'It sounds unnatural, don't it?' returned the daughter, looking coldly on her with her stern, regardless,
hardy, beautiful face; 'but I have thought of it sometimes, in the course of *my* lone years, till I have got
used to it. I have heard some talk about duty first
and last; but it has always been of my duty to other
people. I have wondered now and then—to pass

away the time—whether no one ever owed any duty to me.'

Her mother sat mowing, and mumbling, and shaking her head, but whether angrily, or remorsefully, or in denial, or only in her physical infirmity, did not appear.

'There was a child called Alice Marwood,' said the daughter, with a laugh, and looking down at herself in terrible derision of herself, 'born, among poverty and neglect, and nursed in it. Nobody taught her, nobody stepped forward to help her, nobody cared for her.'

'Nobody!' echoed the mother, pointing to herself, and striking her breast.

'The only care she knew,' returned the daughter, 'was to be beaten, and stinted, and abused sometimes; and she might have done better without that. She lived in homes like this, and in the streets, with a crowd of little wretches like herself; and yet she brought good looks out of this childhood. So much the worse for her. She had better have been hunted and worried to death for ugliness.'

'Go on! go on!' exclaimed the mother.

'I am going on,' returned the daughter. 'There was a girl called Alice Marwood. She was handsome. She was taught too late, and taught all wrong. She was too well cared for, too well trained, too well helped on, too much looked after. You were very fond of her—you were better off then. What came to that girl comes to thousands every year. It was only ruin, and she was born to it.'

'After all these years!' whined the old woman. 'My gal begins with this.'

'She 'll soon have ended,' said the daughter. 'There was a criminal called Alice Marwood—a girl still, but deserted and an outcast. And she was tried, and she was sentenced. And Lord, how the gentlemen in the court talked about it! and how grave the judge was on her duty, and on her having perverted the gifts of nature—as if he didn't know better than anybody there, that they had been made curses to her!—and how he preached about the strong arm of the Law—so very strong to save her, when she was an innocent and helpless little wretch; and how solemn and religious it all was. I have thought of that, many times since, to be sure!'

She folded her arms tightly on her breast, and laughed in a tone that made the howl of the old woman musical.

'So Alice Marwood was transported, mother,' she pursued, 'and was sent to learn her duty, where there was twenty times less duty, and more wickedness, and wrong, and infamy, than here. And Alice Marwood is come back a woman. Such a woman as she ought to be, after all this. In good time, there will be more solemnity, and more fine talk, and more strong arm, most likely, and there will be an end of her; but the gentlemen needn't be afraid of being thrown out of work. There's crowds of little wretches, boy and girl, growing up in any of the streets they live in, that 'll keep them to it till they 've made their fortunes.'

The old woman leaned her elbows on the table, and resting her face upon her two hands, made a show of being in great distress—or really was, perhaps.

'There! I have done, mother,' said the daughter, with a motion of her head, as if in dismissal of the subject. 'I have said enough. Don't let you and I talk of being dutiful, whatever we do. Your childhood was like mine, I suppose. So much the worse for both of us. I don't want to blame you, or to defend myself; why should I? That's all over long ago. But I am a woman—not a girl, now—and you and I needn't make a show of our history, like the gentlemen in the court. *We* know all about it well enough.'

Lost and degraded as she was, there was a beauty in her, both of face and form, which, even in its worst expression, could not but be recognised as such by any one regarding her with the least attention. As she subsided into silence, and her face which had been harshly agitated, quieted down; while her dark eyes, fixed upon the fire, exchanged the reckless light that had animated them, for one that was softened by something like sorrow; there shone through all her wayworn misery and fatigue, a ray of the departed radiance of the fallen angel.

Her mother, after watching her for some time without speaking, ventured to steal her withered hand a little nearer to her across the table; and finding that she permitted this, to touch her face and smooth her hair. With the feeling as it seemed, that the old woman was at least sincere in this show of interest, Alice made no movement to check her; so, advancing by degrees, she bound up her daughter's hair afresh, took off her wet shoes, if they deserved the name, spread something dry upon her shoulders, and hovered humbly about her, muttering to herself, as she recognised her old features and expression more and more.

'You are very poor, mother, I see,' said Alice looking round, when she had sat thus for some time.

'Bitter poor, my deary,' replied the old woman.

She admired her daughter, and was afraid of her. Perhaps her admiration, such as it was, had originated long ago, when she first found anything that was beautiful appearing in the midst of the squalid

fight of her existence. Perhaps her fear was referable, in some sort, to the retrospect she had so lately
heard. Be this as it might, she stood, submissively
and deferentially, before her child, and inclined her
head, as if in a pitiful entreaty to be spared any further reproach.

'How have you lived?'

'By begging, my deary.'

'And pilfering, mother?'

'Sometimes, Ally—in a very small way. I am old
and timid. I have taken trifles from children now
and then, my deary, but not often. I have tramped
about the country, pet, and I know what I know. I
have watched.'

'Watched?' returned the daughter, looking at her.

'I have hung about a family, my deary,' said the
mother, even more humbly and submissively than before.

'What family?'

'Hush, darling. Don't be angry with me, I did it
for the love of you. In memory of my poor gal beyond seas.' She put out her hand deprecatingly, and
drawing it back again, laid it on her lips.

'Years ago, my deary,' she pursued, glancing
timidly at the attentive and stern face opposed to
her. 'I came across his little child by chance.'

'Whose child?'

'Not his, Alice deary; don't look at me like that;
not his. How could it be his? You know he has
none.'

'Whose then?' returned the daughter. 'You said
his.'

'Hush, Ally; you frighten me, deary. Mr. Dombey's—only Mr. Dombey's. Since then, darling, I
have seen them often. I have seen *him*.'

In uttering this last word, the old woman shrunk

and recoiled, as if with a sudden fear that her daughter would strike her. But though the daughter's face was fixed upon her, and expressed the most vehement passion, she remained still: except that she clenched her arms tighter and tighter within each other, on her bosom, as if to restrain them by that means from doing an injury to herself, or some one else, in the blind fury of the wrath that suddenly possessed her.

'Little he thought who I was!' said the old woman, shaking her clenched hand.

'And little he cared!' muttered her daughter, between her teeth.

'But there we were,' said the old woman, 'face to face. I spoke to him, and he spoke to me. I sat and watched him as he went away down a long grove of trees: and at every step he took, I cursed him soul and body.'

'He will thrive in spite of that,' returned the daughter, disdainfully.

'Aye, he is thriving,' said the mother.

She held her peace; for the face and form before her were unshaped by rage. It seemed as if the bosom would burst with the emotions that strove within it. The effort that constrained and held it pent up, was no less formidable than the rage itself: no less bespeaking the violent and dangerous character of the woman who made it. But it succeeded, and she asked, after a silence—

'Is he married?'

'No, deary,' said the mother.

'Going to be?'

'Not that I know of, deary. But his master and friend is married. Oh, we may give him joy! We may give 'em all joy!' cried the old woman, hugging herself with her lean arms in her exultation. 'Nothing but joy to us will come of that marriage. Mind me!'

The daughter looked at her for an explanation.

'But you are wet and tired: hungry and thirsty,' said the old woman, hobbling to the cupboard; 'and there's little here, and little'—diving down into her pocket, and jingling a few halfpence on the table—'little here. Have you any money, Alice, deary?'

The covetous, sharp, eager face with which she asked the question and looked on, as her daughter took out of her bosom the little gift she had so lately received, told almost as much of the history of this parent and child as the child herself had told in words.

'Is that all?' said the mother.

'I have no more. I should not have this, but for charity.'

'But for charity, eh, deary?' said the old woman, bending greedily over the table to look at the money, which she appeared distrustful of her daughter's still retaining in her hand, and gazing on. 'Humph! six and six is twelve and six eighteen—so—we must make the most of it. I'll go buy something to eat and drink.'

With greater alacrity than might have been expected in one of her appearance—for age and misery seemed to have made her as decrepit as ugly—she began to occupy her trembling hands in tying an old bonnet on her head, and folding a torn shawl about herself: still eyeing the money in her daughter's hand, with the same sharp desire.

'What joy is to come to us of this marriage, mother?' asked the daughter. 'You have not told me that.'

'The joy,' she replied, attiring herself, with fumbling fingers, 'of no love at all, and much pride and hate, my deary. The joy of confusion and strife among 'em, proud as they are, and of danger—danger, Alice!'

'What danger?'

'*I* have seen what I have seen. *I* know what I know!' chuckled the mother. 'Let some look to it. Let some be upon their guard. My gal may keep good company yet!'

Then, seeing that in the wondering earnestness with which her daughter regarded her, her hand involuntarily closed upon the money, the old woman made more speed to secure it, and hurriedly added, 'but I 'll go buy something; I 'll go buy something.'

As she stood with her hand stretched out before her daughter, her daughter, glancing again at the money, put it to her lips before parting with it.

'What, Ally! Do you kiss it?' chuckled the old woman. 'That 's like me—I often do. Oh, it 's so good to us!' squeezing her own tarnished halfpence up to her bag of a throat, 'so good to us in everything but not coming in heaps!'

'I kiss it, mother,' said the daughter, 'or I did then —I don't know that I ever did before—for the giver's sake.'

'The giver, eh, deary?' retorted the old woman, whose dimmed eyes glistened as she took it. 'Aye! I 'll kiss it for the giver's sake, too, when the giver can make it go farther. But I 'll go spend it, deary. I 'll be back directly.'

'You seem to say you know a great deal, mother,' said the daughter, following her to the door with her eyes. 'You have grown very wise since we parted.'

'Know!' croaked the old woman, coming back a step or two, 'I know more than you think. I know more than *he* thinks, deary, as I 'll tell you by and by. I know all about him.'

The daughter smiled incredulously.

'I know of his brother, Alice,' said the old woman, stretching out her neck with a leer of malice absolutely frightful, 'who might have been where you have been—for stealing money—and who lives with his sister, over yonder, by the north road out of London.'

'Where?'

'By the north road out of London, deary. You shall see the house if you like. It an't much to boast of, genteel as his own is. No, no, no,' cried the old woman, shaking her head and laughing; for her daughter had started up, 'not now; it's too far off'; it's by the milestone, where the stones are heaped; —to-morrow, deary, if it's fine, and you are in the humour. But I'll go spend—'

'Stop!' and the daughter flung herself upon her, with her former passion raging like a fire. 'The sister is a fair-faced devil, with brown hair?'

The old woman, amazed and terrified, nodded her head.

'I see the shadow of him in her face! It's a red house standing by itself. Before the door there is a small green porch.'

Again the old woman nodded.

'In which I sat to-day! Give me back the money.'

'Alice! Deary!'

'Give me back the money, or you'll be hurt.'

She forced it from the old woman's hand as she spoke, and utterly indifferent to her complainings and entreaties, threw on the garments she had taken off, and hurried out, with headlong speed.

The mother followed, limping after her as she could and expostulating with no more effect upon her than upon the wind and rain and darkness that encompassed them. Obdurate and fierce in her own

purpose, and indifferent to all besides, the daughter
defied the weather and the distance, as if she had
known no travel or fatigue, and made for the house
where she had been relieved.   After some quarter of
an hour's walking, the old woman, spent and out of
breath, ventured to hold by her skirts; but she ventured no more, and they travelled on in silence
through the wet and gloom.   If the mother now and
then uttered a word of complaint, she stifled it lest
her daughter should break away from her and leave
her behind; and the daughter was dumb.

It was within an hour or so of midnight, when they
left the regular streets behind them, and entered on
the deeper gloom of that neutral ground where the
house was situated.   The town lay in the distance,
lurid and lowering; the bleak wind howled over
the open space; all around was black, wild, desolate.

'This is a fit place for me!' said the daughter, stopping to look back.   'I thought so, when I was here
before, to-day!'

'Alice, my deary,' cried the mother, pulling her
gently by the skirt.   'Alice!'

'What now, mother?'

'Don't give the money back, my darling; please
don't.   We can't afford it.   We want supper, deary.
Money is money, whoever gives it.   Say what you
will, but keep the money.'

'See there!' was all the daughter's answer.   'That
is the house I mean.   Is that it?'

The old woman nodded in the affirmative; and a
few more paces brought them to the threshold.   There
was the light of fire and candle in the room where
Alice had sat to dry her clothes; and on her knocking at the door, John Carker appeared from that
room.

He was surprised to see such visitors at such an hour, and asked Alice what she wanted.

'I want your sister,' she said. 'The woman who gave me money to-day.'

At the sound of her raised voice, Harriet came out.

'Oh!' said Alice. 'You are here! Do you remember me?'

'Yes,' she answered, wondering.

The face that had humbled itself before her, looked on her now with such invincible hatred and defiance; and the hand that had gently touched her arm, was clenched with such a show of evil purpose, as if it would gladly strangle her; that she drew close to her brother for protection.

'That I could speak with you, and not know you! That I could come near you, and not feel what blood was running in your veins, by the tingling of my own!' said Alice, with a menacing gesture.

'What do you mean? What have I done?'

'Done!' returned the other. 'You have sat me by your fire; you have given me food and money; you have bestowed your compassion on me! You! whose name I spit upon!'

The old woman, with a malevolence that made her ugliness quite awful, shook her withered hand at the brother and sister in confirmation of her daughter, but plucked her by the skirts again, nevertheless, imploring her to keep the money.

'If I dropped a tear upon your hand, may it wither it up! If I spoke a gentle word in your hearing, may it deafen you! If I touched you with my lips, may the touch be poison to you! A curse upon this roof that gave me shelter! Sorrow and shame upon your head! Ruin upon all belonging to you!'

As she said the words, she threw the money down upon the ground, and spurned it with her foot.

'I tread it in the dust: I wouldn't take it if it paved my way to heaven! I would the bleeding foot that brought me here to-day, had rotted off, before it led me to your house!'

Harriet, pale and trembling, restrained her brother, and suffered her to go on uninterrupted.

'It was well that I should be pitied and forgiven by you, or any one of your name, in the first hour of my return! It was well that you should act the kind good lady to me! I'll thank you when I die; I'll pray for you, and all your race, you may be sure!'

With a fierce action of her hand, as if she sprinkled hatred on the ground, and with it devoted those who were standing there to destruction, she looked up once at the black sky, and strode out into the wild night.

The mother, who had plucked at her skirts again and again in vain, and had eyed the money lying on the threshold with an absorbing greed that seemed to concentrate her faculties upon it, would have prowled about, until the house was dark, and then groped in the mire on the chance of repossessing herself of it. But the daughter drew her away, and they set forth, straight, on their return to their dwelling; the old woman whimpering and bemoaning their loss upon the road, and fretfully bewailing, as openly as she dared, the undutiful conduct of her handsome girl in depriving her of a supper, on the very first night of their reunion.

Supperless to bed she went, saving for a few coarse fragments; and those she sat mumbling and munching over a scrap of fire, long after her undutiful daughter lay asleep.

Were this miserable mother, and this miserable daughter, only the reduction to their lowest grade, of certain social vices sometimes prevailing higher up? In this round world of many circles within circles, do we make a weary journey from the high grade to the low, to find at last that they lie close together, that the two extremes touch, and that our journey's end is but our starting-place? Allowing for great difference of stuff and texture, was the pattern of this woof repeated among gentle blood at all?

Say, Edith Dombey! And Cleopatra, best of mothers, let us have your testimony!

CHAPTER XXXV

THE HAPPY PAIR

THE dark blot on the street is gone. Mr. Dombey's mansion, if it be a gap among the other houses any longer, is only so because it is not to be vied with in its brightness, and haughtily casts them off. The saying is, that home is home, be it never so homely. If it hold good in the opposite contingency, and home is home, be it never so stately, what an altar to the household gods is raised up here!

Lights are sparkling in the windows this evening, and the ruddy glow of fires is warm and bright upon the hangings and soft carpets, and the dinner waits to be served, and the dinner-table is handsomely set forth, though only for four persons, and the sideboard is cumbrous with plate. It is the first time that the house has been arranged for occupation since its late changes, and the happy pair are looked for every minute.

Only second to the wedding morning, in the interest and expectation it engenders among the household, is this evening of the coming home. Mrs. Perch is

in the kitchen taking tea; and has made the tour of
the establishment, and priced the silks and damasks
by the yard, and exhausted every interjection in the
dictionary and out of it expressive of admiration and
wonder.   The upholsterer's foreman, who has left his
hat, with a pocket-handkerchief in it, both smelling
strongly of varnish, under a chair in the hall, lurks
about the house, gazing upwards at the cornices, and
downward at the carpets, and occasionally, in a silent
transport of enjoyment, taking a rule out of his
pocket, and skirmishingly measuring expensive objects, with unutterable feelings.   Cook is in high
spirits, and says give *her* a place where there's plenty
of company (as she'll bet you sixpence there will be
now), for she is of a lively disposition, and she always
was from a child, and she don't mind who knows it;
which sentiment elicits from the breast of Mrs. Perch
a responsive murmur of support and approbation.
All the housemaid hopes is, happiness for 'em—but
marriage is a lottery, and the more she thinks about
it, the more she feels the independence and the safety
of a single life.   Mr. Towlinson is saturnine and
grim, and says that's his opinion too, and give him
war besides, and down with the French—for this
young man has a general impression that every foreigner is a Frenchman, and must be by the laws of
nature.

At each new sound of wheels, they all stop, whatever they are saying, and listen; and more than once
there is a general starting up and a cry of 'Here they
are!'   But here they are not yet; and cook begins to
mourn over the dinner, which has been put back twice,
and the upholsterer's foreman still goes lurking about
the rooms, undisturbed in his blissful reverie!

Florence is ready to receive her father and her new
mamma.   Whether the emotions that are throbbing

in her breast originate in pleasure or in pain, she
hardly knows.   But the fluttering heart sends added
colour to her cheeks, and brightness to her eyes; and
they say downstairs, drawing their heads together—
for they always speak softly when they speak of her
—how beautiful Miss Florence looks to-night, and
what a sweet young lady she has grown, poor dear!
A pause succeeds; and then cook, feeling, as presi-
dent, that her sentiments are waited for, wonders
whether—and there stops.   The housemaid wonders
too, and so does Mrs. Perch, who has the happy social
faculty of always wondering when other people wonder, without being at all particular what she wonders
at.   Mr. Towlinson, who now descries an opportunity
of bringing down the spirits of the ladies to his own
level, says wait and see; he wishes some people were
well out of this.   Cook leads a sigh then, and a murmur of 'Ah, it 's a strange world, it is indeed!' and
when it has gone round the table, adds persuasively,
'but Miss Florence can't well be the worse for any
change, Tom.'   Mr. Towlinson's rejoinder, preg-
nant with frightful meaning, is 'Oh, can't she though!'
and sensible that a mere man can scarcely be more
prophetic, or improve upon that, he holds his peace.

Mrs. Skewton, prepared to greet her darling
daughter and dear son-in-law with open arms, is appropriately attired for that purpose in a very youthful costume, with short sleeves.   At present, however, her ripe charms are blooming in the shade of her
own apartments, whence she has not emerged since
she took possession of them a few hours ago, and
where she is fast growing fretful, on account of the
postponement of dinner.   The maid who ought to
be a skeleton, but is in truth a buxom damsel, is, on
the other hand, in a most amiable state: considering
her quarterly stipend much safer than heretofore, and

foreseeing a great improvement in her board and
lodging.

Where are the happy pair, for whom this brave
home is waiting? Do steam, tide, wind, and horses, all
abate their speed, to linger on such happiness? Does
the swarm of loves and graces hovering about them
retard their progress by its numbers? Are there so
many flowers in their happy path, that they can
scarcely move along, without entanglement in thorn-
less roses, and sweetest brair?

They are here at last! The noise of wheels is
heard, grows louder, and a carriage drives up to the
door! A thundering knock from the obnoxious foreigner anticipates the rush of Mr. Towlinson and
party to open it; and Mr. Dombey and his bride
alight, and walk in arm and arm.

'My sweetest Edith!' cries an agitated voice upon
the stairs. 'My dearest Dombey!' and the short
sleeves wreath themselves about the happy couple in
turn, and embrace them.

Florence had come down to the hall too, but did
not advance: reserving her timid welcome until these
nearer and dearer transports should subside. But the
eyes of Edith sought her out, upon the threshold;
and dismissing her sensitive parent with a slight kiss
on the cheek, she hurried on to Florence and embraced
her.

'How do you do, Florence?' said Mr. Dombey, putting out his hand.

As Florence, trembling, raised it to her lips, she
met his glance. The look was cold and distant
enough, but it stirred her heart to think that she observed in it something more of interest than he had
ever shown before. It even expressed a kind of faint
surprise, and not a disagreeable surprise, at sight of
her. She dared not raise her eyes to his any more;

but she felt that he looked at her once again, and not
less favourably. Oh what a thrill of joy shot through
her, awakened by even this intangible and baseless
confirmation of her hope that she would learn to
win him, through her new and beautiful mamma!

'You will not be long dressing, Mrs. Dombey, I
presume?' said Mr. Dombey.

'I shall be ready immediately.'

'Let them send up dinner in a quarter of an hour.'

With that Mr. Dombey stalked away to his own
dressing-room, and Mrs. Dombey went upstairs to
hers. Mrs. Skewton and Florence repaired to the
drawing-room, where that excellent mother considered
it incumbent on her to shed a few irrepressible tears,
supposed to be forced from her by her daughter's
felicity; and which she was still drying, very gingerly,
with a laced corner of her pocket-handkerchief, when
her son-in-law appeared.

'And how, my dearest Dombey, did you find that
delightfullest of cities, Paris?' she asked, subduing her
emotion.

'It was cold,' returned Mr. Dombey.

'Gay as ever,' said Mrs. Skewton, 'of course.'

'Not particularly. I thought it dull,' said Mr.
Dombey.

'Fie, my dearest Dombey!' archly; 'dull!'

'It made that impression upon me, madam,' said
Mr. Dombey, with grave politeness. 'I believe Mrs.
Dombey found it dull too. She mentioned once or
twice that she thought it so.'

'Why, you naughty girl!' cried Mrs. Skewton, rallying her dear child, who now entered, 'what dreadfully heretical things have you been saying about
Paris?'

Edith raised her eyebrows with an air of weariness;
and passing the folding-doors which were thrown

open to display the suite of rooms in their new and handsome garniture, and barely glancing at them as she passed, sat down by Florence.

'My dear Dombey,' said Mrs. Skewton, 'how charmingly these people have carried out every idea that we hinted. They have made a perfect palace of the house, positively.'

'It is handsome,' said Mr. Dombey, looking round. 'I directed that no expense should be spared; and all that money could do, has been done, I believe.'

'And what can it not do, dear Dombey?' observed Cleopatra.

'It is powerful, madam,' said Mr. Dombey.

He looked in his solemn way towards his wife, but not a word said she.

'I hope, Mrs. Dombey,' addressing her after a moment's silence, with especial distinctness; 'that these alterations meet with your approval.'

'They are as handsome as they can be,' she returned, with haughty carelessness. 'They should be so, of course. And I suppose they are.'

An expression of scorn was habitual to the proud face, and seemed inseparable from it; but the contempt with which it received any appeal to admiration, respect, or consideration on the ground of his riches, no matter how slight or ordinary in itself, was a new and different expression, unequalled in intensity by any other of which it was capable. Whether Mr. Dombey, wrapped in his own greatness, was at all aware of this, or no, there had not been wanting opportunities already for his complete enlightenment; and at that moment it might have been effected by the one glance of the dark eye that lighted on him, after it had rapidly and scornfully surveyed the theme of his self-glorification. He might have read in that one glance that nothing that his wealth could do, though

it were increased ten thousand fold, could win him
for its own sake, one look of softened recognition
from the defiant woman, linked to him, but arrayed
with her whole soul against him. He might have read
in that one glance that even for its sordid and mercenary influence upon herself, she spurned it, while
she claimed its utmost power as her right, her bargain—as the base and worthless recompense for which
she had become his wife. He might have read in
it that, ever baring her own head for the lightning
of her own contempt and pride to strike, the most
innocent allusion to the power of his riches degraded
her anew, sunk her deeper in her own respect, and
made the blight and waste within her more complete.

But dinner was announced, and Mr. Dombey led
down Cleopatra; Edith and his daughter following.
Sweeping past the gold and silver demonstration on
the sideboard as if it were heaped-up dirt, and deign-
ing to bestow no look upon the elegancies around her,
she took her place at his board for the first time, and
sat, like a statue, at the feast.

Mr. Dombey, being a good deal in the statue way
himself, was well enough pleased to see his handsome
wife immoveable and proud and cold. Her deport-
ment being always elegant and graceful, this as a
general behaviour was agreeable and congenial to
him. Presiding, therefore, with his accustomed dignity, and not at all reflecting on his wife by any
warmth or hilarity of his own, he performed his
share of the honours of the table with a cool satisfaction; and the installation dinner, though not regarded
downstairs as a great success, or very promising beginning, passed off, above, in a sufficiently polite, genteel, and frosty manner.

Soon after tea, Mrs. Skewton, who affected to be
quite overcome and worn out by her emotions of

happiness, arising in the contemplation of her dear child united to the man of her heart, but who, there is reason to suppose, found this family party somewhat dull, as she yawned for one hour continually behind her fan, retired to bed. Edith, also, silently withdrew and came back no more. Thus, it happened that Florence, who had been upstairs to have some conversation with Diogenes, returning to the drawing-room with her little work-basket, found no one there but her father, who was walking to and fro, in dreary magnificence.

'I beg your pardon. Shall I go away, papa?' said Florence faintly, hesitating at the door.

'No,' returned Mr. Dombey, looking round over his shoulder; 'you can come and go here, Florence, as you please. This is not my private room.'

Florence entered, and sat down at a distant little table with her work: finding herself for the first time in her life—for the very first time within her memory from her infancy to that hour—alone with her father, as his companion. She, his natural companion, his only child, who in her lonely life and grief had known the suffering of a breaking heart; who, in her rejected love, had never breathed his name to God at night, but with a tearful blessing, heavier on him than a curse; who had prayed to die young, so she might only die in his arms; who had, all through, repaid the agony of slight, and coldness, and dislike, with patient unexacting love, excusing him, and pleading for him, like his better angel!

She trembled, and her eyes were dim. His figure seemed to grow in height and bulk before her as he paced the room: now it was all blurred and indistinct; now clear again, and plain; and now she seemed to think that this had happened, just the same, a multitude of years ago. She yearned towards him, and yet shrunk from his approach. Unnatural emotion in a child innocent of wrong! Unnatural the hand that had directed the sharp plough, which furrowed up her gentle nature for the sowing of its seeds!

Bent upon not distressing or offending him by her distress, Florence controlled herself, and sat quietly at her work. After a few more turns across and across the room, he left off pacing it; and withdrawing into a shadowy corner at some distance, where there was an easy chair, covered his head with a handkerchief, and composed himself to sleep.

It was enough for Florence to sit there watching him; turning her eyes towards his chair from time to time; watching him with her thoughts, when her face was intent upon her work; and sorrowfully glad to think that he *could* sleep, while she was there, and that he was not made restless by her strange and long-forbidden presence.

What would have been her thoughts if she had known that he was steadily regarding her; that the veil upon his face, by accident or by design, was so adjusted that his sight was free, and that it never wandered from her face an instant. That when she looked towards him, in the obscure dark corner, her speaking eyes, more earnest and pathetic in their voiceless speech than all the orators of all the world, and impeaching him more nearly in their mute address, met his, and did not know it. That when she bent her head again over her work, he drew his breath more easily, but with the same attention looked upon her still—upon her white brow and her falling hair, and busy hands; and once attracted, seemed to have no power to turn his eyes away!

And what were his thoughts meanwhile? With what emotions did he prolong the attentive gaze covertly directed on his unknown daughter? Was there

reproach to him in the quiet figure and the mild eyes?
Had he begun to feel her disregarded claims, and did
they touch him home at last, and waken him to some
sense of his cruel injustice?

There are yielding moments in the lives of the
sternest and harshest men, though such men often
keep their secret well. The sight of her in her beauty,
almost changed into a woman without his knowledge,
may have struck out some such moments even in his
life of pride. Some passing thought that he had
had a happy home within his reach—had had a household spirit bending at his feet—had overlooked it in
his stiff-necked sullen arrogance, and wandered away
and lost himself, may have engendered them. Some
simple eloquence distinctly heard, though only uttered in her eyes, unconscious that he read them, as
'By the death-beds I have tended, by the childhood
I have suffered, by our meeting in this dreary house
at midnight, by the cry wrung from me in the anguish
of my heart, oh, father, turn to me and seek a refuge
in my love before it is too late!' may have arrested
them. Meaner and lower thoughts, as that his dead
boy was now superseded by new ties, and he could
forgive the having been supplanted in his affection,
may have occasioned them. The mere association
of her as an ornament, with all the ornament and
pomp about him, may have been sufficient. But as he
looked, he softened to her, more and more. As he
looked, she became blended with the child he had
loved, and he could hardly separate the two. As he
looked, he saw her for an instant by a clearer and a
brighter light, not bending over that child's pillow as
his rival—monstrous thought—but as the spirit of
his home, and in the action tending himself no less,
as he sat once more with his bowed-down head upon
his hand at the foot of the little bed. He felt inclined

to speak to her, and call her to him. The words 'Florence, come here!' were rising to his lips—but slowly and with difficulty, they were so very strange —when they were checked and stifled by a footstep on the stair.

It was his wife's. She had exchanged her dinner dress for a loose robe, and unbound her hair, which fell freely about her neck. But this was not the change in her that startled him.

'Florence, dear,' she said, 'I have been looking for you everywhere.'

As she sat down by the side of Florence, she stooped and kissed her hand. He hardly knew his wife. She was so changed. It was not merely that her smile was new to him—though that he had never seen; but her manner, the tone of her voice, the light of her eyes, the interest, and confidence, and winning wish to please, expressed in all—this was not Edith.

'Softly, dear mamma. Papa is asleep.'

It was Edith now. She looked towards the corner where he was, and he knew that face and manner very well.

'I scarcely thought you could be here, Florence.'

Again, how altered, and how softened, in an instant!

'I left here early,' pursued Edith, 'purposely to sit upstairs and talk with you. But, going to your room, I found my bird was flown, and I have been waiting there ever since, expecting its return.'

If it had been a bird, indeed, she could not have taken it more tenderly and gently to her breast, than she did Florence.

'Come, dear!'

'Papa will not expect to find me, I suppose, when he wakes,' hesitated Florence.

'Do you think he will, Florence?' said Edith, looking full upon her.

Florence drooped her head, and rose, and put up
her work-basket.   Edith drew her hand through her
arm, and they went out of the room like sisters.   Her
very step was different and new to him, Mr. Dombey
thought, as his eyes followed her to the door.

He sat in his shadowy corner so long, that the
church clocks struck the hour three times before he
moved that night.   All that while his face was still
intent upon the spot where Florence had been seated.
The room grew darker, as the candles waned and went
out; but a darkness gathered on his face, exceeding
any that the night could cast, and rested there.

Florence and Edith, seated before the fire in the
remote room where little Paul had died, talked together for a long time.   Diogenes, who was of the
party, had at first objected to the admission of Edith,
and, even in deference to his mistress's wish, had only
permitted it under growling protest.   But emerging by little and little from the ante-room, whither
he had retired in dudgeon, he soon appeared to comprehend, that with the most amiable intentions he
had made one of those mistakes which will occasionally
arise in the best-regulated dogs' minds; as a friendly
apology for which he stuck himself up on end between
the two, in a very hot place in front of the fire, and
sat panting at it, with his tongue out, and a most imbecile expression of countenance, listening to the conversation.

It turned, at first, on Florence's books and favourite
pursuits, and on the manner in which she had beguiled
the interval since the marriage.   The last theme
opened up to her a subject which lay very near her
heart, and she said, with the tears starting to her eyes—

'Oh, mamma! I have had a great sorrow since that day.'

'You a great sorrow, Florence!'

'Yes. Poor Walter is drowned.'

Florence spread her hands before her face, and wept with all her heart. Many as were the secret tears which Walter's fate had cost her, they flowed yet, when she thought or spoke of him.

'But tell me, dear,' said Edith, soothing her. 'Who was Walter? What was he to you?'

'He was my brother, mamma. After dear Paul died, we said we would be brother and sister. I had known him a long time—from a little child. He knew Paul, who liked him very much; Paul said, almost at the last, "Take care of Walter, dear papa! I was fond of him!" Walter had been brought in to see him, and was there then—in this room.'

'And *did* he take care of Walter?' inquired Edith, sternly.

'Papa? He appointed him to go abroad. He was drowned in shipwreck on his voyage,' said Florence, sobbing.

'Does he know that he is dead?' asked Edith.

'I cannot tell, mamma. I have no means of knowing. Dear mamma!' cried Florence, clinging to her as for help, and hiding her face upon her bosom, 'I know that you have seen—'

'Stay! Stop, Florence.' Edith turned so pale, and spoke so earnestly, that Florence did not need her restraining hand upon her lips. 'Tell me all about Walter first; let me understand this history all through.'

Florence related it, and everything belonging to it, even down to the friendship of Mr. Toots, of whom she could hardly speak in her distress without a tearful smile, although she was deeply grateful to him.

When she had concluded her account, to the whole of which Edith, holding her hand, listened with close attention, and when a silence had succeeded, Edith said—

'What is it that you know I have seen, Florence?'

'That I am not,' said Florence, with the same mute appeal, and the same quick concealment of her face as before, 'that I am not a favourite child, mamma. I never have been. I have never known how to be. I have missed the way, and had no one to show it to me. Oh, let me learn from you how to become dearer to papa. Teach me! you, who can so well!' and clinging closer to her, with some broken fervent words of gratitude and endearment, Florence, relieved of her sad secret, wept long, but not as painfully as of yore, within the encircling arms of her new mother.

Pale even to her lips, and with a face that strove for composure until its proud beauty was as fixed as death, Edith looked down upon the weeping girl, and once kissed her. Then gradually disengaging herself, and putting Florence away, she said, stately, and quiet as a marble image, and in a voice that deepened as she spoke, but had no other token of emotion in it—

'Florence, you do not know me! Heaven forbid that you should learn from me!'

'Not learn from you?' echoed Florence, in surprise.

'That I should teach you how to love, or be loved, Heaven forbid!' said Edith. 'If you could teach me, that were better; but it is too late. You are dear to me, Florence. I did not think that anything could ever be so dear to me, as you are in this little time.'

She saw that Florence would have spoken here, so checked her with her hand and went on.

'I will be your true friend always. I will cherish you, as much, if not as well as any one in this world could. You may trust in me,—I know it and I say it, dear—with the whole confidence even of your pure heart. There are hosts of women whom he might have married, better and truer in all other respects than I am, Florence; but there is not one who could come here, his wife, whose heart could beat with greater truth to you than mine does.'

'I know it, dear mamma!' cried Florence. 'From that first most happy day I have known it.'

'Most happy day!' Edith seemed to repeat the words involuntarily, and went on. 'Though the merit is not mine, for I thought little of you until I saw you, let the undeserved reward be mine in your trust and love. And in this—in this, Florence; on the first night of my taking up my abode here; I am led on as it is best I should be, to say it for the first and last time.'

Florence, without knowing why, felt almost afraid to hear her proceed, but kept her eyes riveted on the beautiful face so fixed upon her own.

'Never seek to find in me,' said Edith, laying her hand upon her breast, 'what is not here. Never if you can help it, Florence, fall off from me because it is *not* here. Little by little you will know me better, and the time will come when you will know me, as I know myself. Then, be as lenient to me as you can, and do not turn to bitterness the only sweet remembrance I shall have.'

The tears that were visible in her eyes as she kept them fixed on Florence, showed that the composed face was but as a handsome mask; but she preserved it, and continued—

'I *have* seen what you say, and know how true it is. But believe me—you will soon, if you cannot now—there is no one on this earth less qualified to set it right or help you, Florence, than I. Never ask me

why, or speak to me about it or of my husband, more.
There should be, so far, a division, and a silence between us two, like the grave itself.'

She sat for some time silent; Florence scarcely
venturing to breathe meanwhile, as dim and imperfect
shadows of the truth, and all its daily consequences,
chased each other through her terrified, yet incredulous imagination. Almost as soon as she had ceased
to speak, Edith's face began to subside from its set
composure to that quieter and more relenting aspect,
which it usually wore when she and Florence were
alone together. She shaded it, after this change,
with her hands; and when she arose, and with an affectionate embrace bade Florence good night, went
quickly, and without looking round.

But when Florence was in bed, and the room was
dark except for the glow of the fire, Edith returned,
and saying that she could not sleep, and that her
dressing-room was lonely, drew a chair upon the
hearth, and watched the embers as they died away.
Florence watched them too from her bed, until they,
and the noble figure before them, crowned with its
flowing hair, and in its thoughtful eyes reflecting
back their light, became confused and indistinct, and
finally were lost in slumber.

In her sleep, however, Florence could not lose an
undefined impression of what had so recently passed.
It formed the subject of her dreams, and haunted her;
now in one shape, now in another; but always oppres-
sively; and with a sense of fear. She dreamed of
seeking her father in wildernesses, of following his
track up fearful heights, and down into deep mines
and caverns; of being charged with something that
would release him from extraordinary suffering—
she knew not what, or why—yet never being able to
attain the goal and set him free. Then she saw him

dead, upon that very bed, and in that very room, and knew that he had never loved her to the last, and fell upon his cold breast, passionately weeping. Then a prospect opened, and a river flowed, and a plaintive voice she knew, cried, 'It is running on, Floy! It has never stopped! You are moving with it!' And she saw him at a distance stretching out his arms towards her, while a figure such as Walter's used to be, stood near him, awfully serene and still. In every vision, Edith came and went, sometimes to her joy, sometimes to her sorrow, until they were alone upon the brink of a dark grave, and Edith pointing down, she looked and saw—what!—another Edith lying at the bottom.

In the terror of this dream, she cried out and awoke, she thought. A soft voice seemed to whisper in her ear, 'Florence, dear Florence, it is nothing but a dream!' and stretching out her arms, she returned the caress of her new mamma, who then went out at the door in the light of the grey morning. In a moment, Florence sat up wondering whether this had really taken place or not; but she was only certain that it was grey morning indeed, and that the blackened ashes of the fire were on the hearth, and that she was alone.

So passed the night on which the happy pair came home.

CHAPTER XXXVI

HOUSEWARMING

MANY succeeding days passed in like manner; except that there were numerous visits received and paid, and that Mrs. Skewton held little levees in her own apartments, at which Major Bagstock was a frequent attendant, and that Florence encountered no second look from her father, although she saw him every day. Nor had she much communication in words with her new mamma, who was imperious and proud to all the house but her—Florence could not but observe that—and who, although she always sent for her or went to her when she came home from visiting, and would always go into her own room at night, before retiring to rest, however late the hour, and never lost an opportunity of being with her, was often her silent and thoughtful companion for a long time together.

Florence, who had hoped for so much from this marriage, could not help sometimes comparing the bright house with the faded dreary place out of which it had arisen, and wondering when, in any shape, it would begin to be a home; for that it was no home then, for any one, though everything went on luxuriously and regularly, she had always a secret misgiving. Many an hour of sorrowful reflection by day and night, and many a tear of blighted hope, Florence bestowed upon the assurance her new mamma had given her so strongly, that there was no one on the earth more powerless than herself to teach her how to win her father's heart. And soon Florence began to think—resolved to think would be the truer phrase —that as no one knew so well, how hopeless of being subdued or changed her father's coldness to her was, so she had given her this warning, and forbidden the subject in very compassion. Unselfish here, as in her every act and fancy, Florence preferred to bear the pain of this new wound, rather than encourage any faint foreshadowings of the truth as it concerned her father; tender of him, even in her wandering thoughts. As for his home, she hoped it would become a better

one, when its state of novelty and transition should
be over; and for herself, thought little and lamented
less.

If none of the new family were particularly at
home in private, it was resolved that Mrs. Dombey at
least should be at home in public, without delay. A
series of entertainments in celebration of the late nuptials, and in cultivation of society, were arranged,
chiefly by Mr. Dombey and Mrs. Skewton; and it
was settled that the festive proceedings should com-
mence by Mrs. Dombey's being at home upon a certain evening, and by Mr. and Mrs. Dombey's requesting the honour of the company of a great many
incongruous people to dinner on the same day.

Accordingly, Mr. Dombey produced a list of sundry eastern magnates who were to be bidden to this
feast on his behalf; to which Mrs. Skewton, acting for
her dearest child, who was haughtily careless on the
subject, subjoined a western list, comprising cousin
Feenix, not yet returned to Baden-Baden, greatly to
the detriment of his personal estate; and a variety of
moths of various degrees and ages, who had, at various times, fluttered round the light of her fair daughter, or herself, without any lasting injury to their
wings.   Florence was enrolled as a member of the
dinner-party, by Edith's command—elicited by a moment's doubt and hesitation on the part of Mrs. Skewton; and Florence, with a wondering heart, and with
a quick instinctive sense of everything that grated on
her father in the least, took her silent share in the
proceedings of the day.

The proceedings commenced by Mr. Dombey, in a
cravat of extraordinary height and stiffness walking
restlessly about the drawing-room until the hour appointed for dinner; punctual to which, an East India
Director, of immense wealth, in a waistcoat appar-

ently constructed in serviceable deal by some plain
carpenter, but really engendered in the tailor's art,
and composed of the material called nankeen, arrived,
and was received by Mr. Dombey alone.   The next
stage of the proceedings was Mr. Dombey's sending
his compliments to Mrs. Dombey, with a correct statement of the time; and the next, the East India Director's falling prostrate, in a conversational point of
view, and as Mr. Dombey was not the man to pick
him up, staring at the fire until rescue appeared in
the person of Mrs. Skewton; whom the Director, as
a pleasant start in life for the evening, mistook for
Mrs. Dombey, and greeted with enthusiasm.

The next arrival was a Bank Director, reputed to
be able to buy up anything—human nature generally,
if he should take it in his head to influence the money
market in that direction—but who was a wonderfully
modest spoken man, almost boastfully so, and mentioned his 'little place' at Kingston-upon-Thames, and
its just being barely equal to giving Dombey a bed
and a chop, if he would come and visit it.   Ladies,
he said, it was not for a man who lived in his quiet
way to take upon himself to invite—but if Mrs. Skewton and her daughter, Mrs. Dombey, should ever find
themselves in that direction, and would do him the
honour to look at a little bit of a shrubbery they would
find there, and a poor little flower-bed or so, and a
humble apology for a pinery, and two or three little
attempts of that sort without any pretension, they
would distinguish him very much.   Carrying out his
character, this gentleman was very plainly dressed, in
a wisp of cambric for a neckcloth, big shoes, a coat
that was too loose for him, and a pair of trousers that
were too spare; and mention being made of the Opera
by Mrs. Skewton, he said he very seldom went there,
for he couldn't afford it.   It seemed greatly to de-

light and exhilarate him to say so: and he beamed on his audience afterwards with his hands in his pockets, and excessive satisfaction twinkling in his eyes.

Now Mrs. Dombey appeared, beautiful and proud, and as disdainful and defiant of them all as if the bridal wreath upon her head had been a garland of steel spikes put on to force concession from her which she would die sooner than yield. With her was Florence. When they entered together, the shadow of the night of the return again darkened Mr. Dombey's face. But unobserved: for Florence did not venture to raise her eyes to his, and Edith's indifference was too supreme to take the least heed of him.

The arrivals quickly became numerous. More directors, chairmen of public companies, elderly ladies carrying burdens on their heads for full dress, cousin Feenix, Major Bagstock, friends of Mrs. Skewton, with the same bright bloom on their complexion, and very precious necklaces on very withered necks. Among these, a young lady of sixty-five, remarkably coolly dressed as to her back and shoulders, who spoke with an engaging lisp, and whose eyelids wouldn't keep up well, without a great deal of trouble on her part, and whose manners had that indefinable charm which so frequently attaches to the giddiness of youth. As the greater part of Mr. Dombey's list were disposed to be taciturn, and the greater part of Mrs. Dombey's list were disposed to be talkative, and there was no sympathy between them, Mrs. Dombey's list, by magnetic agreement, entered into a bond of union against Mr. Dombey's list, who, wandering about the rooms in a desolate manner, or seeking refuge in corners, entangled themselves with company coming in, and became barricaded behind sofas, and had doors opened smartly from without against their heads, and underwent every sort of discomfiture.

When dinner was announced, Mr. Dombey took down an old lady like a crimson velvet pincushion stuffed with bank-notes, who might have been the identical old lady of Threadneedle Street, she was so rich, and looked so unaccommodating; cousin Feenix took down Mrs. Dombey; Major Bagstock took down Mrs. Skewton; the young thing with the shoulders was bestowed, as an extinguisher, upon the East India Director; and the remaining ladies were left on view in the drawing-room by the remaining gentlemen, until a forlorn hope volunteered to conduct them downstairs, and those brave spirits with their captives blocked up the dining-room door, shutting out seven mild men in the stony-hearted hall. When all the rest were got in and were seated, one of these mild men still appeared, in smiling confusion, totally destitute and unprovided for, and escorted by the butler, made the complete circuit of the table twice before his chair could be found, which it finally was, on Mrs. Dombey's left hand; after which the mild man never held up his head again.

Now, the spacious dining-room, with the company seated round the glittering table, busy with their glittering spoons, and knives and forks, and plates, might have been taken for a grown-up exposition of Tom Tiddler's ground, where children pick up gold and silver. Mr. Dombey, as Tiddler, looked his character to admiration; and the long plateau of precious metal frosted, separating him from Mrs. Dombey, whereon frosted Cupids offered scentless flowers to each of them, was allegorical to see.

Cousin Feenix was in great force, and looked astonishingly young. But he was sometimes thought-

less in his good-humour—his memory occasionally
wandering like his legs—and on this occasion caused
the company to shudder. It happened thus. The
young lady with the back, who regarded cousin Feenix
with sentiments of tenderness, had entrapped the East
India Director into leading her to the chair next him;
in return for which good office, she immediately abandoned the Director, who, being shaded on the other
side by a gloomy black velvet hat surmounting a bony
and speechless female with a fan, yielded to a depression of spirits and withdrew into himself. Cousin
Feenix and the young lady were very lively and humorous, and the young lady laughed so much at
something cousin Feenix related to her, that Major
Bagstock begged leave to inquire on behalf of Mrs.
Skewton (they were sitting opposite, a little lower
down), whether that might not be considered public
property.

'Why, upon my life,' said cousin Feenix, 'there's
nothing in it; it really is not worth repeating: in point
of fact, it's merely an anecdote of Jack Adams. I
dare say my friend Dombey'; for the general attention was concentrated on cousin Feenix; 'may remember Jack Adams, Jack Adams, not Joe; that was his
brother. Jack—little Jack—man with a cast in his
eye, and slight impediment in his speech—man who
sat for somebody's borough. We used to call him in
my parliamentary time W. P. Adams, in consequence
of his being Warming Pan for a young fellow who
was in his minority. Perhaps my friend Dombey
may have known the man?'

Mr. Dombey, who was as likely to have known Guy
Fawkes, replied in the negative. But one of the
seven mild men unexpectedly leaped into distinction,
by saying *he* had known him, and adding—'always
wore Hessian boots!'

'Exactly,' said cousin Feenix, bending forward to
see the mild man, and smile encouragement at him
down the table. 'That was Jack. Joe wore—'

'Tops!' cried the mild man, rising in public estima-
tion every instant.

'*Of* course,' said cousin Feenix, 'you were intimate
with 'em?'

'I knew them both,' said the mild man. With
whom Mr. Dombey immediately took wine.

'Devilish good fellow, Jack!' said cousin Feenix,
again bending forward, and smiling.

'Excellent,' returned the mild man, becoming bold
on his success. 'One of the best fellows I ever knew.'

'No doubt you have heard the story?' said cousin
Feenix.

'I shall know,' replied the bold mild man, 'when I
have heard your ludship tell it.' With that he leaned
back in his chair and smiled at the ceiling, as knowing
it by heart, and being already tickled.

'In point of fact, it's nothing of a story in itself,'
said cousin Feenix, addressing the table with a smile,
and a gay shake of his head, 'and not worth a word
of preface. But it's illustrative of the neatness of
Jack's humour. The fact is, that Jack was invited
down to a marriage—which I think took place in
Barkshire?'

'Shropshire,' said the bold mild man, finding himself
appealed to.

'Was it? Well! In point of fact it might have
been in any shire,' said cousin Feenix. 'So my friend
being invited down to this marriage in Anyshire,' with
a pleasant sense of the readiness of this joke, 'goes.
Just as some of us, having had the honour of being
invited to the marriage of my lovely and accomplished
relative with my friend Dombey, didn't require to be
asked twice, and were devilish glad to be present on

so interesting an occasion.—Goes—Jack goes. Now, this marriage was, in point of fact, the marriage of an uncommonly fine girl with a man for whom she didn't care a button, but whom she accepted on account of his property, which was immense. When Jack returned to town, after the nuptials, a man he knew, meeting him in the lobby of the House of Commons, says, "Well, Jack, how are the ill-matched couple?" "Ill-matched," says Jack. "Not at all. It's a perfectly fair and equal transaction. *She* is regularly bought, and you may take your oath *he* is as regularly sold!"'

In his full enjoyment of this culminating point of his story the shudder, which had gone all round the table like an electric spark, struck cousin Feenix, and he stopped. Not a smile occasioned by the only general topic of conversation broached that day, appeared on any face. A profound silence ensued; and the wretched mild man, who had been as innocent of any real foreknowledge of the story as the child unborn, had the exquisite misery of reading in every eye that he was regarded as the prime mover of the mischief.

Mr. Dombey's face was not a changeful one, and being cast in its mould of state that day, showed little other apprehension of the story, if any, than that which he expressed when he said solemnly, amidst the silence, that it was 'Very good.' There was a rapid glance from Edith towards Florence, but otherwise she remained, externally, impassive and unconscious.

Through the various stages of rich meats and wines, continual gold and silver, dainties of earth, air, fire, and water, heaped-up fruits, and that unnecessary article in Mr. Dombey's banquets—ice—the dinner slowly made its way: the later stages being achieved to the sonorous music of incessant double-knocks, announcing the arrival of visitors, whose portion of the feast was limited to the smell thereof. When Mrs. Dombey rose, it was a sight to see her lord, with stiff throat and erect head, hold the door open for the withdrawal of the ladies; and to see how she swept past him with his daughter on her arm.

Mr. Dombey was a grave sight, behind the decanters, in a state of dignity; and the East India Director was a forlorn sight near the unoccupied end of the table, in a state of solitude; and the major was a military sight, relating stories of the Duke of York to six of the seven mild men (the ambitious one was utterly quenched); and the Bank Director was a lowly sight, making a plan of his little attempt at a pinery, with dessert-knives, for a group of admirers; and cousin Feenix was a thoughtful sight, as he smoothed his long wristbands and stealthily adjusted his wig. But all these sights were of short duration, being speedily broken up by coffee, and the desertion of the room.

There was a throng in the state-rooms upstairs, increasing every minute; but still Mr. Dombey's list of visitors appeared to have some native impossibility of amalgamation with Mrs. Dombey's list, and no one could have doubted which was which. The single exception to this rule perhaps was Mr. Carker, who now smiled among the company, and who, as he stood in the circle that was gathered about Mrs. Dombey—watchful of her, of them, his chief, Cleopatra and the major, Florence, and everything around—appeared at ease with both divisions of guests, and not marked as exclusively belonging to either.

Florence had a dread of him, which made his presence in the room a nightmare to her. She could not avoid the recollection of it, for her eyes were drawn towards him every now and then, by an attraction of dislike and distrust that she could not resist. Yet her thoughts were busy with other things; for as she sat apart—not unadmired or unsought, but in the gentleness of her quiet spirit—she felt how little part her father had in what was going on, and saw, with pain, how ill at ease he seemed to be, and how little regarded he was as he lingered about near the door, for those visitors whom he wished to distinguish with particular attention, and took them up to introduce them to his wife, who received them with proud coldness, but showed no interest or wish to please, and never, after the bare ceremony of reception, in consultation of his wishes, or in welcome of his friends, opened her lips. It was not the less perplexing or painful to Florence, that she who acted thus, treated her so kindly and with such loving consideration, that it almost seemed an ungrateful return on her part even to know of what was passing before her eyes.

Happy Florence would have been, might she have ventured to bear her father company, by so much as a look; and happy Florence was, in little suspecting the main cause of his uneasiness. But afraid of seeming to know that he was placed at any disadvantage, lest he should be resentful of that knowledge; and divided between her impulse towards him, and her grateful affection for Edith; she scarcely dared to raise her eyes towards either. Anxious and unhappy for them both, the thought stole on her through the crowd, that it might have been better for them if this noise of tongues and tread of feet had never come there,—if the old dulness and decay had never been replaced by novelty and splendour,—if the neglected child had found no friend in Edith, but had lived her solitary life, unpitied and forgotten.

Mrs. Chick had some such thoughts too, but they were not so quietly developed in her mind. This good matron had been outraged in the first instance by not receiving an invitation to dinner.   That blow partially recovered, she had gone to a vast expense to make such a figure before Mrs. Dombey at home, as should dazzle the senses of that lady, and heap mortification, mountains high, on the head of Mrs. Skewton.

'But I am made,' said Mrs. Chick to Mr. Chick, 'of no more account than Florence! Who takes the smallest notice of me? No one!'

'No one, my dear,' assented Mr. Chick, who was seated by the side of Mrs. Chick against the wall, and could console himself, even there, by softly whistling.

'Does it at all appear as if I was wanted here?' exclaimed Mrs. Chick, with flashing eyes.

'No, my dear, I don't think it does,' said Mr. Chick.

'Paul's mad!' said Mrs. Chick.

Mr. Chick whistled.

'Unless you are a monster, which I sometimes think you are,' said Mrs. Chick with candour, 'don't sit there humming tunes. How any one with the most distant feelings of a man, can see that mother-in-law of Paul's, dressed as she is, going on like that, with Major Bagstock, for whom, among other precious things, we are indebted to your Lucretia Tox—'

'*My* Lucretia Tox. my dear!' said Mr. Chick astounded.

'Yes,' retorted Mrs. Chick, with great severity, '*your* Lucretia Tox—I say how anybody can see that mother-in-law of Paul's, and that haughty wife of Paul's, and these indecent old frights with their backs and shoulders, and in short this at home generally, and hum—,' on which word Mrs. Chick laid a scornful emphasis that made Mr. Chick start, 'is, I thank Heaven, a mystery to me!'

Mr. Chick screwed his mouth into a form irreconcilable with humming or whistling, and looked very contemplative.

'But I hope I know what is due to myself,' said Mrs. Chick, swelling with indignation, 'though Paul has forgotten what is due to me. I am not going to sit here, a member of this family, to be taken no notice of. I am not the dirt under Mrs. Dombey's feet, yet—not quite yet,' said Mrs. Chick, as if she expected to become so, about the day after to-morrow. 'And I shall go. I will not say (whatever I may think) that this affair has been got up solely to degrade and insult me. I shall merely go. I shall not be missed!'

Mrs. Chick rose erect with these words, and took the arm of Mr. Chick, who escorted her from the room, after half an hour's shady sojourn there. And it is due to her penetration to observe that she certainly was not missed at all.

But she was not the only indignant guest; for Mr. Dombey's list (still constantly in difficulties) were, as a body, indignant with Mrs. Dombey's list, for looking at them through eye-glasses, and audibly wondering who all those people were; while Mrs. Dombey's list complained of weariness, and the young thing with the shoulders, deprived of the attentions of that gay youth cousin Feenix (who went away from the dinner-table), confidentially alleged to thirty or forty friends that she was bored to death. All the old ladies with the burdens on their heads, had greater or less cause of complaint against Mrs. Dombey; and the Directors and Chairmen coincided in thinking that if Dombey must marry, he had better have married somebody nearer his own age, not quite so handsome, and a little better off. The general opinion among this class of gentlemen was, that it was a weak thing in Dombey, and he'd live to repent it. Hardly anybody there, except the mild men, stayed, or went away, without considering himself or herself neglected and aggrieved by Mr. Dombey or Mrs. Dombey; and the speechless female in the black velvet hat was found to have been stricken mute, because the lady in the crimson velvet had been handed down before her. The nature even of the mild men got corrupted, either from their curdling it with too much lemonade, or from the general inoculation that prevailed; and they made sarcastic jokes to one another, and whispered disparagement on stairs and in by-places. The general dissatisfaction and discomfort so diffused itself, that the assembled footmen in the hall were as well acquainted with it as the company above. Nay, the very linkmen outside got hold of it, and compared the party to a funeral out of mourning, with none of the company remembered in the will.

At last, the guests were all gone, and the linkmen too; and the street, crowded so long with carriages, was clear; and the dying lights showed no one in the rooms, but Mr. Dombey and Mr. Carker, who were talking together apart, and Mrs. Dombey and her mother: the former seated on an ottoman; the latter reclining in the Cleopatra attitude, awaiting the arrival of her maid. Mr. Dombey having finished his communication to Carker, the latter advanced obsequiously to take leave.

'I trust,' he said, 'that the fatigues of this delightful evening will not inconvenience Mrs. Dombey tomorrow.'

'Mrs. Dombey,' said Mr. Dombey, advancing. 'has sufficiently spared herself fatigue, to relieve you from any anxiety of that kind. I regret to say, Mrs. Dombey, that I could have wished you had fatigued yourself a little more on this occasion.'

She looked at him with a supercilious glance, that it seemed not worth her while to protract, and turned away her eyes without speaking.

'I am sorry, madam,' said Mr. Dombey, 'that you should not have thought it your duty—'

She looked at him again.

'Your duty, madam,' pursued Mr. Dombey, 'to have received my friends with a little more deference. Some of those whom you have been pleased to slight to-night in a very marked manner, Mrs. Dombey, confer a distinction upon you, I must tell you, in any visit they pay you.'

'Do you know that there is some one here?' she returned, now looking at him steadily.

'No! Carker! I beg that you do not. I insist that you do not,' cried Mr. Dombey, stopping that noiseless gentleman in his withdrawal. 'Mr. Carker, madam, as you know, possesses my confidence. He is as well acquainted as myself with the subject on which I speak. I beg to tell you, for your information, Mrs. Dombey, that I consider these wealthy and important persons confer a distinction upon *me*': and Mr. Dombey drew himself up, as having now rendered them of the highest possible importance.

'I ask you,' she repeated, bending her disdainful, steady gaze upon him, 'do you know that there is some one here, sir?'

'I must entreat,' said Mr. Carker, stepping forward, 'I must beg, I must demand, to be released. Slight and unimportant as this difference is—'

Mrs. Skewton, who had been intent upon her daughter's face, took him up here.

'My sweetest Edith,' she said, 'and my dearest Dombey; our excellent friend Mr. Carker, for so I am sure I ought to mention him—'

Mr. Carker murmured, 'Too much honour.'

—'has used the very words that were in my mind, and that I have been dying, these ages, for an opportunity of introducing. Slight and unimportant! My sweetest Edith, and my dearest Dombey, do we not know that any difference between you two— No, Flowers; not now.'

Flowers was the maid, who, finding gentlemen present, retreated with precipitation.

'That any difference between you two,' resumed Mrs. Skewton, 'with the Heart you possess in common, and the excessively charming bond of feeling that there is between you, *must* be slight and unimportant? What words could better define the fact? None. Therefore I am glad to take this slight occasion—this trifling occasion, that is so replete with Nature, and your individual characters, and all that— so truly calculated to bring the tears into a parent's eyes—to say that I attach no importance to them in the least, except as developing these minor elements of Soul; and that, unlike most mammas-in-law (that odious phrase, dear Dombey!) as they have been represented to me to exist in this I fear too artificial world, I never shall attempt to interpose between you, at such a time, and never can much regret, after all, such little flashes of the torch of What's-his-name— not Cupid, but the other delightful creature.'

There was a sharpness in the good mother's glance at both her children as she spoke, that may have been expressive of a direct and well-considered purpose hidden between these rambling words. That purpose, providently to detach herself in the beginning from all the clankings of their chain that were to come, and to shelter herself with the fiction of her innocent belief in their mutual affection, and their adaptation to each other.

'I have pointed out to Mrs. Dombey,' said Mr. Dombey, in his most stately manner, 'that in her conduct thus early in our married life, to which I object, and which I request, may be corrected.   Carker,' with a nod of dismissal, 'good night to you!'

Mr. Carker bowed to the imperious form of the bride, whose sparkling eye was fixed upon her husband; and stopping at Cleopatra's couch on his way out, raised to his lips the hand she graciously extended to him, in lowly and admiring homage.

If his handsome wife had reproached him, or even changed countenance, or broken the silence in which she remained, by one word, now that they were alone (for Cleopatra made off with all speed), Mr. Dombey would have been equal to some assertion of his case against her.   But the intense, unutterable, withering scorn, with which, after looking upon him, she dropped her eyes, as if he were too worthless and indifferent to her to be challenged with a syllable— the ineffable disdain and haughtiness in which she sat before him—the cold inflexible resolve with which her every feature seemed to bear him down, and put him by—these he had no resource against; and he left her, with her whole overbearing beauty concentrated on despising him.

Was he coward enough to watch her, an hour afterwards, on the old well staircase, where he had once seen Florence in the moonlight, toiling up with Paul? Or was he in the dark by accident, when, looking up, he saw her coming, with a light, from the room where Florence lay, and marked again the face so changed, which *he* could not subdue?

But it could never alter as his own did.   It never, in its utmost pride and passion, knew the shadow that had fallen on his, in the dark corner, on the night of the return; and often since; and which deepened on it now as he looked up.

CHAPTER XXXVII

MORE WARNINGS THAN ONE

FLORENCE, Edith, and Mrs. Skewton were together next day, and the carriage was waiting at the door to take them out. For Cleopatra had her galley again now, and Withers, no longer the wan, stood upright in a pigeon-breasted jacket and military trousers, behind her wheel-less chair at dinner-time, and butted no more. The hair of Withers was radiant with pomatum, in these days of down, and he wore kid gloves and smelt of the water of Cologne.

They were assembled in Cleopatra's room. The Serpent of old Nile (not to mention her disrespectfully) was reposing on her sofa, sipping her morning chocolate at three o'clock in the afternoon, and Flowers the maid was fastening on her youthful cuffs and frills, and performing a kind of private coronation ceremony on her, with a peach-coloured velvet bonnet; the artificial roses in which nodded to uncommon advantage, as the palsy trifled with them, like a breeze.

'I think I am a little nervous this morning, Flowers,' said Mrs. Skewton. 'My hand quite shakes.'

'You were the life of the party last night, ma'am, you know,' returned Flowers, 'and you suffer for it, to-day, you see.'

Edith, who had beckoned Florence to the window, and was looking out, with her back turned on the toilet of her esteemed mother, suddenly withdrew from it, as if it had lightened.

'My darling child,' cried Cleopatra, languidly, '*you* are not nervous? Don't tell me, my dear Edith, that you, so enviably self-possessed, are beginning to be a martyr too, like your unfortunately constituted mother! Withers, some one at the door.'

'Card, ma'am,' said Withers, taking it towards Mrs. Dombey.

'I am going out,' she said, without looking at it.

'My dear love,' drawled Mrs. Skewton, 'how very odd to send that message without seeing the name! Bring it here, Withers. Dear me, my love; Mr. Carker, too! That very sensible person!'

'I am going out,' repeated Edith, in so imperious a tone that Withers, going to the door, imperiously informed the servant who was waiting, 'Mrs. Dombey is going out. Get along with you,' and shut it on him.

But the servant came back after a short absence, and whispered to Withers again, who once more, and not very willingly, presented himself before Mrs. Dombey.

'If you please, ma'am, Mr. Carker sends his respectful compliments, and begs you will spare him one minute, if you could—for business, ma'am, if you please.'

'Really, my love,' said Mrs. Skewton in her mildest manner; for her daughter's face was threatening; 'if you would allow me to offer a word, I should recommend—'

'Show him this way,' said Edith. As Withers disappeared to execute the command, she added, frowning on her mother, 'As he comes at your recommendation, let him come to your room.'

'May I—shall I go away?' asked Florence, hurriedly.

Edith nodded yes, but on her way to the door, Florence met the visitor coming in. With the same disagreeable mixture of familiarity and forbearance with which he had first addressed her, he addressed

her now in the softest manner—hoped she was quite
well—needed not to ask, with such looks to anticipate
the answer—had scarcely had the honour to know her,.
last night, she was so greatly changed—and held the
door open for her to pass out: with a secret sense of
power in her shrinking from him, that all the deference and politeness of his manner could not quite
conceal.

He then bowed himself for a moment over Mrs.
Skewton's condescending hand, and lastly bowed to
Edith. Coldly returning his salute without looking
at him, neither seating herself, nor inviting him to be
seated, she waited for him to speak.

Entrenched in her pride and power, and with all
the obduracy of her spirit summoned about her, still
her old conviction that she and her mother had been
known by this man in their worst colours, from their
first acquaintance; that every degradation she had
suffered in her own eyes was as plain to him as to herself; that he read her life as though it were a vile
book, and fluttered the leaves before her in slight
looks and tones of voice which no one else could de-
tect; weakened and undermined her. Proudly as she
opposed herself to him, with her commanding face
exacting his humility, her disdainful lip repulsing him,.
her bosom angry at his intrusion, and the dark lashes
of her eyes sullenly veiling their light, that no ray of
it might shine upon him—and submissively as he
stood before her, with an entreating injured manner,
but with complete submission to her will—she knew,
in her own soul, that the cases were reversed, and that
the triumph and superiority were his, and that he
knew it full well.

'I have presumed,' said Mr. Carker, 'to solicit an
interview, and I have ventured to describe it as being
one of business, because—'

'Perhaps you are charged by Mr. Dombey with some message of reproof,' said Edith. 'You possess Mr. Dombey's confidence in such an unusual degree, sir, that you would scarcely surprise me if that were your business.'

'I have no message to the lady who sheds a lustre upon his name,' said Mr. Carker. 'But I entreat that lady, on my own behalf, to be just to a very humble claimant for justice at her hands—a mere dependant of Mr. Dombey's—which is a position of humility; and to reflect upon my perfect helplessness last night, and the impossibility of my avoiding the share that was forced upon me in a very painful occasion.'

'My dearest Edith,' hinted Cleopatra in a low voice, as she held her eye-glasses aside, 'really very charming of Mr. What 's-his-name. And full of heart!'

'For I do,' said Mr. Carker, appealing to Mrs. Skewton with a look of grateful deference,—'I do venture to call it a painful occasion, though merely because it was so to me, who had the misfortune to be present. So slight a difference, as between the principals—between those who love each other with disinterested devotion, and would make any sacrifice of self, in such a cause—is nothing. As Mrs. Skewton herself expressed, with so much truth and feeling last night, it is nothing.'

Edith could not look at him, but she said after a few moments—

'And your business, sir—'

'Edith, my pet,' said Mrs. Skewton, 'all this time Mr. Carker is standing! My dear Mr. Carker, take a seat, I beg.'

He offered no reply to the mother, but fixed his eyes on the proud daughter, as though he would only be bidden by her, and was resolved to be bidden by

her.   Edith, in spite of herself, sat down, and slightly
motioned with her hand to him to be seated too.   No
action could be colder, haughtier, more insolent in its
air of supremacy and disrespect, but she had struggled
against even that concession ineffectually, and it was
wrested from her.   That was enough!   Mr. Carker
sat down.

'May I be allowed, madam,' said Carker, turning his
white teeth on Mrs. Skewton like a light—'a lady of
your excellent sense and quick feeling will give me
credit, for good reason, I am sure—to address what
I have to say, to Mrs. Dombey, and to leave her to
impart it to you who are her best and dearest friend
—next to Mr. Dombey?'

Mrs. Skewton would have retired, but Edith
stopped her.   Edith would have stopped him too, and
indignantly ordered him to speak openly or not at all,
but that he said, in a low voice—'Miss Florence—the
young lady who has just left the room—'

Edith suffered him to proceed.   She looked at him
now.   As he bent forward, to be nearer, with the utmost show of delicacy and respect, and with his teeth
persuasively arrayed, in a self-depreciating smile, she
felt as if she could have struck him dead.

'Miss Florence's position,' he began, 'has been an
unfortunate one.   I have a difficulty in alluding to
it to you, whose attachment to her father is naturally
watchful and jealous of every word that applies to
him.'   Always distinct and soft in speech, no language could describe the extent of his distinctness
and softness, when he said these words, or came to
any others of a similar import.   'But, as one who is
devoted to Mr. Dombey in his different way, and
whose life is passed in admiration of Mr. Dombey's
character, may I say, without offence to your tender-

ness as a wife, that Miss Florence has unhappily been neglected—by her father? May I say by her father?'

Edith replied, 'I know it.'

'You know it!' said Mr. Carker, with a great appearance of relief. 'It removes a mountain from my breast. May I hope you know how the neglect originated; in what an amiable phase of Mr. Dombey's pride—character I mean?'

'You may pass that by, sir,' she returned, 'and come the sooner to the end of what you have to say.'

'Indeed, I am sensible, madam,' replied Carker—'trust me, I am deeply sensible, that Mr. Dombey can require no justification in anything to you. But, kindly judge of my breast by your own, and you will forgive my interest in him, if in its excess, it goes at all astray.'

What a stab to her proud heart, to sit there, face to face with him, and have him tendering her false oath at the altar again and again for her acceptance, and pressing it upon her like the dregs of a sickening cup she could not own her loathing of, or turn away from! How shame, remorse, and passion raged within her, when, upright and majestic in her beauty before him, she knew that in her spirit she was down at his feet!

'Miss Florence,' said Carker, 'left to the care—if one may call it care—of servants and mercenary people, in every way her inferiors, necessarily wanted some guide and compass in her younger days, and, naturally, for want of them, has been indiscreet, and has in some degree forgotten her station. There was some folly about one Walter, a common lad, who is fortunately dead now: and some very undesirable association, I regret to say, with certain coasting sailors, of anything but good repute, and a runaway old bankrupt.'

'I have heard the circumstances, sir,' said Edith, flashing her disdainful glance upon him, 'and I know that you pervert them. You may not know it, I hope so.'

'Pardon me,' said Mr. Carker, 'I believe that nobody knows them so well as I. Your generous and ardent nature, madam—the same nature which is so nobly imperative in vindication of your beloved and honoured husband, and which has blessed him as even his merits deserve—I must respect, defer to, bow before. But, as regards the circumstances, which is indeed the business I presumed to solicit your attention to, I can have no doubt, since, in the execution of my trust as Mr. Dombey's confidential—I presume to say—friend, I have fully ascertained them. In my execution of that trust; in my deep concern which you can so well understand, for everything relating to him, intensified, if you will (for I fear I labour under your displeasure), by the lower motive of desire to prove my diligence, and make myself the more acceptable; I have long pursued these circumstances by myself and trustworthy instruments, and have innumerable and most minute proofs.'

She raised her eyes no higher than his mouth, but she saw the means of mischief vaunted in every tooth it contained.

'Pardon me, madam,' he continued, 'if in my perplexity, I presume to take counsel with you, and to consult your pleasure. I think I have observed that you are greatly interested in Miss Florence?'

What was there in her he had not observed, and did not know? Humbled and yet maddened by the thought, in every new presentment of it, however faint, she pressed her teeth upon her quivering lip to force composure on it, and distantly inclined her head in reply.

'This interest, madam—so touching an evidence of everything associated with Mr. Dombey being dear to you—induces me to pause before I make him acquainted with these circumstances, which, as yet, he does not know. It so far shakes me, if I may make the confession, in my allegiance, that on the intimation of the least desire to that effect from you, I would suppress them.'

Edith raised her head quickly, and starting back, bent her dark glance upon him. He met it with his blandest and most deferential smile, and went on.

'You say that as I describe them, they are perverted. I fear not—I fear not: but let us assume that they are. The uneasiness I have for some time felt on the subject, arises in this: that the mere circumstance of such association often repeated, on the part of Miss Florence, however innocently and confidingly, would be conclusive with Mr. Dombey, already predisposed against her, and would lead him to take some step (I know he has occasionally contemplated it) of separation and alienation of her from his home. Madam, bear with me, and remember my intercourse with Mr. Dombey, and my knowledge of him, and my reverence for him, almost from childhood, when I say that if he has a fault, it is a lofty stubbornness, rooted in that noble pride and sense of power which belong to him, and which we must all defer to; which is not assailable like the obstinacy of other characters; and which grows upon itself from day to day, and year to year.'

She bent her glance upon him still; but, look as steadfast as she would, her haughty nostrils dilated, and her breath came somewhat deeper, and her lip would slightly curl, as he described that in his patron to which they must all bow down. He saw it; and though his expression did not change, she knew he saw it.

'Even so slight an incident as last night's,' he said, 'if I might refer to it once more, would serve to illustrate my meaning, better than a greater one. Dombey and Son know neither time, nor place, nor season, but bear them all down. But I rejoice in its occurrence, for it has opened the way for me to approach Mrs. Dombey with this subject to-day, even if it has entailed upon me the penalty of her temporary displeasure. Madam, in the midst of my uneasiness and apprehension on this subject, I was summoned by Mr. Dombey to Leamington. There I saw you. There I could not help knowing what relation you would shortly occupy towards him—to his enduring happiness and yours. There I resolved to await the time of your establishment at home here, and to do as I have now done. I have, at heart, no fear that I shall be wanting in my duty to Mr. Dombey, if I bury what I know in your breast; for where there is but one heart and mind between two persons—as in such a marriage—one almost represents the other. I can acquit my conscience therefore, almost equally, by confidence, on such a theme, in you or him. For the reasons I have mentioned I would select you. May I aspire to the distinction of believing that my confidence is accepted, and that I am relieved from my responsibility?'

He long remembered the look she gave him—who could see it, and forget it?—and the struggle that ensued within her. At last she said—

'I accept it, sir. You will please to consider this matter at an end, and that it goes no farther.'

He bowed low, and rose. She rose too, and he took leave with all humility. But Withers, meeting him on the stairs, stood amazed at the beauty of his teeth, and at his brilliant smile; and as he rode away upon his white-legged horse, the people took him for a dentist, such was the dazzling show he made. The people took *her,* when she rode out in her carriage presently, for a great lady, as happy as she was rich and fine. But they had not seen her, just before, in her own room with no one by; and they had not heard her utterance of the three words, 'Oh Florence, Florence!'

Mrs. Skewton, reposing on her sofa, and sipping her chocolate, had heard nothing but the low word business, for which she had a mortal aversion, insomuch that she had long banished it from her vocabulary, and had gone nigh, in a charming manner and with an immense amount of heart, to say nothing of soul, to ruin divers milliners and others in consequence. Therefore Mrs. Skewton asked no questions, and showed no curiosity. Indeed, the peach-velvet bonnet gave her sufficient occupation out of doors; for being perched on the back of her head, and the day being rather windy, it was frantic to escape from Mrs. Skewton's company, and would be coaxed into no sort of compromise. When the carriage was closed, and the wind shut out, the palsy played among the artificial roses again like an alms-house-full of superannuated zephyrs; and altogether Mrs. Skewton had enough to do, and got on but indifferently.

She got on no better towards night; for when Mrs. Dombey, in her dressing-room, had been dressed and waiting for her half an hour, and Mr. Dombey, in the drawing-room, had paraded himself into a state of solemn fretfulness (they were all three going out to dinner), Flowers the maid appeared with a pale face to Mrs. Dombey, saying—

'If you please, ma'am, I beg your pardon, but I can't do nothing with missis!'

'What do you mean?' asked Edith.

'Well, ma'am,' replied the frightened maid, 'I hardly know. She's making faces!'

Edith hurried with her to her mother's room. Cleopatra was arrayed in full dress, with the diamonds, short-sleeves, rouge, curls, teeth, and other juvenility all complete; but Paralysis was not to be deceived, had known her for the object of its errand, and had struck her at her glass, where she lay like a horrible doll that had tumbled down.

They took her to pieces in very shame, and put the little of her that was real on a bed. Doctors were sent for, and soon came. Powerful remedies were resorted to; opinions given that she would rally from this shock, but would not survive another; and there she lay speechless, and staring at the ceiling for days; sometimes making inarticulate sounds in answer to such questions as did she know who were present, and the like: sometimes giving no reply either by sign or gesture, or in her unwinking eyes.

At length she began to recover consciousness, and in some degree the power of motion, though not yet of speech. One day the use of her right hand returned; and showing it to her maid who was in attendance on her, and appearing very uneasy in her mind, she made signs for a pencil and some paper. This the maid immediately provided, thinking she was going to make a will, or write some last request; and Mrs. Dombey being from home, the maid awaited the result with solemn feelings.

After much painful scrawling and erasing, and putting in of wrong characters, which seemed to tumble out of the pencil of their own accord, the old woman produced this document—

'Rose-coloured curtains.'

The maid being perfectly transfixed, and with tolerable reason, Cleopatra amended the manuscript by adding two words more, when it stood thus—

'Rose-coloured curtains for doctors.'

The maid now perceived remotely that she wished these articles to be provided for the better presentation of her complexion to the faculty; and as those in the house who knew her best, had no doubt of the correctness of this opinion, which she was soon able to establish for herself, the rose-coloured curtains were added to her bed, and she mended with increased rapidity from that hour. She was soon able to sit up, in curls and a laced cap and night-gown, and to have a little artificial bloom dropped into the hollow caverns of her cheeks.

It was a tremendous sight to see this old woman in her finery leering and mincing at Death, and playing off her youthful tricks upon him as if he had been the major; but an alteration in her mind that ensued on the paralytic stroke was fraught with as much matter for reflection, and was quite as ghastly.

Whether the weakening of her intellect made her more cunning and false than before, or whether it confused her between what she had assumed to be and what she really had been, or whether it had awakened any glimmering of remorse, which could neither struggle into light nor get back into total darkness, or whether, in the jumble of her faculties, a combination of these effects had been shaken up, which is perhaps the more likely supposition, the result was this:—That she became hugely exacting in respect of Edith's affection and gratitude and attention to her; highly laudatory to herself as a most inestimable parent; and very jealous of having any rival in Edith's regard. Further, in place of remembering

that compact made between them for an avoidance
of the subject, she constantly alluded to her daughter's marriage as a proof of her being an incompara-
ble mother; and all this, with the weakness and
peevishness of such a state, always serving for a sarcastic commentary on her levity and youthfulness.

'Where is Mrs. Dombey?' she would say to her
maid.

'Gone out, ma'am.'

'Gone out! Does she go out to shun her mamma,
Flowers?'

'La bless you, no ma'am. Mrs. Dombey has only
gone out for a ride with Miss Florence.'

'Miss Florence. Who's Miss Florence? Don't
tell me about Miss Florence. What's Miss Florence
to her, compared to me?'

The apposite display of the diamonds, or the peach-
velvet bonnet (she sat in the bonnet to receive visitors, weeks before she could stir out of doors), or
the dressing of her up in some gaud or other, usually
stopped the tears that began to flow hereabouts: and
she would remain in a complacent state until Edith
came to see her: when, at a glance of the proud face,
she would relapse again.

'Well, I am sure, Edith!' she would cry, shaking
her head.

'What is the matter, mother?'

'Matter! I really don't know what *is* the matter.
The world is coming to such an artificial and ungrateful state, that I begin to think there's no
Heart—or anything of that sort—left in it, positively. Withers is more a child to me than you are.
He attends to me much more than my own daughter.
I almost wish I didn't look so young—and all that
kind of thing—and then perhaps I should be more
considered.'

'What would you have, mother?'

'Oh, a great deal, Edith,' impatiently.

'Is there anything you want that you have not? It is your own fault if there be.'

'My own fault!' beginning to whimper. 'The parent I have been to you, Edith: making you a companion from your cradle! And when you neglect me, and have no more natural affection for me than if I was a stranger—not a twentieth part of the affection that you have for Florence—but I am only your mother, and should corrupt *her* in a day!—you reproach me with its being my own fault.'

'Mother, mother, I reproach you with nothing. Why will you always dwell on this?'

'Isn't it natural that I should dwell on this, when I am all affection and sensitiveness, and am wounded in the cruelest way, whenever you look at me?'

'I do not mean to wound you, mother. Have you no remembrance of what has been said between us? Let the Past rest.'

'Yes, rest! And let gratitude to me rest; and let affection for me rest; and let *me* rest in my out-of-the-way room, with no society and no attention, while you find new relations to make much of, who have no earthly claim upon you! Good gracious, Edith, do you know what an elegant establishment you are at the head of?'

'Yes. Hush!'

'And that gentlemanly creature, Dombey? Do you know that you are married to him, Edith, and that you have a settlement, and a position, and a carriage, and I don't know what?'

'Indeed, I know it, mother; well.'

'As you would have had with that delightful good soul—what did they call him?—Granger—if he hadn't died. And who have you to thank for all this, Edith?'

'You, mother; you.'

'Then put your arms round my neck, and kiss me; and show me, Edith, that you know there never was a better mamma than I have been to you. And don't let me become a perfect fright with teasing and wearing myself at your ingratitude, or when I 'm out again in society no soul will know me, not even that hateful animal, the major.'

But, sometimes, when Edith went nearer to her, and bending down her stately head, put her cold cheek to hers, the mother would draw back as if she were afraid of her, and would fall into a fit of trembling, and cry out that there was a wandering in her wits. And sometimes she would entreat her, with humility, to sit down on the chair beside her bed, and would look at her (as she sat there brooding) with a face that even the rose-coloured curtains could not make otherwise than seared and wild.

The rose-coloured curtains blushed, in course of time, on Cleopatra's bodily recovery, and on her dress—more juvenile than ever to repair the ravages of illness—and on the rouge, and on the teeth, and on the curls, and on the diamonds, and the short sleeves, and the whole wardrobe of the doll that had tumbled down before the mirror. They blushed, too, now and then, upon an indistinctness in her speech which she turned off with a girlish giggle, and on an occasional failing in her memory, that had no rule in it, but came and went fantastically, as if in mockery of her fantastic self.

But they never blushed upon a change in the new manner of her thought and speech towards her daughter. And though that daughter often came within their influence, they never blushed upon her loveliness irradiated by a smile, or softened by the light of filial love, in its stern beauty.

CHAPTER XXXVIII

MISS TOX IMPROVES AN OLD ACQUAINTANCE

THE forlorn Miss Tox, abandoned by her friend Louisa Chick, and bereft of Mr. Dombey's countenance—for no delicate pair of wedding cards, united by a silver thread, graced the chimney-glass in Princess's Place, or the harpsichord, or any of those little posts of display which Lucretia reserved for holiday occupation—became depressed in her spirits, and suffered much from melancholy. For a time the Bird Waltz was unheard in Princess's Place, the plants were neglected, and dust collected on the miniature of Miss Tox's ancestor with the powdered head and pigtail.

Miss Tox, however, was not of an age or of a disposition long to abandon herself to unavailing regrets. Only two notes of the harpsichord were dumb from disuse when the Bird Waltz again warbled and trilled in the crooked drawing-room: only one slip of geranium fell a victim to imperfect nursing, before she was gardening at her green baskets again, regularly every morning; the powdered-headed ancestor had not been under a cloud for more than six weeks, when Miss Tox breathed on his benignant visage, and polished him up with a piece of washleather.

Still, Miss Tox was lonely, and at a loss. Her attachments, however ludicrously shown, were real and strong; and she was, as she expressed it, 'deeply hurt by the unmerited contumely she had met with from Louisa.' But there was no such thing as anger in Miss Tox's composition. If she had ambled on through life, in her soft-spoken way, without any opinions, she had, at least, got so far without any harsh passions. The mere sight of Louisa Chick in the street one day, at a considerable distance, so overpowered her milky nature, that she was fain to seek immediate refuge in a pastry-cook's, and there, in a musty little back-room usually devoted to the consumption of soups, and pervaded by an ox-tail atmosphere, relieve her feelings by weeping plentifully.

Against Mr. Dombey Miss Tox hardly felt that she had any reason of complaint. Her sense of that gentleman's magnificence was such, that once removed from him, she felt as if her distance always had been immeasurable, and as if he had greatly condescended in tolerating her at all. No wife could be too handsome or too stately for him, according to Miss Tox's sincere opinion. It was perfectly natural that in looking for one, he should look high. Miss Tox with tears laid down this proposition, and fully admitted it, twenty times a day. She never recalled the lofty manner in which Mr. Dombey had made her subservient to his convenience and caprices, and had graciously permitted her to be one of the nurses of his little son. She only thought, in her own words, 'that she had passed a great many happy hours in that house, which she must ever remember with gratification, and that she could never cease to regard Mr. Dombey as one of the most impressive and dignified of men.'

Cut off, however, from the implacable Louisa, and being shy of the major (whom she viewed with some distrust now), Miss Tox found it very irksome to know nothing of what was going on in Mr. Dombey's establishment. And as she really had got into the habit of considering Dombey and Son as the pivot on which the world in general turned, she resolved, rather than be ignorant of intelligence which so strongly interested her, to cultivate her old acquaintance, Mrs. Richards, who she knew, since her last memorable appearance before Mr. Dombey, was in the habit of sometimes holding communication with his servants. Perhaps Miss Tox, in seeking out the Toodle family, had the tender motive hidden in her breast of having somebody to whom she could talk about Mr. Dombey, no matter how humble that somebody might be.

At all events, towards the Toodle habitation Miss Tox directed her steps one evening, what time Mr. Toodle, cindery and swart, was refreshing himself with tea, in the bosom of his family. Mr. Toodle had only three stages of existence. He was either taking refreshments in the bosom just mentioned, or he was tearing through the country at from twenty-five to fifty miles an hour, or he was sleeping after his fatigues. He was always in a whirlwind or a calm, and a peaceable, contented, easy-going man Mr. Toodle was in either state, who seemed to have made over all his own inheritance of fuming and fretting to the engines with which he was connected, which panted, and gasped, and chafed, and wore themselves out, in a most unsparing manner, while Mr. Toodle led a mild and equable life.

'Polly, my gal,' said Mr. Toodle, with a young Toodle on each knee, and two more making tea for him, and plenty more scattered about—Mr. Toodle was never out of children, but always kept a good supply on hand—'You an't seen our Biler lately, have you?'

'No,' replied Polly, 'but he's almost certain to look in to-night. It's his right evening, and he's very regular.'

'I suppose,' said Mr. Toodle, relishing his meal infinitely, 'as our Biler is a doin' now about as well as a boy *can* do, eh, Polly?'

'Oh! he's a doing beautiful!' responded Polly.

'He an't got to be at all secret-like—has he, Polly?' inquired Mr. Toodle.

'No!' said Mrs. Toodle, plumply.

'I'm glad he an't got to be at all secret-like, Polly,' observed Mr. Toodle in his slow and measured way, and shovelling in his bread-and-butter with a clasp knife, as if he were stoking himself, 'because that don't look well; do it, Polly?'

'Why, of course it don't, father. How can you ask?'

'You see, my boys and gals,' said Mr. Toodle, looking round upon his family, 'wotever you're up to in a honest way, it's my opinion as you can't do better than be open. If you find yourselves in cuttings or in tunnels, don't you play no secret games. Keep your whistles going, and let's know where you are.'

The rising Toodles set up a shrill murmur, expressive of their resolution to profit by the paternal advice.

'But what makes you say this along of Rob, father?' asked his wife, anxiously.

'Polly, old 'ooman,' said Mr. Toodle, 'I don't know as I said it partickler along o' Rob, I'm sure. I starts light with Rob only; I comes to a branch; I takes on what I finds there; and a whole train of ideas gets coupled on to him, afore I knows where I am, or where they comes from. What a junction a man's thoughts is,' said Mr. Toodle, 'to-be-sure!'

This profound reflection Mr. Toodle washed down

with a pint mug of tea, and proceeded to solidify with a great weight of bread-and-butter; charging his young daughters meanwhile, to keep plenty of hot water in the pot, as he was uncommon dry, and should take the indefinite quantity of 'a sight of mugs,' before his thirst was appeased.

In satisfying himself, however, Mr. Toodle was not regardless of the younger branches about him, who, although they had made their own evening repast, were on the look-out for irregular morsels, as possessing a relish. These he distributed now and then to the expectant circle, by holding out great wedges of bread-and-butter, to be bitten at by the family in lawful succession, and by serving out small doses of tea in like manner with a spoon; which snacks had such a relish in the mouths of these young Toodles, that, after partaking of the same, they performed private dances of ecstasy among themselves, and stood on one leg a-piece, and hopped, and indulged in other saltatory tokens of gladness. These vents for their excitement found, they gradually closed about Mr. Toodle again, and eyed him hard as he got through more bread-and-butter and tea; affecting, however, to have no further expectations of their own in reference to those viands, but to be conversing on foreign subjects, and whispering confidentially.

Mr. Toodle, in the midst of this family group, and setting an awful example to his children in the way of appetite, was conveying the two young Toodles on his knees to Birmingham by special engine, and was contemplating the rest over a barrier of bread-and-butter, when Rob the Grinder, in his sou'wester hat and mourning slops, presented himself, and was received with a general rush of brothers and sisters.

'Well, mother!' said Rob, dutifully kissing her;
'how are you mother?'

'There's my boy!' cried Polly, giving him a hug
and a pat on the back. 'Secret! Bless you, father,
not he!'

This was intended for Mr. Toodle's private edi-
fication, but Rob the Grinder, whose withers were
not unwrung, caught the words as they were spoken.

'What! father's been a saying something more
again me, has he?' cried the injured innocent. 'Oh,
what a hard thing it is that when a cove has once
gone a little wrong, a cove's own father should be always a throwing it in his face behind his back! It's
enough,' cried Rob, resorting to his coat-cuff in anguish of spirit, 'to make a cove go and do something
out of spite!'

'My poor boy!' cried Polly, 'father didn't mean
anything.'

'If father didn't mean anything,' blubbered the
injured Grinder, 'why did he go and say anything,
mother? Nobody thinks half so bad of me as my
own father does. What a unnatural thing! I wish
somebody'd take and chop my head off. Father
wouldn't mind doing it, I believe, and I'd much
rather he did that than t' other.'

At these desperate words all the young Toodles
shrieked; a pathetic effect, which the Grinder improved by ironically adjuring them not to cry for
him, for they ought to hate him, they ought, if they
was good boys and girls; and this so touched the
youngest Toodle but one, who was easily moved, that
it touched him not only in his spirit but in his wind
too; making him so purple that Mr. Toodle in consternation carried him out to the water-butt, and
would have put him under the tap, but for his being
recovered by the sight of that instrument.

Matters having reached this point, Mr. Toodle explained, and the virtuous feelings of his son being thereby calmed, they shook hands, and harmony reigned again.

'Will you do as I do, Biler, my boy?' inquired his father, returning to his tea with new strength.

'No, thank 'ee, father. Master and I had tea together.'

'And how *is* master, Rob?' said Polly.

'Well, I don't know, mother; not much to boast on. There ain't no bis'ness done, you see. He don't know anything about it, the cap'en don't. There was a man come into the shop this very day, and says, "I want a so-and-so," he says—some hard name or another. "A which?" says the cap'en. "A so-and-so," says the man. "Brother," says the cap'en, "will you take a observation round the shop?" "Well," says the man, "I've done it." "Do you see wot you want?" says the cap'en. "No, I don't," says the man. "Do you know it wen you *do* see it?" says the cap'en. "No, I don't," says the man. "Why, then I tell you wot, my lad," says the cap'en, "you'd better go back and ask wot it's like, outside, for no more don't I!"'

'That ain't the way to make money, though, is it?' said Polly.

'Money, mother! He'll never make money. He has such ways as I never see. He ain't a bad master, though, I'll say that for him. But that ain't much to me, for I don't think I shall stop with him long.'

'Not stop in your place, Rob!' cried his mother; while Mr. Toodle opened his eyes.

'Not in that place, p'raps,' returned the Grinder, with a wink. 'I shouldn't wonder—friends at court you know—but never *you* mind, mother, just now; I'm all right, that's all.'

The indisputable proof afforded in these hints, and in the Grinder's mysterious manner, of his not being subject to that failing which Mr. Toodle had, by implication, attributed to him, might have led to a renewal of his wrongs, and of the sensation in the family, but for the opportune arrival of another visitor, who, to Polly's great surprise, appeared at the door, smiling patronage and friendship on all there.

'How do you do, Mrs. Richards?' said Miss Tox. 'I have come to see you. May I come in?'

The cheery face of Mrs. Richards shone with a hospitable reply, and Miss Tox, accepting the proffered chair, and gracefully recognising Mr. Toodle on her way to it, untied her bonnet-strings, and said that in the first place she must beg the dear children, one and all, to come and kiss her.

The ill-starred youngest Toodle but one, who would appear, from the frequency of his domestic troubles, to have been born under an unlucky planet, was prevented from performing his part in this general salutation by having fixed the sou'wester hat (with which he had been previously trifling) deep on his head, hind-side before, and being unable to get it off again; which accident presenting to his terrified imagination a dismal picture of his passing the rest of his days in darkness, and in hopeless seclusion from his friends and family, caused him to struggle with great violence, and to utter suffocating cries. Being released, his face was discovered to be very hot, and red, and damp; and Miss Tox took him on her lap, much exhausted.

'You have almost forgotten me, sir, I dare say,' said Miss Tox to Mr. Toodle.

'No, ma'am, no,' said Toodle. 'But we've all on us got a little older since then.'

'And how do you find yourself, sir?' inquired Miss Tox, blandly.

'Hearty, ma'am, thank 'ee,' replied Toodle. 'How do *you* find *your*self, ma'am? Do the rheumatics keep off pretty well, ma'am? We must all expect to grow into 'em as we gets on.'

'Thank you,' said Miss Tox. 'I have not felt any inconvenience from that disorder yet.'

'You 're wery fortunate, ma'am,' returned Mr. Toodle. 'Many people at your time of life, ma'am, is martyrs to it. There was my mother—' But catching his wife's eye here, Mr. Toodle judiciously buried the rest in another mug of tea.

'You never mean to say, Mrs. Richards,' cried Miss Tox, looking at Rob, 'that that is your—'

'Eldest, ma'am,' said Polly. 'Yes, indeed, it is. That 's the little fellow, ma'am, that was the innocent cause of so much.'

'This here, ma'am,' said Toodle, 'is him with the short legs—and they was,' said Mr. Toodle, with a touch of poetry in his tone, 'unusual short for leathers —as Mr. Dombey made a Grinder on.'

The recollection almost overpowered Miss Tox. The subject of it had a peculiar interest for her directly. She asked him to shake hands, and congratulated his mother on his frank, ingenuous face. Rob, overhearing her, called up a look, to justify the eulogium, but it was hardly the right look.

'And now, Mrs. Richards,' said Miss Tox,—'and you too, sir,' addressing Toodle—'I 'll tell you, plainly and truly, what I have come here for. You may be aware, Mrs. Richards—and, possibly, you may be aware too, sir—that a little distance has interposed itself between me and some of my friends, and that where I used to visit a good deal, I do not visit now.'

Polly, who, with a woman's tact, understood this

at once, expressed as much in a little look. Mr.
Toodle, who had not the faintest idea of what Miss
Tox was talking about, expressed that also, in a stare.

'Of course,' said Miss Tox, 'how our little coolness has arisen is of no moment, and does not require
to be discussed. It is sufficient for me to say, that
I have the greatest possible respect for, and interest
in, Mr. Dombey'; Miss Tox's voice faltered; 'and
everything that relates to him.'

Mr. Toodle, enlightened, shook his head, and said
he had heerd it said, and, for his own part, he did
think, as Mr. Dombey was a difficult subject.

'Pray don't say so, sir, if you please,' returned Miss
Tox. 'Let me entreat you not to say so, sir, either
now, or at any future time. Such observations cannot but be very painful to me, and to a gentleman,
whose mind is constituted as, I am quite sure yours
is, can afford no permanent satisfaction.'

Mr. Toodle, who had not entertained the least doubt
of offering a remark that would be received with acquiescence, was greatly confounded.

'All that I wish to say, Mrs. Richards,' resumed
Miss Tox,—'and I address myself to you too, sir,—
is this. That any intelligence of the proceedings of
the family, of the welfare of the family, of the health
of the family, that reaches you, will be always most
acceptable to me. That I shall be always very glad
to chat with Mrs. Richards about the family, and
about old times. And as Mrs. Richards and I never
had the least difference (though I could wish now
that we had been better acquainted, but I have no
one but myself to blame for that), I hope she will not
object to our being very good friends now, and to
my coming backwards and forwards here, when I like,
without being a stranger. Now, I really hope, Mrs.
Richards,' said Miss Tox, earnestly, 'that you will

take this, as I mean it, like a good-humoured creature, as you always were.'

Polly was gratified, and showed it. Mr. Toodle didn't know whether he was gratified or not, and preserved a stolid calmness.

'You see, Mrs. Richards,' said Miss Tox—'and I hope you see too, sir—there are many little ways in which I can be slightly useful to you, if you will make no stranger of me; and in which I shall be delighted to be so. For instance, I can teach your children something. I shall bring a few little books, if you 'll allow me, and some work, and of an evening now and then, they 'll learn—dear me, they 'll learn a great deal, I trust, and be a credit to their teacher.'

Mr. Toodle, who had a great respect for learning, jerked his head approvingly at his wife, and moistened his hands with dawning satisfaction.

'Then, not being a stranger, I shall be in nobody's way,' said Miss Tox, 'and everything will go on just as if I were not here. Mrs. Richards will do her mending, or her ironing, or her nursing, whatever it is, without minding me: and you 'll smoke your pipe, too, if you 're so disposed, sir, won't you?'

'Thank 'ee, mum,' said Mr. Toodle. 'Yes; I 'll take my bit of backer.'

'Very good of you to say so, sir,' rejoined Miss Tox, 'and I really do assure you now, unfeignedly, that it will be a great comfort to me, and that whatever good I may be fortunate enough to do the children, you will more than pay back to me, if you 'll enter into this little bargain comfortably, and easily, and good-naturedly, without another word about it.'

The bargain was ratified on the spot; and Miss Tox found herself so much at home already, that without delay she instituted a preliminary examination of the children all round—which Mr. Toodle much admired—and booked their ages, names, and acquirements, on a piece of paper. This ceremony, and a little attendant gossip, prolonged the time until after their usual hour of going to bed, and detained Miss Tox at the Toodle fireside until it was too late for her to walk home alone. The gallant Grinder, however, being still there, politely offered to attend her to her own door; and as it was something to Miss Tox to be seen home by a youth whom Mr. Dombey had first inducted into those manly garments which are rarely mentioned by name, she very readily accepted the proposal.

After shaking hands with Mr. Toodle and Polly, and kissing all the children, Miss Tox left the house, therefore, with unlimited popularity, and carrying away with her so light a heart that it might have given Mrs. Chick offence if that good lady could have weighed it.

Rob the Grinder, in his modesty, would have walked behind, but Miss Tox desired him to keep beside her, for conversational purposes; and, as she afterwards expressed it to his mother, 'drew him out,' upon the road.

He drew out so bright, and clear, and shining, that Miss Tox was charmed with him. The more Miss Tox drew him out, the finer he came—like wire. There never was a better or more promising youth —a more affectionate, steady, prudent, sober, honest, meek, candid young man—than Rob drew out that night.

'I am quite glad,' said Miss Tox, arrived at her own door, 'to know you. I hope you'll consider me your friend, and that you'll come and see me as often as you like. Do you keep a money-box?'

'Yes, ma'am,' returned Rob; 'I'm saving up against I've got enough to put in the bank, ma'am.'

'Very laudable indeed,' said Miss Tox. 'I 'm glad to hear it. Put this half-crown into it, if you please.'

'Oh thank you, ma'am,' replied Rob, 'but really I couldn't think of depriving you.'

'I commend your independent spirit,' said Miss Tox, 'but it 's no deprivation, I assure you. I shall be offended if you don't take it, as a mark of my good-will. Good night, Robin.'

'Good night, ma'am,' said Rob, 'and thank you!'

Who ran sniggering off to get change, and tossed it away with a pieman. But they never taught honour at the Grinders' School, where the system that prevailed was particularly strong in the engendering of hypocrisy. Insomuch, that many of the friends and masters of past Grinders said, if this were what came of education for the common people, let us have none. Some more rational said, let us have a better one. But the governing powers of the Grinders' Company were always ready for *them*, by picking out a few boys who had turned out well, in spite of the system, and roundly asserting that they could have only turned out well because of it. Which settled the business of those objectors out of hand, and established the glory of the Grinders' Institution.

CHAPTER XXXIX

FURTHER ADVENTURES OF CAPTAIN EDWARD CUTTLE, MARINER

TIME, sure of foot and strong of will, had so pressed onward, that the year enjoined by the old instrument-maker, as the term during which his friend should refrain from opening the sealed packet accompanying the letter he had left for him, was now nearly expired, and Captain Cuttle began to look at it, of an evening, with feelings of mystery and uneasiness.

The captain, in his honour, would as soon have thought of opening the parcel one hour before the expiration of the term, as he would have thought of opening himself, to study his own anatomy. He merely brought it out, at a certain stage of his first evening pipe, laid it on the table, and sat gazing at the outside of it, through the smoke, in silent gravity, for two or three hours at a spell. Sometimes, when he had contemplated it thus for a pretty long while, the captain would hitch his chair, by degrees, farther and farther off, as if to get beyond the range of its fascination; but if this were his design, he never succeeded: for even when he was brought up by the parlour wall, the packet still attracted him; or if his eyes, in thoughtful wandering, roved to the ceiling or the fire, its image immediately followed, and posted itself conspicuously among the coals, or took up an advantageous position on the whitewash.

In respect of Heart's Delight, the captain's parental regard and admiration knew no change. But since his last interview with Mr. Carker, Captain Cuttle had come to entertain doubts whether his former intervention in behalf of that young lady and his dear boy Wal'r, had proved altogether so favourable as he could have wished, and as he at the time believed. The captain was troubled with a serious misgiving that he had done more harm than good, in short; and in his remorse and modesty he made the best atonement he could think of, by putting himself out of the way of doing any harm to any one, and, as it were, throwing himself overboard for a dangerous person.

Self-buried, therefore, among the instruments, the

captain never went near Mr. Dombey's house, or reported himself in any way to Florence or Miss Nipper. He even severed himself from Mr. Perch, on the occasion of his next visit, by dryly informing that gentleman, that he thanked him for his company, but had cut himself adrift from all such acquaintance, as he didn't know what magazine he mightn't blow up, without meaning of it. In this self-imposed retirement, the captain passed whole days and weeks without interchanging a word with any one but Rob the Grinder, whom he esteemed as a pattern of disinterested attachment and fidelity. In this retirement, the captain, gazing at the packet of an evening, would sit smoking, and thinking of Florence and poor Walter, until they both seemed to his homely fancy to be dead, and to have passed away into eternal youth, the beautiful and innocent children of his first remembrance.

The captain did not, however, in his musings, neglect his own improvement, or the mental culture of Rob the Grinder. That young man was generally required to read out of some book to the captain, for one hour, every evening; and as the captain implicitly believed that all books were true, he accumulated, by this means, many remarkable facts. On Sunday nights, the captain always read for himself, before going to bed, a certain Divine Sermon once delivered on a Mount; and although he was accustomed to quote the text, without book, after his own manner, he appeared to read it with as reverent an understanding of its heavenly spirit, as if he had got it all by heart in Greek, and had been able to write any number of fierce theological disquisitions on its every phrase.

Rob the Grinder, whose reverence for the inspired writings, under the admirable system of the Grinders' School, had been developed by a perpetual bruising of his intellectual shins against all the proper names of all the tribes of Judah, and by the monotonous repetition of hard verses, especially by way of punishment, and by the parading of him at six years old in leather breeches, three times a Sunday, very high up, in a very hot church, with a great organ buzzing against his drowsy head, like an exceedingly busy bee—Rob the Grinder made a mighty show of being edified when the captain ceased to read, and generally yawned and nodded while the reading was in progress. The latter fact being never so much as suspected by the good captain.

Captain Cuttle, also, as a man of business, took to keeping books. In these he entered observations on the weather, and on the currents of the waggons and other vehicles: which he observed, in that quarter, to set westward in the morning and during the greater part of the day, and eastward towards the evening. Two or three stragglers appearing in one week, who 'spoke him'—so the captain entered it—on the subject of spectacles, and who, without positively purchasing, said they would look in again, the captain decided that the business was improving, and made an entry in the day-book to that effect: the wind then blowing (which he first recorded) pretty fresh, west and by north; having changed in the night.

One of the captain's chief difficulties was Mr. Toots, who called frequently, and who without saying much seemed to have an idea that the little back-parlour was an eligible room to chuckle in, as he would sit and avail himself of its accommodations in that regard by the half-hour together, without at all advancing in intimacy with the captain. The captain, rendered cautious by his late experience, was unable quite to satisfy his mind whether Mr. Toots was the mild subject he appeared to be, or was a profoundly artful

and dissimulating hypocrite. His frequent reference
to Miss Dombey was suspicious; but the captain had
a secret kindness for Mr. Toots's apparent reliance
on him, and forbore to decide against him for the
present; merely eyeing him, with a sagacity not to
be described, whenever he approached the subject that
was nearest to his heart.

'Captain Gills,' blurted out Mr. Toots, one day all
at once, as his manner was, 'do you think you could
think favourably of that proposition of mine, and
give me the pleasure of your acquaintance?'

'Why, I tell you what it is, my lad,' replied the captain, who had at length concluded on a course of
action; 'I 've been turning that there over.'

'Captain Gills, it 's very kind of you,' retorted Mr.
Toots. 'I 'm much obliged to you. Upon my word
and honour, Captain Gills, it would be a charity to
give me the pleasure of your acquaintance. It really
would.'

'You see, brother,' argued the captain, slowly, 'I
don't know you.'

'But you never *can* know me, Captain Gills,' replied
Mr. Toots, steadfast to his point, 'if you don't give
me the pleasure of your acquaintance.'

The captain seemed struck by the originality and
power of this remark, and looked at Mr. Toots as if
he thought there was a great deal more in him than
he had expected.

'Well said, my lad,' observed the captain, nodding
his head thoughtfully; 'and true. Now look 'ee here:
you 've made some observations to me, which gives
me to understand as you admire a certain sweet creetur. Hey?'

'Captain Gills,' said Mr. Toots, gesticulating violently with the hand in which he held his hat, 'admiration is not the word. Upon my honour, you have

no conception what my feelings are. If I could be dyed black, and made Miss Dombey's slave, I should consider it a compliment. If, at the sacrifice of all my property, I could get transmigrated into Miss Dombey's dog—I—I really think I should never leave off wagging my tail. I should be so perfectly happy, Captain Gills!'

Mr. Toots said it with watery eyes, and pressed his hat against his bosom with deep emotion.

'My lad,' returned the captain, moved to compassion, 'if you 're in 'arnest—'

'Captain Gills,' cried Mr. Toots, 'I 'm in such a state of mind, and am so dreadfully in earnest, that if I could swear to it upon a hot piece of iron, or a live coal, or melted lead, or burning sealing-wax, or anything of that sort, I should be glad to hurt myself, as a relief to my feelings.' And Mr. Toots looked hurriedly about the room, as if for some sufficiently painful means of accomplishing his dread purpose.

The captain pushed his glazed hat back upon his head, stroked his face down with his heavy hand—making his nose more mottled in the process—and planting himself before Mr. Toots, and hooking him by the lapel of his coat, addressed him in these words, while Mr. Toots looked up into his face, with much attention and some wonder.

'If you 're in 'arnest, you see, my lad,' said the captain, 'you 're a object of clemency, and clemency is the brightest jewel in the crown of a Briton's head, for which you 'll overhaul the constitution as laid down in Rule Britannia, and, when found, *that* is the charter as them garden angels was a singing of, so many times over. Stand by! This here proposal o' your'n takes me a little aback. And why? Because I holds my own only, you understand, in these here waters, and haven't got no consort, and may be don't wish for none. Steady! You hailed me first, along of a certain young lady, as you was chartered by. Now if you and me is to keep one another's company at all, that there young creetur's name must never be named nor referred to. I don't know what harm mayn't have been done by naming of it too free, afore now, and thereby I brings up short. D' ye make me out pretty clear, brother?'

'Well, you 'll excuse me, Captain Gills,' replied Mr. Toots, 'if I don't quite follow you sometimes. But upon my word I—it 's a hard thing, Captain Gills, not to be able to mention Miss Dombey. I really have got such a dreadful load here!'—Mr. Toots pathetically touched his shirt-front with both hands—'that I feel night and day, exactly as if somebody was sitting upon me.'

'Them,' said the captain, 'is the terms I offer. If they 're hard upon you, brother, as mayhap they are, give 'em a wide berth, sheer off, and part company cheerily!'

'Captain Gills,' returned Mr. Toots, 'I hardly know how it is, but after what you told me when I came here, for the first time, I—I feel that I 'd rather think about Miss Dombey in your society than talk about her in almost anybody else's. Therefore, Captain Gills, if you'll give me the pleasure of your acquaintance, I shall be very happy to accept it on your own conditions. I wish to be honourable, Captain Gills,' said Mr. Toots, holding back his extended hand for a moment, 'and therefore I am obliged to say that I *can not* help thinking about Miss Dombey. It 's impossible for me to make a promise not to think about her.'

'My lad,' said the captain, whose opinion of Mr. Toots was much improved by this candid avowal, 'a man's thoughts is like the winds, and nobody can't answer for 'em for certain, any length of time together. Is it a treaty as to words?'

'As to words, Captain Gills,' returned Mr. Toots, 'I think I can bind myself.'

Mr. Toots gave Captain Cuttle his hand upon it, then and there; and the captain with a pleasant and gracious show of condescension, bestowed his acquaintance upon him formally. Mr. Toots seemed much relieved and gladdened by the acquisition, and chuckled rapturously during the remainder of his visit. The captain, for his part, was not ill pleased to occupy that position of patronage, and was exceedingly well satisfied by his own prudence and foresight.

But rich as Captain Cuttle was in the latter quality, he received a surprise that same evening from a no less ingenuous and simple youth, than Rob the Grinder. That artless lad, drinking tea at the same table, and bending meekly over his cup and saucer, having taken sidelong observations of his master for some time, who was reading the newspaper with great difficulty, but much dignity, through his glasses, broke silence by saying—

'Oh! I beg your pardon, captain, but you mayn't be in want of any pigeons, may you, sir?'

'No, my lad,' replied the captain.

'Because I was wishing to dispose of mine, captain,' said Rob.

'Aye, aye?' cried the captain, lifting up his bushy eyebrows a little.

'Yes; I 'm going, captain, if you please,' said Rob.

'Going? Where are you going?' asked the captain, looking round at him over the glasses.

'What? didn't you know that I was going to leave you, captain?' asked Rob, with a sneaking smile.

The captain put down the paper, took off his spectacles, and brought his eyes to bear on the deserter.

'Oh yes, captain, I am going to give you warning. I thought you 'd have known that beforehand, perhaps,' said Rob, rubbing his hands, and getting up. 'If you could be so good as provide yourself soon, captain, it would be a great convenience to me. You couldn't provide yourself by to-morrow morning, I am afraid, captain: could you, do you think?'

'And you 're a going to desert your colours are you, my lad?' said the captain, after a long examination of his face.

'Oh, it 's very hard upon a cove, captain,' cried the tender Rob, injured and indignant in a moment, 'that he can't give lawful warning, without being frowned at in that way, and called a deserter. You haven't any right to call a poor cove names, captain. It ain't because I 'm a servant and you 're a master, that you 're to go and libel me. What wrong have I done? Come, captain, let me know what my crime is, will you?'

The stricken Grinder wept, and put his coat-cuff in his eye.

'Come, captain,' cried the injured youth, 'give my crime a name! What have I been and done? Have I stolen any of the property? have I set the house afire? If I have, why don't you give me in charge, and try it? But to take away the character of a lad that 's been a good servant to you, because he can't afford to stand in his own light for your good, what a injury it is, and what a bad return for faithful service! This is the way young coves is spiled and drove wrong. I wonder at you, captain, I do.'

All of which the Grinder howled forth in a lachrymose whine, and backing carefully towards the door.

THE MIDSHIPMAN IS BOARDED BY THE ENEMY.

'And so you 've got another berth, have you, my lad?' said the captain, eyeing him intently.

'Yes, captain, since you put it in that shape, I *have* got another berth,' cried Rob, backing more and more; 'a better berth than I 've got here, and one where I don't so much as want your good word, captain, which is fort'nate for me, after all the dirt you 've throw'd at me, because I 'm poor, and can't afford to stand in my own light for your good. Yes, I *have* got another berth; and if it wasn't for leaving you unprovided, captain, I 'd go to it now, sooner than I 'd take them names from you, because I 'm poor, and can't afford to stand in my own light for your good. Why do you reproach me for being poor, and not standing in my own light for your good, captain? How can you so demean yourself?'

'Look ye here, my boy,' replied the peaceful captain, 'don't you pay out no more of them words.'

'Well, then, don't you pay in no more of your words, captain,' retorted the roused innocent, getting louder in his whine, and backing into the shop. 'I 'd sooner you took my blood than my character.'

'Because,' pursued the captain calmly, 'you have heerd, maybe, of such a thing as a rope's end.'

'Oh, have I though, captain?' cried the taunting Grinder. 'No I haven't. I never heerd of any such a article!'

'Well,' said the captain, 'it 's my belief as you 'll know more about it pretty soon, if you don't keep a bright look-out. I can read your signals, my lad. You may go.'

'Oh! I may go at once, may I, captain?' cried Rob, exulting in his success. 'But mind! *I* never asked to go at once, captain. You are not to take away my character again, because you send me off of your own accord. And you're not to stop any of my wages, captain!'

His employer settled the last point by producing the tin canister and telling the Grinder's money out in full upon the table. Rob, snivelling and sobbing, and grievously wounded in his feelings, took up the pieces one by one, with a sob and a snivel for each, and tied them up separately in knots in his pocket-handkerchief; then he ascended to the roof of the house and filled his hat and pockets with pigeons; then, came down to his bed under the counter and made up his bundle, snivelling and sobbing louder as if he were cut to the heart by old associations; then he whined, 'Good night, captain. I leave you without malice!' and then, going out upon the door-step, pulled the little midshipman's nose as a parting indignity, and went away down the street grinning triumph.

The captain, left to himself, resumed his perusal of the news as if nothing unusual or unexpected had taken place, and went reading on with the greatest assiduity. But never a word did Captain Cuttle understand, though he read a vast number, for Rob the Grinder was scampering up one column and down another all through the newspaper.

It is doubtful whether the worthy captain had ever felt himself quite abandoned until now; but now, old Sol Gills, Walter, and Heart's Delight were lost to him indeed, and now Mr. Carker deceived and jeered him cruelly. They were all represented in the false Rob, to whom he had held forth many a time on the recollections that were warm within him; he had believed in the false Rob, and had been glad to believe in him; he had made a companion of him as the last of the old ship's company; he had taken the command of the little midshipman with him at his right hand;

he had meant to do his duty by him, and had felt almost as kindly towards the boy as if they had been shipwrecked and cast upon a desert place together. And now that the false Rob had brought distrust, treachery, and meanness into the very parlour, which was a kind of sacred place, Captain Cuttle felt as if the parlour might have gone down next, and not surprised him much by its sinking, or given him any very great concern.

Therefore Captain Cuttle read the newspaper with profound attention and no comprehension, and therefore Captain Cuttle said nothing whatever about Rob to himself, or admitted to himself that he was thinking about him, or would recognise in the most distant manner that Rob had anything to do with his feeling as lonely as Robinson Crusoe.

In the same composed, business-like way, the captain stepped over to Leadenhall Market in the dusk, and effected an arrangement with a private watchman on duty there, to come and put up and take down the shutters of the wooden midshipman every night and morning. He then called in at the eating-house to diminish by one half the daily rations theretofore supplied to the midshipman, and at the public-house to stop the traitor's beer. 'My young man,' said the captain, in explanation to the young lady at the bar, 'my young man having bettered himself, miss.' Lastly, the captain resolved to take possession of the bed under the counter, and to turn-in there o' nights instead of upstairs, as sole guardian of the property.

From this bed Captain Cuttle daily rose thenceforth, and clapped on his glazed hat at six o'clock in the morning, with the solitary air of Crusoe finishing his toilet with his goat-skin cap; and although his fears of a visitation from the savage tribe, Mac-Stinger, were somewhat cooled, as similar apprehensions on the part of that lone mariner used to be by the lapse of a long interval without any symptoms of the cannibals, he still observed a regular routine of defensive operations, and never encountered a bonnet without previous survey from his castle of retreat. In the meantime (during which he received no call from Mr. Toots, who wrote to say he was out of town) his own voice began to have a strange sound in his ears; and he acquired such habits of profound meditation from much polishing and stowing away of the stock, and from much sitting behind the counter reading, or looking out of window, that the red rim made on his forehead by the hard glazed hat, sometimes ached again with excess of reflection.

The year being now expired, Captain Cuttle deemed it expedient to open the packet; but as he had always designed doing this in the presence of Rob the Grinder, who had brought it to him, and as he had an idea that it would be regular and shipshape to open it in the presence of somebody, he was sadly put to it for want of a witness. In this difficulty, he hailed one day with unusual delight the announcement in the Shipping Intelligence of the arrival of the Cautious Clara, Captain John Bunsby, from a coasting voyage; and to that philosopher immediately despatched a letter by post, enjoining inviolable secrecy as to his place of residence, and requesting to be favoured with an early visit, in the evening season.

Bunsby, who was one of those sages who act upon conviction, took some days to get the conviction thoroughly into his mind, that he had received a letter to this effect. But when he had grappled with the fact, and mastered it, he promptly sent his boy with the message, 'He 's a-coming to-night.' Who being instructed to deliver those words and disappear, fulfilled his mission like a tarry spirit, charged with a mysterious warning.

The captain, well pleased to receive it, made preparation of pipes and rum-and-water, and awaited his visitor in the back-parlour. At the hour of eight, a deep lowing, as of a nautical bull, outside the shop-door, succeeded by the knocking of a stick on the panel, announced to the listening ear of Captain Cuttle, that Bunsby was alongside: whom he instantly admitted, shaggy and loose, and with his stolid mahogany visage, as usual, appearing to have no consciousness of anything before it, but to be attentively observing something that was taking place in quite another part of the world.

'Bunsby,' said the captain, grasping him by the hand, 'what cheer, my lad, what cheer?'

'Shipmet,' replied the voice within Bunsby, unaccompanied by any sign on the part of the commander himself, 'hearty, hearty.'

'Bunsby!' said the captain, rendering irrepressible homage to his genius, 'here you are! a man as can give an opinion as is brighter than di'monds—and give me the lad with the tarry trousers as shines to me like di'monds bright, for which you 'll overhaul the Stanfell's Budget, and when found make a note. Here you are, a man as gave an opinion in this here very place, that has come true, every letter on it,' which the captain sincerely believed.

'Aye, aye?' growled Bunsby.

'Every letter,' said the captain.

'For why?' growled Bunsby, looking at his friend for the first time. 'Which way? If so, why not? Therefore.' With these oracular words—they seemed almost to make the captain giddy; they launched him upon such a sea of speculation and conjecture—the sage submitted to be helped off with his pilot-coat, and accompanied his friend into the back-parlour, where his hand presently alighted on the rum-bottle, from which he brewed a stiff glass of grog; and presently afterwards on a pipe, which he filled, lighted, and began to smoke.

Captain Cuttle, imitating his visitor in the matter of these particulars, though the rapt and imperturbable manner of the great commander was far above his powers, sat in the opposite corner of the fireside, observing him respectfully, and as if he waited for some encouragement or expression of curiosity on Bunsby's part which should lead him to his own affairs. But as the mahogany philosopher gave no evidence of being sentient of anything but warmth and tobacco, except once, when taking his pipe from his lips to make room for his glass, he incidentally remarked with exceeding gruffness, that his name was Jack Bunsby—a declaration that presented but small opening for conversation—the captain bespeaking his attention in a short complimentary exordium, narrated the whole history of uncle Sol's departure, with the change it had produced in his own life and fortunes; and concluded by placing the packet on the table.

After a long pause, Mr. Bunsby nodded his head.

'Open?' said the captain.

Bunsby nodded again.

The captain accordingly broke the seal, and disclosed to view two folded papers, of which he severally read the indorsements, thus: 'Last Will and Testament of Solomon Gills.' 'Letter for Ned Cuttle.'

Bunsby, with his eye on the coast of Greenland, seemed to listen for the contents. The captain therefore hemmed to clear his throat, and read the letter aloud.

' "My dear Ned Cuttle. When I left home for the West Indies—" '

Here the captain stopped, and looked hard at Bunsby, who looked fixedly at the coast of Greenland.

—' "in forlorn search of intelligence of my dear boy, I knew that if you were acquainted with my design, you would thwart it, or accompany me; and therefore I kept it secret. If you ever read this letter, Ned, I am likely to be dead. You will easily forgive an old friend's folly then and will feel for the restlessness and uncertainty in which he wandered away on such a wild voyage. So no more of that. I have little hope that my poor boy will ever read these words, or gladden your eyes with the sight of his frank face any more." No, no; no more,' said Captain Cuttle, sorrowfully meditating; 'no more. There he lays, all his days—'

Mr. Bunsby, who had a musical ear, suddenly bellowed, 'In the Bays of Biscay, O!' which so affected the good captain, as an appropriate tribute to departed worth, that he shook him by the hand in acknowledgment, and was fain to wipe his eyes.

'Well, well!' said the captain with a sigh, as the Lament of Bunsby ceased to ring and vibrate in the skylight. 'Affliction sore, long time he bore, and let us overhaul the wollume, and there find it.'

'Physicians,' observed Bunsby, 'was in vain.'

'Aye, aye, to be sure,' said the captain, 'what's the good o' *them* in two or three hundred fathoms o' water!' Then returning to the letter, he read on: ' "But if he should be by, when it is opened" '; the captain involuntarily looked round, and shook his head; ' "or should know of it at any other time" '; the captain shook his head again; ' "my blessing on him. In case the accompanying paper is not legally

written, it matters very little, for there is no one interested but you and he, and my plain wish is, that
if he is living he should have what little there may
be, and if (as I fear) otherwise, that you should have
it, Ned. You will respect my wish, I know. God
bless you for it, and for all your friendliness besides,
to SOLOMON GILLS." Bunsby!' said the captain, appealing to him solemnly, 'what do you make of this?
There you sit, a man as has had his head broke from
infancy up'ards, and has got a new opinion into it
at every seam as has been opened. Now, what do
you make o' this?'

'If so be,' returned Bunsby, with unusual prompti-
tude, 'as he's dead, my opinion is he won't come back
no more. If so be as he's alive, my opinion is he
will. Do I say he will? No. Why not? Because
the bearings of this obserwation lays in the applica-
tion on it.'

'Bunsby!' said Captain Cuttle, who would seem to
have estimated the value of his distinguished friend's
opinions in proportion to the immensity of the difficulty he experienced in making anything out of them;
'Bunsby,' said the captain, quite confounded by admiration, 'you carry a weight of mind easy, as would
swamp one of my tonnage soon. But in regard o'
this here will, I don't mean to take no steps towards
the property—Lord forbid!—except to keep it for a
more rightful owner; and I hope yet as the rightful
owner, Sol Gills, is living and 'll come back, strange
as it is that he ain't forwarded no dispatches. Now,
what is your opinion, Bunsby, as to stowing of these
here papers away again, and marking outside as they
was opened, such a day, in presence of John Bunsby
and Ed'ard Cuttle?'

Bunsby, descrying no objection, on the coast of
Greenland or elsewhere, to this proposal, it was car-

ried into execution; and that great man, bringing his eye into the present for a moment, affixed his sign-manual to the cover, totally abstaining, with characteristic modesty, from the use of capital letters. Captain Cuttle, having attached his own left-handed signature, and locked up the packet in the iron safe, entreated his guest to mix another glass and smoke another pipe; and doing the like himself, fell a musing over the fire on the possible fortunes of the poor old instrument-maker.

And now a surprise occurred, so overwhelming and terrific that Captain Cuttle, unsupported by the presence of Bunsby, must have sunk beneath it, and been a lost man from that fatal hour.

How the captain, even in the satisfaction of admitting such a guest, could have only shut the door, and not locked it, of which negligence he was undoubtedly guilty, is one of those questions that must for ever remain mere points of speculation, or vague charges against destiny. But by that unlocked door, at this quiet moment, did the fell MacStinger dash into the parlour, bringing Alexander MacStinger in her parental arms, and confusion and vengeance (not to mention Juliana MacStinger, and the sweet child's brother, Charles MacStinger, popularly known about the scenes of his youthful sports, as Chowley) in her train. She came so swiftly and so silently, like a rushing air from the neighbourhood of the East India Docks, that Captain Cuttle found himself in the very act of sitting looking at her, before the calm face with which he had been meditating, changed to one of horror and dismay.

But the moment Captain Cuttle understood the full extent of his misfortune, self-preservation dictated an attempt at flight. Darting at the little door which opened from the parlour on the steep little range of cellar-steps, the captain made a rush, head foremost, at the latter, like a man indifferent to bruises and contusions, who only sought to hide himself in the bowels of the earth. In this gallant effort he would probably have succeeded, but for the affectionate dispositions of Juliana and Chowley, who pinning him by the legs—one of those dear children holding on to each—claimed him as their friend, with lamentable cries. In the meantime, Mrs. MacStinger, who never entered upon any action of importance without previously inverting Alexander MacStinger, to bring him within the range of a brisk battery of slaps, and then sitting him down to cool as the reader first beheld him, performed that solemn rite, as if on this occasion it were a sacrifice to the Furies; and having deposited the victim on the floor, made at the captain with a strength of purpose that appeared to threaten scratches to the interposing Bunsby.

The cries of the two elder MacStingers, and the wailing of young Alexander, who may be said to have passed a piebald childhood, forasmuch as he was black in the face during one half of that fairy period of existence, combined to make this visitation the more awful. But when silence reigned again, and the captain, in a violent perspiration, stood meekly looking at Mrs. MacStinger, its terrors were at their height.

'Oh, Cap'en Cuttle, Cap'en Cuttle!' said Mrs. Mac-Stinger, making her chin rigid, and shaking it in unison with what, but for the weakness of her sex, might be described as a fist. 'Oh, Cap'en Cuttle, Cap'en Cuttle, do you dare to look me in the face, and not be struck down in the herth!'

The captain, who looked anything but daring, feebly muttered 'Stand by!'

'Oh, I was a weak and trusting fool when I took you under *my* roof, Cap'en Cuttle. I was!' cried Mrs.

MacStinger. 'To think of the benefits I 've showered on that man, and the way in which I brought
my children up to love and *honour* him as if he was
a father to 'em, when there an't a 'ousekeeper, no nor
a lodger in our street, don't know that I lost money
by that man, and by his guzzlings and his muzzlings'
—Mrs. MacStinger used the last word for the joint
sake of alliteration and aggravation, rather than for
the expression of any idea—'and when they cried out
one and all, shame upon him for putting upon an
industrious woman, up early and late for the good
of her young family, and keeping her poor place so
clean that a individual might have ate his dinner, yes,
and his tea too, if he was so disposed, off any one of
the floors or stairs, in spite of all his guzzlings *and*
his muzzlings, such was the care and pains bestowed
upon him!'

Mrs. MacStinger stopped to fetch her breath; and
her face flushed with triumph in this second happy
introduction of Captain Cuttle's muzzlings.

'And he runs awa-a-a-ay!' cried Mrs. MacStinger,
with a lengthening out of the last syllable that made
the unfortunate captain regard himself as the meanest of men; 'and keeps away a twelvemonth! From
a woman! Sitch is his conscience! He hasn't the
courage to meet her hi-i-i-igh'; long syllable again;
'but steals away, like a felion. Why, if that baby of
mine,' said Mrs. MacStinger, with sudden rapidity,
'was to offer to go and steal away, I 'd do my duty as
a mother by him, till he was covered with wales!'

The young Alexander, interpreting this into a positive promise, to be shortly redeemed, tumbled over
with fear and grief, and lay upon the floor, exhibiting
the soles of his shoes and making such a deafening
outcry, that Mrs. MacStinger found it necessary to
take him up in her arms, where she quieted him, ever

and anon, as he broke out again, by a shake that
seemed enough to loosen his teeth.

'A pretty sort of a man is Cap'en Cuttle,' said Mrs.
MacStinger, with a sharp stress on the first syllable
of the captain's name, 'to take on for—and to lose
sleep for—and to faint along of—and to think dead
forsooth—and to go up and down the blessed town
like a mad woman, asking questions after! Oh, a
pretty sort of a man! Ha ha ha ha! He's worth
all that trouble and distress of mind, and much more.
That's nothing, bless you! Ha ha ha ha! Cap'en
Cuttle,' said Mrs. MacStinger, with severe reaction
in her voice and manner, 'I wish to know if you're a
coming home.'

The frightened captain looked into his hat, as if
he saw nothing for it but to put it on, and give himself up.

'Cap'en Cuttle,' repeated Mrs. MacStinger, in the
same determined manner, 'I wish to know if you're
a coming home, sir.'

The captain seemed quite ready to go, but faintly
suggested something to the effect of 'not making so
much noise about it.'

'Aye, aye, aye,' said Bunsby, in a soothing tone.
'Awast, my lass, awast!'

'And who may YOU be, if you please!' retorted Mrs.
MacStinger, with chaste loftiness. 'Did you ever
lodge at Number Nine, Brig Place, sir? My memory may be bad, but not with me, I think. There
was a Mrs. Jollson lived at Number Nine before me,
and perhaps you're mistaking me for her. That is
my only ways of accounting for your familiarity, sir.'

'Come, come, my lass, awast, awast!' said Bunsby.

Captain Cuttle could hardly believe it, even of this
great man, though he saw it done with his waking
eyes; but Bunsby, advancing boldly, put his shaggy

blue arm round Mrs. MacStinger, and so softened
her by his magic way of doing it, and by these few
words—he said no more—that she melted into tears,
after looking upon him for a few moments, and observed that a child might conquer her now, she was
so low in her courage.

Speechless and utterly amazed, the captain saw him
gradually persuade this inexorable woman into the
shop, return for rum-and-water and a candle, take
them to her, and pacify her without appearing to
utter one word. Presently he looked in with his pilot-
coat on, and said, 'Cuttle, I 'm a going to act as con-
voy home'; and Captain Cuttle, more to his confusion
than if he had been put in irons himself, for safe
transport to Brig Place, saw the family pacifically
filing off, with Mrs. MacStinger at their head. He
had scarcely time to take down his canister, and
stealthily convey some money into the hands of Juliana MacStinger, his former favourite, and Chowley,
who had the claim upon him that he was naturally
of a maritime build, before the midshipman was abandoned by them all; and Bunsby whispering that he 'd
carry on smart, and hail Ned Cuttle again before he
went aboard, shut the door upon himself, as the last
member of the party.

Some uneasy ideas that he must be walking in his
sleep, or that he had been troubled with phantoms, and
not a family of flesh and blood, beset the captain at
first, when he went back to the little parlour, and
found himself alone. Illimitable faith in, and immeasurable admiration of, the commander of the Cautious Clara, succeeded, and threw the captain into a
wondering trance.

Still, as time wore on, and Bunsby failed to reappear, the captain began to entertain uncomfortable
doubts of another kind. Whether Bunsby had been

artfully decoyed to Brig Place, and was there detained in safe custody as hostage for his friend; in which case it would become the captain, as a man of honour, to release him, by the sacrifice of his own liberty. Whether he had been attacked and defeated by Mrs. MacStinger, and was ashamed to show himself after his discomfiture. Whether Mrs. MacStinger, thinking better of it, in the uncertainty of her temper, had turned back to board the midshipman again, and Bunsby, pretending to conduct her by a short cut, was endeavouring to lose the family amid the wilds and savage places of the City. Above all, what it would behove him, Captain Cuttle, to do, in case of his hearing no more, either of the MacStingers or of Bunsby, which, in these wonderful and unforeseen conjunctions of events, might possibly happen.

He debated all this until he was tired; and still no Bunsby. He made up his bed under the counter, all ready for turning in; and still no Bunsby. At length, when the captain had given him up, for that night at least, and had begun to undress, the sound of approaching wheels was heard, and, stopping at the door, was succeeded by Bunsby's hail.

The captain trembled to think that Mrs. MacStinger was not to be got rid of, and had been brought back in a coach.

But no. Bunsby was accompanied by nothing but a large box, which he hauled into the shop with his own hands, and as soon as he had hauled in, sat upon. Captain Cuttle knew it for the chest he had left at Mrs. MacStinger's house, and looking, candle in hand, at Bunsby more attentively, believed that he was three sheets in the wind, or, in plain words, drunk. It was difficult, however, to be sure of this; the commander having no trace of expression in his face when sober.

'Cuttle,' said the commander, getting off the chest, and opening the lid, 'are these here your traps?'

Captain Cuttle looked in and identified his property.

'Done pretty taut and trim, hey shipmet?' said Bunsby.

The grateful and bewildered captain grasped him by the hand, and was launching into a reply expressive of his astonished feelings, when Bunsby disengaged himself by a jerk of his wrist, and seemed to make an effort to wink with his revolving eye, the only effect of which attempt, in his condition, was nearly to overbalance him. He then abruptly opened the door, and shot away to rejoin the Cautious Clara with all speed—supposed to be his invariable custom, whenever he considered he had made a point.

As it was not his humour to be often sought, Captain Cuttle decided not to go or send to him next day, or until he should make his gracious pleasure known in such wise, or failing that, until some little time should have elapsed. The captain, therefore, renewed his solitary life next morning, and thought profoundly, many mornings, noons, and nights of old Sol Gills, and Bunsby's sentiments concerning him, and the hopes there were of his return. Much of such thinking strengthened Captain Cuttle's hopes; and he humoured them and himself by watching for the instrument-maker at the door as he ventured to do now, in his strange liberty—and setting his chair in its place, and arranging the little parlour as it used to be, in case he should come home unexpectedly. He likewise, in his thoughtfulness, took down a certain little miniature of Walter as a schoolboy, from its accustomed nail, lest it should shock the old man on his return. The captain had his presentiments, too, sometimes, that he would come on such a day; and one particular Sunday, even ordered a double allowance of dinner, he was so sanguine. But come, old Solomon did not; and still the neighbours noticed how the seafaring man in the glazed hat, stood at the shop-door of an evening, looking up and down the street.

CHAPTER XL

DOMESTIC RELATIONS

IT was not in the nature of things that a man of Mr. Dombey's mood, opposed to such a spirit as he had raised against himself, should be softened in the imperious asperity of his temper; or that the cold hard armour of pride in which he lived encased, should be made more flexible by constant collision with haughty scorn and defiance. It is the curse of such a nature—it is a main part of the heavy retribution on itself it bears within itself—that while deference and concession swell its evil qualities, and are the food it grows upon, resistance and a questioning of its exacting claims, foster it too, no less. The evil that is in it finds equally its means of growth and propagation in opposites. It draws support and life from sweets and bitters; bowed down before, or unacknowledged, it still enslaves the breast in which it has its throne; and, worshipped or rejected, is as hard a master as the devil in dark fables.

Towards his first wife, Mr. Dombey, in his cold and lofty arrogance, had borne himself like the removed Being he almost conceived himself to be. He had been 'Mr. Dombey' with her when she first saw him, and he was 'Mr. Dombey' when she died. He had asserted his greatness during their whole married life, and she had meekly recognised it. He had kept

his distant seat of state on the top of his throne, and
she her humble station on its lowest step; and much
good it had done him so to live in solitary bondage
to his one idea! He had imagined that the proud
character of his second wife would have been added
to his own—would have merged into it, and exalted
his greatness. He had pictured himself haughtier
than ever, with Edith's haughtiness subservient to his.
He had never entertained the possibility of its array-
ing itself against him. And now, when he found it
rising in his path at every step and turn of his daily
life, fixing its cold, defiant, and contemptuous face
upon him, this pride of his, instead of withering, or
hanging down its head beneath the shock, put forth
new shoots, became more concentrated and intense,
more gloomy, sullen, irksome, and unyielding, than it
had ever been before.

Who wears such armour, too, bears with him ever
another heavy retribution. It is of proof against
conciliation, love, and confidence! against all gentle
sympathy from without, all trust, all tenderness, all
soft emotion; but to deep stabs in the self-love, it is
as vulnerable as the bare breast to steel; and such tormenting festers rankle there, as follow on no other
wounds, no, though dealt with the mailed hand of
Pride itself, on weaker pride, disarmed and thrown
down.

Such wounds were his. He felt them sharply, in
the solitude of his old rooms; whither he now began
often to retire again, and pass long solitary hours.
It seemed his fate to be ever proud and powerful;
ever humbled and powerless where he would be most
strong. Who seemed fated to work out that doom?

Who? Who was it who could win his wife as she
had won his boy? Who was it who had shown him
that new victory, as he sat in the dark corner? Who

was it whose least word did what his utmost means could not? Who was it who, unaided by his love; regard, or notice, thrived and grew beautiful when those so aided died? Who could it be, but the same child at whom he had often glanced uneasily in her motherless infancy, with a kind of dread, lest he might come to hate her; and of whom his foreboding was fulfilled, for he DID hate her in his heart?

Yes, and he would have it hatred, and he made it hatred, though some sparkles of the light in which she had appeared before him on the memorable night of his return home with his bride, occasionally hung about her still. He knew now that she was beautiful; he did not dispute that she was graceful and winning, and that in the bright dawn of her womanhood she had come upon him, a surprise. But he turned even this against her. In his sullen and unwholesome brooding, the unhappy man, with a dull perception of his alienation from all hearts, and a vague yearning for what he had all his life repelled, made a distorted picture of his rights and wrongs, and justified himself with it against her. The worthier she promised to be of him, the greater claim he was disposed to ante-date upon her duty and submission. When had she ever shown him duty and submission? Did she grace his life—or Edith's? Had her attractions been manifested first to him—or Edith? Why, he and she had never been, from her birth, like father and child! They had always been estranged. She had crossed him every way and everywhere. She was leagued against him now. Her very beauty softened natures that were obdurate to him, and insulted him with an unnatural triumph.

It may have been that in all this there were mutterings of an awakened feeling in his breast, however selfishly aroused by his position of disadvantage, in comparison with what she might have made his life. But he silenced the distant thunder with the rolling of his sea of pride. He would bear nothing but his pride. And in his pride, a heap of inconsistency, and misery, and self-inflicted torment, he hated her.

To the moody, stubborn, sullen demon, that possessed him, his wife opposed her different pride in its full force. They never could have led a happy life together; but nothing could have made it more unhappy, than the wilful and determined warfare of such elements. His pride was set upon maintaining his magnificent supremacy, and forcing recognition of it from her. She would have been racked to death, and turned but her haughty glance of calm inflexible disdain upon him, to the last. Such recognition from Edith! He little knew through what a storm and struggle she had been driven onward to the crowning honour of his hand. He little knew how much she thought she had conceded, when she suffered him to call her wife.

Mr. Dombey was resolved to show her that he was supreme. There must be no will but his. Proud he desired that she should be, but she must be proud for, not against him. As he sat alone, hardening, he would often hear her go out and come home, treading the round of London life with no more heed of his liking or disliking, pleasure or displeasure, than if he had been her groom. Her cold supreme indifference—his own unquestioned attribute usurped—stung him more than any other kind of treatment could have done; and he determined to bend her to his magnificent and stately will.

He had been long communing with these thoughts, when one night he sought her in her own apartment, after he had heard her return home late. She was alone, in her brilliant dress, and had but that moment come from her mother's room. Her face was melancholy and pensive, when he came upon her; but it marked him at the door; for, glancing at the mirror before it, he saw immediately, as in a picture-frame, the knitted brow, and darkened beauty that he knew so well.

'Mrs. Dombey,' he said, entering, 'I must beg leave to have a few words with you.'

'To-morrow,' she replied.

'There is no time like the present, madam,' he returned. 'You mistake your position. I am used to choose my own times; not to have them chosen for me. I think you scarcely understand who and what I am, Mrs. Dombey.'

'I think,' she answered, 'that I understand you very well.'

She looked upon him as she said so, and folding her white arms, sparkling with gold and gems, upon her swelling breast, turned away her eyes.

If she had been less handsome, and less stately in her cold composure, she might not have had the power of impressing him with the sense of disadvantage that penetrated through his utmost pride. But she had the power, and he felt it keenly. He glanced round the room: saw how the splendid means of personal adornment, and the luxuries of dress, were scattered here and there, and disregarded; not in mere caprice and carelessness (or so he thought), but in a steadfast, haughty disregard of costly things: and felt it more and more. Chaplets of flowers, plumes of feathers, jewels, laces, silks and satins; look where he would, he saw riches, despised, poured out, and made of no account. The very diamonds—a marriage gift—that rose and fell impatiently upon her bosom, seemed to pant to break the chain that clasped them round her neck, and roll down on the floor where she might tread upon them.

He felt his disadvantage, and he showed it. Solemn and strange among this wealth of colour and voluptuous glitter, strange and constrained towards its haughty mistress, whose repellent beauty it repeated, and presented all around him, as in so many fragments of a mirror, he was conscious of embarrassment and awkwardness. Nothing that ministered to her disdainful self-possession could fail to gall him. Galled and irritated with himself, he sat down, and went on in no improved humour—

'Mrs. Dombey, it is very necessary that there should be some understanding arrived at between us. Your conduct does not please me, madam.'

She merely glanced at him again, and again averted her eyes; but she might have spoken for an hour, and expressed less.

'I repeat, Mrs. Dombey, does not please me. I have already taken occasion to request that it may be corrected. I now insist upon it.'

'You chose a fitting occasion for your first remonstrance, sir, and you adopt a fitting manner, and a fitting word for your second. *You* insist! To *me!*'

'Madam,' said Mr. Dombey, with his most offensive air of state, 'I have made you my wife. You bear my name. You are associated with my position and my reputation. I will not say that the world in general may be disposed to think you honoured by that association; but I will say that I am accustomed to "insist," to my connections and dependants.'

'Which may you be pleased to consider me?' she asked.

'Possibly I may think that my wife should partake —or does partake, and cannot help herself—of both characters, Mrs. Dombey.'

She bent her eyes upon him steadily, and set her trembling lips. He saw her bosom throb, and saw her face flush and turn white. All this he could know, and did: but he could not know that one word was whispering in the deep recesses of her heart, to keep her quiet; and that the word was Florence.

Blind idiot, rushing to a precipice! He thought she stood in awe of *him!*

'You are too expensive, madam,' said Mr. Dombey. 'You are extravagant. You waste a great deal of money—or what would be a great deal in the pockets of most gentlemen—in cultivating a kind of society that is useless to me, and, indeed, that upon the whole is disagreeable to me. I have to insist upon a total change in all these respects. I know that in the novelty of possessing a tithe of such means as Fortune has placed at your disposal, ladies are apt to run into a sudden extreme. There has been more than enough of that extreme. I beg that Mrs. Granger's very different experiences may now come to the instruction of Mrs. Dombey.'

Still the fixed look, the trembling lips, the throbbing breast, the face now crimson and now white; and still the deep whisper Florence, Florence, speaking to her in the beating of her heart.

His insolence of self-importance dilated as he saw this alteration in her. Swollen no less by her past scorn of him, and his so recent feeling of disadvantage, than by her present submission (as he took it to be), it became too mighty for his breast, and burst all bounds. Why, who could long resist his lofty will and pleasure! He had resolved to conquer her, and look here!

'You will further please, madam,' said Mr. Dombey, in a tone of sovereign command, 'to understand distinctly, that I am to be deferred to and obeyed.

That I must have a positive show and confession of
deference before the world, madam. I am used to
this. I require it as my right. In short I will have
it. I consider it no unreasonable return for the
worldly advancement that has befallen you; and I
believe nobody will be surprised, either at its being
required from you, or at your making it.—To Me—
to Me!' he added with emphasis.

No word from her. No change in her. Her eyes
upon him.

'I have learnt from your mother, Mrs. Dombey,'
said Mr. Dombey, with magisterial importance, 'what
no doubt you know, namely, that Brighton is recommended for her health. Mr. Carker has been so
good—'

She changed suddenly. Her face and bosom
glowed as if the red light of an angry sunset had
been flung upon them. Not unobservant of the
change, and putting his own interpretation upon it,
Mr. Dombey resumed—

'Mr. Carker has been so good as to go down and
secure a house there, for a time. On the return of the
establishment to London, I shall take such steps for
its better management as I consider necessary. One
of these, will be the engagement at Brighton (if it
is to be effected), of a very respectable reduced person there, a Mrs. Pipchin, formerly employed in a
situation of trust in my family, to act as housekeeper.
An establishment like this, presided over but nomi-
nally, Mrs. Dombey, requires a competent head.'

She had changed her attitude before he arrived at
these words, and now sat—still looking at him fixedly
—turning a bracelet round and round upon her arm;
not winding it about with a light, womanly touch,
but pressing and dragging it over the smooth skin,
until the white limb showed a bar of red.

'I observed,' said Mr. Dombey—'and this concludes what I deem it necessary to say to you at present, Mrs. Dombey—I observed a moment ago, madam, that my allusion to Mr. Carker was received in a peculiar manner. On the occasion of my happening to point out to you, before that confidential agent, the objection I had to your mode of receiving my visitors, you were pleased to object to his presence. You will have to get the better of that objection, madam, and to accustom yourself to it very probably on many similar occasions; unless you adopt the remedy which is in your own hands, of giving me no cause of complaint. Mr. Carker,' said Mr. Dombey, who, after the emotion he had just seen, set great store by this means of reducing his proud wife, and who was perhaps sufficiently willing to exhibit his power to that gentleman in a new and triumphant aspect, 'Mr. Carker being in my confidence, Mrs. Dombey, may very well be in yours to such an extent. I hope, Mrs. Dombey,' he continued, after a few moments, during which, in his increasing haughtiness, he had improved on his idea, 'I may not find it necessary ever to intrust Mr. Carker with any message of objection or remonstrance to you; but as it would be derogatory to my position and reputation to be frequently holding trivial disputes with a lady upon whom I have conferred the highest distinction that it is in my power to bestow, I shall not scruple to avail myself of his services if I see occasion.'

'And now,' he thought, rising in his moral magnificence, and rising a stiffer and more impenetrable man than ever, 'she knows me and my resolution.'

The hand that had so pressed the bracelet was laid heavily upon her breast, but she looked at him still, with an unaltered face, and said in a low voice—

'Wait! For God's sake! I must speak to you.'

Why did she not, and what was the inward struggle
that rendered her incapable of doing so, for minutes,
while, in the strong constraint she put upon her face,
it was as fixed as any statue's—looking upon him with
neither yielding nor unyielding, liking nor hatred,
pride nor humility: nothing but a searching gaze.

'Did I ever tempt you to seek my hand? Did I
ever use any art to win you? Was I ever more con-
ciliating to you when you pursued me, than I have
been since our marriage? Was I ever other to you
than I am?'

'It is wholly unnecessary, madam,' said Mr. Dombey, 'to enter upon such discussions.'

'Did you think I loved you? Did you know I did
not? Did you ever care, man! for my heart, or propose to yourself to win the worthless thing? Was
there any poor pretence of any in our bargain?
Upon your side, or on mine?'

'These questions,' said Mr. Dombey, 'are all wide
of the purpose, madam.'

She moved between him and the door to prevent
his going away, and drawing her majestic figure to
its height, looked steadily upon him still.

'You answer each of them. You answer me before
I speak, I see. How can you help it; you who know
the miserable truth as well as I? Now, tell me. If
I loved you to devotion, could I do more than render
up my whole will and being to you, as you have just
demanded? If my heart were pure and all untried,
and you its idol, could you ask more; could you have
more?'

'Possibly not, madam,' he returned coolly.

'You know how different I am. You see me looking on you now, and you can read the warmth of
passion for you that is breathing in my face.' Not a
curl of the proud lip, not a flash of the dark eye,

nothing but the same intent and searching look, accompanied these words. 'You know my general history. You have spoken of my mother. Do you think you can degrade, or bend or break, *me* to submission and obedience?'

Mr. Dombey smiled, as he might have smiled at an inquiry whether he thought he could raise ten thousand pounds.

'If there is anything unusual here,' she said, with a slight motion of her hand before her brow, which did not for a moment flinch from its immoveable and otherwise expressionless gaze, 'as I know there are unusual feelings here,' raising the hand she pressed upon her bosom, and heavily returning it, 'consider that there is no common meaning in the appeal I am going to make you. Yes, for I am going'; she said it as in prompt reply to something in his face; 'to appeal to you.'

Mr. Dombey, with a slightly condescending bend of his chin that rustled and crackled his stiff cravat, sat down on a sofa that was near him, to hear the appeal.

'If you can believe that I am of such a nature now,' —he fancied he saw tears glistening in her eyes, and he thought, complacently, that he had forced them from her, though none fell on her cheek, and she regarded him as steadily as ever,—'as would make what I now say almost incredible to myself, said to any man who had become my husband, but, above all, said to you, you may, perhaps, attach the greater weight to it. In the dark end to which we are tending, and may come, we shall not involve ourselves alone (that might not be much) but others.'

Others! He knew at whom that word pointed, and frowned heavily.

'I speak to you for the sake of others. Also your

own sake; and for mine. Since our marriage, you have been arrogant to me; and I have repaid you in kind. You have shown to me and every one around us, every day and hour, that you think I am graced and distinguished by your alliance. I do not think so, and have shown that too. It seems you do not understand, or (so far as your power can go) intend that each of us shall take a separate course; and you expect from me instead, a homage you will never have.'

Although her face was still the same, there was emphatic confirmation of this 'Never' in the very breath she drew.

'I feel no tenderness towards you; that you know. You would care nothing for it, if I did or could. I know as well that you feel none towards me. But we are linked together; and in the knot that ties us, as I have said, others are bound up. We must both die; we are both connected with the dead already, each by a little child. Let us forbear.'

Mr. Dombey took a long respiration, as if he would have said, Oh! was *this* all!

'There is no wealth,' she went on, turning paler as she watched him, while her eyes grew yet more lustrous in their earnestness, 'that could buy these words of me, and the meaning that belongs to them. Once cast away as idle breath, no wealth or power can bring them back. I mean them; I have weighed them; and I will be true to what I undertake. If you will promise to forbear on your part, I will promise to forbear on mine. We are a most unhappy pair, in whom, from different causes, every sentiment that blesses marriage, or justifies it, is rooted out; but in the course of time, some friendship, or some fitness for each other, may arise between us. I will try to hope so, if you will make the endeavour too; and I will look forward to a better and a happier use of age than I have made of youth or prime.'

Throughout she had spoken in a low plain voice, that neither rose nor fell; ceasing, she dropped the hand with which she had enforced herself to be so passionless and distinct, but not the eyes with which she had so steadily observed him.

'Madam,' said Mr. Dombey, with his utmost dignity, 'I cannot entertain any proposal of this extraordinary nature.'

She looked at him yet, without the least change.

'I cannot,' said Mr. Dombey, rising as he spoke, 'consent to temporise or treat with you, Mrs. Dombey, upon a subject as to which you are in possession of my opinions and expectations. I have stated my *ultimatum,* madam, and have only to request your very serious attention to it.'

To see the face change to its old expression, deepened in intensity! To see the eyes droop as from some mean and odious object! To see the lighting of the haughty brow! To see scorn, anger, indignation, and abhorrence starting into sight, and the pale blank earnestness vanish like a mist! He could not choose but look, although he looked to his dismay.

'Go, sir!' she said, pointing with an imperious hand towards the door. 'Our first and last confidence is at an end. Nothing can make us stranger to each other than we are henceforth.'

'I shall take my rightful course, madam,' said Mr. Dombey, 'undeterred, you may be sure, by any general declamation.'

She turned her back upon him, and, without reply, sat down before her glass.

'I place my reliance on your improved sense of duty, and more correct feeling, and better reflection, madam,' said Mr. Dombey.

She answered not one word. He saw no more expression of any heed of him, in the mirror, than if he had been an unseen spider on the wall, or beetle on the floor, or rather, than if he had been the one or other, seen and crushed when she last turned from him, and forgotten among the ignominious and dead vermin of the ground.

He looked back, as he went out at the door, upon the well-lighted and luxurious room, the beautiful and glittering objects everywhere displayed, the shape of Edith in its rich dress seated before her glass, and the face of Edith as the glass presented it to him; and betook himself to his old chamber of cogitation, carrying away with him a vivid picture in his mind of all these things, and a rambling and unaccountable speculation (such as sometimes comes into a man's head) how they would all look when he saw them next.

For the rest, Mr. Dombey was very taciturn, and very dignified, and very confident of carrying out his purpose; and remained so.

He did not design accompanying the family to Brighton; but he graciously informed Cleopatra at breakfast, on the morning of departure, which arrived a day or two afterwards, that he might be expected down, soon. There was no time to be lost in getting Cleopatra to any place recommended as being salutary; for, indeed, she seemed upon the wane, and turning of the earth, earthy.

Without having undergone any decided second attack of her malady, the old woman seemed to have crawled backward in her recovery from the first. She was more lean and shrunken, more uncertain in her imbecility, and made stranger confusions in her mind and memory. Among other symptoms of this last affliction, she fell into the habit of confounding the names of her two sons-in-law, the living and the deceased; and in general called Mr. Dombey, either 'Grangeby,' or 'Domber,' or indifferently, both.

But she was youthful, very youthful still; and in her youthfulness appeared at breakfast, before going away, in a new bonnet made express, and a travelling robe that was embroidered and braided like an old baby's. It was not easy to put her into a fly-away bonnet now, or to keep the bonnet in its place on the back of her poor nodding head, when it was got on. In this instance, it had not only the extraneous effect of being always on one side, but of being perpetually tapped on the crown by Flowers the maid, who attended in the background during breakfast to perform that duty.

'Now my dearest Grangeby,' said Mrs. Skewton, 'you must posively prom,' she cut some of her words short, and cut out others altogether, 'come down very soon.'

'I said just now, madam,' returned Mr. Dombey, loudly and laboriously, 'that I am coming in a day or two.'

'Bless you, Domber!'

Here the major, who was come to take leave of the ladies, and who was staring through his apoplectic eyes at Mrs. Skewton's face, with the disinterested composure of an immortal being, said—

'Begad, ma'am, you don't ask old Joe to come!'

'Sterious wretch, who's he?' lisped Cleopatra. But a tap on the bonnet from Flowers seeming to jog her memory, she added, 'Oh! You mean yourself, you naughty creature!'

'Devilish queer, sir,' whispered the major to Mr. Dombey. 'Bad case. Never *did* wrap up enough'; the major being buttoned to the chin. 'Why who should J. B. mean by Joe, but old Joe Bagstock—

Joseph—your slave—Joe, ma'am? Here! Here's the man! Here are the Bagstock bellows, ma'am!' cried the major, striking himself a sounding blow on the chest.

'My dearest Edith—Grangeby—it's most trordinry thing,' said Cleopatra, pettishly, 'that Major—'

'Bagstock! J. B.!' cried the major, seeing that she faltered for his name.

'Well, it don't matter,' said Cleopatra. 'Edith, my love, you know I never could remember names—what was it? oh!—most trordinry thing that so many people want to come down to see me. I 'm not going for long. I 'm coming back! Surely they can wait, till I come back!'

Cleopatra looked all round the table as she said it, and appeared very uneasy.

'I won't have visitors—really don't want visitors,' she said; 'little repose—and all that sort of thing—is what I quire. No odious brutes must proach me till I 've shaken off this numbness'; and in a grisly resumption of her coquettish ways, she made a dab at the major with her fan, but overset Mr. Dombey's breakfast-cup instead, which was in quite a different direction.

Then she called for Withers, and charged him to see particularly that word was left about some trivial alterations in her room, which must be all made before she came back, and which must be set about immediately, as there was no saying how soon she might come back; for she had a great many engagements, and all sorts of people to call upon. Withers received these directions with becoming deference, and gave his guarantee for their execution; but when he withdrew a pace or two behind her, it appeared as if he couldn't help looking strangely at the major, who couldn't help looking strangely at Mr. Dombey, who couldn't help looking strangely at Cleopatra, who couldn't help nodding her bonnet over one eye, and rattling her knife and fork upon her plate in using them, as if she were playing castanets.

Edith alone never lifted her eyes to any face at the table, and never seemed dismayed by anything her mother said or did. She listened to her disjointed talk, or at least, turned her head towards her when addressed; replied in a few low words when necessary; and sometimes stopped her when she was rambling, or brought her thoughts back with a monosyllable, to the point from which they had strayed. The mother, however unsteady in other things, was constant in this—that she was always observant of her. She would look at the beautiful face, in its marble stillness and severity, now with a kind of fearful admiration; now in a giggling foolish effort to move it to a smile; now with capricious tears and jealous shakings of her head, as imagining herself neglected by it; always with an attraction towards it, that never fluctuated like her other ideas, but had constant possession of her. From Edith she would sometimes look at Florence, and back again at Edith, in a manner that was wild enough; and sometimes she would try to look elsewhere, as if to escape from her daughter's face; but back to it she seemed forced to come, although it never sought her unless sought, or troubled her with one single glance.

The breakfast concluded, Mrs. Skewton, affecting to lean girlishly upon the major's arm, but heavily supported on the other side by Flowers the maid, and propped up behind by Withers the page, was conducted to the carriage, which was to take her, Florence, and Edith to Brighton.

'And is Joseph absolutely banished?' said the major, thrusting in his purple face over the steps.

'Damme, ma'am, is Cleopatra so hard-hearted as to forbid her faithful Antony Bagstock to approach the presence?'

'Go along!' said Cleopatra, 'I can't bear you. You shall see me when I come back, if you are very good.'

'Tell Joseph, he may live in hope, ma'am,' said the major; 'or he'll die in despair.'

Cleopatra shuddered, and leaned back. 'Edith, my dear,' she said. 'Tell him—'

'What?'

'Such dreadful words,' said Cleopatra. 'He uses such dreadful words!'

Edith signed to him to retire, gave the word to go on, and left the objectionable major to Mr. Dombey. To whom he returned, whistling.

'I'll tell you what, sir,' said the major, with his hands behind him, and his legs very wide asunder, 'a fair friend of ours has removed to Queer Street.'

'What do you mean, major?' inquired Mr. Dombey.

'I mean to say, Dombey,' returned the major, 'that you'll soon be an orphan-in-law.'

Mr. Dombey appeared to relish this waggish description of himself so very little, that the major wound up with the horse's cough, as an expression of gravity.

'Damme, sir,' said the major, 'there is no use in disguising a fact. Joe is blunt, sir. That's his nature. If you take old Josh. at all, you take him as you find him; and a de-vilish rusty, old rasper, of a close-toothed, J. B. file, you *do* find him. Dombey,' said the major, 'your wife's mother is on the move, sir.'

'I fear,' returned Mr. Dombey, with much philosophy, 'that Mrs. Skewton is shaken.'

'Shaken, Dombey!' said the major. 'Smashed!'

'Change, however,' pursued Mr. Dombey, 'and attention may do much yet.'

'Don't believe it, sir,' returned the major. 'Damme, sir, she never wrapped up enough. If a man don't wrap up,' said the major, taking in another button of his buff waistcoat, 'he has nothing to fall back upon. But some people *will* die. They *will* do it. Damme, they *will*. They 're obstinate. I tell you what, Dombey, it may not be ornamental; it may not be refined; it may be rough and tough; but a little of the genuine old English Bagstock stamina, sir, would do all the good in the world to the human breed.'

After imparting this precious piece of information, the major, who was certainly true-blue, whatever other endowments he may have possessed or wanted, coming within the 'genuine old English' classification, which has never been exactly ascertained, took his lobster-eyes and his apoplexy to the club, and choked there all day.

Cleopatra, at one time fretful, at another self-complacent, sometimes awake, sometimes asleep, and at all times juvenile, reached Brighton the same night, fell to pieces as usual, and was put away in bed; where a gloomy fancy might have pictured a more potent skeleton than the maid, who should have been one, watching at the rose-coloured curtains, which were carried down to shed their bloom upon her.

It was settled in high council of medical authority that she should take a carriage airing every day, and that it was important she should get out every day, and walk if she could. Edith was ready to attend her—always ready to attend her, with the same mechanical attention and immoveable beauty—and they drove out alone; for Edith had an uneasiness in the presence of Florence, now that her mother was worse, and told Florence, with a kiss, that she would rather they two went alone.

Mrs. Skewton, on one particular day, was in the irresolute, exacting, jealous temper that had developed itself on her recovery from her first attack. After sitting silent in the carriage watching Edith for some time, she took her hand and kissed it passionately. The hand was neither given nor withdrawn, but simply yielded to her raising of it, and being released, dropped down again, almost as if it were insensible. At this she began to whimper and moan, and say what a mother she had been, and how she was forgotten! This she continued to do at capricious intervals, even when they had alighted: when she herself was halting along with the joint support of Withers and a stick, and Edith was walking by her side, and the carriage slowly following at a little distance.

It was a bleak, lowering, windy day, and they were out upon the Downs with nothing but a bare sweep of land between them and the sky. The mother, with a querulous satisfaction in the monotony of her complaint, was still repeating it in a low voice from time to time, and the proud form of her daughter moved beside her slowly, when there came advancing over a dark ridge before them, two other figures, which in the distance, were so like an exaggerated imitation of their own, that Edith stopped.

Almost as she stopped, the two figures stopped; and that one which to Edith's thinking was like a distorted shadow of her mother, spoke to the other, earnestly, and with a pointing hand towards them. That one seemed inclined to turn back, but the other, in which Edith recognised enough that was like herself to strike her with an unusual feeling, not quite free from fear, came on; and then they came on together.

The greater part of this observation, she made while walking towards them, for her stoppage had been momentary. Nearer observation showed her that they were poorly dressed, as wanderers about the country; that the younger woman carried knitted work or some such goods for sale; and that the old one toiled on empty-handed.

And yet, however far removed she was in dress, in dignity, in beauty, Edith could not but compare the younger woman with herself, still. It may have been that she saw upon her face some traces which she knew were lingering in her own soul, if not yet written on that index; but, as the woman came on, returning her gaze, fixing her shining eyes upon her, undoubtedly presenting something of her own air and stature, and appearing to reciprocate her own thoughts, she felt a chill creep over her, as if the day were darkening, and the wind were colder.

They had now come up. The old woman holding out her hand importunately, stopped to beg of Mrs. Skewton. The younger one stopped too, and she and Edith looked in one another's eyes.

'What is it that you have to sell?' said Edith.

'Only this,' returned the woman, holding out her wares, without looking at them. 'I sold myself long ago.'

'My lady, don't believe her,' croaked the old woman to Mrs. Skewton; 'don't believe what she says. She loves to talk like that. She's my handsome and undutiful daughter. She gives me nothing but reproaches, my lady, for all I have done for her. Look at her now, my lady, how she turns upon her poor old mother with her looks.'

As Mrs. Skewton drew her purse out with a

trembling hand, and eagerly fumbled for some money, which the other old woman greedily watched for—their heads all but touching, in their hurry and decrepitude—Edith interposed—

'I have seen you,' addressing the old woman, 'before.'

'Yes, my lady,' with a curtsey. 'Down in Warwickshire. The morning among the trees. When you wouldn't give me nothing. But the gentleman, *he* give me something! Oh, bless him, bless him!' mumbled the old woman, holding up her skinny hand, and grinning frightfully at her daughter.

'It 's of no use attempting to stay me, Edith!' said Mrs. Skewton, angrily anticipating an objection from her. 'You know nothing about it. I won't be dissuaded. I am sure this is an excellent woman, and a good mother.'

'Yes, my lady, yes,' chattered the old woman, holding out her avaricious hand. 'Thankee, my lady. Lord bless you, my lady. Sixpence more, my pretty lady, as a good mother yourself.'

'And treated undutifully enough, too, my good old creature, sometimes, I assure you,' said Mrs. Skewton, whimpering. 'There! Shake hands with me. You 're a very good old creature—full of what 's-his-name—and all that. You 're all affection and et cetera, an't you?'

'Oh, yes, my lady!'

'Yes, I 'm sure you are; and so 's that gentlemanly creature Grangeby. I must really shake hands with you again. And now you can go, you know; and I hope,' addressing the daughter, 'that you 'll show more gratitude, and natural what 's-its-name, and all the rest of it—but I never *did* remember names—for there never was a better mother than the good old creature 's been to you. Come, Edith!'

As the ruin of Cleopatra tottered off whimpering, and wiping its eyes with a gingerly remembrance of rouge in their neighbourhood, the old woman hobbled another way, mumbling and counting her money. Not one word more, nor one other gesture, had been exchanged between Edith and the younger woman, but neither had removed her eyes from the other for a moment. They had remained confronted until now, when Edith, as awakening from a dream, passed slowly on.

'You 're a handsome woman,' muttered her shadow, looking after her; 'but good looks won't save us. And you 're a proud woman; but pride won't save us. We had need to know each other when we meet again!'

CHAPTER XLI

NEW VOICES IN THE WAVES

ALL is going on as it was wont. The waves are hoarse with repetition of their mystery: the dust lies piled upon the shore; the sea-birds soar and hover; the winds and clouds go forth upon their trackless flight; the white arms beckon, in the moonlight, to the invisible country far away.

With a tender melancholy pleasure, Florence finds herself again on the old ground so sadly trodden, yet so happily, and thinks of him in the quiet place, where he and she have many and many a time conversed together, with the water welling up about his couch. And now, as she sits pensive there, she hears in the wild low murmur of the sea, his little story told again, his very words repeated; and finds that all her life, and hopes, and griefs, since—in the solitary house, and in the pageant it has changed to—have a portion in the burden of the marvellous song.

And gentle Mr. Toots, who wanders at a distance, looking wistfully towards the figure that he dotes upon, and has followed there, but cannot in his delicacy disturb at such a time, likewise hears the requiem of little Dombey on the waters, rising and falling in the lulls of their eternal madrigal in praise of Florence.   Yes! and he faintly understands, poor Mr. Toots, that they are saying something of a time when he was sensible of being brighter and not addlebrained; and the tears rising in his eyes when he fears that he is dull and stupid now, and good for little but to be laughed at, diminish his satisfaction in their soothing reminder that he is relieved from present responsibility to the Chicken, by the absence of that game head of poultry in the country, training (at Toots's cost) for his great mill with the Larkey Boy.

But Mr. Toots takes courage, when they whisper a kind thought to him; and by slow degrees and with many indecisive stoppages on the way, approaches Florence.   Stammering and blushing, Mr. Toots affects amazement when he comes near her, and says (having followed close on the carriage in which she travelled, every inch of the way from London, loving even to be choked by the dust of its wheels) that he never was so surprised in all his life.

'And you've brought Diogenes, too, Miss Dombey!' says Mr. Toots, thrilled through and through by the touch of the small hand so pleasantly and frankly given him.

No doubt Diogenes is there, and no doubt Mr. Toots has reason to observe him, for he comes straight way at Mr. Toots's legs, and tumbles over himself in the desperation with which he makes at him, like a very Dog of Montargis. But he is checked by his sweet mistress.

'Down, Di, down. Don't you remember who first made us friends, Di? For shame!'

Oh! Well may Di lay his loving cheek against her hand, and run off, and run back, and run round her, barking, and run headlong at anybody coming by, to show his devotion. Mr. Toots would run headlong at anybody, too. A military gentleman goes past, and Mr. Toots would like nothing better than to run at him, full tilt.

'Diogenes is quite in his native air, isn't he, Miss Dombey?' says Mr. Toots.

Florence assents, with a grateful smile.

'Miss Dombey,' says Mr. Toots, 'beg your pardon, but if you would like to walk to Blimber's, I—I 'm going there.'

Florence puts her arm in that of Mr. Toots without a word, and they walk away together, with Diogenes going on before. Mr. Toots's legs shake under him; and though he is splendidly dressed, he feels misfits, and sees wrinkles, in the masterpieces of Burgess and Co., and wishes he had put on that brightest pair of boots.

Doctor Blimber's house, outside, has as scholastic and studious an air as ever: and up there is the window where she used to look for the pale face, and where the pale face brightened when it saw her, and the wasted little hand waved kisses as she passed. The door is opened by the same weak-eyed young man, whose imbecility of grin at sight of Mr. Toots is feebleness of character personified. They are shown into the Doctor's study, where blind Homer and Minerva give them audience as of yore, to the sober ticking of the great clock in the hall; and where the globes stand still in their accustomed places, as if the world were stationary too, and nothing in it ever perished in obedience to the universal law, that, while it keeps it on the roll, calls everything to earth.

And here is Doctor Blimber, with his learned legs; and here is Mrs. Blimber, with her sky-blue cap; and here is Cornelia, with her sandy little row of curls, and her bright spectacles, still working like a sexton in the graves of languages. Here is the table upon which he sat forlorn and strange, the 'new boy' of the school; and hither comes the distant cooing of the old boys, at their old lives in the old room on the old principle!

'Toots,' says Doctor Blimber, 'I am very glad to see you, Toots.'

Mr. Toots chuckles in reply.

'Also to see you, Toots, in such good company,' says Doctor Blimber.

Mr. Toots, with a scarlet visage, explains that he has met Miss Dombey by accident, and that Miss Dombey wishing, like himself, to see the old place, they have come together.

'You will like,' says Doctor Blimber, 'to step among our young friends, Miss Dombey, no doubt. All fellow-students of yours, Toots, once. I think we have no new disciples in our little portico, my dear,' says Doctor Blimber to Cornelia, 'since Mr. Toots left us.'

'Except Bitherstone,' returns Cornelia.

'Aye, truly,' says the Doctor. 'Bitherstone is new to Mr. Toots.'

New to Florence, too, almost; for, in the school-room, Bitherstone—no longer Master Bitherstone of Mrs. Pipchin's—shows in collars and a neckcloth, and wears a watch. But Bitherstone, born beneath some Bengal star of ill-omen, is extremely inky; and his lexicon has got so dropsical from constant reference, that it won't shut, and yawns as if it really could not bear to be so bothered. So does Bitherstone its master, forced at Doctor Blimber's highest pressure; but in the yawn of Bitherstone there is malice and snarl, and he has been heard to say that he wishes he could catch 'old Blimber' in India. He 'd precious soon find himself carried up the country by a few of his (Bitherstone's) coolies, and handed over to the Thugs; he can tell him that.

Briggs is still grinding in the mill of knowledge; and Tozer, too; and Johnson, too; and all the rest; the older pupils being principally engaged in forgetting, with prodigious labour, everything they knew when they were younger. All are as polite and as pale as ever; and among them, Mr. Feeder, B.A., with his bony hand and bristly head, is still hard at it: with his Herodotus stop on just at present, and his other barrels on a shelf behind him.

A mighty sensation is created, even among these grave young gentlemen, by a visit from the emancipated Toots; who is regarded with a kind of awe, as one who has passed the Rubicon, and is pledged never to come back, and concerning the cut of whose clothes, and fashion of whose jewellery, whispers go about, behind hands; the bilious Bitherstone, who is not of Mr. Toots's time, affecting to despise the latter to the smaller boys, and saying he knows better, and that he should like to see him coming that sort of thing in Bengal, where his mother has got an emerald belonging to him that was taken out of the footstool of a rajah. Come now!

Bewildering emotions are awakened also by the sight of Florence, with whom every young gentleman immediately falls in love, again: except, as aforesaid, the bilious Bitherstone, who declines to do

so, out of contradiction. Black jealousies of Mr.
Toots arise, and Briggs is of opinion that he an't
so very old after all. But this disparaging insinuation is speedily made nought by Mr. Toots saying
aloud to Mr. Feeder, B.A., 'How are you, Feeder?'
and asking him to come and dine with him to-day
at the Bedford; in right of which feats he might set
up as Old Parr, if he chose, unquestioned.

There is much shaking of hands, and much bowing
and a great desire on the part of each young gentleman to take Toots down in Miss Dombey's good
graces; and then, Mr. Toots having bestowed a
chuckle on his old desk, Florence and he withdraw
with Mrs. Blimber and Cornelia; and Doctor Blimber is heard to observe behind them as he comes out
last, and shuts the door, 'Gentlemen, we will now resume our studies.' For that and little else is what
the Doctor hears the sea say, or has heard it saying
all his life.

Florence then steals away and goes upstairs to the
old bedroom with Mrs. Blimber and Cornelia; Mr.
Toots, who feels that neither he nor anybody else is
wanted there, stands talking to the Doctor at the
study-door, or rather hearing the Doctor talk to him,
and wondering how he ever thought the study a great
sanctuary, and the Doctor, with his round turned legs,
like a clerical pianoforte, an awful man. Florence
soon comes down and takes leave; Mr. Toots takes
leave; and Diogenes, who has been worrying the
weak-eyed young man pitilessly all the time, shoots
out at the door, and barks a glad defiance down
the cliff; while 'Melia, and another of the Doctor's
female domestics, look out of an upper window,
laughing 'at that there Toots,' and saying of Miss
Dombey, 'But really though, now—ain't she like her
brother, only prettier?'

Mr. Toots, who saw when Florence came down that there were tears upon her face, is desperately anxious and uneasy, and at first fears that he did wrong in proposing the visit. But he is soon relieved by her saying she is very glad to have been there again, and by her talking quite cheerfully about it all, as they walked on by the sea. What with the voices there, and her sweet voice, when they come near Mr. Dombey's house, and Mr. Toots must leave her, he is so enslaved that he has not a scrap of free-will left; when she gives him her hand at parting, he cannot let it go.

'Miss Dombey, I beg your pardon,' says Mr. Toots, in a sad fluster, 'but if you would allow me to—to—'

The smiling and unconscious look of Florence brings him to a dead stop.

'If you would allow me to—if you would not consider it a liberty, Miss Dombey, if I was to—without any encouragement at all, if I was to hope, you know,' says Mr. Toots.

Florence looks at him inquiringly.

'Miss Dombey,' says Mr. Toots, who feels that he is in for it now, 'I really am in that state of adoration of you that I don't know what to do with myself. I am the most deplorable wretch. If it wasn't at the corner of the square at present, I should go down on my knees, and beg and entreat of you, without any encouragement at all, just to let me hope that I may —may think it possible that you—'

'Oh, if you please, don't!' cried Florence, for the moment quite alarmed and distressed. 'Oh, pray don't, Mr. Toots. Stop, if you please. Don't say any more. As a kindness and a favour to me, don't.'

Mr. Toots is dreadfully abashed, and his mouth opens.

'You have been so good to me,' says Florence, 'I

am so grateful to you, I have such reason to like you
for being a kind friend to me, and I do like you so
much'; and here the ingenuous face smiles upon him
with the pleasantest look of honesty in the world; 'that
I am sure you are only going to say good-bye!'

'Certainly, Miss Dombey,' says Mr. Toots, 'I—I
—That's exactly what I mean. It's of no consequence.'

'Good-bye!' cries Florence.

'Good-bye, Miss Dombey!' stammers Mr. Toots.
'I hope you won't think anything about it. It's—
it's of no consequence, thank you. It's not of the
least consequence in the world.'

Poor Mr. Toots goes home to his hotel in a state
of desperation, locks himself into his bedroom, flings
himself upon his bed, and lies there for a long time;
as if it were of the greatest consequence, nevertheless. But Mr. Feeder, B.A., is coming to dinner,
which happens well for Mr. Toots, or there is no
knowing when he might get up again. Mr. Toots is
obliged to get up to receive him, and to give him hospitable entertainment.

And the generous influence of that social virtue,
hospitality (to make no mention of wine and good
cheer), opens Mr. Toots's heart, and warms him to
conversation. He does not tell Mr. Feeder, B.A.,
what passed at the corner of the square; but when
Mr. Feeder asks him 'When it is to come off?' Mr.
Toots replies, 'that there are certain subjects'—which
brings Mr. Feeder down a peg or two immediately.
Mr. Toots adds, that he don't know what right Blimber had to notice his being in Miss Dombey's company, and that if he thought he meant impudence by
it, he'd have him out, Doctor or no Doctor; but he
supposes it's only his ignorance. Mr. Feeder says
he has no doubt of it.

Mr. Feeder, however, as an intimate friend, is not excluded from the subject. Mr. Toots merely requires that it should be mentioned mysteriously, and with feeling. After a few glasses of wine, he gives Miss Dombey's health, observing, 'Feeder, you have no idea of the sentiments with which I propose tha. toast.' Mr. Feeder replies, 'Oh, yes, I have, my dear Toots; and greatly they redound to your honour, old boy.' Mr. Feeder is then agitated by friendship, and shakes hands; and says, if ever Toots wants a brother he knows where to find him, either by post or parcel. Mr. Feeder likewise says, that if he may advise, he would recommend Mr. Toots to learn the guitar, or, at least the flute; for women like music, when you are paying your addresses to 'em, and he has found the advantage of it himself.

This brings Mr. Feeder, B.A., to the confession that he has his eye upon Cornelia Blimber. He informs Mr. Toots that he don't object to spectacles, and that if the Doctor were to do the handsome thing and give up the business, why, there they are—provided for. He says it's his opinion that when a man has made a handsome sum by his business, he is bound to give it up; and that Cornelia would be an assistance in it which any man might be proud of. Mr. Toots replies by launching wildly out into Miss Dombey's praises, and by insinuations that sometimes he thinks he should like to blow his brains out. Mr. Feeder strongly urges that it would be a rash attempt, and shows him, as a reconcilement to existence, Cornelia's portrait, spectacles and all.

Thus these quiet spirits pass the evening; and when it has yielded place to night, Mr. Toots walks home with Mr. Feeder, and parts with him at Doctor Blimber's door. But Mr. Feeder only goes up the steps, and when Mr. Toots is gone, comes down again, to stroll upon the beach alone, and think about his prospects. Mr. Feeder plainly hears the waves informing him, as he loiters along, that Doctor Blimber will give up the business; and he feels a soft romantic pleasure in looking at the outside of the house, and thinking that the Doctor will first paint it, and put it into thorough repair.

Mr. Toots is likewise roaming up and down, outside the casket that contains his jewel; and in a deplorable condition of mind, and not unsuspected by the police, gazes at a window where he sees a light, and which he has no doubt is Florence's. But it is not, for that is Mrs. Skewton's room; and while Florence, sleeping in another chamber, dreams lovingly, in the midst of the old scenes, and their old associations live again, the figure which in grim reality is substituted for the patient boy's on the same theatre, once more to connect it—but how differently! —with decay and death, is stretched there, wakeful and complaining. Ugly and haggard it lies upon its bed of unrest; and by it, in the terror of her unimpassioned loveliness—for it *has* terror in the sufferer's failing eyes—sits Edith. What do the waves say, in the stillness of the night, to them!

'Edith, what is that stone arm raised to strike me? Don't you see it?'

'There is nothing, mother, but your fancy.'

'But my fancy? Everything is my fancy. Look! Is it possible that you don't see it?'

'Indeed, mother, there is nothing. Should I sit unmoved, if there were any such thing there?'

'Unmoved?' looking wildly at her—'it 's gone now —and why are you so unmoved? That is not my fancy, Edith. It turns me cold to see you sitting at my side.'

'I am sorry, mother.'

'Sorry! You seem always sorry. But it is not for me!'

With that, she cries; and tossing her restless head from side to side upon her pillow, runs on about neglect, and the mother she has been, and the mother the good old creature was, whom they met, and the cold return the daughters of such mothers make. In the midst of her incoherence, she stops, looks at her daughter, cries out that her wits are going, and hides her face upon her bed.

Edith, in compassion, bends over her and speaks to her. The sick old woman clutches her round the neck, and says, with a look of horror—

'Edith! we are going home soon; going back. You mean that I shall go home again?'

'Yes, mother, yes.'

'And what he said—what's his name, I never could remember names—Major—that dreadful word, when we came away—it's not true? Edith!' with a shriek and a stare, 'it's not *that* that is the matter with me.'

Night after night, the light burns in the window, and the figure lies upon the bed, and Edith sits beside it, and the restless waves are calling to them both the whole night long. Night after night, the waves are hoarse with repetition of their mystery; the dust lies piled upon the shore; the sea-birds soar and hover; the winds and clouds are on their trackless flight; the white arms beckon, in the moonlight, to the invisible country far away.

And still the sick old woman looks into the corner, where the stone arm—part of a figure of some tomb, she says—is raised to strike her. At last it falls; and then a dumb old woman lies upon the bed, and she is crooked and shrunk up, and half of her is dead.

Such is the figure, painted and patched for the sun to mock, that is drawn slowly through the crowd from day to day; looking, as it goes, for the good old creature who was such a mother, and making mouths as it peers among the crowd in vain. Such is the figure that is often wheeled down to the margin of the sea, and stationed there; but on which no wind can blow freshness, and for which the murmur of the ocean has no soothing word. She lies and listens to it by the hour; but its speech is dark and gloomy to her, and a dread is on her face, and when her eyes wander over the expanse, they see but a broad stretch of desolation between earth and heaven.

Florence she seldom sees, and when she does, is angry with and mows at. Edith is beside her always, and keeps Florence away; and Florence, in her bed at night, trembles at the thought of death in such a shape, and often wakes and listens, thinking it has come. No one attends on her but Edith. It is better that few eyes should see her; and her daughter watches alone by the bedside.

A shadow even on that shadowed face, a sharpening even of the sharpened features, and a thickening of the veil before the eyes into a pall that shuts out the dim world, is come. Her wandering hands upon the coverlet join feebly palm to palm, and move towards her daughter; and a voice not like hers, not like any voice that speaks our mortal language—says, 'For I nursed you!'

Edith, without a tear, kneels down to bring her voice closer to the sinking head, and answers—

'Mother, can you hear me?'

Staring wide, she tries to nod in answer.

'Can you recollect the night before I married?'

The head is motionless, but it expresses somehow that she does.

'I told you then that I forgave your part in it, and prayed God to forgive my own. I told you that the

past was at an end between us. I say so now, again.
Kiss me, mother.'

Edith touches the white lips, and for a moment all
is still. A moment afterwards, her mother, with her
girlish laugh, and the skeleton of the Cleopatra manner, rises in her bed.

Draw the rose-coloured curtains. There is something else upon its flight besides the wind and clouds.
Draw the rose-coloured curtains close!

Intelligence of the event is sent to Mr. Dombey in
town, who waits upon cousin Feenix (not yet able to
make up his mind for Baden-Baden), who has just
received it too. A good-natured creature like cousin
Feenix is the very man for a marriage or a funeral,
and his position in the family renders it right that he
should be consulted.

'Dombey,' said cousin Feenix, 'upon my soul, I am
very much shocked to see you on such a melancholy
occasion. My poor aunt! She was a devilish lively
woman.'

Mr. Dombey replies, 'Very much so.'

'And made up,' says cousin Feenix, 'really young,
you know, considering. I am sure, on the day of your
marriage, I thought she was good for another twenty
years. In point of fact, I said so to a man at Brooks's
—little Billy Joper—you know him, no doubt—man
with a glass in his eye?'

Mr. Dombey bows a negative. 'In reference to
the obsequies,' he hints, 'whether there is any suggestion—'

'Well, upon my life,' says cousin Feenix, stroking
his chin, which he has just enough of hand below his
wristbands to do; 'I really don't know. There's a
mausoleum down at my place, in the park, but I'm
afraid it's in bad repair, and, in point of fact, in a

devil of a state. But for being a little out at
elbows, I should have had it put to rights; but I believe
the people come and make picnic parties there inside
the iron railings.

Mr. Dombey is clear that this won't do.

'There's an uncommon good church in the village,'
says cousin Feenix, thoughtfully; 'pure specimen of
the Anglo-Norman style, and admirably well sketched
too by Lady Jane Finchbury—woman with tight stays
—but they've spoilt it with whitewash, I understand,
and it's a long journey.'

'Perhaps Brighton itself,' Mr. Dombey suggests.

'Upon my honour, Dombey, I don't think we could
do better,' says cousin Feenix. 'It's on the spot, you
see, and a very cheerful place.'

'And when,' hints Mr. Dombey, 'would it be convenient?'

'I shall make a point,' says cousin Feenix, 'of pledg-
ing myself for any day you think best. I shall have
great pleasure (melancholy pleasure, of course) in following my poor aunt to the confines of the—in point
of fact, to the grave,' says cousin Feenix, failing in
the other turn of speech.

'Would Monday do for leaving town?' says Mr.
Dombey.

'Monday would suit me to perfection,' replies cousin
Feenix. Therefore Mr. Dombey arranges to take
cousin Feenix down on that day, and presently takes
his leave, attended to the stairs by cousin Feenix, who
says, at parting, 'I'm really excessively sorry, Dombey, that you should have so much trouble about it';
to which Mr. Dombey answers, 'Not at all.'

At the appointed time, cousin Feenix and Mr. Dombey meet, and go down to Brighton, and representing,
in their two selves, all the other mourners for the deceased lady's loss, attend her remains to their place of

rest. Cousin Feenix, sitting in the mourning-coach, recognises innumerable acquaintances on the road, but takes no other notice of them, in decorum, than checking them off aloud, as they go by, for Mr. Dombey's information, as 'Tom Johnson. Man with cork leg from White's. What, are *you* here, Tommy? Foley on a blood mare. The Smalder girls—' and so forth. At the ceremony cousin Feenix is depressed, observing, that these are the occasions to make a man think, in point of fact, that he is getting shaky; and his eyes are really moistened, when it is over. But he soon recovers; and so do the rest of Mrs. Skewton's relatives and friends, of whom the major continually tells the club that she never did wrap up enough; while the young lady with the back, who has so much trouble with her eyelids, says, with a little scream, that she must have been enormously old, and that she died of all kinds of horrors, and you mustn't mention it.

So Edith's mother lies unmentioned of her dear friends, who are deaf to the waves that are hoarse with repetition of their mystery, and blind to the dust that is piled upon the shore, and to the white arms that are beckoning, in the moonlight, to the invisible country far away. But all goes on as it was wont, upon the margin of the unknown sea; and Edith standing there alone, and listening to its waves, has dank weed cast up at her feet, to strew her path in life withal.

CHAPTER XLII

CONFIDENTIAL AND ACCIDENTAL

ATTIRED no more in Captain Cuttle's sable slops and sou'wester hat, but dressed in a substantial suit of brown livery, which, while it affected to be a very

sober and demure livery indeed, was really as self-sat-
isfied and confident a one as tailor need desire to make,
Rob the Grinder, thus transformed as to his outer man,
and all regardless within of the captain and the midshipman, except when he devoted a few minutes of
his leisure time to crowing over those inseparable
worthies, and recalling, with much applauding music
from that brazen instrument, his conscience, the triumphant manner in which he had disembarrassed himself of their company, now served his patron, Mr.
Carker. Inmate of Mr. Carker's house, and serving
about his person, Rob kept his round eyes on the white
teeth with fear and trembling, and felt that he had
need to open them wider than ever.

He could not have quaked more, through his whole
being, before the teeth, though he had come into the
service of some powerful enchanter, and they had been
his strongest spell. The boy had a sense of power
and authority in this patron of his that engrossed his
whole attention and exacted his most implicit submission and obedience. He hardly considered himself
safe in thinking about him when he was absent, lest
he should feel himself immediately taken by the throat
again, as on the morning when he first became bound
to him, and should see every one of the teeth finding
him out, and taxing him with every fancy of his mind.
Face to face with him, Rob had no more doubt that
Mr. Carker read his secret thoughts, or that he could
read them by the least exertion of his will if he were
so inclined, than he had that Mr. Carker saw him
when he looked at him. The ascendancy was so complete, and held him in such enthralment, that, hardly
daring to think at all, but with his mind filled with
a constantly dilating impression of his patron's irresistible command over him, and power of doing anything
with him, he would stand watching his pleasure, and

trying to anticipate his orders, in a state of mental suspension, as to all other things.

Rob had not informed himself perhaps—in his then state of mind it would have been an act of no common temerity to inquire—whether he yielded so completely to this influence in any part, because he had floating suspicions of his patron's being a master of certain treacherous arts in which he had himself been a poor scholar at the Grinders' School. But certainly Rob admired him, as well as feared him. Mr. Carker, perhaps, was better acquainted with the sources of his power, which lost nothing by his management of it.

On the very night when he left the captain's service, Rob, after disposing of his pigeons, and even making a bad bargain in his hurry, had gone straight down to Mr. Carker's house, and hotly presented himself before his new master with a glowing face that seemed to expect commendation.

'What, scapegrace!' said Mr. Carker, glancing at his bundle. 'Have you left your situation and come to me?'

'Oh if you please, sir,' faltered Rob, 'you said, you know, when I come here last—'

'*I* said,' returned Mr. Carker, 'what did I say?'

'If you please, sir, you didn't say nothing at all, sir,' returned Rob, warned by the manner of this inquiry, and very much disconcerted.

His patron looked at him with a wide display of gums, and shaking his forefinger, observed—

'You 'll come to an evil end, my vagabond friend, I foresee. There 's ruin in store for you.'

'Oh if you please, don't, sir!' cried Rob, with his legs trembling under him. 'I 'm sure, sir, I only want to work for you, sir, and to wait upon you, sir, and to do faithful whatever I 'm bid, sir.'

'You had better do faithfully whatever you are bid,'

returned his patron, 'if you have anything to do with me.'

'Yes, I know that, sir,' pleaded the submissive Rob; 'I 'm sure of that, sir. If you 'll only be so good as try me, sir! And if ever you find me out, sir, doing anything against your wishes, I give you leave to kill me.'

'You dog!' said Mr. Carker, leaning back in his chair, and smiling at him serenely. 'That 's nothing to what I 'd do to you, if you tried to deceive me.'

'Yes, sir,' replied the abject Grinder, 'I 'm sure you would be down upon me dreadful, sir. I wouldn't attempt for to go and do it, sir, not if I was bribed with golden guineas.'

Thoroughly checked in his expectations of commendation, the crestfallen Grinder stood looking at his patron, and vainly endeavouring not to look at him, with the uneasiness which a cur will often manifest in a similar situation.

'So you have left your old service, and come here to ask me to take you into mine, eh?' said Mr. Carker.

'Yes, if you please, sir,' returned Rob, who, in doing so, had acted on his patron's own instructions, but dared not justify himself by the least insinuation to that effect.

'Well!' said Mr. Carker. 'You know me, boy?'

'Please, sir, yes, sir,' returned Rob, fumbling with his hat, and still fixed by Mr. Carker's eye, and fruitlessly endeavouring to unfix himself.

Mr. Carker nodded. 'Take care, then!'

Rob expressed in a number of short bows his lively understanding of this caution, and was bowing himself back to the door, greatly relieved by the prospect of getting on the outside of it, when his patron stopped him.

'Halloa!' he cried, calling him roughly back. 'You have been—shut that door.'

Rob obeyed as if his life had depended on his alacrity.

'You have been used to eavesdropping. Do you know what that means?'

'Listening, sir?' Rob hazarded, after some embarrassed reflection.

His patron nodded. 'And watching, and so forth.'

'I wouldn't do such a thing here, sir,' answered Rob; 'upon my word and honour, I wouldn't, sir, I wish I may die if I would, sir, for anything that could be promised to me. I should consider it is as much as all the world was worth, to offer to do such a thing, unless I was ordered, sir.'

'You had better not. You have been used, too, to babbling and tattling,' said his patron with perfect coolness. 'Beware of that here, or you're a lost rascal,' and he smiled again, and again cautioned him with his forefinger.

The Grinder's breath came short and thick with consternation. He tried to protest the purity of his intentions, but could only stare at the smiling gentleman in a stupor of submission, with which the smiling gentleman seemed well enough satisfied, for he ordered him downstairs, after observing him for some moments in silence, and gave him to understand that he was retained in his employment.

This was the manner of Rob the Grinder's engagement by Mr. Carker, and his awe-stricken devotion to that gentleman had strengthened and increased, if possible, with every minute of his service.

It was a service of some months' duration, when early one morning, Rob opened the garden gate to Mr. Dombey, who was come to breakfast with his master, by appointment. At the same moment his master himself came, hurrying forth to receive the distinguished guest, and give him welcome with all his teeth.

'I never thought,' said Carker, when he had assisted him to alight from his horse, 'to see you here, I'm sure. This is an extraordinary day in my calendar. No occasion is very special to a man like you, who may do anything; but to a man like me, the case is widely different.'

'You have a tasteful place here, Carker,' said Mr. Dombey, condescending to stop upon the lawn, to look about him.

'You can afford to say so,' returned Carker. 'Thank you.'

'Indeed,' said Mr. Dombey, in his lofty patronage, 'any one might say so. As far as it goes, it is a very commodious and well-arranged place—quite elegant.'

'As far as it goes, truly,' returned Carker, with an air of disparagement. 'It wants that qualification. Well! we have said enough about it; and though you can afford to praise it, I thank you none the less. Will you walk in?'

Mr. Dombey, entering the house, noticed, as he had reason to do, the complete arrangement of the rooms, and the numerous contrivances for comfort and effect that abounded there. Mr. Carker, in his ostentation of humility, received this notice with a deferential smile, and said he understood its delicate meaning, and appreciated it, but in truth the cottage was good enough for one in his position—better, perhaps, than such a man should occupy, poor as it was.

'But perhaps to you, who are so far removed, it really does look better than it is,' he said, with his false mouth distended to its fullest stretch. 'Just as monarchs imagine attractions in the lives of beggars.'

He directed a sharp glance and a sharp smile at

Mr. Dombey as he spoke, and a sharper glance, and a sharper smile yet, when Mr. Dombey, drawing himself up before the fire, in the attitude so often copied by his second in command, looked round at the pictures on the walls. Cursorily as his cold eye wandered over them, Carker's keen glance accompanied his, and kept pace with his, marking exactly where it went, and what it saw. As it rested on one picture in particular, Carker hardly seemed to breathe, his sidelong scrutiny was so catlike and vigilant, but the eye of his great chief passed from that, as from the others, and appeared no more impressed by it than by the rest.

Carker looked at it—it was the picture that resembled Edith—as if it were a living thing; and with a wicked, silent laugh upon his face, that seemed in part addressed to it, though it was all derisive of the great man standing so unconscious beside him. Breakfast was soon set upon the table: and, inviting Mr. Dombey to a chair which had its back towards this picture, he took his own seat opposite to it as usual.

Mr. Dombey was even graver than it was his custom to be, and quite silent. The parrot, swinging in the gilded hoop within her gaudy cage, attempted in vain to attract notice, for Carker was too observant of his visitor to heed her; and the visitor, abstracted in meditation, looked fixedly, not to say sullenly, over his stiff neckcloth, without raising his eyes from the tablecloth. As to Rob, who was in attendance, all his faculties and energies were so locked up in observation of his master, that he scarcely ventured to give shelter to the thought that the visitor was the great gentleman before whom he had been carried as a certificate of the family health, in his childhood, and to whom he had been indebted for his leather smalls.

'Allow me,' said Carker suddenly, 'to ask how Mrs. Dombey is?'

He leaned forward obsequiously, as he made the inquiry, with his chin resting on his hand; and at the same time his eyes went up to the picture, as if he said to it, 'Now, see, how I will lead him on!'

Mr. Dombey reddened as he answered—

'Mrs. Dombey is quite well. You remind me, Carker, of some conversation that I wish to have with you.'

'Robin, you can leave us,' said his master, at whose mild tones Robin started and disappeared, with his eyes fixed on his patron to the last. 'You don't remember that boy, of course?' he added, when the immeshed Grinder was gone.

'No,' said Mr. Dombey, with magnificent indifference.

'Not likely that a man like you would. Hardly possible,' murmured Carker. 'But he is one of that family from whom you took a nurse. Perhaps you may remember having generously charged yourself with his education?'

'Is it that boy?' said Mr. Dombey, with a frown. 'He does little credit to his education, I believe.'

'Why, he is a young rip, I am afraid,' returned Carker, with a shrug. 'He bears that character. But the truth is, I took him into my service because, being able to get no other employment, he conceived (had been taught at home, I dare say) that he had some sort of claim upon you, and was constantly trying to dog your heels with his petition. And although my defined and recognised connection with your affairs is merely of a business character, still I have that spontaneous interest in everything belonging to you, that—'

He stopped again, as if to discover whether he had

led Mr. Dombey far enough yet. And again, with his chin resting on his hand, he leered at the picture.

'Carker,' said Mr. Dombey, 'I am sensible that you do not limit your—'

'Service,' suggested his smiling entertainer.

'No; I prefer to say your regard,' observed Mr. Dombey; very sensible, as he said so, that he was paying him a handsome and flattering compliment, 'to our mere business relations. Your consideration for my feelings, hopes, and disappointments, in the little instance you have just now mentioned, is an example in point. I am obliged to you, Carker.'

Mr. Carker bent his head slowly, and very softly rubbed his hands, as if he were afraid by any action to disturb the current of Mr. Dombey's confidence.

'Your allusion to it is opportune,' said Mr. Dombey, after a little hesitation; 'for it prepares the way to what I was beginning to say to you, and reminds me that that involves no absolutely new relations between us, although it may involve more personal confidence on my part than I have hitherto—'

'Distinguished me with,' suggested Carker, bending his head again: 'I will not say to you how honoured I am; for a man like you well knows how much honour he has in his power to bestow at pleasure.'

'Mrs. Dombey and myself,' said Mr. Dombey, passing this compliment with august self-denial, 'are not quite agreed upon some points. We do not appear to understand each other yet. Mrs. Dombey has something to learn.'

'Mrs. Dombey is distinguished by many rare attractions; and has been accustomed, no doubt, to receive much adulation,' said the smooth, sleek watcher of his slightest look and tone. 'But where there is affection, duty, and respect, any little mistakes engendered by such causes are soon set right.'

Mr. Dombey's thoughts instinctively flew back to the face that had looked at him in his wife's dressing-room, when an imperious hand was stretched towards the door; and remembering the affection, duty, and respect, expressed in it, he felt the blood rush to his own face quite as plainly as the watchful eyes upon him saw it there.

'Mrs. Dombey and myself,' he went on to say, 'had some discussion, before Mrs. Skewton's death, upon the causes of my dissatisfaction; of which you will have formed a general understanding from having been a witness of what passed between Mrs. Dombey and myself on the evening when you were at our— at my house.'

'When I so much regretted being present,' said the smiling Carker. 'Proud as a man in my position necessarily must be of your familiar notice—though I give you no credit for it; you may do anything you please without losing caste—and honoured as I was by an early presentation to Mrs. Dombey, before she was made eminent by bearing your name, I almost regretted that night, I assure you, that I had been the object of such especial good fortune.'

That any man could, under any possible circumstances, regret the being distinguished by his condescension and patronage, was a moral phenomenon which Mr. Dombey could not comprehend. He therefore responded, with a considerable accession of dignity. 'Indeed! And why, Carker?'

'I fear,' returned the confidential agent, 'that Mrs. Dombey, never very much disposed to regard me with favourable interest—one in my position could not expect that, from a lady naturally proud, and whose pride becomes her so well—may not easily forgive my innocent part in that conversation Your displeasure is no light matter, you must remember; and to be visited with it before a third party—'

'Carker,' said Mr. Dombey, arrogantly; 'I presume that *I* am the first consideration?'

'Oh! Can there be a doubt about it?' replied the other, with the impatience of a man admitting a notorious and incontrovertible fact.

'Mrs. Dombey becomes a secondary consideration, when we are both in question, I imagine,' said Mr. Dombey. 'Is that so?'

'Is it so?' returned Carker. 'Do you know better than any one, that you have no need to ask?'

'Then I hope, Carker,' said Mr. Dombey, 'that your regret in the acquisition of Mrs. Dombey's displeasure, may be almost counterbalanced by your satisfaction in retaining *my* confidence and good opinion.'

'I have the misfortune, I find,' returned Carker, 'to have incurred that displeasure. Mrs. Dombey has expressed it to you?'

'Mrs. Dombey has expressed various opinions,' said Mr. Dombey, with majestic coldness and indifference, 'in which I do not participate, and which I am not inclined to discuss, or to recall. I made Mrs. Dombey acquainted, some time since, as I have already told you, with certain points of domestic deference and submission on which I felt it necessary to insist. I failed to convince Mrs. Dombey of the expediency of her immediately altering her conduct in those respects, with a view to her own peace and welfare, and my dignity; and I informed Mrs. Dombey that if I should find it necessary to object or remonstrate again, I should express my opinion to her through yourself, my confidential agent.'

Blended with the look that Carker bent upon him, was a devilish look at the picture over his head, that struck upon it like a flash of lightning.

'Now, Carker,' said Mr. Dombey, 'I do not hesitate to say to you that I *will* carry my point. I am not to be trifled with. Mrs. Dombey must understand that my will is law, and that I cannot allow of one exception to the whole rule of my life. You will have the goodness to undertake this charge, which, coming from me, is not unacceptable to you, I hope, whatever regret you may politely profess—for which I am obliged to you on behalf of Mrs. Dombey; and you will have the goodness, I am persuaded, to discharge it as exactly as any other commission.'

'You know,' said Mr. Carker, 'that you have only to command me.'

'I know,' said Mr. Dombey, with a majestic indication of assent, 'that I have only to command you. It is necessary that I should proceed in this. Mrs. Dombey is a lady undoubtedly highly qualified, in many respects, to—'

'To do credit even to your choice,' suggested Carker, with a fawning show of teeth.

'Yes; if you please to adopt that form of words,' said Mr. Dombey, in his tone of state; 'and at present I do not conceive that Mrs. Dombey does that credit to it, to which it is entitled. There is a principle of opposition in Mrs. Dombey that must be eradicated; that must be overcome: Mrs. Dombey does not appear to understand,' said Mr. Dombey, forcibly, 'that the idea of opposition to Me is monstrous and absurd.'

'We, in the City, know you better,' replied Carker, with a smile from ear to ear.

'You know me better,' said Mr. Dombey. 'I hope so. Though, indeed, I am bound to do Mrs. Dombey the justice of saying, however inconsistent it may seem with her subsequent conduct (which remains unchanged), that on my expressing my disapproba- tion and determination to her, with some severity, on the occasion to which I have referred, my admonition appeared to produce a very powerful effect.' Mr. Dombey delivered himself of those words with most portentous stateliness. 'I wish you to have the good- ness, then, to inform Mrs. Dombey, Carker, from me, that I must recall our former conversation to her re- membrance, in some surprise that it has not yet had its effect. That I must insist upon her regulating her conduct by the injunctions laid upon her in that conversation. That I am not satisfied with her con- duct. That I am greatly dissatisfied with it. And that I shall be under the very disagreeable necessity of making you the bearer of yet more unwelcome and explicit communications, if she has not the good sense and the proper feeling to adapt herself to my wishes, as the first Mrs. Dombey did, and, I believe I may add, as any other lady in her place would.'

'The first Mrs. Dombey lived very happily,' said Carker.

'The first Mrs. Dombey had great good sense,' said Mr. Dombey, in a gentlemanly toleration of the dead, 'and very correct feeling.'

'Is Miss Dombey like her mother, do you think?' said Carker.

Swiftly and darkly, Mr. Dombey's face changed His confidential agent eyed it keenly.

'I have approached a painful subject,' he said, in a soft regretful tone of voice, irreconcilable with his eager eye. 'Pray forgive me. I forget these chains of association in the interest I have. Pray forgive me.'

But for all he said, his eager eye scanned Mr. Dom-

bey's downcast face none the less closely; and then it
shot a strange triumphant look at the picture, as
appealing to it to bear witness how he led him on
again, and what was coming.

'Carker,' said Mr. Dombey, looking here and there
upon the table, and speaking in a somewhat altered
and more hurried voice, and with a paler lip, 'there
is no occasion for apology. You mistake. The association is with the matter in hand, and not with any
recollection, as you suppose. I do not approve of
Mrs. Dombey's behaviour towards my daughter.'

'Pardon me,' said Mr. Carker, 'I don't quite understand.'

'Understand then,' returned Mr. Dombey, 'that
you may make that—that you *will* make that, if you
please—matter of direct objection from me to Mrs.
Dombey. You will please to tell her that her show
of devotion for my daughter is disagreeable to me.
It is likely to be noticed. It is likely to induce people to contrast Mrs. Dombey in her relation towards
my daughter, with Mrs. Dombey in her relation towards myself. You will have the goodness to let
Mrs. Dombey know, plainly, that I object to it; and
that I expect her to defer, immediately, to my objection. Mrs. Dombey may be in earnest, or she may
be pursuing a whim, or she may be opposing me; but
I object to it in any case, and in every case. If Mrs.
Dombey is in earnest, so much the less reluctant should
she be to desist; for she will not serve my daughter
by any such display. If my wife has any superfluous gentleness and duty over and above her proper
submission to me, she may bestow them where she
pleases, perhaps; but I will have submission first!—
Carker,' said Mr. Dombey, checking the unusual
emotion with which he had spoken, and falling into
a tone more like that in which he was accustomed to

assert his greatness, 'you will have the goodness not to omit or slur this point, but to consider it a very important part of your instructions.'

Mr. Carker bowed his head, and rising from the table, and standing thoughtfully before the fire, with his hand to his smooth chin, looked down at Mr. Dombey with the evil slyness of some monkish carving, half human and half brute; or like a leering face on an old water-spout. Mr. Dombey, recovering his composure by degrees, or cooling his emotion in his sense of having taken a high position, sat gradually stiffening again, and looking at the parrot as she swung to and fro, in her great wedding ring.

'I beg your pardon,' said Carker, after a silence, suddenly resuming his chair, and drawing it opposite to Mr. Dombey's, 'but let me understand. Mrs. Dombey is aware of the probability of your making me the organ of your displeasure?'

'Yes,' replied Mr. Dombey. 'I have said so.'

'Yes,' rejoined Carker, quickly; 'but why?'

'Why!' Mr. Dombey repeated, not without hesitation. 'Because I told her.'

'Aye,' replied Carker. 'But why did you tell her? You see,' he continued with a smile, and softly laying his velvet hand, as a cat might have laid its sheathed claws, on Mr. Dombey's arm; 'if I perfectly understand what is in your mind, I am so much more likely to be useful, and to have the happiness of being effectually employed. I think I *do* understand. I have not the honour of Mrs. Dombey's good opinion. In my position, I have no reason to expect it; but I take the fact to be, that I have not got it?'

'Possibly not,' said Mr. Dombey.

'Consequently,' pursued Carker, 'your making these communications to Mrs. Dombey, through me, is sure to be particularly unpalatable to that lady?'

'It appears to me,' said Mr. Dombey, with haughty reserve, and yet with some embarrassment, 'that Mrs. Dombey's views upon the subject form no part of it as it presents itself to you and me, Carker. But it may be so.'

'And—pardon me—do I misconceive you,' said Carker, 'when I think you descry in this, a likely means of humbling Mrs. Dombey's pride—I use the word as expressive of a quality which, kept within due bounds, adorns and graces a lady so distinguished for her beauty and accomplishments—and, not to say of punishing her, but of reducing her to the submission you so naturally and justly require?'

'I am not accustomed, Carker, as you know,' said Mr. Dombey, 'to give such close reasons for any course of conduct I think proper to adopt, but I will gainsay nothing of this. If you have any objection to found upon it, that is indeed another thing, and the mere statement that you have one will be sufficient. But I have not supposed, I confess, that any confidence I could intrust to you, would be likely to degrade you—'

'Oh! *I* degraded!' exclaimed Carker. 'In *your* service!'

'—or to place you,' pursued Mr. Dombey, 'in a false position.'

'*I* in a false position!' exclaimed Carker. 'I shall be proud—delighted—to execute your trust. I could have wished, I own, to have given the lady at whose feet I would lay my humble duty and devotion—for is she not your wife?—no new cause of dislike; but a wish from you is, of course, paramount to every other consideration on earth. Besides, when Mrs. Dombey is converted from these little errors of judgment, incidental, I would presume to say, to the novelty of her situation, I shall hope that she will perceive in the slight part I take, only a grain—my removed and different sphere gives room for little more—of the respect for you, and sacrifice of all considerations to you, of which it will be her pleasure and privilege to garner up a great store every day.'

Mr. Dombey seemed, at the moment, again to see her with her hand stretched out towards the door, and again to hear through the mild speech of his confidential agent an echo of the words, 'Nothing can make us stranger to each other than we are henceforth!' But he shook off the fancy, and did not shake in his resolution, and said, 'Certainly, no doubt.'

'There is nothing more,' quoth Carker, drawing his chair back to its old place—for they had taken little breakfast as yet—and pausing for an answer before he sat down.

'Nothing,' said Mr. Dombey, 'but this. You will be good enough to observe, Carker, that no message to Mrs. Dombey with which you are or may be charged, admits of reply. You will be good enough to bring me no reply. Mrs. Dombey is informed that it does not become me to temporise or treat upon any matter that is at issue between us, and that what I say is final.'

Mr. Carker signified his understanding of these credentials, and they fell to breakfast with what appetite they might. The Grinder also, in due time, reappeared, keeping his eyes upon his master without a moment's respite, and passing the time in a reverie of worshipful terror. Breakfast concluded, Mr. Dombey's horse was ordered out again, and Mr. Carker mounting his own, they rode off for the City together.

Mr. Carker was in capital spirits, and talked much. Mr. Dombey received his conversation with the sovereign air of a man who had a right to be talked to, and occasionally condescended to throw in a few words to carry on the conversation. So they rode on characteristically enough. But Mr. Dombey, in his dignity, rode with very long stirrups, and a very loose rein, and very rarely deigned to look down to see where his horse went. In consequence of which it happened that Mr. Dombey's horse, while going at a round trot, stumbled on some loose stones, threw him, rolled over him, and lashing out with his iron-shod feet, in his struggles to get up, kicked him.

Mr. Carker, quick of eye, steady of hand, and a good horseman, was afoot, and had the struggling animal upon his legs and by the bridle, in a moment. Otherwise that morning's confidence would have been Mr. Dombey's last. Yet even with the flush and hurry of this action red upon him, he bent over his prostrate chief with every tooth disclosed, and muttered as he stooped down, 'I have given good cause of offence to Mrs. Dombey *now,* if she knew it!'

Mr. Dombey being insensible, and bleeding from the head and face, was carried by certain menders of the road, under Carker's direction, to the nearest public-house, which was not far off, and where he was soon attended by divers surgeons, who arrived in quick succession from all parts, and who seemed to come by some mysterious instinct, as vultures are said to gather about a camel who dies in the desert. After being at some pains to restore him to consciousness, these gentlemen examined into the nature of his injuries. One surgeon who lived hard by was strong for a compound fracture of the leg, which was the landlord's opinion also; but two surgeons who lived at a distance, and were only in that neighbourhood by accident, combated this opinion so disinterestedly, that it was decided at last that the patient, though severely cut and bruised, had broken no bones but a lesser rib or so, and might be carefully taken home before night. His injuries being dressed and bandaged, which was a long operation, and he at length left to repose, Mr. Carker mounted his horse again, and rode away to carry the intelligence home.

Crafty and cruel as his face was at the best of times, though it was a sufficiently fair face as to form and regularity of feature, it was at its worst when he set forth on this errand; animated by the craft and cruelty of thoughts within him, suggestions of remote possibility rather than of design or plot, that made him ride as if he hunted men and women. Drawing rein at length, and slackening in his speed, as he came into the more public roads, he checked his white-legged horse into picking his way along as usual, and hid himself beneath his sleek, hushed, crouched manner, and his ivory smile, as he best could.

He rode direct to Mr. Dombey's house, alighted at the door, and begged to see Mrs. Dombey on an affair of importance. The servant who showed him to Mr. Dombey's own room, soon returned to say that it was not Mrs. Dombey's hour for receiving visitors, and that he begged pardon for not having mentioned it before.

Mr. Carker, who was quite prepared for a cold reception, wrote upon a card that he must take the liberty of pressing for an interview, and that he would not be so bold as to do so, *for the second time* (this he underlined), if he were not equally sure of the occasion being sufficient for his justification. After a trifling delay, Mrs. Dombey's maid appeared, and conducted him to a morning room upstairs, where Edith and Florence were together.

He had never thought Edith half so beautiful before. Much as he admired the graces of her face and form, and freshly as they dwelt within his sensual remembrance, he had never thought her half so beautiful.

Her glance fell haughtily upon him in the doorway; but he looked at Florence—though only in the act of bending his head, as he came in—with some irrepressible expression of the new power he held; and it was his triumph to see the glance droop and falter, and to see that Edith half rose up to receive him.

He was very sorry, he was deeply grieved; he couldn't say with what unwillingness he came to prepare her for the intelligence of a very slight accident. He entreated Mrs. Dombey to compose herself. Upon his sacred word of honour, there was no cause of alarm. But Mr. Dombey—'

Florence uttered a sudden cry. He did not look at her, but at Edith. Edith composed and reassured her. *She* uttered no cry of distress. No, no.

Mr. Dombey had met with an accident in riding. His horse had slipped, and he had been thrown.

Florence wildly exclaimed that he was badly hurt; that he was killed!

No. Upon his honour, Mr. Dombey, though stunned at first, was soon recovered, and though certainly hurt was in no kind of danger. If this were not the truth, he, the distressed intruder, never could have had the courage to present himself before Mrs. Dombey. It was the truth indeed, he solemnly assured her.

All this he said as if he were answering Edith, and not Florence, and with his eyes and his smile fastened on Edith.

He then went on to tell her where Mr. Dombey was lying, and to request that a carriage might be placed at his disposal to bring him home.

'Mamma,' faltered Florence in tears, 'if I might venture to go!'

Mr. Carker, having his eyes on Edith when he heard these words, gave her a secret look and slightly shook his head. He saw how she battled with herself before she answered him with her handsome eyes, but he wrested the answer from her—he showed her that he would have it, or that he would speak and cut Florence to the heart—and she gave it to him. As he had looked at the picture in the morning, so he looked at her afterwards, when she turned her eyes away.

'I am directed to request,' he said, 'that the new housekeeper—Mrs. Pipchin, I think is the name—'

Nothing escaped him. He saw in an instant, that she was another slight of Mr. Dombey's on his wife.

'—may be informed that Mr. Dombey wishes to have his bed prepared in his own apartments downstairs, as he prefers those rooms to any other. I shall return to Mr. Dombey almost immediately. That every possible attention has been paid to his comfort, and that he is the object of every possible solicitude, I need not assure you, madam. Let me again say, there is no cause for the least alarm. Even you may be quite at ease, believe me.'

He bowed himself out, with his extremest show of deference and conciliation; and having returned to Mr. Dombey's room, and there arranged for a carriage being sent after him to the City, mounted his horse again, and rode slowly thither. He was very thoughtful as he went along, and very thoughtful there, and very thoughtful in the carriage on his way back to the place where Mr. Dombey had been left. It was only when sitting by that gentleman's couch that he was quite himself again, and conscious of his teeth.

About the time of twilight, Mr. Dombey, grievously afflicted with aches and pains, was helped into

his carriage, and propped with cloaks and pillows on
one side of it, while his confidential agent bore him
company upon the other.   As he was not to be shaken,
they moved at little more than a foot-pace; and hence
it was quite dark when he was brought home.   Mrs.
Pipchin, bitter and grim, and not oblivious of the
Peruvian mines, as the establishment in general had
good reason to know, received him at the door, and
freshened the domestics with several little sprinklings
of wordy vinegar, while they assisted in conveying
him to his room.   Mr. Carker remained in attendance
until he was safe in bed, and then, as he declined to
receive any female visitor, but the excellent ogress
who presided over his household, waited on Mrs. Dombey once more, with his report on her lord's condition.

He again found Edith alone with Florence, and he
again addressed the whole of his soothing speech to
Edith, as if she were a prey to the liveliest and most
affectionate anxieties.   So earnest he was in his respectful sympathy, that on taking leave, he ventured
—with one more glance towards Florence at the moment—to take her hand, and bending over it, to touch
it with his lips.

Edith did not withdraw the hand, nor did she strike
his fair face with it, despite the flush upon her cheek,
the bright light in her eyes, and the dilation of her
whole form.   But when she was alone in her own
room, she struck it on the marble chimney-shelf, so
that, at one blow, it was bruised, and bled; and held
it from her, near the shining fire, as if she could have
thrust it in and burned it.

Far into the night she sat alone, by the sinking
blaze, in dark and threatening beauty, watching the
murky shadows looming on the wall, as if her thoughts
were tangible and cast them there.   Whatever shapes
of outrage and affront, and black foreshadowings of

things that might happen, flickered, indistinct and giant-like, before her, one resented figure marshalled them against her. And that figure was her husband.

CHAPTER XLIII

THE WATCHES OF THE NIGHT

FLORENCE, long since awakened from her dream, mournfully observed the estrangement between her father and Edith, and saw it widen more and more, and knew that there was greater bitterness between them every day. Each day's added knowledge deepened the shade upon her love and hope, roused up the old sorrow that had slumbered for a little time, and made it even heavier to bear than it had been before.

It had been hard—how hard may none but Florence ever know!—to have the natural affection of a true and earnest nature turned to agony; and slight, or stern repulse, substituted for the tenderest protection and the dearest care. It had been hard to feel in her deep heart what she had felt, and never know the happiness of one touch of response. But it was much more hard to be compelled to doubt either her father or Edith, so affectionate and dear to her, and to think of her love for each of them, by turns, with fear, distrust, and wonder.

Yet Florence now began to do so; and the doing of it was a task imposed upon her by the very purity of her soul, as one she could not fly from. She saw her father cold and obdurate to Edith, as to her; hard, inflexible, unyielding. Could it be, she asked herself with starting tears, that her own dear mother had been made unhappy by such treatment, and had pined away and died? Then she would think how proud and stately Edith was to every one but her, with what disdain she treated him, how distantly she kept apart from him, and what she had said on the night when she came home; and quickly it would come on Florence, almost as a crime, that she loved one who was set in opposition to her father, and that her father knowing of it, must think of her in his solitary room as the unnatural child who added this wrong to the old fault, so much wept for, of never having won his fatherly affection from her birth. The next kind word from Edith, the next kind glance, would shake these thoughts again, and make them seem like black ingratitude; for who but she had cheered the drooping heart of Florence, so lonely and so hurt, and been its best of comforters! Thus, with her gentle nature yearning to them both, feeling the misery of both, and whispering doubts of her own duty to both, Florence in her wider and expanded love, and by the side of Edith, endured more than when she had hoarded up her undivided secret in the mournful house, and her beautiful mamma had never dawned upon it.

One exquisite unhappiness that would have far out-weighed this, Florence was spared. She never had the least suspicion that Edith by her tenderness for her widened the separation from her father, or gave him new cause of dislike. If Florence had conceived the possibility of such an effect being wrought by such a cause, what grief she would have felt, what sacrifice she would have tried to make, poor loving girl, how fast and sure her quiet passage might have been beneath it to the presence of that higher Father who does not reject his children's love, or spurn their tried and broken hearts, Heaven knows! But it was otherwise, and that was well.

No word was ever spoken between Florence and

Edith now, on these subjects. Edith had said there ought to be between them, in that wise, a division and a silence like the grave itself: and Florence felt that she was right.

In this state of affairs her father was brought home suffering and disabled: and gloomily retired to his own rooms, where he was tended by servants, not approached by Edith, and had no friend or companion but Mr. Carker, who withdrew near midnight.

'And nice company *he* is, Miss Floy,' said Susan Nipper. 'Oh, he's a precious piece of goods! If ever he wants a character don't let him come to me whatever he does, that's all I tell him.'

'Dear Susan,' urged Florence, 'don't.'

'Oh, it's very well to say "don't" Miss Floy,' returned the Nipper, much exasperated; 'but raly begging your pardon we're coming to such passes that it turns all the blood in a person's body into pins and needles, with their pints all ways. Don't mistake me, Miss Floy, I don't mean nothing again your ma-in-law who has always treated me as a lady should though she is rather high I must say not that I have any right to object to that particular, but when we come to Mrs. Pipchinses and having them put over us and keeping guard at your pa's door like crocodiles (only make us thankful that they lay no eggs!) we are growing too outrageous!'

'Papa thinks well of Mrs. Pipchin, Susan,' returned Florence, 'and has a right to choose his housekeeper, you know. Pray don't!'

'Well Miss Floy,' returned the Nipper, 'when you say don't, I never do I hope but Mrs. Pipchin acts like early gooseberries upon me miss, and nothing less.'

Susan was unusually emphatic and destitute of punctuation in her discourse on this night, which was the night of Mr. Dombey's being brought home, because, having been sent downstairs by Florence to inquire after him, she had been obliged to deliver her message to her mortal enemy Mrs. Pipchin; who, without carrying it in to Mr. Dombey, had taken upon herself to return what Miss Nipper called a huffish answer, on her own responsibility. This, Susan Nipper construed into presumption on the part of that exemplary sufferer by the Peruvian mines, and a deed of disparagement upon her young lady, that was not to be forgiven; and so far her emphatic state was special. But she had been in a condition of greatly increased suspicion and distrust, ever since the marriage; for, like most persons, of her quality of mind, who form a strong and sincere attachment to one in the different station which Florence occupied, Susan was very jealous, and her jealousy naturally attached to Edith, who divided her old empire, and came between them. Proud and glad as Susan Nipper truly was, that her young mistress should be advanced towards her proper place in the scene of her old neglect, and that she should have her father's handsome wife for her companion and protectress, she could not relinquish any part of her own dominion to the handsome wife, without a grudge and a vague feeling of ill-will, for which she did not fail to find a disinterested justification in her sharp perception of the pride and passion of the lady's character. From the background to which she had necessarily retired somewhat, since the marriage, Miss Nipper looked on, therefore, at domestic affairs in general, with a resolute conviction that no good would come of Mrs. Dombey: always being very careful to publish on all possible occasions, that she had nothing to say against her.

'Susan,' said Florence, who was sitting thoughtfully at her table, 'it is very late. I shall want nothing more to-night.'

'Ah, Miss Floy!' returned the Nipper, 'I 'm sure I often wish for them old times when I sat up with you hours later than this and fell asleep through being tired out when you was as broad awake as spectacles, but you 've ma's-in-law to come and sit with you now Miss Floy and I 'm thankful for it I 'm sure. I 've not a word to say against 'em.'

'I shall not forget who was my old companion when I had none, Susan,' returned Florence, gently, 'never!' And looking up, she put her arm around the neck of her humble friend, drew her face down to hers, and bidding her good night, kissed it; which so mollified Miss Nipper, that she fell a sobbing.

'Now my dear Miss Floy,' said Susan, 'let me go downstairs again and see how your pa is, I know you 're wretched about him, do let me go downstairs again and knock at his door my own self.'

'No,' said Florence, 'go to bed. We shall hear more in the morning. I will inquire myself in the morning. Mamma has been down, I dare say'; Florence blushed, for she had no such hope; 'or is there now, perhaps. Good night!'

Susan was too much softened to express her private opinion on the probability of Mrs. Dombey's being in attendance on her husband; and silently withdrew. Florence left alone, soon hid her head upon her hands as she had often done in other days, and did not restrain the tears from coursing down her face. The misery of this domestic discord and unhappiness; the withered hope she cherished now, if hope it could be called, of ever being taken to her father's heart; her doubts and fears between the two; the yearning of her innocent breast to both; the heavy disappointment and regret of such an end as this, to what had been a vision of bright hope and promise to her; all crowded on her mind and made her tears flow fast. Her mother and her brother dead, her father unmoved towards her, Edith opposed to him and casting him away, but loving her, and loved by her, it seemed as if her affection could never prosper, rest where it would. That weak thought was soon hushed, but the thoughts in which it had arisen were too true and strong to be dismissed with it; and they made the night desolate.

Among such reflections there rose up, as there had risen up all day, the image of her father, wounded and in pain, alone in his room, untended by those who should be nearest to him, and passing the tardy hours in lonely suffering. A frightened thought which made her start and clasp her hands—though it was not a new one in her mind—that he might die, and never see her or pronounce her name, thrilled her whole frame. In her agitation she thought, and trembled while she thought, of once more stealing downstairs, and venturing to his door.

She listened at her own. The house was quiet, and all the lights were out. It was a long, long time, she thought, since she used to make her nightly pilgrimages to his door! It was a long, long time, she tried to think, since she had entered his room at midnight, and he had led her back to the stair-foot!

With the same child's heart within her, as of old: even with the child's sweet timid eyes and clustering hair: Florence, as strange to her father in her early maiden bloom, as in her nursery time, crept down the staircase listening as she went, and drew near to his room. No one was stirring in the house. The door was partly open to admit air; and all was so still within, that she could hear the burning of the fire, and count the ticking of the clock that stood upon the chimney-piece.

She looked in. In that room, the housekeeper

wrapped in a blanket was fast asleep in an easy-chair before the fire. The doors between it and the next were partly closed, and a screen was drawn before them; but there was a light there, and it shone upon the cornice of his bed. All was so very still that she could hear from his breathing that he was asleep. This gave her courage to pass round the screen, and look into his chamber.

It was as great a start to come upon his sleeping face as if she had not expected to see it. Florence stood arrested on the spot, and if he had awakened then, must have remained there.

There was a cut upon his forehead, and they had been wetting his hair, which lay bedabbled and entangled on the pillow. One of his arms, resting outside the bed, was bandaged up, and he was very white. But it was not this, that after the first quick glance, and first assurance of his sleeping quietly, held Florence rooted to the ground. It was something very different from this, and more than this, that made him look so solemn in her eyes.

She had never seen his face in all her life, but there had been upon it—or she fancied so—some disturbing consciousness of her. She had never seen his face in all her life, but hope had sunk within her, and her timid glance had drooped before its stern, unloving, and repelling harshness. As she looked upon it now, she saw it, for the first time, free from the cloud that had darkened her childhood. Calm, tranquil night was reigning in its stead. He might have gone to sleep, for anything she saw there, blessing her.

Awake, unkind father! Awake, now, sullen man! The time is flitting by; the hour is coming with an angry tread. Awake!

There was no change upon his face; and as she watched it, awfully, its motionless repose recalled the faces that were gone. So they looked, so would he; so she, his weeping child, who should say when! so all the world of love and hatred and indifference around them! When that time should come, it would not be the heavier to him, for this that she was going to do; and it might fall something lighter upon her.

She stole close to the bed, and drawing in her breath bent down, and softly kissed him on the face, and laid her own for one brief moment by its side, and put the arm, with which she dared not touch him, round about him on the pillow.

Awake, doomed man, while she is near. The time is flitting by; the hour is coming with an angry tread; its foot is in the house. Awake!

In her mind, she prayed to God to bless her father, and to soften him towards her, if it might be so; and if not, to forgive him if he was wrong, and pardon her the prayer which almost seemed impiety. And doing so, and looking back at him with blinded eyes, and stealing timidly away, passed out of his room, and crossed the other, and was gone.

He may sleep on now. He may sleep on while he may. But let him look for that slight figure when he wakes, and find it near him when the hour is come!

Sad and grieving was the heart of Florence, as she crept upstairs. The quiet house had grown more dismal since she came down. The sleep she had been looking on, in the dead of night, had the solemnity to her of death and life in one. The secrecy and silence of her own proceeding made the night secret, silent, and oppressive. She felt unwilling, almost unable, to go on to her own chamber; and turning into the drawing-rooms, where the clouded moon was shining through the blinds, looked out into the empty streets.

The wind was blowing drearily. The lamps looked

pale, and shook as if they were cold. There was a distant glimmer of something that was not quite darkness, rather than of light, in the sky; and foreboding night was shivering and restless, as the dying are who make a troubled end. Florence remembered how, as a watcher, by a sick bed, she had noted this bleak time, and felt its influence, as if in some hidden natural antipathy to it; and now it was very, very gloomy.

Her mamma had not come to her room that night, which was one cause of her having sat late out of her bed. In her general uneasiness, no less than in her ardent longing to have somebody to speak to, and to break the spell of gloom and silence, Florence directed her steps towards the chamber where she slept.

The door was not fastened within, and yielded smoothly to her hesitating hand. She was surprised to find a bright light burning; still more surprised, on looking in, to see that her mamma, but partially undressed, was sitting near the ashes of the fire, which had crumbled and dropped away. Her eyes were intently bent upon the air; and in their light, and in her face, and in her form, and in the grasp with which she held the elbows of her chair as if about to start up, Florence saw such fierce emotion that it terrified her.

'Mamma!' she cried, 'what is the matter!'

Edith started; looking at her with such a strange dread in her face, that Florence was more frightened than before.

'Mamma!' said Florence, hurriedly advancing. 'Dear mamma! what is the matter!'

'I have not been well,' said Edith, shaking, and still looking at her in the same strange way. 'I have had bad dreams, my love.'

'And not yet been to bed, mamma?'

'No,' she returned. 'Half-waking dreams.'

Her features gradually softened; and suffering Florence to come close to her, within her embrace, she said in a tender manner, 'But what does my bird do here? What does my bird do here?'

'I have been uneasy, mamma, in not seeing you to-night, and in not knowing how papa was; and I—'

Florence stopped there, and said no more.

'Is it late?' asked Edith, fondly putting back the curls that mingled with her own dark hair, and strayed upon her face.

'Very late. Near day.'

'Near day!' she repeated in surprise.

'Dear mamma, what have you done to your hand?' said Florence.

Edith drew it suddenly away, and, for a moment, looked at her with the same strange dread (there was a sort of wild avoidance in it) as before; but she presently said, 'Nothing, nothing. A blow.' And then she said, 'My Florence!' and then her bosom heaved, and she was weeping passionately.

'Mamma!' said Florence. 'Oh mamma, what can I do, what should I do, to make us happier? Is there anything?'

'Nothing,' she replied.

'Are you sure of that? Can it never be? If I speak now of what is in my thoughts, in spite of what we have agreed,' said Florence, 'you will not blame me, will you?'

'It is useless,' she replied, 'useless. I have told you, dear, that I have had bad dreams. Nothing can change them, or prevent their coming back.'

'I do not understand,' said Florence, gazing on her agitated face, which seemed to darken as she looked.

'I have dreamed,' said Edith in a low voice, 'of a pride that is all powerless for good, all powerful for evil; of a pride that has been galled and goaded,

through many shameful years, and has never recoiled
except upon itself: a pride that has debased its owner
with the consciousness of deep humiliation, and never
helped its owner boldly to resent it or avoid it, or to
say, "This shall not be!" a pride that, rightly guided,
might have led perhaps to better things, but which,
misdirected and perverted, like all else belonging to
the same possessor, has been self-contempt, mere
hardihood, and ruin.'

She neither looked nor spoke to Florence now, but
went on as if she were alone.

'I have dreamed,' she said, 'of such indifference
and callousness, arising from this self-contempt; this
wretched, inefficient, miserable pride; that it has gone
on with listless steps even to the altar, yielding to the
old, familiar, beckoning finger,—oh mother, oh
mother!—while it spurned it; and willing to be hateful to itself for once and for all, rather than to be
stung daily in some new form.   Mean, poor thing!'

And now with gathering and darkening emotion,
she looked as she had looked when Florence entered.

'And I have dreamed,' she said, 'that in a first late
effort to achieve a purpose, it has been trodden on,
and trodden down by a base foot, but turns and looks
upon him.   I have dreamed that it is wounded,
hunted, set upon by dogs, but that it stands at bay,
and will not yield; no, that it cannot if it would; but
that it is urged on to hate him, rise against him, and
defy him!'

Her clenched hand tightened on the trembling arm
she had in hers, and as she looked down on the alarmed
and wondering face, her own subsided. 'Oh Florence!' she said, 'I think I have been nearly mad to-
night!' and humbled her proud head upon her neck,
and wept again.

'Don't leave me! be near me! I have no hope but in you!' These words she said a score of times.

Soon she grew calmer, and was full of pity for the tears of Florence, and for her waking at such untimely hours. And the day now dawning, Edith folded her in her arms and laid her down upon her bed, and, not lying down herself, sat by her, and bade her try to sleep.

'For you are weary, dearest, and unhappy, and should rest.'

'I am indeed unhappy, dear mamma, to-night,' said Florence. 'But you are weary and unhappy, too.'

'Not when you lie asleep so near me, sweet.'

They kissed each other, and Florence, worn out, gradually fell into a gentle slumber; but as her eyes closed on the face beside her, it was so sad to think upon the face downstairs, that her hand drew closer to Edith for some comfort; yet, even in the act, it faltered, lest it should be deserting him. So, in her sleep, she tried to reconcile the two together, and to show them that she loved them both, but could not do it, and her waking grief was part of her dreams.

Edith, sitting by, looked down at the dark eyelashes lying wet on the flushed cheeks, and looked with gentleness and pity, for she knew the truth. But no sleep hung upon her own eyes. As the day came on she still sat watching and waking, with the placid hand in hers, and sometimes whispered, as she looked at the hushed face, 'Be near me, Florence, I have no hope but in you!'

CHAPTER XLIV

A SEPARATION

WITH the day, though not so early as the sun, uprose Miss Susan Nipper. There was a heaviness in this young maiden's exceedingly sharp black eyes, that abated somewhat of their sparkling, and suggested—which was not their usual character—the possibility of their being sometimes shut. There was likewise a swollen look about them, as if they had been crying overnight. But the Nipper, so far from being cast down, was singularly brisk and bold, and all her energies appeared to be braced up for some great feat. This was noticeable even in her dress, which was much more tight and trim than usual; and in occasional twitches of her head as she went about the house, which were mightily expressive of determination.

In a word, she had formed a determination, and an aspiring one: it being nothing less than this—to penetrate to Mr. Dombey's presence, and have speech of that gentleman alone. 'I have often said I would,' she remarked, in a threatening manner, to herself, that morning, with many twitches of her head, 'and now I *will!*'

Spurring herself on to the accomplishment of this desperate design, with a sharpness that was peculiar to herself, Susan Nipper haunted the hall and staircase during the whole forenoon, without finding a favourable opportunity for the assault. Not at all baffled by this discomfiture, which indeed had a stimulating effect, and put her on her mettle, she diminished nothing of her vigilance; and at last discovered, towards evening, that her sworn foe Mrs. Pipchin, under pretence of having sat up all night, was dozing in her own room, and that Mr. Dombey was lying on his sofa, unattended.

With a twitch—not of her head merely, this time, but of her whole self—the Nipper went on tiptoe to Mr. Dombey's door, and knocked. 'Come in!' said Mr. Dombey. Susan encouraged herself with a final twitch, and went in.

Mr. Dombey, who was eyeing the fire, gave an amazed look at his visitor, and raised himself a little on his arm. The Nipper dropped a curtsey.

'What do you want?' said Mr. Dombey.

'If you please, sir, I wish to speak to you,' said Susan.

Mr. Dombey moved his lips as if he were repeating the words, but he seemed so lost in astonishment at the presumption of the young woman as to be incapable of giving them utterance.

'I have been in your service, sir,' said Susan Nipper, with her usual rapidity, 'now twelve year a waiting on Miss Floy my own young lady who couldn't speak plain when I first come here and I was old in this house when Mrs. Richards was new, I may not be Meethosalem, but I am not a child in arms.'

Mr. Dombey, raised upon his arm and looking at her, offered no comment on this preparatory statement of facts.

'There never was a dearer or a blesseder young lady than is my young lady, sir,' said Susan, 'and I ought to know a great deal better than some for I have seen her in her grief and I have seen her in her joy (there's not been much of it) and I have seen her with her brother and I have seen her in her loneliness and some have never seen her, and I say to some and all—I do!' and here the black-eyed shook her head, and slightly stamped her foot; 'that she's the blessedest and dearest angel is Miss Floy that ever drew the breath of life, the more that I was torn to pieces sir the more I 'd say it though I may not be a Fox's martyr.'

Mr. Dombey turned yet paler than his fall had made him, with indignation and astonishment; and kept his eyes upon the speaker as if he accused them, and his ears too, of playing him false.

'No one could be anything but true and faithful to Miss Floy, sir,' pursued Susan, 'and I take no merit for my service of twelve year, for I love her—yes, I say to some and all I do!'—and here the black-eyed shook her head again, and slightly stamped her foot again, and checked a sob; 'but true and faithful service gives me right to speak I hope, and speak I must and will now, right or wrong.'

'What do you mean, woman?' said Mr. Dombey, glaring at her. 'How do you dare?'

'What I mean, sir, is to speak respectful and without offence, but out, and how I dare I know not but I do!' said Susan. 'Oh! you don't know my young lady sir you don't indeed, you 'd never know so little of her, if you did.'

Mr. Dombey, in a fury, put his hand out for the bell-rope; but there was no bell-rope on that side of the fire, and he could not rise and cross to the other without assistance. The quick eye of the Nipper detected his helplessness immediately, and now, as she afterwards observed, she felt she had got him.

'Miss Floy,' said Susan Nipper, 'is the most devoted and most patient and most dutiful and beautiful of daughters, there an't no gentleman, no sir, though as great and rich as all the greatest and richest of England put together, but might be proud of her and would and ought. If he knew her value right, he 'd rather lose his greatness and his fortune piece by piece and beg his way in rags from door to door, I say to some and all, he would!' cried Susan Nipper, bursting into tears, 'than bring the sorrow on her tender heart that I have seen it suffer in this house!'

'Woman,' cried Mr. Dombey, 'leave the room.'

'Begging your pardon, not even if I am to leave the situation, sir,' replied the steadfast Nipper, 'in which I have been so many years and seen so much—although I hope you 'd never have the heart to send me from Miss Floy for such a cause—will I go now till I have said the rest, I may not be a Indian widow sir and I am not and I would not so become but if I once made up my mind to burn myself alive, I 'd do it! And I 've made my mind up to go on.'

Which was rendered no less clear by the expression of Susan Nipper's countenance, than by her words.

'There an't a person in your service, sir,' pursued the black-eyed, 'that has always stood more in awe of you than me and you may think how true it is when I make so bold as say that I have hundreds and hundreds of times thought of speaking to you and never been able to make my mind up to it till last night, but last night decided of me.'

Mr. Dombey, in a paroxysm of rage, made another grasp at the bell-rope that was not there, and, in its absence, pulled his hair rather than nothing.

'I have seen,' said Susan Nipper, 'Miss Floy strive and strive when nothing but a child so sweet and patient that the best of women might have copied from her, I 've seen her sitting nights together half the night through to help her delicate brother with his learning, I 've seen her helping him and watching him at other times—some well know when—I 've seen her, with no encouragement and no help, grow up to be a lady, thank God! that is the grace and pride of every company she goes in, and I 've always seen her cruelly neglected and keenly feeling of it—I say to some and all, I have!—and never said one word, but order-

ing one's self lowly and reverently towards one's bet-
ters, is not to be a worshipper of graven images, and
I will and must speak!'

'Is there anybody there?' cried Mr. Dombey, calling
out. 'Where are the men? where are the women? Is
there no one there?'

'I left my dear young lady out of bed late last
night,' said Susan, nothing checked, 'and I knew why,
for you was ill sir and she didn't know how ill and
that was enough to make her wretched as I saw it did.
I may not be a peacock; but I have my eyes—and I
sat up a little in my own room thinking she might be
lonesome and might want me, and I saw her steal
downstairs and come to this door as if it was a guilty
thing to look at her own pa, and then steal back again
and go into them lonely drawing-rooms, a crying so,
that I could hardly bear to hear it. I *can not* bear to
hear it,' said Susan Nipper, wiping her black eyes,
and fixing them undauntingly on Mr. Dombey's in-
furiated face. 'It's not the first time I have heard
it, not by many and many a time you don't know your
own daughter, sir, you don't know what you're doing,
sir, I say to some and all,' cried Susan Nipper, in a
final burst, 'that it's a sinful shame!'

'Why, hoity toity!' cried the voice of Mrs. Pipchin,
as the black bombazeen garments of that fair Peruvian
miner swept into the room. 'What's this, indeed?'

Susan favoured Mrs. Pipchin with a look she had
invented expressly for her when they first became acquainted, and resigned the reply to Mr. Dombey.

'What's this?' repeated Mr. Dombey, almost foam-
ing. 'What's this, madam? You who are at the
head of this household, and bound to keep it in
order, have reason to inquire. Do you know this
woman?'

'I know very little good of her, sir,' croaked Mrs.

Pipchin. 'How dare you come here, you hussy? Go along with you!'

But the inflexible Nipper, merely honouring Mrs. Pipchin with another look, remained.

'Do you call it managing this establishment, madam,' said Mr. Dombey, 'to leave a person like this at liberty to come and talk to *me?* A gentleman —in his own house—in his own room—assailed with the impertinences of women servants!'

'Well, sir,' returned Mrs. Pipchin, with vengeance in her hard grey eye, 'I exceedingly deplore it; nothing can be more irregular; nothing can be more out of all bounds and reason; but I regret to say sir, that this young woman is quite beyond control. She has been spoiled by Miss Dombey, and is amenable to nobody. You know you 're not,' said Mrs. Pipchin, sharply, and shaking her head at Susan Nipper. 'For shame, you hussy! Go along with you!'

'If you find people in my service who are not to be controlled, Mrs. Pipchin,' said Mr. Dombey, turning back towards the fire, 'you know what to do with them, I presume. You know what you are here for? Take her away!'

'Sir, I know what to do,' retorted Mrs. Pipchin, 'and of course shall do it. Susan Nipper,' snapping her up particularly short, 'a month's warning from this hour.'

'Oh, indeed!' cried Susan, loftily.

'Yes,' returned Mrs. Pipchin, 'and don't smile at me, you minx, or I 'll know the reason why! Go along with you this minute!'

'I intend to go this minute, you may rely upon it,' said the voluble Nipper. 'I have been in this house waiting on my young lady a dozen year and I won't stop in it one hour under notice from a person owning to the name of Pipchin, trust me, Mrs. P.'

'A good riddance of bad rubbish!' said that wrathful old lady. 'Get along with you, or I 'll have you carried out!'

'My comfort is,' said Susan, looking back at Mr. Dombey, 'that I have told a piece of truth this day which ought to have been told long before and can't be told too often or too plain and that no amount of Pipchinses—I hope the number of 'em mayn't be great' (here Mrs. Pipchin uttered a very sharp 'Go along with you!' and Miss Nipper repeated the look) 'can unsay what I have said, though they gave a whole year full of warnings beginning at ten o'clock in the forenoon and never leaving off till twelve at night and died of the exhaustion which would be a Jubilee!'

With these words, Miss Nipper preceded her foe out of the room; and walking upstairs to her own apartment in great state, to the choking exasperation of the ireful Pipchin sat down among her boxes and began to cry.

From this soft mood she was soon aroused, with a very wholesome and refreshing effect, by the voice of Mrs. Pipchin outside the door.

'Does that bold-faced slut,' said the fell Pipchin, 'intend to take her warning, or does she not?'

Miss Nipper replied from within that the person described did not inhabit that part of the house, but that her name was Pipchin, and she was to be found in the housekeeper's room.

'You saucy baggage!' retorted Mrs. Pipchin, rattling at the handle of the door. 'Go along with you this minute. Pack up your things directly! How dare you talk in this way to a gentlewoman who has seen better days?'

To which Miss Nipper rejoined from her castle, that she pitied the better days that had seen Mrs. Pipchin; and that for her part she considered the worst days in the year to be about that lady's mark, except that they were much too good for her.

'But you needn't trouble yourself to make a noise at my door,' said Susan Nipper, 'nor to contaminate the key-hole with your eye, I'm packing up and going you may take your affidavit.'

The dowager expressed her lively satisfaction at this intelligence, and with some general opinions upon young hussies as a race, and especially upon their demerits after being spoiled by Miss Dombey, withdrew to prepare the Nipper's wages. Susan then bestirred herself to get her trunks in order, that she might take an immediate and dignified departure; sobbing heartily all the time, as she thought of Florence.

The object of her regret was not long in coming to her, for the news soon spread over the house that Susan Nipper had had a disturbance with Mrs. Pipchin, and that they had both appealed to Mr. Dombey, and that there had been an unprecedented piece of work in Mr. Dombey's room, and that Susan was going. The latter part of this confused rumour, Florence found to be so correct, that Susan had locked the last trunk and was sitting upon it with her bonnet on, when she came into her room.

'Susan!' cried Florence. 'Going to leave me! You!'

'Oh for goodness gracious sake, Miss Floy,' said Susan, sobbing, 'don't speak a word to me or I shall demean myself before them Pi-i-ipchinses, and I wouldn't have 'em see me cry Miss Floy for worlds!'

'Susan!' said Florence. 'My dear girl, my old friend! What shall I do without you? Can you bear to go away so?'

'No-n-o-o, my darling dear Miss Floy, I can't in-deed,' sobbed Susan. 'But it can't be helped, I've done my duty miss, I have indeed. It's no fault of mine. I am quite resi-igned. I couldn't stay my month or I could never leave you then my darling and I must at last as well as at first, don't speak to me Miss Floy, for though I'm pretty firm I'm not a marble doorpost, my own dear.'

'What is it! Why is it?' said Florence. 'Won't you tell me?' For Susan was shaking her head.

'No-n-no, my darling,' returned Susan. 'Don't ask me, for I mustn't, and whatever you do don't put in a word for me to stop, for it couldn't be, and you'd only wrong yourself, and so God bless you my own precious and forgive me any harm I have done, or any temper I have showed in all these many years!'

With which entreaty, very heartily delivered, Susan hugged her mistress in her arms.

'My darling there's a many that may come to serve you and be glad to serve you and who'll serve you well and true,' said Susan, 'but there can't be one who'll serve you so affectionate as me or love you half so dearly, that's my comfort. Go-ood-bye, sweet Miss Floy!'

'Where will you go, Susan?' asked her weeping mistress.

'I've got a brother down in the country miss—a farmer in Essex,' said the heart-broken Nipper, 'that keeps ever so many co-o-ows and pigs and I shall go down there by the coach and sto-op with him, and don't mind me, for I've got money in the savings' bank my dear, and needn't take another service just yet, which I couldn't, couldn't, couldn't do, my heart's own mistress!' Susan finished with a burst of sorrow, which was opportunely broken by the voice of Mrs. Pipchin talking downstairs; on hearing which, she dried her red and swollen eyes, and made a melancholy feint of calling jauntily to Mr. Towlinson to fetch a cab and carry down her boxes.

Florence, pale and hurried and distressed, but withheld from useless interference even here, by her dread of causing any new division between her father and his wife (whose stern, indignant face had been a warning to her a few moments since), and by her apprehension of being in some way unconsciously connected already with the dismissal of her old servant and friend, followed, weeping, downstairs to Edith's dressing-room, whither Susan betook herself to make her parting curtsey.

'Now, here's the cab, and here's the boxes, get along with you, do!' said Mrs. Pipchin, presenting herself at the same moment. 'I beg your pardon, ma'am, but Mr. Dombey's orders are imperative.'

Edith, sitting under the hands of her maid—she was going out to dinner—preserved her haughty face, and took not the least notice.

'There's your money,' said Mrs. Pipchin, who in pursuance of her system, and in recollection of the mines, was accustomed to rout the servants about, as she had routed her young Brighton boarders; to the everlasting acidulation of Master Bitherstone, 'and the sooner this house sees your back the better.'

Susan had no spirits even for the look that belonged to Mrs. Pipchin by right; so she dropped her curtsey to Mrs. Dombey (who inclined her head without one word, and whose eye avoided every one but Florence), and gave one last parting hug to her young mistress, and received her parting embrace in return. Poor Susan's face at this crisis, in the intensity of her feelings and the determined suffocation of her sobs, lest one should become audible and be a triumph to Mrs. Pipchin, presented a series of the most extraordinary physiognomical phenomena ever witnessed.

'I beg your pardon, miss, I 'm sure,' said Towlin-son, outside the door with the boxes, addressing Florence, 'but Mr. Toots is in the drawing-room, and sends his compliments, and begs to know how Diogenes and master is.'

Quick as thought, Florence glided out and hastened downstairs, where Mr. Toots, in the most splendid vestments, was breathing very hard with doubt and agitation on the subject of her coming.

'Oh, how de do, Miss Dombey,' said Mr. Toots, 'God bless my soul!'

This last ejaculation was occasioned by Mr. Toots's deep concern at the distress he saw in Florence's face; which caused him to stop short in a fit of chuckles, and become an image of despair.

'Dear Mr. Toots,' said Florence, 'you are so friendly to me, and so honest, that I am sure I may ask a favour of you.'

'Miss Dombey,' returned Mr. Toots, 'if you 'll only name one, you 'll—you 'll give me an appetite. To which,' said Mr. Toots, with some sentiment, 'I have long been a stranger.'

'Susan, who is an old friend of mine, the oldest friend I have,' said Florence, 'is about to leave here suddenly, and quite alone, poor girl. She is going home, a little way into the country. Might I ask you to take care of her until she is in the coach?'

'Miss Dombey,' returned Mr. Toots, 'you really do me an honour and a kindness. This proof of your confidence, after the manner in which I was beast enough to conduct myself at Brighton—'

'Yes,' said Florence, hurriedly—'no—don't think of that. Then would you have the kindness to—to go? and to be ready to meet her when she comes out? Thank you a thousand times! You ease my mind so much. She doesn't seem so desolate. You cannot think how grateful I feel to you, or what a good friend I am sure you are!' And Florence in her earnestness, thanked him again and again; and Mr. Toots, in *his* earnestness, hurried away—but backwards, that he might lose no glimpse of her.

Florence had not the courage to go out, when she saw poor Susan in the hall, with Mrs. Pipchin driving her forth, and Diogenes jumping about her, and terrifying Mrs. Pipchin to the last degree by making snaps at her bombazeen skirts, and howling with anguish at the sound of her voice—for the good duenna was the dearest and most cherished aversion of his breast. But she saw Susan shake hands with the servants all round, and turn once to look at her old home; and she saw Diogenes bound out after the cab, and want to follow it, and testify an impossibility of conviction that he had no longer any property in the fare; and the door was shut, and the hurry over, and her tears flowed fast for the loss of an old friend, whom no one could replace. No one. No one.

Mr. Toots, like the leal and trusty soul he was, stopped the cabriolet in a twinkling, and told Susan Nipper of his commission, at which she cried more than before.

'Upon my soul and body!' said Mr. Toots, taking his seat beside her, 'I feel for you. Upon my word and honour I think you can hardly know your own feelings better than I imagine them. I can conceive nothing more dreadful than to have to leave Miss Dombey.'

Susan abandoned herself to her grief now, and it really was touching to see her.

'I say,' said Mr. Toots, 'now, don't! at least I mean now do, you know!'

'Do what, Mr. Toots?' cried Susan.

'Why, come home to my place, and have some dinner before you start,' said Mr. Toots. 'My cook 's a most respectable woman—one of the most motherly people I ever saw—and she 'll be delighted to make you comfortable. Her son,' said Mr. Toots, as an additional recommendation, 'was educated in the Blue-coat School, and blown up in a powder-mill.'

Susan accepting this kind offer, Mr. Toots conducted her to his dwelling, where they were received by the matron in question, who fully justified his character of her, and by the Chicken, who at first supposed, on seeing a lady in the vehicle, that Mr. Dombey had been doubled up, agreeably to his old recommendation, and Miss Dombey abducted. This gentleman awakened in Miss Nipper some considerable astonishment; for, having been defeated by the Larkey Boy, his visage was in a state of such great dilapidation, as to be hardly presentable in society with comfort to the beholders. The Chicken himself attributed this punishment to his having had the misfortune to get into Chancery early in the proceedings, when he was severely fibbed by the Larkey One, and heavily grassed. But it appeared from the published records of that great contest that the Larkey Boy had had it all his own way from the beginning, and that the Chicken had been tapped, and bunged, and had received pepper, and had been made groggy, and had come up piping, and had endured a complication of similar strange inconveniences, until he had been gone into and finished.

After a good repast, and much hospitality, Susan set out for the coach-office in another cabriolet, with Mr. Toots inside, as before, and the Chicken on the box, who, whatever distinction he conferred on the little party by the moral weight and heroism of his character, was scarcely ornamental to it, physically speaking, on account of his plasters; which were numerous. But the Chicken had registered a vow, in secret, that he would never leave Mr. Toots (who was secretly pining to get rid of him), for any less consideration than the goodwill and fixtures of a public-house; and being ambitious to go into that line, and drink himself to death as soon as possible, he felt it his cue to make his company unacceptable.

The night-coach by which Susan was to go, was on the point of departure. Mr. Toots having put her inside, lingered by the window, irresolutely, until the driver was about to mount; when, standing on the step, and putting in a face that by the light of the lamp was anxious and confused, he said abruptly—

'I say, Susan! Miss Dombey, you know—'

'Yes, sir.'

'Do you think she could—you know—eh?'

'I beg your pardon, Mr. Toots,' said Susan, 'but I don't hear you.'

'Do you think she could be brought, you know—not exactly at once, but in time—in a long time—to—to love me, you know! There!' said poor Mr. Toots.

'Oh dear no': returned Susan, shaking her head. 'I should say, never. Ne—ver!'

'Thank 'ee!' said Mr. Toots. 'It's of no consequence. Good night. It's of no consequence, thank 'ee!'

CHAPTER XLV

THE TRUSTY AGENT

EDITH went out alone that day, and returned home early. It was but a few minutes after ten o'clock, when her carriage rolled along the street in which she lived.

There was the same enforced composure on her face, that there had been when she was dressing; and the wreath upon her head encircled the same cold and steady brow. But it would have been better to have seen its leaves and flowers reft into fragments by her passionate hand, or rendered shapeless by the fitful searches of a throbbing and bewildered brain for any resting-place, than adorning such tranquillity. So obdurate, so unapproachable, so unrelenting, one would have thought that nothing could soften such a woman's nature, and that everything in life had hardened it.

Arrived at her own door, she was alighting, when some one coming quietly from the hall, and standing bareheaded, offered her his arm. The servant being thrust aside, she had no choice but to touch it; and she then knew whose arm it was.

'How is your patient, sir?' she said, with a curled lip.

'He is better,' returned Carker. 'He is doing very well. I have left him for the night.'

She bent her head, and was passing up the staircase, when he followed, and said, speaking at the bottom—

'Madam! May I beg the favour of a minute's audience?'

She stopped and turned her eyes back. 'It is an unreasonable time, sir, and I am fatigued. Is your business urgent?'

'It is very urgent,' returned Carker. 'As I am so fortunate as to have met you, let me press my petition.'

She looked down for a moment at his glistening mouth; and he looked up at her, standing above him in her stately dress, and thought, again, how beautiful she was.

'Where is Miss Dombey?' she asked the servant, aloud.

'In the morning-room, ma'am.'

'Show the way there!' Turning her eyes again on the attentive gentleman at the bottom of the stairs, and informing him with a slight motion of her head, that he was at liberty to follow, she passed on.

'I beg your pardon! Madam! Mrs. Dombey!' cried the soft and nimble Carker at her side in a moment. 'May I be permitted to entreat that Miss Dombey is not present?'

She confronted him, with a quick look, but with the same self-possession and steadiness.

'I would spare Miss Dombey,' said Carker, in a low voice, 'the knowledge of what I have to say. At least, madam, I would leave it to you to decide whether she shall know of it or not. I owe that to you. It is my bounden duty to you. After our former interview, it would be monstrous in me if I did otherwise.'

She slowly withdrew her eyes from his face, and turning to the servant, said, 'Some other room.' He led the way to a drawing-room, which he speedily lighted up and then left them. While he remained, not a word was spoken. Edith enthroned herself upon a couch by the fire; and Mr. Carker, with his hat in his hand and his eyes bent upon the carpet, stood before her, at some little distance.

'Before I hear you, sir,' said Edith, when the door was closed, 'I wish you to hear me.'

'To be addressed by Mrs. Dombey,' he returned, 'even in accents of unmerited reproach, is an honour I so greatly esteem, that although I were not her servant in all things, I should defer to such a wish, most readily.'

'If you are charged by the man whom you have just now left, sir'; Mr. Carker raised his eyes, as if he were going to counterfeit surprise, but she met them, and stopped him, if such were his intention; 'with any message to me, do not attempt to deliver it, for I will not receive it. I need scarcely ask you if you are come on such an errand. I have expected you some time.'

'It is my misfortune,' he replied, 'to be here, wholly against my will, for such a purpose. Allow me to say that I am here for two purposes. That is one.'

'That one, sir,' she returned, 'is ended. Or, if you return to it—'

'Can Mrs. Dombey believe,' said Carker, coming nearer, 'that I would return to it in the face of her prohibition? It is possible that Mrs. Dombey, having no regard to my unfortunate position, is so determined to consider me inseparable from my instructor as to do me great and wilful injustice?'

'Sir,' returned Edith, bending her dark gaze full upon him, and speaking with a rising passion that inflated her proud nostril and her swelling neck, and stirred the delicate white down upon a robe she wore, thrown loosely over shoulders that could bear its snowy neighbourhood, 'Why do you present yourself to me, as you have done, and speak to me of love and duty to my husband, and pretend to think that I am happily married, and that I honour him? How dare you venture so to affront me, when you know—*I* do not know better, sir: I have seen it in your every glance, and heard it in your every word—that in place of affection between us there is aversion and contempt, and that I despise him hardly less than I despise myself for being his! Injustice! If I had done justice to the torment you have made me feel, and to my sense of the insult you have put upon me, I should have slain you!'

She had asked him why he did this. Had she not been blinded by her pride and wrath, and self-humiliation,—which she was, fiercely as she bent her gaze upon him,—she would have seen the answer in his face. To bring her to this declaration.

She saw it not, nor cared not whether it was there or no. She saw only the indignities and struggles she had undergone, and had to undergo, and was writhing under them. As she sat looking fixedly at them, rather than at him, she plucked the feathers from a pinion of some rare and beautiful bird, which hung from her wrist by a golden thread, to serve her as a fan, and rained them on the ground.

He did not shrink beneath her gaze, but stood, until such outward signs of her anger as had escaped her control subsided, with the air of a man who had his sufficient reply in reserve and would presently deliver it. And he then spoke, looking straight into her kindling eyes.

'Madam,' he said, 'I know, and knew before to-day, that I have found no favour with you; and I knew why. Yes. I knew why. You have spoken so openly to me; I am so relieved by the possession of your confidence—'

'Confidence!' she repeated, with disdain.

He passed it over.

'—that I will make no pretence of concealment. I *did* see from the first, that there was no affection on your part for Mr. Dombey—how could it possibly exist between such different subjects! And I *have* seen, since, that stronger feelings than indifference have been engendered in your breast—how could that possibly be otherwise, either, circumstanced as you have been? But was it for me to presume to avow this knowledge to you in so many words?'

'Was it for you, sir,' she replied, 'to feign that other belief, and audaciously to thrust it on me day by day?'

'Madam, it was,' he eagerly retorted. 'If I had done less, if I had done anything but that, I should not be speaking to you thus; and I foresaw—who could better foresee, for who has had greater experience of Mr. Dombey than myself?—that unless your character should prove to be as yielding and obedient as that of his first submissive lady, which I did not believe—'

A haughty smile gave him reason to observe that he might repeat this.

'I say, which I did not believe,— the time was likely to come, when such an understanding as we have now arrived at, would be serviceable.'

'Serviceable to whom, sir?' she demanded scornfully.

'To you. I will not add to myself, as warning me to refrain even from that limited commendation of Mr. Dombey, in which I can honestly indulge, in order that I may not have the misfortune of saying anything distasteful to one whose aversion and contempt,' with great expression, 'are so keen.'

'It is honest in you, sir,' said Edith, 'to confess to your "limited commendation," and to speak in that tone of disparagement, even of him: being his chief counsellor and flatterer!'

'Counsellor,—yes,' said Carker. 'Flatterer,—no. A little reservation I fear I must confess to. But our interest and convenience commonly oblige many of us to make professions that we cannot feel. We have partnerships of interest and convenience, friendships of interest and convenience, dealings of interest and convenience, marriages of interest and convenience, every day.'

She bit her blood-red lip; but without wavering in the dark, stern watch she kept upon him.

'Madam,' said Mr. Carker, sitting down in a chair that was near her, with an air of the most profound and most considerate respect, 'why should I hesitate now, being altogether devoted to your service, to speak plainly! It was natural that a lady, endowed as you are, should think it feasible to change her husband's character in some respects, and mould him to a better form.'

'It was not natural to *me*, sir,' she rejoined. 'I had never any expectation or intention of that kind.'

The proud undaunted face showed him it was resolute to wear no mask he offered, but was set upon a reckless disclosure of itself, indifferent to any aspect in which it might present itself to such as he.

'At least it was natural,' he resumed, 'that you should deem it quite possible to live with Mr. Dombey as his wife, at once without submitting to him, and without coming into such violent collision with him. But, madam, you did not know Mr. Dombey (as you have since ascertained), when you thought that. You did not know how exacting and how proud he is, or how he is, if I may say so, the slave of his own greatness, and goes yoked to his own triumphal car like a beast of burden, with no idea on earth but that it is behind him and is to be drawn on, over everything and through everything.'

His teeth gleamed through his malicious relish of this conceit, as he went on talking:

'Mr. Dombey is really capable of no more true consideration for you, madam, than for me. The comparison is an extreme one; I intend it to be so; but quite just. Mr. Dombey, in the plenitude of his power, asked me—I had it from his own lips yesterday morning—to be his go-between to you, because he knows I am not agreeable to you, and because he intends that I shall be a punishment for your contumacy; and besides that, because he really does consider, that I, his paid servant, am an ambassador whom it is derogatory to the dignity—not of the lady to whom I have the happiness of speaking; she has no existence in his mind—but of his wife, a part of himself, to receive. You may imagine how regardless of me, how obtuse to the possibility of my having any individual sentiment or opinion he is, when he tells me, openly, that I am so employed. You know how perfectly indifferent to your feelings he is, when he threatens you with such a messenger. As you, of course, have not forgotten that he did.'

She watched him still attentively. But he watched her too; and he saw that this indication of a knowledge on his part, of something that had passed between herself and her husband, rankled and smarted in her haughty breast, like a poisoned arrow.

'I do not recall all this to widen the breach between yourself and Mr. Dombey, madam—Heaven forbid! what would it profit me?—but as an example of the hopelessness of impressing Mr. Dombey with a sense that anybody is to be considered when he is in question. We who are about him have, in our various positions, done our part, I dare say, to confirm him in his way of thinking; but if we had not done so, others would—or they would not have been about him; and it has always been from the beginning, the very staple of his life. Mr. Dombey has had to deal, in short, with none but submissive and dependent persons, who have bowed the knee, and bent the neck, before him. He has never known what it is to have angry pride and strong resentment opposed to him.'

'But he will know it now!' she seemed to say; though her lips did not part, nor her eyes falter. He saw the soft down tremble once again, and he saw her lay the plumage of the beautiful bird against her bosom for a moment; and he unfolded one more ring of the coil into which he had gathered himself.

'Mr. Dombey, though a most honourable gentleman,' he said, 'is so prone to pervert even facts to his own view, when he is at all opposed, in consequence of the warp in his mind, that he—can I give a better instance than this!—he sincerely believes (you will excuse the folly of what I am about to say; it not being mine) that his severe expression of opinion to his present wife, on a certain special occasion she may remember, before the lamented death of Mrs. Skewton, produced a withering effect, and for the moment quite subdued her!'

Edith laughed. How harshly and unmusically need not be described. It is enough that he was glad to hear her.

'Madam,' he resumed, 'I have done with this. Your own opinions are so strong, and, I am persuaded, so unalterable,' he repeated those words slowly and with great emphasis, 'that I am almost afraid to incur your displeasure anew, when I say that in spite of these defects and my full knowledge of them, I have become habituated to Mr. Dombey, and esteem him. But when I say so, it is not, believe me, for the mere sake of vaunting a feeling that is so utterly at variance with your own, and for which you can have no sympathy'—oh how distinct and plain and emphasised this was! 'but to give you an assurance of the zeal with which, in this unhappy matter, I am yours, and the indignation with which I regard the part I am required to fill!'

She sat as if she were afraid to take her eyes from his face.

And now to unwind the last ring of the coil!

'It is growing late,' said Carker, after a pause, 'and you are, as you said, fatigued. But the second object of this interview, I must not forget. I must recommend you, I must entreat you in the most earnest manner, for sufficient reasons that I have, to be cautious in your demonstrations of regard for Miss Dombey.'

'Cautious! What do you mean?'

'To be careful how you exhibit too much affection for that young lady.'

'Too much affection, sir!' said Edith, knitting her broad brow and rising. 'Who judges my affection, or measures it out? You?'

'It is not I who do so.' He was, or feigned to be, perplexed.

'Who then?'

'Can you not guess who then?'

'I do not choose to guess,' she answered.

'Madam,' he said after a little hesitation; meantime they had been and still were, regarding each other as before; 'I am in a difficulty here. You have told me you will receive no message, and you have forbidden me to return to that subject; but the two subjects are so closely entwined, I find, that unless you will accept this vague caution from one who has now the honour to possess your confidence, though the way to it has been through your displeasure, I must violate the injunction you have laid upon me.'

'You know that you are free to do so, sir,' said Edith. 'Do it.'

So pale, so trembling, so impassioned! He had not miscalculated the effect then!

'His instructions were,' he said, in a low voice, 'that I should inform you that your demeanour towards Miss Dombey is not agreeable to him. That it suggests comparisons to him which are not favourable to himself. That he desires it may be wholly changed; and that if you are in earnest, he is confident it will be; for your continued show of affection will not benefit its object.'

'That is a threat,' she said.

'That is a threat,' he answered in his voiceless manner of assent: adding aloud, 'but not directed against you.'

Proud, erect, and dignified, as she stood confronting him; and looking through him as she did, with her full bright flashing eye; and smiling, as she was, with scorn and bitterness; she sunk as if the ground had dropped beneath her, and in an instant would have fallen on the floor, but that he caught her in his arms. As instantaneously she threw him off, the moment that he touched her, and, drawing back, confronted him again, immoveable, with her hand stretched out.

'Please to leave me. Say no more to-night.'

'I feel the urgency of this,' said Mr. Carker, 'because it is impossible to say what unforeseen consequences might arise, or how soon, from your being unacquainted with his state of mind. I understand Miss Dombey is concerned, now, at the dismissal of her old servant, which is likely to have been a minor consequence in itself. You don't blame me for requesting that Miss Dombey might not be present. May I hope so?'

'I do not. Please to leave me, sir.'

'I knew that your regard for the young lady, which is very sincere and strong, I am well pursuaded, would render it a great unhappiness to you, ever to be a prey to the reflection that you had injured her position and ruined her future hopes,' said Carker hurriedly, but eagerly.

'No more to-night. Leave me, if you please.'

'I shall be here constantly in my attendance upon him, and in the transaction of business matters. You will allow me to see you again, and to consult what should be done, and learn your wishes?'

She motioned him towards the door.

'I cannot even decide whether to tell him I have spoken to you yet; or to lead him to suppose that I have deferred doing so, for want of opportunity, or for any other reason. It will be necessary that you should enable me to consult with you very soon.'

'At any time but now,' she answered.

'You will understand, when I wish to see you, that Miss Dombey it not to be present; and that I seek an interview as one who has the happiness to possess your confidence, and who comes to render you every assistance in his power, and, perhaps, on many occasions, to ward off evil from her?'

Looking at him still with the same apparent dread of releasing him for a moment from the influence of her steady gaze, whatever that might be, she answered, 'Yes!' and once more bade him go.

He bowed, as if in compliance; but turning back, when he had nearly reached the door, said—

'I am forgiven, and have explained my fault. May I—for Miss Dombey's sake—and for my own —take your hand before I go?'

She gave him the gloved hand she had maimed last night. He took it in one of his, and kissed it, and withdrew. And when he had closed the door, he waved the hand with which he had taken hers, and thrust it in his breast.

CHAPTER XLVI

RECOGNISANT AND REFLECTIVE

AMONG sundry minor alterations in Mr. Carker's life and habits that began to take place at this time, none was more remarkable than the extraordinary diligence with which he applied himself to business, and the closeness with which he investigated every detail that the affairs of the House laid open to him. Always active and penetrating in such matters, his lynx-eyed vigilance now increased twenty-fold. Not only did his weary watch keep pace with every present point that every day presented to him in some new form, but in the midst of these engrossing occupations he found leisure—that is, he made it—to review the past transactions of the Firm, and his share in them, during a long series of years. Frequently when the clerks were all gone, the offices dark and empty, and all similar places of business shut up, Mr. Carker, with the whole anatomy of the iron room laid bare before him, would explore the mysteries of books and papers, with the patient progress of a man who was dissecting the minutest nerves and fibres of his subject. Perch, the messenger, who usually remained on these occasions, to entertain himself with the perusal of the Price Current by the light of one candle, or to doze over the fire in the outer office, at the imminent risk every moment of diving head foremost into the coal box, could not withhold the tribute of his admiration from this zealous conduct, although it much contracted his domestic enjoyments; and again, and again, expatiated to Mrs. Perch (now nursing twins) on the industry and acuteness of their managing gentleman in the City.

The same increased and sharp attention that Mr. Carker bestowed on the business of the House, he applied to his own personal affairs. Though not a partner in the concern—a distinction hitherto reserved solely to inheritors of the great name of Dombey— he was in the receipt of some per centage on its dealings; and, participating in all its facilities for the employment of money to advantage, was considered, by the minnows among the tritons of the East, a rich man. It began to be said, among these shrewd observers, that Jem Carker, of Dombey's, was looking about him to see what he was worth; and that he was calling in his money at a good time, like the long-headed fellow he was; and bets were even offered on the Stock Exchange that Jem was going to marry a rich widow.

Yet these cares did not in the least interfere with Mr. Carker's watching of his chief, or with his cleanness, neatness, sleekness, or any cat-like quality he possessed. It was not so much that there was a change in him, in reference to any of his habits, as that the whole man was intensified. Everything that had been observable in him before, was observable now, but with a greater amount of concentration. He did each single thing, as if he did nothing else—a pretty certain indication in a man of that range of ability and purpose, that he is doing something which sharpens and keeps alive his keenest powers.

The only decided alteration in him was, that as he rode to and fro along the streets, he would fall into deep fits of musing, like that in which he had come away from Mr. Dombey's house, on the morning of that gentleman's disaster. At such times, he would keep clear of the obstacles in his way, mechanically; and would appear to see and hear nothing until arrival at his destination, or some sudden chance or effort roused him.

Walking his white-legged horse thus, to the counting-house of Dombey and Son one day, he was as unconscious of the observation of two pairs of women's eyes, as of the fascinated orbs of Rob the Grinder, who, in waiting a street's length from the appointed place, as a demonstration of punctuality, vainly touched and retouched his hat to attract attention, and trotted along on foot, by his master's side, prepared to hold his stirrup when he should alight.

'See where he goes!' cried one of these two women, an old creature, who stretched out her shrivelled arm to point him out to her companion, a young woman, who stood close beside her, withdrawn like herself into a gateway.

Mrs. Brown's daughter looked out, at this bidding on the part of Mrs. Brown; and there were wrath and vengeance in her face.

'I never thought to look at him again,' she said, in a low voice; 'but it's well I should, perhaps. I see. I see!'

'Not changed!' said the old woman, with a look of eager malice.

'*He* changed!' returned the other. 'What for? What has *he* suffered? There is change enough for twenty in me. Isn't that enough?'

'See where he goes!' muttered the old woman, watching her daughter with her red eyes; 'so easy and so trim, a' horseback, while we are in the mud—'

'And of it,' said her daughter impatiently. 'We are mud, underneath his horse's feet. What should we be?'

In the intentness with which she looked after him again, she made a hasty gesture with her hand when the old woman began to reply, as if her view could be obstructed by mere sound. Her mother watching her, and not him, remained silent; until her kindling glance subsided, and she drew a long breath, as if in the relief of his being gone.

'Deary!' said the old woman then. 'Alice! Handsome gal! Ally!' She gently shook her sleeve to arouse her attention. 'Will you let him go like that, when you can wring money from him? Why, it 's a wickedness, my daughter.'

'Haven't I told you, that I will not have money from him?' she returned. 'And don't you yet believe me? Did I take his sister's money? Would I touch a penny, if I knew it, that had gone through his white hands—unless, it was, indeed, that I could poison it, and send it back to him? Peace, mother, and come away.'

'And him so rich?' murmured the old woman. 'And us so poor!'

'Poor in not being able to pay him any of the harm we owe him,' returned her daughter. 'Let him give me that sort of riches, and I 'll take them from him, and use them. Come away. It 's no good looking at his horse. Come away, mother!'

But the old woman, for whom the spectacle of Rob the Grinder returning down the street, leading the riderless horse, appeared to have some extraneous interest that it did not possess in itself, surveyed that young man with the utmost earnestness; and seeming to have whatever doubts she entertained, resolved as he drew nearer, glanced at her daughter with brightened eyes and with her finger on her lip, and emerging from the gateway at the moment of his passing, touched him on the shoulder.

'Why, where 's my sprightly Rob been, all this time!' she said, as he turned round.

The sprightly Rob, whose sprightliness was very much diminished by the salutation, looked exceedingly dismayed, and said, with the water rising in his eyes—

'Oh! why can't you leave a poor cove alone, Misses Brown, when he's getting an honest livelihood and conducting himself respectable? What do you come and deprive a cove of his character for, by talking to him in the streets, when he's taking his master's horse to a honest stable—a horse you'd go and sell for cats' and dogs' meat if you had your way? Why, I thought,' said the Grinder, producing his concluding remark as if it were the climax of all his injuries, 'that you was dead long ago!'

'This is the way,' cried the old woman, appealing to her daughter, 'that he talks to me, who knew him weeks and months together, my deary, and have stood his friend many and many a time among the pigeon-fancying tramps and bird-catchers.'

'Let the birds be, will you, Misses Brown?' retorted Rob, in a tone of the acutest anguish. 'I think a cove had better have to do with lions than them little creeturs, for they're always flying back in your face when you least expect it. Well, how d'ye do and what do you want?' These polite inquiries the Grinder uttered, as it were under protest, and with great exasperation and vindictiveness.

'Hark how he speaks to an old friend, my deary!' said Mrs. Brown, again appealing to her daughter. 'But there's some of his old friends not so patient as me. If I was to tell some that he knows, and has sported and cheated with, where to find him—'

'Will you hold your tongue, Misses Brown?' interrupted the miserable Grinder, glancing quickly round, as though he expected to see his master's teeth shining at his elbow. 'What do you take a

pleasure in ruining a cove for? At your time of life
too! when you ought to be thinking of a variety of
things!'

'What a gallant horse!' said the old woman, patting the animal's neck.

'Let him alone, will you, Misses Brown?' cried
Rob, pushing away her hand. 'You're enough to
drive a penitent cove mad!'

'Why, what hurt do I do him, child?' returned the
old woman.

'Hurt?' said Rob. 'He's got a master that would
find it out if he was touched with a straw.' And he
blew upon the place where the old woman's hand had
rested for a moment, and smoothed it gently with
his finger, as if he seriously believed what he said.

The old woman looking back to mumble and mouth
at her daughter, who followed, kept close to Rob's
heels as he walked on with the bridle in his hand; and
pursued the conversation.

'A good place, Rob, eh?' said she. 'You're in
luck, my child.'

'Oh don't talk about luck, Misses Brown,' retorted
the wretched Grinder, facing round and stopping.
'If you'd never come, or if you'd go away, then
indeed a cove might be considered tolerably lucky.
Can't you go along, Misses Brown, and not foller
me!' blubbered Rob, with sudden defiance. 'If the
young woman's a friend of yours, why don't she take
you away, instead of letting you make yourself so
disgraceful?'

'What?' croaked the old woman, putting her face
close to his, with a malevolent grin upon it that puck-
ered up the loose skin down in her very throat. 'Do
you deny your old chum? Have you lurked to my
house fifty times, and slept sound in a corner when
you had no other bed but the paving-stones, and do

you talk to *me* like this? Have I bought and sold
with you, and helped you in my way of business,
school-boy, sneak, and what not, and do you tell *me*
to go along? Could I raise a crowd of old company
about you to-morrow morning, that would follow you
to ruin like copies of your own shadow, and do you
turn on *me* with your bold looks! I 'll go. Come,
Alice.'

'Stop, Misses Brown!' cried the distracted Grinder.
'What are you doing of? Don't put yourself in a
passion! Don't let her go, if you please. I haven't
meant any offence. I said "How d' ye do," at first,
didn't I? But you wouldn't answer. How *do* you
do? Besides,' said Rob piteously, 'look here! How
can a cove stand talking in the street with his master's prad a wanting to be took to be rubbed down,
and his master up to every individgle thing that
happens?'

The old woman made a show of being partially
appeased, but shook her head, and mouthed and muttered still.

'Come along to the stables, and have a glass of
something that 's good for you, Misses Brown, can't
you?' said Rob, 'instead of going on, like that, which
is no good to you, nor anybody else? Come along
with her, will you be so kind?' said Rob. 'I 'm sure
I 'm delighted to see her, if it wasn't for the horse!'

With this apology, Rob turned away, a rueful
picture of despair, and walked his charge down a bye-
street. The old woman, mouthing at her daughter,
followed close upon him. The daughter followed.

Turning into a silent little square or court-yard
that had a great church tower rising above it, and a
packer's warehouse, and a bottle-maker's warehouse,
for its places of business, Rob the Grinder delivered
the white-legged horse to the hostler of a quaint

stable at the corner; and inviting Mrs. Brown and her daughter to seat themselves upon a stone bench at the gate of that establishment, soon reappeared from a neighbouring public-house with a pewter measure and a glass.

'Here's master—Mr. Carker, child!' said the old woman, slowly, as her sentiment before drinking. 'Lord bless him!'

'Why, I didn't tell you who he was?' observed Rob, with staring eyes.

'We know him by sight,' said Mrs. Brown, whose working mouth and nodding head stopped for the moment, in the fixedness of her attention. 'We saw him pass this morning, afore he got off his horse; when you were ready to take it.'

'Aye, aye?' returned Rob, appearing to wish that his readiness had carried him to any other place.— 'What's the matter with her? Won't she drink?'

This inquiry had reference to Alice, who, folded in her cloak, sat a little apart profoundly inattentive to his offer of the replenished glass.

The old woman shook her head. 'Don't mind her,' she said; 'she's a strange creetur, if you know'd her, Rob. But Mr. Carker—'

'Hush!' said Rob, glancing cautiously up at the packer's, and at the bottle-maker's, as if, from any one of the tiers of warehouses, Mr. Carker might be looking down. 'Softly.'

'Why, he ain't here!' cried Mrs. Brown.

'I don't know that,' muttered Rob, whose glance even wandered to the church tower, as if he might be there, with a supernatural power of hearing.

'Good master?' inquired Mrs. Brown.

Rob nodded; and added in a low voice, 'Precious sharp.'

'Lives out of town, don't he, lovey?' said the old woman.

'When he's at home,' returned Rob; 'but we don't live at home just now.'

'Where then?' asked the old woman.

'Lodgings; up near Mr. Dombey's,' returned Rob.

The younger woman fixed her eyes so searchingly upon him, and so suddenly, that Rob was quite confounded, and offered the glass again, but with no more effect upon her than before.

'Mr. Dombey—you and I used to talk about him, sometimes, you know,' said Rob to Mrs. Brown. 'You used to get me to talk about him.'

The old woman nodded.

'Well, Mr. Dombey, he's had a fall from his horse,' said Rob unwillingly; 'and my master has to be up there, more than usual, either with him, or Mrs. Dombey, or some of 'em; and so we've come to town.'

'Are they good friends, lovey?' asked the old woman.

'Who?' retorted Rob.

'He and she?'

'What, Mr. and Mrs. Dombey?' said Rob. 'How should I know!'

'Not them—Master and Mrs. Dombey, chick,' replied the old woman, coaxingly.

'I don't know,' said Rob, looking round him again. 'I suppose so. How curious you are, Misses Brown! Least said, soonest mended.'

'Why there's no harm in it!' exclaimed the old woman, with a laugh, and a clap of her hands. 'Sprightly Rob has grown tame since he has been well off! There's no harm in it.'

'No, there's no harm in it, I know,' returned Rob,

with the same distrustful glance at the packer's and the bottle-maker's, and the church; 'but blabbing, if it's only about the number of buttons on my master's coat, won't do. I tell you it won't do with him. A cove had better drown himself. He says so. I shouldn't have so much as told you what his name was, if you hadn't known it. Talk about somebody else.'

As Rob took another cautious survey of the yard, the old woman made a secret motion to her daughter. It was momentary, but the daughter, with a slight look of intelligence, withdrew her eyes from the boy's face, and sat folded in her cloak as before.

'Rob, lovey!' said the old woman, beckoning him to the other end of the bench. 'You were always a pet and favourite of mine. Now, weren't you? Don't you know we were?'

'Yes, Misses Brown,' replied the Grinder, with a very bad grace.

'And you could leave me!' said the old woman, flinging her arms about his neck. 'You could go away, and grow almost out of knowledge, and never come to tell your poor old friend how fortunate you were, proud lad! Oho oho!'

'Oh here's a dreadful go for a cove that's got a master wide-awake in the neighbourhood!' exclaimed the wretched Grinder. 'To be howled over like this here!'

'Won't you come and see me, Robby?' cried Mrs. Brown. 'Oho, won't you ever come and see me?'

'Yes, I tell you! Yes, I will!' returned the Grinder.

'That's my own Rob! That's my lovey!' said Mrs. Brown, drying the tears upon her shrivelled face, and giving him a tender squeeze. 'At the old place, Rob?'

'Yes,' replied the Grinder.

'Soon, Robby dear?' cried Mrs. Brown: 'and often?'

'Yes. Yes. Yes,' replied Rob. 'I will indeed, upon my soul and body.'

'And then,' said Mrs. Brown, with her arms uplifted towards the sky, and her head thrown back and shaking, 'if he's true to his word, I'll never come a-near him, though I know where he is, and never breathe a syllable about him! Never!'

This ejaculation seemed a drop of comfort to the miserable Grinder, who shook Mrs. Brown by the hand upon it, and implored her with tears in his eyes to leave a cove and not destroy his prospects. Mrs. Brown, with another fond embrace, assented; but in the act of following her daughter, turned back, with her finger stealthily raised, and asked in a hoarse whisper for some money.

'A shilling, dear!' she said, with her eager avaricious face, 'or sixpence! For old acquaintance sake. I'm so poor. And my handsome gal'—looking over her shoulder—'she's my gal, Rob—half starves me.'

But as the reluctant Grinder put it in her hand, her daughter, coming quietly back, caught the hand in hers, and twisted out the coin.

'What?' she said, 'mother! always money! money from the first, and to the last. Do you mind so little what I said but now? Here. Take it!'

The old woman uttered a moan as the money was restored, but without in any other way opposing its restoration, hobbled at her daughter's side out of the yard, and along the bye-street upon which it opened. The astonished and dismayed Rob staring after them, saw that they stopped, and fell to earnest conversation very soon; and more than once observed a darkly threatening action of the younger woman's hand (obviously having reference to some one of whom they spoke), and a crooning feeble imitation of it on the part of Mrs. Brown, that made him earnestly hope he might not be the subject of their discourse.

With the present consolation that they were gone, and with the prospective comfort that Mrs. Brown could not live for ever, and was not likely to live long to trouble him, the Grinder, not otherwise regretting his misdeeds than as they were attended with such disagreeable incidental consequences, composed his ruffled features to a more serene expression by thinking of the admirable manner in which he had disposed of Captain Cuttle (a reflection that seldom failed to put him in a flow of spirits), and went to the Dombey counting-house to receive his master's orders.

There his master, so subtle and vigilant of eye, that Rob quaked before him, more than half expecting to be taxed with Mrs. Brown, gave him the usual morning's box of papers for Mr. Dombey, and a note for Mrs. Dombey: merely nodding his head as an enjoinder to be careful, and to use despatch—a mysterious admonition, fraught in the Grinder's imagination with dismal warnings and threats; and more powerful with him than any words.

Alone again, in his own room, Mr. Carker applied himself to work, and worked all day. He saw many visitors; overlooked a number of documents; went in and out, to and from, sundry places of mercantile resort; and indulged in no more abstraction until the day's business was done. But, when the usual clearance of papers from his table was made at last, he fell into his thoughtful mood once more.

He was standing in his accustomed place and attitude, with his eyes intently fixed upon the ground, when his brother entered to bring back some letters that had been taken out in the course of the day. He put them quietly on the table, and was going immediately, when Mr. Carker the manager, whose eyes had rested on him, on his entrance, as if they had all this time had him for the subject of their contemplation, instead of the office-floor, said—

'Well, John Carker, and what brings *you* here?'

His brother pointed to the letters, and was again withdrawing.

'I wonder,' said the manager, 'that you can come and go, without inquiring how our master is.'

'We had word this morning in the counting-house, that Mr. Dombey was doing well,' replied his brother.

'You are such a meek fellow,' said the manager, with a smile, '—but you have grown so, in the course of years—that if any harm came to him, you'd be miserable, I dare swear now.'

'I should be truly sorry, James,' returned the other.

'He would be sorry!' said the manager, pointing at him, as if there were some other person present to whom he was appealing. 'He would be truly sorry! This brother of mine! This junior of the place, this slighted piece of lumber, pushed aside with his face to the wall, like a rotten picture, and left so, for Heaven knows how many years; *he's* all gratitude and respect, and devotion too, he would have me believe!'

'I would have you believe nothing, James,' returned the other. 'Be as just to me as you would to any other man below you. You ask a question, and I answer it.'

'And have you nothing, Spaniel,' said the manager, with unusual irascibility, 'to complain of in him? No proud treatment to resent, no insolence, no foolery of state, no exaction of any sort? What the devil! are you man or mouse?'

'It would be strange if any two persons could be together for so many years, especially as superior and inferior, without each having something to complain of in the other—as he thought, at all events,' replied John Carker. 'But apart from my history here—'

'His history here!' exclaimed the manager. 'Why, there it is. The very fact that makes him an extreme case, puts him out of the whole chapter! Well?'

'Apart from that, which, as you hint, gives me a reason to be thankful that I alone (happily for all the rest) possess, surely there is no one in the House who would not say and feel at least as much. You do not think that anybody here would be indifferent to a mischance or misfortune happening to the head of the House, or anything than truly sorry for it?'

'You have good reason to be bound to him too!' said the manager, contemptuously. 'Why, don't you believe that you are kept here, as a cheap example, and a famous instance of the clemency of Dombey and Son, redounding to the credit of the illustrious House?'

'No,' replied his brother, mildly, 'I have long believed that I am kept here for more kind and disinterested reasons.'

'But you were going,' said the manager, with the snarl of a tiger-cat, 'to recite some Christian precept, I observed.'

'Nay, James,' returned the other, 'though the tie of brotherhood between us has been long broken and thrown away—'

'Who broke it, good sir?' said the manager.

'I, by my misconduct. I do not charge it upon you.'

The manager replied, with that mute action of his bristling mouth, 'Oh, you don't charge it upon me!' and bade him go on.

'I say, though there is not that tie between us, do not, I entreat, assail me with unnecessary taunts, or misinterpret what I say, or would say. I was only going to suggest to you that it would be a mistake to suppose that it is only you, who have been selected here, above all others, for advancement, confidence and distinction (selected, in the beginning, I know, for your great ability and trustfulness), and who communicate more freely with Mr. Dombey than any one, and stand, it may be said, on equal terms with him, and have been favoured and enriched by him— that it would be a mistake to suppose that it is only you who are tender of his welfare and reputation. There is no one in the House, from yourself down to the lowest, I sincerely believe, who does not participate in that feeling.'

'You lie!' said the manager, red with sudden anger. 'You 're a hypocrite, John Carker, and you lie!'

'James!' cried the other, flushing in his turn. 'What do you mean by these insulting words? Why do you so basely use them to me, unprovoked?'

'I tell you,' said the manager, 'that your hypocrisy and meekness—that all the hypocrisy and meekness of this place—is not worth *that* to me,' snapping his thumb and finger, 'and that I see through it as if it were air! There is not a man employed here, standing between myself and the lowest in place (of whom you are very considerate, and with reason, for he is not far off), who wouldn't be glad at heart to see his master humbled: who does not hate him, secretly: who does not wish him evil rather than good: and who would not turn upon him, if he had the power and boldness. The nearer to his favour, the nearer to his

insolence; the closer to him, the farther from him.
That's the creed here!'

'I don't know,' said his brother, whose roused feelings had soon yielded to surprise, 'who may have
abused your ear with such representations; or why
you have chosen to try me, rather than another. But
that you have been trying me, and tampering with me,
I am now sure. You have a different manner and a
different aspect from any that I ever saw in you. I
will only say to you, once more, you are deceived.'

'I know I am,' said the manager. 'I have told you
so.'

'Not by me,' returned his brother. 'By your in-
formant, if you have one. If not, by your own
thoughts and suspicions.'

'I have no suspicions,' said the manager. 'Mine
are certainties. You pusillanimous, abject, cringing
dogs! All making the same show, all canting the
same story, all whining the same professions, all har-
bouring the same transparent secret.'

His brother withdrew, without saying more, and
shut the door as he concluded. Mr. Carker the manager drew a chair close before the fire, and fell to
beating the coals softly with the poker.

'The faint-hearted, fawning knaves,' he muttered,
with his two shining rows of teeth laid bare.
'There's not one among them, who wouldn't feign to
be so shocked and outraged—! Bah! There's not
one among them, but if he had at once the power, and
the wit and daring to use it, would scatter Dombey's
pride and lay it low, as ruthlessly as I rake out these
ashes.'

As he broke them up and strewed them in the
grate, he looked on with a thoughtful smile at what
he was doing. 'Without the same queen beckoner
too!' he added presently; 'and there is pride there,

not to be forgotten—witness our own acquaintance!'
With that he fell into a deeper reverie, and sat pondering over the blackening grate, until he rose up
like a man who had been absorbed in a book, and
looking round him took his hat and gloves, went to
where his horse was waiting, mounted, and rode away
through the lighted streets, for it was evening.

He rode near Mr. Dombey's house; and falling
into a walk as he approached it, looked up at the windows. The window where he had once seen Florence
sitting with her dog, attracted his attention first,
though there was no light in it; but he smiled as he
carried his eyes up the tall front of the house, and
seemed to leave that object superciliously behind.

'Time was,' he said, 'when it was well to watch
even your rising little star, and know in what quarter
there were clouds, to shadow you if needful. But a
planet has arisen, and you are lost in its light.'

He turned the white-legged horse round the street-
corner, and sought one shining window from among
those at the back of the house. Associated with it
was a certain stately presence, a gloved hand, the remembrance how the feathers of a beautiful bird's
wing had been showered down upon the floor, and
how the light white down upon a robe had stirred and
rustled, as in the rising of a distant storm. These
were the things he carried with him as he turned away
again, and rode through the darkening and deserted
parks at a quick rate.

In fatal truth, these were associated with a woman,
a proud woman, who hated him, but who by slow and
sure degrees had been led on by his craft, and her
pride and resentment, to endure his company, and
little by little to receive him as one who had the privilege to talk to her of her own defiant disregard of her
own husband, and her abandonment of high consid-

eration for herself. They were associated with a woman who hated him deeply, and who knew him, and who mistrusted him because she knew him, and because he knew her; but who fed her fierce resentment by suffering him to draw nearer and yet nearer to her every day, in spite of the hate she cherished for him. In spite of it! For that very reason; since its depths, too far down for her threatening eye to pierce, though she could see into them dimly, lay the dark retaliation, whose faintest shadow seen once and shuddered at, and never seen again, would have been sufficient stain upon her soul.

Did the phantom of such a woman flit about him on his ride; true to the reality, and obvious to him?

Yes. He saw her in his mind, exactly as she was. She bore him company with her pride, resentment, hatred, all as plain to him as her beauty; with nothing plainer to him than her hatred of him. He saw her sometimes haughty and repellent at his side, and sometimes down among his horse's feet, fallen and in the dust. But he always saw her as she was, without disguise, and watched her on the dangerous way that she was going.

And when his ride was over, and he was newly dressed, and came into the light of her bright room with his bent head, soft voice, and soothing smile, he saw her yet as plainly. He even suspected the mystery of the gloved hand, and held it all the longer in his own for that suspicion. Upon the dangerous way that she was going, he was still; and not a footprint did she mark upon it, but he set his own there, straight.

CHAPTER XLVII

THE THUNDERBOLT

THE barrier between Mr. Dombey and his wife was
not weakened by time. Ill-assorted couple, unhappy
in themselves and in each other, bound together by no
tie but the manacle that joined their fettered hands,
and straining that so harshly, in their shrinking
asunder, that it wore and chafed to the bone, Time,
consoler of affliction and softener of anger, could do
nothing to help them. Their pride, however different in kind and object, was equal in degree; and, in
their flinty opposition, struck out fire between them
which might smoulder or might blaze, as circumstances were, but burned up everything within their
mutual reach, and made their marriage way a road of
ashes.

Let us be just to him: In the monstrous delusion
of his life, swelling with every grain of sand that
shifted in its glass, he urged her on, he little thought
to what, or considered how; but still his feeling towards her, such as it was, remained as at first. She
had the grand demerit of unaccountably putting herself in opposition to the recognition of his vast importance, and to the acknowledgment of her complete
submission to it, and so far it was necessary to correct
and reduce her; but otherwise he still considered her,
in his cold way, a lady capable of doing honour, if she
would, to his choice and name, and of reflecting credit
on his proprietorship.

Now, she, with all her might of passionate and
proud resentment, bent her dark glance from day to
day, and hour to hour—from that night in her own
chamber, when she had sat gazing at the shadows on

the wall, to the deeper night fast coming—upon one
figure directing a crowd of humiliations and exas-
perations against her; and that figure, still her husband's.

Was Mr. Dombey's master-vice, that ruled him so
inexorably, an unnatural characteristic? It might be
worth while, sometimes, to inquire what Nature is,
and how men work to change her, and whether, in the
enforced distortions so produced, it is not natural to
be unnatural. Coop any son or daughter of our
mighty mother within narrow range, and bind the
prisoner to one idea, and foster it by servile worship
of it on the part of the few timid or designing people
standing round, and what is nature to the willing
captive who has never risen up upon the wings of a
free mind—drooping and useless soon—to see her
in her comprehensive truth?

Alas! are there so few things in the world, about
us, most unnatural, and yet most natural in being so?
Hear the magistrate or judge admonish the unnatural
outcasts of society; unnatural in brutal habits, unnatural in want of decency, unnatural in losing and
confounding all distinctions between good and evil;
unnatural in ignorance, in vice, in recklessness, in contumacy, in mind, in looks, in everything. But follow
the good clergyman or doctor, who, with his life im-
perilled at every breath he draws, goes down into their
dens, lying within the echoes of our carriage-wheels
and daily tread upon the pavement stones. Look
round upon the world of odious sights—millions of
immortal creatures have no other world on earth—at
the lightest mention of which humanity revolts, and
dainty delicacy living in the next street, stops her
ears, and lisps 'I don't believe it!' Breathe the polluted air, foul with every impurity that is poisonous
to health and life; and have every sense, conferred

upon our race for its delight and happiness, offended,
sickened and disgusted, and made a channel by which
misery and death alone can enter. Vainly attempt
to think of any simple plant, or flower, or wholesome
weed, that, set in this fœtid bed, could have its natural
growth, or put its little leaves off to the sun as God
designed it. And then, calling up some ghastly child,
with stunted form and wicked face, hold forth on
its unnatural sinfulness, and lament its being, so early,
far away from Heaven—but think a little of its having been conceived, and born and bred, in Hell!

Those who study the physical sciences, and bring
them to bear upon the health of man, tell us that if the
noxious particles that rise from vitiated air were pal-
pable to the sight, we should see them lowering in a
dense black cloud above such haunts, and rolling slowly
on to corrupt the better portions of a town. But if
the moral pestilence that rises with them, and in the
eternal laws of outraged Nature, is inseparable from
them, could be made discernible too, how terrible the
revelation! Then should we see depravity, impiety,
drunkenness, theft, murder, and a long train of nameless sins against the natural affections and repulsions
of mankind, overhanging the devoted spots, and
creeping on, to blight the innocent and spread con-
tagion among the pure. Then should we see how the
same poisoned fountains that flow into our hospitals
and lazar-houses, inundate the gaols, and make the
convict-ships swim deep, and roll across the seas, and
overrun vast continents with crime. Then should we
stand appalled to know, that where we generate dis-
ease to strike our children down and entail itself on
unborn generations, there also we breed, by the same
certain process, infancy that knows no innocence,
youth without modesty or shame, maturity that is
mature in nothing but in suffering and guilt, blasted

old age that is a scandal on the form we bear. Unnatural humanity! When we shall gather grapes from thorns, and figs from thistles; when fields of grain shall spring up from the offal in the bye-ways of our wicked cities, and roses bloom in the fat church-yards that they cherish; then we may look for natural humanity and find it growing from such seed.

Oh for a good spirit who would take the house-tops off, with a more potent and benignant hand than the lame demon in the tale, and show a Christian people what dark shapes issue from amidst their homes, to swell the retinue of the Destroying Angel as he moves forth among them! For only one night's view of the pale phantoms rising from the scenes of our too-long neglect; and from the thick and sullen air where Vice and Fever propagate together, raining the tremendous social retributions which are ever pouring down, and ever coming thicker! Bright and blest the morning that should rise on such a night: for men, delayed no more by stumbling-blocks of their own making, which are but specks of dust upon the path between them and eternity, would then apply themselves, like creatures of one common origin, owing one duty to the Father of one family, and tending to one common end, to make the world a better place!

Not the less bright and blest would that day be for rousing some who never have looked out upon the world of human life around them, to a knowledge of their own relation to it, and for making them acquainted with a perversion of nature in their own contracted sympathies and estimates; as great, and yet as natural in its development when once begun, as the lowest degradation known.

But no such day had ever dawned on Mr. Dombey, or his wife; and the course of each was taken.

Through six months that ensued upon his accident,

they held the same relations one towards the other.
A marble rock could not have stood more obdurately
in his way than she; and no chilled spring, lying un-
cheered by any ray of light in the depths of a deep
cave, could be more sullen or more cold than he.

The hope that had fluttered within her when the
promise of her new home dawned, was quite gone
from the heart of Florence now. That home was
nearly two years old; and even the patient trust that
was in her, could not survive the daily blight of such
experience. If she had any lingering fancy in the
nature of hope left, that Edith and her father might
be happier together, in some distant time, she had
none, now, that her father would ever love her. The
little interval in which she had imagined that she saw
some small relenting in him, was forgotten in the long
remembrance of his coldness since and before, or only
remembered as a sorrowful delusion.

Florence loved him still, but, by degrees, had come to
love him rather as some dear one who had been, or who
might have been, than as the hard reality before her
eyes. Something of the softened sadness with which
she loved the memory of little Paul, or of her mother,
seemed to enter now into her thoughts of him, and to
make them, as it were, a dear remembrance. Whether
is was that he was dead to her, and that partly for
this reason, partly for his share in those old objects
of her affection, and partly for the long association
of him with hopes that were withered and tenderness
he had frozen, she could not have told; but the father
whom she loved began to be a vague and dreamy idea
to her: hardly more substantially connected with her
real life, than the image she would sometimes conjure
up, of her dear brother yet alive, and growing to be
a man, who would protect and cherish her.

The change, if it may be called one, had stolen on

her like the change from childhood to womanhood, and had come with it. Florence was almost seventeen, when, in her lonely musings, she was conscious of these thoughts.

She was often alone now, for the old association between her and her mamma was greatly changed. At the time of her father's accident, and when he was lying in his room downstairs, Florence had first observed that Edith avoided her. Wounded and shocked, and yet unable to reconcile this with her affection when they did meet, she sought her in her own room at night, once more.

'Mamma,' said Florence, stealing softly to her side, 'have I offended you?'

Edith answered 'No.'

'I must have done something,' said Florence. 'Tell me what it is. You have changed your manner to me, dear mamma. I cannot say how instantly I feel the least change; for I love you with my whole heart.'

'As I do you,' said Edith. 'Ah, Florence, believe me never more than now!'

'Why do you go away from me so often, and keep away?' asked Florence. 'And why do you sometimes look so strangely on me, dear mamma? You do so, do you not?'

Edith signified assent with her dark eyes.

'Why?' returned Florence imploringly. 'Tell me why, that I may know how to please you better; and tell me this shall not be so any more.'

'My Florence,' answered Edith, taking the hand that embraced her neck, and looking into the eyes that looked into hers so lovingly, as Florence knelt upon the ground before her; 'why it is, I cannot tell you. It is neither for me to say, nor you to hear; but that it is, and that it must be, I know. Should I do it if I did not?'

'Are *we* to be estranged, mamma?' asked Florence, gazing at her like one frightened.

Edith's silent lips formed 'Yes.'

Florence looked at her with increasing fear and wonder, until she could see her no more through the blinding tears that ran down her face.

'Florence! my life!' said Edith, hurriedly, 'listen to me. I cannot bear to see this grief. Be calmer. You see that I am composed, and is it nothing to me?'

She resumed her steady voice and manner as she said the latter words, and added presently—

'Not wholly estranged. Partially: and only that, in appearance, Florence, for in my own breast I am still the same to you, and ever will be. But what I do is not done for myself.'

'Is it for me, mamma?' asked Florence.

'It is enough,' said Edith, after a pause, 'to know what it is; why, matters little. Dear Florence, it is better—it is necessary—it must be—that our association should be less frequent. The confidence there has been between us must be broken off.'

'When?' cried Florence. 'Oh, mamma, when?'

'Now,' said Edith.

'For all time to come?' asked Florence.

'I do not say that,' answered Edith. 'I do not know that. Nor will I say that companionship between us is, at the best, an ill-assorted and unholy union, of which I might have known no good could come. My way here has been through paths that you will never tread, and my way henceforth may lie— God knows—I do not see it—'

Her voice died away into silence; and she sat looking at Florence, and almost shrinking from her, with the same strange dread and wild avoidance that Florence had noticed once before. The same dark pride and rage succeeded, sweeping over her form and features like an angry chord across the strings of a wild harp. But no softness or humility ensued on that. She did not lay her head down now, and weep, and say that she had no hope but in Florence. She held it up as if she were a beautiful Medusa, looking on him, face to face, to strike him dead. Yes, and she would have done it, if she had had the charm.

'Mamma,' said Florence, anxiously, 'there is a change in you, in more than what you say to me, which alarms me. Let me stay with you a little.'

'No,' said Edith, 'no, dearest. I am best left alone now, and I do best to keep apart from you, of all else. Ask me no questions, but believe that what I am when I seem fickle or capricious to you, I am not of my own will, or for myself. Believe, though we are stranger to each other than we have been, that I am unchanged to you within. Forgive me for having ever darkened your dark home—I am a shadow on it, I know well—and let us never speak of this again.'

'Mamma,' sobbed Florence, 'we are not to part?'

'We do this that we may not part,' said Edith. 'Ask no more. Go, Florence! My love and my remorse go with you!'

She embraced her, and dismissed her; and as Florence passed out of her room, Edith looked on the retiring figure, as if her good angel went out in that form, and left her to the haughty and indignant passions that now claimed her for their own, and set their seal upon her brow.

From that hour, Florence and she were, as they had been, no more. For days together, they would seldom meet, except at table, and when Mr. Dombey was present. Then Edith, imperious, inflexible, and silent, never looked at her. Whenever Mr. Carker was of the party, as he often was, during the progress of

Mr. Dombey's recovery, and afterwards, Edith held herself more removed from her, and was more distant towards her, than at other times. Yet she and Florence never encountered, when there was no one by, but she would embrace her as affectionately as of old, though not with the same relenting of her proud aspect; and often, when she had been out late, she would steal up to Florence's room, as she had been used to do, in the dark, and whisper 'good night,' on her pillow. When unconscious, in her slumber, of such visits, Florence would sometimes awake, as from a dream of those words, softly spoken, and would seem to feel the touch of lips upon her face. But less and less often as the months went on.

And now the void in Florence's own heart began again, indeed, to make a solitude around her. As the image of the father whom she loved had insensibly become a mere abstraction, so Edith, following the fate of all the rest about whom her affections had entwined themselves, was fleeting, fading, growing paler in the distance, every day. Little by little, she receded from Florence, like the retiring ghost of what she had been; little by little, the chasm between them widened and seemed deeper; little by little, all the power of earnestness and tenderness she had shown, was frozen up in the bold, angry hardihood with which she stood, upon the brink of a deep precipice unseen by Florence, daring to look down.

There was but one consideration to set against the heavy loss of Edith, and though it was slight comfort to her burdened heart, she tried to think it some relief. No longer divided between her affection and duty to the two, Florence could love both and do no injustice to either. As shadows of her fond imagination, she could give them equal place in her own bosom. and wrong them with no doubts.

So she tried to do.   At times, and often too, wondering speculations on the cause of this change in Edith would obtrude themselves upon her mind and frighten her; but in the calm of its abandonment once more to silent grief and loneliness, it was not a curious mind.   Florence had only to remember that her star of promise was clouded in the general gloom that hung upon the house, and to weep and be resigned.

Thus living, in a dream wherein the overflowing love of her young heart expended itself on airy forms, and in a real world where she had experienced little but the rolling back of that strong tide upon itself, Florence grew to be seventeen.   Timid and retiring as her solitary life had made her, it had not embittered her sweet temper, or her earnest nature.   A child in innocent simplicity; a woman in her modest self-reliance, and her deep intensity of feeling; both child and woman seemed at once expressed in her fair face and fragile delicacy of shape, and gracefully to mingle there;—as if the spring should be unwilling to depart when summer came, and sought to blend the earlier beauties of the flowers with their bloom.   But in her thrilling voice, in her calm eyes, sometimes in a strange ethereal light that seemed to rest upon her head, and always in a certain pensive air upon her beauty, there was an expression, such as had been seen in the dead boy; and the council in the servants' hall whispered so among themselves, and shook their heads, and ate and drank the more, in a closer bond of good-fellowship.

This observant body had plenty to say of Mr. and Mrs. Dombey, and of Mr. Carker, who appeared to be a mediator between them, and who came and went as if he were trying to make peace, but never could. They all deplored the uncomfortable state of affairs, and all agreed that Mrs. Pipchin (whose unpopularity was not to be surpassed) had some hand in it; but, upon the whole, it was agreeable to have so good a subject for a rallying point, and they made a great deal of it, and enjoyed themselves very much.

The general visitors who came to the house, and those among whom Mr. and Mrs. Dombey visited, thought it a pretty equal match, as to haughtiness, at all events, and thought nothing more about it. The young lady with the back did not appear for some time after Mrs. Skewton's death; observing to some particular friends, with her usual engaging little scream, that she couldn't separate the family from a notion of tombstones, and horrors of that sort; but when she did come, she saw nothing wrong, except Mr. Dombey's wearing a bunch of gold seals to his watch, which shocked her very much, as an exploded superstition. This youthful fascinator considered a daughter-in-law objectionable in principle; otherwise, she had nothing to say against Florence, but that she sadly wanted 'style'—which might mean back, perhaps. Many, who only came to the house on state occasions, hardly knew who Florence was, and said, going home, 'Indeed, was *that* Miss Dombey, in the corner? Very pretty, but a little delicate and thoughtful in appearance!'

None the less so, certainly, for her life of the last six months, Florence took her seat at the dinner-table, on the day before the second anniversary of her father's marriage to Edith (Mrs. Skewton had been lying stricken with paralysis when the first came round), with an uneasiness, amounting to dread. She had no other warrant for it, than the occasion, the expression of her father's face, in the hasty glance she caught of it, and the presence of Mr. Carker, which, always unpleasant to her, was more so on this day, than she had ever felt it before.

Edith was richly dressed, for she and Mr. Dombey were engaged in the evening to some large assembly, and the dinner-hour that day was late. She did not appear until they were seated at table, when Mr. Carker rose and led her to her chair. Beautiful and lustrous as she was, there was that in her face and air which seemed to separate her hopelessly from Florence, and from every one, for ever more. And yet, for an instant, Florence saw a beam of kindness in her eyes, when they were turned on her, that made the distance to which she had withdrawn herself, a greater cause of sorrow and regret than ever.

There was very little said at dinner. Florence heard her father speak to Mr. Carker sometimes on business matters, and heard him softly reply, but she paid little attention to what they said, and only wished the dinner at an end. When the dessert was placed upon the table, and they were left alone with no servant in attendance, Mr. Dombey, who had been several times clearing his throat in a manner that augured no good, said—

'Mrs. Dombey, you know, I suppose, that I have instructed the housekeeper that there will be some company to dinner here to-morrow.'

'I do not dine at home,' she answered.

'Not a large party,' pursued Mr. Dombey, with an indifferent assumption of not having heard her; 'merely some twelve or fourteen. My sister, Major Bagstock, and some others whom you know but slightly.'

'I do not dine at home,' she repeated.

'However doubtful reason I may have, Mrs. Dombey,' said Mr. Dombey, still going majestically on, as if she had not spoken, 'to hold the occasion in very pleasant remembrance just now, there are appearances in these things which must be maintained before the world. If you have no respect for yourself, Mrs. Dombey—'

'I have none,' she said.

'Madam,' cried Mr. Dombey, striking his hand upon the table, 'hear me if you please. I say, if you have no respect for yourself—'

'And *I* say I have none,' she answered.

He looked at her; but the face she showed him in return would not have changed, if death itself had looked.

'Carker,' said Mr. Dombey, turning more quietly to that gentleman, 'as you have been my medium of communication with Mrs. Dombey on former occasions, and as I choose to preserve the decencies of life, so far as I am individually concerned, I will trouble you to have the goodness to inform Mrs. Dombey that if she has no respect for herself, I have some respect for *my*self, and therefore insist on my arrangements for to-morrow.'

'Tell your sovereign master, sir,' said Edith, 'that I will take leave to speak to him on this subject by-and-by, and that I will speak to him alone.'

'Mr. Carker, madam,' said her husband, 'being in possession of the reason which obliges me to refuse you that privilege, shall be absolved from the delivery of any such message.' He saw her eyes move, while he spoke, and followed them with his own.

'Your daughter is present, sir,' said Edith.

'My daughter will remain present,' said Mr. Dombey.

Florence, who had risen, sat down again, hiding her face in her hands, and trembling.

'My daughter, madam'—began Mr. Dombey.

But Edith stopped him, in a voice which, although not raised in the least, was so clear, emphatic, and distinct, that it might have been heard in a whirlwind.

'I tell you I will speak to you alone,' she said. 'If you are not mad, heed what I say.'

'I have authority to speak to you, madam,' returned her husband, 'when and where I please; and it is my pleasure to speak here and now.'

She rose up as if to leave the room; but sat down again, and looking at him with all outward composure, said, in the same voice—

'You shall!'

'I must tell you first, that there is a threatening appearance in your manner, madam,' said Mr. Dombey, 'which does not become you.'

She laughed. The shaken diamonds in her hair started and trembled. There are fables of precious stones that would turn pale, their wearer being in danger. Had these been such, their imprisoned rays of light would have taken flight that moment, and they would have been as dull as lead.

Carker listened, with his eyes cast down.

'As to my daughter, madam,' said Mr. Dombey, resuming the thread of his discourse, 'it is by no means inconsistent with her duty to me, that she should know what conduct to avoid. At present you are a very strong example to her of this kind, and I hope she may profit by it.'

'I would not stop you now,' returned his wife, immoveable in eye, and voice, and attitude; 'I would not rise and go away, and save you the utterance of one word, if the room were burning.'

Mr. Dombey moved his head, as if in a sarcastic acknowledgment of the attention, and resumed. But not with so much self-possession as before; for Edith's quick uneasiness in reference to Florence, and Edith's indifference to him and his censure, chafed and galled him like a stiffening wound.

'Mrs. Dombey,' said he, 'it may not be inconsistent

with my daughter's improvement to know how very much to be lamented, and how necessary to be corrected, a stubborn disposition is, especially when it is indulged in—unthankfully indulged in, I will add—after the gratification of ambition and interest. Both of which, I believe, had some share in inducing you to occupy your present station at this board.'

'No! I would not rise, and go away, and save you the utterance of one word,' she repeated, exactly as befort, 'if the room were burning.'

'It may be natural enough, Mrs. Dombey,' he pursued, 'that you should be uneasy in the presence of any auditors of these disagreeable truths; though why—' he could not hide his real feelings here, or keep his eyes from glancing gloomily at Florence—'why any one can give them greater force and point than myself, whom they so nearly concern, I do not pretend to understand. It may be natural enough that you should object to hear, in anybody's presence, that there is a rebellious principle within you which you cannot curb too soon; which you must curb, Mrs. Dombey; and which, I regret to say, I remember to have seen manifested—with some doubt and displeasure, on more than one occasion before our marriage—towards your deceased mother. But you have the remedy in your own hands. I by no means forgot, when I began, that my daughter was present, Mrs. Dombey. I beg *you* will not forget, to-morrow, that there are several persons present; and that, with some regard to appearances, you will receive your company in a becoming manner.'

'So it is not enough,' said Edith, 'that you know what has passed between yourself and me; it is not enough that you can look here,' pointing at Carker, who still listened, with his eyes cast down, 'and be reminded of the affronts you have put upon me; it

is not enough that you can look here,' pointing to
Florence with a hand that slightly trembled for the
first and only time, 'and think of what you have done,
and of the ingenious agony, daily, hourly, constant,
you have made me feel in doing it; it is not enough
that this day, of all others in the year, is memorable
to me for a struggle (well-deserved, but not conceiv-
able by such as you) in which I wish I had died!
You add to all this, do you, the last crowning meanness of making *her* a witness of the depth to which I
have fallen; when you know that you have made me
sacrifice to her peace, the only gentle feeling and interest of my life, when you know that for her sake,
I would now if I could—but I *can not,* my soul recoils
from you too much—submit myself wholly to your
will and be the meekest vassal that you have!'

This was not the way to minister to Mr. Dombey's
greatness. The old feeling was roused by what she
said, into a stronger and fiercer existence than it had
ever had. Again, his neglected child, at this rough
passage of his life, put forth by even this rebellious
woman, as powerful where he was powerless, and
everything where he was nothing!

He turned on Florence, as if it were she who had
spoken, and bade her leave the room. Florence with
her covered face obeyed, trembling and weeping as she
went.

'I understand, madam,' said Mr. Dombey, with an
angry flush of triumph, 'the spirit of opposition that
turned your affections in that channel, but they have
been met, Mrs. Dombey; they have been met, and
turned back!'

'The worse for you!' she answered, with her voice
and manner still unchanged. 'Aye!' for he turned
sharply when she said so, 'what is the worse for me, is

twenty million times the worse for you. Heed that, if you heed nothing else.'

The arch of diamonds spanning her dark hair, flashed and glittered like a starry bridge. There was no warning in them, or they would have turned as dull and dim as tarnished honour. Carker still sat and listened, with his eyes cast down.

'Mrs. Dombey,' said Mr. Dombey, resuming as much as he could of his arrogant composure, 'you will not conciliate me, or turn me from any purpose, by this course of conduct.'

'It is the only true although it is a faint expression of what is within me,' she replied. 'But if I thought it would conciliate you, I would repress it, if it were repressible by any human effort. I will do nothing that you ask.'

'I am not accustomed to ask, Mrs. Dombey,' he observed; 'I direct.'

'I will hold no place in your house to-morrow, or on any recurrence of to-morrow. I will be exhibited to no one, as the refractory slave you purchased, such a time. If I kept my marriage-day, I would keep it as a day of shame. Self-respect! appearances before the world! what are these to me? You have done all you can to make them nothing to me, and they *are* nothing.'

'Carker,' said Mr. Dombey, speaking with knitted brows, and after a moment's consideration, 'Mrs. Dombey is so forgetful of herself and me in all this, and places me in a position so unsuited to my character, that I must bring this state of matters to a close.'

'Release me, then,' said Edith, immoveable in voice, in look, and bearing, as she had been throughout, 'from the chain by which I am bound. Let me go.'

'Madam?' exclaimed Mr. Dombey.

'Loose me. Set me free!'

'Madam?' he repeated, 'Mrs. Dombey?'

'Tell him,' said Edith, addressing her proud face to Carker, 'that I wish for a separation between us. That there had better be one. That I recommend it to him. Tell him it may take place on his own terms —his wealth is nothing to me—but that it cannot be too soon.'

'Good heaven, Mrs. Dombey!' said her husband, with supreme amazement, 'do you imagine it possible that I could ever listen to such a proposition? Do you know who I am, madam? Do you know what I represent? Did you ever hear of Dombey and Son? People to say that Mr. Dombey—Mr. Dombey!— was separated from his wife! Common people to talk of Mr. Dombey and his domestic affairs! Do you seriously think, Mrs. Dombey, that I would permit my name to be handed about in such connection? Pooh, pooh, madam! Fie for shame! You're absurd.' Mr. Dombey absolutely laughed.

But not as she did. She had better have been dead than laugh as she did, in reply, with her intent look fixed upon him. He had better have been dead, than sitting there, in his magnificence, to hear her.

'No, Mrs. Dombey,' he resumed, 'No, madam. There is no possibility of separation between you and me, and therefore I the more advise you to be awakened to a sense of duty. And, Carker, as I was about to say to you—'

Mr. Carker, who had sat and listened all this time, now raised his eyes, in which there was a bright unusual light.

—'As I was about to say to you,' resumed Mr. Dombey, 'I must beg you, now that matters have come to this, to inform Mrs. Dombey, that it is not the rule of my life to allow myself to be thwarted by

anybody—anybody, Carker—or to suffer anybody to
be paraded as a stronger motive for obedience in
those who owe obedience to me than I am myself.
The mention that has been made of my daughter,
and the use that is made of my daughter, in opposition to me, are unnatural.   Whether my daughter is
in actual concert with Mrs. Dombey, I do not know,
and do not care; but after what Mrs. Dombey has said
to-day, and my daughter has heard to-day, I beg you
to make known to Mrs. Dombey, that if she continues
to make this house the scene of contention it has become, I shall consider my daughter responsible in
some degree, on that lady's own avowal, and shall
visit her with my severe displeasure.   Mrs. Dombey
has asked "whether it is not enough," that she had
done this and that.   You will please to answer no, it
is not enough.'

'A moment!' cried Carker, interposing, 'permit
me! painful as my position is, at the best, and unusually painful in seeming to entertain a different
opinion from you,' addressing Mr. Dombey, 'I must
ask, had you not better reconsider the question of a
separation?   I know how incompatible it appears
with your high public position, and I know how determined you are when you give Mrs. Dombey to
understand'—the light in his eyes fell upon her as
he separated his words each from each, with the distinctness of so many bells—'that nothing but death
can ever part you.   Nothing else.   But when you
consider that Mrs. Dombey, by living in this house,
and making it as you have said, a scene of contention,
not only has her part in that contention, but compro-
mises Miss Dombey every day (for I know how
determined you are), will you not relieve her from a
continual irritation of spirit, and a continual sense of
being unjust to another, almost intolerable?   Does

this not seem like—I do not say it is—sacrificing Mrs. Dombey to the preservation of your pre-eminent and unassailable position?'

Again the light in his eyes fell upon her, as she stood looking at her husband: now with an extraordinary and awful smile upon her face.

'Carker,' returned Mr. Dombey, with a supercilious frown, and in a tone that was intended to be final, 'you mistake your position in offering advice to me on such a point, and you mistake me (I am surprised to find) in the character of your advice. I have no more to say.'

'Perhaps,' said Carker, with an unusual and inde-finable taunt in his air, '*you* mistook my position, when you honoured me with the negotiations in which I have been engaged here'—with a motion of his hand towards Mrs. Dombey.

'Not at all, sir, not at all,' returned the other haughtily. 'You were employed—'

'Being an inferior person, for the humiliation of Mrs. Dombey. I forgot. Oh, yes, it was expressly understood!' said Carker. 'I beg your pardon!'

As he bent his head to Mr. Dombey, with an air of deference that accorded ill with his words, though they were humbly spoken, he moved it round towards her, and kept his watching eyes that way.

She had better have turned hideous and dropped dead, than have stood up with such a smile upon her face, in such a fallen spirit's majesty of scorn and beauty. She lifted her hand to the tiara of bright jewels radiant on her head, and, plucking it off with a force that dragged and strained her rich black hair with heedless cruelty, and brought it tumbling wildly on her shoulders, cast the gems upon the ground. From each arm, she unclasped a diamond bracelet, flung it down, and trod upon the glittering heap.

Without a word, without a shadow on the fire of her bright eye, without abatement of her awful smile, she looked on Mr. Dombey to the last, in moving to the door; and left him.

Florence had heard enough before quitting the room, to know that Edith loved her yet; that she had suffered for her sake; and that she had kept her sacrifices quiet, lest they should trouble her peace. She did not want to speak to her of this—she could not, remembering to whom she was opposed—but she wished, in one silent and affectionate embrace, to assure her that she felt it all, and thanked her.

Her father went out alone, that evening, and Florence issuing from her own chamber soon afterwards, went about the house in search of Edith, but unavailingly. She was in her own rooms, where Florence had long ceased to go, and did not dare to venture now, lest she should unconsciously engender new trouble. Still Florence hoping to meet her before going to bed, changed from room to room, and wandered through the house so splendid and so dreary, without remaining anywhere.

She was crossing a gallery of communication that opened at some little distance on the staircase, and was only lighted on great occasions, when she saw, through the opening, which was an arch, the figure of a man coming down some few stairs opposite. Instinctively apprehensive of her father, whom she supposed it was, she stopped, in the dark, gazing through the arch into the light. But it was Mr. Carker coming down alone, and looking over the railing into the hall. No bell was rung to announce his departure, and no servant was in attendance. He went down quietly, opened the door for himself, glided out, and shut it softly after him.

Her invincible repugnance to this man, and perhaps the stealthy act of watching any one, which, even under such innocent circumstances, is in a manner guilty and oppressive, made Florence shake from head to foot. Her blood seemed to run cold. As soon as she could—for at first she felt an insurmountable dread of moving—she went quickly to her own room and locked her door; but even then, shut in with her dog beside her, felt a chill sensation of horror, as if there were danger brooding somewhere near her.

It invaded her dreams and disturbed the whole night. Rising in the morning, unrefreshed, and with a heavy recollection of the domestic unhappiness of the preceding day, she sought Edith again in all the rooms, and did so, from time to time, all the morning. But she remained in her own chamber, and Florence saw nothing of her. Learning, however, that the projected dinner at home was put off, Florence thought it likely that she would go out in the evening to fulfil the engagement she had spoken of; and resolved to try and meet her, then, upon the staircase.

When the evening had set in, she heard, from the room in which she sat on purpose, a footstep on the stairs that she thought to be Edith's. Hurrying out, and up towards her room, Florence met her immediately, coming down alone.

What was Florence's affright and wonder when, at sight of her, with her tearful face, and outstretched arms, Edith recoiled and shrieked!

'Don't come near me!' she cried. 'Keep away! Let me go by!'

'Mamma!' said Florence.

'Don't call me by that name! Don't speak to me! Don't look at me!—Florence!' shrinking back, as Florence moved a step towards her, 'don't touch me!'

As Florence stood transfixed before the haggard

FLORENCE AND EDITH ON THE STAIRCASE.

face and staring eyes, she noted, as in a dream, that Edith spread her hands over them, and shuddering through all her form, and crouching down against the wall, crawled by her like some lower animal, sprang up, and fled away.

Florence dropped upon the stairs in a swoon; and was found there by Mrs. Pipchin, she supposed. She knew nothing more, until she found herself lying on her own bed, with Mrs. Pipchin and some servants standing round her.

'Where is mamma?' was her first question.

'Gone out to dinner,' said Mrs. Pipchin.

'And papa?'

'Mr. Dombey is in his own room, Miss Dombey,' said Mrs. Pipchin, 'and the best thing you can do, is to take off your things and go to bed this minute.' This was the sagacious woman's remedy for all complaints, particularly lowness of spirits and inability to sleep; for which offences, many young victims in the days of the Brighton Castle had been committed to bed at ten o'clock in the morning.

Without promising obedience, but on the plea of desiring to be very quiet, Florence disengaged herself, as soon as she could, from the ministration of Mrs. Pipchin and her attendants. Left alone, she thought of what had happened on the staircase, at first in doubt of its reality; then with tears; then with an indescribable and terrible alarm, like that she had felt the night before.

She determined not to go to bed until Edith returned, and if she could not speak to her, at least to be sure that she was safe at home. What indistinct and shadowy dread moved Florence to this resolution, she did not know, and did not dare to think. She only knew that until Edith came back, there was no repose for her aching head or throbbing heart.

The evening deepened into night: midnight came; no Edith.

Florence could not read, or rest a moment. She paced her own room, opened the door, and paced the staircase-gallery outside, looked out of window on the night, listened to the wind blowing and the rain falling, sat down and watched the faces in the fire, got up and watched the moon flying like a storm-driven ship through the sea of clouds.

All the house was gone to bed, except two servants who were waiting the return of their mistress, downstairs.

One o'clock. The carriages that rumbled in the distance, turned away, or stopped short, or went past; the silence gradually deepened, and was more and more rarely broken, save by a rush of wind or sweep of rain. Two o'clock. No Edith!

Florence, more agitated, paced her room, and paced the gallery outside; and looked out at the night, blurred and wavy with the rain drops on the glass, and the tears in her own eyes; and looked up at the hurry in the sky, so different from the repose below, and yet so tranquil and solitary. Three o'clock. There was a terror in every ash that dropped out of the fire. No Edith yet.

More and more agitated, Florence paced her room, and paced the gallery, and looked out at the moon with a new fancy of her likeness to a pale fugitive hurrying away and hiding her guilty face. Four struck! Five! No Edith yet.

But now there was some cautious stir in the house; and Florence found that Mrs. Pipchin had been awakened by one of those who sat up, had risen and had gone down to her father's door. Stealing lower down the stairs, and observing what passed, she saw her father come out in his morning gown, and start when he was told his wife had not come home. He despatched a messenger to the stables to inquire whether the coachman was there; and while the man was gone, dressed himself very hurriedly.

The man came back, in great haste, bringing the coachman with him, who said he had been at home and in bed since ten o'clock. He had driven his mistress to her old house in Brook Street, where she had been met by Mr. Carker—

Florence stood upon the very spot where she had seen him coming down. Again she shivered with the nameless terror of that sight, and had hardly steadiness enough to hear and understand what followed.

—Who had told him, the man went on to say, that his mistress would not want the carriage to go home in; and had dismissed him.

She saw her father turn white in the face, and heard him ask in a quick, trembling voice for Mrs. Dombey's maid. The whole house was roused; for she was there, in a moment, very pale too, and speaking incoherently.

She said she had dressed her mistress early—full two hours before she went out—and had been told, as she often was, that she would not be wanted at night. She had just come from her mistress's rooms, but—

'But what! what was it?' Florence heard her father demand like a madman.

'But the inner dressing-room was locked, and the key gone.'

Her father seized a candle that was flaming on the ground—some one had put it down there, and forgotten it—and came running upstairs with such fury, that Florence, in her fear, had hardly time to fly before him. She heard him striking in the door as she

ran on, with her hands widely spread, and her hair
streaming, and her face like a distracted person's,
back to her own room.

When the door yielded, and he rushed in, what did
he see there? No one knew. But thrown down in a
costly mass upon the ground, was every ornament she
had had, since she had been his wife: every dress
she had worn; and everything she had possessed.
This was the room in which he had seen, in yonder
mirror, the proud face discard him. This was the
room in which he had wondered, idly, how these things
would look when he should see them next!

Heaping them back into the drawers, and locking
them up in a rage of haste, he saw some papers on
the table. The deed of settlement he had executed
on the marriage, and a letter. He read that she was
gone. He read that he was dishonoured. He read
that she had fled, upon her shameful wedding-day,
with the man whom he had chosen for her humiliation; and he tore out of the room, and out of the
house, with a frantic idea of finding her yet, at the
place to which she had been taken, and beating all
trace of beauty out of the triumphant face with his
bare hand.

Florence, not knowing what she did, put on a shawl
and bonnet, in a dream of running through the streets
until she found Edith, and then clasping her in her
arms, to save and bring her back. But when she
hurried out upon the staircase, and saw the frightened servants going up and down with lights, and
whispering together, and falling away from her
father as he passed down, she awoke to a sense of
her own powerlessness: and hiding in one of the great
rooms that had been made gorgeous for *this*, felt as
if her heart would burst with grief.

Compassion for her father was the first distinct

emotion that made head against the flood of sorrow which overwhelmed her. Her constant nature turned to him in his distress, as fervently and faithfully, as if, in his prosperity, he had been the embodiment of that idea which had gradually become so faint and dim. Although she did not know, otherwise than through the suggestions of a shapeless fear, the full extent of his calamity, he stood before her wronged and deserted; and again her yearning love impelled her to his side.

He was not long away: for Florence was yet weeping in the great room and nourishing these thoughts, when she heard him come back. He ordered the servants to set about their ordinary occupations, and went into his own apartment, where he trod so heavily that she could hear him walking up and down from end to end.

Yielding at once to the impulse of her affection, timid at all other times, but bold in its truth to him in his adversity, and undaunted by past repulse, Florence, dressed as she was, hurried downstairs. As she set her light foot in the hall, he came out of his room. She hastened towards him unchecked, with her arms stretched out, and crying 'Oh dear, dear papa!' as if she would have clasped him round the neck.

And so she would have done. But in his frenzy, he lifted up his cruel arm, and struck her, crosswise, with that heaviness, that she tottered on the marble floor; and as he dealt the blow, he told her what Edith was, and bade her follow her, since they had always been in league.

She did not sink down at his feet; she did not shut out the sight of him with her trembling hands; she did not weep; she did not utter one word of reproach. But she looked at him, and a cry of desolation issued from her heart. For as she looked, she saw him murdering that fond idea to which she had held in spite of him. She saw his cruelty, neglect, and hatred dominant above it, and stamping it down. She saw she had no father upon earth, and ran out, orphaned, from his house.

Ran out of his house. A moment, and her hand was on the lock, the cry was on her lips, his face was there, made paler by the yellow candles hastily put down and guttering away, and by the daylight coming in above the door. Another moment, and the close darkness of the shut-up house (forgotten to be opened, though it was long since day) yielded to the unexpected glare and freedom of the morning; and Florence, with her head bent down to hide her agony of tears, was in the streets.

CHAPTER XLVIII

THE FLIGHT OF FLORENCE

In the wildness of her sorrow, shame, and terror, the forlorn girl hurried through the sunshine of a bright morning, as if it were the darkness of a winter night. Wringing her hands and weeping bitterly, insensible to everything but the deep wound in her breast, stunned by the loss of all she loved, left like the sole survivor on a lonely shore from the wreck of a great vessel, she fled without a thought, without a hope, without a purpose, but to fly somewhere—anywhere.

The cheerful vista of the long street, burnished by the morning light, the sight of the blue sky and airy clouds, the vigorous freshness of the day, so flushed and rosy in its conquest of the night, awakened no responsive feelings in her so hurt bosom. Some-

where, anywhere, to hide her head! somewhere, anywhere, for refuge, never more to look upon the place
from which she fled!

But there were people going to and fro; there were
opening shops, and servants at the doors of houses;
there was the rising clash and roar of the day's struggle. Florence saw surprise and curiosity in the faces
flitting past her; saw long shadows coming back upon
the pavement; and heard voices that were strange to
her asking her where she went, and what the matter
was; and though these frightened her the more at
first, and made her hurry on the faster, they did her
the good service of recalling her in some degree to
herself, and reminding her of the necessity of great
composure.

Where to go? Still somewhere, anywhere! still
going on; but where! She thought of the only other
time she had been lost in the wide wilderness of London—though not lost as now—and went that way.
To the home of Walter's uncle.

Checking her sobs, and drying her swollen eyes,
and endeavouring to calm the agitation of her manner, so as to avoid attracting notice, Florence, resolving to keep to the more quiet streets as long as she
could, was going on more quietly herself, when a
familiar little shadow darted past upon the sunny
pavement, stopped short, wheeled about, came close
to her, made off again, bounded round and round
her, and Diogenes, panting for breath, and yet making the street ring with his glad bark, was at her feet.

'Oh, Di! oh, dear, true, faithful Di, how did you
come here? How could I ever leave you, Di, who
would never leave me?'

Florence bent down on the pavement, and laid his
rough, old, loving, foolish head against her breast, and
they got up together, and went on together; Di more

off the ground than on it, endeavouring to kiss his mistress flying, tumbling over and getting up again without the least concern, dashing at big dogs in a jocose defiance of his species, terrifying with touches of his nose young housemaids who were cleaning doorsteps, and continually stopping, in the midst of a thousand extravagances, to look back at Florence, and bark until all the dogs within hearing answered, and all the dogs who could come out, came out to stare at him.

With this last adherent, Florence hurried away in the advancing morning, and the strengthening sunshine, to the City. The roar soon grew more loud, the passengers more numerous, the shops more busy, until she was carried onward in a stream of life setting that way, and flowing, indifferently, past marts and mansions, prisons, churches, market-places, wealth, poverty, good, and evil, like the broad river side by side with it, awakened from its dreams of rushes, willows, and green moss, and rolling on, turbid and troubled, among the works and cares of men, to the deep sea.

At length the quarters of the little midshipman arose in view. Nearer yet, and the little midshipman himself was seen upon his post, intent as ever, on his observations. Nearer yet, and the door stood open, inviting her to enter. Florence, who had again quickened her pace, as she approached the end of her journey, ran across the road (closely followed by Diogenes, whom the bustle had somewhat confused), ran in, and sank upon the threshold of the well-remembered little parlour.

The captain, in his glazed hat, was standing over the fire, making his morning's cocoa, with that elegant trifle, his watch, upon the chimney-piece, for easy reference during the progress of the cookery. Hearing a footstep and the rustle of a dress, the captain turned with a palpitating remembrance of the dreadful Mrs. MacStinger, at the instant when Florence made a motion with her hand towards him, reeled, and fell upon the floor.

The captain, pale as Florence, pale in the very knobs upon his face, raised her like a baby, and laid her on the same old sofa upon which she had slumbered long ago.

'It's Heart's Delight!' said the captain, looking intently in her face. 'It's the sweet creetur grow'd a woman!'

Captain Cuttle was so respectful of her, and had such a reverence for her, in this new character, that he would not have held her in his arms, while she was unconscious, for a thousand pounds.

'My Heart's Delight!' said the captain, withdrawing to a little distance, with the greatest alarm and sympathy depicted on his countenance. 'If you can hail Ned Cuttle with a finger, do it!'

But Florence did not stir.

'My Heart's Delight!' said the trembling captain. 'For the sake of Wal'r drownded in the briny deep, turn to, and histe up something or another, if able.'

Finding her insensible to this impressive adjuration also, Captain Cuttle snatched from his breakfast-table a basin of cold water, and sprinkled some upon her face. Yielding to the urgency of the case, the captain then, using his immense hand with extraordinary gentleness, relieved her of her bonnet, moistened her lips and forehead, put back her hair, covered her feet with his own coat which he pulled off for the purpose, patted her hand—so small in his, that he was struck with wonder when he touched it

—and seeing that her eyelids quivered, and that her lips began to move, continued these restorative applications with a better heart.

'Cheerily,' said the captain. 'Cheerily! Stand by, my pretty one, stand by! There! You 're better now. Steady 's the word, and steady it is. Keep her so! Drink a little drop o' this here,' said the captain. 'There you are! What cheer now, my pretty, what cheer now?'

At this stage of her recovery, Captain Cuttle, with an imperfect association of a watch with a physician's treatment of a patient, took his own down from the mantel-shelf, and holding it out on his hook, and taking Florence's hand in his, looked steadily from one to the other, as expecting the dial to do something.

'What cheer, my pretty?' said the captain. 'What cheer now? You 've done her some good, my lad, I believe,' said the captain, under his breath, and throwing an approving glance upon his watch. 'Put you back half an hour every morning, and about another quarter towards the afternoon, and you 're a watch as can be ekalled by few and excelled by none. What cheer, my lady lass!'

'Captain Cuttle! Is it you?' exclaimed Florence, raising herself a little.

'Yes, yes, my lady lass,' said the captain, hastily deciding in his own mind upon the superior elegance of that form of address, as the most courtly he could think of.

'Is Walter's uncle here?' asked Florence.

'Here, pretty!' returned the captain. 'He an't been here this many a long day. He an't been heerd on, since he sheered off arter poor Wal'r. But,' said the captain, as a quotation, 'Though lost to sight, to memory dear, and England, home, and beauty!'

'Do you live here?' asked Florence.

'Yes, my lady lass,' returned the captain.

'Oh Captain Cuttle!' cried Florence, putting her hands together, and speaking wildly. 'Save me! keep me here! Let no one know where I am! I 'll tell you what has happened by and by, when I can. I have no one in the world to go to. Do not send me away!'

'Send *you* away, my lady lass!' exclaimed the captain. '*You*, my Heart's Delight! Stay a bit! We 'll put up this here dead-light, and take a double turn on the key!'

With these words, the captain, using his one hand and his hook with the greatest dexterity, got out the shutter of the door, put it up, made it all fast, and locked the door itself.

When he came back to the side of Florence, she took his hand, and kissed it. The helplessness of the action, the appeal it made to him, the confidence it expressed, the unspeakable sorrow in her face, the pain of mind she had too plainly suffered, and was suffering then, his knowledge of her past history, her present lonely, worn, and unprotected appearance, all so rushed upon the good captain together, that he fairly overflowed with compassion and gentleness.

'My lady lass,' said the captain, polishing the bridge of his nose with his arm until it shone like burnished copper, 'don't you say a word to Ed'ard Cuttle, until such times as you finds yourself a riding smooth and easy; which won't be to-day, nor yet to-morrow. And as to giving of you up, or reporting where you are, yes verily, and by God's help, so I won't, Church catechism, make a note on!'

This the captain said, reference and all, in one breath, and with much solemnity; taking off his hat at 'yes verily,' and putting it on again, when he had quite concluded.

Florence could do but one thing more to thank him, and to show him how she trusted in him; and she did it. Clinging to this rough creature as the last asylum of her bleeding heart, she laid her head upon his honest shoulder, and clasped him round his neck, and would have kneeled down to bless him, but that he divined her purpose, and held her up like a true man.

'Steady!' said the captain. 'Steady! You're too weak to stand, you see, my pretty, and must lie down here again. There, there!' To see the captain lift her on the sofa, and cover her with his coat, would have been worth a hundred state sights. 'And now,' said the captain, 'you must take some breakfast, lady lass, and the dog shall have some too. And arter that you shall go aloft to old Sol Gills's room, and fall asleep there, like a angel.'

Captain Cuttle patted Diogenes when he made allusion to him, and Diogenes met that overture graciously, half-way. During the administration of the restoratives he had clearly been in two minds whether to fly at the captain or to offer him his friendship, and he had expressed that conflict of feeling by alternate waggings of his tail, and displays of his teeth, with now and then a growl or so. But by this time his doubts were all removed. It was plain that he considered the captain one of the most amiable of men, and a man whom it was an honour to a dog to know.

In evidence of these convictions, Diogenes attended on the captain while he made some tea and toast, and showed a lively interest in his housekeeping. But it was in vain for the kind captain to make such preparations for Florence, who sorely tried to do some honour to them, but could touch nothing, and could only weep and weep again.

'Well, well!' said the compassionate captain, 'arter turning in, my Heart's Delight, you'll get more way

upon you.   Now, I'll serve out your allowance, my
lad.'   To Diogenes.   'And you shall keep guard on
your mistress aloft.'

Diogenes, however, although he had been eyeing
his intended breakfast with a watering mouth and
glistening eyes, instead of falling to, ravenously,
when it was put before him, pricked up his ears,
darted to the shop-door, and barked there furiously:
burrowing with his head at the bottom, as if he were
bent on mining his way out.

'Can there be anybody there!' asked Florence, in
alarm.

'No, my lady lass,' returned the captain.   'Who'd
stay there, without making any noise!   Keep up a
good heart, pretty.   It's only people going by.'

But for all that, Diogenes barked and barked, and
burrowed and burrowed, with pertinacious fury; and
whenever he stopped to listen, appeared to receive
some new conviction into his mind, for he set to, barking and burrowing again, a dozen times.   Even when
he was persuaded to return to his breakfast, he came
jogging back to it, with a very doubtful air; and was
off again, in another paroxysm, before touching a
morsel.

'If there should be some one listening and watching,' whispered Florence.   'Some one who saw me
come—who followed me, perhaps.'

'It an't the young woman, lady lass, is it?' said the
captain, taken with a bright idea.

'Susan?' said Florence, shaking her head.   'Ah no!
Susan has been gone from me a long time.'

'Not deserted, I hope?' said the captain.   'Don't
say that there young woman's run, my pretty!'

'Oh, no, no!' cried Florence.   'She is one of the
truest hearts in the world!'

The captain was greatly relieved by this reply, and

expressed his satisfaction by taking off his hard glazed hat, and dabbing his head all over with his handkerchief, rolled up like a ball, observing several times, with infinite complacency, and with a beaming countenance, that he know'd it.

'So you 're quiet now, are you, brother?' said the captain to Diogenes. 'There warn't nobody there, my lady lass, bless you!'

Diogenes was not so sure of that. The door still had an attraction for him at intervals; and he went snuffing about it, and growling to himself, unable to forget the subject. This incident, coupled with the captain's observation of Florence's fatigue and faintness, decided him to prepare Sol Gills's chamber as a place of retirement for her immediately. He therefore hastily betook himself to the top of the house, and made the best arrangement of it that his imagination and his means suggested.

It was very clean already; and the captain being an orderly man, and accustomed to make things shipshape, converted the bed into a couch, by covering it all over with a clean white drapery. By a similar contrivance, the captain converted the little dressing-table into a species of altar, on which he set forth two silver teaspoons, a flower-pot, a telescope, his celebrated watch, a pocket-comb, and a song-book, as a small collection of rarities, that made a choice appearance. Having darkened the window, and straightened the pieces of carpet on the floor, the captain surveyed these preparations with great delight, and descended to the little parlour again, to bring Florence to her bower.

Nothing would induce the captain to believe that it was possible for Florence to walk upstairs. If he could have got the idea into his head, he would have considered it an outrageous breach of hospitality to allow her to do so. Florence was too weak to dispute the point, and the captain carried her up out of hand, laid her down, and covered her with a great watch-coat.

'My lady lass!' said the captain, 'you 're as safe here as if you was at the top of St. Paul's Cathedral, with the ladder cast off. Sleep is what you want, afore all other things, and may you be able to show yourself smart with that there balsam for the still small woice of a wownded mind! When there 's anything you want, my Heart's Delight, as this here humble house or town can offer, pass the word to Ed'ard Cuttle, as 'll stand off and on outside that door, and that there man will wibrate with joy.' The captain concluded by kissing the hand that Florence stretched out to him, with the chivalry of any old knight-errant, and walking on tip-toe out of the room.

Descending to the little parlour, Captain Cuttle, after holding a hasty council with himself, decided to open the shop-door for a few minutes, and satisfy himself that now, at all events, there was no one loitering about it. Accordingly he set it open, and stood upon the threshold, keeping a bright look-out, and sweeping the whole street with his spectacles.

'How de do, Captain Gills?' said a voice beside him. The captain, looking down, found that he had been boarded by Mr. Toots while sweeping the horizon.

'How are you, my lad?' replied the captain.

'Well, I 'm pretty well, thank 'ee, Captain Gills,' said Mr. Toots. 'You know I 'm never quite what I could wish to be, now. I don't expect that I ever shall be any more.'

Mr. Toots never approached any nearer than this to the great theme of his life when in conversation with Captain Cuttle, on account of the agreement between them.

'Captain Gills,' said Mr. Toots, 'if I could have the pleasure of a word with you, it 's—it 's rather particular.'

'Why, you see, my lad,' replied the captain, leading the way into the parlour, 'I an't what you may call exactly free this morning; and therefore if you can clap on a bit, I should take it kindly.'

'Certainly, Captain Gills,' replied Mr. Toots, who seldom had any notion of the captain's meaning. 'To clap on, is exactly what I could wish to do. Naturally.'

'If so be, my lad,' returned the captain, 'do it!'

The captain was so impressed by the possession of his tremendous secret—by the fact of Miss Dombey being at that moment under his roof, while the innocent and unconscious Toots sat opposite to him—that a perspiration broke out on his forehead, and he found it impossible while slowly drying the same, glazed hat in hand, to keep his eyes off Mr. Toots's face. Mr. Toots, who himself appeared to have some secret reasons for being in a nervous state, was so unspeakably disconcerted by the captain's stare, that after looking at him vacantly for some time in silence, and shifting uneasily on his chair, he said—

'I beg your pardon, Captain Gills, but you don't happen to see anything particular in me, do you?'

'No, my lad,' returned the captain. 'No.'

'Because you know,' said Mr. Toots with a chuckle, 'I KNOW I 'm wasting away. You needn't at all mind alluding to that. I—I should like it. Burgess and Co. have altered my measure, I 'm in that state of thinness. It 's a gratification to me. I—I 'm glad of it. I—I 'd a great deal rather go into a decline, if I could. I 'm a mere brute you know, grazing upon the surface of the earth, Captain Gills.'

The more Mr. Toots went on in this way, the more the captain was weighed down by his secret, and stared at him. What with this cause of uneasiness, and his desire to get rid of Mr. Toots, the captain was in such a scared and strange condition, indeed, that if he had been in conversation with a ghost, he could hardly have evinced greater discomposure.

'But I was going to say, Captain Gills,' said Mr. Toots. 'Happening to be this way early this morning—to tell you the truth, I was coming to breakfast with you. As to sleep, you know, I never sleep now. I might be a watchman, except that I don't get any pay, and he's got nothing on his mind.'

'Carry on, my lad!' said the captain, in an admonitory voice.

'Certainly, Captain Gills,' said Mr. Toots. 'Perfectly true! Happening to be this way early this morning (an hour or so ago), and finding the door shut—'

'What! were *you* waiting there, brother?' demanded the captain.

'Not at all, Captain Gills,' returned Mr. Toots. 'I didn't stop a moment. I thought you were out. But the person said—by the bye you *don't* keep a dog *do* you, Captain Gills?'

The captain shook his head.

'To be sure,' said Mr. Toots, 'that's exactly what I said. I knew you didn't. There *is* a dog, Captain Gills, connected with—but excuse me. That's forbidden ground.'

The captain stared at Mr. Toots until he seemed to swell to twice his natural size; and again the perspiration broke out on the captain's forehead, when he thought of Diogenes taking it into his head to come down and make a third in the parlour.

'The person said,' continued Mr. Toots, 'that he had heard a dog barking in the shop: which I knew couldn't be, and I told him so. But he was as positive as if he had seen the dog.'

'What person, my lad?' inquired the captain.

'Why, you see there it is, Captain Gills,' said Mr. Toots, with a perceptible increase in the nervousness of his manner. 'It's not for me to say what may have taken place, or what may not have taken place. Indeed, I don't know. I get mixed up with all sorts of things that I don't quite understand, and I think there's something rather weak in my—in my head, in short.'

The captain nodded his own, as a mark of assent.

'But the person said, as we were walking away,' continued Mr. Toots, 'that you knew what, under existing circumstances, *might* occur—he said "might," very strongly—and that if you were requested to prepare yourself, you would, no doubt, come prepared.'

'Person, my lad?' the captain repeated.

'I don't know what person, I'm sure, Captain Gills,' replied Mr. Toots, 'I haven't the least idea. But coming to the door, I found him waiting there; and he said was I coming back again, and I said yes; and he said did I know you, and I said yes, I had the pleasure of your acquaintance—you had given me the pleasure of your acquaintance, after some persuasion; and he said, if that was the case, would I say to you what I *have* said, about existing circumstances and and coming prepared, and as soon as ever I saw you, would I ask you to step round the corner, if it was only for one minute, on most important business, to Mr. Brogley's the broker's. Now, I tell you what, Captain Gills—whatever it is, I am convinced it's very important; and if you like to step round, now, I'll wait here till you come back.'

The captain, divided between his fear of compromising Florence in some way by not going, and his horror of leaving Mr. Toots in possession of the house with a chance of finding out the secret, was a spectacle of mental disturbance that even Mr. Toots could not be blind to. But that young gentleman, considering his nautical friend as merely in a state of preparation for the interview he was going to have, was quite satisfied, and did not review his own discreet conduct without chuckles.

At length the captain decided, as the lesser of two evils, to run round to Brogley's the broker's: previously locking the door that communicated with the upper part of the house, and putting the key in his pocket. 'If so be,' said the captain to Mr. Toots, with not a little shame and hesitation, 'as you'll excuse my doing of it, brother.'

'Captain Gills,' returned Mr. Toots, 'whatever you do, is satisfactory to me.'

The captain thanked him heartily, and promising to come back in less than five minutes, went out in quest of the person who had intrusted Mr. Toots with this mysterious message. Poor Toots, left to himself, lay down upon the sofa, little thinking who had reclined there last, and, gazing up at the skylight and resigning himself to visions of Miss Dombey, lost all heed of time and place.

It was as well that he did so; for although the captain was not gone long, he was gone much longer than he had proposed. When he came back, he was very pale indeed, and greatly agitated, and even looked as if he had been shedding tears. He seemed to have lost the faculty of speech, until he had been to the cupboard and taken a dram of rum from the case-bottle, when he fetched a deep breath, and sat down in a chair with his hand before his face.

'Captain Gills,' said Toots, kindly, 'I hope and trust there's nothing wrong?'

'Thank 'ee, my lad, not a bit,' said the captain. 'Quite contrary.'

'You have the appearance of being overcome, Captain Gills,' observed Mr. Toots.

'Why, my lad, I *am* took aback,' the captain admitted. 'I am.'

'Is there anything I can do, Captain Gills?' inquired Mr. Toots. 'If there is, make use of me.'

The captain removed his hand from his face, looked at him with a remarkable expression of pity and tenderness, and took him by the hand and shook it hard.

'No, thank 'ee,' said the captain. 'Nothing. Only I'll take is as a favour if you'll part company for the present. I believe, brother,' wringing his hand again, 'that, after Wal'r, and on a different model, you're as good a lad as ever stepped.'

'Upon my word and honour, Captain Gills,' returned Mr. Toots, giving the captain's hand a preliminary slap before shaking it again, 'it's delightful to me to possess your good opinion. Thank 'ee.'

'And bear a hand and cheer up,' said the captain, patting him on the back. 'What! There's more than one sweet creetur in the world!'

'Not to me, Captain Gills,' replied Mr. Toots gravely. 'Not to me, I assure you. The state of my feelings towards Miss Dombey is of that unspeakable description, that my heart is a desert island, and she lives in it alone. I'm getting more used up every day, and I'm proud to be so. If you could see my legs when I take my boots off, you'd form some idea of what unrequited affection is. I have been prescribed bark, but I don't take it, for I don't wish to have any tone whatever given to my constitution.

I 'd rather not. This, however, is forbidden ground. Captain Gills, good-bye!'

Captain Cuttle cordially reciprocating the warmth of Mr. Toots's farewell, locked the door behind him, and shaking his head with the same remarkable expression of pity and tenderness as he had regarded him with before, went up to see if Florence wanted him.

There was an entire change in the captain's face as he went upstairs. He wiped his eyes with his handkerchief, and he polished the bridge of his nose with his sleeve as he had done already that morning, but his face was absolutely changed. Now, he might have been thought supremely happy; now, he might have been thought sad, but the kind of gravity that sat upon his features was quite new to them, and was as great an improvement to them as if they had undergone some sublimating process.

He knocked softly, with his hook, at Florence's door, twice or thrice; but, receiving no answer, ventured first to peep in, and then to enter: emboldened to take the latter step, perhaps, by the familiar recognition of Diogenes, who, stretched upon the ground by the side of her couch, wagged his tail, and winked his eyes at the captain, without being at the trouble of getting up.

She was sleeping heavily, and moaning in her sleep; and Captain Cuttle, with a perfect awe of her youth and beauty, and her sorrow, raised her head, and adjusted the coat that covered her, where it had fallen off, and darkened the window a little more that she might sleep on, and crept out again, and took his post of watch upon the stairs. All this, with a touch and tread as light as Florence's own.

Long may it remain in this mixed world a point not

easy of decision, which is the more beautiful evidence
of the Almighty's goodness—the delicate fingers that
are formed for sensitiveness and sympathy of touch,
and made to minister to pain and grief, or the rough
hard Captain Cuttle hand, that the heart teaches,
guides, and softens in a moment!

Florence slept upon her couch, forgetful of her
homelessness and orphanage, and Captain Cuttle
watched upon the stairs. A louder sob or moan than
usual, brought him sometimes to her door; but by
degrees she slept more peacefully, and the captain's
watch was undisturbed.

CHAPTER XLIX

THE MIDSHIPMAN MAKES A DISCOVERY

It was long before Florence awoke. The day was
in its prime, the day was in its wane, and still, uneasy
in mind and body, she slept on; unconscious of her
strange bed, of the noise and turmoil in the street, and
of the light that shone outside the shaded window.
Perfect unconsciousness of what had happened in the
home that existed no more, even the deep slumber of
exhaustion could not produce. Some undefined and
mournful recollection of it, dozing uneasily but never
sleeping, pervaded all her rest. A dull sorrow, like
a half-lulled sense of pain, was always present to
her; and her pale cheek was oftener wet with tears
than the honest captain, softly putting in his head
from time to time at the half-closed door, could have
desired to see it.

The sun was getting low in the west, and, glancing out of a red mist, pierced with its rays opposite
loop-holes and pieces of fretwork in the spires of city

churches, as if with golden arrows that struck through
and through them—and far away athwart the river
and its flat banks, it was gleaming like a path of fire
—and out at sea it was irradiating sails of ships—
and, looked towards, from quiet churchyards, upon
hill-tops in the country, it was steeping distant prospects in a flush and glow that seemed to mingle earth
and sky together in one glorious suffusion—when
Florence, opening her heavy eyes, lay at first, looking
without interest or recognition at the unfamiliar walls
around her, and listening in the same regardless manner to the noises in the street. But presently she
started up upon her couch, gazed round with a surprised and vacant look, and recollected all.

'My pretty,' said the captain, knocking at the door,
'what cheer!'

'Dear friend,' cried Florence, hurrying to him, 'is
it you?'

The captain felt so much pride in the name, and
was so pleased by the gleam of pleasure in her face,
when she saw him, that he kissed his hook, by way of
reply, in speechless gratification.

'What cheer, bright di'mond!' said the captain.

'I have surely slept very long,' returned Florence.
'When did I come here? Yesterday?'

'This here blessed day, my lady lass,' replied the
captain.

'Has there been no night? Is it still day?' asked
Florence.

'Getting on for evening now, my pretty,' said the
captain, drawing back the curtain of the window.
'See!'

Florence, with her hand upon the captain's arm, so
sorrowful and timid, and the captain with his rough
face and burly figure, so quietly protective of her,
stood in the rosy light of the bright evening sky, with-

out saying a word. However strange the form of
speech into which he might have fashioned the feeling,
if he had had to give it utterance, the captain felt,
as sensibly as the most eloquent of men could have
done, that there was something in the tranquil time
and in its softened beauty that would make the
wounded heart of Florence overflow; and that it was
better that such tears should have their way. So not
a word spake Captain Cuttle. But when he felt his
arm clasped closer, and when he felt the lonely head
come nearer to it, and lay itself against his homely
coarse blue sleeve, he pressed it gently with his rugged
hand, and understood it, and was understood.

'Better now, my pretty!' said the captain.
'Cheerily, cheerily; I'll go down below, and get some
dinner ready. Will you come down of your own
self, arterwards, pretty, or shall Ed'ard Cuttle come
and fetch you?'

As Florence assured him that she was quite able
to walk downstairs, the captain, though evidently
doubtful of his own hospitality in permitting it, left
her to do so, and immediately set about roasting a
fowl at the fire in the little parlour. To achieve his
cookery with the greater skill, he pulled off his coat,
tucked up his wristbands, and put on his glazed hat,
without which assistant he never applied himself to
any nice, or difficult undertaking.

After cooling her aching head and burning face in
the fresh water which the captain's care had provided
for her while she slept, Florence went to the little mirror to bind up her disordered hair. Then she knew—
in a moment, for she shunned it instantly—that on her
breast there was the darkening mark of an angry hand.

Her tears burst forth afresh at the sight; she was
ashamed and afraid of it; but it moved her to no
anger against him. Homeless and fatherless, she for-

gave him everything; hardly thought that she had
need to forgive him, or that she did; but she fled from
the idea of him as she had fled from the reality, and
he was utterly gone and lost. There was no such
being in the world.

What to do, or where to live, Florence—poor, inexperienced girl!—could not yet consider. She had
indistinct dreams of finding, a long way off, some
little sisters to instruct, who would be gentle with her,
and to whom, under some feigned name, she might
attach herself, and who would grow up in their happy
home, and marry, and be good to their old governess,
and perhaps intrust her, in time, with the education
of their own daughters. And she thought how
strange and sorrowful it would be, thus to become a
grey-haired woman, carrying her secret to the grave,
when Florence Dombey was forgotten. But it was
all dim and clouded to her now. She only knew that
she had no Father upon earth, and she said so, many
times, with her suppliant head hidden from all, but her
Father who was in Heaven.

Her little stock of money amounted to but a few
guineas. With a part of this, it would be necessary
to buy some clothes, for she had none but those she
wore. She was too desolate to think how soon her
money would be gone—too much a child in worldly
matters to be greatly troubled on that score yet, even
if her other trouble had been less. She tried to calm
her thoughts and stay her tears; to quiet the hurry
in her throbbing head, and bring herself to believe
that what had happened were but the events of a few
hours ago, instead of weeks or months, as they appeared; and went down to her kind protector.

The captain had spread the cloth with great care,
and was making some egg-sauce in a little saucepan;
basting the fowl from time to time during the process

with a strong interest, as it turned and browned on a string before the fire. Having propped Florence up with cushions on the sofa, which was already wheeled into a warm corner for her greater comfort, the captain pursued his cooking with extraordinary skill, making hot gravy in a second little saucepan, boiling a handful of potatoes in a third, never forgetting the egg-sauce in the first, and making an impartial round of basting and stirring with the most useful of spoons every minute. Besides these cares, the captain had to keep his eye on a diminutive frying-pan, in which some sausages were hissing and bubbling in a most musical manner; and there was never such a radiant cook as the captain looked, in the height and heat of these functions: it being impossible to say whether his face or his glazed hat shone the brighter.

The dinner being at length quite ready, Captain Cuttle dished and served it up, with no less dexterity than he had cooked it. He then dressed for dinner, by taking off his glazed hat and putting on his coat. That done, he wheeled the table close against Florence on the sofa, said grace, unscrewed his hook, screwed his fork into its place, and did the honours of the table.

'My lady lass,' said the captain, 'cheer up, and try to eat a deal. Stand by, my deary! Liver wing it is. Sarse it is. Sassage it is. And potato!' all which the captain ranged symmetrically on a plate, and pouring hot gravy on the whole with the useful spoon, set before his cherished guest.

'The whole row o' dead lights is up, for'ard, lady lass,' observed the captain, encouragingly, 'and everythink is made snug. Try and pick a bit, my pretty. If Wal'r was here—'

'Ah! If I had him for my brother now?' cried Florence.

'Don't! don't take on, my pretty!' said the captain,
'awast to obleege me! He *was* your nat'ral born
friend like, warn't he, pet?'

Florence had no words to answer with. She only
said, 'Oh, dear, dear Paul! oh, Walter!'

'The wery planks she walked on,' murmured the
captain, looking at her drooping face, 'was as high
esteemed by Wal'r, as the water brooks is by the hart
which never rejices! I see him now, the wery day as
he was rated on them Dombey books, a speaking of
her with his face a glistening with doo—leastways
with his modest sentiments—like a new blowed rose,
at dinner. Well, well! If our poor Wal'r was here,
my lady lass—or if he could be—for he's drownded,
an't he?'

Florence shook her head.

'Yes, yes; drownded,' said the captain, soothingly;
'as I was saying, if he could be here he'd beg and
pray of you, my precious, to pick a leetle bit, with a
look-out for your own sweet health. Whereby, hold
your own, my lady lass, as if it was for Wal'r's sake,
and lay your pretty head to the wind.'

Florence essayed to eat a morsel, for the captain's
pleasure. The captain, meanwhile, who seemed to
have quite forgotten his own dinner, laid down his
knife and fork, and drew his chair to the sofa.

'Wal'r was a trim lad, warn't he, precious?' said
the captain, after sitting for some time silently rubbing his chin, with his eyes fixed upon her, 'and a
brave lad, and a good lad?'

Florence tearfully assented.

'And he's drownded, beauty, an't he?' said the captain, in a soothing voice.

Florence could not but assent again.

'He was older than you, my lady lass,' pursued the

captain, 'but you was like two children together, at first; warn't you?'

Florence answered 'Yes.'

'And Wal'r's drownded,' said the captain. 'An't he?'

The repetition of this inquiry was a curious source of consolation, but it seemed to be one to Captain Cuttle, for he came back to it again and again. Florence, fain to push from her her untasted dinner, and to lie back on her sofa, gave him her hand, feeling that she had disappointed him, though truly wishing to have pleased him after all his trouble, but he held it in his own (which shook as he held it), and appearing to have quite forgotten all about the dinner and her want of appetite, went on growling at intervals, in a ruminating tone of sympathy, 'Poor Wal'r. Aye, aye! Drownded. An't he?' And always waited for her answer, in which the great point of these singular reflections appeared to consist.

The fowl and sausages were cold, and the gravy and the egg-sauce stagnant, before the captain remembered that they were on the board, and fell to with the assistance of Diogenes, whose united efforts quickly despatched the banquet. The captain's delight and wonder at the quiet housewifery of Florence in assisting to clear the table, arrange the parlour, and sweep up the hearth—only to be equalled by the fervency of his protest when she began to assist him— were gradually raised to that degree, that at last he could not choose but do nothing himself, and stand looking at her as if she were some fairy, daintily performing these offices for him; the red rim on his forehead glowing again, in his unspeakable admiration.

But when Florence, taking down his pipe from the mantel-shelf gave it into his hand, and entreated him to smoke it, the good captain was so bewildered by her

attention that he held it as if he had never held a pipe
in all his life.   Likewise, when Florence, looking into
the little cupboard, took out the case-bottle and mixed
a perfect glass of grog for him, unasked, and set it
at his elbow, his ruddy nose turned pale he felt himself so graced and honoured.   When he had filled his
pipe in an absolute reverie of satisfaction, Florence
lighted it for him—the captain having no power to
object, or to prevent her—and resuming her place
on the old sofa, looked at him with a smile so loving
and so grateful, a smile that showed him so plainly
how her forlorn heart turned to him, as her face did,
through grief, that the smoke of the pipe got into the
captain's throat and made him cough, and got into
the captain's eyes, and make them blink and water.

The manner in which the captain tried to make believe that the cause of these effects lay hidden in the
pipe itself, and the way in which he looked into the
bowl for it, and not finding it there, pretended to blow
it out of the stem, was wonderfully pleasant.   The
pipe soon getting into better condition, he fell into
that state of repose becoming a good smoker; but sat
with his eyes fixed on Florence, and, with a beaming
placidity not to be described, and stopping every now
and then to discharge a little cloud from his lips,
slowly puffed it forth, as if it were a scroll coming
out of his mouth, bearing the legend 'Poor Wal'r, aye
aye.   Drownded, an't he?' after which he would resume his smoking with infinite gentleness.

Unlike as they were externally—and there could
scarcely be a more decided contrast than between
Florence in her delicate youth and beauty, and Captain Cuttle with his knobby face, his great broad
weather-beaten person, and his gruff voice—in simple
innocence of the world's ways and the world's per-
plexities and dangers, they were nearly on a level.

No child could have surpassed Captain Cuttle in inexperience of everything but wind and weather; in simplicity, credulity, and generous trustfulness. Faith, hope, and charity, shared his whole nature among them.   An odd sort of romance, perfectly unimaginative, yet perfectly unreal, and subject to no considerations of worldly prudence or practicability, was the only partner they had in his character.   As the captain sat, and smoked, and looked at Florence, God knows what impossible pictures, in which she was the principal figure, presented themselves to his mind. Equally vague and uncertain, though not so sanguine, were her own thoughts of the life before her; and even as her tears made prismatic colours in the light she gazed at, so, through her new and heavy grief, she already saw a rainbow faintly shining in the far-off sky.   A wandering princess and a good monster in a story-book might have sat by the fireside, and talked as Captain Cuttle and poor Florence thought —and not have looked very much unlike them.

The captain was not troubled with the faintest idea of any difficulty in retaining Florence, or of any responsibility thereby incurred.   Having put up the shutters and locked the door, he was quite satisfied on this head.   If she had been a ward in Chancery, it would have made no difference at all to Captain Cuttle.   He was the last man in the world to be troubled by any such considerations.

So the captain smoked his pipe very comfortably, and Florence and he meditated after their own manner.   When the pipe was out, they had some tea; and then Florence entreated him to take her to some neighbouring shop, where she could buy the few necessaries she immediately wanted.   It being quite dark, the captain consented: peeping carefully out first, as he had been wont to do in his time of hiding from

Mrs. MacStinger; and arming himself with his large stick, in case of an appeal to arms being rendered necessary by any unforeseen circumstance.

The pride Captain Cuttle had, in giving his arm to Florence, and escorting her some two or three hundred yards, keeping a bright look-out all the time, and attracting the attention of every one who passed them, by his great vigilance and numerous precautions, was extreme. Arrived at the shop, the captain felt it a point of delicacy to retire during the making of the purchases, as they were to consist of wearing apparel; but he previously deposited his tin canister on the counter, and informing the young lady of the establishment that it contained fourteen pound two, requested her, in case that amount of property should not be sufficient to defray the expenses of his niece's little outfit—at the word 'niece,' he bestowed a most significant look on Florence, accompanied with pantomime, expressive of sagacity and mystery—to have the goodness to 'sing out,' and he would make up the difference from his pocket. Casually consulting his big watch, as a deep means of dazzling the establishment, and impressing it with a sense of property, the captain then kissed his hook to his niece, and retired outside the window, where it was a choice sight to see his great face looking in from time to time, among the silks and ribbons, with an obvious misgiving that Florence had been spirited away by a back door.

'Dear Captain Cuttle,' said Florence, when she came out with a parcel, the size of which greatly disappointed the captain, who had expected to see a porter following with a bale of goods, 'I don't want this money, indeed. I have not spent any of it. I have money of my own.'

'My lady lass,' returned the baffled captain, looking straight down the street before them, 'take care on it for me, will you be so good, till such time as I ask ye for it?'

'May I put it back in its usual place,' said Florence, 'and keep it there?'

The captain was not at all gratified by this proposal, but he answered, 'Aye, aye, put it anywheres, my lady lass, so long as you know where to find it again. It an't o' no use to *me*,' said the captain. 'I wonder I haven't chucked it away afore now.'

The captain was quite disheartened for the moment, but he revived at the first touch of Florence's arm, and they returned with the same precautions as they had come; the captain opening the door of the little midshipman's berth, and diving in, with a suddenness which his great practice only could have taught him. During Florence's slumber in the morning, he had engaged the daughter of an elderly lady, who usually sat under a blue umbrella in Leadenhall Market, selling poultry, to come and put her room in order, and render her any little services she required; and this damsel now appearing, Florence found everything about her as convenient and orderly, if not as handsome, as in the terrible dream she had once called home.

When they were alone again, the captain insisted on her eating a slice of dry toast, and drinking a glass of spiced negus (which he made to perfection); and, encouraging her with every kind word and inconsequential quotation he could possibly think of, led her upstairs to her bedroom. But he too had something on his mind, and was not easy in his manner.

'Good night, dear heart,' said Captain Cuttle to her at her chamber door.

Florence raised her lips to his face, and kissed him.

At any other time the captain would have been overbalanced by such a token of her affection and gratitude; but now, although he was very sensible of it, he looked in her face with even more uneasiness than he had testified before, and seemed unwilling to leave her.

'Poor Wal'r!' said the captain.

'Poor, poor Walter!' sighed Florence.

'Drownded, an't he?' said the captain.

Florence shook her head, and sighed.

'Good night, my lady lass!' said Captain Cuttle, putting out his hand.

'God bless you, dear, kind friend!'

But the captain lingered still.

'Is anything the matter, dear Captain Cuttle?' said Florence, easily alarmed in her then state of mind. 'Have you anything to tell me?'

'To tell you, lady lass?' replied the captain, meeting her eyes in confusion. 'No, no; what should I have to tell you, pretty! You don't expect as I've got anything good to tell you, sure?'

'No!' said Florence, shaking her head.

The captain looked at her wistfully, and repeated 'No,'—still lingering, and still showing embarrassment.

'Poor Wal'r!' said the captain. 'My Wal'r, as I used to call you! Old Sol Gills's nevy! Welcome to all as knowed you, as the flowers in May! Where are you got to, brave boy! Drownded, an't he?'

Concluding his apostrophe with this abrupt appeal to Florence, the captain bade her good night, and descended the stairs, while Florence remained at the top, holding the candle out to light him down. He was lost in the obscurity, and, judging from the sound of his receding footsteps, was in the act of turning into the little parlour, when his head and shoulders unexpectedly emerged again, as from the deep, apparently for no other purpose than to repeat, 'Drownded, an't he, pretty?' For when he had said that in a tone of tender condolence, he disappeared.

Florence was very sorry that she should unwittingly, though naturally, have awakened these associations in the mind of her protector, by taking refuge there; and sitting down before the little table where the captain had arranged the telescope and song-book, and those other rarities, thought of Walter, and of all that was connected with him in the past, until she could have almost wished to lie down on her bed and fade away. But in her lonely yearning to the dead whom she had loved, no thought of home—no possibility of going back—no presentation of it as yet existing, or as sheltering her father—once entered her thoughts. She had seen the murder done. In the last lingering natural aspect in which she had cherished him through so much, he had been torn out of her heart, defaced and slain. The thought of it was so appalling to her, that she covered her eyes, and shrunk trembling from the least remembrance of the deed, or of the cruel hand that did it. If her fond heart could have held his image after that, it must have broken; but it could not; and the void was filled with a wild dread that fled from all confronting with its shattered fragments—with such a dread as could have risen out of nothing but the depths of such a love, so wronged.

She dared not look into the glass; for the sight of the darkening mark upon her bosom made her afraid of herself, as if she bore about her something wicked. She covered it up, with a hasty, faltering hand, and in the dark; and laid her weary head down, weeping.

The captain did not go to bed for a long time. He walked to and fro in the shop and in the little parlour, for a full hour, and, appearing to have composed himself by that exercise, sat down with a grave

and thoughtful face, and read out of a Prayer-book
the forms of prayer appointed to be used at sea.
These were not easily disposed of; the good captain
being a mighty slow, gruff reader, and frequently
stopping at a hard word to give himself such encouragement as 'Now, my lad! With a will!' or, 'Steady,
Ed'ard Cuttle, steady!' which had a great effect in
helping him out of any difficulty. Moreover, his
spectacles greatly interfered with his powers of vision. But notwithstanding these drawbacks, the captain, being heartily in earnest, read the service to the
very last line, and with genuine feeling too; and approving of it very much when he had done, turned
in under the counter (but not before he had been
upstairs, and listened at Florence's door), with a
serene breast and a most benevolent visage.

The captain turned out several times in the course
of the night to assure himself that his charge was resting quietly; and once, at daybreak, found that she
was awake: for she called to know if it were he, on
hearing footsteps near her door.

'Yes, my lady lass,' replied the captain, in a growling whisper. 'Are you all right, di'mond?'

Florence thanked him, and said 'Yes.'

The captain could not lose so favourable an opportunity of applying his mouth to the keyhole, and calling through it like a hoarse breeze, 'Poor Wal'r!
Drownded, an't he?' After which he withdrew, and
turning in again, slept till seven o'clock.

Nor was he free from his uneasy and embarrassed
manner all that day; though Florence, being busy with
her needle in the little parlour, was more calm and
tranquil than she had been on the day preceding. Almost always when she raised her eyes from her work,
she observed the captain looking at her, and thoughtfully stroking his chin; and he so often hitched his

arm-chair close to her, as if he were going to say something very confidential, and hitched it away again, as not being able to make up his mind how to begin, that in the course of the day he cruised completely round the parlour in that frail bark, and more than once went ashore against the wainscot or the closet door, in a very distressed condition.

It was not until the twilight that Captain Cuttle, fairly dropping anchor, at last, by the side of Florence, began to talk at all connectedly. But when the light of the fire was shining on the walls and ceiling of the little room, and on the tea-board and the cups and saucers that were ranged upon the table, and on her calm face turned towards the flame, and reflecting it in the tears that filled her eyes, the captain broke a long silence thus—

'You never was at sea, my own?'

'No,' replied Florence.

'Aye,' said the captain, reverentially; 'it's a almighty element. There's wonders in the deep, my pretty. Think on it when the winds is roaring and the waves is rowling. Think on it when the stormy nights is so pitch dark,' said the captain, solemnly holding up his hook, 'as you can't see your hand afore you, excepting when the wiwid lightning reweals the same; and when you drive, drive, drive through the storm and dark, as if you was a driving, head on, to the world without end, evermore, amen, and when found making a note of. Them's the times, my beauty, when a man may say to his messmate (previously a overhauling of the wollume), "A stiff norwester's blowing, Bill; hark, don't you hear it roar now! Lord help 'em, how I pitys all unhappy folks ashore now!"' Which quotation, as particularly applicable to the terrors of the ocean, the captain deliv-

ered in a most impressive manner, concluding with a
sonorous 'Stand by!'

'Were *you* ever in a dreadful storm?' asked Florence.

'Why aye, my lady lass, I 've seen my share of bad
weather,' said the captain, tremulously wiping his
head, 'and I 've had my share of knocking about; but
—but it ain't of myself as I was a meaning to speak.
Our dear boy,' drawing closer to her, 'Wal'r, darling,
as was drownded.'

The captain spoke in such a trembling voice, and
looked at Florence with a face so pale and agitated,
that she clung to his hand in affright.

'Your face is changed,' cried Florence. 'You are
altered in a moment. What is it? Dear Captain
Cuttle, it turns me cold to see you!'

'What! Lady lass,' returned the captain, support-
ing her with his hand, 'don't be took aback. No, no!
All 's well, all 's well, my dear. As I was a saying—
Wal'r—he 's—he 's drownded. An't he?'

Florence looked at him intently; her colour came
and went; and she laid her hand upon her breast.

'There 's perils and dangers on the deep, my
beauty,' said the captain: 'and over many a brave ship,
and many and many a bould heart, the secret waters
has closed up, and never told no tales. But there 's
escapes upon the deep, too, and sometimes one man out
of a score,—ah! may be out of a hundred, pretty,—
has been saved by the mercy of God, and come home
after being given over for dead, and told of all hands
lost. I—I know a story, Heart's Delight,' stammered the captain, 'o' this natur, as was told to me
once; and being on this here tack, and you and me
sitting alone by the fire, maybe you 'd like to hear
me tell it. Would you, deary?'

Florence, trembling with agitation which she could not control or understand, involuntarily followed his glance, which went behind her into the shop, where a lamp was burning. The instant that she turned her head, the captain sprang out of his chair, and interposed his hand.

'There's nothing there, my beauty,' said the captain. 'Don't look there.'

'Why not?' asked Florence.

The captain murmured something about its being dull that way, and about the fire being cheerful. He drew the door ajar, which had been standing open until now, and resumed his seat. Florence followed him with her eyes, and looked intently in his face.

'The story was about a ship, my lady lass,' began the captain, 'as sailed out of the port of London, with a fair wind and in fair weather, bound for—don't be took aback, my lady lass, she was only out'ard bound, pretty, only out'ard bound!'

The expression on Florence's face alarmed the captain, who was himself very hot and flurried, and showed scarcely less agitation than she did.

'Shall I go on, beauty?' said the captain.

'Yes, yes, pray!' cried Florence.

The captain made a gulp as if to get down something that was sticking in his throat, and nervously proceeded—

'That there unfort'nate ship met with such foul weather, out at sea, as don't blow once in twenty year, my darling. There was hurricanes ashore as tore up forests and blowed down towns, and there was gales at sea in them latitudes, as not the stoutest wessel ever launched could live in. Day arter day that there unfort'nate ship behaved noble, I'm told, and did her duty brave, my pretty, but at one blow a'most her bulwarks was stove in, her masts and rudder carried

away, her best men swept overboard, and she left to
the mercy of the storm as had no mercy but blowed
harder and harder yet, while the waves dashed over
her, and beat her in, and every time they come a thundering at her, broke her like a shell. Every black
spot in every mountain of water that rolled away was
a bit o' the ship's life or a living man, and so she went
to pieces, beauty, and no grass will never grow upon
the graves of them as manned that ship.'

'They were not all lost!' cried Florence. 'Some
were saved!—Was one?'

'Aboard o' that there unfort'nate wessel,' said the
captain, rising from his chair, and clenching his hand
with prodigious energy and exultation, 'was a lad, a
gallant lad—as I 've heerd tell—that had loved, when
he was a boy, to read and talk about brave actions
in shipwrecks—I 've heerd him! I 've heerd him!—
and he remembered of 'em in his hour of need; for
when the stoutest hearts and oldest hands was hove
down, he was firm and cheery. It warn't the want
of objects to like and love ashore that gave him courage, it was his nat'ral mind. I 've seen it in his face,
when he was no more than a child—aye, many a time!
—and when I thought it nothing but his good looks,
bless him!'

'And was he saved?' cried Florence. 'Was he
saved?'

'That brave lad,' said the captain—'look at me,
pretty! Don't look round—'

Florence had hardly power to repeat, 'Why not?'

'Because there 's nothing there, my deary,' said the
captain. 'Don't be took aback, pretty creetur!
Don't, for the sake of Wal'r, as was dear to all on us!
That there lad,' said the captain, 'arter working with
the best, and standing by the faint-hearted, and never
making no complaint nor sign of fear, and keeping

up a spirit in all hands that made 'em honour him as
if he 'd been a admiral—that lad, along with the
second-mate and one seaman, was left, of all the
beatin' hearts that went aboard that ship, the only
living creeturs—lashed to a fragment of the wreck,
and driftin' on the stormy sea.'

'Were they saved?' cried Florence.

'Days and nights they drifted on them endless
waters,' said the captain, 'until at last—No! Don't
look that way, pretty!—a sail bore down upon 'em,
and they was, by the Lord's mercy, took aboard; two
living and one dead.'

'Which of them was dead?' cried Florence.

'Not the lad I speak on,' said the captain.

'Thank God! oh thank God!'

'Amen!' returned the captain hurriedly. 'Don't be
took aback! A minute more, my lady lass! with a
good heart!—aboard that ship, they went a long voyage, right away across the chart (for there warn't no
touching nowhere), and on that voyage the seaman as
was picked up with him died. But he was spared,
and—'

The captain, without knowing what he did, had
cut a slice of bread from the loaf, and put it on his
hook (which was his usual toasting-fork), on which
he now held it to the fire; looking behind Florence
with great emotion in his face, and suffering the bread
to blaze and burn like fuel.

'Was spared,' repeated Florence, 'and—?'

'And come home in that ship,' said the captain, still
looking in the same direction, 'and—don't be frightened, pretty—and landed; and one morning come cautiously to his own door to take a obserwation, knowing
that his friends would think him drownded, when he
sheered off at the unexpected—'

'At the unexpected barking of a dog?' cried Florence, quickly.

'Yes,' roared the captain. 'Steady, darling! courage! Don't look round yet. See there! upon the wall!'

There was the shadow of a man upon the wall close to her. She started up, looked round, and with a piercing cry, saw Walter Gay behind her!

She had no thought of him but as a brother, a brother rescued from the grave; a shipwrecked brother saved and at her side; and rushed into his arms. In all the world, he seemed to be her hope, her comfort, refuge, natural protector. 'Take care of Walter, I was fond of Walter!' The dear remembrance of the plaintive voice that said so, rushed upon her soul, like music in the night. 'Oh welcome home, dear Walter! Welcome to this stricken breast!' She felt the words, although she could not utter them, and held him in her pure embrace.

Captain Cuttle, in a fit of delirium, attempted to wipe his head with the blackened toast upon his hook: and finding it an uncongenial substance for the purpose, put it into the crown of his glazed hat, put the glazed hat on with some difficulty, essayed to sing a verse of Lovely Peg, broke down at the first word, and retired into the shop, whence he presently came back, express, with a face all flushed and besmeared, and the starch completely taken out of his shirt-collar to say these words—

'Wal'r, my lad, here is a little bit of property as I should wish to make over, jintly!'

The captain hastily produced the big watch, the tea-spoons, the sugar-tongs, and the canister, and laying them on the table, swept them with his great hand into Walter's hat; but in handing that singular strong box

to Walter, he was so overcome again, that he was fain
to make another retreat into the shop, and absent himself for a longer space of time than on his first retirement.

But Walter sought him out, and brought him back;
and then the captain's great apprehension was, that
Florence would suffer from this new shock.   He felt
it so earnestly, that he turned quite rational, and positively interdicted any further allusion to Walter's ad-
ventures for some days to come.   Captain Cuttle then
became sufficiently composed to relieve himself of the
toast in his hat, and to take his place at the tea-board;
but finding Walter's grasp upon his shoulder, on one
side, and Florence whispering her tearful congratulations on the other, the captain suddenly bolted again,
and was missing for a good ten minutes.

But never in all his life had the captain's face so
shone and glistened, as when at last, he sat stationary
at the tea-board, looking from Florence to Walter,
and from Walter to Florence.   Nor was this effect
produced or at all heightened by the immense quantity
of polishing he had administered to his face with his
coat-sleeve during the last half-hour.   It was solely
the effect of his internal emotions.   There was a glory
and delight within the captain that spread itself over
his whole visage, and made a perfect illumination
there.

The pride with which the captain looked upon the
bronzed cheek and the courageous eyes of his recovered boy; with which he saw the generous fervour of
his youth, and all its frank and hopeful qualities, shining once more, in the fresh, wholesome manner, and
the ardent face, would have kindled something of this
light in his countenance.   The admiration and sympathy with which he turned his eyes on Florence,
whose beauty, grace, and innocence could have won

THE SHADOW IN THE LITTLE PARLOUR.

THE SHADOW IN THE LITTLE TAILOR.

no truer or more zealous champion than himself, would
have had an equal influence upon him. But the fulness of the glow he shed around him could only have
been engendered in his contemplation of the two together, and in all the fancies springing out of that
association, that came sparkling and beaming into his
head, and danced about it.

How they talked of poor old uncle Sol, and dwelt
on every little circumstance relating to his disappearance; how their joy was moderated by the old man's
absence and by the misfortunes of Florence; how they
released Diogenes, whom the captain had decoyed upstairs some time before, lest he should bark again; the
captain, though he was in one continual flutter, and
made many more short plunges into the shop, fully
comprehended. But he no more dreamed that
Walter looked on Florence, as it were, from a new
and far-off place; that while his eyes often sought
the lovely face, they seldom met its open glance of
sisterly affection, but withdrew themselves when hers
were raised towards him; than he believed that it was
Walter's ghost who sat beside him. He saw them
there together in their youth and beauty, and he knew
the story of their younger days, and he had no inch
of room beneath his great blue waistcoat for anything
save admiration of such a pair, and gratitude for their
being reunited.

They sat thus, until it grew late. The captain
would have been content to sit so for a week. But
Walter rose, to take leave for the night.

'Going, Walter!' said Florence. 'Where?'

'He slings his hammock for the present, lady lass,'
said Captain Cuttle, 'round at Brogley's. Within
hail, Heart's Delight.'

'I am the cause of your going away, Walter,' said
Florence. 'There is a houseless sister in your place.'

'Dear Miss Dombey,' replied Walter, hesitating—
'if it is not too bold to call you so—'

'—Walter!' she exclaimed, surprised.

'If anything could make me happier in being allowed to see and speak to you, would it not be the discovery that I had any means on earth of doing you a moment's service! Where would I not go, what would I not do for your sake?'

She smiled, and called him brother.

'You are so changed,' said Walter—

'I changed!' she interrupted.

'To me,' said Walter, softly, as if he were thinking aloud, 'changed to me. I left you such a child, and find you—oh! something so different—'

'But your sister, Walter. You have not forgotten what we promised each other, when we parted?'

'Forgotten!' But he said no more.

'And if you had—if suffering and danger had driven it from your thoughts—which it has not—you would remember it now, Walter, when you find me poor and abandoned, with no home but this, and no friends but the two who hear me speak!'

'I would! Heaven knows I would!' said Walter.

'Oh, Walter,' exclaimed Florence, through her sobs and tears. 'Dear brother! Show me some way through the world—some humble path that I may take alone, and labour in, and sometimes think of you as one who will protect and care for me as for a sister! Oh, help me, Walter, for I need help so much!'

'Miss Dombey! Florence! I would die to help you. But your friends are proud and rich. Your father—'

'No, no! Walter!' She shrieked, and put her hands up to her head, in an attitude of terror that transfixed him where he stood. 'Don't say that word!'

He never from that hour, forgot the voice and look

with which she stopped him at the name.   He felt that
if he were to live a hundred years, he never could
forget it.

Somewhere—anywhere—but   never   home! All
past, all gone, all lost, and broken up!   The whole
history of her untold slight and suffering was in the
cry and look; and he felt he never could forget it,
and he never did.

She laid her gentle face upon the captain's shoulder, and related how and why she had fled.   If every
sorrowing tear she shed in doing so, had been a curse
upon the head of him she never named or blamed, it
would have been better for him, Walter thought, with
awe, than to be renounced out of such a strength and
might of love.

'There, precious!' said the captain, when she ceased;
and deep attention the captain had paid to her while
she spoke; listening, with his glazed hat all awry and
his mouth wide open. 'Awast, awast, my eyes!
Wal'r, dear lad, sheer off for to-night, and leave the
pretty one to me!'

Walter took her hand in both of his, and put it to
his lips, and kissed it.   He knew now that she was,
indeed, a homeless wandering fugitive; but, richer to
him so, than in all the wealth and pride of her right
station, she seemed farther off than even on the height
that had made him giddy in his boyish dreams.

Captain Cuttle, perplexed by no such meditations,
guarded Florence to her room, and watched at intervals upon the charmed ground outside her door—for
such it truly was to him—until he felt sufficiently easy
in his mind about her, to turn in under the counter.
On abandoning his watch for that purpose, he could
not help calling once, rapturously, through the key-
hole, 'Drownded.   An't he, pretty?—or, when he got
downstairs, making another trial at that verse of

Lovely Peg. But it stuck in his throat somehow, and he could make nothing of it; so he went to bed, and dreamed that old Sol Gills was married to Mrs. Mac-Stinger, and kept prisoner by that lady in a secret chamber on a short allowance of victuals.

CHAPTER L

MR. TOOTS'S COMPLAINT

THERE was an empty room above-stairs at the wooden midshipman's, which, in days of yore, had been Walter's bedroom. Walter, rousing up the captain betimes in the morning, proposed that they should carry thither such furniture out of the little parlour as would grace it best, so that Florence might take possession of it when she rose. As nothing could be more agreeable to Captain Cuttle than making himself very red and short of breath in such a cause, he turned to (as he himself said) with a will; and, in a couple of hours, this garret was transformed into a species of land-cabin, adorned with all the choicest moveables out of the parlour, inclusive even of the Tartar frigate, which the captain hung up over the chimney-piece with such extreme delight, that he could do nothing for half an hour afterwards but walk backward from it, lost in admiration.

The captain could be induced by no persuasion of Walter's to wind up the big watch, or to take back the canister, or to touch the sugar-tongs and tea-spoons. 'No, no, my lad'; was the captain's invariable reply to any solicitation of the kind, 'I 've made that there little property over, jintly.' These words he repeated with great unction and gravity, evidently believing that they had the virtue of an Act of Parliament, and that unless he committed himself by some new admission of ownership, no flaw could be found in such a form of conveyance.

It was an advantage of the new arrangement, that besides the greater seclusion it afforded Florence, it admitted of the midshipman being restored to his usual post of observation, and also of the shop shutters being taken down. The latter ceremony, however little importance the unconscious captain attached to it, was not wholly superfluous; for, on the previous day, so much excitement had been occasioned in the neighbourhood, by the shutters remaining unopened, that the instrument-maker's house had been honoured with an unusual share of public observation, and had been intently stared at from the opposite side of the way, by groups of hungry gazers, at any time between sunrise and sunset. The idlers and vagabonds had been particularly interested in the captain's fate; constantly grovelling in the mud to apply their eyes to the cellar-grating, under the shop-window, and delighting their imaginations with the fancy that they could see a piece of his coat as he hung in a corner; though this settlement of him was stoutly disputed by an opposite faction, who were of opinion that he lay murdered with a hammer, on the stairs. It was not without exciting some discontent, therefore, that the subject of these rumours was seen early in the morning standing at his shop-door as hale and hearty as if nothing had happened; and the beadle of that quarter, a man of ambitious character, who had expected to have the distinction of being present at the breaking open of the door, and of giving evidence in full uniform before the coroner, went so far as to say to an opposite neighbour, that the chap in the glazed hat had better not try it on there—without more particularly mentioning what—and further, that he, the beadle, would keep his eye upon him.

'Captain Cuttle,' said Walter, musing, when they stood resting from their labours at the shop-door, looking down the old familiar street; it being still early in the morning; 'nothing at all of uncle Sol, in all that time?'

'Nothing at all, my lad,' replied the captain, shaking his head.

'Gone in search of me, dear, kind old man,' said Walter: 'yet never write to you! But why not? He says, in effect, in this packet that you gave me,' taking the paper from his pocket, which had been opened in the presence of the enlightened Bunsby, 'that if you never hear from him before opening it, you may believe him dead. Heaven forbid! But you would have heard *of* him, even if he *were* dead! Some one would have written, surely, by his desire, if he could not; and have said, "on such a day, there died in my house," or "under my care," or so forth, "Mr. Solomon Gills of London, who left this last remembrance and this last request to you." '

The captain, who had never climbed to such a clear height of probability before, was greatly impressed by the wide prospect it opened, and answered, with a thoughtful shake of his head, 'Well said, my lad; wery well said.'

'I have been thinking of this, or, at least,' said Walter, colouring, 'I have been thinking of one thing and another, all through a sleepless night, and I cannot believe, Captain Cuttle, but that my uncle Sol (Lord bless him!) is alive, and will return. I don't so much wonder at his going away, because, leaving out of consideration that spice of the marvellous which was always in his character, and his great affection

for me, before which every other consideration of his
life became nothing, as no one ought to know so well
as I who had the best of fathers in him,'—Walter's
voice was indistinct and husky here, and he looked
away, along the street,—'leaving that out of consideration, I say, I have often read and heard of people
who, having some near and dear relative, who was supposed to be shipwrecked at sea, have gone down to
live on that part of the sea-shore where any tidings of
the missing ship might be expected to arrive though
only an hour or two sooner than elsewhere, or have
even gone upon her track to the place whither she was
bound, as if their going would create intelligence.   I
think I should do such a thing myself, as soon as another, or sooner than many, perhaps.   But why my
uncle shouldn't write to you, when he so clearly intended to do so, or how he should die abroad, and you
not know it through some other hand, I cannot make
out.'

Captain Cuttle observed, with a shake of his head,
that Jack Bunsby himself hadn't made it out, and
that he was a man as could give a pretty taut opinion
too.

'If my uncle had been a heedless young man, likely
to be entrapped by jovial company to some drinking-
place, where he was to be got rid of for the sake of
what money he might have about him,' said Walter;
'or if he had been a reckless sailor, going ashore with
two or three months' pay in his pocket, I could understand his disappearing, and leaving no trace behind.
But, being what he was—and, is, I hope—I can't believe it.'

'Wal'r, my lad,' inquired the captain, wistfully
eyeing him as he pondered and pondered, 'what do you
make of it, then?'

'Captain Cuttle,' returned Walter, 'I don't know

what to make of it. I suppose he never *has* written? There is no doubt about that?'

'If so be as Sol Gills wrote, my lad,' replied the captain argumentatively, 'where 's his despatch?'

'Say that he intrusted it to some private hand,' suggested Walter, 'and that it has been forgotten, or carelessly thrown aside, or lost. Even that is more probable to me, than the other event. In short, I not only cannot bear to contemplate that other event, Captain Cuttle, but I can't, and won't.'

'Hope, you see, Wal'r,' said the captain, sagely, 'Hope. It 's that as animates you. Hope is a buoy, for which you overhaul your Little Warbler, sentimental diwision, but Lord, my lad, like any other buoy, it only floats; it can't be steered nowhere. Along with the figure-head of Hope,' said the captain, 'there 's a anchor; but what 's the good of my having a anchor, if I can't find no bottom to let it go in.'

Captain Cuttle said this rather in his character of a sagacious citizen and householder, bound to impart a morsel from his stores of wisdom to an inexperienced youth, than in his own proper person. Indeed, his face was quite luminous as he spoke, with new hope, caught from Walter; and he appropriately concluded by slapping him on the back; and saying, with enthusiasm, 'Hooroar, my lad! Indiwidually, I'm o' your opinion.'

Walter, with this cheerful laugh, returned the salutation, and said—

'Only one word more about my uncle at present, Captain Cuttle. I suppose it is impossible that he can have written in the ordinary course—by mail packet, or ship letter, you understand—'

'Aye, aye, my lad,' said the captain approvingly.

'—And that you have missed the letter anyhow?'

'Why, Wal'r,' said the captain, turning his eyes upon him with a faint approach to a severe expression, 'an't I been on the look-out for any tidings of that man o' science, old Sol Gills, your uncle, day and night, ever since I lost him? An't my heart been heavy and watchful always, along of him and you? Sleeping and waking, an't I been upon my post, and wouldn't I scorn to quit it while this here midshipman held together?'

'Yes, Captain Cuttle,' replied Walter, grasping his hand, 'I know you would, and I know how faithful and earnest all you say and feel is. I am sure of it. You don't doubt that I am as sure of it as I am that my foot is again upon this doorstep, or that I again have hold of this true hand? Do you?'

'No, no, Wal'r,' returned the captain, with his beaming face.

'I 'll hazard no more conjectures,' said Walter, fervently shaking the hard hand of the captain, who shook his with no less good-will. 'All I will add is, Heaven forbid that I should touch my uncle's possessions, Captain Cuttle! Everything that he left here, shall remain in the care of the truest of stewards and kindest of men—and if his name is not Cuttle, he has no name! Now, best of friends, about—Miss Dombey.'

There was a change in Walter's manner, as he came to these two words; and when he uttered them, all his confidence and cheerfulness appeared to have deserted him.

'I thought, before Miss Dombey stopped me when I spoke of her father last night,' said Walter, '—you remember how?'

The captain well remembered, and shook his head.

'I thought,' said Walter, 'before that, that we had but one hard duty to perform, and that it was, to prevail upon her to communicate with her friends, and to return home.'

The captain muttered a feeble 'Awast!' or a 'Stand by!' or something or other, equally pertinent to the occasion; but it was rendered so extremely feeble by the total discomfiture with which he received this announcement, that what it was, is mere matter of conjecture.

'But,' said Walter, 'that is over. I think so no longer. I would sooner be put back again upon that piece of wreck, on which I have so often floated, since my preservation, in my dreams, and there left to drift, and drive, and die!'

'Hooroar, my lad!' exclaimed the captain, in a burst of uncontrollable satisfaction. 'Hooroar! hooroar! hooroar!'

'To think that she, so young, so good, and beautiful,' said Walter, 'so delicately brought up, and born to such a different fortune, should strive with the rough world! But we have seen the gulf that cuts off all behind her, though no one but herself can know how deep it is; and there is no return.'

Captain Cuttle, without quite understanding this, greatly approved of it, and observed, in a tone of strong corroboration, that the wind was quite abaft.

'She ought not to be alone here; ought she, Captain Cuttle?' said Walter, anxiously.

'Well, my lad,' replied the captain, after a little sagacious consideration. 'I don't know. You being here to keep her company, you see, and you two being jintly—'

'Dear Captain Cuttle!' remonstrated Walter. 'I being here! Miss Dombey, in her guileless innocent heart, regards me as her adopted brother; but what would the guile and guilt of *my* heart be, if I pretended to believe that I had any right to approach her, familiarly, in that character—if I pretended to forget that I am bound, in honour, not to do it?'

'Wal'r, my lad,' hinted the captain, with some revival of his discomfiture, 'an't there no other character as—'

'Oh!' returned Walter, 'would you have me die in her esteem—in such esteem as hers—and put a veil between myself and her angel's face for ever, by taking advantage of her being here for refuge, so trusting and so unprotected, to endeavour to exalt myself into her lover? What do I say? There is no one in the world who would be more opposed to me if I could do so, than you.'

'Wal'r, my lad,' said the captain, drooping more and more, 'prowiding as there is any just cause or impediment why two persons should not be jined together in the house of bondage, for which you 'll overhaul the place and make a note, I hope I should declare it as promised and wowed in the banns. So there an't no other character; an't there, my lad?'

Walter briskly waved his hand in the negative.

'Well, my lad,' growled the captain slowly, 'I won't deny but what I find myself wery much down by the head, along o' this here, or but what I 've gone clean about. But as to lady lass, Wal'r, mind you, wot 's respect and duty to her is respect and duty in my articles, howsumwer disapinting; and therefore I follows in your wake, my lad, and feel as you are, no doubt, acting up to yourself. And there an't *no* other character, an't there?' said the captain, musing over the ruins of his fallen castle with a very despondent face.

'Now, Captain Cuttle,' said Walter, starting a fresh point with a gayer air, to cheer the captain up —but nothing could do that; he was too much concerned—'I think we should exert ourselves to find

some one who would be a proper attendant for Miss
Dombey while she remains here, and who may be
trusted. None of her relations may. It 's clear Miss
Dombey feels that they are all subservient to her
father. What has become of Susan?'

'The young woman?' returned the captain. 'It 's
my belief as she was sent away again the will of
Heart's Delight. I made a signal for her when lady
lass first come, and she rated of her wery high, and
said she had been gone a long time.'

'Then,' said Walter, 'do you ask Miss Dombey
where she 's gone, and we 'll try to find her. The
morning 's getting on, and Miss Dombey will soon be
rising. You are her best friend. Wait for her upstairs, and leave me to take care of all down here.'

The captain, very crest-fallen indeed, echoed the
sigh with which Walter said this, and complied.
Florence was delighted with her new room, anxious
to see Walter, and overjoyed at the prospect of greeting her old friend Susan. But Florence could not
say where Susan was gone, except that it was in
Essex, and no one could say, she remembered, unless
it were Mr. Toots.

With this information the melancholy captain returned to Walter, and gave him to understand that
Mr. Toots was the young gentleman whom he had
encountered on the door-step, and that he was a friend
of his, and that he was a young gentleman of property, and that he hopelessly adored Miss Dombey.
The captain also related how the intelligence of
Walter's supposed fate had first made him acquainted
with Mr. Toots, and how there was solemn treaty and
compact between them, that Mr. Toots should be
mute upon the subject of his love.

The question then was, whether Florence could
trust Mr. Toots; and Florence saying, with a smile,

'Oh, yes, with her whole heart!' it became important to find out where Mr. Toots lived. This Florence didn't know, and the captain had forgotten; and the captain was telling Walter, in the little parlour, that Mr. Toots was sure to be there soon, when in came Mr. Toots himself.

'Captain Gills,' said Mr. Toots, rushing into the parlour without any ceremony, 'I 'm in a state of mind bordering on distraction!'

Mr. Toots had discharged these words, as from a mortar, before he observed Walter, whom he recognised with what may be described as a chuckle of misery.

'You 'll excuse me, sir,' said Mr. Toots, holding his forehead, 'but I 'm at present in that state that my brain is going, if not gone, and anything approaching to politeness in an individual so situated would be a hollow mockery. Captain Gills, I beg to request the favour of a private interview.'

'Why, brother,' returned the captain, taking him by the hand, 'you are the man as we was on the lookout for.'

'Oh, Captain Gills,' said Mr. Toots, 'what a lookout that must be, of which *I* am the object! I haven't dared to shave, I 'm in that rash state. I haven't had my clothes brushed. My hair is matted together. I told the Chicken that if he offered to clean my boots, I 'd stretch him a corpse before me!'

All these indications of a disordered mind were verified in Mr. Toots's appearance, which was wild and savage.

'See here, brother,' said the captain. 'This here 's old Sol Gills's nevy Wal'r. Him as was supposed to have perished at sea.'

Mr. Toots took his hand from his forehead, and stared at Walter.

'Good gracious me!' stammered Mr. Toots. 'What a complication of misery! How-de-do? I— I—I'm afraid you must have got very wet. Captain Gills, will you allow me a word in the shop?'

He took the captain by the coat, and going out with him whispered—

'That then, Captain Gills, is the party you spoke of, when you said that he and Miss Dombey were made for one another?'

'Why, aye, my lad,' replied the disconsolate captain: 'I was of that mind once.'

'And at this time!' exclaimed Mr. Toots, with his hand to his forehead again. 'Of all others!—a hated rival! At least, he an't a hated rival,' said Mr. Toots, stopping short, on second thoughts, and taking away his hand; 'what should I hate him for? No. If my affection has been truly disinterested, Captain Gills, let me prove it now!'

Mr. Toots shot back abruptly into the parlour, and said, wringing Walter by the hand—

'How-de-do? I hope you didn't take any cold. I —I shall be very glad if you'll give me the pleasure of your acquaintance. I wish you many happy returns of the day. Upon my word and honour,' said Mr. Toots, warming as he became better acquainted with Walter's face and figure, 'I'm very glad to see you!'

'Thank you, heartily,' said Walter. 'I couldn't desire a more genuine and genial welcome.'

'Couldn't you, though?' said Mr. Toots, still shaking his hand. 'It's very kind of you. I'm much obliged to you. How-de-do? I hope you left everybody quite well over the—that is, upon the—I mean wherever you came from last, you know.'

All these good wishes, and better intentions, Walter responded to manfully.

'Captain Gills,' said Mr. Toots, 'I should wish to be strictly honourable; but I trust I may be allowed now, to allude to a certain subject that—'

'Aye, aye, my lad,' returned the captain. 'Freely, freely.'

'Then, Captain Gills,' said Mr. Toots, 'and Lieutenant Walters, are you aware that the most dreadful circumstances have been happening at Mr. Dombey's house, and that Miss Dombey herself has left her father, who, in my opinion,' said Mr. Toots, with great excitement, 'is a brute, that it would be a flattery to call a—a marble monument, or a bird of prey, —and that she is not to be found, and has gone no one knows where?'

'May I ask how you heard this?' inquired Walter.

'Lieutenant Walters,' said Mr. Toots, who had arrived at that appellation by a process peculiar to himself; probably by jumbling up his Christian name with the seafaring profession, and supposing some relationship between him and the captain, which would extend, as a matter of course, to their titles; 'Lieutenant Walters, I can have no objection to make a straightforward reply. The fact is, that feeling extremely interested in everything that relates to Miss Dombey—not for any selfish reason, Lieutenant Walters, for I am well aware that the most agreeable thing I could do for all parties would be to put an end to my existence, which can only be regarded as an inconvenience—I have been in the habit of bestowing a trifle now and then upon a footman; a most respectable young man, of the name of Towlinson, who has lived in the family some time; and Towlinson informed me, yesterday evening, that this was the state of things. Since which, Captain Gills —and Lieutenant Walters—I have been perfectly frantic, and have been lying down on the sofa all night, the ruin you behold.'

'Mr. Toots,' said Walter, 'I am happy to be able to relieve your mind. Pray calm yourself. Miss Dombey is safe and well.'

'Sir!' cried Mr. Toots, starting from his chair and shaking hands with him anew, 'the relief is so excessive, and unspeakable, that if you were to tell me now that Miss Dombey was married even, I could smile. Yes, Captain Gills,' said Mr. Toots appealing to him, 'upon my soul and body, I really think, whatever I might do to myself immediately afterwards, that I could smile, I am so relieved.'

'It will be a greater relief and delight still, to such a generous mind as yours,' said Walter, not at all slow in returning his greeting, 'to find that you can render service to Miss Dombey. Captain Cuttle, will you have the kindness to take Mr. Toots upstairs?'

The captain beckoned to Mr. Toots, who followed him with a bewildered countenance, and, ascending to the top of the house, was introduced, without a word of preparation from his conductor, into Florence's new retreat.

Poor Mr. Toots's amazement and pleasure at sight of her were such, that they could find a vent in nothing but extravagance. He ran up to her, seized her hand, kissed it, dropped it, seized it again, fell upon one knee, shed tears, chuckled, and was quite regardless of his danger of being pinned by Diogenes, who, inspired by the belief that there was something hostile to his mistress in these demonstrations, worked round and round him, as if only undecided at what particular point to go in for the assault, but quite resolved to do him a fearful mischief.

'Oh Di, you bad, forgetful dog! Dear Mr. Toots, I am so rejoiced to see you!'

'Thankee,' said Mr. Toots, 'I am pretty well, I 'm much obliged to you, Miss Dombey. I hope all the family are the same.'

Mr. Toots said this without the least notion of what he was talking about, and sat down on a chair, staring at Florence with the liveliest contention of delight and despair going on in his face that any face could exhibit.

'Captain Gills and Lieutenant Walters have mentioned, Miss Dombey,' gasped Mr. Toots, 'that I can do you some service. If I could by any means wash out the remembrance of that day at Brighton, when I conducted myself—much more like a parricide than a person of independent property,' said Mr. Toots, with severe self-accusation, 'I should sink into the silent tomb with a gleam of joy.'

'Pray, Mr. Toots,' said Florence, 'do not wish me to forget anything in our acquaintance. I never can, believe me. You have been far too kind and good to me, always.'

'Miss Dombey,' returned Mr. Toots, 'your consideration for my feelings is a part of your angelic character. Thank you a thousand times. It 's of no consequence at all.'

'What we thought of asking you,' said Florence, 'is, whether you remember where Susan, whom you were so kind as to accompany to the coach-office when she left me, is to be found.'

'Why I do not certainly, Miss Dombey,' said Mr. Toots, after a little consideration, 'remember the exact name of the place that was on the coach; and I do recollect that she said she was not going to stop there, but was going farther on. But Miss Dombey, if your object is to find her, and to have her here, myself and the Chicken will produce her with every despatch that devotion on my part, and great intelligence on the Chicken's, can insure.'

Mr. Toots was so manifestly delighted and revived by the prospect of being useful, and the disinterested sincerity of his devotion was so unquestionable, that it would have been cruel to refuse him. Florence, with an instinctive delicacy, forbore to urge the least obstacle, though she did not forbear to overpower him with thanks; and Mr. Toots proudly took the commission upon himself for immediate execution.

'Miss Dombey,' said Mr. Toots, touching her proffered hand, with a pang of hopeless love visibly shooting through him, and flashing out in his face, 'Good-bye! Allow me to take the liberty of saying, that your misfortunes make me perfectly wretched, and that you may trust me, next to Captain Gills himself. I am quite aware, Miss Dombey, of my own deficiencies—they 're not of the least consequence, thank you—but I am entirely to be relied upon, I do assure you, Miss Dombey.'

With that Mr. Toots came out of the room, again accompanied by the captain, who, standing at a little distance, holding his hat under his arm and arranging his scattered locks with his hook, had been a not uninterested witness of what passed. And when the door closed behind them, the light of Mr. Toots's life was darkly clouded again.

'Captain Gills,' said that gentleman, stopping near the bottom of the stairs, and turning round, 'to tell you the truth, I am not in a frame of mind at the present moment, in which I could see Lieutenant Walters with that entirely friendly feeling towards him that I should wish to harbour in my breast. We cannot always command our feelings, Captain Gills, and I should take it as a particular favour if you'd let me out at the private door.'

'Brother,' returned the captain, 'you shall shape your own course. Wotever course you take, is plain and seamanlike, I'm wery sure.'

'Captain Gills,' said Mr. Toots, 'you're extremely kind. Your good opinion is a consolation to me. There is one thing,' said Mr. Toots, standing in the passage, behind the half-opened door, 'that I hope you'll bear in mind, Captain Gills, and that I should wish Lieutenant Walters to be made acquainted with. I have quite come into my property now, you know, and—and I don't know what to do with it. If I could be at all useful in a pecuniary point of view, I should glide into the silent tomb with ease and smoothness.'

Mr. Toots said no more, but slipped out quietly and shut the door upon himself, to cut the captain off from any reply.

Florence thought of this good creature, long after he had left her, with mingled emotions of pain and pleasure. He was so honest and warm-hearted, that to see him again and be assured of his truth to her in her distress, was a joy and comfort beyond all price; but for that very reason, it was so affecting to think that she caused him a moment's unhappiness, or ruffled, by a breath, the harmless current of his life, that her eyes filled with tears, and her bosom overflowed with pity. Captain Cuttle, in his different way, thought much of Mr. Toots too; and so did Walter; and when the evening came, and they were all sitting together in Florence's new room, Walter praised him in a most impassioned manner, and told Florence what he had said on leaving the house, with every graceful setting-off in the way of comment and appreciation that his own honesty and sympathy could surround it with.

Mr. Toots did not return upon the next day, or the next, or for several days; and in the meanwhile Florence, without any new alarm, lived like a quiet bird in a cage, at the top of the old instrument-maker's house. But Florence drooped and hung her head more and more plainly, as the days went on; and the expression that had been seen in the face of the dead child, was often turned to the sky from her high window, as if it sought his angel out, on the bright shore of which he had spoken: lying on his little bed.

Florence had been weak and delicate of late, and the agitation she had undergone was not without its influences on her health. But it was no bodily illness that affected her now. She was distressed in mind; and the cause of her distress was Walter.

Interested in her, anxious for her, proud and glad to serve her, and showing all this with the enthusiasm and ardour of his character, Florence saw that he avoided her. All the long day through, he seldom approached her room. If she asked for him, he came, again for the moment as earnest and as bright as she remembered him when she was a lost child in the staring streets; but he soon became so constrained —her quick affection was too watchful not to know it—and uneasy, and soon left her. Unsought, he never came, all day, between the morning and the night. When the evening closed in, he was always there, and that was her happiest time, for then she half believed that the old Walter of her childhood was not changed. But, even then, some trivial word, look, or circumstance would show her that there was

an indefinable division between them which could not
be passed.

And she could not but see that these revealings of
a great alteration in Walter manifested themselves in
despite of his utmost efforts to hide them. In his consideration for her, she thought, and in the earnestness
of his desire to spare her any wound from his kind
hand, he resorted to innumerable little artifices and
disguises. So much the more did Florence feel the
greatness of the alteration in him; so much the oftener
did she weep at this estrangement of her brother.

The good captain—her untiring, tender, ever zealous friend—saw it, too, Florence thought, and it
pained him. He was less cheerful and hopeful than
he had been at first, and would steal looks at her and
Walter, by turns, when they were all three together
of an evening, with quite a sad face.

Florence resolved, at last, to speak to Walter. She
believed she knew now what the cause of his estrangement was, and she thought it would be a relief to her
full heart, and would set him more at ease, if she told
him she had found it out, and quite submitted to it,
and did not reproach him.

It was on a certain Sunday afternoon, that
Florence took this resolution. The faithful captain,
in an amazing shirt-collar, was sitting by her, reading with his spectacles on, and she asked him where
Walter was.

'I think he 's down below, my lady lass,' returned
the captain.

'I should like to speak to him,' said Florence, rising
hurriedly as if to go downstairs.

'I 'll rouse him up here, beauty,' said the captain,
'in a trice.'

Thereupon the captain, with much alacrity, shouldered his book—for he made it a point of duty to read none but very large books on a Sunday, as having a more staid appearance: and had bargained, years ago, for a prodigious volume at a book-stall, five lines of which utterly confounded him at any time, insomuch that he had not yet ascertained of what subject it treated—and withdrew. Walter soon appeared.

'Captain Cuttle tells me, Miss Dombey,' he eagerly began on coming in—but stopped when he saw her face.

'You are not so well to-day. You look distressed. You have been weeping.'

He spoke so kindly, and with such a fervent tremor in his voice, that the tears gushed into her eyes at the sound of his words.

'Walter,' said Florence, gently, 'I am not quite well, and I have been weeping. I want to speak to you.'

He sat down opposite to her, looking at her beautiful and innocent face; and his own turned pale, and his lips trembled.

'You said, upon the night when I knew that you were saved—and oh! dear Walter, what I felt that night, and what I hoped!'—

He put his trembling hand upon the table between them, and sat looking at her.

—'that I was changed. I was surprised to hear you say so, but I understand, now, that I am. Don't be angry with me, Walter. I was too much overjoyed to think of it, then.'

She seemed a child to him again. It was the ingenuous, confiding, loving child he saw and heard. Not the dear woman, at whose feet he would have laid the riches of the earth.

'You remember the last time I saw you, Walter, before you went away?'

He put his hand into his breast, and took out a little
purse.

'I have always worn it round my neck! If I had
gone down in the deep, it would have been with me at
the bottom of the sea.'

'And you will wear it still, Walter, for my old
sake?'

'Until I die!'

She laid her hand on his, as fearlessly and simply,
as if not a day had intervened since she gave him the
little token of remembrance.

'I am glad of that. I shall be always glad to
think so, Walter. Do you recollect that a thought
of this change seemed to come into our minds at the
same time that evening, when we were talking together?'

'No!' he answered, in a wondering tone.

'Yes, Walter. I had been the means of injuring
your hopes and prospects even then. I feared to
think so, then, but I know it now. If you were able,
then, in your generosity, to hide from me that you
knew it too, you cannot do so now, although you try
as generously as before. You *do*. I thank you for
it, Walter, deeply, truly; but you cannot succeed.
You have suffered too much in your own hardships,
and in those of your dearest relation, quite to over-
look the innocent cause of all the peril and affliction
that has befallen you. You cannot quite forget me
in that character, and we can be brother and sister
no longer. But, dear Walter, do not think that I
complain of you in this. I might have known it—
ought to have known it—but forgot it in my joy.
All I hope is that you may think of me less irksomely

when this feeling is no more a secret one; and all I ask is, Walter, in the name of the poor child who was your sister once, that you will not struggle with yourself, and pain yourself, for my sake, now that I know all!'

Walter had looked upon her while she said this, with a face so full of wonder and amazement, that it had room for nothing else. Now he caught up the hand that touched his, so entreatingly, and held it between his own.

'Oh, Miss Dombey,' he said, 'is it possible that while I have been suffering so much, in striving with my sense of what is due to you, and must be rendered to you, I have made you suffer what your words disclose to me. Never, never, before Heaven, have I thought of you but as the single, bright, pure, blessed recollection of my boyhood and my youth. Never have I from the first, and never shall I to the last, regard your part in my life, but as something sacred, never to be lightly thought of, never to be esteemed enough, never, until death, to be forgotten. Again to see you look, and hear you speak, as you did on that night when we parted, is happiness to me that there are no words to utter; and to be loved and trusted as your brother, is the next great gift I could receive and prize!'

'Walter,' said Florence, looking at him earnestly, but with a changing face, 'what is that which is due to me, and must be rendered to me, at the sacrifice of all this?'

'Respect,' said Walter, in a low tone. 'Reverence.'

The colour dawned in her face, and she timidly and thoughtfully withdrew her hand; still looking at him with unabated earnestness.

'I have not a brother's right,' said Walter. 'I have

not a brother's claim. I left a child. I find a
woman.'

The colour overspread her face. She made a
gesture as if of entreaty that he would say no more,
and her face dropped upon her hands.

They were both silent for a time: she weeping.

'I owe it to a heart so trusting, pure, and good,'
said Walter, 'even to tear myself from it, though I
rend my own. How dare I say it is my sister's!'

She was weeping still.

'If you had been happy; surrounded as you should
be by loving and admiring friends, and by all that
makes the station you were born to enviable,' said
Walter; 'and if you had called me brother, then, in
your affectionate remembrance of the past, I could
have answered to the name from my distant place,
with no inward assurance that I wronged your spot-
less truth by doing so. But here—and now!'—

'O thank you, thank you, Walter! Forgive my
having wronged you so much. I had no one to advise me. I am quite alone.'

'Florence!' said Walter, passionately. 'I am hurried on to say, what I thought, but a few moments
ago, nothing could have forced from my lips. If I
had been prosperous; if I had any means or hope
of being one day able to restore you to a station near
your own; I would have told you that there was one
name you might bestow upon me—a right above all
others, to protect and cherish you—that I was worthy
of in nothing but the love and honour that I bore
you, and in my whole heart being yours. I would
have told you that it was the only claim that you
could give me to defend and guard you, which I
dare accept and dare assert; but that if I had that
right, I would regard it as a trust so precious and so

priceless, that the undivided truth and fervour of my life would poorly acknowledge its worth.'

The head was still bent down, the tears still falling, and the bosom swelling with its sobs.

'Dear Florence! Dearest Florence! whom I called so in my thoughts before I could consider how presumptuous and wild it was. One last time let me call you by your own dear name, and touch this gentle hand in token of your sisterly forgetfulness of what I have said.'

She raised her head, and spoke to him with such a solemn sweetness in her eyes; with such a calm, bright, placid smile shining on him through her tears; with such a low, soft tremble in her frame and voice; that the innermost chords of his heart were touched, and his sight was dim as he listened.

'No, Walter, I cannot forget it. I would not forget it, for the world. Are you—are you very poor?'

'I am but a wanderer,' said Walter, 'making voyages to live across the sea. That is my calling now.'

'Are you soon going away again, Walter?'

'Very soon.'

She sat looking at him for a moment; then timidly put her trembling hand in his.

'If you will take me for your wife, Walter, I will love you dearly. If you will let me go with you, Walter, I will go to the world's end without fear. I can give up nothing for you—I have nothing to resign, and no one to forsake; but all my love and life shall be devoted to you, and with my last breath I will breathe your name to God if I have sense and memory left.'

He caught her to his heart, and laid her cheek against his own, and now, no more repulsed, no more forlorn, she wept indeed, upon the breast of her dear lover.

Blessed Sunday bells, ringing so tranquilly in their entranced and happy ears! Blessed Sunday peace and quiet, harmonising with the calmness in their souls, and making holy air around them! Blessed twilight stealing on, and shading her so soothingly and gravely, as she falls asleep, like a hushed child, upon the bosom she has clung to!

Oh load of love and trustfulness that lies so lightly there! Aye, look down on the closed eyes, Walter, with a proudly tender gaze; for in all the wide wide world they seek but thee now—only thee!

The captain remained in the little parlour until it was quite dark. He took the chair on which Walter had been sitting, and looked up at the skylight, until the day, by little and little, faded away, and the stars peeped down. He lighted a candle, lighted a pipe, smoked it out, and wondered what on earth was going on upstairs, and why they didn't call him to tea.

Florence came to his side while he was in the height of his wonderment.

'Aye! lady lass!' cried the captain. 'Why, you and Wal'r have had a long spell o' talk, my beauty.'

Florence put her little hand round one of the great buttons of his coat, and said, looking down into his face—

'Dear Captain, I want to tell you something, if you please.'

The captain raised his head pretty smartly, to hear what it was. Catching by this means a more distinct view of Florence, he pushed back his chair, and himself with it as far as they could go.

'What! Heart's Delight!' cried the captain, suddenly elated. 'Is it that?'

'Yes!' said Florence, eagerly.

'Wal'r! Husband! THAT?' roared the captain, tossing up his glazed hat into the skylight.

'Yes!' cried Florence, laughing and crying together.

The captain immediately hugged her; and then, picking up the glazed hat and putting it on, drew her arm through his, and conducted her upstairs again; where he felt that the great joke of his life was now to be made.

'What, Wal'r my lad!' said the captain, looking in at the door, with his face like an amiable warming-pan. 'So there ain't NO other character, ain't there?'

He had like to have suffocated himself with this pleasantry, which he repeated at least forty times during tea; polishing his radiant face with the sleeve of his coat, and dabbing his head all over with his pocket-handkerchief, in the intervals. But he was not without a graver source of enjoyment to fall back upon, when so disposed, for he was repeatedly heard to say in an under-tone, as he looked with ineffable delight at Walter and Florence—

'Ed'ard Cuttle, my lad, you never shaped a better course in your life, than when you made that there little property over, jintly!'

CHAPTER LI

MR. DOMBEY AND THE WORLD

WHAT is the proud man doing, while the days go by? Does he ever think of his daughter, or wonder where she is gone? Does he suppose she has come home, and is leading her old life in the weary house? No one can answer for him. He has never uttered her name, since. His household dread him too much to approach a subject on which he is resolutely dumb; and the only person who dare question him, he silences immediately.

'My dear Paul!' murmurs his sister, sidling into the room, on the day of Florence's departure, 'your wife! that upstart woman! Is it possible that what I hear confusedly, is true, and that this is her return for your unparalleled devotion to her; extending, I am sure, even to the sacrifice of your own relations, to her caprices and haughtiness? My poor brother?'

With this speech, feelingly reminiscent of her not having been asked to dinner on the day of the first party, Mrs. Chick makes great use of her pocket-handkerchief, and falls on Mr. Dombey's neck. But Mr. Dombey frigidly lifts her off, and hands her to a chair.

'I thank you, Louisa,' he says, 'for this mark of your affection; but desire that our conversation may refer to any other subject. When I bewail my fate, Louisa, or express myself as being in want of consolation, you can offer it, if you will have the goodness.'

'My dear Paul,' rejoins his sister, with her handkerchief to her face, and shaking her head, 'I know your great spirit, and will say no more upon a theme so painful and revolting'; on the heads of which two adjectives, Mrs. Chick visits scathing indignation; 'but pray let me ask you—though I dread to hear something that will shock and distress me—that unfortunate child Florence—'

'Louisa!' says her brother, sternly, 'silence. Not another word of this!'

Mrs. Chick can only shake her head, and use her handkerchief, and moan over degenerate Dombeys, who are no Dombeys. But whether Florence has been inculpated in the flight of Edith, or has followed her, or has done too much, or too little, or anything, or nothing, she has not the least idea.

He goes on, without deviation, keeping his thoughts and feelings close within his own breast, and imparting them to no one. He makes no search for his daughter. He may think that she is with his sister, or that she is under his own roof. He may think of her constantly, or he may never think about her. It is all one for any sign he makes.

But this is sure; he does *not* think that he has lost her. He has no suspicion of the truth. He has lived too long shut up in his towering supremacy, seeing her, a patient gentle creature, in the path below it, to have any fear of that. Shaken as he is by his disgrace, he is not yet humbled to the level earth. The root is broad and deep, and in the course of years its fibres have spread out and gathered nourishment from everything around it. The tree is struck, but not down.

Though he hide the world within him from the world without—which he believes has but one purpose for the time, and that, to watch him eagerly wherever he goes—he cannot hide those rebel traces of it, which escape in hollow eyes and cheeks, a haggard forehead, and a moody, brooding air. Impenetrable as before, he is still an altered man: and, proud as ever, he is humbled, or those marks would not be there.

The world. What the world thinks of him, how it looks at him, what it sees in him, and what it says— this is the haunting demon of his mind. It is everywhere where he is; and, worse than that, it is everywhere where he is not. It comes out with him among his servants, and yet he leaves it whispering behind; he sees it pointing after him in the street; it is waiting for him in his counting-house: it leers over the shoulders of rich men among the merchants; it goes beckoning and babbling among the crowd; it always anticipates him, in every place; and is always busiest he knows, when he has gone away. When he is shut up in his room at night, it is in his house, outside it, audible in footsteps on the pavement, visible in print upon the table, steaming to and fro on railroads and in ships: restless and busy everywhere, with nothing else but him.

It is not a phantom of his imagination. It is as active in other people's minds as in his. Witness cousin Feenix, who comes from Baden-Baden, purposely to talk to him. Witness Major Bagstock, who accompanies cousin Feenix on that friendly mission.

Mr. Dombey receives them with his usual dignity, and stands erect, in his old attitude, before the fire. He feels that the world is looking at him out of their eyes. That it is in the stare of the pictures. That Mr. Pitt, upon the book-case, represents it. That there are eyes in its own map, hanging on the wall.

'An unusually cold spring,' says Mr. Dombey—to deceive the world.

'Damme, sir,' says the major, in the warmth of friendship, 'Joseph Bagstock is a bad hand at a counterfeit. If you want to hold your friends off, Dombey, and to give them the cold shoulder, J. B. is not the man for your purpose. Joe is ough and tough, sir; blunt, sir, blunt, is Joe. His royal Highness the late Duke of York did me the honour to say, deservedly or undeservedly—never mind that—"If there is a man in the service on whom I can depend for coming to the point, that man is Joe—Joe Bagstock."'

Mr. Dombey intimates his acquiescence.

'Now, Dombey,' says the major, 'I am a man of

the world. Our friend Feenix—if I may presume to—'

'Honoured, I am sure,' says cousin Feenix.

'—is,' proceeds the major, with a wag of his head, 'also a man of the world, Dombey, *you* are a man of the world. Now, when three men of the world meet together, and are friends—as I believe'—again appealing to cousin Feenix.

'I am sure,' says cousin Feenix, 'most friendly.'

'—and are friends,' resumes the major, 'Old Joe's opinion is (J. may be wrong), that the opinion of the world on any particular subject, is very easily got at.'

'Undoubtedly,' says cousin Feenix. 'In point of fact, it's quite a self-evident sort of thing. I am extremely anxious, major, that my friend Dombey should hear me express my very great astonishment and regret, that my lovely and accomplished relative, who was possessed of every qualification to make a man happy, should have so far forgotten what was due to—in point of fact, to the world—as to commit herself in such a very extraordinary manner. I have been in a devilish state of depression ever since; and said indeed to Long Saxby last night—man of six foot ten, with whom my friend Dombey is probably acquainted—that it had upset me in a confounded way, and made me bilious. It induces a man to reflect, this kind of fatal catastrophe,' says cousin Feenix, 'that events do occur in quite a providential manner; for if my aunt had been living at the time, I think the effect upon a devilish lively woman like herself, would have been prostration, and that she would have fallen, in point of fact, a victim.'

'Now, Dombey!—' says the major, resuming his discourse with great energy.

'I beg your pardon,' interposes cousin Feenix.

'Allow me another word. My friend Dombey will permit me to say, that if any circumstance could have added to the most infernal state of pain in which I find myself on this occasion, it would be the natural amazement of the world at my lovely and accomplished relative (as I must still beg leave to call her) being supposed to have so committed herself with a person—man with white teeth, in point of fact—of very inferior station to her husband. But while I must, rather peremptorily, request my friend Dombey not to criminate my lovely and accomplished relative until her criminality is perfectly established, I beg to assure my friend Dombey that the family I represent, and which is now almost extinct (devilish sad reflection for a man!), will interpose no obstacle in his way, and will be happy to assent to any honourable course of proceeding, with a view to the future, that he may point out. I trust my friend Dombey will give me credit for the intentions by which I am animated in this very melancholy affair, and—a—in point of fact, I am not aware that I need trouble my friend Dombey with any further observations.'

Mr. Dombey bows, without raising his eyes, and is silent.

'Now, Dombey,' says the major, 'our friend Feenix having, with an amount of eloquence that old Joe B. has never heard surpassed—no, by the Lord, sir! never!'—says the major, very blue, indeed, and grasping his cane in the middle—'stated the case as regards the lady, I shall presume upon our friendship, Dombey, to offer a word on another aspect of it. Sir,' says the major, with the horse's cough, 'the world in these things has opinions, which must be satisfied.'

'I know it,' rejoins Mr. Dombey.

'Of course you know it, Dombey,' says the major.

'Damme, sir, I know you know it. A man of your calibre is not likely to be ignorant of it.'

'I hope not,' replies Mr. Dombey.

'Dombey!' says the major, 'you will guess the rest. I speak out—prematurely, perhaps—because the Bagstock breed have always spoken out. Little, sir, have they ever got by doing it; but it's in the Bagstock blood. A shot is to be taken at this man. You have J. B. at your elbow. He claims the name of friend. God bless you!'

'Major,' returns Mr. Dombey, 'I am obliged. I shall put myself in your hands when the time comes. The time not being come, I have forborne to speak to you.'

'Where is the fellow, Dombey?' inquires the major, after gasping and looking at him, for a minute.

'I don't know.'

'Any intelligence of him?' asks the major.

'Yes.'

'Dombey, I am rejoiced to hear it,' says the major. 'I congratulate you.'

'You will excuse—even you, major,' replies Mr. Dombey, 'my entering into any further detail at present. The intelligence is of a singular kind, and singularly obtained. It may turn out to be valueless; it may turn out to be true; I cannot say at present. My explanation must stop here.'

Although this is but a dry reply to the major's purple enthusiasm, the major receives it graciously, and is delighted to think that the world has such a fair prospect of soon receiving its due. Cousin Feenix is then presented with his meed of acknowledgment by the husband of his lovely and accomplished relative, and cousin Feenix and Major Bagstock retire, leaving that husband to the world again, and to ponder at leisure on their representation of its state of mind concerning his affairs, and on its just and reasonable expectations.

But who sits in the housekeeper's room, shedding tears, and talking to Mrs. Pipchin in a low tone, with uplifted hands? It is a lady with her face concealed in a very close black bonnet, which appears not to belong to her. It is Miss Tox, who has borrowed this disguise from her servant, and comes from Princess's Place, thus secretly, to revive her old acquaintance with Mrs. Pipchin, in order to get certain information of the state of Mr. Dombey.

'How does he bear it, my dear creature?' asks Miss Tox.

'Well,' says Mrs. Pipchin, in her snappish way, 'he's pretty much as usual.'

'Externally,' suggests Miss Tox. 'But what he feels within!'

Mrs. Pipchin's hard grey eye looks doubtful as she answers, in three distinct jerks, 'Ah! Perhaps. I suppose so.'

'To tell you my mind, Lucretia,' says Mrs. Pipchin; she still calls Miss Tox Lucretia, on account of having made her first experiments in the child-quelling line of business on that lady, when an unfortunate and weazen little girl of tender years; 'to tell you my mind, Lucretia, I think it's a good riddance. I don't want any of your brazen faces here, myself!'

'Brazen indeed! Well may you say brazen, Mrs. Pipchin!' returns Miss Tox. 'To leave him! Such a noble figure of a man!' And here Miss Tox is overcome.

'I don't know about noble, I'm sure,' observes Mrs. Pipchin, irascibly rubbing her nose. 'But I know this—that when people meet with trials, they must bear 'em. Hoity, toity! I have had enough to bear myself, in my time! What a fuss there is! She's gone and well got rid of. Nobody wants her back, I should think!'

This hint of the Peruvian mines, causes Miss Tox to rise to go away; when Mrs. Pipchin rings the bell for Towlinson to show her out. Mr. Towlinson, not having seen Miss Tox for ages, grins, and hopes she's well; observing that he didn't know her at first, in that bonnet.

'Pretty well, Towlinson, I thank you,' says Miss Tox. 'I beg you'll have the goodness, when you happen to see me here, not to mention it. My visits are merely to Mrs. Pipchin.'

'Very good, miss,' says Towlinson.

'Shocking circumstances occur, Towlinson,' says Miss Tox.

'Very much so indeed, miss,' rejoins Towlinson.

'I hope, Towlinson,' says Miss Tox, who, in her instruction of the Toodle family, has acquired an admonitorial tone, and a habit of improving passing occasions, 'that what has happened here, will be a warning to you, Towlinson.'

'Thank you, miss, I'm sure,' says Towlinson.

He appears to be falling into a consideration of the manner in which this warning ought to operate in his particular case, when the vinegary Mrs. Pipchin, suddenly stirring him up with a 'What are you doing? Why don't you show the lady to the door?' he ushers Miss Tox forth. As she passes Mr. Dombey's room, she shrinks into the inmost depths of the black bonnet, and walks on tiptoe; and there is not another atom in the world which haunts him so, that feels such sorrow and solicitude about him, as Miss Tox takes out under the black bonnet into the street, and tries to carry home shadowed from the newly-lighted lamps.

But Miss Tox is not a part of Mr. Dombey's world.

She comes back every evening at dusk; adding clogs and an umbrella to the bonnet on wet nights; and bears the grins of Towlinson, and the huffs and rebuffs of Mrs. Pipchin, and all to ask how he does, and how he bears his misfortune: but she has nothing to do with Mr. Dombey's world. Exacting and harassing as ever, it goes on without her; and she, a by no means bright or particular star, moves in her little orbit in the corner of another system, and knows it quite well, and comes, and cries, and goes away, and is satisfied. Verily Miss Tox is easier of satisfaction than the world that troubles Mr. Dombey so much!

At the counting-house, the clerks discuss the great disaster in all its lights and shades, but chiefly wonder who will get Mr. Carker's place. They are generally of opinion that it will be shorn of some of its emoluments, and made uncomfortable by newly devised checks and restrictions; and those who are beyond all hope of it, are quite sure they would rather not have it, and don't at all envy the person for whom it may prove to be reserved. Nothing like the prevailing sensation has existed in the counting-house since Mr. Dombey's little son died; but all such excitements there take a social, not to say a jovial turn, and lead to the cultivation of good-fellowship. A reconciliation is established on this propitious occasion between the acknowledged wit of the counting-house and an aspiring rival, with whom he has been at deadly feud for months; and a little dinner being proposed, in commemoration of their happily restored amity, takes place at a neighbouring tavern; the wit in the chair; the rival acting as vice-president. The orations following the removal of the cloth are opened by the chair, who says, Gentlemen, he can't disguise from himself that this is not a time for private dissensions.

Recent occurrences to which he need not more particularly allude, but which have not been altogether without notice in some Sunday papers, and in a daily paper which he need not name (here every other member of the company names it in an audible murmur), have caused him to reflect; and he feels that for him and Robinson to have any personal differences at such a moment, would be for ever to deny that good feeling in the general cause, for which he has reason to think and hope that the gentlemen in Dombey's House have always been distinguished. Robinson replies to this like a man and a brother; and one gentleman who has been in the office three years, under continual notice to quit on account of lapses in his arithmetic, appears in a perfectly new light, suddenly bursting out with a thrilling speech, in which he says, May their respected chief never again know the desolation which has fallen on his hearth! and says a great variety of things, beginning with 'May he never again,' which are received with thunders of applause. In short, a most delightful evening is passed, only interrupted by a difference between two juniors, who, quarrelling about the probable amount of Mr. Carker's late receipts per annum, defy each other with decanters, and are taken out greatly excited. Soda water is in general request at the office next day, and most of the party deem the bill an imposition.

As to Perch, the messenger, he is in a fair way of being ruined for life. He finds himself again constantly in bars of public-houses, being treated and lying dreadfully. It appears that he met everybody concerned in the late transaction, everywhere, and said to them, 'sir,' or 'madam,' as the case was, 'why do you look so pale?' at which each shuddered from head to foot, and said, 'Oh, Perch!' and ran away. Either the consciousness of these enormities, or the reaction consequent on liquor, reduced Mr. Perch to an extreme state of low spirits at that hour of the evening when he usually seeks consolation in the society of Mrs. Perch at Balls Pond; and Mrs. Perch frets a good deal, for she fears his confidence in woman is shaken now, and that he half expects on coming home at night to find her gone off with some viscount.

Mr. Dombey's servants are becoming, at the same time, quite dissipated, and unfit for other service. They have hot suppers every night, and 'talk it over' with smoking drinks upon the board. Mr. Towlinson is always maudlin after half-past ten, and frequently begs to know whether he didn't say that no good would ever come of living in a corner house? They whisper about Miss Florence, and wonder where she is; but agree that if Mr. Dombey don't know, Mrs. Dombey does. This brings them to the latter, of whom cook says, She had a stately way though, hadn't she? But she was too high! They all agree that she was too high, and Mr. Towlinson's old flame, the housemaid (who is very virtuous), entreats that you will never talk to her any more about people who holds their heads up, as if the ground wasn't good enough for 'em.

Everything that is said and done about it, except by Mr. Dombey, is done in chorus. Mr. Dombey and the world are alone together.

CHAPTER LII

SECRET INTELLIGENCE

Good Mrs. Brown and her daughter Alice, kept silent company together, in their own dwelling. It was early in the evening, and late in the spring. But a

few days had elapsed since Mr. Dombey had told
Major Bagstock of his singular intelligence, singularly obtained, which might turn out to be valueless,
and might turn out to be true; and the world was not
satisfied yet.

The mother and daughter sat for a long time without interchanging a word: almost without motion.
The old woman's face was shrewdly anxious and expectant; that of her daughter was expectant too, but
in a less sharp degree, and sometimes it darkened, as
if with gathering disappointment and incredulity.
The old woman, without heeding these changes in its
expression, though her eyes were often turned towards it, sat mumbling and munching, and listening
confidently.

Their abode, though poor and miserable, was not so
utterly wretched as in the days when only Good Mrs.
Brown inhabited it. Some few attempts at cleanli-
ness and order were manifest, though made in a reckless, gipsy way, that might have connected them, at
a glance, with the younger woman. The shades of
evening thickened and deepened as the two kept
silence, until the blackened walls were nearly lost in
the prevailing gloom.

Then Alice broke the silence which had lasted so
long, and said—

'You may give him up, mother. He'll not come
here.'

'Death give him up!' returned the old woman, impatiently. 'He *will* come here.'

'We shall see,' said Alice.

'We shall see *him*,' returned her mother.

'And doomsday,' said the daughter.

'You think I'm in my second childhood, I know!'
croaked the old woman. 'That's the respect and duty

that I get from my own gal, but I 'm wiser than you take me for. He 'll come. T' other day when I touched his coat in the street, he looked round as if I was a toad. But Lord, to see him when I said their names, and asked him if he 'd like to find out where they was!'

'Was it so angry?' asked her daughter, roused to interest in a moment.

'Angry? ask if it was bloody. That 's more like the word. Angry? Ha, ha! To call that only angry!' said the old woman, hobbling to the cupboard, and lighting a candle, which displayed the workings of her mouth to ugly advantage, as she brought it to the table. 'I might as well call your face only angry, when you think or talk about 'em.'

It was something different from that, truly, as she sat as still as a crouched tigress, with her kindling eyes.

'Hark!' said the old woman, triumphantly. 'I hear a step coming. It 's not the tread of any one that lives about here, or comes this way often. We don't walk like that. We should grow proud on such neighbours! Do you hear him?'

'I believe you are right, mother,' replied Alice, in a low voice. 'Peace! open the door.'

As she drew herself within her shawl, and gathered it about her, the old woman complied; and peering out, and beckoning, gave admission to Mr. Dombey, who stopped when he had set his foot within the door, and looked distrustfully around.

'It 's a poor place for a great gentleman like your worship,' said the old woman, curtseying and chattering. 'I told you so, but there 's no harm in it.'

'Who is that?' asked Mr. Dombey, looking at her companion.

'That's my handsome daughter,' said the old woman. 'Your worship won't mind her. She knows all about it.'

A shadow fell upon his face not less expressive than if he had groaned aloud, 'Who does not know all about it?' but he looked at her steadily, and she, without any acknowledgment of his presence, looked at him. The shadow on his face was darker when he turned his glance away from her; and even then it wandered back again, furtively, as if he were haunted by her bold eyes, and some remembrance they inspired.

'Woman,' said Mr. Dombey to the old witch who was chuckling and leering close at his elbow, and who, when he turned to address her, pointed stealthily at her daughter, and rubbed her hands, and pointed again, 'Woman! I believe that I am weak and forgetful of my station in coming here, but you know why I come, and what you offered when you stopped me in the street the other day. What is it that you have to tell me concerning what I want to know; and how does it happen that I can find voluntary intelligence in a hovel like this,' with a disdainful glance about him, 'when I have exerted my power and means to obtain it in vain? I do not think,' he said, after a moment's pause, during which he had observed her, sternly, 'that you are so audacious as to mean to trifle with me, or endeavour to impose on me. But if you have that purpose, you had better stop on the threshold of your scheme. My humour is not a trifling one, and my acknowledgment will be severe.'

'Oh a proud, hard gentleman!' chuckled the old woman, shaking her head, and rubbing her shrivelled hands, 'oh hard, hard, hard! But your worship shall see with your own eyes and hear with your own ears; not with ours—and if your worship's put upon their track, you won't mind paying something for it, will you, honourable deary?'

'Money,' returned Mr. Dombey, apparently relieved, and reassured by this inquiry, 'will bring about unlikely things, I know. It may turn even means as unexpected and unpromising as these, to account. Yes. For any reliable information I receive, I will pay. But I must have the information first, and judge for myself of its value.'

'Do you know nothing more powerful than money?' asked the younger woman, without rising or altering her attitude.

'Not here, I should imagine,' said Mr. Dombey.

'You should know of something that is more powerful elsewhere, as I judge,' she returned. 'Do you know nothing of a woman's anger?'

'You have a saucy tongue, jade,' said Mr. Dombey.

'Not usually,' she answered, without any show of emotion: 'I speak to you now, that you may understand us better, and rely more on us. A woman's anger is pretty much the same here, as in your fine house. I am angry. I have been so, many years. I have as good cause for my anger as you have for yours, and its object is the same man.'

He started, in spite of himself, and looked at her with astonishment.

'Yes,' she said, with a kind of laugh. 'Wide as the distance may seem between us, it is so. How it is so, is no matter; that is my story, and I keep my story to myself. I would bring you and him together, because I have a rage against him. My mother there, is avaricious and poor; and she would sell any tidings she could glean, or anything, or anybody, for money. It is fair enough perhaps, that you should pay her some, if she can help you to what you want to know. But that is not my motive. I have told you what mine is, and it would be as strong and all sufficient with me if you haggled and bargained with her for a sixpence. I have done. My saucy tongue says no more, if you wait here till sunrise to-morrow.'

The old woman who had shown great uneasiness during this speech, which had a tendency to depreciate her expected gains, pulled Mr. Dombey softly by the sleeve, and whispered to him not to mind her. He glanced at them both, by turns, with a haggard look, and said, in a deeper voice than was usual with him—

'Go on—what do you know?'

'Oh, not so fast, your worship! we must wait for some one,' answered the old woman. 'It's to be got from some one else—wormed out—screwed and twisted from him.'

'What do you mean?' said Mr. Dombey.

'Patience,' she croaked, laying her hand, like a claw, upon his arm. 'Patience I'll get at it. I know I can! If he was to hold it back from me,' said Good Mrs. Brown, crooking her ten fingers, 'I'd tear it out of him!'

Mr. Dombey followed her with his eyes as she hobbled to the door, and looked out again: and then his glance sought her daughter; but she remained impassive, silent, and regardless of him.

'Do you tell me, woman,' he said, when the bent figure of Mrs. Brown came back, shaking its head and chattering to itself, 'that there is another person expected here?'

'Yes!' said the old woman, looking up into his face, and nodding.

'From whom you are to exact the intelligence that is to be useful to me?'

'Yes,' said the old woman, nodding again.

'A stranger?'

'Chut!' said the old woman, with a shrill laugh. 'What signifies! Well, well; no. No stranger to your worship. But he won't see you. He'd be afraid of you and wouldn't talk. You'll stand behind that door, and judge him for yourself. We don't ask to be believed on trust. What? Your worship doubts the room behind the door? Oh the suspicion of you rich gentlefolks! Look at it, then.'

Her sharp eye had detected an involuntary expression of this feeling on his part, which was not unreasonable under the circumstances. In satisfaction of it she now took the candle to the door she spoke of. Mr. Dombey looked in; assured himself that it was an empty, crazy room; and signed to her to put the light back in its place.

'How long,' he asked, 'before this person comes?'

'Not long,' she answered. 'Would your worship sit down for a few odd minutes?'

He made no answer; but began pacing the room with an irresolute air, as if he were undecided whether to remain or depart, and as if he had some quarrel with himself for being there at all. But soon his tread grew slower and heavier, and his face more sternly thoughtful: as the object with which he had come, fixed itself in his mind, and dilated there again.

While he thus walked up and down with his eyes on the ground, Mrs. Brown, in the chair from which she had risen to receive him, sat listening anew. The monotony of his step, or the uncertainty of age, made her so slow of hearing, that a footfall without had sounded in her daughter's ears for some moments, and she had looked up hastily to warn her mother of its approach, before the old woman was roused by it. But then she started from her seat, and whispering 'Here he is!' hurried her visitor to his place of observation, and put a bottle and glass upon the table, with such alacrity as to be ready to fling her arms round the neck of Rob the Grinder on his appearance at the door.

'And here's my bonny boy,' cried Mrs. Brown, 'at last!—oho, oho! You're like my own son, Robby!'

'Oh! Misses Brown!' remonstrated the Grinder. 'Don't! Can't you be fond of a cove without squeedging and throttling of him? Take care of the birdcage in my hand, will you?'

'Thinks of a birdcage, afore me!' cried the old woman, apostrophising the ceiling. 'Me that feels more than a mother for him!'

'Well, I'm sure I'm very much obliged to you, Misses Brown,' said the unfortunate youth, greatly aggravated; 'but you're so jealous of a cove. I'm very fond of you myself, and all that, of course; but I don't smother you, do I, Misses Brown?'

He looked and spoke as if he would have been far from objecting to do so, however, on a favourable occasion.

'And to talk about birdcages, too!' whimpered the Grinder. 'As if that was a crime! Why, look 'ee here! Do you know who this belongs to?'

'To master, dear?' said the old woman with a grin.

'Ah!' replied the Grinder, lifting a large cage tied up in a wrapper, on the table, and untying it with his teeth and hands. 'It's our parrot, this is.'

'Mr. Carker's parrot, Rob?'

'Will you hold your tongue, Misses Brown?' returned the goaded Grinder. 'What do you go naming names for? I'm blest,' said Rob, pulling his hair with both hands in the exasperation of his feelings, 'if she an't enough to make a cove run wild!'

'What? Do you snub me, thankless boy?' cried the old woman, with ready vehemence.

'Good gracious, Misses Brown, no!' returned the Grinder, with tears in his eyes. 'Was there ever such a!— Don't I dote upon you, Misses Brown?'

'Do you, sweet Rob? Do you truly, chickabiddy?' With that, Mrs. Brown held him in her fond embrace once more; and did not release him until he had made several violent and ineffectual struggles with his legs, and his hair was standing on end all over his head.

'Oh!' returned the Grinder, 'what a thing it is to be perfectly pitched into with affection like this here. I wish she was— How have you been, Misses Brown?'

'Ah! Not here since this night week!' said the old woman, contemplating him with a look of reproach.

'Good gracious, Misses Brown,' returned the Grinder, 'I said to-night's a week, that I'd come to-night, didn't I? And here I am. How you do go on! I wish you'd be a little rational, Misses Brown. I'm hoarse with saying things in my defence, and my very face is shiny with being hugged.' He rubbed it hard with his sleeve, as if to remove the tender polish in question.

'Drink a little drop to comfort you, my Robin,' said the old woman, filling the glass from the bottle and giving it to him.

'Thank 'ee, Misses Brown,' returned the Grinder. 'Here's your health. And long may you—et ceterer.' Which to judge from the expression of his face, did not include any very choice blessings. 'And here's *her* health,' said the Grinder, glancing at Alice, who sat with her eyes fixed, as it seemed to him, on the wall behind him, but in reality on Mr. Dombey's face at the door, 'and wishing her the same and many of 'em!'

He drained the glass to these two sentiments, and set it down.

'Well, I say, Misses Brown!' he proceeded. 'To go on a little rational now. You 're a judge of birds, and up to their ways, as I know to my cost.'

'Cost!' repeated Mrs. Brown.

'Satisfaction, I mean,' returned the Grinder. 'How you do take up a cove, Misses Brown! You 've put it all out of my head again.'

'Judge of birds, Robby,' suggested the old woman.

'Ah!' said the Grinder. 'Well, I 've got to take care of this parrot—certain things being sold, and a certain establishment broke up—and as I don't want no notice took at present, I wish you 'd attend to her for a week or so, and give her board and lodging, will you? If I *must* come backwards and forwards,' mused the Grinder with a dejected face, 'I may as well have something to come for.'

'Something to come for?' screamed the old woman.

'Besides you, I mean, Misses Brown,' returned the craven Rob. 'Not that I want any inducement but yourself, Misses Brown, I 'm sure. Don't begin again, for goodness' sake.'

'He don't care for me! He don't care for me, as I care for him!' cried Mrs. Brown, lifting up her skinny hands. 'But I 'll take care of his bird.'

'Take good care of it too, you know, Mrs. Brown,' said Rob, shaking his head. 'If you was so much as to stroke its feathers once the wrong way, I believe it would be found out.'

'Ah, so sharp as that, Rob?' said Mrs. Brown, quickly.

'Sharp, Misses Brown!' repeated Rob. 'But this is not to be talked about.'

Checking himself abruptly, and not without a fearful glance across the room, Rob filled the glass again, and having slowly emptied it, shook his head, and began to draw his fingers across and across the wires of

SECRET INTELLIGENCE.

SECRET INTELLIGENCE.

the parrot's cage by way of a diversion from the dangerous theme that had just been broached.

The old woman eyed him slily, and hitching her chair nearer his, and looking in at the parrot, who came down from the gilded dome at her call, said—

'Out of place now, Robby?'

'Never *you* mind, Misses Brown,' returned the Grinder, shortly.

'Board wages, perhaps, Rob?' said Mrs. Brown.

'Pretty Polly!' said the Grinder.

The old woman darted a glance at him that might have warned him to consider his ears in danger, but it was his turn to look in at the parrot now, and however expressive his imagination may have made her angry scowl, it was unseen by his bodily eyes.

'I wonder master didn't take you with him, Rob,' said the old woman, in a wheedling voice, but with increased malignity of aspect.

Rob was so absorbed in contemplation of the parrot, and in trolling his forefinger on the wires, that he made no answer.

The old woman had her clutch within a hair's breadth of his shock of hair as it stooped over the table; but she restrained her fingers, and said, in a voice that choked with its efforts to be coaxing—

'Robby, my child.'

'Well, Misses Brown,' returned the Grinder.

'I say I wonder master didn't take you with him, dear.'

'Never *you* mind, Misses Brown,' returned the Grinder.

Mrs. Brown instantly directed the clutch of her right hand at his hair, and the clutch of her left hand at his throat, and held on to the object of her fond affection with such extraordinary fury, that his face began to blacken in a moment.

'Misses Brown!' exclaimed the Grinder, 'let go, will you? What are you doing of? Help, young woman! Misses Brow—Brow—!'

The young woman, however, equally unmoved by his direct appeal to her, and by his inarticulate utterance, remained quite neutral, until, after struggling with his assailant into a corner, Rob disengaged himself, and stood there panting and fenced in by his own elbows, while the old woman, panting too, and stamping with rage and eagerness, appeared to be collecting her energies for another swoop upon him. At this crisis Alice interposed her voice, but not in the Grinder's favour, by saying—

'Well done, mother. Tear him to pieces!'

'What, young woman!' blubbered Rob; 'are you against me too? What have I been and done? What am I to be tore to pieces for, I should like to know? Why do you take and choke a cove who has never done you any harm, neither of you? Call yourselves females, too!' said the frightened and afflicted Grinder, with his coat-cuff at his eye. 'I'm surprised at you! Where's your feminine tenderness?'

'You thankless dog!' gasped Mrs. Brown. 'You impudent insulting dog!'

'What have I been and done to go and give you offence, Misses Brown?' retorted the tearful Rob. 'You was very much attached to me a minute ago.'

'To cut me off with his short answers and his sulky words,' said the old woman. 'Me! Because I happen to be curious to have a little bit of gossip about master and the lady, to dare to play at fast and loose with me! But I'll talk to you no more, my lad. Now go!'

'I'm sure, Misses Brown,' returned the abject Grinder, 'I never insiniwated that I wished to go. Don't talk like that, Misses Brown, if you please.'

'I won't talk at all,' said Mrs. Brown, with an action of her crooked fingers that made him shrink into half his natural compass in the corner. 'Not another word with him shall pass my lips. He's an ungrateful hound. I cast him off. Now let him go! And I'll slip those after him that shall talk too much; that won't be shook away; that'll hang to him like leeches, and slink arter him like foxes. What? He knows 'em. He knows his old games and his old ways. If he's forgotten 'em, they'll soon remind him. Now let him go, and see how he'll do master's business, and keep master's secrets, with such company always following him up and down. Ha, ha, ha! He'll find 'em a different sort from you and me, Ally; close as he is with you and me. Now let him go, now let him go!'

The old woman, to the unspeakable dismay of the Grinder, walked her twisted figure round and round, in a ring of some four feet in diameter, constantly repeating these words, and shaking her fist above her head, and working her mouth about.

'Misses Brown,' pleaded Rob, coming a little out of his corner, 'I'm sure you wouldn't injure a cove, on second thoughts, and in cold blood, would you?'

'Don't talk to me,' said Mrs. Brown, still wrathfully pursuing her circle. 'Now let him go, now let him go!'

'Misses Brown,' urged the tormented Grinder, 'I didn't mean to—Oh, what a thing it is for a cove to get into such a line as this!—I was only careful of talking, Misses Brown, because I always am, on account of his being up to everything; but I might have known it wouldn't have gone any further. I'm sure I'm quite agreeable,' with a wretched face, 'for any little bit of gossip, Misses Brown. Don't go on like this, if you please. Oh, couldn't you have the goodness to put in a word for a miserable cove, here?' said the Grinder, appealing in desperation to the daughter.

'Come, mother, you hear what he says,' she interposed, in her stern voice, and with an impatient action of her head; 'try him once more, and if you fall out with him again, ruin him, if you like, and have done with him.'

Mrs. Brown, moved as it seemed by this very tender exhortation, presently began to howl; and softening by degrees, took the apologetic Grinder to her arms, who embraced her with a face of unutterable woe, and like a victim as he was, resumed his former seat, close by the side of his venerable friend, whom he suffered, not without much constrained sweetness of countenance, combating very expressive physiognomical revelations of an opposite character, to draw his arm through hers, and keep it there.

'And how 's master, deary dear?' said Mrs. Brown, when, sitting in this amicable posture, they had pledged each other.

'Hush! If you 'd be so good, Misses Brown, as to speak a little lower,' Rob implored. 'Why, he 's pretty well, thank 'ee, I suppose.'

'You 're not out of place, Robby?' said Mrs. Brown in a wheedling tone.

'Why, I 'm not exactly out of place, nor in,' faltered Rob. 'I—I 'm still in pay, Misses Brown.'

'And nothing to do, Rob?'

'Nothing particular to do just now, Misses Brown, but to—keep my eyes open,' said the Grinder, rolling them in a forlorn way.

'Master abroad, Rob?'

'Oh, for goodness' sake, Misses Brown, couldn't you gossip with a cove about anything else?' cried the Grinder, in a burst of despair.

The impetuous Mrs. Brown rising directly, the tortured Grinder detained her, stammering 'Ye-es, Misses Brown, I believe he's abroad. What's she staring at?' he added, in allusion to the daughter, whose eyes were fixed upon the face that now again looked out behind him.

'Don't mind her, lad,' said the old woman, holding him closer to prevent his turning round. 'It's her way—her way. Tell me, Rob. Did you ever see the lady, deary?'

'Oh, Misses Brown, what lady?' cried the Grinder in a tone of piteous supplication.

'What lady?' she retorted. 'The lady; Mrs. Dombey.'

'Yes, I believe I see her once,' replied Rob.

'The night she went away, Robby, eh?' said the old woman in his ear, and taking note of every change in his face. 'Aha! I know it was that night.'

'Well, if you know it was that night, you know, Mrs. Brown,' replied Rob, 'it's no use putting pinchers into a cove to make him say so.'

'Where did they go that night, Rob? Straight away? How did they go? Where did you see her? Did she laugh? Did she cry? Tell me all about it,' cried the old hag, holding him closer yet, patting the hand that was drawn through his arm against her other hand, and searching every line in his face with her bleared eyes. 'Come! Begin! I want to be told all about it. What, Rob boy! you and me can keep a secret together, eh? We've done so before now. Where did they go first, Rob?'

The wretched Grinder made a gasp, and a pause.

'Are you dumb?' said the old woman, angrily.

'Lord, Misses Brown, no! You expect a cove to be a flash of lightning. I wish I *was* the electric fluency,' muttered the bewildered Grinder. 'I'd have a shock at somebody, that would settle their business.'

'What do you say?' asked the old woman, with a grin.

'I'm wishing my love to you, Misses Brown,' returned the false Rob, seeking consolation in the glass. 'Where did they go to first, was it? Him and her do you mean?'

'Ah!' said the old woman, eagerly. 'Them two.'

'Why, they didn't go nowhere—not together, I mean,' answered Rob.

The old woman looked at him, as though she had a strong impulse upon her to make another clutch at his head, and throat, but was restrained by a certain dogged mystery in his face.

'That was the art of it,' said the reluctant Grinder; 'that's the way nobody saw 'em go, or has been able to say how they did go. They went different ways, I tell you, Misses Brown.'

'Ay, ay, ay! To meet at an appointed place,' chuckled the old woman, after a moment's silent and keen scrutiny of his face.

'Why, if they weren't a going to meet somewhere, I suppose they might as well have stayed at home, mightn't they, Misses Brown?' returned the unwilling Grinder.

'Well, Rob? Well?' said the old woman, drawing his arm yet tighter through her own, as if, in her eagerness, she were afraid of his slipping away.

'What, haven't we talked enough yet, Misses Brown?' returned the Grinder, who, between his sense of injury, his sense of liquor, and his sense of being on the rack, had become so lachrymose, that at almost every answer he scooped his coat-cuff into one or other of his eyes, and uttered an unavailing whine of remonstrance. 'Did she laugh that night, was it? Didn't you ask if she laughed, Misses Brown?'

'Or cried?' added the old woman, nodding assent.

'Neither,' said the Grinder. 'She kept as steady when she and me—oh, I see you *will* have it out of me, Misses Brown! But take your solemn oath now, that you 'll never tell anybody.'

This Mrs. Brown very readily did: being naturally Jesuitical; and having no other intention in the matter than that her concealed visitor should hear for himself.

'She kept as steady, then, when she and me went down to Southampton,' said the Grinder, 'as a image. In the morning she was just the same, Misses Brown. And when she went away in the packet before daylight, by herself—me pretending to be her servant, and seeing her safe aboard—she was just the same. *Now,* are you contented, Mrs. Brown?'

'No, Rob. Not yet,' answered Mrs. Brown, decisively.

'Oh, here 's a woman for you!' cried the unfortunate Rob, in an outburst of feeble lamentation over his own helplessness. 'What do you wish to know next, Misses Brown?'

'What became of master? Where did he go?' She inquired, still holding him tight, and looking close into his face, with her sharp eyes.

'Upon my soul, I don't know, Misses Brown,' answered Rob. 'Upon my soul, I don't know what he did, nor where he went, nor anything about him. I only know what he said to me as a caution to hold my tongue, when we parted; and I tell you this, Mrs. Brown, as a friend, that sooner than ever repeat a word of what we 're saying now, you had better take and shoot yourself, or shut yourself up in this house, and set it afire, for there 's nothing he wouldn't do, to be revenged upon you. You don't know him half as well as I do, Misses Brown. You're never safe from him, I tell you.'

'Haven't I taken an oath,' retorted the old woman, 'and won't I keep it?'

'Well, I'm sure I hope you will, Misses Brown,' returned Rob, somewhat doubtfully, and not without a latent threatening in his manner. 'For your own sake quite as much as mine.'

He looked at her as he gave her this friendly caution, and emphasised it with a nodding of his head; but finding it uncomfortable to encounter the yellow face with its grotesque action, and the ferret eyes with their keen old wintry gaze, so close to his own, he looked down uneasily and sat shuffling in his chair, as if he were trying to bring himself to a sullen declaration that he would answer no more questions. The old woman, still holding him as before, took this opportunity of raising the forefinger of her right hand, in the air, as a stealthy signal to the concealed observer to give particular attention to what was about to follow.

'Rob,' she said, in her most coaxing tone.

'Good gracious, Misses Brown, what's the matter now?' returned the exasperated Grinder.

'Rob! where did the lady and master appoint to meet?'

Rob shuffled more and more, and looked up and looked down, and bit his thumb, and dried it on his waistcoat, and finally said, eyeing his tormentor askant, 'How should *I* know, Misses Brown?'

The old woman held up her finger again, as before, and replying, 'Come, lad! It's no use leading me to that, and there leaving me. I want to know'—waited for his answer.

Rob, after a discomfited pause, suddenly broke out

with, 'How can I pronounce the names of foreign places, Misses Brown? What an unreasonable woman you are!'

'But you have heard it said, Robby,' she retorted firmly, 'and you knew what it sounded like. Come!'

'I never heard it said, Misses Brown,' returned the Grinder.

'Then,' retorted the old woman quickly, 'you have seen it written, and you can spell it.'

Rob, with a petulant exclamation between laughing and crying—for he was penetrated with some admiration of Mrs. Brown's cunning, even through this persecution—after some reluctant fumbling in his waistcoat pocket, produced from it a little piece of chalk. The old woman's eyes sparkled when she saw it between his thumb and finger, and hastily clearing a space on the deal table, that he might write the word there, she once more made her signal with a shaking hand.

'Now I tell you beforehand what it is, Misses Brown,' said Rob, 'it's no use asking me anything else. I won't answer anything else; I can't. How long it was to be before they met, or whose plan it was that they was to go away alone, I don't know no more than you do. I don't know any more about it. If I was to tell you how I found out this word, you'd believe that. Shall I tell you, Misses Brown?'

'Yes, Rob.'

'Well then, Misses Brown. The way—now you won't ask any more, you know?' said Rob, turning his eyes, which were now fast getting drowsy and stupid, upon her.

'Not another word,' said Mrs. Brown.

'Well then, the way was this. When a certain person left the lady with me, he put a piece of paper with a direction on it in the lady's hand, saying it was in case she should forget. She wasn't afraid of forgetting, for she tore it up as soon as his back was turned, and when I put up the carriage steps, I shook out one of the pieces—she sprinkled the rest out of the window, I suppose, for there was none there afterwards, though I looked for 'em. There was only one word on it, and that was this, if you must and will know. But remember! You're upon your oath, Misses Brown!'

Mrs. Brown knew that, she said. Rob, having nothing more to say, began to chalk, slowly, and laboriously, on the table.

' "D," ' the old woman read aloud, when he had formed the letter.

'Will you hold your tongue, Misses Brown?' he exclaimed, covering it with his hand, and turning impatiently upon her, 'I won't have it read out. Be quiet, will you!'

'Then write large, Rob,' she returned, repeating her secret signal; 'for my eyes are not good, even at print.'

Muttering to himself, and returning to his work with an ill will, Rob went on, with the word. As he bent his head down, the person for whose information he so unconsciously laboured, moved from the door behind him to within a short stride of his shoulder, and looked eagerly towards the creeping track of his hand upon the table. At the same time, Alice, from her opposite chair, watched it narrowly as it shaped the letters, and repeated each one on her lips as he made it, without articulating it aloud. At the end of every letter her eyes and Mr. Dombey's met, as if each of them sought to be confirmed by the other; and thus they both spelt D. I. J. O. N.

'There!' said the Grinder, moistening the palm of his hand hastily, to obliterate the word; and not content with smearing it out, rubbing and planing all trace of it away with his coat-sleeve, until the very colour of the chalk was gone from the table. 'Now, I hope you 're contented, Misses Brown!'

The old woman, in token of her being so, released his arm and patted his back; and the Grinder, overcome with mortification, cross-examination, and liquor, folded his arms on the table, laid his head upon them, and fell asleep.

Not until he had been heavily asleep some time, and was snoring roundly, did the old woman turn towards the door, where Mr. Dombey stood concealed, and beckon him to come through the room, and pass out. Even then, she hovered over Rob, ready to blind him with her hands, or strike his head down, if he should raise it while the secret step was crossing to the door. But though her glance took sharp cognisance of the sleeper, it was sharp too for the waking man; and when he touched her hand with his, and in spite of all his caution, made a chinking, golden sound, it was as bright and greedy as a raven's.

The daughter's dark gaze followed him to the door, and noted well how pale he was, and how his hurried tread indicated that the least delay was an insupportable restraint upon him, and how he was burning to be active and away. As he closed the door behind him, she looked round at her mother. The old woman trotted to her; opened her hand to show what was within; and, tightly closing it again in her jealousy and avarice, whispered—

'What will he do, Ally?'

'Mischief,' said the daughter.

'Murder?' asked the old woman.

'He 's a madman, in his wounded pride, and may do that, for anything we can say, or he either.'

Her glance was brighter than her mother's, and

the fire that shone in it was fiercer; but her face was colourless, even to her lips.

They said no more, but sat apart; the mother communing with her money; the daughter with her thoughts; the glance of each, shining in the gloom of the feebly lighted room. Rob slept and snored. The disregarded parrot only was in action. It twisted and pulled at the wires of its cage, with its crooked beak, and crawled up to the dome, and along its roof like a fly, and down again head foremost, and shook, and bit, and rattled at every slender bar, as if it knew its master's danger, and was wild to force a passage out, and fly away to warn him of it.

CHAPTER LIII

MORE INTELLIGENCE

THERE were two of the traitor's own blood—his renounced brother and sister—on whom the weight of his guilt rested almost more heavily, at this time, than on the man whom he had so deeply injured. Prying and tormenting as the world was, it did Mr. Dombey the service of nerving him to pursuit and revenge. It roused his passion, stung his pride, twisted the one idea of his life into a new shape, and made some gratification of his wrath, the object into which his whole intellectual existence resolved itself. All the stubbornness and implacability of his nature, all its hard impenetrable quality, all its gloom and moroseness, all its exaggerated sense of personal importance, all its jealous disposition to resent the least flaw in the ample recognition of his importance by others, set this way like many streams united into one, and bore him on upon their tide. The most impetuously passionate and violently impulsive of mankind would have been a milder enemy to encounter than the sullen Mr. Dombey wrought to this. A wild beast would have been easier turned or soothed than the grave gentleman without a wrinkle in his starched cravat.

But the very intensity of his purpose became almost a substitute for action in it. While he was yet uninformed of the traitor's retreat, it served to divert his mind from his own calamity, and to entertain it with another prospect. The brother and sister of his false favourite had no such relief; everything in their history, past and present, gave his delinquency a more afflicting meaning to them.

The sister may have sometimes sadly thought that if she had remained with him, the companion and friend she had been once, he might have escaped the crime into which he had fallen. If she ever thought so, it was still without regret for what she had done, without the least doubt of her duty, without any pricing or enhancing of her self-devotion. But when this possibility presented itself to the erring and repentant brother, as it sometimes did, it smote upon his heart with such a keen, reproachful touch as he could hardly bear. No idea of retort upon his cruel brother came into his mind. New accusation of himself, fresh inward lamentings over his own unworthiness, and the ruin in which it was at once his consolation and his self-reproach that he did not stand alone, were the sole kind of reflections to which the discovery gave rise in him.

It was on the very same day whose evening set upon the last chapter, and when Mr. Dombey's world was busiest with the elopement of his wife, that the window of the room in which the brother and sister sat at their early breakfast, was darkened by the unexpected shadow of a man coming to the little porch: which man was Perch the messenger.

'I've stepped over from Balls Pond at a early hour,' said Mr. Perch, confidentially looking in at the room door, and stopping on the mat to wipe his shoes all round, which had no mud upon them, 'agreeable to my instructions last night. They was, to be sure and bring a note to you, Mr. Carker, before you went out in the morning. I should have been here a good hour and a half ago,' said Mr. Perch, meekly, 'but for the state of health of Mrs. P., who I thought I should have lost in the night, I do assure you, five distinct times.'

'Is your wife so ill?' asked Harriet.

'Why, you see,' said Mr. Perch, first turning round to shut the door carefully, 'she takes what has happened in our House so much to heart, miss. Her nerves is so very delicate, you see, and soon unstrung. Not but what the strongest nerves had good need to be shook, I'm sure. You feel it very much yourself, no doubts.'

Harriet repressed a sigh, and glanced at her brother.

'I'm sure I feel it myself, in my humble way,' Mr. Perch went on to say, with a shake of his head, 'in a manner I couldn't have believed if I hadn't been called upon to undergo. It has almost the effect of drink upon me. I literally feels every morning as if I had been taking more than was good for me overnight.'

Mr. Perch's appearance corroborated this recital of his symptoms. There was an air of feverish lassitude about it, that seemed referable to drams; and which, in fact, might no doubt have been traced to those numerous discoveries of himself in the bars of

public-houses, being treated and questioned, which
he was in the daily habit of making.

'Therefore I can judge,' said Mr. Perch, shaking
his head again, and speaking in a silvery murmur,
'of the feelings of such as is at all peculiarly sitiwated
in this most painful rewelation.'

Here Mr. Perch waited to be confided in; and receiving no confidence, coughed behind his hand.
This leading to nothing, he coughed behind his hat;
and that leading to nothing, he put his hat on the
ground and sought in his breast-pocket for the letter.

'If I rightly recollect, there was no answer,' said
Mr. Perch, with an affable smile; 'but perhaps you 'll
be so good as cast your eye over it, sir.'

John Carker broke the seal, which was Mr. Dombey's, and possessing himself of the contents, which
were very brief, replied, 'No. No answer is expected.'

'Then I shall wish you good morning, miss,' said
Perch, taking a step toward the door, 'and hoping,
I 'm sure, that you 'll not permit yourself to be more
reduced in mind than you can help, by the late painful rewelation. The papers,' said Mr. Perch, taking
two steps back again, and comprehensively addressing both the brother and the sister in a whisper of
increased mystery, 'is more eager for news of it
than you 'd suppose possible. One of the Sunday
ones, in a blue cloak and a white hat, that had previously offered for to bribe me—need I say with
what success?—was dodging about our court last
night as late as twenty minutes after eight o'clock.
I see him myself, with his eye at the counting-house
keyhole, which being patent is impervious. Another
one,' said Mr. Perch, 'with milintary frogs, is in the
parlour of the King's Arms all the blessed day. I

happened, last week, to let a little obserwation fall there, and next morning, which was Sunday, I see it worked up in print, in a most surprising manner.'

Mr. Perch resorted to his breast-pocket, as if to produce the paragraph, but receiving no encouragement, pulled out his beaver gloves, picked up his hat, and took his leave; and before it was high noon, Mr. Perch had related to several select audiences at the King's Arms and elsewhere, how Miss Carker, bursting into tears, had caught him by both hands, and said, 'Oh! dear dear Perch, the sight of you is all the comfort I have left!' and how Mr. John Carker had said, in an awful voice, 'Perch, I disown him. Never let me hear him mentioned as a brother more!'

'Dear John,' said Harriet, when they were left alone, and had remained silent for some few moments. 'There are bad tidings in that letter.'

'Yes. But nothing unexpected,' he replied. 'I saw the writer yesterday.'

'The writer?'

'Mr. Dombey. He passed twice through the counting-house while I was there. I had been able to avoid him before, but of course could not hope to do that long. I know how natural it was that he should regard my presence as something offensive; I felt it must be so, myself.'

'He did not say so?'

'No; he said nothing: but I saw that his glance rested on me for a moment, and I was prepared for what would happen—for what *has* happened. I am dismissed!'

She looked as little shocked and as hopeful as she could, but it was distressing news, for many reasons.

' "I need not tell you," ' said John Carker, reading the letter, ' "why your name would henceforth have an unnatural sound, in however remote a connection with mine, or why the daily sight of any one who bears it, would be unendurable to me. I have to notify the cessation of all engagements between us, from this date, and to request that no renewal of any communication with me, or my establishment, be ever attempted by you."—Enclosed is an equivalent in money to a generously long notice, and this is my discharge. Heaven knows, Harriet, it is a lenient and considerate one, when we remember all!'

'If it be lenient and considerate to punish you at all, John, for the misdeed of another,' she replied gently, 'yes.'

'We have been an ill-omened race to him,' said John Carker. 'He has reason to shrink from the sound of our name, and to think that there is something cursed and wicked in our blood. I should almost think it too, Harriet, but for you.'

'Brother, don't speak like this. If you have any special reason, as you say you have, and think you have—though I say, No!—to love me, spare me the hearing of such wild mad words!'

He covered his face with both his hands; but soon permitted her, coming near him, to take one in her own.

'After so many years, this parting is a melancholy thing, I know,' said his sister, 'and the cause of it is dreadful to us both. We have to live, too, and must look about us for the means. Well, well! We can do so, undismayed. It is our pride, not our trouble, to strive, John, and to strive together!'

A smile played on her lips, as she kissed his cheek, and entreated him to be of good cheer.

'Oh, dearest sister! Tied, of your own noble will,

to a ruined man! whose reputation is blighted; who has no friend himself, and has driven every friend of yours away!'

'John!' she laid her hand hastily upon his lips, 'for my sake! In remembrance of our long companionship!' He was silent. 'Now, let me tell you, dear,' quietly sitting by his side, 'I have, as you have, expected this; and when I have been thinking of it, and fearing that it would happen, and preparing myself for it, as well as I could, I have resolved to tell you, if it should be so, that I have kept a secret from you, and that we *have* a friend.'

'What's our friend's name, Harriet?' he answered with a sorrowful smile.

'Indeed, I don't know, but he once made a very earnest protestation to me of his friendship and his wish to serve us: and to this day I believe him.'

'Harriet!' exclaimed her wondering brother, 'where does this friend live?'

'Neither do I know that,' she returned. 'But he knows us both, and our history—all our little history, John. That is the reason why, at his own suggestion, I have kept the secret of his coming here, from you, lest his acquaintance with it should distress you.'

'Here! Has he been here, Harriet?'

'Here, in this room. Once.'

'What kind of man?'

'Not young. "Grey-headed," as he said, "and fast growing greyer." But generous, and frank, and good, I am sure.'

'And only seen once, Harriet?'

'In this room only once,' said his sister, with the slightest and most transient glow upon her cheek; 'but when here, he entreated me to suffer him to see me once a week as he passed by, in token of our being well, and continuing to need nothing at his hands.

For I told him, when he proffered us any service he could render—which was the object of his visit—that we needed nothing.'

'And once a week—'

'Once every week since then, and always on the same day, and at the same hour, he has gone past; always on foot; always going in the same direction —towards London; and never pausing longer than to bow to me, and wave his hand cheerfully, as a kind guardian might. He made that promise when he proposed these curious interviews, and has kept it so faithfully and pleasantly, that if I ever felt any trifling uneasiness about them in the beginning (which I don't think I did, John; his manner was so plain and true) it very soon vanished, and left me quite glad when the day was coming. Last Monday—the first since this terrible event—he did not go by; and I have wondered whether his absence can have been in any way connected with what has happened.'

'How?' inquired her brother.

'I don't know how. I have only speculated on the coincidence; I have not tried to account for it. I feel sure he will return. When he does, dear John, let me tell him that I have at last spoken to you, and let me bring you together. He will certainly help us to a new livelihood. His entreaty was that he might do something to smooth my life and yours; and I gave him my promise that if we ever wanted a friend, I would remember him. Then his name was to be no secret.'

'Harriet,' said her brother, who had listened with close attention, 'describe this gentleman to me. I surely ought to know one who knows me so well.'

His sister painted, as vividly as she could, the features, stature, and dress of her visitor; but John

Carker, either from having no knowledge of the original, or from some fault in her description, or from some abstraction of his thoughts as he walked to and fro, pondering, could not recognise the portrait she presented to him.

However, it was agreed between them that he should see the original when he next appeared. This concluded, the sister applied herself, with a less anxious breast, to her domestic occupations; and the grey-haired man, late Junior of Dombey's, devoted the first day of his unwonted liberty to working in the garden.

It was quite late at night, and the brother was reading aloud while the sister plied her needle, when they were interrupted by a knocking at the door. In the atmosphere of vague anxiety and dread that lowered about them in connection with their fugitive brother, this sound, unusual there, became almost alarming. The brother going to the door, the sister sat and listened timidly. Some one spoke to him, and he replied and seemed surprised; and after a few words, the two approached together.

'Harriet,' said her brother, lighting in their late visitor, and speaking in a low voice, 'Mr. Morfin—the gentleman so long in Dombey's house with James.'

His sister started back, as if a ghost had entered. In the doorway stood the unknown friend, with the dark hair sprinkled with grey, the ruddy face, the broad clear brow, and hazel eyes, whose secret she had kept so long!'

'John!' she said, half-breathless. 'It is the gentleman I told you of, to-day!'

'The gentleman, Miss Harriet,' said the visitor, coming in—for he had stopped a moment in the doorway, 'is greatly relieved to hear you say that:

he has been devising ways and means, all the way here, of explaining himself, and has been satisfied with none. Mr. John, I am not quite a stranger here. You were stricken with astonishment when you saw me at your door just now. I observe you are more astonished at present. Well! That's reasonable enough under existing circumstances. If we were not such creatures of habit as we are, we shouldn't have reason to be astonished half so often.'

By this time, he had greeted Harriet with that agreeable mingling of cordiality and respect which she recollected so well, and had sat down near her, pulled off his gloves, and thrown them into his hat upon the table.

'There's nothing astonishing,' he said, 'in my having conceived a desire to see your sister, Mr. John, or in my having gratified it in my own way. As to the regularity of my visits since (which she may have mentioned to you), there is nothing extraordinary in that. They soon grew into a habit; and we are creatures of habit—creatures of habit!'

Putting his hands into his pockets, and leaning back in his chair, he looked at the brother and sister as if it were interesting to him to see them together; and went on to say, with a kind of irritable thoughtfulness: 'It's this same habit that confirms some of us, who are capable of better things, in Lucifer's own pride and stubbornness—that confirms and deepens others of us in villainy—more of us in indifference—that hardens us from day to day, according to the temper of our clay, like images, and leaves us as susceptible as images to new impressions and convictions. You shall judge of its influence on me, John. For more years than I need name, I had my small, and exactly defined share, in the management of Dombey's house, and saw your brother (who

has proved himself a scoundrel! Your sister will
forgive my being obliged to mention it) extending
and extending his influence, until the business and
its owner were his football; and saw you toiling at
your obscure desk every day; and was quite content
to be as little troubled as I might be, out of my own
strip of duty, and to let everything about me go on,
day by day, unquestioned, like a great machine—
that was its habit and mine—and to take it all for
granted, and consider it all right. My Wednesday
nights came regularly round, our quartette parties
came regularly off, my violoncello was in good tune,
and there was nothing wrong in my world—or if
anything not much—or little or much, it was no affair of mine.'

'I can answer for your being more respected and
beloved during all that time than anybody in the
house, sir,' said John Carker.

'Pooh! Good-natured and easy enough, I dare
say,' returned the other, 'a habit I had. It suited the
manager; it suited the man he managed: it suited
me best of all. I did what was allotted to me to
do, made no court to either of them, and was glad
to occupy a station in which none was required. So
I should have gone on till now, but that my room
had a thin wall. You can tell your sister that it was
divided from the manager's room by a wainscot par-
tition.'

'They were adjoining rooms; had been one, perhaps, originally; and were separated, as Mr. Morfin
says,' said her brother, looking back to him for the
resumption of his explanation.

'I have whistled, hummed tunes, gone accurately
through the whole of Beethoven's Sonata in B, to let
him know that I was within hearing,' said Mr.
Morfin; 'but he never heeded me. It happened sel-

dom enough that I was within hearing of anything
of a private nature, certainly. But when I was,
and couldn't otherwise avoid knowing something of
it, I walked out. I walked out once, John, during
a conversation between two brothers, to which, in the
beginning, young Walter Gay was a party. But I
overheard some of it before I left the room. You
remember it sufficiently, perhaps, to tell your sister
what its nature was?'

'It referred, Harriet,' said her brother in a low
voice, 'to the past, and to our relative positions in the
House.'

'Its matter was not new to me, but was presented
in a new aspect. It shook me in my habit—the
habit of nine-tenths of the world—of believing that
all was right about me, because I was used to it,'
said their visitor; 'and induced me to recall the history of the two brothers, and to ponder on it. I
think it was almost the first time in my life when
I fell into this train of reflection—how will many
things that are familiar, and quite matters of course
to us now, look when we come to see them from that
new and distant point of view which we must all take
up, one day or other? I was something less good-
natured, as the phrase goes, after that morning, less
easy and complacent altogether.'

He sat for a minute or so, drumming with one
hand on the table; and resumed in a hurry, as if he
were anxious to get rid of his confession.

'Before I knew what to do, or whether I could do
anything, there was a second conversation between
the same two brothers, in which their sister was mentioned. I had no scruples of conscience in suffering all the waifs and strays of that conversation to
float to me as freely as they would. I considered
them mine by right. After that, I came here to see

the sister for myself. The first time I stopped at the garden gate, I made a pretext of inquiring into the character of a poor neighbour; but I wandered out of that track, and I think Miss Harriet mistrusted me. The second time I asked leave to come in; came in; and said what I wished to say. Your sister showed me reasons which I dared not dispute, for receiving no assistance from me then; but I established a means of communication between us, which remained unbroken until within these few days, when I was prevented, by important matters that have lately devolved upon me, from maintaining them.'

'How little I have suspected this,' said John Carker, 'when I have seen you every day, sir! If Harriet could have guessed your name—'

'Why, to tell you the truth, John,' interposed the visitor, 'I kept it to myself for two reasons. I don't know that the first might have been binding alone; but one has no business to take credit for good intentions, and I made up my mind, at all events, not to disclose myself until I should be able to do you some real service or other. My second reason was, that I always hoped there might be some lingering possibility of your brother's relenting towards you both; and in that case, I felt that where there was the chance of a man of his suspicious, watchful character, discovering that you had been secretly befriended by me, there was the chance of a new and fatal cause of division. I resolved, to be sure, at the risk of turning his displeasure against myself— which would have been no matter—to watch my opportunity of serving you with the head of the house; but the distractions of death, courtship, marriage, and domestic unhappiness, have left us no head but your brother for this long, long time. And it would have been better for us,' said the visitor, dropping his voice, 'to have been a lifeless trunk.'

He seemed conscious that these latter words had escaped him against his will, and stretching out a hand to the brother, and a hand to the sister, continued—

'All I could desire to say, and more, I have now said. All I mean goes beyond words, as I hope you understand and believe. The time has come, John —though most unfortunately and unhappily come— when I may help you without interfering with that redeeming struggle, which has lasted through so many years; since you were discharged from it to-day by no act of your own. It is late; I need say no more to-night. You will guard the treasure you have here, without advice or reminder from me.'

With these words he rose to go.

'But go you first, John,' he said good-humouredly, 'with a light, without saying what you want to say, whatever that may be'; John Carker's heart was full, and he would have relieved it in speech, if he could; 'and let me have a word with your sister. We have talked alone before, and in this room too; though it looks more natural with you here.'

Following him out with his eyes, he turned kindly to Harriet, and said in a lower voice, and with an altered and graver manner—

'You wish to ask me something of the man whose sister it is your misfortune to be.'

'I dread to ask,' said Harriet.

'You have looked so earnestly at me more than once,' rejoined the visitor, 'that I think I can divine your question. Has he taken money? Is it that?'

'Yes.'

'He has not.'

'I thank Heaven!' said Harriet.   'For the sake of John.'

'That he has abused his trust in many ways,' said Mr. Morfin; 'that he has oftener dealt and speculated to advantage for himself, than for the House he represented; that he has led the House on, to prodigious ventures, often resulting in enormous losses; that he has always pampered the vanity and ambition of his employer, when it was his duty to have held them in check, and shown, as it was in his power to do, to what they tended here or there; will not, perhaps, surprise you now.   Undertakings have been entered on, to swell the reputation of the House for vast resources, and to exhibit it in magnificent contrast to other merchants' houses, of which it requires a steady head to contemplate the possibly—a few disastrous changes of affairs might render them the probably—ruinous consequences.   In the midst of the many transactions of the House, in most parts of the world: a great labyrinth of which only he has held the clue: he has had the opportunity, and he seems to have used it, of keeping the various results afloat, when ascertained, and substituting estimates and generalities for facts.   But latterly—you follow me, Miss Harriet?'

'Perfectly, perfectly,' she answered, with her frightened face fixed on his.   'Pray tell me all the worst at once.'

'Latterly, he appears to have devoted the greatest pains to making these results so plain and clear, that reference to the private books enables one to grasp them, numerous and varying as they are, with extraordinary ease.   As if he had resolved to show his employer at one broad view what has been brought upon him by ministration to his ruling passion!

That it has been his constant practice to minister to that passion basely, and to flatter it corruptly, is indubitable. In that, his criminality, as it is connected with the affairs of the House, chiefly consists.'

'One other word before you leave me, dear sir,' said Harriet. 'There is no danger in all this?'

'How danger?' he returned, with a little hesitation.

'To the credit of the House?'

'I cannot help answering you plainly, and trusting you completely,' said Mr. Morfin, after a moment's survey of her face.

'You may. Indeed you may!'

'I am sure I may. Danger to the House's credit? No; none. There may be difficulty, greater or less difficulty, but no danger, unless—unless, indeed—the head of the House, unable to bring his mind to the reduction of its enterprises, and positively refusing to believe that it is, or can be, in any position but the position in which he has always represented it to himself, should urge it beyond its strength. Then it would totter.'

'But there is no apprehension of that?' said Harriet.

'There shall be no half-confidence,' he replied, shaking her hand, 'between us. Mr. Dombey is unapproachable by any one, and his state of mind is haughty, rash, unreasonable, and ungovernable, now. But he is disturbed and agitated now beyond all common bounds, and it may pass. You now know all, both worst and best. No more to-night, and good night!'

With that he kissed her hand, and, passing out to the door where her brother stood awaiting his coming, put him cheerfully aside when he essayed to speak; told him that, as they would see each other soon and often, he might speak at another time, if he would, but there was no leisure for it then; and went away at a round pace, in order that no word of gratitude might follow him.

The brother and sister sat conversing by the fireside, until it was almost day; made sleepless by this glimpse of the new world that opened before them, and feeling like two people shipwrecked long ago, upon a solitary coast, to whom a ship had come at last, when they were old in resignation, and had lost all thought of any other home. But another and different kind of disquietude kept them waking too. The darkness out of which this light had broken on them gathered around; and the shadow of their guilty brother was in the house where his foot had never trod.

Nor was it to be driven out, nor did it fade before the sun. Next morning it was there; at noon; at night. Darkest and most distinct at night, as is now to be told.

John Carker had gone out, in pursuance of a letter of appointment from their friend, and Harriet was left in the house alone. She had been alone some hours. A dull, grave evening, and a deepening twilight, were not favourable to the removal of the oppression on her spirits. The idea of this brother, long unseen and unknown, flitted about her in frightful shapes. He was dead, dying, calling to her, staring at her, frowning on her. The pictures in her mind were so obtrusive and exact that, as the twilight deepened, she dreaded to raise her head and look at the dark corners of the room, lest his wraith, the offspring of her excited imagination, should be waiting there, to startle her. Once she had such a fancy of his being in the next room, hiding—though she knew quite well what a distempered fancy it was,

and had no belief in it—that she forced herself to go
there, for her own conviction. But in vain. The
room resumed its shadowy terrors, the moment she
left it; and she had no more power to divest herself
of these vague impressions of dread, than if they had
been stone giants, rooted in the solid earth.

It was almost dark, and she was sitting near the
window, with her head upon her hand, looking down,
when, sensible of a sudden increase in the gloom of
the apartment, she raised her eyes, and uttered an
involuntary cry. Close to the glass, a pale scared
face gazed in; vacantly, for an instant, as searching
for an object; then the eyes rested on herself, and
lighted up.

'Let me in! Let me in! I want to speak to you!'
and the hand rattled on the glass.

She recognised immediately the woman with the
long dark hair, to whom she had given warmth, food,
and shelter, one wet night. Naturally afraid of her,
remembering her violent behaviour, Harriet, retreat-
ing a little from the window, stood undecided and
alarmed.

'Let me in! Let me speak to you! I am thankful—quiet—humble—anything you like. But let
me speak to you.'

The vehement manner of the entreaty, the earnest
expression of the face, the trembling of the two hands
that were raised imploringly, a certain dread and terror in the voice akin to her own condition at the
moment, prevailed with Harriet. She hastened to
the door and opened it.

'May I come in, or shall I speak here?' said the
woman, catching at her hand.

'What is it that you want? What is it that you
have to say?'

'Not much, but let me say it out, or I shall never

say it. I am tempted now to go away. There seem to be hands dragging me from the door. Let me come in, if you can trust me for this once!'

Her energy again prevailed, and they passed into the firelight of the little kitchen, where she had before sat, and ate, and dried her clothes.

'Sit there,' said Alice, kneeling down beside her, 'and look at me. You remember me?'

'I do.'

'You remember what I told you I had been, and where I came from, ragged and lame, with the fierce wind and weather beating on my head?'

'Yes.'

'You know how I came back that night, and threw your money in the dirt, and cursed you and your race. Now, see me here, upon my knees. Am I less earnest now, than I was then?'

'If what you ask,' said Harriet, gently, 'is forgiveness—'

'But it's not!' returned the other, with a proud fierce look. 'What I ask is to be believed. Now you shall judge if I am worthy of belief, both as I was, and as I am.'

Still upon her knees, and with her eyes upon the fire, and the fire shining on her ruined beauty and her wild black hair, one long tress of which she pulled over her shoulder, and wound about her hand, and thoughtfully bit and tore while speaking, she went on—

'When I was young and pretty, and this,' plucking contemptuously at the hair she held, 'was only handled delicately, and couldn't be admired enough, my mother, who had not been very mindful of me as a child, found out my merits, and was fond of me, and proud of me. She was covetous and poor, and thought to make a sort of property of me. No

great lady ever thought that of a daughter yet, I 'm
sure, or acted as if she did—it 's never done, we all
know—and that shows that the only instances of
mothers bringing up their daughters wrong, and evil
coming of it, are among such miserable folks as us.'

Looking at the fire, as if she were forgetful, for
the moment, of having any auditor, she continued in
a dreamy way, as she wound the long tress of hair
tight round and round her hand.

'What came of that, I needn't say. Wretched
marriages don't come of such things, in our degree;
only wretchedness and ruin. Wretchedness and ruin
came on me—came on me.'

Raising her eyes swiftly from their moody gaze
upon the fire, to Harriet's face, she said—

'I am wasting time, and there is none to spare; yet
if I hadn't thought of all, I shouldn't be here now.
Wretchedness and ruin came on me, I say. I was
made a short-lived toy, and flung aside more cruelly
and carelessly than even such things are. By whose
hand do you think?'

'Why do you ask me?' said Harriet.

'Why do you tremble?' rejoined Alice, with an
eager look. 'His usage made a devil of me. I sunk
in wretchedness and ruin, lower and lower yet. I was
concerned in a robbery—in every part of it but the
gains—and was found out, and sent to be tried,
without a friend, without a penny. Though I was
but a girl, I would have gone to death, sooner than
ask him for a word, if a word of his could have saved
me. I would! To any death that could have been
invented. But my mother, covetous always, sent to
him in my name, told the true story of my case, and
humbly prayed and petitioned for a small last gift
—for not so many pounds as I have fingers on this
hand. Who was it, do you think, who snapped his

fingers at me in my misery, lying, as he believed, at his feet, and left me without even this poor sign of remembrance; well satisfied that I should be sent abroad, beyond the reach of further trouble to him, and should die, and rot there? Who was this, do you think?'

'Why do you ask me?' repeated Harriet.

'Why do you tremble?' said Alice, laying her hand upon her arm, and looking in her face, 'but that the answer is on your lips! It was your brother James.'

Harriet trembled more and more, but did not avert her eyes from the eager look that rested on them.

'When I knew you were his sister—which was on that night—I came back, weary and lame, to spurn your gift. I felt that night as if I could have travelled weary and lame, over the whole world, to stab him, if I could have found him in a lonely place with no one near. Do you believe that I was earnest in all that?'

'I do! Good Heaven, why are you come again?'

'Since then,' said Alice, with the same grasp of her arm, and the same look in her face, 'I have seen him! I have followed him with my eyes, in the broad day. If any spark of my resentment slumbered in my bosom, it sprung into a blaze when my eyes rested on him. You know he has wronged a proud man, and made him his deadly enemy. What if I had given information of him to that man?'

'Information!' repeated Harriet.

'What if I had found out one who knew your brother's secret; who knew the manner of his flight; who knew where he and the companion of his flight were gone? What if I had made him utter all his knowledge, word by word, before his enemy, concealed to hear it? What if I had sat by at the time, looking into this enemy's face, and seeing it change till it was scarcely human? What if I had seen him rush away, mad, in pursuit? What if I knew, now, that he was on his road, more fiend than man, and must, in so many hours, come up with him?'

'Remove your hand!' said Harriet, recoiling. 'Go away! Your touch is dreadful to me!'

'I have done this,' pursued the other, with her eager look, regardless of the interruption. 'Do I speak and look as if I really had? Do you believe what I am saying?'

'I fear I must. Let my arm go!'

'Not yet. A moment more. You can think what my revengeful purpose must have been, to last so long, and urge me to do this?'

'Dreadful!' said Harriet.

'Then when you see me now,' said Alice hoarsely, 'here again, kneeling quietly on the ground, with my touch upon your arm, with my eyes upon your face, you may believe that there is no common earnestness in what I say, and that no common struggle has been battling in my breast. I am ashamed to speak the words, but I relent. I despise myself; I have fought with myself all day, and all last night; but I relent towards him without reason, and wish to repair what I have done, if it is possible. I wouldn't have them come together while his pursuer is so blind and headlong. If you had seen him as he went out last night, you would know the danger better.'

'How shall it be prevented! What can I do!' cried Harriet.

'All night long,' pursued the other, hurriedly, 'I had dreams of him—and yet I didn't sleep—in his blood. All day, I have had him near me.'

'What can I do!' cried Harriet, shuddering at these words.

'If there is any one who 'll write, or send, or go to

him, let them lose no time. He is at Dijon. Do you
know the name, and where it is?'

'Yes.'

'Warn him that the man he has made his enemy is
in a frenzy, and that he doesn't know him if he makes
light of his approach. Tell him that he is on the
road—I know he is!—and hurrying on. Urge him
to get away while there is time—if there *is* time—and
not to meet him yet. A month or so will make years
of difference. Let them not encounter, through me.
Anywhere but there! Any time but now! Let his
foe follow him, and find him for himself, but not
through me! There is enough upon my head without.'

The fire ceased to be reflected in her jet black hair,
uplifted face, and eager eyes; her hand was gone
from Harriet's arm; and the place where she had been
was empty.

CHAPTER LIV

THE FUGITIVES

THE time, an hour short of midnight; the place, a
French apartment, comprising some half-dozen rooms;
—a dull cold hall or corridor, a dining-room, a drawing-room, a bed-chamber, and an inner drawing room,
or boudoir, smaller and more retired than the rest.
All these shut in by one large pair of doors on the main
staircase, but each room provided with two or three
pairs of doors of its own, establishing several means
of communication with the remaining portion of the
apartment, or with certain small passages within the
wall, leading, as is not unusual in such houses, to some
back-stairs with an obscure outlet below. The whole

situated on the first floor of so large an hotel, that it did not absorb one entire row of windows upon one side of the square courtyard in the centre, upon which the whole four sides of the mansion looked.

An air of splendour, sufficiently faded to be melancholy, and sufficiently dazzling to clog and embarrass the details of life with a show of state, reigned in these rooms. The walls and ceilings were gilded and painted; the floors were waxed and polished; crimson drapery hung in festoons from window, door, and mirror; candelabra, gnarled and intertwisted, like the branches of trees, or horns of animals, stuck out from the panels of the wall. But in the day-time, when the lattice-blinds (now closely shut) were opened, and the light let in, traces were discernible among this finery, of wear and tear and dust, of sun and damp and smoke, and lengthened intervals of want of use and habitation, when such shows and toys of life seem sensitive like life, and waste as men shut up in prison do. Even night, and clusters of burning candles, could not wholly efface them, though the general glitter threw them in the shade.

The glitter of bright tapers, and their reflection in looking-glasses, scraps of gilding and gay colours, were confined, on this night, to one room—that smaller room within the rest, just now enumerated. Seen from the hall, where a lamp was feebly burning, through the dark perspective of open doors, it looked as shining and precious as a gem. In the heart of its radiance sat a beautiful woman—Edith.

She was alone. The same defiant, scornful woman still. The cheek a little worn, the eye a little larger in appearance, and more lustrous, but the haughty bearing just the same. No shame upon her brow; no late repentance bending her disdainful neck. Im-

perious and stately yet, and yet regardless of herself
and of all else, she sat with her dark eyes cast down,
waiting for some one.

No book, no work, no occupation of any kind but
her own thoughts, beguiled the tardy time. Some
purpose, strong enough to fill up any pause, possessed her. With her lips pressed together, and
quivering if for a moment she released them from
her control; with her nostril inflated; her hands
clasped in one another; and her purpose swelling in
her breast; she sat, and waited.

At the sound of a key in the outer door, and a
footstep in the hall, she started up, and cried 'Who's
that?' The answer was in French, and two men
came in with jingling trays, to make preparation for
supper.

'Who had bade them to do so?' she asked.

'Monsieur had commanded it, when it was his
pleasure to take the apartment. Monsieur had said,
when he stayed there for an hour, *en route*, and left
the letter for madame—madame had received it
surely?'

'Yes.'

'A thousand pardons! The sudden apprehension
that it might have been forgotten had struck him';
a bald man, with a large beard, from a neighbouring *restaurant:* 'with despair! Monsieur had said
that supper was to be ready at that hour: also that
he had forewarned madame of the commands he had
given, in his letter. Monsieur had done the Golden
Head the honour to request that the supper should be
choice and delicate. Monsieur would find that his
confidence in the Golden Head was not misplaced.'

Edith said no more, but looked on thoughtfully
while they prepared the table for two persons, and
set the wine upon it. She arose before they had fin-

ished, and taking a lamp, passed into the bed-chamber and into the drawing-room, where she hurriedly
but narrowly examined all the doors; particularly
one in the former room that opened on the passage
in the wall. From this she took the key, and put it
on the outer side. She then came back.

The men—the second of whom was a dark, bilious
subject, in a jacket, close shaved, and with a black
head of hair close cropped—had completed their preparation of the table, and were standing looking at
it. He who had spoken before, inquired whether
madame thought it would be long before monsieur
arrived?

'She couldn't say. It was all one.'

'Pardon! There was the supper! It should be
eaten on the instant. Monsieur (who spoke French
like an angel—or a Frenchman—it was all the same)
had spoken with great emphasis of his punctuality.
But the English nation had so grand a genius for
punctuality. Ah! what noise! Great Heaven, here
was monsieur. Behold him!'

In effect, monsieur, admitted by the other of the
two, came, with his gleaming teeth, through the dark
rooms, like a mouth; and arriving in that sanctuary
of light and colour, a figure at full length, embraced
madame, and addressed her in the French tongue as
his charming wife.

'My God! Madame is going to faint. Madame
is overcome with joy!' The bald man with the beard
observed it, and cried out.

Madame had only shrunk and shivered. Before
the words were spoken, she was standing with her
hand upon the velvet back of a great chair; her figure drawn up to its full height, and her face immoveable.

'François has flown over to the Golden Head for

supper. He flies on these occasions like an angel or a bird. The baggage of monsieur is in his room. All is arranged. The supper will be here this moment.' These facts the bald man notified with bows and smiles, and presently the supper came.

The hot dishes were on a chafing-dish; the cold already set forth, with the change of service on a sideboard. Monsieur was satisfied with this arrangement. The supper table being small, it pleased him very well. Let them set the chafing-dish upon the floor, and go. He would remove the dishes with his own hands.

'Pardon!' said the bald man, politely. 'It was impossible!'

Monsieur was of another opinion. He required no further attendance that night.

'But madame'—the bald man hinted.

'Madame,' replied monsieur, 'had her own maid. It was enough.'

'A million pardons! No! Madame had no maid!'

'I came here alone,' said Edith. 'It was my choice to do so. I am well used to travelling; I want no attendance. They need send nobody to me.'

Monsieur accordingly, persevering in his first proposed impossibility, proceeded to follow the two attendants to the outer door, and secure it after them for the night. The bald man turning round to bow, as he went out, observed that madame still stood with her hand upon the velvet back of the great chair, and that her face was quite regardless of him, though she was looking straight before her.

As the sound of Carker's fastening the door resounded through the intermediate rooms, and seemed to come hushed and stifled into that last distant one, the sound of the cathedral clock striking twelve mingled with it, in Edith's ears. She heard him

pause as if he heard it too and listened; and then
came back towards her, laying a long train of footsteps through the silence, and shutting all the doors
behind him as he came along.   Her hand, for a moment, left the velvet chair to bring a knife within her
reach upon the table; then she stood as she had stood
before.

'How strange to come here by yourself, my love,'
he said as he entered.

'What?' she returned.

Her tone was so harsh; the quick turn of her head
so fierce; her attitude so repellent; and her frown
so black; that he stood, with the lamp in his hand,
looking at her, as if she had struck him motionless.

'I say,' he at length repeated, putting down the
lamp, and smiling his most courtly smile, 'how strange
to come here alone! It was unnecessary caution
surely, and might have defeated itself.   You were to
have engaged an attendant at Havre or Rouen, and
have had abundance of time for the purpose, though
you had been the most capricious and difficult (as
you are the most beautiful, my love) of women.'

Her eyes gleamed strangely on him, but she stood
with her hand resting on the chair, and said not a
word.

'I have never,' resumed Carker, 'seen you look so
handsome, as you do to-night. Even the picture I
have carried in my mind during this cruel probation,
and which I have contemplated night and day, is
exceeded by the reality.'

Not a word. Not a look. Her eyes completely
hidden by their drooping lashes, but her head held
up.

'Hard, unrelenting terms they were!' said Carker,
with a smile, 'but they are all fulfilled and passed, and
make the present more delicious and more safe.

Sicily shall be the place of our retreat. In the idlest
and easiest part of the world, my soul, we 'll both
seek compensation for old slavery.'

He was coming gaily towards her, when, in an
instant, she caught the knife up from the table, and
started one pace back.

'Stand still!' she said, 'or I shall murder you!'

The sudden change in her, the towering fury and
intense abhorrence sparkling in her eyes and lighting
up her brow, made him stop as if a fire had stopped
him.

'Stand still!' she said, 'come no nearer me, upon
your life!'

They both stood looking at each other. Rage and
astonishment were in his face, but he controlled them,
and said lightly—

'Come, come! Tush, we are alone, and out of
everybody's sight and hearing. Do you think to
frighten me with these tricks of virtue?'

'Do you think to frighten *me,*' she answered
fiercely, 'from any purpose that I have, and any course
I am resolved upon, by reminding me of the solitude
of this place, and there being no help near? Me, who
am here alone, designedly? If I feared you, should
I not have avoided you? If I feared you, should I
be here, in the dead of night, telling you to your face
what I am going to tell?'

'And what is that,' he said, 'you handsome shrew?
Handsomer so, than any other woman in her best
humour?'

'I tell you nothing,' she returned, 'until you go
back to that chair—except this, once again—Don't
come near me! Not a step nearer. I tell you, if
you do, as Heaven sees us, I shall murder you!'

'Do you mistake me for your husband?' he retorted, with a grin.

Disdaining to reply, she stretched her arm out, pointing to the chair. He bit his lip, frowned, laughed, and sat down in it, with a baffled, irresolute, impatient air, he was unable to conceal; and biting his nail nervously, and looking at her sideways, with bitter discomfiture, even while he feigned to be amazed by her caprice.

She put the knife down upon the table, and touching her bosom with her hand, said—

'I have something lying here that is no love trinket; and sooner than endure your touch once more, I would use it on you—and you know it, while I speak —with less reluctance than I would on any other creeping thing that lives.'

He affected to laugh jestingly, and entreated her to act her play out quickly, for the supper was growing cold. But the secret look with which he regarded her, was more sullen and lowering, and he struck his foot once upon the floor with a muttered oath.

'How many times,' said Edith, bending her darkest glance upon him, 'has your bold knavery assailed me with outrage and insult? How many times in your smooth manner, and mocking words and looks, have I been twitted with my courtship and my marriage? How many times have you laid bare my wound of love for that sweet, injured girl, and lacerated it? How often have you fanned the fire on which, for two years, I have writhed; and tempted me to take a desperate revenge, when it has most tortured me?'

'I have no doubt, ma'am,' he replied, 'that you have kept a good account, and that it's pretty accurate. Come, Edith. To your husband, poor wretch, this was well enough—'

'Why, if,' she said, surveying him with a haughty contempt and disgust, that he shrunk under, let him

brave it as he would, 'if all my other reasons for despising him could have been blown away like feathers,
his having you for his counsellor and favourite, would
have almost been enough to hold their place.'

'Is that a reason why you have run away with me?'
he asked her, tauntingly.

'Yes, and why we are face to face for the last time.
Wretch! We meet to-night, and part to-night. For
not one moment after I have ceased to speak, will I
stay here.'

He turned upon her with his ugliest look, and
griped the table with his hand; but neither rose, nor
otherwise answered or threatened her.

'I am a woman,' she said, confronting him steadfastly, 'who from her very childhood has been shamed
and steeled. I have been offered and rejected, put up
and appraised, until my very soul has sickened. I
have not had an accomplishment or grace that might
have been a resource to me, but it has been paraded and
vended to enhance my value, as if the common crier
had called it through the streets. My poor, proud
friends, have looked on and approved; and every tie
between us has been deadened in my breast. There
is not one of them for whom I care, as I could care
for a pet-dog. I stand alone in the world, remembering well what a hollow world it has been to me, and
what a hollow part of it I have been myself. You
know this, and you know that my fame with it is
worthless to me.'

'Yes; I imagined that,' he said.

'And calculated on it,' she rejoined, 'and so pursued me. Grown too indifferent for any opposition
but indifference, to the daily working of the hands
that had moulded me to this; and knowing that my
marriage would at least prevent their hawking of
me up and down; I suffered myself to be sold as

infamously as any woman with a halter round her neck is sold in any market-place. You know that.'

'Yes,' he said, showing all his teeth. 'I know that.'

'And calculated on it,' she rejoined once more, 'and so pursued me. From my marriage day, I found myself exposed to such new shame—to such solicitation and pursuit (expressed as clearly as if it had been written in the coarsest words, and thrust into my hand at every turn) from one mean villain, that I felt as if I had never known humiliation till that time. This shame my husband fixed upon me; hemmed me round with, himself; steeped me in, with his own hands, and of his own act, repeated hundreds of times. And thus—forced by the two from every point of rest I had—forced by the two to yield up the last retreat of love and gentleness within me, or to be a new misfortune on its innocent object— driven from each to each, and beset by one when I escaped the other—my anger rose almost to distraction against both. I do not know against which it rose higher—the master or the man!'

He watched her closely, as she stood before him in the very triumph of her indignant beauty. She was resolute, he saw; undauntable; with no more fear of him than of a worm.

'What should I say of honour or of chastity to you?' she went on. 'What meaning would it have to you; what meaning would it have from me? But if I tell you that the lightest touch of your hand makes my blood cold with antipathy; that from the hour when I first saw and hated you, to now, when my instinctive repugnance is enhanced by every minute's knowledge of you I have since had, you have been a loathsome creature to me which has not its like on earth; how then?'

He answered, with a faint laugh, 'Aye! How then, my queen?'

'On that night, when, emboldened by the scene you had assisted at, you dared come to my room and speak to me,' she said, 'what passed?'

He shrugged his shoulders, and laughed again.

'What passed?' she said.

'Your memory is so distinct,' he returned, 'that I have no doubt you can recall it.'

'I can,' she said. 'Hear it! Proposing then, this flight—not this flight, but the flight you thought it —you told me that in the having given you that meeting, and leaving you to be discovered there, if you so thought fit; and in the having suffered you to be alone with me many times before,—and having made the opportunities, you said,—and in the having openly avowed to you that I had no feeling for my husband but aversion, and no care for myself—I was lost; I had given you the power to traduce my name; and I lived, in virtuous reputation, at the pleasure of your breath.'

'All stratagems in love—' he interrupted, smiling. 'The old adage—'

'On that night,' said Edith, 'and then the struggle that I long had had with something that was not respect for my good fame—that was I know not what—perhaps the clinging to that last retreat—was ended. On that night, and then, I turned from everything but passion and resentment. I struck a blow that laid your lofty master in the dust, and set you there, before me, looking at me now, and knowing what I mean.'

He sprung up from his chair with a great oath. She put her hand into her bosom, and not a finger trembled, not a hair upon her head was stirred. He stood still: she too: the table and chair between them.

'When I forget that this man put his lips to mine that night, and held me in his arms as he has done again to-night,' said Edith, pointing at him; 'when I forget the taint of his kiss upon my cheek—the cheek that Florence would have laid her guiltless face against—when I forget my meeting with her, while that taint was hot upon me, and in what a flood the knowledge rushed upon me when I saw her, that in releasing her from the persecution I had caused by my love, I brought a shame and degradation on her name through mine, and in all time to come should be the solitary figure representing in her mind her first avoidance of a guilty creature—then, husband from whom I stand divorced henceforth, I will forget these last two years, and undo what I have done, and undeceive you!'

Her flashing eyes, uplifted for a moment, lighted again on Carker, and she held some letters out in her left hand.

'See these!' she said, contemptuously. 'You have addressed these to me in the false name you go by; one here, some elsewhere on my road. The seals are unbroken. Take them back!'

She crunched them in her hand, and tossed them to his feet. And as she looked upon him now, a smile was on her face.

'We meet and part to-night,' she said. 'You have fallen on Sicilian days and sensual rest, too soon. You might have cajoled, and fawned, and played your traitor's part, a little longer, and grown richer. You purchase your voluptuous retirement dear!'

'Edith!' he retorted, menacing her with his hand. 'Sit down! Have done with this! What devil possesses you?'

'Their name is Legion,' she replied, uprearing her proud form as if she would have crushed him; 'you and your master have raised them in a fruitful house, and they shall tear you both. False to him, false to his innocent child, false every way and everywhere, go forth and boast of me, and gnash your teeth for once to know that you are lying!'

He stood before her muttering and menacing, and scowling round as if for something that would help him to conquer her; but with the same indomitable spirit she opposed him, without faltering.

'In every vaunt you make,' she said, 'I have my triumph. I single out in you the meanest man I know, the parasite and tool of the proud tyrant, that his wound may go the deeper and may rankle more. Boast, and revenge me on him! You know how you came here to-night; you know how you stand cowering there; you see yourself in colours quite as despicable, if not as odious, as those in which I see you. Boast then, and revenge me on yourself.'

The foam was on his lips; the wet stood on his forehead. If she would have faltered once for only one half-moment, he would have pinioned her; but she was as firm as rock, and her searching eyes never left him.

'We don't part so,' he said. 'Do you think I am drivelling, to let you go in your mad temper?'

'Do you think,' she answered, 'that I am to be stayed?'

'I'll try, my dear,' he said, with a ferocious gesture of his head.

'God's mercy on you, if you try by coming near me!' she replied.

'And what,' he said, 'if there are none of these same boasts and vaunts on my part? What if I were to turn too? Come!' and his teeth fairly shone again. 'We must make a treaty of this or I may take some unexpected course. Sit down, sit down!'

'Too late!' she cried, with eyes that seemed to sparkle fire. 'I have thrown my fame and good name to the winds! I have resolved to bear the shame that will attach to me—resolved to know that it attaches falsely—that you know it too—and that he does not, never can, and never shall. I 'll die, and make no sign. For this I am here alone with you, at the dead of night. For this I have met you here, in a false name, as your wife. For this, I have been seen here by those men, and left here. Nothing can save you now.'

He would have sold his soul to root her, in her beauty, to the floor, and make her arms drop at her sides, and have her at his mercy. But he could not look at her, and not be afraid of her. He saw strength within her that was resistless. He saw that she was desperate, and that her unquenchable hatred of him would stop at nothing. His eyes followed the hand that was put with such rugged uncongenial purpose into her white bosom, and he thought that if it struck at him, and failed, it would strike there, just as soon.

He did not venture, therefore, to advance towards her; but the door by which he had entered was behind him, and he stepped back to lock it.

'Lastly, take my warning! Look to yourself!' she said, and smiled again. 'You have been betrayed, as all betrayers are. It has been made known that you are in this place, or were to be, or have been. If I live, I saw my husband in a carriage in the street to-night!'

'Strumpet, it 's false!' cried Carker.

At the moment, the bell rang loudly in the hall. He turned white, as she held her hand up like an enchantress, at whose invocation the sound had come.

'Hark! do you hear it?'

He set his back against the door; for he saw a change in her, and fancied she was coming on to pass him. But, in a moment, she was gone through the opposite doors communicating with the bed-chamber, and they shut upon her.

Once turned, once changed in her inflexible unyielding look, he felt that he could cope with her. He thought a sudden terror, occasioned by this night-alarm, had subdued her; not the less readily, for her overwrought condition. Throwing open the doors, he followed, almost instantly.

But the room was dark; and as she made no answer to his call, he was fain to go back for the lamp. He held it up, and looked round everywhere, expecting to see her crouching in some corner; but the room was empty. So, into the drawing-room and dining-room he went, in succession, with the uncertain steps of a man in a strange place; looking fearfully about, and prying behind screens and couches; but she was not there. No, nor in the hall, which was so bare that he could see that, at a glance.

All this time, the ringing at the bell was constantly renewed; and those without were beating at the door. He put his lamp down at a distance, and going near it, listened. There were several voices talking together: at least two of them in English; and though the door was thick, and there was great confusion, he knew one of these too well to doubt whose voice it was.

He took up his lamp again, and came back quickly through all the rooms, stopping as he quitted each, and looking round for her, with the light raised above his head. He was standing thus in the bed-chamber, when the door, leading to the little passage in the wall, caught his eye. He went to it, and found it fastened on the other side; but she had dropped a veil in going through, and shut it in the door.

All this time the people on the stairs were ringing at the bell, and knocking with their hands and feet.

He was not a coward: but these sounds; what had gone before; the strangeness of the place, which had confused him, even in his return from the hall; the frustration of his schemes (for, strange to say, he would have been much bolder, if they had succeeded); the unseasonable time; the recollection of having no one near to whom he could appeal for any friendly office; above all, the sudden sense, which made even his heart beat like lead, that the man whose confidence he had outraged, and whom he had so treacherously deceived, was there to recognise and challenge him with his mask plucked off his face, struck a panic through him. He tried the door in which the veil was shut, but couldn't force it. He opened one of the windows, and looked down through the lattice of the blind, into the courtyard; but it was a high leap, and the stones were pitiless.

The ringing and knocking still continuing—his panic too—he went back to the door in the bed-chamber, and with some new efforts each more stubborn than the last, wrenched it open. Seeing the little staircase not far off, and feeling the night-air coming up, he stole back for his hat and coat, made the door as secure after him as he could, crept down lamp in hand, extinguished it on seeing the street, and having put it in a corner, went out where the stars were shining.

CHAPTER LV

ROB THE GRINDER LOSES HIS PLACE

THE porter at the iron gate which shut the court-yard from the street, had left the little wicket of his house open, and was gone away; no doubt to mingle in the distant noise at the door of the great stair-case. Lifting the latch softly, Carker crept out, and shutting the jangling gate after him with as little noise as possible, hurried off.

In the fever of his mortification and unavailing rage, the panic that had seized upon him mastered him completely. It rose to such a height that he would have blindly encountered almost any risk, rather than meet the man of whom, two hours ago, he had been utterly regardless. His fierce arrival, which he had never expected; the sound of his voice; their having been so near a meeting, face to face, he would have braved out this, after the first momentary shock of alarm, and would have put as bold a front upon his guilt as any villain. But the springing of his mine upon himself, seemed to have rent and shiv-ered all his hardihood and self-reliance. Spurned like any reptile; entrapped and mocked; turned upon, and trodden down by the proud woman whose mind he had slowly poisoned, as he thought, until she had sunk into the mere creature of his pleasure; unde-ceived in his deceit, and with his fox's hide stripped off, he sneaked away, abashed, degraded, and afraid.

Some other terror came upon him quite removed from this of being pursued, suddenly, like an electric shock, as he was creeping through the streets. Some visionary terror, unintelligible and inexplicable, as-sociated with a trembling of the ground,—a rush and sweep of something through the air, like Death upon the wing. He shrunk, as if to let the thing go by. It was not gone, it never had been there, yet what a startling horror it had left behind.

He raised his wicked face, so full of trouble, to the night sky, where the stars, so full of peace, were shining on him as they had been when he first stole out into the air; and stopped to think what he should do. The dread of being hunted in a strange remote place, where the laws might not protect him—the novelty of the feeling that it *was* strange and remote, originating in his being left alone so suddenly amid the ruins of his plans—his greater dread of seeking refuge now, in Italy or in Sicily, where men might be hired to assassinate him, he thought, at any dark street corner—the waywardness of guilt and fear— perhaps some sympathy of action with the turning back of all his schemes—impelled him to turn back too, and go to England.

'I am safer there, in any case. If I should not decide,' he thought, 'to give this fool a meeting, I am less likely to be traced there, than abroad here, now. And if I should (this cursed fit being over), at least I shall not be alone, without a soul to speak to, or advise with, or stand by me. I shall not be run in upon and worried like a rat.'

He muttered Edith's name, and clenched his hand. As he crept along, in the shadow of the massive buildings, he set his teeth, and muttered dreadful imprecations on her head, and looked from side to side, as if in search of her. Thus, he stole on to the gate of an inn-yard. The people were abed; but his ringing at the bell soon produced a man with a lantern, in company with whom he was presently in a dim coachhouse, bargaining for the hire of an old phaeton, to Paris.

The bargain was a short one; and the horses were soon sent for. Leaving word that the carriage was to follow him when they came, he stole away again, beyond the town, past the old ramparts, out on the open road, which seemed to glide away along the dark plain, like a stream.

Whither did it flow? What was the end of it? As he paused, with some suggestion within him, looking over the gloomy flat where the slender trees marked out the way, again that flight of Death came rushing up, again went on, impetuous and resistless, again was nothing but a horror in his mind, dark as the scene and undefined as its remotest verge.

There was no wind; there was no passing shadow on the deep shade of the night; there was no noise. The city lay behind him, lighted here and there, and starry worlds were hidden by the masonry of spire and roof that hardly made out any shapes against the sky. Dark and lonely distance lay around him everywhere, and the clocks were faintly striking two.

He went forward for what appeared a long time, and a long way; often stopping to listen. At last the ringing of horses' bells greeted his anxious ears. Now softer, and now louder, now inaudible, now ringing very slowly over bad ground, now brisk and merry, it came on; until with a loud shouting and lashing, a shadowy postilion muffled to the eyes, checked his four struggling horses at his side.

'Who goes there? Monsieur?'

'Yes.'

'Monsieur has walked a long way in the dark midnight.'

'No matter. Every one to his taste. Were there any other horses ordered at the post-house?'

'A thousand devils!—and pardons! other horses? at this hour? No.'

'Listen, my friend. I am much hurried. Let us see how fast we can travel! The faster, the more money there will be to drink. Off we go then! Quick!'

'Halloa! whoop! Halloa! Hi!' Away, at a gallop, over the black landscape, scattering the dust and dirt like spray!

The clatter and commotion echoed to the hurry and discordance of the fugitive's ideas. Nothing clear without, and nothing clear within. Objects flitting past, merging into one another, dimly descried, confusedly lost sight of, gone! Beyond the changing scraps of fence and cottage immediately upon the road, a lowering waste. Beyond the shifting images that rose up in his mind and vanished as they showed themselves, a black expanse of dread and rage and baffled villainy. Occasionally, a sigh of mountain air came from the distant Jura, fading along the plain. Sometimes that rush which was so furious and horrible, again came sweeping through his fancy, passed away, and left a chill upon his blood.

The lamps, gleaming on the medley of horses' heads, jumbled with the shadowy driver, and the fluttering of his cloak, made a thousand indistinct shapes, answering to his thoughts. Shadows of familiar people, stooping at their desks and books, in their remembered attitudes; strange apparitions of the man whom he was flying from, or of Edith; repetitions in the ringing bells and rolling wheels, of words that had been spoken; confusions of time and place, making last night a month ago, a month ago last night— home now distant beyond hope, now instantly accessible; commotion, discord, hurry, darkness, and confusion in his mind, and all around him.—Hallo! Hi! away at a gallop over the black landscape; dust and dirt flying like spray, the smoking horses snorting and plunging as if each of them were ridden by a demon, away in a frantic triumph on the dark road —whither?

Again the nameless shock comes speeding up, and as it passes, the bells ring in the ears 'whither?' The wheels roar in his ears 'whither?' All the noise and rattle shapes itself into that cry. The lights and shadows dance upon the horses' heads like imps. No stopping now: no slackening! On, on! Away with him upon the dark road wildly!

He could not think to any purpose. He could not separate one subject of reflection from another, sufficiently to dwell upon it, by itself, for a minute at a time. The crash of his project for the gaining of a voluptuous compensation for past restraint; the overthrow of his treachery to one who had been true and generous to him, but whose least proud word and look he had treasured up, at interest, for years—for false and subtle men will always secretly despise and dislike the object upon which they fawn, and always resent the payment and receipt of homage that they know to be worthless; these were the themes uppermost in his mind. A lurking rage against the woman who had so entrapped him and avenged herself was always there; crude and misshapen schemes of retaliation upon her, floated in his brain; but nothing was distinct. A hurry and contradiction pervaded all his thoughts. Even while he was so busy with this fevered, ineffectual thinking, his one constant idea was, that he would postpone reflection until some indefinite time.

Then, the old days before the second marriage rose up in his remembrance. He thought how jealous he had been of the boy, how jealous he had been of the girl, how artfully he had kept intruders at a distance, and drawn a circle round his dupe that none but himself should cross; and then he thought, had he done all this to be flying now, like a scared thief, from only the poor dupe?

He could have laid hands upon himself for his cowardice, but it was the very shadow of his defeat, and could not be separated from it. To have his confidence in his own knavery, so shattered at a blow— to be within his own knowledge such a miserable tool —was like being paralysed. With an impotent ferocity he raged at Edith, and hated Mr. Dombey and hated himself, but still he fled, and could do nothing else.

Again and again he listened for the sound of wheels behind. Again and again his fancy heard it, coming on louder and louder. At last he was so persuaded of this, that he cried out, 'Stop!' preferring even the loss of ground to such uncertainty.

The word soon brought carriage, horses, driver, all in a heap together, across the road.

'The devil!' cried the driver, looking over his shoulder. 'What's the matter?'

'Hark! What's that?'

'What?'

'That noise.'

'Ah Heaven, be quiet, cursed brigand!' to a horse who shook his bells. 'What noise?'

'Behind. Is it not another carriage at a gallop? There! what's that?'

'Miscreant with a pig's head, stand still!' to another horse, who bit another, who frightened the other two, who plunged and backed. 'There is nothing coming.'

'Nothing?'

'No, nothing but the day yonder.'

'You are right, I think. I hear nothing now, indeed. Go on!'

The entangled equipage, half hidden in the reeking cloud from the horses, goes on slowly at first, for the driver, checked unnecessarily in his progress, sulkily takes out a pocket-knife, and puts a new lash to his whip. Then 'Hallo, whoop! Hallo, hi!' Away once more, savagely.

And now the stars faded, and the day glimmered, and standing in the carriage, looking back, he could discern the track by which he had come, and see that there was no traveller within view, on all the heavy expanse. And soon it was broad day, and the sun began to shine on corn-fields and vineyards; and solitary labourers, risen from little temporary huts by heaps of stones upon the road, were, here and there, at work repairing the highway, or eating bread. By and by, there were peasants going to their daily labour, or to market, or lounging at the doors of poor cottages, gazing idly at him as he passed. And then there was a post-yard, ankle-deep in mud, with steaming dunghills and vast outhouses half ruined; and looking on this dainty prospect, an immense, old, shadeless, glaring, stone chateau, with half its windows blinded, and green damp crawling lazily over it, from the balustraded terrace to the taper tips of the extinguishers upon the turrets.

Gathered up moodily in a corner of the carriage, and only intent on going fast—except when he stood up, for a mile together, and looked back; which he would do whenever there was a piece of open country—he went on, still postponing thought indefinitely, and still always tormented with thinking to no purpose.

Shame, disappointment, and discomfiture gnawed at his heart; a constant apprehension of being overtaken, or met—for he was groundlessly afraid even of travellers, who came towards him by the way he

was going—oppressed him heavily. The same intolerable awe and dread that had come upon him in
the night, returned unweakened in the day. The
monotonous ringing of the bells and tramping of the
horses; the monotony of his anxiety, and useless rage;
the monotonous wheel of fear, regret, and passion,
he kept turning round and round; made the journey
like a vision, in which nothing was quite real but his
own torment.

It was a vision of long roads; that stretched away
to a horizon, always receding and never gained; of
ill-paved towns, up hill and down, where faces came
to dark doors and ill-glazed windows, and where rows
of mud-bespattered cows and oxen were tied up for
sale in the long narrow streets, butting and lowing,
and receiving blows on their blunt heads from
bludgeons that might have beaten them in; of
bridges, crosses, churches, post-yards, new horses being put in against their wills, and the horses of the
last stage reeking, panting, and laying their drooping
heads together dolefully at stable-doors; of little ceme-
teries with black crosses settled sideways in the graves,
and withered wreathes upon them dropping away;
again of long, long roads, dragging themselves out,
up hill and down, to the treacherous horizon.

Of morning, noon, and sunset; night, and the rising of an early moon. Of long roads temporarily
left behind, and a rough pavement reached; of bat-
tering and clattering over it, and looking up, among
house-roofs, at a great church-tower; of getting out
and eating hastily, and drinking draughts of wine
that had no cheering influence; of coming forth afoot,
among a host of beggars—blind men with quivering
eyelids, led by old women holding candles to their
faces; idiot girls; the lame, the epileptic, and the palsied—of passing through the clamour, and looking

from his seat at the upturned countenances and outstretched hands, with a hurried dread of recognising some pursuer pressing forward—of galloping away again, upon the long, long road, gathered up, dull and stunned, in his corner, or rising to see where the moon shone faintly on a patch of the same endless road miles away, or looking back to see who followed.

Of never sleeping, but sometimes dozing with unclosed eyes, and springing up with a start, and a reply aloud to an imaginary voice. Of cursing himself for being there, for having fled, for having let her go, for not having confronted and defied him. Of having a deadly quarrel with the whole world, but chiefly with himself. Of blighting everything with his black mood as he was carried on and away.

It was a fevered vision of things past and present all confounded together; of his life and journey blended into one. Of being madly hurried somewhere, whither he must go. Of old scenes starting up among the novelties through which he travelled. Of musing and brooding over what was past and distant, and seeming to take no notice of the actual objects he encountered, but with a wearisome exhausting consciousness of being bewildered by them, and having their images all crowded in his hot brain after they were gone.

A vision of change upon change, and still the same monotony of bells and wheels, and horses' feet, and no rest. Of town and country, post-yards, horses, drivers, hill and valley, light and darkness, road and pavement, height and hollow, wet weather and dry, and still the some monotony of bells and wheels, and horses' feet, and no rest. A vision of tending on at last, towards the distant capital, by busier roads, and sweeping round, by old cathedrals, and dashing through small towns and villages, less thinly scattered on the road than formerly, and sitting shrouded in his corner, with his cloak up to his face, as people passing by looked at him.

Of rolling on and on, always postponing thought, and always racked with thinking; of being unable to reckon up the hours he had been upon the road, or to comprehend the points of time and place in his journey. Of being parched and giddy, and half mad. Of pressing on, in spite of all, as if he could not stop, and coming into Paris, where the turbid river held its swift course undisturbed, between two brawling streams of life and motion.

A troubled vision, then, of bridges, quays, interminable streets; of wine-shops, water-carriers, great crowds of people, soldiers, coaches, military drums, arcades. Of the monotony of bells and wheels and horses' feet being at length lost in the universal din and uproar. Of the gradual subsidence of that noise as he passed out in another carriage by a different barrier from that by which he had entered. Of the restoration, as he travelled on towards the sea-coast, of the monotony of bells and wheels, and horses' feet, and no rest.

Of sunset once again, and nightfall. Of long roads again, and dead of night, and feeble lights in windows by the roadside; and still the old monotony of bells and wheels, and horses' feet, and no rest. Of dawn, and daybreak, and the rising of the sun. Of toiling slowly up a hill, and feeling on its top the fresh sea-breeze; and seeing the morning light upon the edges of the distant waves. Of coming down into a harbour when the tide was at its full, and seeing fishing-boats float in, and glad women and children waiting for them. Of nets and seamen's clothes spread out to dry upon the shore; of busy sailors, and their voices high among ships' masts and rigging; of the buoyancy and brightness of the water, and the universal sparkling.

Of receding from the coast, and looking back upon it from the deck when it was a haze upon the water, with here and there a little opening of bright land where the sun struck. Of the swell, and flash, and murmur of the calm sea. Of another grey line on the ocean, on the vessel's track, fast growing clearer and higher. Of cliffs and buildings, and a windmill, and a church, becoming more and more visible upon it. Of steaming on at last into smooth water, and mooring to a pier whence groups of people looked down, greeting friends on board. Of disembarking, passing among them quickly, shunning every one; and of being at last again in England.

He had thought, in his dream, of going down into a remote country-place he knew, and lying quiet there, while he secretly informed himself of what transpired, and determined how to act. Still in the same stunned condition, he remembered a certain station on the railway, where he would have to branch off to his place of destination, and where there was a quiet inn. Here, he indistinctly resolved to tarry and rest.

With this purpose he slunk into a railway carriage as quickly as he could, and lying there wrapped in his cloak as if he were asleep, was soon borne far away from the sea, and deep into the inland green. Arrived at his destination he looked out, and surveyed it carefully. He was not mistaken in his impression of the place. It was a retired spot, on the borders of a little wood. Only one house, newly built or altered for the purpose, stood there, surrounded by its neat garden; the small town that was nearest, was some miles away. Here he alighted then; and going straight into the tavern, unobserved by any one, secured two rooms upstairs communicating with each other, and sufficiently retired.

His object was to rest, and recover the command of himself, and the balance of his mind. Imbecile discomfiture and rage—so that, as he walked about his room, he ground his teeth—had complete possession of him. His thoughts, not to be stopped or directed, still wandered where they would, and dragged him after them. He was stupefied, and he was wearied to death.

But, as if there were a curse upon him that he should never rest again, his drowsy senses would not lose their consciousness. He had no more influence with them in this regard, than if they had been another man's. It was not that they forced him to take note of present sounds and objects, but that they would not be diverted from the whole hurried vision of his journey. It was constantly before him all at once. She stood there, with her dark disdainful eyes again upon him; and he was riding on nevertheless, through town and country, light and darkness, wet weather and dry, over road and pavement, hill and valley, height and hollow, jaded and scared by the monotony of bells, and wheels, and horses' feet, and no rest.

'What day is this?' he asked of the waiter, who was making preparations for his dinner.

'Day, sir?'

'Is it Wednesday?'

'Wednesday, sir? No, sir. Thursday, sir.'

'I forgot. How goes the time? My watch is unwound.'

'Wants a few minutes of five o'clock, sir. Been travelling a long time, sir, perhaps?'

'Yes.'

'By rail, sir?'

'Yes.'

'Very confusing, sir. Not much in the habit of travelling by rail myself, sir, but gentlemen frequently say so.'

'Do many gentlemen come here?'

'Pretty well, sir, in general. Nobody here at present. Rather slack just now, sir. Everything *is* slack, sir.'

He made no answer; but had risen into a sitting posture on the sofa where he had been lying, and leaned forward with an arm on each knee, staring at the ground. He could not master his own attention for a minute together. It rushed away where it would, but it never, for an instant, lost itself in sleep.

He drank a quantity of wine after dinner, in vain. No such artificial means would bring sleep to his eyes. His thoughts, more incoherent, dragged him more unmercifully after them—as if a wretch, condemned to such expiation, were drawn at the heels of wild horses. No oblivion, and no rest.

How long he sat, drinking and brooding, and being dragged in imagination hither and thither, no one could have told less correctly than he. But he knew that he had been sitting a long time by candlelight, when he started up and listened, in a sudden terror.

For now, indeed, it was no fancy. The ground shook, the house rattled, the fierce impetuous rush was in the air! He felt it come up, and go darting by; and even when he had hurried to the window, and saw what it was, he stood, shrinking from it, as if it were not safe to look.

A curse upon the fiery devil, thundering along so smoothly, tracked through the distant valley by a glare of light and lurid smoke, and gone! He felt as if he had been plucked out of its path, and saved from being torn asunder. It made him shrink and shudder even now, when its faintest hum was hushed, and when the lines of iron road he could trace in the moonlight, running to a point, were as empty and as silent as a desert.

Unable to rest, and irresistibly attracted—or he thought so—to this road, he went out and lounged on the brink of it, marking the way the train had gone, by the yet smoking cinders that were lying in its track. After a lounge of some half-hour in the direction by which it had disappeared, he turned and walked the other way—still keeping to the brink of the road—past the inn garden, and a long way down; looking curiously at the bridges, signals, lamps, and wondering when another devil would come by.

A trembling of the ground, and quick vibration in his ears; a distant shriek; a dull light advancing, quickly changed to two red eyes, and a fierce fire, dropping glowing coals; an irresistible bearing on of a great roaring and dilating mass; a high wind, and a rattle—another come and gone, and he holding to a gate, as if to save himself!

He waited for another, and for another. He walked back to his former point, and back again to that, and still through the wearisome vision of his journey, looked for these approaching monsters. He loitered about the station, waiting until one should stay to call there; and when one did, and was detached for water, he stood parallel with it, watching its heavy wheels and brazen front, and thinking what a cruel power and might it had. Ugh! To see the great wheels slowly turning, and to think of being run down and crushed!

Disordered with wine and want of rest—that want which nothing, although he was so weary, would appease—these ideas and objects assumed a diseased importance in his thoughts. When he went back to his room, which was not until near midnight, they still haunted him, and he sat listening for the coming of another.

So in his bed, whither he repaired with no hope of sleep. He still lay listening; and when he felt the trembling and vibration, got up and went to the window, to watch (as he could from its position) the dull light changing to the two red eyes, and the fierce fire dropping glowing coals, and the rush of the giant as it fled past, and the track of glare and smoke along the valley. Then he would glance in the direction by which he intended to depart at sunrise, as there was no rest for him there; and would lie down again, to be troubled by the vision of his journey, and the old monotony of bells and wheels and horses' feet, until another came. This lasted all night. So far from resuming the mastery of himself, he seemed, if possible, to lose it more and more, as the night crept on. When the dawn appeared, he was still tormented with thinking, still postponing thought until he should be in a better state; the past, present, and future, all floated confusedly before him, and he had lost all power of looking steadily at any one of them.

'At what time,' he asked the man who had waited on him over-night, now entering with a candle, 'do I leave here, did you say?'

'About a quarter after four, sir. Express comes through at four, sir.—It don't stop.'

He passed his hand across his throbbing head, and looked at his watch. Nearly half-past three.

'Nobody going with you, sir, probably,' observed the man. 'Two gentlemen here, sir, but they 're waiting for the train to London.'

'I thought you said there was nobody here,' said

Carker, turning upon him with the ghost of his old smile, when he was angry or suspicious.

'Not then, sir. Two gentlemen came in the night by the short train that stops here, sir. Warm water, sir?'

'No; and take away the candle. There's day enough for me.'

Having thrown himself upon the bed, half-dressed, he was at the window as the man left the room. The cold light of morning had succeeded to night, and there was already, in the sky, the red suffusion of the coming sun. He bathed his head and face with water —there was no cooling influence in it for him—hurriedly put on his clothes, paid what he owed, and went out.

The air struck chill and comfortless as it breathed upon him. There was a heavy dew; and, hot as he was, it made him shiver. After a glance at the place where he had walked last night, and at the signal-lights burning feebly in the morning, and bereft of their significance, he turned to where the sun was rising, and beheld it, in its glory, as it broke upon the scene.

So awful, so transcendent in its beauty, so divinely solemn. As he cast his faded eyes upon it, where it rose, tranquil and serene, unmoved by all the wrong and wickedness on which its beams had shone since the beginning of the world, who shall say that some weak sense of virtue upon earth, and its reward in heaven, did not manifest itself, even to him? If ever he remembered sister or brother with a touch of tenderness and remorse, who shall say it was not then?

He needed some such touch then. Death was on him. He was marked off from the living world, and going down into his grave.

He paid the money for his journey to the country-place he had thought of; and was walking to and fro, alone, looking along the lines of iron, across the valley in one direction, and towards a dark bridge near at hand in the other; when, turning in his walk, where it was bounded by one end of the wooden stage on which he paced up and down, he saw the man from whom he had fled, emerging from the door by which he himself had entered there. And their eyes met.

In the quick unsteadiness of the surprise, he staggered, and slipped on to the road below him. But recovering his feet immediately, he stepped back a pace or two upon that road, to interpose some wider space between them, and looked at his pursuer, breathing short and quick.

He heard a shout—another—saw the face change from its vindictive passion to a faint sickness and terror—felt the earth tremble—knew in a moment that the rush was come—uttered a shriek—looked round—saw the red eyes, bleared and dim, in the daylight, close upon him—was beaten down, caught up, and whirled away upon a jagged mill, that spun him round and round and struck him limb from limb, and licked his stream of life up with its fiery heat, and cast his mutilated fragments in the air.

When the traveller, who had been recognised, recovered from a swoon, he saw them bringing from a distance something covered, that lay heavy and still, upon a board, between four men, and saw that others drove some dogs away that sniffed upon the road, and soaked his blood up, with a train of ashes.

CHAPTER LVI

SEVERAL PEOPLE DELIGHTED, AND THE
GAME CHICKEN DISGUSTED

THE midshipman was all alive. Mr. Toots and
Susan had arrived at last. Susan had run upstairs
like a young woman bereft of her senses, and Mr.
Toots and the Chicken had gone into the parlour.

'Oh my own pretty darling sweet Miss Floy!' cried
the Nipper, running into Florence's room, 'to think
that it should come to this and I should find you here
my own dear dove with nobody to wait upon you and
no home to call your own but never never will I go
away again Miss Floy for though I may not gather
moss I'm not a rolling-stone nor is my heart a stone or
else it wouldn't bust as it is busting now oh dear oh
dear!'

Pouring out these words, without the faintest indication of a stop, of any sort, Miss Nipper, on her
knees beside her mistress, hugged her close.

'Oh love!' cried Susan, 'I know all that's past I
know it all my tender pet and I'm a choking give me
air!'

'Susan, dear good Susan!' said Florence.

'Oh bless her! I that was her little maid when she
was a little child! and is she really, really truly going
to be married?' exclaimed Susan, in a burst of pain
and pleasure, pride and grief, and Heaven knows
how many other conflicting feelings.

'Who told you so?' said Florence.

'Oh gracious me! that innocentest creetur Toots,'
returned Susan hysterically. 'I knew he must be
right my dear because he took on so. He's the de-
votedest and innocentest infant! And is my darling,'

pursued Susan, with another close embrace and burst of tears, 'really really going to be married!'

The mixture of compassion, pleasure, tenderness, protection, and regret with which the Nipper constantly recurred to this subject, and at every such recurrence, raised her head to look in the young face and kiss it, and then laid her head again upon her mistress's shoulder, caressing her and sobbing, was as womanly and good a thing, in its way, as ever was seen in the world.

'There, there!' said the soothing voice of Florence presently. 'Now you 're quite yourself, dear Susan!'

Miss Nipper, sitting down upon the floor, at her mistress's feet, laughing and sobbing, holding her pocket-handkerchief to her eyes with one hand, and patting Diogenes with the other as he licked her face, confessed to being more composed, and laughed and cried a little more in proof of it.

'I—I—I never did see such a creetur as that Toots,' said Susan, 'in all my born days never!'

'So kind,' suggested Florence.

'And so comic!' Susan sobbed. 'The way he 's been going on inside with me with that disrespectable Chicken on the box!'

'About what, Susan?' inquired Florence timidly.

'Oh about Lieutenant Walters, and Captain Gills, and you my dear Miss Floy, and the silent tomb,' said Susan.

'The silent tomb!' repeated Florence.

'He says,' here Susan burst into a violent hysterical laugh, 'that he 'll go down into it now immediately and quite comfortable, but bless your heart my dear Miss Floy he won't, he 's a great deal too happy in seeing other people happy for that, he may not be a Solomon,' pursued the Nipper, with her usual volubility, 'nor do I say he is but this I do say a less selfish human creature human nature never knew!'

Miss Nipper being still hysterical, laughed immoderately after making this energetic declaration, and then informed Florence that he was waiting below to see her; which would be a rich repayment for the trouble he had had in his late expedition.

Florence entreated Susan to beg of Mr. Toots as a favour that she might have the pleasure of thanking him for his kindness; and Susan, in a few moments, produced that young gentleman, still very much dishevelled in appearance, and stammering exceedingly.

'Miss Dombey,' said Mr. Toots. 'To be again permitted to—to—gaze—at least, not to gaze, but—I don't exactly know what I was going to say, but it's of no consequence.'

'I have to thank you so often,' returned Florence, giving him both her hands, with all her innocent gratitude beaming in her face, 'that I have no words left, and don't know how to do it.'

'Miss Dombey,' said Mr. Toots, in an awful voice, 'if it was possible that you could, consistently with your angelic nature, curse me, you would—if I may be allowed to say so—floor me infinitely less, than by these undeserved expressions of kindness. Their effect upon me—is—but,' said Mr. Toots, abruptly, 'this is a digression, and's of no consequence at all.'

As there seemed to be no means of replying to this, but by thanking him again, Florence thanked him again.

'I could wish,' said Mr. Toots, 'to take this opportunity, Miss Dombey, if I might, of entering into a word of explanation. I should have had the pleasure of—of returning with Susan at an earlier period; but, in the first place, we didn't know the name of the relation to whose house she had gone, and, in the second, as she had left that relation's and gone to another at a distance, I think that scarcely anything short of the sagacity of the Chicken, would have found her out in the time.'

Florence was sure of it.

'This, however,' said Mr. Toots, 'is not the point. The company of Susan has been, I assure you, Miss Dombey, a consolation and satisfaction to me, in my state of mind, more easily conceived than described. The journey has been its own reward. That, however, still, is not the point. Miss Dombey, I have before observed that I know I am not what is considered a quick person. I am perfectly aware of that. I don't think anybody could be better acquainted with his own—if it was not too strong an expression, I should say with the thickness of his own head—than myself. But, Miss Dombey, I do, notwithstanding, perceive the state of—of things—with Lieutenant Walters. Whatever agony that state of things may have caused me (which is of no consequence at all), I am bound to say, that Lieutenant Walters is a person who appears to be worthy of the blessing that has fallen on his—on his brow. May he wear it long, and appreciate it, as a very different, and very unworthy individual, that it is of no consequence to name, would have done! That, however, still, is not the point. Miss Dombey, Captain Gills is a friend of mine; and during the interval that is now elapsing, I believe it would afford Captain Gills pleasure to see me occasionally coming backwards and forwards here. It would afford me pleasure so to come. But I cannot forget that I once committed myself, fatally, at the corner of the square at Brighton; and if my presence will be, in the least degree, unpleasant to you, I only ask you to name it to me now, and assure you that I shall perfectly understand you. I shall not consider it at all unkind, and shall only be too delighted and happy to be honoured with your confidence.'

'Mr. Toots,' returned Florence, 'if you, who are so old and true a friend of mine, were to stay away from this house now, you would make me very unhappy. It can never, never, give me any feeling but pleasure to see you.'

'Miss Dombey,' said Mr. Toots, taking out his pocket-handkerchief, 'if I shed a tear, it is a tear of joy. It is of no consequence, and I am very much obliged to you. I may be allowed to remark, after what you have so kindly said, that it is not my intention to neglect my person any longer.'

Florence received this intimation with the prettiest expression of perplexity possible.

'I mean,' said Mr. Toots, 'that I shall consider it my duty as a fellow-creature generally, until I am claimed by the silent tomb, to make the best of myself, and to—to have my boots as brightly polished, as—as circumstances will admit of. This is the last time, Miss Dombey, of my intruding any observation of a private and personal nature. I thank you very much indeed. If I am not, in a general way, as sensible as my friends could wish me to be, or as I could wish myself, I really am, upon my word and honour, particularly sensible of what is considerate and kind. I feel,' said Mr. Toots, in an impassioned tone, 'as if I could express my feelings, at the present moment, in a most remarkable manner, if—if—I could only get a start.'

Appearing not to get it, after waiting a minute or two to see if it would come, Mr. Toots took a hasty leave, and went below to seek the captain, whom he found in the shop.

'Captain Gills,' said Mr. Toots, 'what is now to take place between us, takes place under the sacred

seal of confidence. It is the sequel, Captain Gills, of
what has taken place between myself and Miss Dombey, upstairs.'

'Alow and aloft, eh, my lad?' murmured the captain.

'Exactly so, Captain Gills,' said Mr. Toots, whose
fervour of acquiescence was greatly heightened by his
entire ignorance of the captain's meaning. 'Miss
Dombey, I believe, Captain Gills, is to be shortly
united to Lieutenant Walters?'

'Why, aye, my lad. We're all shipmets here—
Wal'r and sweetheart will be jined together in the
house of bondage, as soon as the askings is over,'
whispered Captain Cuttle, in his ear.

'The askings, Captain Gills?' repeated Mr. Toots.

'In the church, down yonder,' said the captain,
pointing his thumb over his shoulder.

'Oh! Yes!' returned Mr. Toots.

'And then,' said the captain, in his hoarse whisper,
and tapping Mr. Toots on the chest with the back of
his hand, and falling from him with a look of infinite
admiration, 'what follers? That there pretty creetur,
as delicately brought up as a foreign bird, goes away
upon the roaring main with Wal'r on a woyage to
China!'

'Lord, Captain Gills!' said Mr. Toots.

'Aye!' nodded the captain. 'The ship as took him
up, when he was wrecked in the hurricane that had
drove her clean out of her course, was a China trader,
and Wal'r made the woyage, and got into favour,
aboard and ashore—being as smart and good a lad as
ever stepped—and so, the supercargo dying at Can-
ton, he got made (having acted as clerk afore), and
now he's supercargo aboard another ship, same owners. And so, you see,' repeated the captain, thought-

fully, 'the pretty creetur goes away upon the roaring main with Wal'r, on a woyage to China.'

Mr. Toots and Captain Cuttle heaved a sigh in concert.

'What then?' said the captain. 'She loves him true. He loves her true. Them as should have loved and tended of her, treated of her like the beasts as perish. When she, cast out of home, come here to me, and dropped upon them planks, her wounded heart was broke. I know it. I, Ed'ard Cuttle, see it. There's nowt but true, kind, steady love, as can ever piece it up again. If so be I didn't know that, and didn't know as Wal'r was her true love, brother, and she his, I'd have these here blue arms and legs chopped off, afore I'd let her go. But I *do* know it, and what then? Why, then, I say, Heaven go with 'em both, and so it will! Amen!'

'Captain Gills,' said Mr. Toots, 'let me have the pleasure of shaking hands. You've a way of saying things, that gives me an agreeable warmth, all up my back. *I* say Amen. You are aware, Captain Gills, that I, too, have adored Miss Dombey.'

'Cheer up!' said the captain, laying his hand on Mr. Toots's shoulder. 'Stand by, boy!'

'It is my intention, Captain Gills,' returned the spirited Mr. Toots, '*to* cheer up. Also to stand by, as much as possible. When the silent tomb shall yawn, Captain Gills, I shall be ready for burial; not before. But not being certain, just at present, of my power over myself, what I wish to say to you, and what I shall take it as a particular favour if you will mention to Lieutenant Walters, is as follows.'

'Is as follers,' echoed the captain. 'Steady!'

'Miss Dombey being so inexpressibly kind,' continued Mr. Toots with watery eyes, 'as to say that my presence is the reverse of disagreeable to her, and you and everybody here being no less forbearing and tolerant towards one who—who certainly,' said Mr. Toots, with momentary dejection, 'would appear to have been born by mistake, I shall come backwards and forwards of an evening, during the short time we can all be together. But what I ask is this. If, at any moment, I find that I cannot endure the contemplation of Lieutenant Walter's bliss, and should rush out, I hope, Captain Gills, that you and he will both consider it as my misfortune and not my fault, or the want of inward conflict. That you'll feel convinced I bear no malice to any living creature—least of all to Lieutenant Walters himself—and that you'll casually remark that I have gone out for a walk, or probably to see what o'clock it is by the Royal Exchange. Captain Gills, if you could enter into this arrangement, and could answer for Lieutenant Walters, it would be a relief to my feelings that I should think cheap at the sacrifice of a considerable portion of my property.'

'My lad,' returned the captain, 'say no more. There ain't a colour you can run up, as won't be made out, and answered to, by Wal'r and self.'

'Captain Gills,' said Mr. Toots, 'my mind is greatly relieved. I wish to preserve the good opinion of all here. I—I—mean well, upon my honour, however badly I may show it. You know,' said Mr. Toots, 'it's exactly as if Burgess and Co. wished to oblige a customer with a most extraordinary pair of trousers, and could not cut out what they had in their minds.'

With this opposite illustration, of which he seemed a little proud, Mr. Toots gave Captain Cuttle his blessing and departed.

The honest captain, with his Heart's Delight in

the house, and Susan tending her, was a beaming and a happy man. As the days flew by, he grew more beaming and more happy, every day. After some conferences with Susan (for whose wisdom the captain had a profound respect, and whose valiant precipitation of herself on Mrs. MacStinger he could never forget), he proposed to Florence that the daughter of the elderly lady who usually sat under the blue umbrella in Leadenhall Market, should, for prudential reasons and considerations of privacy, be superseded in the temporary discharge of the household duties, by some one who was not unknown to them, and in whom they could safely confide. Susan, being present, then named, in furtherance of a suggestion she had previously offered to the captain, Mrs. Richards. Florence brightened at the name. And Susan, setting off that very afternoon to the Toodle domicile, to sound Mrs. Richards, returned in triumph the same evening, accompanied by the identical rosy-cheeked, apple-faced Polly, whose demonstrations, when brought into Florence's presence, were hardly less affectionate than those of Susan Nipper herself.

This piece of generalship accomplished; from which the captain derived uncommon satisfaction, as he did, indeed, from everything else that was done, whatever it happened to be; Florence had next to prepare Susan for their approaching separation. This was a much more difficult task, as Miss Nipper was of a resolute disposition, and had fully made up her mind that she had come back never to be parted from her old mistress any more.

'As to wages, dear Miss Floy,' she said, 'you wouldn't hint and wrong me so as think of naming them, for I've put money by and wouldn't sell my love and duty at a time like this even if the savings' bank and me were total strangers or the banks were broke to pieces, but you 've never been without me darling from the time your poor dear ma was took away, and though I 'm nothing to be boasted of you 're used to me and oh my own dear mistress through so many years don't think of going anywhere without me, for it mustn't and can't be!'

'Dear Susan, I am going on a long, long voyage.'

'Well Miss Floy, and what of that? the more you 'll want me. Lengths of voyages ain't an object in my eyes, thank God!' said the impetuous Susan Nipper.

'But, Susan, I am going with Walter, and I would go with Walter anywhere—everywhere! Walter is poor, and I am very poor, and I must learn, now, both to help myself, and help him.'

'Dear Miss Floy!' cried Susan, bursting out afresh, and shaking her head violently, 'it 's nothing new to you to help yourself and others too and be the patientest and truest of noble hearts, but let me talk to Mr. Walter Gay and settle it with him, for suffer you to go away across the world alone I cannot, and I won't.'

'Alone, Susan?' returned Florence. 'Alone? and Walter taking me with him!' Ah, what a bright, amazed, enraptured smile was on her face!—He should have seen it. 'I am sure you will not speak to Walter if I ask you not,' she added tenderly; 'and pray don't, dear.'

Susan sobbed 'Why not, Miss Floy?'

'Because,' said Florence, 'I am going to be his wife, to give him up my whole heart, and to live with him and die with him. He might think, if you said to him what you have said to me, that I am afraid of what is before me, or that you have some cause to be afraid for me. Why, Susan dear, I love him!'

Miss Nipper was so much affected by the quiet

fervour of these words, and the simple, heartfelt, all-pervading earnestness expressed in them, and making the speaker's face more beautiful and pure than ever, that she could only cling to her again, crying, Was her little mistress really, really going to be married, and pitying, caressing, and protecting her, as she had done before.

But the Nipper, though susceptible of womanly weaknesses, was almost as capable of putting constraint upon herself as of attacking the redoubtable MacStinger. From that time, she never returned to the subject, but was always cheerful, active, bustling, and hopeful. She did, indeed, inform Mr. Toots privately, that she was only 'keeping up' for the time, and that when it was all over, and Miss Dombey was gone, she might be expected to become a spectacle distressful; and Mr. Toots did also express that it was his case too, and that they would mingle their tears together; but she never otherwise indulged her private feelings in the presence of Florence or within the precincts of the midshipman.

Limited and plain as Florence's wardrobe was—what a contrast to that prepared for the last marriage in which she had taken part!—there was a good deal to do in getting it ready, and Susan Nipper worked away at her side, all day, with the concentrated zeal of fifty sempstresses. The wonderful contributions Captain Cuttle would have made to this branch of the outfit, if he had been permitted—as pink parasols, tinted silk stockings, blue shoes, and other articles no less necessary on shipboard—would occupy some space in the recital. He was induced, however, by various fraudulent representations, to limit his contributions to a work-box and dressing-case, of each of which he purchased the very largest specimen that could be got for money. For ten days or a fortnight

afterwards, he generally sat during the greater part
of the day, gazing at these boxes; divided between
extreme admiration of them, and dejected misgivings
that they were not gorgeous enough, and frequently
diving out into the street to purchase some wild article that he deemed necessary to their completeness.
But his master-stroke was the bearing of them both
off, suddenly, one morning, and getting the two
words FLORENCE GAY engraved upon a brass heart
inlaid over the lid of each. After this, he smoked
four pipes successively in the little parlour by himself, and was discovered chuckling, at the expiration
of as many hours.

Walter was busy and away all day, but came there
every morning early to see Florence, and always
passed the evening with her. Florence never left her
high rooms but to steal downstairs to wait for him
when it was his time to come, or, sheltered by his
proud encircling arm, to bear him company to the
door again and sometimes peep into the street. In
the twilight they were always together. Oh blessed
time! Oh wandering heart at rest! Oh deep, ex-
haustless, mighty well of love, in which so much was
sunk!

The cruel mark was on her bosom yet. It rose
against her father with the breath she drew, it lay
between her and her lover when he pressed her to his
heart. But she forgot it. In the beating of that
heart for her, and in the beating of her own for him,
all harsher music was unheard, all stern unloving
hearts forgotten. Fragile and delicate she was, but
with a might of love within her that could, and did,
create a world to fly to, and to rest in, out of his one
image.

How often did the great house, and the old days,
come before her in the twilight time, when she was

sheltered by the arm, so proud, so fond, and creeping closer to him, shrunk within it at the recollection! How often, from remembering the night when she went down to that room and met the never-to-be-forgotten look, did she raise her eyes to those that watched her with such loving earnestness, and weep with happiness in such a refuge! The more she clung to it, the more the dear dead child was in her thoughts: but as if the last time she had seen her father, had been when he was sleeping and she kissed his face, she always left him so, and never, in her fancy, passed that hour.

'Walter, dear,' said Florence, one evening, when it was almost dark. 'Do you know what I have been thinking to-day?'

'Thinking how the time is flying on, and how soon we shall be upon the sea, sweet Florence?'

'I don't mean that, Walter, though I think of that too. I have been thinking what a charge I am to you.'

'A precious, sacred charge, dear heart! Why I think that sometimes.'

'You are laughing, Walter. I know that's much more in your thoughts than mine. But I mean a cost.'

'A cost, my own?'

'In money, dear. All these preparations that Susan and I are busy with—I have been able to purchase very little for myself. You were poor before. But how much poorer I shall make you, Walter!'

'And how much richer, Florence!'

Florence laughed and shook her head.

'Besides,' said Walter, 'long ago—before I went to sea—I had a little purse presented to me, dearest, which had money in it.'

'Ah!' returned Florence, laughing sorrowfully,

'very little! Very little, Walter! But, you must not think,' and here she laid her light hand on his shoulder, and looked into his face, 'that I regret to be this burden on you. No, dear love, I am glad of it. I am happy in it. I wouldn't have it otherwise for all the world!'

'Nor I, indeed, dear Florence.'

'Aye! but Walter, you can never feel it as I do. I am so proud of you! It makes my heart swell with such delight to know that those who speak of you must say you married a poor disowned girl, who had taken shelter here; who had no other home, no other friends; who had nothing—nothing! Oh, Walter, if I could have brought you millions, I never could have been so happy for your sake, as I am!'

'And you, dear Florence? are you nothing?' he returned.

'No, nothing, Walter. Nothing but your wife.' The light hand stole about his neck, and the voice came nearer—nearer. 'I am nothing any more, that is not you. I have no earthly hope any more, that is not you. I have nothing dear to me any more, that is not you.'

Oh! well might Mr. Toots leave the little company that evening, and twice go out to correct his watch by the Royal Exchange, and once to keep an appointment with a banker which he suddenly remembered, and once to take a little turn to Aldgate Pump and back!

But before he went upon these expeditions, or indeed before he came, and before lights were brought, Walter said—

'Florence, love, the lading of our ship is nearly finished, and probably on the very day of our marriage she will drop down the river. Shall we go

away that morning, and stay in Kent until we go on
board at Gravesend within a week?'

'If you please, Walter. I shall be happy anywhere. But—'

'Yes, my life?'

'You know,' said Florence, 'that we shall have no
marriage party, and that nobody will distinguish us
by our dress from other people. As we leave the
same day, will you—will you take me somewhere that
morning, Walter—early—before we go to church?'

Walter seemed to understand her, as so true a lover
so truly loved should, and confirmed his ready promise
with a kiss—with more than one perhaps, or two or
three, or five or six; and in the grave, peaceful evening, Florence was very happy.

Then into the quiet room came Susan Nipper and
the candles; shortly afterwards, the tea, the captain,
and the excursive Mr. Toots, who, as above mentioned, was frequently on the move afterwards, and
passed but a restless evening. This, however, was
not his habit: for he generally got on very well, by
dint of playing at cribbage with the captain under
the advice and guidance of Miss Nipper, and dis-
tracting his mind with the calculations incidental to
the game; which he found to be a very effectual means
of utterly confounding himself.

The captain's visage on these occasions presented
one of the finest examples of combination and succession of expression ever observed. His instinctive
delicacy and his chivalrous feeling towards Florence,
taught him that it was not a time for any boisterous
jollity, or violent display of satisfaction. Certain
floating reminiscences of Lovely Peg, on the other
hand, were constantly struggling for a vent, and
urging the captain to commit himself by some irrep-

arable demonstration. Anon, his admiration of Florence and Walter—well-matched, truly, and full of grace and interest in their youth, and love, and good looks, as they sat apart—would take such complete possession of him, that he would lay down his cards, and beam upon them, dabbing his head all over with his pocket-handkerchief; until warned, perhaps, by the sudden rushing forth of Mr. Toots, that he had unconsciously been very instrumental, indeed, in making that gentleman miserable. This reflection would make the captain profoundly melancholy, until the return of Mr. Toots; when he would fall to his cards again, with many side winks and nods, and polite waves of his hook at Miss Nipper, importing that he wasn't going to do so any more. The state that ensued on this, was, perhaps, his best; for then, endeavouring to discharge all expression from his face, he would sit, staring round the room, with all these expressions conveyed into it at once, and each wrestling with the other. Delighted admiration of Florence and Walter always overthrew the rest, and remained victorious and undisguised, unless Mr. Toots made another rush into the air, and then the captain would sit, like a remorseful culprit, until he came back again, occasionally calling upon himself, in a low reproachful voice, to 'Stand by!' or growling some remonstrance to 'Ed'ard Cuttle, my lad,' on the want of caution observable in his behaviour.

One of Mr. Toots's hardest trials, however, was of his own seeking. On the approach of the Sunday which was to witness the last of those askings in church of which the captain had spoken, Mr. Toots thus stated his feelings to Susan Nipper.

'Susan,' said Mr. Toots, 'I am drawn towards the building. The words which cut me off from Miss Dombey for ever, will strike upon my ears like a knell

you know, but upon my word and honour, I feel that
I must hear them. Therefore,' said Mr. Toots, 'will
you accompany me to-morrow, to the sacred edifice?'

Miss Nipper expressed her readiness to do so, if
that would be any satisfaction to Mr. Toots, but besought him to abandon his idea of going.

'Susan,' returned Mr. Toots, with much solemnity,
'before my whiskers began to be observed by anybody but myself, I adored Miss Dombey. While yet
a victim to the thraldom of Blimber, I adored Miss
Dombey. When I could no longer be kept out of
my property, in a legal point of view, and—and accordingly came into it—I adored Miss Dombey.
The banns which consign her to Lieutenant Walters,
and me to—to Gloom, you know,' said Mr. Toots,
after hesitating for a strong expression, 'may be
dreadful, *will* be dreadful: but I feel that I should
wish to hear them spoken. I feel that I should wish
to know that the ground was certainly cut from under
me, and that I hadn't a hope to cherish, or a—or a leg,
in short, to—to go upon.'

Susan Nipper could only commiserate Mr. Toots's
unfortunate condition, and agree, under these circumstances, to accompany him; which she did next
morning.

The church Walter had chosen for the purpose,
was a mouldy old church in a yard, hemmed in by
a labyrinth of back streets and courts, with a little
burying-ground round it, and itself buried in a kind
of vault, formed by the neighbouring houses, and
paved with echoing stones. It was a great dim,
shabby pile, with high old oaken pews, among which
about a score of people lost themselves every Sunday; while the clergyman's voice drowsily resounded
through the emptiness, and the organ rumbled and
rolled as if the church had got the colic, for want of

a congregation to keep the wind and damp out. But so far was this city church from languishing for the company of other churches, that spires were clustered round it, as the masts of shipping cluster on the river. It would have been hard to count them from its steeple-top, they were so many. In almost every yard and blind-place near, there was a church. The confusion of bells when Susan and Mr. Toots betook themselves towards it on the Sunday morning, was deafening. There were twenty churches close together, clamouring for people to come in.

The two stray sheep in question were penned by a beadle in a commodious pew, and, being early, sat for some time counting the congregation, listening to the disappointed bell high up in the tower, or looking at a shabby little old man in the porch behind the screen, who was ringing the same, like the bull in Cock Robin, with his foot in a stirrup. Mr. Toots, after a lengthened survey of the large books on the reading-desk, whispered Miss Nipper that he wondered where the banns were kept, but that young lady merely shook her head and frowned; repelling for the time all approaches of a temporal nature.

Mr. Toots, however, appearing unable to keep his thoughts from the banns, was evidently looking out for them during the whole preliminary portion of the service. As the time for reading them approached, the poor young gentleman manifested great anxiety and trepidation, which was not diminished by the unexpected apparition of the captain in the front row of the gallery. When the clerk handed up a list to the clergyman, Mr. Toots, being then seated, held on by the seat of the pew; but when the names of Walter Gay and Florence Dombey were read aloud as being in the third and last stage of that association, he was so entirely conquered by his feelings as

to rush from the church without his hat, followed by
the beadle and pew-opener, and two gentlemen of the
medical profession, who happened to be present; of
whom the first-named presently returned for that
article, informing Miss Nipper in a whisper that she
was not to make herself uneasy about the gentleman,
as the gentleman said his indisposition was of no consequence.

Miss Nipper, feeling that the eyes of that integral
portion of Europe which lost itself weekly among
the high-backed pews, were upon her, would have
been sufficiently embarrassed by this incident, though
it had terminated here; the more so, as the captain
in the front row of the gallery, was in a state of
unmitigated consciousness which could hardly fail to
express to the congregation that he had some mysterious connection with it.   But the extreme restlessness
of Mr. Toots painfully increased and protracted the
delicacy of her situation.   That young gentleman,
incapable, in his state of mind, of remaining alone
in the churchyard, a prey to solitary meditation, and
also desirous, no doubt, of testifying his respect for
the offices he had in some measure interrupted, suddenly returned—not coming back to the pew, but
stationing himself on a free seat in the aisle, between
two elderly females who were in the habit of receiving their portion of a weekly dole of bread then set
forth on a shelf in the porch.   In this conjunction
Mr. Toots remained, greatly disturbing the congregation, who felt it impossible to avoid looking at him,
until his feelings overcame him again, when he departed silently and suddenly.   Not venturing to
trust himself in the church any more, and yet wishing
to have some social participation in what was going
on there, Mr. Toots was, after this, seen from time
to time, looking in, with a lorn aspect, at one or other

of the windows; and as there were several windows accessible to him from without, and as his restlessness was very great, it not only became difficult to conceive at which window he would appear next, but likewise became necessary, as it were, for the whole congregation to speculate upon the chances of the different windows, during the comparative leisure afforded them by the sermon. Mr. Toots's movements in the churchyard were so eccentric, that he seemed generally to defeat all calculation, and to appear, like the conjuror's figure, where he was least expected; and the effect of these mysterious presentations was much increased by its being difficult to him to see in, and easy to everybody else to see out: which occasioned his remaining, every time, longer than might have been expected, with his face close to the glass, until he all at once became aware that all eyes were upon him, and vanished.

These proceedings on the part of Mr. Toots, and the strong individual consciousness of them that was exhibited by the captain, rendered Miss Nipper's position so responsible a one, that she was mightily relieved by the conclusion of the service; and was hardly so affable to Mr. Toots as usual, when he informed her and the captain, on the way back, that now he was sure he had no hope, you know, he felt more comfortable—at least not exactly more comfortable, but more comfortably and completely miserable.

Swiftly now, indeed, the time flew by until it was the evening before the day appointed for the marriage. They were all assembled in the upper room at the midshipman's, and had no fear of interruption; for there were no lodgers in the house now, and the midshipman had it all to himself. They were grave and quiet in the prospect of to-morrow, but moderately cheerful too. Florence, with Walter close beside her, was finishing a little piece of work intended as a parting gift to the captain. The captain was playing cribbage with Mr. Toots. Mr. Toots was taking counsel as to his hand, of Susan Nipper. Miss Nipper was giving it, with all due secrecy and circumspection. Diogenes was listening, and occasionally breaking out into a gruff half-smothered fragment of a bark, of which he afterwards seemed half-ashamed, as if he doubted having any reason for it.

'Steady, steady!' said the captain to Diogenes, 'what's amiss with you? You don't seem easy in your mind to-night, my boy!'

Diogenes wagged his tail, but pricked up his ears immediately afterwards, and gave utterance to another fragment of a bark; for which he apologised to the captain, by again wagging his tail.

'It's my opinion, Di,' said the captain, looking thoughtfully at his cards, and stroking his chin with his hook, 'as you have your doubts of Mrs. Richards; but if you're the animal I take you to be, you'll think better o' that; for her looks is her commission. Now, brother': to Mr. Toots: 'if so be as you're ready, heave ahead.'

The captain spoke with all composure and attention to the game, but suddenly his cards dropped out of his hand, his mouth and eyes opened wide, his legs drew themselves up and stuck out in front of his chair, and he sat staring at the door with blank amazement. Looking round upon the company, and seeing that none of them observed him or the cause of his astonishment, the captain recovered himself with a great gasp, struck the table a tremendous blow, cried in a stentorian roar, 'Sol Gills ahoy!' and tumbled into the arms of a weather-beaten pea-coat that had come with Polly into the room.

In another moment, Walter was in the arms of the weather-beaten pea-coat. In another moment, Florence was in the arms of the weather-beaten pea-coat. In another moment, Captain Cuttle had embraced Mrs. Richards and Miss Nipper, and was violently shaking hands with Mr. Toots, exclaiming, as he waved his hook above his head, 'Hooroar, my lad, hooroar!' To which Mr. Toots, wholly at a loss to account for these proceedings, replied with great politeness, 'Certainly, Captain Gills, whatever you think proper!'

The weather-beaten pea-coat, and a no less weather-beaten cap and comforter belonging to it, turned from the captain and from Florence back to Walter, and sounds came from the weather-beaten pea-coat, cap, and comforter, as of an old man sobbing underneath them; while the shaggy sleeves clasped Walter tight. During this pause, there was a universal silence, and the captain polished his nose with great diligence. But when the pea-coat, cap, and comforter lifted themselves up again, Florence gently moved towards them; and she and Walter taking them off, disclosed the old instrument-maker, a little thinner and more careworn than of old, in his old Welsh wig and his old coffee-coloured coat and basket buttons, with his old infallible chronometer ticking away in his pocket.

'Chock full o' science,' said the radiant captain, 'as ever he was! Sol Gills, Sol Gills, what have you been up to, for this many a long day, my ould boy?'

'I'm half blind, Ned,' said the old man, 'and almost deaf and dumb with joy.'

'His wery woice,' said the captain, looking round with an exultation to which even his face could hardly render justice—'his wery woice as chock full o' science as ever it was! Sol Gills, lay to, my lad, upon your

own wines and fig-trees, like a taut ould patriark as
you are, and overhaul them there adwentures o'
yourn, in your own formilior woice. 'Tis *the* woice,'
said the captain, impressively, and announcing a
quotation with his hook, 'of the sluggard, I heerd
him complain, you have woke me too soon, I must
slumber again. Scatter his ene-mies, and make 'em
fall!'

The captain sat down with the air of a man who
had happily expressed the feeling of everybody
present, and immediately rose again to present Mr.
Toots, who was much disconcerted by the arrival of
anybody, appearing to prefer a claim to the name of
Gills.

'Although,' stammered Mr. Toots, 'I had not the
pleasure of your acquaintance, sir, before you were—
you were—'

'Lost to sight, to memory dear,' suggested the
captain, in a low voice.

'Exactly so, Captain Gills!' assented Mr. Toots.
'Although I had not the pleasure of your acquaintance, Mr.—Mr. Sols,' said Toots, hitting on that
name in the inspiration of a bright idea, 'before that
happened, I have the greatest pleasure, I assure you,
in—you know, in knowing you. I hope,' said Mr.
Toots, 'that you're as well as can be expected.'

With these courteous words, Mr. Toots sat down
blushing and chuckling.

The old instrument-maker, seated in a corner between Walter and Florence, and nodding at Polly,
who was looking on, all smiles and delight, answered
the captain thus—

'Ned Cuttle, my dear boy, although I have heard
something of the changes of events here, from my
pleasant friend there—what a pleasant face she has
to be sure, to welcome a wanderer home!' said the old

man, breaking off, and rubbing his hands in his old dreamy way.

'Hear him!' cried the captain gravely. ''Tis woman as seduces all mankind. For which,' aside to Mr. Toots, 'you'll overhaul your Adam and Eve, brother.'

'I shall make a point of doing so, Captain Gills,' said Mr. Toots.

'Although I have heard something of the changes of events, from her,' resumed the instrument-maker, taking his old spectacles from his pocket, and putting them on his forehead in his old manner, 'they are so great and unexpected, and I am so overpowered by the sight of my dear boy, and by the,'— glancing at the downcast eyes of Florence, and not attempting to finish the sentence—'that I—I can't say much to-night. But my dear Ned Cuttle, why didn't you write?'

The astonishment depicted in the captain's features positively frightened Mr. Toots, whose eyes were quite fixed by it, so that he could not withdraw them from his face.

'Write!' echoed the captain. 'Write, Sol Gills?'

'Aye,' said the old man, 'either to Barbados, or Jamaica, or Demerara. That was what I asked.'

'What you asked, Sol Gills?' repeated the captain.

'Aye,' said the old man. 'Don't you know, Ned? Sure you have not forgotten? Every time I wrote to you.'

The captain took off his glazed hat, hung it on his hook, and smoothing his hair from behind with his hand, sat gazing at the group around him: a perfect image of wondering resignation.

'You don't appear to understand me, Ned!' observed old Sol.

'Sol Gills,' returned the captain, after staring at

him and the rest for a long time, without speaking,
'I'm gone about and adrift. Pay out a word or two
respecting them adwentures, will you! Can't I bring
up, nohows? Nohows?' said the captain, ruminating
and staring all round.

'You know, Ned,' said Sol Gills, 'why I left here.
Did you open my packet, Ned?'

'Why, aye, aye,' said the captain. 'To be sure, I
opened the packet.'

'And read it?' said the old man.

'And read it,' answered the captain, eyeing him
attentively, and proceeding to quote it from memory.
'"My dear Ned Cuttle, when I left home for the
West Indies in forlorn search of intelligence of my
dear—" There he sits! There's Wal'r!' said the
captain, as if he were relieved by getting hold of
anything that was real and indisputable.

'Well, Ned. Now attend a moment!' said the old
man. 'When I wrote first—that was from Barbados—I said that though you would receive that
letter long before the year was out, I should be glad
if you would open the packet, as it explained the
reason of my going away. Very good, Ned. When
I wrote the second, third, and perhaps the fourth
times—that was from Jamaica—I said I was in just
the same state, couldn't rest, and couldn't come away
from that part of the world, without knowing that
my boy was lost or saved. When I wrote next—
that, I think, was from Demerara, wasn't it?'

'That he thinks was from Demerara, warn't it?'
said the captain, looking hopelessly round.

'—I said,' proceeded old Sol, 'that still there was
no certain information got yet. That I found many
captains and others, in that part of the world, who
had known me for years, and who assisted me with
a passage here and there, and for whom I was able,

now and then, to do a little in return, in my own craft. That every one was sorry for me, and seemed to take a sort of interest in my wanderings; and that I began to think it would be my fate to cruise about in search of tidings of my boy until I died.'

'Began to think as how he was a scientific Flying Dutchman!' said the captain, as before, and with great seriousness.

'But when the news come one day, Ned,—that was to Barbados, after I got back there,—that a China trader home'ard bound had been spoke, that had my boy aboard, then, Ned, I took passage in the next ship and came home! and arrived at home to-night to find it true, thank God!' said the old man, devoutly.

The captain, after bowing his head with great reverence, stared all round the circle, beginning with Mr. Toots, and ending with the instrument-maker: then gravely said—

'Sol Gills! The observation as I 'm a going to make is calc'lated to blow every stitch of sail as you can carry, clean out of the bolt-ropes, and bring you on your beam-ends with a lurch. Not one of them letters was ever delivered to Ed'ard Cuttle. Not one o' them letters,' repeated the captain, to make his declaration the more solemn and impressive, 'was ever delivered unto Ed'ard Cuttle, mariner, of England, as lives at home at ease, and doth improve each shining hour!'

'And posted by my own hand! And directed by my own hand, Number nine Brig Place!' exclaimed old Sol.

The colour all went out of the captain's face, and all came back again in a glow.

'What do you mean, Sol Gills, my friend, by Number nine Brig Place?' inquired the captain.

'Mean? Your lodgings, Ned,' returned the old man. 'Mrs. What's-her-name! I shall forget my own name next, but I am behind the present time—I always was, you recollect—and very much confused. Mrs.—'

'Sol Gills!' said the captain, as if he were putting the most improbable case in the world, 'it ain't the name of MacStinger as you 're a trying to remember?'

'Of course it is!' exclaimed the instrument-maker. 'To be sure, Ned. Mrs. MacStinger!'

Captain Cuttle, whose eyes were now as wide open as they could be, and the knobs upon whose face were perfectly luminous, gave a long shrill whistle of a most melancholy sound, and stood gazing at everybody in a state of speechlessness.

'Overhaul that there again, Sol Gills, will you be so kind?' he said at last.

'All these letters,' returned uncle Sol, beating time with the forefinger of his right hand upon the palm of his left, with a steadiness and distinctness that might have done honour, even to the infallible chronometer in his pocket, 'I posted with my own hand, and directed with my own hand, to Captain Cuttle, at Mrs. MacStinger's, Number nine Brig Place.'

The captain took his glazed hat off his hook, looked into it, put it on, and sat down.

'Why, friends all,' said the captain, staring round in the last state of discomfiture, 'I cut and run from there!'

'And no one knew where you were gone, Captain Cuttle?' cried Walter hastily.

'Bless your heart, Wal'r,' said the captain, shaking his head, 'she 'd never have allowed o' my coming to take charge o' this here property. Nothing could be done but cut and run. Lord love you, Wal'r!' said the captain, 'you 've only seen her in a calm! But see her when her angry passions rise—and make a note on!'

'*I* 'd give it her!' remarked the Nipper, softly.

'Would you, do you think, my dear?' returned the captain with feeble admiration. 'Well, my dear, it does you credit. But there ain't no wild animal I would sooner face myself. I only got my chest away by means of a friend as nobody 's a match for. It was no good sending any letter there. *She* wouldn't take in any letter, bless you,' said the captain, 'under them circumstances! Why, you could hardly make it worth a man's while to be the postman!'

'Then it 's pretty clear, Captain Cuttle, that all of us, and you and uncle Sol especially,' said Walter, 'may thank Mrs. MacStinger for no small anxiety.'

The general obligation in this wise to the determined relict of the late Mr. MacStinger, was so apparent, that the captain did not contest the point; but being in some measure ashamed of his position, though nobody dwelt upon the subject, and Walter especially avoided it, remembering the last conversation he and the captain had held together respecting it, he remained under a cloud for nearly five minutes —an extraordinary period for him—when that sun, his face, broke out once more, shining on all beholders with extraordinary brilliancy; and he fell into a fit of shaking hands with everybody over and over again.

At an early hour, but not before uncle Sol and Walter had questioned each other at some length about their voyages and dangers, they all, except Walter, vacated Florence's room, and went down to the parlour. Here they were soon afterwards joined by Walter, who told them Florence was a little sorrowful and heavy-hearted, and had gone to

bed.   Though they could not have disturbed her with
their voices down there, they all spoke in a whisper
after this: and each, in his different way, felt very
lovingly and gently towards Walter's fair young
bride: and a long explanation there was of everything relating to her, for the satisfaction of uncle
Sol; and very sensible Mr. Toots was of the delicacy
with which Walter made his name and services important, and his presence necessary to their little
council.

'Mr. Toots,' said Walter, on parting with him at
the house door, 'we shall see each other to-morrow
morning?'

'Lieutenant Walters,' returned Mr. Toots, grasping his hand fervently, 'I shall certainly be present.'

'This is the last night we shall meet for a long time
—the last night we may ever meet,' said Walter.
'Such a noble heart as yours, must feel, I think, when
another heart is bound to it.   I hope you know that
I am very grateful to you.'

'Walters,' replied Mr. Toots, quite touched, 'I
should be glad to feel that you had reason to be so.'

'Florence,' said Walter, 'on this last night of her
bearing her own name, has made me promise—it was
only just now, when you left us together—that I
would tell you—with her dear love—'

Mr. Toots laid his hand upon the doorpost, and his
eyes upon his hand.

'—with her dear love,' said Walter, 'that she can
never have a friend whom she will value above you.
That the recollection of your true consideration for
her always, can never be forgotten by her.   That she
remembers you in her prayers to-night, and hopes
that you will think of her when she is far away.
Shall I say anything for you?'

'Say, Walters,' replied Mr. Toots, indistinctly,

'that I shall think of her every day, but never without feeling happy to know that she is married to the man she loves, and who loves her. Say, if you please, that I am sure her husband deserves her—even her! —and that I am glad of her choice.'

Mr. Toots got more distinct as he came to these last words, and raising his eyes from the doorpost, said them stoutly. He then shook Walter's hand again with a fervour that Walter was not slow to return, and started homeward.

Mr. Toots was accompanied by the Chicken, whom he had of late brought with him every evening, and left in the shop, with an idea that unforeseen circumstances might arise from without, in which the prowess of that distinguished character would be of service to the midshipman. The Chicken did not appear to be in a particularly good humour on this occasion. Either the gas-lamps were treacherous, or he cocked his eye in a hideous manner, and likewise distorted his nose, when Mr. Toots, crossing the road, looked back over his shoulder at the room where Florence slept. On the road home, he was more demonstrative of aggressive intentions against the other foot-passengers, than comported with a professor of the peaceful art of self-defence. Arrived at home, instead of leaving Mr. Toots in his apartments when he had escorted him thither, he remained before him weighing his white hat in both hands by the brim, and twitching his head and nose (both of which had been many times broken, and but indifferently repaired), with an air of decided disrespect.

His patron being much engaged with his own thoughts, did not observe this for some time, nor indeed until the Chicken, determined not to be overlooked, had made divers clicking sounds with his tongue and teeth, to attract attention.

'Now, master,' said the Chicken, doggedly, when he, at length, caught Mr. Toots's eye, 'I want to know whether this here gammon is to finish it, or whether you 're a going in to win?'

'Chicken,' returned Mr. Toots, 'explain yourself.'

'Why then, here 's all about it, master,' said the Chicken. 'I ain't a cove to chuck a word away. Here 's wot it is. Are any on 'em to be doubled up?'

When the Chicken put this question he dropped his hat, made a dodge and a feint with his left hand, hit a supposed enemy a violent blow with his right, shook his head smartly, and recovered himself.

'Come, master,' said the Chicken. 'Is it to be gammon or pluck? Which?'

'Chicken,' returned Mr. Toots, 'your expressions are coarse, and your meaning is obscure.'

'Why, then, I tell you what, master,' said the Chicken. 'This is where it is. It 's mean.'

'What is mean, Chicken?' asked Mr. Toots.

'*It* is,' said the Chicken, with a frightful corrugation of his broken nose. 'There! Now, master! Wot! Wen you could go and blow on this here match to the stiff 'un'; by which depreciatory appellation it has since supposed that the Game One intended to signify Mr. Dombey; 'and when you could knock the winner and all the kit of 'em dead out o' wind and time, are you going to give in? To *give in?*' said the Chicken, with contemptuous emphasis. 'Wy, it 's mean!'

'Chicken,' said Mr. Toots, severely, 'you 're a perfect vulture! Your sentiments are atrocious.'

'My sentiments is game and fancy, master,' returned the Chicken. 'That 's wot my sentiments is. I can't abear a meanness. I 'm afore the public, I 'm to be heerd on at the bar of the Little Helephant, and no gov'ner o' mine mustn't go and do what's mean. Wy, it's mean,' said the Chicken, with increased expression. 'That's where it is. It's mean.'

'Chicken!' said Mr. Toots, 'you disgust me.'

'Master,' returned the Chicken, putting on his hat, 'there's a pair on us, then. Come! Here's a offer! You've spoke to me more than once't or twice't about the public line. Never mind! Give me a fi'typunnote to-morrow, and let me go.'

'Chicken,' returned Mr. Toots, 'after the odious sentiments you have expressed, I shall be glad to part on such terms.'

'Done then,' said the Chicken. 'It's a bargain. This here conduct of yourn, won't suit *my* book, master. Wy it's mean,' said the Chicken; who seemed equally unable to get beyond that point, and to stop short of it. 'That's where it is; it's mean!'

So Mr. Toots and the Chicken agreed to part on this incompatibility of moral perception; and Mr. Toots, lying down to sleep, dreamed happily of Florence, who had thought of him as her friend upon the last night of her maiden life, and who had sent him her dear love.

CHAPTER LVII

ANOTHER WEDDING

MR. SOWNDS the beadle, and Mrs. Miff the pew-opener, are early at their posts in the fine church where Mr. Dombey was married. A yellow-faced old gentleman from India, is going to take unto himself a young wife this morning, and six carriages full of company are expected, and Mrs. Miff has been informed that the yellow-faced old gentleman could pave the road to church with diamonds and hardly miss them. The nuptial benediction is to be a superior one, proceeding from a very reverend, a dean, and the lady is to be given away, as an extraordinary present, by somebody who comes express from the Horse Guards.

Mrs. Miff is more intolerant of common people this morning, than she generally is; and she has always strong opinions on that subject, for it is associated with free sittings. Mrs. Miff is not a student of political economy (she thinks the science is connected with dissenters; 'Baptists or Wesleyans, or some o' them,' she says), but she can never understand what business your common folks have to be married. 'Drat 'em,' says Mrs. Miff, 'you read the same things over 'em, and instead of sovereigns get sixpences!'

Mr. Sownds the beadle is more liberal than Mrs. Miff—but then he is not a pew-opener. 'It must be done, ma'am,' he says. 'We must marry 'em. We must have our national schools to walk at the head of, and we must have our standing armies. We must marry 'em, ma'am,' says Mr. Sownds, 'and keep the country going.'

Mr. Sownds is sitting on the steps and Mrs. Miff is dusting in the church, when a young couple, plainly dressed, come in. The mortified bonnet of Mrs. Miff is sharply turned towards them, for she espies in this early visit indications of a runaway match. But they don't want to be married—'Only,' says the gentleman, 'to walk round the church.' And as he slips a genteel compliment into the palm of Mrs. Miff, her vinegary face relaxes, and her mortified bonnet and her spare dry figure dip and crackle.

Mrs. Miff resumes her dusting and plumps up her

cushions—for the yellow-faced old gentleman is reported to have tender knees—but keeps her glazed,
pew-opening eye on the young couple who are walking round the church. 'Ahem,' coughs Mrs. Miff,
whose cough is drier than the hay in any hassock in
her charge, 'you 'll come to us one of these mornings,
my dears, unless I 'm much mistaken!'

They are looking at a tablet on the wall, erected
to the memory of some one dead. They are a long
way off from Mrs. Miff, but Mrs. Miff can see with
half an eye how she is leaning on his arm, and how
his head is bent down over her. 'Well, well,' says
Mrs. Miff, 'you might do worse. For you 're a tidy
pair.'

There is nothing personal in Mrs. Miff's remark.
She merely speaks of stock in trade. She is hardly
more curious in couples than in coffins. She is such
a spare, straight, dry old lady—such a pew of a woman
—that you should find as many individual sympathies
in a chip. Mr. Sownds, now, who is fleshy, and has
scarlet in his coat, is of a different temperament. He
says, as they stand upon the steps watching the young
couple away, that she has a pretty figure, hasn't she,
and as well as he could see (for she held her head
down coming out), an uncommon pretty face. 'Altogether, Mrs. Miff,' says Mr. Sownds with a relish,
'she is what you may call a rosebud.'

Mrs. Miff assents with a spare nod of her mortified
bonnet; but approves of this so little, that she in-
wardly resolves she wouldn't be the wife of Mr.
Sownds for any money he could give her, beadle as he
is.

And what are the young couple saying as they
leave the church, and go out at the gate?

'Dear Walter, thank you! I can go away, now,
happy.'

'And when we come back, Florence, we will come and see his grave again.'

Florence lifts her eyes, so bright with tears, to his kind face; and clasps her disengaged hand on that other modest little hand which clasps his arm.

'It is very early, Walter, and the streets are almost empty yet. Let us walk.'

'But you will be to tired, my love.'

'Oh, no! I was very tired the first time that we ever walked together, but I shall not be so to-day.'

And thus—not much changed—she, as innocent and earnest-hearted—he, as frank, as hopeful and more proud of her—Florence and Walter, on their bridal morning, walk through the streets together.

Not even in that childish walk of long ago, were they so far removed from all the world about them as to-day. The childish feet of long ago, did not tread such enchanted ground as theirs do now. The confidence and love of children may be given many times, and will spring up in many places; but the woman's heart of Florence, with its undivided treasure, can be yielded only once, and under slight or change, can only droop and die.

They take the streets that are the quietest, and do not go near that in which her old home stands. It is a fair, warm summer morning, and the sun shines on them, as they walk towards the darkening mist that overspreads the city. Riches are uncovering in shops; jewels, gold, and silver flash in the goldsmiths' sunny windows; and great houses cast a stately shade upon them as they pass. But through the light, and through the shade, they go on lovingly together, lost to everything around; thinking of no other riches, and no prouder home, than they have now in one another.

Gradually they come into the darker, narrower streets, where the sun, now yellow, and now red, is seen through the mist, only at street corners, and in small open spaces where there is a tree, or one of the innumerable churches, or a paved way and a flight of steps, or a curious little patch of garden, or a burying-ground, where the few tombs and tombstones are almost black. Lovingly and trustfully, through all the narrow yards and alleys and the shady streets, Florence goes, clinging to his arm, to be his wife.

Her heart beats quicker now, for Walter tells her that their church is very near. They pass a few great stacks of warehouses, with waggons at the doors, and busy carmen stopping up the way—but Florence does not see or hear them—and then the air is quiet, and the day is darkened, and she is trembling in a church which has a strange smell like a cellar.

The shabby little old man, ringer of the disappointed bell, is standing in the porch, and has put his hat in the font—for he is quite at home there, being sexton. He ushers them into an old brown, panelled, dusty vestry, like a corner-cupboard with the shelves taken out; where the wormy registers diffuse a smell like faded snuff, which has set the tearful Nipper sneezing.

Youthful, and how beautiful, the young bride looks, in this old dusty place, with no kindred object near her but her husband. There is a dusty old clerk, who keeps a sort of evaporated news-shop underneath an archway opposite, behind a perfect fortification of posts. There is a dusty old pew-opener who only keeps herself, and finds that quite enough to do. There is a dusty old beadle (these are Mr. Toots's beadle and pew-opener of last Sunday), who has something to do with a Worshipful Company who have got a hall in the next yard, with a stained-glass window in it that no mortal ever saw.

There are dusty wooden ledges and cornices poked in and out over the altar, and over the screen and round the gallery, and over the inscription about what the master and wardens of the Worshipful Company did in one thousand six hundred and ninety-four. There are dusty old sounding-boards over the pulpit and reading-desk, looking like lids to be let down on the officiating ministers, in case of their giving offence. There is every possible provision for the accommodation of dust, except in the churchyard, where the facilities in that respect are very limited.

The captain, uncle Sol, and Mr. Toots are come; the clergyman is putting on his surplice in the vestry, while the clerk walks round him, blowing the dust off it; and the bride and bridegroom stand before the altar. There is no bridesmaid, unless Susan Nipper is one; and no better father than Captain Cuttle. A man with a wooden leg, chewing a faint apple and carrying a blue bag in his hand, looks in to see what is going on; but finding it nothing entertaining, stumps off again, and pegs his way among the echoes out of doors.

No gracious ray of light is seen to fall on Florence, kneeling at the altar with her timid head bowed down. The morning luminary is built out, and don't shine there. There is a meagre tree outside, where the sparrows are chirping a little; and there is a blackbird in an eyelet-hole of sun in a dyer's garret, over against the window, who whistles loudly whilst the service is performing; and there is the man with the wooden leg stumping away. The amens of the dusty clerk appear, like Macbeth's, to stick in his throat a little; but Captain Cuttle helps him out, and does it with so much good-will that he interpolates three entirely new responses of that word, never introduced into the service before.

They are married, and have signed their names in one of the old sneezy registers, and the clergyman's surplice is restored to the dust, and the clergyman is gone home. In a dark corner of the dark church, Florence has turned to Susan Nipper, and is weeping in her arms. Mr. Toots's eyes are red. The captain lubricates his nose. Uncle Sol has pulled down his spectacles from his forehead, and walked out to the door.

'God bless you, Susan; dearest Susan! If you ever can bear witness to the love I have for Walter, and the reason that I have to love him, do it for his sake. Good-bye! Good-bye!'

They have thought it better not to go back to the midshipman, but to part so; a coach is waiting for them, near at hand.

Miss Nipper cannot speak; she only sobs and chokes, and hugs her mistress. Mr. Toots advances, urges her to cheer up, and takes charge of her. Florence gives him her hand—gives him, in the fulness of her heart, her lips—kisses uncle Sol, and Captain Cuttle, and is borne away by her young husband.

But Susan cannot bear that Florence should go away with a mournful recollection of her. She had meant to be so different, that she reproaches herself bitterly. Intent on making one last effort to redeem her character, she breaks from Mr. Toots and runs away to find the coach, and show a parting smile. The captain, divining her object, sets off after her; for he feels it his duty also to dismiss them with a cheer, if possible. Uncle Sol and Mr. Toots are left behind together, outside the church, to wait for them.

The coach is gone, but the street is steep, and narrow, and blocked up, and Susan can see it at a standstill in the distance, she is sure. Captain Cuttle follows her as she flies down the hill, and waves his glazed hat as a general signal, which may attract the right coach and which may not.

Susan outstrips the captain, and comes up with it. She looks in at the window, sees Walter, with the gentle face beside him, and claps her hands and screams—

'Miss Floy, my darling! look at me! We are all so happy now, dear! One more good-bye, my precious, one more!'

How Susan does it, she don't know, but she reaches to the window, kisses her, and has her arms about her neck, in a moment.

'We are all so—so happy now, my dear Miss Floy!' says Susan, with a suspicious catching in her breath. 'You, you won't be angry with me now. Now *will* you?'

'Angry, Susan!'

'No, no; I am sure you won't. I say you won't, my pet, my dearest!' exclaims Susan; 'and here 's the captain, too—your friend the captain, you know— to say good-bye once more!'

'Hooroar, my Heart's Delight!' vociferates the captain, with a countenance of strong emotion. 'Hooroar, Wal'r, my lad. Hooroar! Hooroar!'

What with the young husband at one window, and the young wife at the other; the captain hanging on at this door, and Susan Nipper holding fast by that; the coach obliged to go on whether it will or no, and all the other carts and coaches turbulent because it hesitates; there never was so much confusion on four wheels. But Susan Nipper gallantly maintains her point. She keeps a smiling face upon her mistress, smiling through her tears, until the last. Even when she is left behind, the captain continues to appear and disappear at the door crying 'Hooroar, my lad! Hooroar, my Heart's Delight!' with his shirt collar in a violent state of agitation, until it is hopeless to attempt to keep up with the coach any longer. Finally, when the coach is gone, Susan Nipper, being rejoined by the captain, falls into a state of insensibility, and is taken into a baker's shop to recover.

Uncle Sol and Mr. Toots wait patiently in the churchyard, sitting on the coping-stone of the railings, until Captain Cuttle and Susan come back. Neither being at all desirous to speak, or to be spoken to, they are excellent company, and quite satisfied. When they all arrive again at the little midshipman, and sit down to breakfast, nobody can touch a morsel. Captain Cuttle makes a feint of being voracious about toast, but gives it up as a swindle. Mr. Toots says, after breakfast, he will come back in the evening; and goes wandering about the town all day, with a vague sensation upon him as if he hadn't been to bed for a fortnight.

There is a strange charm in the house, and in the room, in which they have been used to be together, and out of which so much is gone. It aggravates, and yet it soothes, the sorrow of the separation. Mr. Toots tells Susan Nipper when he comes at night, that he hasn't been so wretched all day long, and yet he likes it. He confides in Susan Nipper, being alone with her, and tells her what his feelings were when she gave him that candid opinion as to the probability of Miss Dombey's ever loving him. In the vein of confidence engendered by these common recollections, and their tears, Mr. Toots proposes that they shall go out together, and buy something for supper. Miss Nipper assenting, they buy a good many little things; and, with the aid of Mrs. Richards, set the supper out quite showily before the captain and old Sol came home.

The captain and old Sol have been on board the

ship, and have established Di there, and have seen
the chests put aboard. They have much to tell about
the popularity of Walter, and the comforts he will
have about him, and the quiet way in which it seems
he has been working early and late, to make his cabin
what the captain calls 'a picter,' to surprise his little
wife. 'A admiral's cabin, mind you,' says the captain, 'ain't more trim.'

But one of the captain's chief delights is, that he
knows the big watch, and the sugar-tongs, and tea-
spoons, are on board; and again and again he murmurs to himself, 'Ed'ard Cuttle, my lad, you never
shaped a better course in your life than when you
made that there little property over jintly. *You* see
how the land bore, Ed'ard,' says the captain, 'and it
does you credit, my lad.'

The old instrument-maker is more distraught and
misty than he used to be, and takes the marriage and
the parting very much to heart. But he is greatly
comforted by having his old ally, Ned Cuttle, at
his side; and he sits down to supper with a grateful
and contented face.

'My boy has been preserved and thrives,' says old
Sol Gills, rubbing his hands. 'What right have I
to be otherwise than thankful and happy!'

The captain, who has not yet taken his seat at the
table, but who has been fidgeting about for some time,
and now stands hesitating in his place, looks doubtfully at Mr. Gills, and says—

'Sol! There's the last bottle of the old Madeira
down below. Would you wish to have it up to-night,
my boy, and drink to Wal'r and his wife?'

The instrument-maker, looking wistfully at the
captain, puts his hand into the breast-pocket of his
coffee-coloured coat, brings forth his pocket-book,
and takes a letter out.

'To Mr. Dombey,' says the old man. 'From Walter. To be sent in three weeks' time. I'll read it.'

' "Sir. I am married to your daughter. She is gone with me upon a distant voyage. To be devoted to her is to have no claim on her or you, but God knows that I am.

' "Why, loving her beyond all earthly things, I have yet, without remorse, united her to the uncertainties and dangers of my life, I will not say to you. You know why, and you are her father.

' "Do not reproach her. She has never reproached you.

' "I do not think or hope that you will ever forgive me. There is nothing I expect less. But if an hour should come when it will comfort you to believe that Florence has some one ever near her, the great charge of whose life is to cancel her remembrance of past sorrow, I solemnly assure you, you may, in that hour, rest in that belief." '

Solomon puts back the letter carefully in his pocket-book, and puts back his pocket-book in his coat.

'We won't drink the last bottle of the old Madeira yet, Ned,' says the old man thoughtfully. 'Not yet.'

'Not yet,' assents the captain. 'No. Not yet.'

Susan and Mr. Toots are of the same opinion. After a silence they all sit down to supper, and drink to the young husband and wife in something else; and the last bottle of old Madeira still remains among its dust and cobwebs undisturbed.

A few days have elapsed, and a stately ship is out at sea, spreading its white wings to the favouring wind.

Upon the deck, image to the roughest man on board of something that is graceful, beautiful, and harmless —something that it is good and pleasant to have there, and that should make the voyage prosperous—is Florence. It is night, and she and Walter sit alone, watching the solemn path of light upon the sea between them and the moon.

At length she cannot see it plainly, for the tears that fill her eyes; and then she lays her head down on his breast, and puts her arms around his neck, saying, 'Oh Walter, dearest love, I am so happy!'

Her husband holds her to his heart, and they are very quiet, and the stately ship goes on serenely.

'As I hear the sea,' says Florence, 'and sit watching it, it brings so many days into my mind. It makes me think so much—'

'Of Paul, my love. I know it does.'

Of Paul and Walter. And the voices in the waves are always whispering to Florence, in their ceaseless murmuring, of love—of love, eternal and illimitable, not bounded by the confines of this world, or by the end of time, but ranging still, beyond the sea, beyond the sky, to the invisible country far away!

CHAPTER LVIII

AFTER A LAPSE

THE sea had ebbed and flowed, through a whole year. Through a whole year, the winds and clouds had come and gone; the ceaseless work of Time had been performed, in storm and sunshine. Through a whole year, the tides of human chance and change had set in their allotted courses. Through a whole year, the famous house of Dombey and Son had fought a fight for life, against cross accidents, doubtful rumours, unsuccessful ventures, unpropitious times, and most of all, against the infatuation of its head, who would not contract its enterprises by a hair's breadth, and would not listen to a word of warning that the ship he strained so hard against the storm, was weak, and could not bear it.

The year was out, and the great House was down.

One summer afternoon; a year, wanting some odd days, after the marriage in the city church; there was a buzz and whisper upon 'Change of a great failure. A certain cold proud man, well known there, was not there, nor was he represented there. Next day it was noised abroad that Dombey and Son had stopped, and next night there was a list of bankrupts published, headed by that name.

The world was very busy now, in sooth, and had a deal to say. It was an innocently credulous and a much ill-used world. It was a world in which there was no other sort of bankruptcy whatever. There were no conspicuous people in it, trading far and wide on rotten banks of religion, patriotism, virtue, honour. There was no amount worth mentioning of mere paper in circulation, on which anybody lived pretty handsomely, promising to pay great sums of goodness with no effects. There were no shortcomings anywhere, in anything but money. The world was very angry indeed; and the people especially, who, in a worse world, might have been supposed to be bankrupt traders themselves in shows and pretences, were observed to be mightily indignant.

Here was a new inducement to dissipation, presented to that sport of circumstances, Mr. Perch the messenger! It was apparently the fate of Mr. Perch to be always waking up, and finding himself famous. He had but yesterday, as one might say, subsided into private life from the celebrity of the elopement and the events that followed it; and now he was made a more important man than ever, by the bankruptcy.

Gliding from his bracket in the outer office where he now sat, watching the strange faces of accountants and others, who quickly superceded nearly all the old clerks, Mr. Perch had but to show himself in the court outside, or, at farthest, in the bar of the King's Arms, to be asked a multitude of questions, almost certain to include that interesting question, what would he take to drink? Then would Mr. Perch descant upon the hours of acute uneasiness he and Mrs. Perch had suffered out at Balls Pond, when they first suspected 'things was going wrong.' Then would Mr. Perch relate to gaping listeners, in a low voice, as if the corpse of the deceased House were lying unburied in the next room, how Mrs. Perch had first come to surmise that things *was* going wrong by hearing him (Perch) moaning in his sleep, 'twelve and ninepence in the pound, twelve and ninepence in the pound!' Which act of somnambulism he supposed to have originated in the impression made upon him by the change in Mr. Dombey's face. Then would he inform them how he had once said, 'Might I make so bold as ask, sir, are you unhappy in your mind?' and how Mr. Dombey had replied, 'My faithful Perch—but no, it cannot be!' and with that had struck his hand upon his forehead, and said, 'Leave me, Perch!' Then, in short, would Mr. Perch, a victim to his position, tell all manner of lies; affecting himself to tears by those that were of a moving nature, and really believing that the inventions of yesterday had, on repetition, a sort of truth about them to-day.

Mr. Perch always closed these conferences by meekly remarking, That, of course, whatever his suspicions might have been (as if he had ever had any!) it wasn't for *him* to betray his trust, was it? Which sentiment (there never being any creditors present) was re-

ceived as doing great honour to his feelings. Thus,
he generally brought away a soothed conscience and
left an agreeable impression behind him, when he returned to his bracket: again to sit watching the strange
faces of the accountants and others, making so free
with the great mysteries, the books; or now and then
to go on tip-toe into Mr. Dombey's empty room, and
stir the fire; or to take an airing at the door, and have
a little more doleful chat with any straggler whom
he knew; or to propitiate, with various small attentions, the head accountant: from whom Mr. Perch had
expectations of a messengership in a fire office, when
the affairs of the House should be wound up.

To Major Bagstock, the bankruptcy was quite
a calamity. The major was not a sympathetic character—his attention being wholly concentrated on J.
B.—nor was he a man subject to lively emotions,
except in the physical regards of gasping and choking. But he had so paraded his friend Dombey at the
club; had so flourished him at the heads of the members in general, and so put them down by continual
assertion of his riches; that the club, being but human,
was delighted to retort upon the major, by asking
him, with a show of great concern, whether this tremendous smash had been at all expected, and how his
friend Dombey bore it. To such questions, the
major, waxing very purple, would reply that it was
a bad world, sir, altogether; that Joey knew a thing
or two, but had been done, sir, done like an infant;
that if you had foretold this, sir, to J. Bagstock,
when he went abroad with Dombey and was chasing
that vagabond up and down France, J. Bagstock
would have pooh-pooh'd you—would have pooh-
pooh'd you, sir, by the Lord! That Joe had been deceived, sir, taken in, hoodwinked, blindfolded, but
was broad awake again and staring; insomuch, sir,

that if Joe's father were to rise up from the grave
to-morrow, he wouldn't trust the old blade with a
penny piece, but would tell him that his son Josh
was too old a soldier to be done again, sir. That he
was a suspicious, crabbed, cranky, used-up, J. B.
infidel, sir; and that if it were consistent with the dignity of a rough and tough old major, of the old school,
who had had the honour of being personally known
to, and commended by, their late Royal Highnesses the
Dukes of Kent and York, to retire to a tub and live
in it, by Gad! sir, he'd have a tub in Pall Mall to-
morrow, to show his contempt for mankind!

Of all this, and many variations of the same tune,
the major would deliver himself with so many apoplectic symptoms, such rollings of his head, and such
violent growls of ill usage and resentment, that the
younger members of the club surmised he had in-
vested money in his friend Dombey's house, and lost
it; though the older soldiers and deeper dogs, who
knew Joe better, wouldn't hear of such a thing. The
unfortunate native, expressing no opinion, suffered
dreadfully; not merely in his moral feelings, which
were regularly fusilladed by the major every hour
in the day, and riddled through and through, but in
his sensitiveness to bodily knocks and bumps, which
was kept continually on the stretch. For six entire
weeks after the bankruptcy, this miserable foreigner
lived in a rainy season of boot-jacks and brushes.

Mrs. Chick had three ideas upon the subject of the
terrible reverse. The first was that she could not
understand it. The second, that her brother had not
made an effort. The third, that if she had been invited to dinner on the day of that first party, it never
would have happened; and that she had said so, at
the time.

Nobody's opinion stayed the misfortune, lightened

it, or made it heavier. It was understood that the affairs of the House were to be wound up as they best could be; that Mr. Dombey freely resigned everything he had, and asked for no favour from any one. That any resumption of the business was out of the question, as he would listen to no friendly negotiation having that compromise in view; that he had relinquished every post of trust or distinction he had held, as a man respected among merchants; that he was dying, according to some; that he was going melancholy mad, according to others; that he was a broken man, according to all.

The clerks dispersed after holding a little dinner of condolence among themselves, which was enlivened by comic singing, and went off admirably. Some took places abroad, and some engaged in other Houses at home; some looked up relations in the country, for whom they suddenly remembered they had a particular affection; and some advertised for employment in the newspapers. Mr. Perch alone remained of all the late establishment, sitting on his bracket looking at the accountants, or starting off it, to propitiate the head accountant, who was to get him into the fire office. The counting-house soon got to be dirty and neglected. The principal slipper and dogs'-collar seller, at the corner of the court, would have doubted the propriety of throwing up his forefinger to the brim of his hat, any more, if Mr. Dombey had appeared there now; and the ticket porter, with his hands under his white apron, moralised good sound morality about ambition, which (he observed) was not, in his opinion, made to rhyme to perdition, for nothing.

Mr. Morfin, the hazel-eyed bachelor, with the hair and whiskers sprinkled with grey, was perhaps the only person within the atmosphere of the House— its head, of course, excepted—who was heartily and deeply affected by the disaster that had befallen it. He had treated Mr. Dombey with due respect and deference through many years, but he had never disguised his natural character, or meanly truckled to him, or pampered his master-passion for the advancement of his own purposes. He had, therefore, no self-disrespect to avenge; no long-tightened springs to release with a quick recoil. He worked early and late to unravel whatever was complicated or difficult in the records of the transactions of the House; was always in attendance to explain whatever required explanation; sat in his old room sometimes very late at night, studying points by his mastery of which he could spare Mr. Dombey the pain of being personally referred to; and then would go home to Islington, and calm his mind by producing the most dismal and forlorn sounds out of his violoncello before going to bed.

He was solacing himself with this melodious grumbler one evening, and, having been much dispirited by the proceedings of the day, was scraping consolation out of its deepest notes, when his landlady (who was fortunately deaf, and had no other consciousness of these performances than a sensation of something rumbling in her bones) announced a lady.

'In mourning,' she said.

The violoncello stopped immediately; and the performer, laying it on the sofa with great tenderness and care, made a sign that the lady was to come in. He followed directly, and met Harriet Carker on the stair.

'Alone!' he said, 'and John here this morning! Is there anything the matter, my dear? But no,' he added, 'your face tells quite another story.'

'I am afraid it is a selfish revelation that you see there, then,' she answered.

'It is a very pleasant one,' said he; 'and, if selfish, a novelty too, worth seeing in you. But I don't believe that.'

He had placed a chair for her by this time, and sat down opposite; the violoncello lying snugly on the sofa between them.

'You will not be surprised at my coming alone, or at John's not having told you I was coming,' said Harriet; 'and you *will* believe that, when I tell you why I have come. May I do so now?'

'You can do nothing better.'

'You were not busy?'

He pointed to the violoncello lying on the sofa, and said, 'I have been, all day. Here's my witness. I have been confiding all my cares to it. I wish I had none but my own to tell.'

'Is the House at an end?' said Harriet, earnestly.

'Completely at an end.'

'Will it never be resumed?'

'Never.'

The bright expression of her face was not overshadowed as her lips silently repeated the word. He seemed to observe this with some little involuntary surprise: and said again—

'Never. You remember what I told you. It has been, all along, impossible to convince him; impossible to reason with him; sometimes, impossible even to approach him. The worst has happened; and the House has fallen, never to be built up any more.'

'And Mr. Dombey, is he personally ruined?'

'Ruined.'

'Will he have no private fortune left? Nothing?'

A certain eagerness in her voice, and something that was almost joyful in her look, seemed to surprise him more and more; to disappoint him too, and jar discordantly against his own emotions. He drummed with the fingers of one hand on the table, looking wistfully at her, and shaking his head, said, after a pause—

'The extent of Mr. Dombey's resources is not accurately within my knowledge; but though they are doubtless very large, his obligations are enormous. He is a gentleman of high honour and integrity. Any man in his position could, and many a man in his position would, have saved himself, by making terms which would have very slightly, almost insensibly, increased the losses of those who had had dealings with him, and left him a remnant to live upon. But he is resolved on payment to the last farthing of his means. His own words are, that they will clear, or nearly clear, the House, and that no one can lose much. Ah Miss Harriet, it would do us no harm to remember oftener than we do, that vices are sometimes only virtues carried to excess! His pride shows well in this.'

She heard him with little or no change in her expression, and with a divided attention that showed her to be busy with something in her own mind. When he was silent, she asked him hurriedly—

'Have you seen him lately?'

'No one sees him. When this crisis of his affairs renders it necessary for him to come out of his house, he comes out for the occasion, and again goes home, and shuts himself up, and will see no one. He has written me a letter, acknowledging our past connection in higher terms than it deserved, and parting from me. I am delicate of obtruding myself upon him now, never having had much intercourse with him in better times; but I have tried to do so. I have written, gone there, entreated. Quite in vain.'

He watched her, as in the hope that she would testify some greater concern than she had yet shown;

and spoke gravely and feelingly, as if to impress her the more; but there was no change in her.

'Well, well, Miss Harriet,' he said, with a disappointed air, 'this is not to the purpose. You have not come here to hear this. Some other and pleasanter theme is in your mind. Let it be in mine, too, and we shall talk upon more equal terms. Come!'

'No, it is the same theme,' returned Harriet, with frank and quick surprise. 'Is it not likely that it should be? Is it not natural that John and I should have been thinking and speaking very much of late of these great changes? Mr. Dombey, whom he served so many years—you know upon what terms —reduced, as you describe; and we quite rich!'

Good, true face, as that face of hers was, and pleasant as it had been to him, Mr. Morfin, the hazel-eyed bachelor, since the first time he had ever looked upon it, it pleased him less at that moment, lighted with a ray of exultation, than it had ever pleased him before.

'I need not remind you,' said Harriet, casting down her eyes upon her black dress, 'through what means our circumstances changed. You have not forgotten that out brother James, upon that dreadful day, left no will, no relations but ourselves.'

The face was pleasanter to him now, though it was pale and melancholy, than it had been a moment since. He seemed to breathe more cheerily.

'You know,' she said, 'our history, the history of both my brothers, in connection with the unfortunate, unhappy gentleman, of whom you have spoken so truly. You know how few our wants are—John's and mine—and what little use we have for money, after the life we have led together for so many years; and now that he is earning an income that is ample for us, through your kindness. You are not unprepared to hear what favour I have come to ask of you?'

'I hardly know. I was, a minute ago. Now, I think, I am not.'

'Of my dead brother I say nothing. If the dead know what we do—but you understand me. Of my living brother I could say much: but what need I say more, than that this act of duty, in which I have come to ask your indispensable assistance, is his own, and that he cannot rest until it is performed!'

She raised her eyes again; and the light of exultation in her face began to appear beautiful, in the observant eyes that watched her.

'Dear sir,' she went on to say, 'it must be done very quietly and secretly. Your experience and knowledge will point out a way of doing it. Mr. Dombey may, perhaps, be led to believe that it is something saved, unexpectedly, from the wreck of his fortunes; or that it is a voluntary tribute to his honourable and upright character, from some of those with whom he has had great dealings; or that it is some old lost debt repaid. There must be many ways of doing it. I know you will choose the best. The favour I have come to ask is, that you will do it for us in your own kind, generous, considerate manner. That you will never speak of it to John, whose chief happiness in this act of restitution is to do it secretly, unknown, and unapproved of: that only a very small part of the inheritance may be reserved to us, until Mr. Dombey shall have possessed the interest of the rest for the remainder of his life; that you will keep our secret, faithfully—but that I am sure you will; and that, from this time, it may seldom be whispered, even between you and me, but may live in my thoughts only as a new reason for thankfulness to Heaven, and joy and pride in my brother.'

Such a look of exultation there may be on angels'
faces, when the one repentant sinner enters heaven,
among ninety-nine just men.   It was not dimmed
or tarnished by the joyful tears that filled her eyes,
but was the brighter for them.

'My dear Harriet,' said Mr. Morfin, after a silence,
'I was not prepared for this. Do I understand you
that you wish to make your own part in the inheritance available for your good purpose, as well as
John's?'

'Oh yes,' she returned. 'When we have shared
everything together for so long a time, and have had
no care, hope, or purpose apart, could I bear to be
excluded from my share in this?   May I not urge
a claim to be my brother's partner and companion to
the last?'

'Heaven forbid that I should dispute it!' he replied.

'We may rely on your friendly help?' she said.   'I
knew we might!'

'I should be a worse man than,—than I hope I
am, or would willingly believe myself, if I could not
give you that assurance from my heart and soul.
You may, implicitly.   Upon my honour, I will keep
your secret.   And if it should be found that Mr.
Dombey is so reduced as I fear he will be, acting on
a determination that there seem to be no means of in-
fluencing, I will assist you to accomplish the design, on
which you and John are jointly resolved.'

She gave him her hand, and thanked him with a
cordial, happy face.

'Harriet,' he said, detaining it in his.   'To speak
to you of the worth of any sacrifice that you can
make now—above all, of any sacrifice of mere money
—would be idle and presumptuous.   To put before
you any appeal to reconsider your purpose or to set

narrow limits to it would be, I feel, not less so. I have no right to mar the great end of a great history, by any obtrusion of my own weak self. I have every right to bend my head before what you confide to me, satisfied that it comes from a higher and better source of inspiration than my poor worldly knowledge. I will say only this: I am your faithful steward; and I would rather be so, and your chosen friend, than I would be anybody in the world, except yourself.'

She thanked him again, cordially, and wished him good night.

'Are you going home?' he said. 'Let me go with you.'

'Not to-night. I am not going home now; I have a visit to make alone. Will you come to-morrow?'

'Well, well,' said he. 'I 'll come to-morrow. In the meantime, I 'll think of this, and how we can best proceed. And perhaps *you 'll* think of it, dear Harriet, and—and—think of me a little in connection with it.'

He handed her down to a coach she had in waiting at the door; and if his landlady had not been deaf, she would have heard him muttering as he went back upstairs, when the coach had driven off, that we were creatures of habit, and it was a sorrowful habit to be an old bachelor.

The violoncello lying on the sofa between the two chairs, he took it up, without putting away the vacant chair, and sat droning on it, and slowly shaking his head at the vacant chair, for a long, long time. The expression he communicated to the instrument at first, though monstrously pathetic and bland, was nothing to the expression he communicated to his own face, and bestowed upon the empty chair: which was so sincere, that he was obliged to have recourse to Captain Cuttle's remedy more than once, and to rub his face with his sleeve. By degrees, however, the violoncello, in unison with his own frame of mind, glided melodiously into the Harmonious Blacksmith, which he played over and over again, until his ruddy and serene face gleamed like true metal on the anvil of a veritable blacksmith. In fine, the violoncello and the empty chair were the companions of his bachelor-hood until nearly midnight; and when he took his supper, the violoncello set up on end in the sofa cor-ner, big with the latent harmony of a whole foundry full of harmonious blacksmiths, seemed to ogle the empty chair out of its crooked eyes, with unutterable intelligence.

When Harriet left the house, the driver of her hired coach, taking a course that was evidently no new one to him, went in and out by bye-ways through that part of the suburbs, until he arrived at some open ground, where there were a few quiet little old houses standing among gardens. At the garden-gate of one of these he stopped, and Harriet alighted.

Her gentle ringing at the bell was responded to by a dolorous-looking woman, of light complexion, with raised eyebrows, and head dropping on one side, who curtseyed at sight of her, and conducted her across the garden to the house.

'How is your patient, nurse, to-night?' said Har-riet.

'In a poor way, miss, I am afraid. Oh how she do remind me, sometimes, of my uncle's Betsy Jane!' returned the woman of the light complexion, in a sort of doleful rapture.

'In what respect?' asked Harriet.

'Miss, in all respects,' replied the other, 'except that she's grown up, and Betsy Jane, when at death's door, was but a child.'

'But you have told me she recovered,' observed Harriet mildly; 'so there is the more reason for hope, Mrs. Wickham.'

'Ah, miss, hope is an excellent thing for such as has the spirits to bear it!' said Mrs. Wickham, shaking her head. 'My own spirits is not equal to it, but I don't owe it any grudge. I envys them that is so blest!'

'You should try to be more cheerful,' remarked Harriet.

'Thank you, miss, I'm sure,' said Mrs. Wickham grimly. 'If I was so inclined, the loneliness of this situation—you'll excuse my speaking so free—would put it out of my power in four and twenty hours; but I an't at all. I'd rather not. The little spirits that I ever had, I was bereaved of at Brighton some few years ago, and I think I feel myself the better for it.'

In truth, this was the very Mrs. Wickham who had superseded Mrs. Richards as the nurse of little Paul, and who considered herself to have gained the loss in question, under the roof of the amiable Pipchin. The excellent and thoughtful old system, hallowed by long prescription, which has usually picked out from the rest of mankind the most dreary and uncomfortable people that could possibly be laid hold of, to act as instructors of youth, finger-posts to the virtues, matrons, monitors, attendants on sick beds, and the like, had established Mrs. Wickham in very good business as a nurse, and had led to her serious qualities being particularly commended by an admiring and numerous connection.

Mrs. Wickham, with her eyebrows elevated, and her head on one side, lighted the way upstairs to a clean, neat chamber, opening on another chamber, dimly lighted, where there was a bed. In the first room, an old woman sat mechanically staring out at the open window, on the darkness. In the second, stretched upon the bed, lay the shadow of a figure that had spurned the wind and rain, one wintry night; hardly to be recognised now, but by the long black hair that showed so very black against the colourless face, and all the white things about it.

Oh, the strong eyes, and the weak frame! The eyes that turned so eagerly and brightly to the door when Harriet came in; the feeble head that could not raise itself, and moved so slowly round upon its pillow!

'Alice!' said the visitor's mild voice, 'am I late to-night?'

'You always seem late, but are always early.'

Harriet had sat down by the bedside now, and put her hand upon the thin hand lying there.

'You are better?'

Mrs. Wickham, standing at the foot of the bed, like a disconsolate spectre, most decidedly and forcibly shook her head to negative this position.

'It matters very little!' said Alice, with a faint smile. 'Better or worse to-day, is but a day's difference—perhaps not so much.'

Mrs. Wickham, as a serious character, expressed her approval with a groan; and having made some cold dabs at the bottom of the bedclothes, as feeling for the patient's feet and expecting to find them stony, went clinking among the medicine-bottles on the table, as who should say, 'while we *are* here, let us repeat the mixture as before.'

'No,' said Alice, whispering to her visitor, 'evil courses, and remorse, travel, want, and weather, storm within, and storm without, have worn my life away. It will not last much longer.'

She drew the hand up as she spoke, and laid her face against it.

'I lie here, sometimes, thinking I should like to live until I had had a little time to show you how grateful I could be! It is a weakness, and soon passes. Better for you as it is. Better for me!'

How different her hold upon the hand, from what it had been when she took it by the fireside on the bleak winter evening! Scorn, rage, defiance, recklessness, look here! This is the end.

Mrs. Wickham having clinked sufficiently among the bottles, now produced the mixture. Mrs. Wickham looked hard at her patient in the act of drinking, screwed her mouth up tight, her eyebrows also, and shook her head, expressing that tortures shouldn't make her say it was a hopeless case. Mrs. Wickham then sprinkled a little cooling-stuff about the room, with the air of a female grave-digger, who was strewing ashes on ashes, dust on dust—for she was a serious character—and withdrew to partake of certain funeral baked meats downstairs.

'How long is it,' asked Alice, 'since I went to you and told you what I had done, and when you were advised it was too late for any one to follow?'

'It is a year and more,' said Harriet.

'A year and more,' said Alice, thoughtfully intent upon her face. 'Months upon months since you brought me here!'

Harriet answered 'Yes.'

'Brought me here, by force of gentleness and kindness. Me!' said Alice, shrinking with her face behind her hand, 'and made me human by woman's looks and words, and angel's deeds!'

Harriet bending over her, composed and soothed her. By and by, Alice lying as before, with the hand against her face, asked to have her mother called.

Harriet called to her more than once, but the old woman was so absorbed looking out at the open window on the darkness, that she did not hear. It was not until Harriet went to her and touched her, that she rose up, and came.

'Mother,' said Alice, taking the hand again, and fixing her lustrous eyes lovingly upon her visitor, while she merely addressed a motion of her finger to the old woman, 'tell her what you know.'

'To-night, my deary?'

'Aye, mother,' answered Alice, faintly and solemnly, 'to-night!'

The old woman, whose wits appeared disordered by alarm, remorse, or grief, came creeping along the side of the bed, opposite to that on which Harriet sat; and kneeling down, so as to bring her withered face upon a level with the coverlet, and stretching out her hand, so as to touch her daughter's arm, began—

'My handsome gal—'

Heaven what a cry was that, with which she stopped there, gazing at the poor form lying on the bed!

'Changed, long ago, mother! Withered, long ago,' said Alice, without looking at her. 'Don't grieve for that now.'

—'My daughter,' faltered the old woman, 'my gal who 'll soon get better, and shame 'em all with her good looks.'

Alice smiled mournfully at Harriet, and fondled her hand a little closer, but said nothing.

'Who 'll soon get better, I say,' repeated the old woman, menacing the vacant air with her shrivelled fist, 'and who 'll shame 'em all with her good looks —she will. I say she will! she shall!'—as if she were in passionate contention with some unseen opponent at the bed-side, who contradicted her—'my daughter has been turned away from, and cast out, but she could boast relationship to proud folks too, if she chose! Ah! To proud folks! There 's relation-

ship without your clergy and your wedding rings—
they may make it, but they can't break it—and my
daughter's well related. Show me Mrs. Dombey,
and I'll show you my Alice's first cousin.'

Harriet glanced from the old woman to the lustrous
eyes intent upon her face, and derived corroboration
from them.

'What!' cried the old woman, her nodding head
bridling with a ghastly vanity. 'Though I am old
and ugly now,—much older by life and habit than
years though,—I was once as young as any. Ah! as
pretty too, as many! I was a fresh country wench
in my time, darling,' stretching out her arm to Harriet, across the bed, 'and looked it, too. Down in
my country, Mrs. Dombey's father and his brother
were the gayest gentlemen and the best-liked that
came a visiting from London—they have long been
dead, though! Lord, Lord, this long while! The
brother, who was my Ally's father, longest of the
two.'

She raised her head a little, and peered at her
daughter's face; as if from the remembrance of her
own youth, she had flown to the remembrance of her
child's. Then, suddenly, she laid her face down on
the bed, and shut her head up in her hands and arms.

'They were as like,' said the old woman, without
looking up, 'as you could see two brothers, so near
an age—there wasn't much more than a year between
them, as I recollect—and if you could have seen my
gal, as I have seen her once, side by side with the
other's daughter, you'd have seen, for all the difference of dress and life, that they were like each other.
Oh! is the likeness gone, and is it my gal—only my
gal—that's to change so?'

'We shall all change, mother, in our turn,' said
Alice.

'Turn!' cried the old woman, 'but why not hers as soon as my gal's? The mother must have changed— she looked as old as me, and full as wrinkled through her paint—but *she* was handsome. What have *I* done, I, what have *I* done worse than her, that only my gal is to lie there fading?'

With another of those wild cries, she went running out into the room from which she had come; but immediately, in her uncertain mood, returned, and creeping up to Harriet, said—

'That's what Alice bade me tell you, deary. That's all. I found it out when I began to ask who she was, and all about her, away in Warwickshire there, one summer time. Such relations was no good to me, then. They wouldn't have owned me, and had nothing to give me. I should have asked 'em maybe, for a little money, afterwards, if it hadn't been for my Alice; she'd a'most have killed me, if I had, I think. She was as proud as t' other in her way,' said the old woman, touching the face of her daughter fearfully, and withdrawing her hand, 'for all she's so quiet now; but she'll shame 'em with her good looks yet. Ha, ha! *She'll* shame 'em, will my handsome daughter!'

Her laugh, as she retreated, was worse than her cry; worse than the burst of imbecile lamentation in which it ended; worse than the doting air with which she sat down in her old seat, and stared out at the darkness.

The eyes of Alice had all this time been fixed on Harriet, whose hand she had never released. She said now—

'I have felt, lying here, that I should like you to know this. It might explain, I have thought, something that used to help to harden me. I had heard so much, in my wrong-doing, of my neglected duty, that I took up with the belief that duty had not been done to me, and that as the seed was sown, the harvest grew. I somehow made it out that when ladies had bad homes and mothers, they went wrong in their way, too; but that their way was not so foul a one as mine, and they had need to bless God for it. That is all past. It is like a dream, now, which I cannot quite remember or understand. It has been more and more like a dream, every day, since you began to sit here, and to read to me. I only tell it you, as I can recollect it. Will you read to me a little more?'

Harriet was withdrawing her hand to open the book, when Alice detained it for a moment.

'You will not forget my mother? I forgive her, if I have any cause. I know that she forgives me, and is sorry in her heart. You will not forget her?'

'Never, Alice!'

'A moment yet. Lay my head so, dear, that as you read I may see the words in your kind face.'

Harriet complied and read—read the eternal book for all the weary and the heavy-laden; for all the wretched, fallen, and neglected of this earth—read the blessed history, in which the blind lame palsied beggar, the criminal, the woman stained with shame, the shunned of all our dainty clay, has each a portion, that no human pride, indifference, or sophistry, through all the ages that this world shall last, can take away, or by the thousandth atom of a grain reduce—read the ministry of Him who, through the round of human life, and all its hopes and griefs, from birth to death, from infancy to age, had sweet compassion for, and interest in, its every scene and stage, its every suffering and sorrow.

'I shall come,' said Harriet, when she shut the book, 'very early in the morning.'

The lustrous eyes, yet fixed upon her face, closed

for a moment, then opened; and Alice kissed and blest her.

The same eyes followed her to the door; and in their light, and on the tranquil face, there was a smile when it was closed.

They never turned away. She laid her hand upon her breast, murmuring the sacred name that had been read to her; and life passed from her face, like light removed.

Nothing lay there, any longer, but the ruin of the mortal house on which the rain had beaten, and the black hair that had fluttered in the wintry wind.

CHAPTER LIX

RETRIBUTION

CHANGES have come again upon the great house in the long dull street, once the scene of Florence's childhood and loneliness. It is a great house still, proof against wind and weather, without breaches in the roof, or shattered windows, or dilapidated walls; but it is a ruin none the less, and the rats fly from it.

Mr. Towlinson and company are, at first, incredulous in respect of the shapeless rumours that they hear. Cook says our people's credit ain't so easy shook as that comes to, thank God; and Mr. Towlinson expects to hear it reported that the Bank of England's a going to break, or the jewels in the Tower to be sold up. But, next come the Gazette, and Mr. Perch: and Mr. Perch brings Mrs. Perch to talk it over in the kitchen, and to spend a pleasant evening.

As soon as there is no doubt about it, Mr. Towlinson's main anxiety is that the failure should be a good round one—not less than a hundred thousand pound.

Mr. Perch don't think himself that a hundred thousand pound will nearly cover it. The women, led by Mrs. Perch and cook, often repeat 'a hun-dred thousand pound!' with awful satisfaction—as if handling the words were like handling the money; and the housemaid, who has her eye on Mr. Towlinson, wishes she had only a hundredth part of the sum to bestow on the man of her choice. Mr. Towlinson, still mindful of his old wrong, opines that a foreigner would hardly know what to do with so much money, unless he spent it on his whiskers, which bitter sarcasm causes the housemaid to withdraw in tears.

But not to remain long absent; for cook, who has the reputation of being extremely good-hearted, says, whatever they do, let 'em stand by one another now, Towlinson, for there 's no telling how soon they may be divided. They have been in that house (says cook) through a funeral, a wedding, and a running-away; and let it not be said that they couldn't agree among themselves at such a time as the present. Mrs. Perch is immensely affected by this moving address, and openly remarks that cook is an angel. Mr. Towlinson replies to cook, far be it from him to stand in the way of that good feeling which he could wish to see; and adjourning in quest of the housemaid, and presently returning with that young lady on his arm, informs the kitchen that foreigners is only his fun, and that him and Anne have now resolved to take one another for better for worse, and to settle in Oxford Market in the general greengrocery and herb and leech line, where your kind favours is particular requested. This announcement is received with acclamation; and Mrs. Perch projecting her soul into futurity, says, 'girls,' in cook's ear, in a solemn whisper.

Misfortune in the family without feasting, in these

lower regions, couldn't be. Therefore cook tosses up a hot dish or two for supper, and Mr. Towlinson compounds a lobster salad to be devoted to the same hospitable purpose. Even Mrs. Pipchin, agitated by the occasion, rings her bell, and sends down word that she requests to have that little bit of sweet-bread that was left, warmed up for her supper, and sent to her on a tray with about a quarter of a tumblerful of mulled sherry; for she feels poorly.

There is a little talk about Mr. Dombey, but very little. It is chiefly speculation as to how long he has known that this was going to happen. Cook says shrewdly, 'Oh a long time, bless you! Take your oath of that.' And reference being made to Mr. Perch, he confirms her view of the case. Somebody wonders what he 'll do, and whether he 'll go out in any situation. Mr. Towlinson thinks not, and hints at a refuge in one of them gen-teel almshouses of the better kind. 'Ah, where he 'll have his little garden you know,' says cook plaintively, 'and bring up sweet peas in the spring.' 'Exactly so,' says Mr. Towlinson, 'and be one of the brethren of something or another.' 'We are all brethren,' says Mrs. Perch, in a pause of her drink. 'Except the sisters,' says Mr. Perch. 'How are the mighty fallen!' remarks cook. 'Pride shall have a fall, and it always was and will be so!' observes the housemaid.

It is wonderful how good they feel, in making these reflections; and what a Christian unanimity they are sensible of, in bearing the common shock with resignation. There is only one interruption to this excellent state of mind, which is occasioned by a young kitchenmaid of inferior rank—in black stockings—who, having sat with her mouth open for a long time, unexpectedly discharges from it words to this effect, 'Suppose the wages shouldn't be paid!' The company sit for a moment speechless; but cook recovering first, turns upon the young woman, and requests to know how she dares insult the family, whose bread she eats, by such a dishonest supposition, and whether she thinks that anybody, with a scrap of honour left, could deprive poor servants of their pittance? 'Because if *that* is your religious feelings, Mary Daws,' says cook warmly, 'I don't know where you mean to go to.'

Mr. Towlinson don't know either; nor anybody; and the young kitchenmaid, appearing not to know exactly, herself, and scouted by the general voice, is covered with confusion, as with a garment.

After a few days, strange people begin to call at the house, and to make appointments with one another in the dining-room, as if they lived there. Especially, there is a gentleman, of a Mosaic Arabian cast of countenance, with a very massive watch-guard, who whistles in the drawing-room, and, while he is waiting for the other gentleman, who always has pen and ink in his pocket, asks Mr. Towlinson (by the easy name of 'Old Cock,') if he happens to know what the figure of them crimson and gold hangings might have been, when new bought. The callers and appointments in the dining-room become more numerous every day, and every gentleman seems to have pen and ink in his pocket, and to have some occasion to use it. At last it is said that there is going to be a sale; and then more people arrive, with pen and ink in their pockets, commanding a detachment of men with carpet-caps, who immediately begin to pull up the carpets, and knock the furniture about, and to print off thousands of impressions of their shoes upon the hall and staircase.

The council downstairs are in full conclave all this time, and, having nothing to do, perform perfect feats of eating. At length, they are one day summoned in a body to Mrs. Pipchin's room, and thus addressed by the fair Peruvian—

'Your master's in difficulties,' says Mrs. Pipchin, tartly. 'You know that, I suppose?'

Mr. Towlinson, as spokesman, admits a general knowledge of that fact.

'And you're all on the look-out for yourselves, I warrant you,' says Mrs. Pipchin, shaking her head at them.

A shrill voice from the rear exclaims, 'No more than yourself!'

'That's your opinion, Mrs. Impudence, is it?' says the ireful Pipchin, looking with a fiery eye over the intermediate heads.

'Yes, Mrs. Pipchin, it is,' replies cook, advancing. 'And what then, pray?'

'Why, then you may go as soon as you like,' says Mrs. Pipchin. 'The sooner the better; and I hope I shall never see your face again.'

With this the doughty Pipchin produces a canvas bag; and tells her wages out to that day, and a month beyond it: and clutches the money tight until a receipt for the same is duly signed, to the last up-stroke; when she grudgingly lets it go. This form of proceeding Mrs. Pipchin repeats with every member of the household, until all are paid.

'Now those that choose can go about their business,' says Mrs. Pipchin, 'and those that choose can stay here on board wages for a week or so, and make themselves useful. Except,' says the inflammable Pipchin, 'that slut of a cook, who'll go immediately.'

'That,' says the cook, 'she certainly will! I wish you good day, Mrs. Pipchin, and sincerely wish I could compliment you on the sweetness of your appearance!'

'Get along with you,' says Mrs. Pipchin, stamping her foot.

Cook sails off with an air of beneficent dignity, highly exasperating to Mrs. Pipchin, and is shortly joined below-stairs by the rest of the confederation.

Mr. Towlinson then says that, in the first place, he would beg to propose a little snack of something to eat; and over that snack would desire to offer a suggestion which he thinks will meet the position in which they find themselves. The refreshment being produced, and very heartily partaken of, Mr. Towlinson's suggestion is, in effect, that cook is going, and that if we are not true to ourselves, nobody will be true to us. That they have lived in that house a long time, and exerted themselves very much to be sociable together. (At this, cook says, with emotion, 'Hear, hear!' and Mrs. Perch, who is there again, and full to the throat, sheds tears.) And that he thinks, at the present time, the feeling ought to be 'Go one, go all!' The housemaid is much affected at this generous sentiment, and warmly seconds it. Cook says she feels it's right, and only hopes it's not done as a compliment to her, but from a sense of duty. Mr. Towlinson replies, from a sense of duty; and that now he is driven to express his opinions, he will openly say, that he does not think it over-respectable to remain in a house where sales and such-like are carrying forwards. The housemaid is sure of it; and relates, in confirmation, that a strange man, in a carpet-cap, offered this very morning to kiss her on the stairs. Hereupon, Mr. Towlinson is starting from his chair, to seek and 'smash' the offender; when he is laid hold of by the ladies, who beseech him to calm himself, and to reflect that it is easier and wiser to leave the scene of such indecencies at once. Mrs. Perch, presenting the case in a new light, even shows

that delicacy towards Mr. Dombey, shut up in his
own rooms, imperatively demands precipitate retreat.
'For what,' says the good woman, 'must his feelings
be, if he was to come upon any of the poor servants
that he once deceived into thinking him immensely
rich!' Cook is so struck by this moral consideration
that Mrs. Perch improves it with several pious axioms,
original and selected. It becomes a clear case that
they must all go. Boxes are packed, cabs fetched,
and at dusk that evening there is not one member of
the party left.

The house stands, large and weather-proof, in the
long dull street; but it is a ruin, and the rats fly
from it.

The men in the carpet-caps go on tumbling the
furniture about; and the gentlemen with the pens and
ink make out inventories of it, and sit upon pieces of
furniture never made to be sat upon, and eat bread
and cheese from the public-house on other pieces of
furniture never made to be eaten on, and seem to have
a delight in appropriating precious articles to strange
uses. Chaotic combinations of furniture also take
place. Mattresses and bedding appear in the dining-
room; the glass and china get into the conservatory;
the great dinner service is set out in heaps on the
long divan in the large drawing-room; and the stair-
wires, made into fasces, decorate the marble chimney-
pieces. Finally, a rug, with a printed bill upon it,
is hung out from the balcony; and a similar appendage
graces either side of the hall-door.

Then, all day long, there is a retinue of mouldy
gigs and chaise-carts in the street; and herds of
shabby vampires, Jew and Christian, overrun the
house, sounding the plate-glass mirrors with their
knuckles, striking discordant octaves on the grand

piano, drawing wet forefingers over the pictures, breathing on the blades of the best dinner-knives, punching the squabs of chairs and sofas with their dirty fists, touzling the featherbeds, opening and shutting all the drawers, balancing the silver spoons and forks, looking into the very threads of the drapery and linen, and disparaging everything. There is not a secret place in the whole house. Fluffy and snuffy strangers stare into the kitchen-range as curiously as into the attic clothes-press. Stout men with napless hats on, look out of the bedroom windows, and cut jokes with friends in the streets. Quiet, calculating spirits withdraw into the dressing-rooms with catalogues, and make marginal notes thereon, with stumps of pencils. The brokers invade the very fire-escape, and take a panoramic survey of the neighbourhood from the top of the house. The swarm and buzz, and going up and down, endure for days. The Capital Modern Household Furniture, etc., is on view.

Then there is a palisade of tables made in the best drawing-room; and on the capital, french-polished, extending, telescopic range of Spanish mahogany dining-tables with turned legs, the pulpit of the auctioneer is erected; and the herds of shabby vampires, Jew and Christian, the strangers fluffy and snuffy, and the stout men with the napless hats, congregate about it and sit upon everything within reach, mantel-pieces included, and begin to bid. Hot, humming, and dusty are the rooms all day; and—high above the heat, hum, and dust—the head and shouders, voice and hammer, of the auctioneer, are ever at work; the men in the carpet-caps get flustered and vicious with tumbling the lots about, and still the lots are going, going, gone; still coming on. Sometimes there is joking and a general roar.   This lasts all day and three days following.   The Capital Modern Household Furniture, etc., is on sale.

Then the mouldy gigs and chaise-carts reappear; and with them come spring-vans and waggons, and an army of porters with knots.   All day long, the men with carpet-caps are screwing at screw-drivers and bed-winches, or staggering by the dozen together on the staircase under heavy burdens, or upheaving perfect rocks of Spanish mahogany, best rosewood, or plate-glass, into the gigs and chaise-carts, vans and waggons.   All sorts of vehicles of burden are in attendance, from a tilted waggon to a wheelbarrow. Poor Paul's little bedstead is carried off in a donkey-tandem.   For nearly a whole week, the Capital Modern Household Furniture, etc., is in course of removal.

At last it is all gone.   Nothing is left about the house but scattered leaves of catalogues, littered scraps of straw and hay, and a battery of pewter pots behind the hall-door.   The men with the carpet-caps gather up their screw-drivers and bed-winches into bags, shoulder them, and walk off.   One of the pen and ink gentlemen goes over the house as a last attention; sticking up bills in the windows respecting the lease of this desirable family mansion, and shutting the shutters.   At length he follows the men with the carpet-caps.   None of the invaders remain.   The house is a ruin, and the rats fly from it.

Mrs. Pipchin's apartments, together with those locked rooms on the ground-floor where the window-blinds are drawn down close, have been spared the general devastation.   Mrs. Pipchin has remained austere and stony during the proceedings in her own room; or has occasionally looked in at the sale to see what the goods are fetching, and to bid for one particular easy-chair.   Mrs. Pipchin has been the highest bidder for the easy-chair, and sits upon her property when Mrs. Chick comes to see her.

'How is my brother, Mrs. Pipchin?' says Mrs. Chick.

'I don't know any more than the deuce,' said Mrs. Pipchin. 'He never does me the honour to speak to me. He has his meat and drink put in the next room to his own; and what he takes, he comes out and takes when there's nobody there. It's no use asking me. I know no more about him than the man in the south who burnt his mouth by eating cold plum porridge.'

This the acrimonious Pipchin says with a flounce.

'But good gracious me!' cries Mrs. Chick blandly, 'How long is this to last! If my brother will not make an effort, Mrs. Pipchin, what is to become of him? I am sure I should have thought he had seen enough of the consequences of *not* making an effort, by this time, to be warned against that fatal error.'

'Hoity toity!' says Mrs. Pipchin, rubbing her nose. 'There's a great fuss, I think, about it. It an't so wonderful a case. People have had misfortunes before now, and been obliged to part with their furniture. I'm sure *I* have!'

'My brother,' pursues Mrs. Chick profoundly, 'is so peculiar—so strange a man. He is the most peculiar man *I* ever saw. Would any one believe that when he received news of the marriage and emigration of that unnatural child—it's a comfort to me, now, to remember that I always said there was something extraordinary about that child: but nobody minds me—would anybody believe, I say, that he should then turn round upon me and say he had supposed, from my manner, that she had come to my house? Why, my gracious! And would anybody believe that when I merely say to him, "Paul, I may be very foolish, and I have no doubt I am, but I cannot understand how your affairs can have got into this state," he should actually fly at me, and request that I will come to see him no more until he asks me? Why, my goodness!'

'Ah!' says Mrs. Pipchin. 'It's a pity he hadn't a little more to do with mines. They'd have tried his temper for him.'

'And what,' resumes Mrs. Chick, quite regardless of Mrs. Pipchin's observations, 'is it to end in? That's what I want to know. What does my brother mean to do? He must do something. It's of no use remaining shut up in his own rooms. Business won't come to him. No. He must go to it. Then why don't he go? He knows where to go, I suppose, having been a man of business all his life. Very good. Then why not go there?'

Mrs. Chick, after forging this powerful chain of reasoning, remains silent for a minute to admire it.

'Besides,' says the discreet lady, with an argumentative air, 'who ever heard of such obstinacy as his staying shut up here through all these dreadful disagreeables? It's not as if there was no place for him to go to. Of course he could have come to our house. He knows he is at home there, I suppose? Mr. Chick has perfectly bored about it, and I said with my own lips, "Why surely, Paul, you don't imagine that because your affairs have got into this state, you are the less at home to such near relatives as ourselves? You don't imagine that we are like the rest of the world?" But no; here he stays all through, and here he is. Why, good gracious me, suppose the house was to be let! What would he do then? He couldn't remain here, then. If he attempted to do so, there would be an ejectment, an action for Doe, and all sorts of things; and then he *must* go. Then why not go at first instead of at last? And that brings me back to what I said just now, and I naturally ask what is to be the end of it?'

'I know what's to be the end of it, as far as *I* am concerned,' replies Mrs. Pipchin, 'and that's enough for me. I'm going to take *my*self off in a jiffy.'

'In a which, Mrs. Pipchin?' says Mrs. Chick.

'In a jiffy,' retorts Mrs. Pipchin sharply.

'Ah, well! really I can't blame you, Mrs. Pipchin,' said Mrs. Chick, with frankness.

'It would be pretty much the same to me, if you could,' replies the sardonic Pipchin. 'At any rate I'm going. I can't stop here. I should be dead in a week. I had to cook my own pork chop yesterday, and I'm not used to it. My constitution will be giving way next. Besides, I had a very fair connection at Brighton when I came here—little Pankey's folks alone were worth a good eighty pounds a year to me —and I can't afford to throw it away. I've written to my niece, and she expects me by this time.'

'Have you spoken to my brother?' inquires Mrs. Chick.

'Oh, yes, it's very easy to say speak to him,' retorts Mrs. Pipchin. 'How is it done! I called out to him yesterday, that I was no use here, and that he had better let me send for Mrs. Richards. He grunted something or other that meant yes, and I sent! Grunt indeed! If he had been Mr. Pipchin, he'd have had some reason to grunt. Yah! I've no patience with it!'

Here this exemplary female, who has pumped up so much fortitude and virtue from the depths of the Peruvian mines, rises from her cushioned property to see Mrs. Chick to the door. Mrs. Chick, deploring to the last the peculiar character of her brother, noiselessly retires, much occupied with her own sagacity and clearness of head.

In the dusk of the evening Mr. Toodle, being off duty, arrives with Polly and a box, and leaves them, with a sounding kiss, in the hall of the empty house, the retired character of which affects Mr. Toodle's spirits strongly.

'I tell you what, Polly, my dear,' says Mr. Toodle, 'being now an ingein-driver, and well to do in the world, I shouldn't allow of your coming here, to be made dull-like, if it warn't for favours past. But favours past, Polly, is never to be forgot. To them which is in adversity, besides, your face is a cord'l. So let's have another kiss on it, my dear. You wish no better than to do a right act, I know; and my views is, that it's right and dutiful to do this. Good night, Polly!'

Mrs. Pipchin by this time looms dark in her black bombazeen skirts, black bonnet, and shawl; and has her personal property packed up; and has her chair (late a favourite chair of Mr. Dombey's and the dead bargain of the sale) ready near the street door; and is only waiting for a fly van, going to-night to Brighton on private service, which is to call for her, by private contract, and convey her home.

Presently it comes. Mrs. Pipchin's wardrobe being handed in and stowed away, Mrs. Pipchin's chair is next handed in, and placed in a convenient corner among certain trusses of hay; it being the intention of the amiable woman to occupy the chair during her journey. Mrs. Pipchin herself is next handed in, and grimly takes her seat. There is a snaky gleam in her hard grey eye, as of anticipated rounds of buttered toast, relays of hot chops, worryings and quellings of young children, sharp snappings at poor

Berry, and all the other delights of her ogress's castle. Mrs. Pipchin almost laughs as the fly van drives off, and she composes her black bombazeen skirts, and settles herself among the cushions of her easy-chair.

The house is such a ruin that the rats have fled, and there is not one left.

But Polly, though alone in the deserted mansion —for there is no companionship in the shut-up rooms in which its late master hides his head—is not alone long. It is night; and she is sitting at work in the housekeeper's room, trying to forget what a lonely house it is, and what a history belongs to it; when there is a knock at the hall-door, as loud-sounding as any knock can be, striking into such an empty place. Opening it, she returns across the echoing hall, accompanied by a female figure in a close black bonnet. It is Miss Tox, and Miss Tox's eyes are red.

'Oh, Polly,' says Miss Tox, 'when I looked in to have a little lesson with the children just now, I got the message that you left for me; and as soon as I could recover my spirits at all, I came on after you. Is there no one here but you?'

'Ah! not a soul,' says Polly.

'Have you seen him?' whispers Miss Tox.

'Bless you,' returns Polly, 'no; he has not been seen this many a day. They tell me he never leaves his room.'

'Is he said to be ill?' inquires Miss Tox.

'No, ma'am, not that I know of,' returns Polly, 'except in his mind. He must be very bad there, poor gentleman!'

Miss Tox's sympathy is such that she can scarcely speak. She is no chicken, but she has not grown tough with age and celibacy. Her heart is very tender, her compassion very genuine, her homage very

real. Beneath the locket with the fishy eye in it,
Miss Tox bears better qualities than many a less
whimsical outside; such qualities as will outlive, by
many courses of the sun, the best outsides and brightest husks that fall in the harvest of the great reaper.

It is long before Miss Tox goes away, and before
Polly, with a candle flaring on the blank stairs, looks
after her, for company, down the street, and feels
unwilling to go back into the dreary house, and jar
its emptiness with the heavy fastenings of the door,
and glide away to bed. But all this Polly does; and
in the morning sets in one of those darkened rooms
such matters as she has been advised to prepare, and
then retires and enters them no more until next morning at the same hour. There are bells there, but they
never ring; and though she can sometimes hear a footfall going to and fro, it never comes out.

Miss Tox returns early in the day. It then begins
to be Miss Tox's occupation to prepare little dainties
—or what are such to her—to be carried into these
rooms next morning. She derives so much satisfaction from the pursuit, that she enters on it regularly
from that time; and brings daily in her little basket,
various choice condiments selected from the scanty
stores of the deceased owner of the powdered head
and pigtail. She likewise brings, in sheets of curl
paper, morsels of cold meats, tongues of sheep, halves
of fowls, for her own dinner; and sharing these col-
lations with Polly, passes the greater part of her time
in the ruined house that the rats have fled from: hiding, in a fright at every sound, stealing in and out
like a criminal; only desiring to be true to the fallen
object of her admiration, unknown to him, unknown
to all the world but one poor simple woman.

The major knows it; but no one is the wiser for
that, though the major is much the merrier. The

major, in a fit of curiosity, has charged the native
to watch the house sometimes, and find out what becomes of Dombey. The native has reported Miss
Tox's fidelity, and the major has nearly choked himself dead with laughter. He is permanently bluer
from that hour, and constantly wheezes to himself, his
lobster eyes starting out of his head, 'Damme, sir, the
woman's a born idiot!'

And the ruined man. How does he pass the hours,
alone?

'Let him remember it in that room, years to come!'
He did remember it. It was heavy on his mind now;
heavier than all the rest.

'Let him remember it in that room, years to come!
The rain that falls upon the roof, the wind that
mourns outside the door, may have foreknowledge
in their melancholy sound. Let him remember it in
that room, years to come!'

He did remember it. In the miserable night he
thought of it; in the dreary day, the wretched dawn,
the ghostly, memory-haunted twilight. He did remember it. In agony, in sorrow, in remorse, in
despair! 'Papa! papa! Speak to me, dear papa!'
He heard the words again, and saw the face. He
saw it fall upon the trembling hands, and heard the
one prolonged cry go upward.

He was fallen, never to be raised up any more.
For the night of his worldly ruin there was no to-
morrow's sun; for the stain of his domestic shame
there was no purification; nothing, thank Heaven,
could bring his dead child back to life. But that
which he might have made so different in all the past
—which might have made the past itself so different,
though this he hardly thought of now—that which
was his own work, that which he could so easily have
wrought into a blessing, and had set himself so stead-

ily for years to form into a curse; that was the sharp grief of his soul.

Oh! He did remember it! The rain that fell upon the roof, the wind that mourned outside the door that night, had had foreknowledge in their melancholy sound. He knew, now, what he had done. He knew, now, that he had called down that upon his head, which bowed it lower than the heaviest stroke of fortune. He knew, now, what it was to be rejected and deserted; now, when every loving blossom he had withered in his innocent daughter's heart was snowing down in ashes on him.

He thought of her, as she had been that night when he and his bride came home. He thought of her as she had been, in all the home-events of the abandoned house. He thought, now, that of all around him, she alone had never changed. His boy had faded into dust, his proud wife had sunk into a polluted creature, his flatterer and friend had been transformed into the worst of villains, his riches had melted away, the very walls that sheltered him looked on him as a stranger; she alone had turned the same mild gentle look upon him always. Yes, to the latest and the last. She had never changed to him—nor had he ever changed to her—and she was lost.

As, one by one, they fell away before his mind—his baby-hope, his wife, his friend, his fortune—oh how the mist, through which he had seen her, cleared, and showed him her true self! Oh, how much better than this that he had loved her as he had his boy, and lost her as he had his boy, and laid them in their early grave together!

In his pride—for he was proud yet—he let the world go from him freely. As it fell away, he shook it off. Whether he imagined its face as expressing pity for him, or indifference to him, he shunned it alike. It was in the same degree to be avoided, in either aspect. He had no idea of any one companion in his misery, but the one he had driven away. What he would have said to her, or what consolation submitted to receive from her, he never pictured to himself. But he always knew she would have been true to him, if he had suffered her. He always knew she would have loved him better now, than at any other time: he was as certain that it was in her nature, as he was that there was a sky above him; and he sat thinking so, in his loneliness, from hour to hour. Day after day uttered this speech; night after night showed him this knowledge.

It began, beyond all doubt (however slowly it advanced for some time), in the receipt of her young husband's letter, and the certainty that she was gone. And yet—so proud he was in his ruin, or so reminiscent of her, only as something that might have been his, but was lost beyond redemption—that if he could have heard her voice in an adjoining room, he would not have gone to her. If he could have seen her in the street, and she had done no more than look at him as she had been used to look, he would have passed on with his old cold unforgiving face, and not addressed her, or relaxed it, though his heart should have broken soon afterwards. However turbulent his thoughts, or harsh his anger had been, at first, concerning her marriage, or her husband, that was all past now. He chiefly thought of what might have been, and what was not. What was, was all summed up in this: that she was lost, and he bowed down with sorrow and remorse.

And now he felt that he had had two children born to him in that house, and that between him and the bare wide empty walls there was a tie, mournful, but hard to rend asunder, connected with a double childhood, and a double loss. He had thought to leave the house—knowing he must go, not knowing whither —upon the evening of the day on which this feeling first struck root in his breast; but he resolved to stay another night, and in the night to ramble through the rooms once more.

He came out of his solitude when it was the dead of night, and with a candle in his hand went softly up the stairs. Of all the footmarks there, making them as common as the common street, there was not one, he thought, but had seemed at the time to set itself upon his brain while he had kept close, listening. He looked at their number, and their hurry, and contention—foot treading foot out, and upward track and downward jostling one another—and thought, with absolute dread and wonder, how much he must have suffered during that trial, and what a changed man he had cause to be. He thought, besides, oh was there, somewhere in the world, a light footstep that might have worn out in a moment half those marks!—and bent his head, and wept as he went up.

He almost saw it, going on before. He stopped, looked up towards the skylight; and a figure, childish itself, but carrying a child, and singing as it went, seemed to be there again. Anon, it was the same figure, alone, stopping for an instant, with suspended breath; the bright hair clustering loosely round its tearful face; and looking back at him.

He wandered through the rooms: lately so luxurious; now so bare and dismal and so changed, apparently, even in their shape and size. The press of footsteps was as thick here; and the same consideration of the suffering he had had, perplexed and terrified him. He began to fear that all this intricacy in his brain would drive him mad; and that his thoughts already lost coherence as the footprints did, and were pieced on to one another, with the same trackless involutions, and varieties of indistinct shapes.

He did not so much as know in which of these rooms she had lived, when she was alone. He was glad to leave them, and go wandering higher up. Abundance of associations were here, connected with his false wife, his false friend and servant, his false grounds of pride; but he put them all by now, and only recalled miserably, weakly, fondly, his two children.

Everywhere, the footsteps! They had had no respect for the old room high up, where the little bed had been; he could hardly find a clear space there, to throw himself down, on the floor, against the wall, poor broken man, and let his tears flow as they would. He had shed so many tears here, long ago, that he was less ashamed of his weakness in this place than in any other—perhaps, with that consciousness, had made excuses to himself for coming here. Here, with stooping shoulders, and his chin dropped on his breast, he had come. Here, thrown upon the bare boards, in the dead of night, he wept, alone—a proud man, even then; who, if a kind hand could have been stretched out, or a kind face could have looked in, would have risen up, and turned away, and gone down to his cell.

When the day broke he was shut up in his rooms again. He had meant to go away to-day, but clung to this tie in the house as the last and only thing left to him. He would go to-morrow. To-morrow came. He would go to-morrow. Every night, within the knowledge of no human creature, he came forth, and wandered through the despoiled house like a ghost. Many a morning when the day broke, his altered face, drooping behind the closed blind in his window, imperfectly transparent to the light as yet, pondered on the loss of his two children. It was one child no more. He reunited them in his thoughts, and they were never asunder. Oh, that he could have united them in his past love, and in death, and that one had not been so much worse than dead!

Strong mental agitation and disturbance was no novelty to him, even before his late sufferings. It never is, to obstinate and sullen natures; for they struggle hard to be such. Ground, long undermined, will often fall down in a moment; what was undermined here in so many ways, weakened, and crumbled, little by little, more and more, as the hand moved on the dial.

At last, he began to think he need not go at all. He might yet give up what his creditors had spared him (that they had not spared him more, was his own act), and only sever the tie between him and the ruined house, by severing that other link—

It was then that his footfall was audible in the late housekeeper's room, as he walked to and fro; but not audible in its true meaning, or it would have had an appalling sound.

The world was very busy and restless about him. He became aware of that again. It was whispering and babbling. It was never quiet. This, and the intricacy and complication of the footsteps, harassed him to death. Objects began to take a bleared and russet colour in his eyes. Dombey and Son was no more—his children no more. This must be thought of, well, to-morrow.

He thought of it to-morrow; and sitting thinking in his chair, saw in the glass, from time to time, this picture—

A spectral, haggard, wasted likeness of himself, brooded and brooded over the empty fireplace. Now it lifted up its head, examining the lines and hollows in its face; now hung it down again, and brooded afresh. Now it rose and walked about; now passed into the next room, and came back with something from the dressing-table in its breast. Now, it was looking at the bottom of the door, and thinking.

—Hush! what?

It was thinking that if blood were to trickle that way, and to leak out into the hall, it must be a long time going so far. It would move so stealthily and slowly, creeping on, with here a lazy little pool, and there a start, and then another little pool, that a desperately wounded man could only be discovered through its means, either dead or dying. When it had thought of this a long while, it got up again, and walked to and fro with its hand in its breast. He glanced at it occasionally, very curious to watch its motions, and he marked how wicked and murderous that hand looked.

Now it was thinking again! What was it thinking?

Whether they would tread in the blood when it crept so far, and carry it about the house among those many prints of feet, or even out into the street.

It sat down with its eyes upon the empty fireplace, and as it lost itself in thought there shone into the room a gleam of light; a ray of sun. It was quite unmindful, and sat thinking. Suddenly it rose, with a terrible face, and that guilty hand grasping what was in its breast. Then it was arrested by a cry—a wild, loud, piercing, loving, rapturous cry—and he only saw his own reflection in the glass, and at his knees, his daughter!

Yes. His daughter! Look at her! Look here! Down upon the ground, clinging to him, calling to him, folding her hands, praying to him.

'Papa! Dearest papa! Pardon me, forgive me!

I have come back to ask forgiveness on my knees. I never can be happy more, without it!'

Unchanged still. Of all the world, unchanged. Raising the same face to his, as on that miserable night. Asking *his* forgiveness!

'Dear papa, oh don't look strangely on me! I never meant to leave you. I never thought of it before or afterwards. I was frightened when I went away, and could not think. Papa, dear, I am changed. I am penitent. I know my fault. I know my duty better now. Papa, don't cast me off, or I shall die!'

He tottered to his chair. He felt her draw his arms about her neck; he felt her put her own round his; he felt her kisses on his face; he felt her wet cheek laid against his own; he felt—oh, how deeply!— all that he had done.

Upon the breast that he had bruised, against the heart that he had almost broken, she laid his face, now covered with his hands, and said, sobbing—

'Papa, love, I am a mother. I have a child who will soon call Walter by the name by which I call you. When it was born, and when I knew how much I loved it, I knew what I had done in leaving you. Forgive me, dear papa! oh say God bless me, and my little child!'

He would have said it, if he could. He would have raised his hands and besought her for pardon, but she caught them in her own, and put them down, hurriedly.

'My little child was born at sea, papa. I prayed to God (and so did Walter for me) to spare me, that I might come home. The moment I could land, I came back to you. Never let us be parted any more, papa!'

His head, now grey, was encircled by her arm; and

he groaned to think that never, never, had it rested
so before.

'You will come home with me, papa, and see my
baby? A boy, papa. His name is Paul. I think—
I hope—he 's like—'

Her tears stopped her.

'Dear papa, for the sake of my child, for the sake
of the name we have given him, for my sake, pardon
Walter. He is so kind and tender to me. I am so
happy with him. It was not his fault that we were
married. It was mine. I loved him so much.'

She clung closer to him, more endearing and more
earnest.

'He is the darling of my heart, papa. I would
die for him. He will love and honour you as I will.
We will teach our little child to love and honour you;
and we will tell him, when he can understand, that
you had a son of that name once, and that he died,
and you were very sorry; but that he is gone to
Heaven, where we all hope to see him when our time
for resting comes. Kiss me, papa, as a promise that
you will be reconciled to Walter—to my dearest husband—to the father of the little child who taught me
to come back, papa. Who taught me to come back!'

As she clung closer to him, in another burst of
tears, he kissed her on her lips, and lifting up his
eyes, said, 'Oh my God, forgive me, for I need it very
much!'

With that he dropped his head again, lamenting
over and caressing her, and there was not a sound in
all the house for a long, long time; they remaining
clasped in one another's arms, in the glorious sunshine that had crept in with Florence.

He dressed himself for going out, with a docile
submission to her entreaty; and walking with a feeble
gait, and looking back, with a tremble, at the room

in which he had been so long shut up, and where he had seen the picture in the glass, passed out with her into the hall. Florence, hardly glancing round her, lest she should remind him freshly of their last parting—for their feet were on the very stones where he had struck her in his madness—and keeping close to him, with her eyes upon his face, and his arm about her, led him out to a coach that was waiting at the door, and carried him away.

Then, Miss Tox and Polly came out of their concealment, and exulted tearfully. And then they packed his clothes, and books, and so forth, with great care; and consigned them in due course to certain persons sent by Florence in the evening, to fetch them. And then they took a last cup of tea in the lonely house.

'And so Dombey and Son, as I observed upon a certain sad occasion,' said Miss Tox, winding up a host of recollections, 'is indeed a daughter, Polly, after all.'

'And a good one!' exclaimed Polly.

'You are right,' said Miss Tox; 'and it's a credit to you, Polly, that you were always her friend when she was a little child. You were her friend long before I was, Polly,' said Miss Tox; 'and you're a good creature, Robin!'

Miss Tox addressed herself to a bullet-headed young man, who appeared to be in but indifferent circumstances, and in depressed spirits, and who was sitting in a remote corner. Rising, he disclosed to view the form and features of the Grinder.

'Robin,' said Miss Tox, 'I have just observed to your mother, as you may have heard, that she is a good creature.'

'And so she is, miss,' quoth the Grinder, with some feeling.

'Very well, Robin,' said Miss Tox, 'I am glad to hear you say so. Now, Robin, as I am going to give you a trial, at your urgent request, as my domestic, with a view to your restoration to respectability, I will take this impressive occasion of remarking that I hope you will never forget that you have, and have always had, a good mother, and that you will endeavour so to conduct yourself as to be a comfort to her.'

'Upon my soul I will, miss,' returned the Grinder. 'I have come through a good deal, and my intentions is now as straight for'ard, miss, as a cove's—'

'I must get you to break yourself of that word, Robin, if you please,' interposed Miss Tox, politely.

'If you please, miss, as a chap's—'

'Thankee, Robin, no,' returned Miss Tox. 'I should prefer individual.'

'As a indiwiddle's,' said the Grinder.

'Much better,' remarked Miss Tox, complacently; 'infinitely more expressive!'

'—can be,' pursued Rob. 'If I hadn't been and got made a Grinder on, miss and mother, which was a most unfortunate circumstance for a young co—indiwiddle.'

'Very good indeed,' observed Miss Tox, approvingly.

'—and if I hadn't been led away by birds, and then fallen into a bad service,' said the Grinder, 'I hope I might have done better. But it's never too late for a—'

'Indi—' suggested Miss Tox.

'widdle,' said the Grinder, 'to mend; and I hope to mend, miss, with your kind trial; and wishing, mother, my love to father, and brothers and sisters, and saying of it.'

'I am very glad indeed to hear it,' observed Miss

Tox. 'Will you take a little bread and butter, and a cup of tea, before we go, Robin?'

'Thankee, miss,' returned the Grinder; who immediately began to use his own personal grinders in a most remarkable manner, as if he had been on very short allowance for a considerable period.

Miss Tox being, in good time, bonneted and shawled, and Polly too, Rob hugged his mother, and followed his new mistress away; so much to the hopeful admiration of Polly, that something in her eyes made luminous rings round the gas-lamps as she looked after him. Polly then put out her light, locked the house-door, delivered the key at an agent's hard by, and went home as fast as she could go; rejoicing in the shrill delight that her unexpected arrival would occasion there. The great house, dumb as to all that had been suffered in it, and the changes it had witnessed, stood frowning like a dark mute on the street; baulking any nearer inquiries with the staring announcement that the lease of this desirable family mansion was to be disposed of.

CHAPTER LX

CHIEFLY MATRIMONIAL

THE grand half-yearly festival holden by Doctor and Mrs. Blimber, on which occasion they requested the pleasure of the company of every young gentleman pursuing his studies in that genteel establishment, at an early party, when the hour was half-past seven o'clock, and when the object was quadrilles, had duly taken place, about this time; and the young gentlemen, with no unbecoming demonstrations of levity, had betaken themselves, in a state of scholastic repletion, to their own homes. Mr. Skettles had repaired abroad, permanently to grace the establishment of his father, Sir Barnet Skettles, whose popular manners had obtained him a diplomatic appointment, the honours of which were discharged by himself and Lady Skettles, to the satisfaction even of their own countrymen and countrywomen: which was considered almost miraculous. Mr. Tozer, now a young man of lofty stature, in Wellington boots, was so extremely full of antiquity as to be nearly on a par with a genuine ancient Roman in his knowledge of English: a triumph that affected his good parents with the tenderest emotions, and caused the father and mother of Mr. Briggs (whose learning, like ill-arranged luggage, was so tightly packed that he couldn't get at anything he wanted) to hide their diminished heads. The fruit laboriously gathered from the tree of knowledge by this latter young gentleman, in fact, had been subjected to so much pressure, that it had become a kind of intellectual Norfolk Biffin, and had nothing of its original form or flavour remaining. Master Bitherstone now, on whom the forcing system had the happier and not uncommon effect of leaving no impression whatever, when the forcing apparatus ceased to work, was in a much more comfortable plight; and being then on shipboard, bound for Bengal, found himself forgetting, with such admirable rapidity, that it was doubtful whether his declensions of noun-substantives would hold out to the end of the voyage.

When Dr. Blimber, in pursuance of the usual course, would have said to the young gentlemen, on the morning of the party, 'Gentlemen, we will resume our studies on the twenty-fifth of next month,' he departed from the usual course, and said, 'Gentlemen, when our friend Cincinnatus retired to his farm, he did not present to the senate any Roman whom he sought to nominate as his successor. But there is a Roman here,' said Doctor Blimber, laying his hand on the shoulder of Mr. Feeder, B.A., '*adolescens imprimis gravis et doctus*, gentlemen, whom I, a retiring Cincinnatus, wish to present to *my* little senate, as their future Dictator. Gentlemen, we will resume our studies on the twenty-fifth of next month, under the auspices of Mr. Feeder, B.A.' At this (which Dr. Blimber had previously called upon all the parents, and urbanely explained), the young gentlemen cheered; and Mr. Tozer, on behalf of the rest, instantly presented the Doctor with a silver inkstand, in a speech containing very little of the mother-tongue, but fifteen quotations from the Latin, and seven from the Greek, which moved the younger of the young gentlemen to discontent and envy: they remarking, 'Oh, ah! It was all very well for old Tozer, but they didn't subscribe money for old Tozer to show off with, they supposed; did they? What business was it of old Tozer's more than anybody else's? It wasn't *his* inkstand. Why couldn't he leave the boys' property alone?' and murmuring other expressions of their dissatisfaction, which seemed to find a greater relief in calling him old Tozer, than in any other available vent.

Not a word had been said to the young gentlemen, nor a hint dropped, of anything like a contemplated marriage between Mr. Feeder, B.A., and the fair Cornelia Blimber. Doctor Blimber, especially, seemed to take pains to look as if nothing would surprise him more; but it was perfectly well known to all the young gentlemen nevertheless, and when they departed for the society of their relations and friends, they took leave of Mr. Feeder with awe.

Mr. Feeder's most romantic visions were fulfilled.

The Doctor had determined to paint the house outside, and put it in thorough repair; and to give up the
business, and to give up Cornelia. The painting and
repairing began upon the very day of the young
gentlemen's departure, and now behold! the wedding
morning was come, and Cornelia, in a new pair of
spectacles, was waiting to be led to the hymeneal
altar.

The Doctor with his learned legs, and Mrs. Blimber in a lilac bonnet, and Mr. Feeder, B.A., with his
long knuckles and his bristly head of hair, and Mr.
Feeder's brother, the Reverend Alfred Feeder, M.A.,
who was to perform the ceremony, were all assembled
in the drawing-room, and Cornelia with her orange-
flowers and bridesmaids had just come down, and
looked, as of old, a little squeezed in appearance, but
very charming, when the door opened, and the weak-
eyed young man, in a loud voice, made the following
proclamation—

'MR. AND MRS. TOOTS!'

Upon which there entered Mr. Toots, grown extremely stout, and on his arm a lady very handsomely
and becomingly dressed, with very bright black eyes.

'Mrs. Blimber,' said Mr. Toots, 'allow me to present my wife.'

Mrs. Blimber was delighted to receive her. Mrs.
Blimber was a little condescending, but extremely
kind.

'And as you've known me for a long time, you
know,' said Mr. Toots, 'let me assure you that she is
one of the most remarkable women that ever lived.'

'My dear!' remonstrated Mrs. Toots.

'Upon my word and honour she is,' said Mr. Toots.
'I—I assure you, Mrs. Blimber, she's a most extraordinary woman.'

Mrs. Toots laughed merrily, and Mrs. Blimber led

her to Cornelia. Mr. Toots having paid his respects in that direction, and having saluted his old preceptor, who said, in allusion to his conjugal state, 'Well Toots, well Toots! So you are one of us, are you, Toots?'—retired with Mr. Feeder, B.A., into a window.

Mr. Feeder, B.A., being in great spirits, made a spar at Mr. Toots, and tapped him skilfully with the back of his hand on the breastbone.

'Well, old buck!' said Mr. Feeder with a laugh. 'Well! Here we are! Taken in and done for. Eh?'

'Feeder,' returned Mr. Toots. 'I give you joy. If you're as—as—as perfectly blissful in a matrimonial life, as I am myself, you'll have nothing to desire.'

'I don't forget *my* old friends, you see,' said Mr. Feeder. 'I ask 'em to *my* wedding, Toots.'

'Feeder,' replied Mr. Toots gravely, 'the fact is, that there were several circumstances which prevented me from communicating with you until after my marriage had been solemnised. In the first place, I had made a perfect brute of myself to you, on the subject of Miss Dombey; and I felt that if you were asked to any wedding of mine, you would naturally expect that it was *with* Miss Dombey, which involved explanations, that upon my word and honour, at that crisis, would have knocked me completely over. In the second place, our wedding was strictly private; there being nobody present but one friend of myself and Mrs. Toots's, who is a captain in—I don't exactly know in what,' said Mr. Toots, 'but it's of no consequence. I hope, Feeder, that in writing a statement of what had occurred before Mrs. Toots and myself went abroad upon our foreign tour, I fully discharged the offices of friendship.'

'Toots, my boy,' said Mr. Feeder, shaking his hands, 'I was joking.'

'And now Feeder,' said Mr. Toots, 'I should be glad to know what you think of my union.'

'Capital!' returned Mr. Feeder.

'You think it's capital, do you, Feeder?' said Mr. Toots solemnly, 'Then how capital must it be to Me. For *you* can never know what an extraordinary woman that is.'

Mr. Feeder was willing to take it for granted. But Mr. Toots shook his head, and wouldn't hear of that being possible.

'You see,' said Mr. Toots, 'what *I* wanted in a wife was—in short, was sense. Money, Feeder, I had. Sense I—I had not, particularly.'

Mr. Feeder murmured, 'Oh, yes, you had, Toots!' But Mr. Toots said—

'No, Feeder, I had *not*. Why should I disguise it? I had *not*. I knew that sense was there,' said Mr. Toots, stretching out his hand towards his wife, 'in perfect heaps. I had no relation to object or be offended, on the score of station; for I had no relation. I have never had anybody belonging to me but my guardian, and him, Feeder, I have always considered as a pirate and a corsair. Therefore, you know it was not likely,' said Mr. Toots, 'that I should take *his* opinion.'

'No,' said Mr. Feeder.

'Accordingly,' resumed Mr. Toots, 'I acted on my own. Bright was the day on which I did so! Feeder! Nobody but myself can tell what the capacity of that woman's mind is. If ever the Rights of Women, and all that kind of thing, are properly attended to, it will be through her powerful intellect. —Susan, my dear!' said Mr. Toots, looking abruptly out of the window-curtains, 'pray do not exert yourself!'

'My dear,' said Mrs. Toots, 'I was only talking.'

'But my love,' said Mr. Toots, 'pray do not exert yourself. You really must be careful. Do not, my dear Susan, exert yourself. She's so easily excited,' said Mr. Toots, apart to Mrs. Blimber, 'and then she forgets the medical man altogether.'

Mrs. Blimber was impressing on Mrs. Toots the necessity of caution, when Mr. Feeder, B.A., offered her his arm, and led her down to the carriages that were in waiting to go to church. Doctor Blimber escorted Mrs. Toots. Mr. Toots escorted the fair bride, around whose lambent spectacles two gauzy little bridesmaids fluttered like moths. Mr. Feeder's brother, Mr. Alfred Feeder, M.A., had already gone on, in advance, to assume his official functions.

The ceremony was performed in an admirable manner, Cornelia, with her crisp little curls, 'went in,' as the Chicken might have said, with great composure; and Doctor Blimber gave her away, like a man who had quite made up his mind to it. The gauzy little bridesmaids appeared to suffer most. Mrs. Blimber was affected, but gently so; and told the Reverend Mr. Alfred Feeder, M.A., on the way home, that if she could only have seen Cicero in his retirement at Tusculum, she would not have had a wish, now, ungratified.

There was a breakfast afterwards, limited to the same small party; at which the spirits of Mr. Feeder, B.A., were tremendous, and so communicated themselves to Mrs. Toots that Mr. Toots was several times heard to observe, across the table, 'My dear Susan, *don't* exert yourself!' The best of it was, that Mr. Toots felt it incumbent on him to make a speech; and in spite of a whole code of telegraphic dissuasions from Mrs. Toots, appeared on his legs for the first time in his life.

'I really,' said Mr. Toots, 'in this house, where whatever was done to me in the way of—of any mental confusion sometimes—which is of no consequence and I impute to nobody—I was always treated like one of Doctor Blimber's family, and had a desk to myself for a considerable period—can—not—allow—my friend Feeder to be—'

Mrs. Toots suggested 'married.'

'It may not be inappropriate to the occasion, or altogether uninteresting,' said Mr. Toots with a delighted face, 'to observe that my wife is a most extraordinary woman, and would do this much better than myself—allow my friend Feeder to be married—especially to—'

Mrs. Toots suggested 'to Miss Blimber.'

'To Mrs. Feeder, my love!' said Mr. Toots, in a subdued tone of private discussion: '"whom God hath joined," you know, "let no man"—don't you know? I cannot allow my friend, Feeder, to be married—especially to Mrs. Feeder—without proposing their—their—toasts; and may,' said Mr. Toots, fixing his eyes on his wife, as if for inspiration in a high flight, 'may the torch of Hymen be the beacon of joy, and may the flowers we have this day strewed in their path, be the—the banishers of—of gloom!'

Doctor Blimber, who had a taste for metaphor, was pleased with this, and said, 'Very good, Toots! Very well said, indeed, Toots!' and nodded his head and patted his hands. Mr. Feeder made in reply, a comic speech chequered with sentiment. Mr. Alfred Feeder, M.A., was afterwards very happy on Doctor and Mrs. Blimber; Mr. Feeder, B.A., scarcely less so, on the gauzy little bridesmaids. Doctor Blimber then, in a sonorous voice, delivered a few thoughts in the pastoral style, relative to the rushes among which it was the intention of himself and Mrs. Blimber to dwell, and the bee that would hum around their cot. Shortly after which, as the Doctor's eyes were twinkling in a remarkable manner, and his son-in-law had already observed that time was made for slaves, and had inquired whether Mrs. Toots sang, the discreet Mrs. Blimber dissolved the sitting, and sent Cornelia away, very cool and comfortable, in a post-chaise, with the man of her heart.

Mr. and Mrs. Toots withdrew to the Bedford (Mrs. Toots had been there before in old times, under her maiden name of Nipper), and there found a letter, which it took Mr. Toots such an enormous time to read, that Mrs. Toots was frightened.

'My dear Susan,' said Mr. Toots, 'fright is worse than exertion. Pray be calm!'

'Who is it from?' asked Mrs. Toots.

'Why, my love,' said Mr. Toots, 'it's from Captain Gills. Do not excite yourself. Walters and Miss Dombey are expected home!'

'My dear,' said Mrs. Toots, raising herself quickly from the sofa, very pale, 'don't try to deceive me, for it's no use, they're come home—I see it plainly in your face!'

'She's a most extraordinary woman!' exclaimed Mr. Toots, in rapturous admiration. 'You're perfectly right, my love, they have come home. Miss Dombey has seen her father, and they are reconciled!'

'Reconciled!' cried Mrs. Toots, clapping her hands.

'My dear,' said Mr. Toots; 'pray do not exert yourself. Do remember the medical man! Captain Gills says—at least he don't say, but I imagine, from what I can make out, he means—that Miss Dombey has brought her unfortunate father away from his

old house, to one where she and Walters are living;
that he is lying very ill there—supposed to be dying;
and that she attends upon him night and day.'

Mrs. Toots began to cry quite bitterly.

'My dearest Susan,' replied Mr. Toots, 'do, do, if
you possibly can, remember the medical man! If you
can't, it's of no consequence—but do endeavour to!'

His wife, with her old manner suddenly restored,
so pathetically entreated him to take her to her precious pet, her little mistress, her own darling, and the
like, that Mr. Toots, whose sympathy and admiration were of the strongest kind, consented from his
very heart of hearts; and they agreed to depart immediately, and present themselves in answer to the
captain's letter.

Now some hidden sympathies of things, or some
coincidences, had that day brought the captain himself (towards whom Mr. and Mrs. Toots were soon
journeying), into the flowery train of wedlock; not
as a principal, but as an accessory. It happened ac-
cidentally, and thus—

The captain, having seen Florence and her baby
for a moment, to his unbounded content, and having
had a long talk with Walter, turned out for a walk;
feeling it necessary to have some solitary meditation
on the changes of human affairs, and to shake his
glazed hat profoundly over the fall of Mr. Dombey,
for whom the generosity and simplicity of his nature
were awakened in a lively manner. The captain
would have been very low, indeed, on the unhappy
gentleman's account, but for the recollection of the
baby; which afforded him such intense satisfaction
whenever it arose, that he laughed aloud as he went
along the street, and, indeed, more than once, in a
sudden impulse of joy, threw up his glazed hat and
caught it again; much to the amazement of the spec-

tators. The rapid alternations of light and shade to which these two conflicting subjects of reflection exposed the captain, were so very trying to his spirits, that he felt a long walk necessary to his composure; and as there is a great deal in the influence of harmonious associations, he chose, for the scene of this walk, his old neighbourhood, down among the mast, oar, and blockmakers, ship-biscuit bakers, coal-whippers, pitch-kettles, sailors, canals, docks, swing-bridges, and other soothing objects.

These peaceful scenes, and particularly the region of Limehouse Hole and thereabouts, were so influential in calming the captain, that he walked on with restored tranquillity, and was, in fact, regaling himself under his breath, with the ballad of Lovely Peg, when, on turning a corner, he was suddenly transfixed and rendered speechless by a triumphant procession that he beheld advancing towards him.

This awful demonstration was headed by that determined woman, Mrs. MacStinger, who, preserving a countenance of inexorable resolution, and wearing conspicuously attached to her obdurate bosom a stupendous watch and appendages, which the captain recognised at a glance as the property of Bunsby, conducted under her arm no other than that sagacious mariner; he, with the distraught and melancholy visage of a captive borne into a foreign land, meekly resigning himself to her will. Behind them appeared the young MacStingers, in a body, exulting. Behind them, two ladies of a terrible and steadfast aspect, leading between them a short gentleman in a tall hat, who likewise exulted. In the wake, appeared Bunsby's boy, bearing umbrellas. The whole were in good marching order; and a dreadful smartness that pervaded the party would have sufficiently announced, if the intrepid countenances of the ladies had been wanting, that it was a procession of sacrifice, and that the victim was Bunsby.

The first impulse of the captain was to run away. This also appeared to be the first impulse of Bunsby, hopeless as its execution must have proved. But a cry of recognition proceeding from the party, and Alexander MacStinger running up to the captain with open arms, the captain struck.

'Well, Cap'en Cuttle!' said Mrs. MacStinger. 'This is indeed a meeting! I bear no malice now. Cap'en Cuttle—you needn't fear that I'm a going to cast any reflections. I hope to go to the altar in another spirit.' Here Mrs. MacStinger paused, and drawing herself up, and inflating her bosom with a long breath, said, in allusion to the victim, 'My 'usband, Cap'en Cuttle!'

The abject Bunsby looked neither to the right nor to the left, nor at his bride, nor at his friend, but straight before him at nothing. The captain putting out his hand, Bunsby put out his; but, in answer to the captain's greeting, spake no word.

'Cap'en Cuttle,' said Mrs. MacStinger, 'if you would wish to heal up past animosities, and to see the last of your friend, my 'usband, as a single person, we should be 'appy of your company to chapel. Here is a lady here,' said Mrs. MacStinger, turning round to the more intrepid of the two, 'my bridesmaid, that will be glad of your protection, Cap'en Cuttle.'

The short gentleman in the tall hat, who it appeared was the husband of the other lady, and who evidently exulted at the reduction of a fellow-creature to his own condition, gave place at this, and resigned the lady to Captain Cuttle. The lady immediately seized him, and, observing that there was no time to lose, gave the word, in a strong voice, to advance.

The captain's concern for his friend, not un-
mingled, at first, with some concern for himself—
for a shadowy terror that he might be married by
violence, possessed him, until his knowledge of the
service came to his relief, and remembering the legal
obligation of saying, 'I will,' he felt himself personally safe so long as he resolved, if asked any
question, distinctly to reply 'I won't'—threw him into
a profuse perspiration; and rendered him, for a time,
insensible to the movements of the procession, of
which he now formed a feature, and to the conversation of his fair companion. But as he became less
agitated, he learnt from this lady that she was the
widow of a Mr. Bokum, who had held an employment in the Custom House; that she was the dearest
friend of Mrs. MacStinger, whom she considered a
pattern for her sex; that she had often heard of the
captain, and now hoped he had repented of his past
life; that she trusted Mr. Bunsby knew what a blessing he had gained, but that she feared men seldom
did know what such blessings were, until they had
lost them; with more to the same purpose.

All this time, the captain could not but observe that
Mrs. Bokum kept her eyes steadily on the bridegroom, and that whenever they came near a court or
other narrow turning which appeared favourable for
flight, she was on the alert to cut him off if he attempted to escape. The other lady, too, as well as
her husband, the short gentleman with the tall hat,
was plainly on guard, according to a preconcerted
plan; and the wretched man was so secured by Mrs.
MacStinger, that any effort at self-preservation by
flight was rendered futile. This, indeed, was apparent to the mere populace, who expressed their perception of the fact by jeers and cries; to all of which,
the dread MacStinger was inflexibly indifferent,

while Bunsby himself appeared in a state of unconsciousness.

The captain made many attempts to accost the philosopher, if only in a monosyllable or a signal; but always failed, in consequence of the vigilance of the guard, and the difficulty, at all times peculiar to Bunsby's constitution, of having his attention aroused by any outward and visible sign whatever. Thus they approached the chapel, a neat whitewashed edifice, recently engaged by the Reverend Melchisedech Howler, who had consented, on very urgent solicitation, to give the world another two years of existence, but had informed his followers that, then, it must positively go.

While the Reverend Melchisedech was offering up some extemporary orisons, the captain found an opportunity of growling in the bridegroom's ear—

'What cheer, my lad, what cheer?'

To which Bunsby replied, with a forgetfulness of the Reverend Melchisedech, which nothing but his desperate circumstances could have excused—

'D—d bad.'

'Jack Bunsby,' whispered the captain, 'do you do this here, o' your own free will?'

Mr. Bunsby answered 'No.'

'Why do you do it, then, my lad?' inquired the captain, not unnaturally.

Bunsby, still looking, and always looking with an immoveable countenance, at the opposite side of the world, made no reply.

'Why not sheer off?' said the captain.

'Eh?' whispered Bunsby, with a momentary gleam of hope.

'Sheer off,' said the captain.

'Where's the good?' retorted the forlorn sage. 'She'd capter me agen.'

'Try!' replied the captain. 'Cheer up! Come! Now's your time. Sheer off, Jack Bunsby!'

Jack Bunsby, however, instead of profiting by the advice, said in a doleful whisper—

'It all began in that there chest o' yourn. Why did I ever conwoy her into port that night?'

'My lad,' faltered the captain, 'I thought as you had come over her; not as she had come over you. A man as has got such opinions as you have!'

Mr. Bunsby merely uttered a suppressed groan.

'Come!' said the captain, nudging him with his elbow, 'now's your time! Sheer off! I'll cover your retreat. The time's a flying. Bunsby! It's for liberty. Will you once?'

Bunsby was immoveable.

'Bunsby!' whispered the captain, 'will you twice?'

Bunsby wouldn't twice.

'Bunsby!' urged the captain, 'it's for liberty; will you three times? Now or never!'

Bunsby didn't then, and didn't ever; for Mrs. MacStinger immediately afterwards married him.

One of the most frightful circumstances of the ceremony to the captain, was the deadly interest exhibited therein by Juliana MacStinger; and the fatal concentration of her faculties, with which that promising child, already the image of her parent, observed the whole proceedings. The captain saw in this a succession of man-traps stretching out infinitely; a series of ages of oppression and coercion, through which the seafaring line was doomed. It was a more memorable sight than the unflinching steadiness of Mrs. Bokum and the other lady, the exultation of the short gentleman in the tall hat, or even the fell inflexibility of Mrs. MacStinger. The Master MacStingers understood little of what was going on, and cared less; being chiefly engaged, during the cere-

mony, in treading on one another's half-boots; but
the contrast afforded by those wretched infants only
set off and adorned the precocious woman in Juliana.
Another year or two, the captain thought, and to
lodge where that child was, would be destruction.

The ceremony was concluded by a general spring
of the young family on Mr. Bunsby, whom they
hailed by the endearing name of father, and from
whom they solicited halfpence. These gushes of affection over, the procession was about to issue forth
again, when it was delayed for some little time by
an unexpected transport on the part of Alexander
MacStinger. That dear child, it seemed, connecting
a chapel with tombstones, when it was entered for
any purpose apart from the ordinary religious exercises, could not be persuaded but that his mother
was now to be decently interred, and lost to him for
ever. In the anguish of this conviction, he screamed
with astonishing force, and turned black in the face.
However touching these marks of a tender disposition were to his mother, it was not in the character
of that remarkable woman to permit her recognition
of them to degenerate into weakness. Therefore,
after vainly endeavouring to convince his reason by
shakes, pokes, bawlings-out, and similar applications
to his head, she led him into the air, and tried another
method; which was manifested to the marriage party
by a quick succession of sharp sounds, resembling
applause, and subsequently, by their seeing Alexander in contact with the coolest paving-stone in the
court, greatly flushed, and loudly lamenting.

The procession being then in a condition to form
itself once more, and repair to Brig Place, where a
marriage feast was in readiness, returned as it had
come: not without the receipt, by Bunsby, of many
humorous congratulations from the populace on his

recently-acquired happiness. The captain accompanied it as far as the house-door, but, being made uneasy by the gentler manner of Mrs. Bokum, who, now that she was relieved from her engrossing duty —for the watchfulness and alacrity of the ladies sensibly diminished when the bridegroom was safely married—had greater leisure to show an interest in his behalf, there left it and the captive; faintly pleading an appointment, and promising to return presently. The captain had another cause for uneasiness, in remorsefully reflecting that he had been the first means of Bunsby's entrapment, though certainly without intending it, and through his unbounded faith in the resources of that philosopher.

To go back to old Sol Gills at the wooden midshipman's, and not first go round to ask how Mr. Dombey fared—albeit the house where he lay was out of London, and away on the borders of a fresh heath—was quite out of the captain's course. So he got a lift when he was tired, and made out the journey gaily.

The blinds were pulled down, and the house so quiet, that the captain was almost afraid to knock; but listening at the door, he heard low voices within, very near it, and, knocking softly, was admitted by Mr. Toots. Mr. Toots and his wife had, in fact, just arrived there; having been at the midshipman's to seek him, and having there obtained the address.

They were not so recently arrived, but that Mrs. Toots had caught the baby from somebody, taken it in her arms, and sat down on the stairs, hugging and fondling it. Florence was stooping down beside her; and no one could have said which Mrs. Toots was hugging and fondling most, the mother or the child, or which was the tenderer, Florence of Mrs. Toots, or Mrs. Toots of her, or both of the baby; it was such a little group of love and agitation.

'And is your pa very ill, my darling dear Miss Floy?' asked Susan.

'He is very, very ill,' said Florence. 'But Susan, dear, you must not speak to me as you used to speak. And what's this?' said Florence, touching her clothes, in amazement. 'Your old dress, dear? Your old cap, curls, and all?'

Susan burst into tears, and showered kisses on the little hand that had touched her so wonderingly.

'My dear Miss Dombey,' said Mr. Toots, stepping forward, 'I'll explain. She's the most extraordinary woman. There are not many to equal her! She has always said—she said before we were married, and has said to this day—that whenever you came home, she'd come to you in no dress but the dress she used to serve you in, for fear she might seem strange to you, and you might like her less. I admire the dress myself,' said Mr. Toots, 'of all things. I adore her in it! My dear Miss Dombey, she'll be your maid again, your nurse, all that she ever was, and more. There's no change in her. But Susan, my dear,' said Mr. Toots, who had spoken with great feeling and high admiration, 'all I ask is, that you'll remember the medical man, and not exert yourself too much.'

CHAPTER LXI

RELENTING

FLORENCE had need of help. Her father's need of it was sore, and made the aid of her old friend invaluable. Death stood at his pillow. A shade, already, of what he had been, shattered in mind, and perilously sick in body, he laid his weary head down on the bed his daughter's hands prepared for him, and had never raised it since.

She was always with him. He knew her, generally; though, in the wandering of his brain, he often confused the circumstances under which he spoke to her. Thus he would address her, sometimes, as if his boy were newly dead; and would tell her, that although he had said nothing of her ministering at the little bedside, yet he had seen it—he had seen it; and then would hide his face and sob, and put out his worn hand. Sometimes he would ask her for herself. 'Where is Florence?'—'I am here, papa, I am here.' 'I don't know her!' he would cry. 'We have been parted so long, that I don't know her!' and then a staring dread would be upon him, until she could soothe his perturbation; and recall the tears she tried so hard, at other times, to dry.

He rambled through the scenes of his old pursuits —through many where Florence lost him as she listened—sometimes for hours. He would repeat that childish question, 'What is money?' and ponder on it, and think about it, and reason with himself, more or less connectedly, for a good answer; as if it had never been proposed to him until that moment. He would go on with a musing repetition of the title of his old firm twenty thousand times, and at every one of them, would turn his head upon his pillow. He would count his children—one—two—stop, and go back, and begin again in the same way.

But this was when his mind was in its most distracted state. In all the other phases of its illness, and in those to which it was most constant, it always turned on Florence. What he would oftenest do was this: he would recall that night he had so recently remembered, the night on which she came down to his room, and would imagine that his heart smote him, and that he went out after her, and up the stairs to seek her. Then, confounding that time with the later days of the many footsteps, he would be amazed at their number, and begin to count them as he followed her. Here, of a sudden, was a bloody footstep going on among the others; and after it there began to be, at intervals, doors standing open, through which certain terrible pictures were seen, in mirrors, of haggard men, concealing something in their breasts. Still, among the many footsteps and the bloody footsteps here and there, was the step of Florence. Still she was going on before. Still the restless mind went, following and counting, ever farther, ever higher, as to the summit of a mighty tower that it took years to climb.

One day he inquired if that were not Susan who had spoken a long while ago.

Florence said 'Yes, dear papa'; and asked him would he like to see her.

He said 'very much.' And Susan, with no little trepidation, showed herself at his bedside.

It seemed a great relief to him. He begged her not to go; to understand that he forgave her what she had said; and that she was to stay. Florence and he were very different now, he said, and very happy. Let her look at this! He meant his drawing the gentle head to his pillow, and laying it beside him.

He remained like this for days and weeks. At length, lying, the faint feeble semblance of a man, upon his bed, and speaking in a voice so low that they could only hear him by listening very near to his lips, he became quiet. It was dimly pleasant to him now, to lie there, with the window open, looking out at the summer sky and the trees; and, in the evening, at the sunset. To watch the shadows of the clouds and leaves, and seem to feel a sympathy with shadows. It was natural that he should. To him, life and the world were nothing else.

He began to show now that he thought of Florence's fatigue: and often taxed his weakness to whisper to her, 'Go and walk, my dearest, in the sweet air. Go to your good husband!' One time when Walter was in his room, he beckoned him to come near, and to stoop down; and pressing his hand, whispered an assurance to him that he knew he could trust him with his child when he was dead.

It chanced one evening, towards sunset, when Florence and Walter were sitting in his room together, as he liked to see them, that Florence, having her baby in her arms, began in a low voice to sing to the little fellow, and sang the old tune she had so often sung to the dead child. He could not bear it at the time; he held up his trembling hand, imploring her to stop; but next day he asked her to repeat it, and to do so often of an evening: which she did. He listening, with his face turned away.

Florence was sitting on a certain time by his window, with her work-basket between her and her old attendant, who was still her faithful companion. He had fallen into a doze. It was a beautiful evening, with two hours of light to come yet; and the tranquillity and quiet made Florence very thoughtful. She was lost to everything for the moment, but the occasion when the so altered figure on the bed had first presented her to her beautiful mamma; when a touch from Walter leaning on the back of her chair, made her start.

'My dear,' said Walter, 'there is some one downstairs who wishes to speak to you.'

She fancied Walter looked grave, and asked him if anything had happened.

'No, no, my love!' said Walter, 'I have seen the gentleman myself, and spoken with him. Nothing has happened. Will you come?'

Florence put her arm through his; and confiding her father to the black-eyed Mrs. Toots, who sat as brisk and smart at her work as black-eyed woman could, accompanied her husband downstairs. In the pleasant little parlour opening on the garden, sat a gentleman, who rose to advance towards her when she came in, but turned off, by reason of some peculiarity in his legs, and was only stopped by the table.

Florence then remembered cousin Feenix, whom she had not at first recognised in the shade of the leaves. Cousin Feenix took her hand, and congratulated her upon her marriage.

'I could have wished, I am sure,' said cousin Feenix, sitting down as Florence sat, 'to have had an earlier opportunity of offering my congratulations; but, in point of fact, so many painful occurrences have happened, treading, as a man may say, on one another's heels, that I have been in a devil of a state myself, and perfectly unfit for every description of society. The only description of society I have kept, has been my own; and it certainly is anything but flattering to a man's good opinion of his own resources, to know that, in point of fact, he has the capacity of boring himself to a perfectly unlimited extent.'

Florence divined, from some indefinable constraint and anxiety in this gentleman's manner—which was always a gentleman's, in spite of the harmless little eccentricities that attached to it—and from Walter's manner no less, that something more immediately tending to some object was to follow this.

'I have been mentioning to my friend Mr. Gay, if I may be allowed to have the honour of calling him so,' said cousin Feenix, 'that I am rejoiced to hear that my friend Dombey is very decidedly mending. I trust my friend Dombey will not allow his mind to be too much preyed upon, by any mere loss of fortune. I cannot say that I have ever experienced any very great loss of fortune myself: never having had, in point of fact, any great amount of fortune to lose. But as much as I could lose, I have lost; and I don't find that I particularly care about it. I know my friend Dombey to be a devilish honourable man; and it 's calculated to console my friend Dombey very much, to know, that this is the universal sentiment. Even Tommy Screwzer,—a man of an extremely bilious habit, with whom my friend Gay is probably acquainted—cannot say a syllable in disputation of the fact.'

Florence felt, more than ever, that there was something to come; and looked earnestly for it. So earnestly, that cousin Feenix answered, as if she had spoken.

'The fact is,' said cousin Feenix, 'that my friend Gay and myself have been discussing the propriety of entreating a favour at your hands; and that I have the consent of my friend Gay—who has met me in an exceedingly kind and open manner, for which I am very much indebted to him—to solicit it. I am sensible that so amiable a lady as the lovely and accomplished daughter of my friend Dombey, will not require much urging; but I am happy to know, that I am supported by my friend Gay's influence and approval. As in my parliamentary time, when a man had a motion to make of any sort—which happened seldom in those days, for we were kept very tight in hand, the leaders on both sides being regular mar-

tinets, which was a devilish good thing for the rank
and file, like myself, and prevented our exposing ourselves continually, as a great many of us had a feverish anxiety to do—as, in my parliamentary time, I was
about to say, when a man had leave to let off any little
private popgun, it was always considered a great point
for him to say that he had the happiness of believing
that his sentiments were not without an echo in the
breast of Mr. Pitt; the pilot, in point of fact, who had
weathered the storm. Upon which, a devilish large
number of fellows immediately cheered, and put him
in spirits. Though the fact is, that these fellows, being under orders to cheer most excessively whenever
Mr. Pitt's name was mentioned, became so proficient
that it always woke 'em. And they were so entirely
innocent of what was going on, otherwise, that it used
to be commonly said by Conversation Brown—four
bottle man at the Treasury Board, with whom the
father of my friend Gay was probably acquainted,
for it was before my friend Gay's time—that if a man
had risen in his place, and said that he regretted to
inform the house that there was an honourable member in the last stage of convulsions in the lobby, and
that the honourable member's name was Pitt, the approbation would have been vociferous.'

This postponement of the point, put Florence in a
flutter; and she looked from cousin Feenix to Walter, in increasing agitation.

'My love,' said Walter, 'there is nothing the matter.'

'There is nothing the matter, upon my honour,' said
cousin Feenix; 'and I am deeply distressed at being
the means of causing you a moment's uneasiness. I
beg to assure you that there is nothing the matter.
The favour that I have to ask is, simply—but it really
does seem so exceeding singular, that I should be in
the last degree obliged to my friend Gay if he would

have the goodness to break the—in point of fact, the ice,' said cousin Feenix.

Walter thus appealed to, and appealed to no less in the look that Florence turned towards him, said—

'My dearest, it is no more than this. That you will ride to London with this gentleman, whom you know.'

'And my friend Gay, also—I beg your pardon!' interrupted cousin Feenix.

'—And with me—and make a visit somewhere.'

'To whom?' asked Florence, looking from one to the other.

'If I might entreat,' said cousin Feenix, 'that you would not press for an answer to that question, I would venture to take the liberty of making the request.'

'Do *you* know, Walter?' said Florence.

'Yes.'

'And think it right?'

'Yes. Only because I am sure that you would too. Though there may be reasons I very well understand, which make it better that nothing more should be said beforehand.'

'If papa is still asleep, or can spare me if he is awake, I will go immediately,' said Florence. And rising quietly, and glancing at them with a look that was a little alarmed but perfectly confiding, left the room.

When she came back, ready to bear them company, they were talking together, gravely, at the window; and Florence could not but wonder what the topic was, that had made them so well acquainted in so short a time. She did not wonder at the look of pride and love with which her husband broke off as she entered; for she never saw him, but that rested on her.

'I will leave,' said cousin Feenix, 'a card for my friend Dombey, sincerely trusting that he will pick

up health and strength with every returning hour.
And I hope my friend Dombey will do me the favour
to consider me a man who has a devilish warm admiration of his character, as, in point of fact, a British
merchant and a devilish upright gentleman. My
place in the country is in a most confounded state of
dilapidation, but if my friend Dombey should require
a change of air, and would take up his quarters there,
he would find it a remarkably healthy spot—as it need
be, for it's amazingly dull. If my friend Dombey
suffers from bodily weakness, and would allow me to
recommend what has frequently done myself good,
as a man who has been extremely queer at times, and
who lived pretty freely in the days when men lived
very freely, I should say, let it be in point of fact the
yolk of an egg, beat up with sugar and nutmeg, in
a glass of sherry, and taken in the morning with a
slice of dry toast. Jackson, who kept the boxing-
rooms in Bond Street—man of very superior qualifi-
cations, with whose reputation my friend Gay is no
doubt acquainted—used to mention that in training
for the ring they substituted rum for sherry. I
should recommend sherry in this case, on account of
my friend Dombey being in an invalided condition;
which might occasion rum to fly—in point of fact to
his head—and throw him into a devil of a state.'

Of all this, cousin Feenix delivered himself with
an obviously nervous and discomposed air. Then,
giving his arm to Florence, and putting the strongest possible constraint upon his wilful legs which
seemed determined to go out into the garden, he led her
to the door, and handed her into a carriage that was
ready for her reception.

Walter entered after him, and they drove away.

Their ride was six or eight miles long. When they
drove through certain dull and stately streets, lying

westward in London, it was growing dusk. Florence had, by this time, put her hand in Walter's; and was looking very earnestly, and with increasing agitation, into every new street into which they turned.

When the carriage stopped, at last, before that house in Brook Street, where his father's unhappy marriage had been celebrated, Florence said, 'Walter, what is this? Who is here?' Walter cheering her, and not replying, she glanced up at the house-front, and saw that all the windows were shut, as if it were uninhabited. Cousin Feenix had by this time alighted, and was offering his hand.

'Are you not coming, Walter?'

'No, I will remain here. Don't tremble! there is nothing to fear, dearest Florence.'

'I know that, Walter, with you so near. I am sure of that, but—'

The door was softly opened, without any knock, and cousin Feenix led her out of the summer evening air into the close dull house. More sombre and brown than ever, it seemed to have been shut up from the wedding-day, and to have hoarded darkness and sadness ever since.

Florence ascended the dusky staircase, trembling; and stopped, with her conductor, at the drawing-room door. He opened it, without speaking, and signed an entreaty to her to advance into the inner room, while he remained there. Florence, after hesitating an instant, complied.

Sitting by the window at a table, where she seemed to have been writing or drawing, was a lady, whose head, turned away towards the dying light, was resting on her hand. Florence advancing, doubtfully, all at once stood still, as if she had lost the power of motion. The lady turned her head.

'Great Heaven!' she said, 'what is this?'

'No, no!' cried Florence, shrinking back as she rose up, and putting out her hands to keep her off. 'Mamma!'

They stood looking at each other. Passion and pride had worn it, but it was the face of Edith, and beautiful and stately yet. It was the face of Florence, and through all the terrified avoidance it expressed, there was pity in it, sorrow, a grateful tender memory. On each face, wonder and fear were painted vividly; each so still and silent, looking at the other over the black gulf of the irrevocable past.

Florence was the first to change. Bursting into tears, she said from her full heart, 'Oh, mamma, mamma! why do we meet like this? Why were you ever kind to me when there was no one else, that we should meet like this?'

Edith stood before her, dumb and motionless. Her eyes were fixed upon her face.

'I dare not think of that,' said Florence, 'I am come from papa's sick bed. We are never asunder now; we never shall be, any more. If you would have me ask his pardon, I will do it, mamma. I am almost sure he will grant it now, if I ask him. May Heaven grant it to you, too, and comfort you!'

She answered not a word.

'Walter—I am married to him, and we have a son' —said Florence, timidly, 'is at the door, and has brought me here. I will tell him that you are repentant; that you are changed,' said Florence, looking mournfully upon her; 'and he will speak to papa with me, I know. Is there anything but this that I can do?'

Edith, breaking her silence, without moving eye or limb, answered slowly—

'The stain upon your name, upon your husband's, on your child's. Will that ever be forgiven, Florence?'

'Will it ever be, mamma? It is! Freely, freely, both by Walter and by me. If that is any consolation to you, there is nothing that you may believe more certainly. You do not—you do not,' faltered Florence, 'speak of papa; but I am sure you wish that I should ask him for his forgiveness. I am sure you do.'

She answered not a word.

'I will!' said Florence. 'I will bring it you, if you will let me; and then, perhaps, we may take leave of each other, more like what we used to be to one another. I have not,' said Florence very gently, and drawing nearer to her, 'I have not shrunk back from you, mamma, because I fear you, or because I dread to be disgraced by you. I only wish to do my duty to papa. I am very dear to him, and he is very dear to me. But I never can forget that you were very good to me. Oh, pray to Heaven,' cried Florence, falling on her bosom, 'pray to Heaven, mamma, to forgive you all this sin and shame, and to forgive me if I cannot help doing this (if it is wrong), when I remember what you used to be!'

Edith, as if she fell beneath her touch, sunk down on her knees, and caught her round the neck.

'Florence!' she cried. 'My better angel! Before I am mad again, before my stubbornness comes back and strikes me dumb, believe me, upon my soul I am innocent.'

'Mamma!'

'Guilty of much! Guilty of that which sets a waste between us evermore. Guilty of what must separate me, through the whole remainder of my life, from purity and innocence—from you, of all the earth. Guilty of a blind and passionate resentment, of which I do not, cannot, will not, even now, repent; but not guilty with that dead man. Before God!'

Upon her knees upon the ground, she held up both her hands, and swore it.

'Florence!' she said, 'purest and best of natures,— whom I love—who might have changed me long ago, and did for a time work some change even in the woman that I am,—believe me, I am innocent of that; and once more, on my desolate heart, let me lay this dear head, for the last time!'

She was moved and weeping. Had she been of- tener thus in older days, she had been happier now.

'There is nothing else in all the world,' she said, 'that would have wrung denial from me. No love, no hatred, no hope, no threat. I said that I would die, and make no sign. I could have done so, and I would, if we had never met, Florence.'

'I trust,' said cousin Feenix, ambling in at the door, and speaking, half in the room, and half out of it, 'that my lovely and accomplished relative will excuse my having, by a little stratagem, effected this meet- ing. I cannot say that I was, at first, wholly incredu- lous as to the possibility of my lovely and accom- plished relative having, very unfortunately, commit- ted herself with the deceased person with white teeth; because, in point of fact, one does see, in this world —which is remarkable for devilish strange arrange- ments, and for being decidedly the most unintelligible thing within a man's experience—very odd conjunc- tions of that sort. But as I mentioned to my friend Dombey, I could not admit the criminality of my lovely and accomplished relative until it was perfectly established. And feeling, when the deceased per- son was, in point of fact, destroyed in a devilish hor- rible manner, that her position was a very painful

one—and feeling besides that our family had been
a little to blame in not paying more attention to her,
and that we are a careless family—and also that my
aunt, though a devilish lively woman, had perhaps
not been the very best of mothers—I took the liberty
of seeking her in France, and offering her such protection as a man very much out at elbows could offer.
Upon which occasion, my lovely and accomplished
relative did me the honour to express that she believed
I was, in my way, a devilish good sort of fellow; and
that therefore she put herself under my protection.
Which in point of fact I understood to be a kind
thing on the part of my lovely and accomplished relative as I am getting extremely shaky, and have derived great comfort from her solicitude.'

Edith, who had taken Florence to a sofa, made a
gesture with her hand as if she would have begged
him to say no more.

'My lovely and accomplished relative,' resumed
cousin Feenix, still ambling about at the door, 'will
excuse me, if, for her satisfaction, and my own, and
that of my friend Dombey, whose lovely and accomplished daughter we so much admire, I complete the
thread of my observations. She will remember that,
from the first, she and I have never alluded to the
subject of her elopement. My impression, certainly,
has always been, that there was a mystery in the affair which she could explain if so inclined. But my
lovely and accomplished relative being a devilish
resolute woman, I knew that she was not, in point of
fact, to be trifled with, and therefore did not involve
myself in any discussions. But observing lately, that
her accessible point did appear to be a very strong
description of tenderness for the daughter of my
friend Dombey, it occurred to me that if I could
bring about a meeting, unexpected on both sides, it

might lead to beneficial results. Therefore, we being in London, in the present private way, before going to the South of Italy, there to establish ourselves, in point of fact, until we go to our long homes, which is a devilish disagreeable reflection for a man, I applied myself to the discovery of the residence of my friend Gay—handsome man of an uncommonly frank disposition, who is probably known to my lovely and accomplished relative—and had the happiness of bringing his amiable wife to the present place. And now,' said cousin Feenix, with a real and genuine earnestness shining through the levity of his manner and his slipshod speech, 'I do conjure my relative, not to stop half-way, but to set right, as far as she can, whatever she has done wrong—not for the honour of her family, not for her own fame, not for any of those considerations which unfortunate circumstances have induced her to regard as hollow, and in point of fact, as approaching to humbug—but because it *is* wrong, and not right.'

Cousin Feenix's legs consented to take him away after this; and leaving them alone together, he shut the door.

Edith remained silent for some minutes, with Florence sitting close beside her. Then she took from her bosom a sealed paper.

'I debated with myself a long time,' she said in a low voice, 'whether to write this at all, in case of dying suddenly or by accident, and feeling the want of it upon me. I have deliberated, ever since, when and how to destroy it. Take it, Florence. The truth is written in it.'

'Is it for papa?' asked Florence.

'It is for whom you will,' she answered. 'It is given to you, and is obtained by you. He never could have had it otherwise.'

Again they sat silent, in the deepening darkness.

'Mamma,' said Florence, 'he has lost his fortune; he has been at the point of death; he may not recover, even now. Is there any word that I shall say to him from you?'

'Did you tell me,' asked Edith, 'that you were very dear to him?'

'Yes!' said Florence in a thrilling voice.

'Tell him I am sorry that we ever met.'

'No more?' said Florence after a pause.

'Tell him if he asks, that I do not repent of what I have done—not yet—for if it were to do again to-morrow, I should do it. But if he is a changed man—'

She stopped. There was something in the silent touch of Florence's hand that stopped her.

—'But that being a changed man, he knows, now, it would never be. Tell him I wish it never had been.'

'May I say,' said Florence, 'that you grieved to hear of the afflictions he has suffered?'

'Not,' she replied, 'if they have taught him that his daughter is very dear to him. He will not grieve for them himself, one day, if they have brought that lesson, Florence.'

'You wish well to him, and would have him happy. I am sure you would!' said Florence. 'Oh! let me be able, if I have the occasion at some future time, to say so?'

Edith sat with her dark eyes gazing steadfastly before her, and did not reply until Florence had repeated her entreaty; when she drew her hand within her arm, and said, with the same thoughtful gaze upon the night outside—

'Tell him that if, in his own present, he can find any reason to compassionate my past, I sent word that I asked him to do so. Tell him that if, in his own present, he can find a reason to think less bitterly of me, I asked him to do so. Tell him, that, dead as we are to one another, never more to meet on this side of eternity, he knows there is one feeling in common between us now, that there never was before.'

Her sternness seemed to yield, and there were tears in her dark eyes.

'I trust myself to that,' she said, 'for his better thoughts of me, and mine of him. When he loves his Florence most, he will hate me least. When he is most proud and happy in her and her children, he will be most repentant of his own part in the dark vision of our married life. At that time, I will be repentant too—let him know it then—and think that when I thought so much of all the causes that had made me what I was, I needed to have allowed more for the causes that had made him what he was. I will try, then, to forgive him his share of blame. Let him try to forgive me mine!'

'Oh mamma!' said Florence. 'How it lightens my heart, even in such a meeting and parting, to hear this!'

'Strange words in my own ears,' said Edith, 'and foreign to the sound of my own voice! But even if I had been the wretched creature I have given him occasion to believe me, I think I could have said them still, hearing that you and he were very dear to one another. Let him, when you are dearest, ever feel that he is most forbearing in his thoughts of me— that I am most forbearing in my thoughts of him! Those are the last words I send him! Now, good-bye, my life!'

She clasped her in her arms, and seemed to pour out all her woman's soul of love and tenderness at once.

'This kiss for your child! These kisses for a blessing on your head! My own dear Florence, my sweet girl, farewell!'

'To meet again!' cried Florence.

'Never again! Never again! When you leave me in this dark room, think that you have left me in the grave. Remember only that I was once, and that I loved you!'

And Florence left her, seeing her face no more, but accompanied by her embraces and caresses to the last.

Cousin Feenix met her at the door, and took her down to Walter in the dingy dining-room: upon whose shoulder she laid her head weeping.

'I am devilish sorry,' said cousin Feenix, lifting his wristbands to his eyes in the simplest manner possible, and without the least concealment, 'that the lovely and accomplished daughter of my friend Dombey and amiable wife of my friend Gay, should have had her sensitive nature so very much distressed and cut up by the interview which is just concluded. But I hope and trust I have acted for the best, and that my honourable friend Dombey will find his mind relieved by the disclosures which have taken place. I exceedingly lament that my friend Dombey should have got himself, in point of fact, into the devil's own state of conglomeration by an alliance with our family; but am strongly of opinion that if it hadn't been for the infernal scoundrel Carker—man with white teeth—everything would have gone on pretty smoothly. In regard to my relative who does me the honour to have formed an uncommonly good opinion of myself, I can assure the amiable wife of my friend Gay, that she may rely on my being, in point of fact, a father to her. And in regard to the changes of human life, and the extraordinary manner in which we are perpetually conducting ourselves, all I can say is, with my friend Shakespeare—man who wasn't for

an age but for all time, and with whom my friend
Gay is no doubt acquainted—that it 's like the shadow
of a dream.'

CHAPTER LXII

FINAL

A BOTTLE that has been long excluded from the light
of day, and is hoary with dust and cobwebs, has been
brought into the sunshine; and the golden wine within
it sheds a lustre on the table.

It is the last bottle of the old Madeira.

'You are quite right, Mr. Gills,' says Mr. Dombey.
'This is a very rare and most delicious wine.'

The captain, who is of the party, beams with joy.
There is a very halo of delight round his glowing
forehead.

'We always promised ourselves, sir,' observes Mr.
Gills, 'Ned and myself, I mean—'

Mr. Dombey nods at the captain, who shines more
and more with speechless gratification.

—'that we would drink this, one day or other, to
Walter safe at home: though such a home we never
thought of.   If you don't object to our old whim, sir,
let us devote this first glass to Walter and his wife.'

'To Walter and his wife!' says Mr. Dombey.
'Florence, my child'—and turns to kiss her.

'To Walter and his wife!' says Mr. Toots.

'To Wal'r and his wife!' exclaims the captain.
'Hooroar!' and the captain exhibiting a strong desire
to clink his glass against some other glass, Mr. Dombey, with a ready hand, holds out his.   The others follow; and there is a blithe and merry ringing, as of a
little peal of marriage bells.

Other buried wine grows older, as the old Madeira did in its time; and dust and cobwebs thicken on the bottles.

Mr. Dombey is a white-haired gentleman, whose face bears heavy marks of care and suffering; but they are traces of a storm that has passed on for ever, and left a clear evening in its track.

Ambitious projects trouble him no more. His only pride is in his daughter and her husband. He has a silent, thoughtful, quiet manner, and is always with his daughter. Miss Tox is not unfrequently of the family party, and is quite devoted to it, and a great favourite. Her admiration of her once stately patron is, and has been ever since the morning of her shock in Princess's Place, platonic, but not weakened in the least.

Nothing has drifted to him from the wreck of his fortunes, but a certain annual sum that comes he knows not how, with an earnest entreaty that he will not seek to discover, and with the assurance that it is a debt, and an act of reparation. He has consulted with his old clerk about this, who is clear it may be honourably accepted, and has no doubt it arises out of some forgotten transaction in the times of the old House.

That hazel-eyed bachelor, a bachelor no more, is married now, and to the sister of the grey-haired Junior. He visits his old chief sometimes, but seldom. There is a reason in the grey-haired Junior's history, and yet a stronger reason in his name, why he should keep retired from his old employer; and as he lives with his sister and her husband, they participate in that retirement. Walter sees them sometimes—Florence too—and the pleasant house resounds with profound duets arranged for the piano-forte and violoncello, and with the labours of Harmonious Blacksmiths.

And how goes the wooden midshipman in these changed days? Why, here he still is, right leg foremost, hard at work upon the hackney coaches, and more on the alert than ever, being newly-painted from his cocked hat to his buckled shoes; and up above him, in golden characters these names shine refulgent, GILLS AND CUTTLE.

Not another stroke of business does the midshipman achieve beyond his usual easy trade. But they do say, in a circuit of some half-mile round the blue umbrella in Leadenhall Market, that some of Mr. Gills's old investments are coming out wonderfully well; and that instead of being behind the time in those respects, as he supposed, he was, in truth, a little before it, and had to wait the fulness of the time and the design. The whisper is that Mr. Gills's money has begun to turn itself, and that it is turning itself over and over pretty briskly. Certain it is that, standing at his shop-door, in his coffee-coloured suit, with his chronometer in his pocket, and his spectacles on his forehead, he don't appear to break his heart at customers not coming, but looks very jovial and contented, though full as misty as of yore.

As to his partner, Captain Cuttle, there is a fiction of a business in the captain's mind which is better than any reality. The captain is as satisfied of the midshipman's importance to the commerce and navigation of the country, as he could possibly be, if no ship left the port of London without the midshipman's assistance. His delight in his own name over the door, is inexhaustible. He crosses the street, twenty times a day, to look at it from the other side of the way; and invariably says, on these occasions, 'Ed'ard Cuttle, my lad, if your mother could ha' knowed as you would ever be a man o' science, the good old creetur would ha' been took aback in-deed!'

But here is Mr. Toots descending on the midshipman with violent rapidity, and Mr. Toots's face is very red as he bursts into the little parlour.

'Captain Gills,' says Mr. Toots, 'and Mr. Sols, I am happy to inform you that Mrs. Toots has had an increase to her family.'

'And it does her credit!' cries the captain.

'I give you joy, Mr. Toots!' says old Sol.

'Thank 'ee,' chuckles Mr. Toots, 'I 'm very much obliged to you.   I knew that you 'd be glad to hear, and so I came down myself.   We 're positively getting on, you know.   There 's Florence, and Susan, and now here 's another little stranger.'

'A female stranger?' inquires the captain.

'Yes, Captain Gills,' says Mr. Toots, 'and I 'm glad of it.   The oftener we can repeat that most extraordinary woman, my opinion is, the better!'

'Stand by!' says the captain, turning to the old case-bottle with no throat—for it is evening, and the midshipman's usual moderate provision of pipes and glasses is on the board.   'Here 's to her, and may she have ever so many more!'

'Thank 'ee, Captain Gills,' says the delighted Mr. Toots.   'I echo the sentiment.   If you 'll allow me, as my so doing cannot be unpleasant to anybody, under the circumstances, I think I 'll take a pipe.'

Mr. Toots begins to smoke, accordingly, and in the openness of his heart is very loquacious.

'Of all the remarkable instances that that delightful woman has given of her excellent sense, Captain Gills and Mr. Sols,' says Toots, 'I think none is more remarkable than the perfection with which she has understood my devotion to Miss Dombey.'

Both his auditors assent.

'Because you know,' says Mr. Toots, '*I* have never changed my sentiments towards Miss Dombey.

They are the same as ever. She is the same bright
vision to me, at present, that she was before I made
Walters's acquaintance. When Mrs. Toots and myself first began to talk of—in short, of the tender
passion, you know, Captain Gills.'

'Aye, aye, my lad,' says the captain, 'as makes us
all slue round—for which you 'll overhaul the book—'

'I shall certainly do so, Captain Gills,' says Mr.
Toots, with great earnestness; 'when we first began to
mention such subjects, I explained that I was what
you may call a blighted flower, you know.'

The captain approves of this figure greatly; and
murmurs that no flower as blows, is like the rose.

'But Lord bless me,' pursues Mr. Toots, 'she was
as entirely conscious of the state of my feelings as
I was myself. There was nothing I could tell *her*.
She was the only person who could have stood between me and the silent tomb, and she did it, in a
manner to command my everlasting admiration. She
knows that there 's nobody in the world I look up to,
as I do to Miss Dombey. She knows that there 's
nothing on earth I wouldn't do for Miss Dombey.
She knows that I consider Miss Dombey the most
beautiful, the most amiable, the most angelic of her
sex. What is her observation upon that? The perfection of sense. "My dear, you 're right. *I* think
so too." '

'And so do I!' says the captain.

'So do I,' says Sol Gills.

'Then,' resumes Mr. Toots, after some contemplative pulling at his pipe, during which his visage
has expressed the most contented reflection, 'what an
observant woman my wife is! What sagacity she
possesses! What remarks she makes! It was only
last night, when we were sitting in the enjoyment of
connubial bliss—which, upon my word and honour,

is a feeble term to express my feelings in the society of my wife—that she said how remarkable it was to consider the present position of our friend Walters. "Here," observes my wife, "he is, released from sea-going, after that first long voyage with his young bride"—as you know he was, Mr. Sols.'

'Quite true,' says the old instrument-maker, rubbing his hands.

' "Here he is," says my wife, "released from that, immediately; appointed by the same establishment to a post of great trust and confidence at home; showing himself again worthy; mounting up the ladder with the greatest expedition; beloved by everybody; assisted by his uncle at the very best possible time of his fortunes"—which I think is the case, Mr. Sols? My wife is always correct.'

'Why yes, yes—some of our lost ships, freighted with gold, have come home, truly,' returns old Sol, laughing. 'Small craft, Mr. Toots, but serviceable to my boy!'

'Exactly so,' says Mr. Toots. 'You'll never find my wife wrong. "Here he is," says that most remarkable woman, "so situated,—and what follows? What follows?" observed Mrs. Toots. Now pray remark, Captain Gills, and Mr. Sols, the depth of my wife's penetration. "Why that, under the very eye of Mr. Dombey, there is a foundation going on, upon which a—an edifice"; that was Mrs. Toots's word,' says Mr. Toots exultingly, ' "is gradually rising, perhaps to equal, perhaps excel, that of which he was once the head, and the small beginnings of which (a common fault, but a bad one, Mrs. Toots said) escaped his memory. Thus," said my wife, "from his daughter, after all, another Dombey and Son will ascend"—no "rise"; that was Mrs. Toots's word—"triumphant." '

Mr. Toots, with the assistance of his pipe—which he is extremely glad to devote to oratorical purposes, as its proper use affects him with a very uncomfortable sensation—does such grand justice to this prophetic sentence of his wife's, that the captain, throwing away his glazed hat in a state of the greatest excitement, cries—

'Sol Gills, you man of science and my ould pardner, what did I tell Wal'r to overhaul on that there night when he first took to business? Was it this here quotation, "Turn again Whittington Lord Mayor of London, and when you are old you will never depart from it"? Was it them words, Sol Gills?'

'It certainly was, Ned,' replied the old instrument-maker. 'I remember well.'

'Then I tell you what,' says the captain, leaning back in his chair, and composing his chest for a prodigious roar. 'I'll give you Lovely Peg right through; and stand by, both on you, for the chorus!'

Buried wine grows older, as the old Madeira did, in its time; and dust and cobwebs thicken on the bottles.

Autumn days are shining, and on the sea-beach there are often a young lady, and a white-haired gentleman. With them, or near them, are two children: boy and girl. And an old dog is generally in their company.

The white-haired gentleman walks with the little boy, talks with him, helps him in his play, attends upon him, watches him, as if he were the object of his life. If he be thoughtful, the white-haired gentleman is thoughtful too; and sometimes when the child is sitting by his side, and looks up in his face, asking him questions, he takes the tiny hand in his, and holding it, forgets to answer. Then the child says—

'What, grandpapa! Am I so like my poor little uncle again?'

'Yes, Paul. But he was weak, and you are very strong.'

'Oh yes, I am very strong.'

'And he lay on a little bed beside the sea, and you can run about.'

And so they range away again, busily, for the white-haired gentleman likes best to see the child free and stirring; and as they go about together, the story of the bond between them goes about, and follows them.

But no one, except Florence, knows the measure of the white-haired gentleman's affection for the girl. That story never goes about. The child herself almost wonders at a certain secrecy he keeps in it. He hoards her in his heart. He cannot bear to see a cloud upon her face. He cannot bear to see her sit apart. He fancies that she feels a slight, when there is none. He steals away to look at her, in her sleep. It pleases him to have her come, and wake him in the morning. He is fondest of her and most loving to her, when there is no creature by. The child says then, sometimes—

'Dear grandpapa, why do you cry when you kiss me?'

He only answers 'Little Florence! Little Florence!' and smooths away the curls that shade her earnest eyes.

THE END